D0916569

REDWOOD
LIBRARY

Now Voyagers:
The Night Sea

TURTLE POINT PRESS NEW YORK

NOW VOYAGERS: THE NIGHT SEA JOURNEY

Journey

SOME DIVISIONS OF THE SAGA OF MAWRDEW CZGOWCHWZ, OLTRANO. AUTHENTICATED BY PERSONS REPRESENTED THEREIN. BOOK ONE.

James McCourt

ISBN 978-1-933527-08-6
LCCN 2006906039
Design and composition by
Wilsted & Taylor Publishing Services

In glad remembrance of my parents,
Jim McCourt and Kitty Moore

I

"*There was a time*," she then said, "*time out of mind*."

"So to begin," he replied, "at the beginning alike of the story and its solemn telling. Only what we're actually up to here in this stately room as the hour of the wolf approaches is more in the nature of the good old Invocation in Medias Résumé. And so far from our topos being of a time time out of mind, we've got it on both our minds big time and why not, so? Aristotle says, *After this comes the construction of Plot, which some rank first one with a double story*. That's us front and center, right down the line.

"But yes, for the listening world the standard model of the universe of fable always kicks in with *Fado, fado*, once-upon-a-time, *Il y a, Es war, Ci-fu*—all requisite portal tropes of children's stories, of creation fables, of foundation protocols, and the sonorous sagas of the impossibly valiant. Nice to know we're in with the right crowd, anyway, so far as posterity goes—although enforst, parfit, whilom, and eftsoons we must forcibly abjure, lest we tip our hand too early and queer the pitch altogether. How does that sound? Yawpish enough, think you, for the general populace?"

"You've captured my attention—but the story is you always have."

The clock of the Metropolitan Life Insurance Company Tower four blocks away on Madison Square had just struck eight familiar tones, signaling the half hour, in this instance half past eleven on the signal evening of June 16, 2004. In the front parlor of 47 Gramercy Park North, two old friends had sat down together at an old walnut oval Sheraton table to regroup their forces: S.D.J. (The) O'Maurigan and the woman once known (as she would have it, but in truth known still to the knowing world such as it was) as Mawrdew Czgowchwz, oltrano diva of the twentieth century, lately registered in the civic directory as Maev Cohalen, MAPA, psychoanalyst at New York's Center for Modern Psychoanalytic Studies and psychotherapist for the cadets and teaching staff at the Police Academy on East Twentieth Street.

The friends, elected affinities and denizens both of the night and the city, had just come in from an evening at Symphony Space on Upper Broadway, having participated in the boisterous Bloomsday centennial reading of James Joyce's *Ulysses*. (He had enacted Simon Dedalus from "The Wandering Rocks" and she Gertie MacDowell from "Nausicaa.") Now, in their one-room preceptory they had begun the work of the midnight hour, the examination of a collection of tapes dating back forty-seven years to the nineteen fifty-six–fifty-seven theatrical season, and a dusty manuscript entitled MNOPQR *STUVWXYZ*, unearthed earlier in the day from what they called the press, a large mahogany cupboard on the top floor of the town house. Each looked to the other uncertainly, wondering what had they done, what were they about to do?

"Here," he then said, "is a definite beginning, lest our plan be accused of lacking the most defining characteristics of a strategy—forethought, preparation, a definite objective in mind. A manuscript in the form of an extended telegram, entailing the allegorized matter of an epic fable, has been dislodged after many decades from its hiding place in an old cupboard, and the following story, correcting the fable and forging its corrected elements into a fragment of a history is, by many separate voices, told in full, or as nearly as can be. Ought to be enough for anybody is our feeling."

"You hurried down that same evening of the sailing and had the thing dispatched shore to ship."

"Yes, *There was a time, time out of mind*—the opening words of the offering we found uncanny, the offering called MNOPQR *STUVXYZ*, unpronounceable, but immediately recognizable and clocked for what it was, that sent us on a season's merry chase after means, motives, opportunities, and mischiefs.

"The whole of it, entirely in majuscule. The longest telegram on record, dispatched from the Western Union office across Broadway from the old house, up the block from Longchamps. Shore to ship—although come to think of it now, Leo Lerman always called Manhattan itself a great ocean liner, so possibly ship to ship. And even now, understanding much that youth and ignorance caused me at the time to remark without comprehending, I find it hard to disentangle the ... etcetera. Yes, *there was a time, time out of mind* ... so there was."

The woman who had been Mawrdew Czgowchwz, oltrano, took up the long telegram of the allegorical text (representing her as Mnopqr Stuvwxyz) she had first read another life ago (or so it seemed, without exaggeration) while crossing the Atlantic with her then companion Jacob Beltane, oltrano, on the *Queen Mary* in late September, nineteen fifty-six.

THERE WAS A TIME TIME OUT OF MIND IN THE SEMPITERNAL PROGRESS OF ITAL DIVADIENST AT THAT SUSPENSORY PAUSE JUST PRIOR TO THE ADVENT OF WHAT CAME TO BE KNOWN AS MNOPQR-DOLATRY OR IN CERTAIN QUARTERS ITAL STUVWXYZCHINA WHEN THE CULT OF NIRVANA MORI FLOURISHED IN THE HOTHOUSE AMBIENCE OF THE CROSSROADS CAFE ON 42ND STREET ACROSS BROADWAY FROM THE VERY HOTEL WHERE IN THE GREAT DAYS CARUSO HAD IN SOMETHING LIKE THE SACRAMENTAL SENSE RECEIVED DESTINN WHOSE PALMY LOBBY ONCE ORMOLU MARBLE AND VELVET HAD BEEN TRANSFORMED INTO A VAST DRUGSTORE AND WHERE LATELY IN CARUSOS SUITE A PODIATRIST INSTALLED STOP THERE AT THE CROSSROADS CAFE IN THE SHADOW OF THE TIMES BUILDING NOVEMBER TO NOVEMBER FOR MORI WAS A DEAD CENTER SCORPIO THE GREAT WORLDS RAW CONCERNS WERE FLATLY IGNORED

The Crossroads Café: if Manhattan was a great ocean liner, the Crossroads Café was one of the places you could cross from first down to third—to social steerage. In that it resembled a chapel, didn't it, and even if you think of it a swimming pool—other places on board for crossing up or down.

"Crossing up, crossing down: dress stage. Passing ships—there's an idea, if not quite—"

"Original. It was a dark and stormy—"

"No, it was nothing like a dark and stormy night. There was a moon."

"That there was, waning from full, viewed from ship's deck in Manhattan as well—shining across the Great Meadow in the Park. This night, though dark enough here on the street where you live, isn't stormy, not yet. But then in New York lit up the way it is, on such languid summer nights how often come torrential rain and crashing thunder, too, like on the event-driven night of the first Bloomsday itself, when and while in the aftermath of old hurts new-enacted, two famously unlikely companions . . . but they've likely not yet gotten to Eumaeus uptown, so let's bide our time in sultry air and set about our business, the drawing up of blueprints for a biosphere."

"You wrote a poem about that waning moon."

> *"It was that cool, clear late September evening*
> *on the day they sailed away, when we looked up*
> *and saw Pagliaccio in the moon—on the wane*
> *from full to gibbous. The wan expression on him—*
> *that moue, the oval mouth, sad eyes. Who was it*
> *said,* 'Look at him—he's singing "*Plaisir d'amour*"
> and he's just come to "*ne dure qu'un moment.*" '

"And on it went, detailing how the face in the moon, eyes, nose, mouth, is formed by the shadows cast upon the light-reflecting whole by the so-called *maria*, specifically the . . . but of course I don't remember.

"And from there on to parallel imagined voyages across those seas whose names I don't recall, to the voyage out of the second line, employing every sort of word Arisotle designated—well, there are eight of those, and I do, or could recall them and what they had to do with the words of '*Plaisir d'amour*' in relation to the poet's sorrow of the moment—but why now? More important surely to consider the ambiguity of Pound's *news that stays news* in view of the two immediately available meanings of *stay*—leaving out the one that had to do with whalebone corsets. *Stay* as in 'Linger awhile, thou art so fair!' and *stay* as in stop any further thing from happening and let us have an end to news."

"The poet is clairvoyant. '*Ne dure qu'un moment*'—and our moment had only just gotten under way."

"Yes, well, it's easy to make predictions, is it not—especially concerning the future."

"Yogi Berra. We had a yogi on board."

"And yet one insists there must be more to it all—*pictura loquens*—than *tick-tock*, *Tag aus*, *Tag ein*, *E pluribus unum* and ashes, ashes, all fall down. The cultured young cry out, 'Do tell us about—we want to hear allabouteveryfucking-lastoneofem, *Notes and queries*, Q. and A., relating to the many consequential initiatives with which they became closely involved. The laughs the frowns, the upsandowns all first nature to them then and not in short, in long, the *works*. And unlike some in the city we do have all night.

"But unlike the authors of the long dispatch again to hand—who saw themselves, it seems, not as the bowler-and-stick vaudevillians they were, but as twin rhapsodes of mock-epic caliber, exuberantly flinging out their random paradoxical teasers as substitutes for Apollonian objects of contemplation, their fiery emotional effects as substitutes for Dionysian enchantment.

"For they were clever ones, as we soon discovered. Students of Comparative Literature no less, possessed, we saw at once, as we read through their unsettling text, of adroit, cool, and penetrating insight into theme, motivation, and character, keen in their primitive, exuberant ambition to *get it*.

"Fresh as paint their grasp of ideas introduced in Auerbach's *Mimesis*, and wielding an altogether more subtle knife than those blades thrust into the hands of the slashers recruited by the semiotic vogue. Determined to represent by annotating the fluctuations of their attitudes, as well as what they perpetrate and undergo, men's characters, and women's, too.

"Cruising our ranks in unobtrusive fashion during the intermissions, then later at the Crossroads Café dissecting us all down to the bone as an experiment in adaptation and exploitation. And if as it turned out what they were not so good at as they were at allegory and the grand design was smoking out a tail, and thus did finally fall into our clutches, their like never did come about again on the line."

"Don't you think they wanted to be caught out all along? I always did."

"That they made us making them? I suppose so, except that what they seemed to think they were up to the whole time was making us *up*. The *crust*!

"That said, we, all these years later making ourselves making them making us do not unroll our design in transparently allegorical fashion. Rather we allow them to unfold themselves as does life itself, which can be either tracked or lived, but never both simultaneously, according to both the uncertainty principle and the phenomenon of self-similarity. In this we are in our fashion true to our many darlings and also appropriately postcontemporary chaotic.

"We care little for plot or for the thudding sameness and strained expectation imbedded in it, seeking to reduce all experience to a carefully tabulated, weighed, and balanced succession of ratified incidents—one fucking thing after another, culminating in the uncovering and publication of the truth that will rock the world . . . right to sleep.

"For us such schemes have been weighed in the balance and found wanting, as were police reports and journalism for Sherlock Holmes. For in general it may be said of postmodern writing of serious intent that in it, the function of the narrator is just that, no less, no more—to fucking narrate, all right? To describe the fluctuations of movement. He is permitted speculation in time-slip chronicles solely on approximations of distance and duration, and of necessity, that he may be seen as anything but omniscient, on his own infirmities of character and intellect, especially those concerned with the illusion of self-determination, as they are the very ones that tend to support the more preposterous asseverations benighted readers have been encouraged to believe they have been vouchsafed as gospel, beware of the dog.

"Nothing reported concerning the fluctuations of gesture, no speculation on the motivation, or lack of same, in any character—so many spinning in an ever-narrowing gyre—may be confidently taken as read, merely as read about—*candidates must write on one side of the paper only; this margin to be left blank for the examiner.*

"That also said, in mitigation directly concerning the exercise of free will, and mindful of the conditions that must necessarily obtain in order that our narrator may competently answer the decorum of a legend, any and all remarks acknowledging the constant presence-in-absence of the distant, the strange, the far-out, and further typifications of the scarcely known must be accommodated—*imprimatur, nihil obstat*—so long that is, as no notion of roman à clef is entertained. We're out for ummediated, unadorned truth here, and not for floods of spurious verisimilitude—dreaded analog to the symptom of flooding in a psychosis.

"And a good thing at that, given the tendency of tropes to mutate—indeed mutate into life itself, taking command of the text altogether, making its story their story—so that it may be said of certain texts not so much that they are lifelike as that the reading of them is like the experience of living. No book can live two lives, *mar dhea*.

"Because for the slab of a thing to be read as a true roman à clef, according to the latest postmodern formulation *forensic multiples: a survey*, they'd want to have more keys on their turnkeys' rings than are turned clockwise on any given day up the Hudson at Sing-Sing—and that's straight from the source, sparkling and bottled on the premises in clear glass.

"Moreover, we don't care what people do—in fact they can do it in the streets if they like—alarums and excursions galore, fife and drum, and the monkey wrapped his tale around a flagpole. More power and good luck to them now there are no more horses likely to be frightened by them—certainly not the noble steeds of the mounted police. Our attitude will remain that of still, calm, tranquil contemplation with open eyes, gaze unaverted, a state which beholds the images boldly presented to it and declares 'just so.' "

"Still and all," she observed, "whoever they turn out to be, they should be doing something worthy of note to attract the world's indulgent attention—something, indeed, besides vibrating."

"Agreed, and with the proviso that we shall remain less interested in what they are up to just then than in what they are thinking of getting up to or remembering what they've gotten up to before, we don't wish to stop them, or see them stopped.

"Not for long anyway. Only long enough to freeze-frame and cut into them, to examine in cross section their motives, means, and opportunities, to arrive at some sense of their origins beyond the bounds of sense—should anybody anywhere anytime wish to know *just what's going on*—the accurate depiction of primal conflicts being ever better served by allegory than romance. And then, somehow, to reinstigate fluency from what has been halted.

"And in their own words, not in the words of avid narrative adepts whose accounts inevitably climax with hair-raising escapes for some—all colors and lengths of hair at that—leaving hearts beating out of chests all around the town, and for unfortunate others, catapulted bodies splayed at unnatural angles on outcroppings of jagged rock. Absolutely not. Our inspiration is drawn from Maupertuis and his principle of least action, forerunner of quantum mechanics."

"In their own words."

"A debriefing."

"Had they a brief?"

"We know they did—to follow the lead of Mawrdew Czgowchwz."

"Where to?"

"Where to. Well, in the end I see us all together at the Grand Hotel, each in his own room, reading the emergency instructions on the back of the door, prior to dressing for the coming occasion, then going down in the elevator to the lobby to await her descent down the great staircase to get into the limousine, us following along in taxis—"

"Not you, you always rode in the car."

"Didn't I just. In any event, surely to the opera house."

"And what is she singing?"

"What else but Minnie, of course, her favorite role."

"It was—still is. You know, in murder mysteries, I've always liked best the ones with everybody gathered in one place and they each and all have a motive."

"Interesting projection."

"Oh?"

"What else, when it was yourself up there on the stage slaying them all."

"You've forgotten not for the first time either."

"How neglectful—not for the first time either."

"Like a serial killer."

"That said, and since you bring the matter up, both the knack for plotting ghastly murders and skillful thriller trade craft are worthy attributes, indeed, providing richly enjoyable, sophisticated, and beguiling entertainment on the middlebrow commodities exchange by the filling up of volume after volume with savage, implacable killers, chilling conspiracies, terrifying histories—such as you yourself in the company of both heroes and villains have experienced and endured in actual world and time.

"Not to mention the heartening generosity with which those adept at these significant tasks spring into action to thank their editors, agents and publishers, spouses, partners, otherwise significant others, friends providing assistance selflessly, and, importantly, certain specialists for reading their manuscripts with the utmost forensic intensity and for providing the answers to certain crucial questions at crucial times, particularly for setting them on the right road from the start with commonsense advice concerning the properties of blood, and all the while combining meticulous attention to detail with a watchful eye on continuity. Ought to be enough for anybody, don't you think?"

"Quite enough—although it must occur to you as it does to me that we might take a leaf from the book of your adepts by acknowledging, if only—"

"To ourselves the debt we would owe to our own small army of so many more than fourteen holy helpers of varying degrees of intimacy and so forth, all working together for decades on the Open-Unsolved Unit, for there are no cold cases only cold hearts. Deriving satisfaction from the work itself without anyone in particular outside the circle knowing they were doing it."

"Rather like benign witches."

"Not, as we now say, getting off on the attention by the casual dropping of the throwaway remark—wanting no attention, their fulfillment self-contained, needing no public component."

"Again like a particular species of serial killer. That said, however, were we at all sore beset by a terror of death, the idea of reliving any portion of the eventful lives we lived by reliving them in the guise of richly enjoyable, cunningly sophisticated, and beguiling entertainment would add a new terror to it, absolutely."

"I suppose I agree. If one were sentenced to relive all the recording, elaboration, veiling, and titillating fan-dance peekaboos of terrible secrets in the real world, the world of history—to endure again the horrors of recorded time: it was all a contemptible lie, and the conniving bastards knew it was all along. Century upon century upon century, countless wars, all of it a lie, and they knew it all along. Secrets so terrible, ranging over a whole spate of disorienting predictions on the fate of mankind as dominated by disaster, death, and horror, that upon their revelation young heads of hair would go white overnight.

"Not to mention the necessity of doing so by representing in language of a certain prolixity and complexity some approximation—quite impossible to realize by means of the routine deployment of the ostensibly simpler and more direct syntactical constructions—of the tessellated and polyphonic texture of even the least educated, inquisitive, and sophisticated human natures' interior colloquies, almost never attempted in present times by either the writing of history or the fictionalization of it—"

"Well, it has taken fifty years for our hair to go white—clearly our secrets were—"

"Never so terrible. Not as such, no, but the secret revealed to us before the voyage home, that we did solemnly swear to keep—that was no recipe for—"

"Fish soup. Indeed not—and the agents never did discover it."

" 'Now this is to die with you, because you see, it was to die with me.' "

"Indeed. You know, one of the codices in the *Book of Ballymote* was called 'Vexation of a Poet's Heart.' Apt. And now we sit in the Crib Room of advancing age hoping for that lightning flash of inspiration, the simple plaintext of wisdom: *so* that *was it*! Hoping for it today, or tomorrow, or soon. Nietzsche called today an impossible book, poorly written, ponderous, with fantastic and confused imagery, uneven in tempo, lacking any impulse for logical clarity, extremely self-confident, and thus dispensing with evidence, like a book for the initiated."

"And they continued, did they not, your schoolboys, recording our words—or rather yours in New York; we'd by then sailed away. It was their tried and true method, how they'd cooked up their fantasy in the first place and became a sensation for a season, the season under review."

"Yes, and then disappeared, never picking up the story with *On the day her destiny returned to claim her, Mnopqr Stuvwxyz* . . . whatever. They never trespassed again, disappearing without trace. It was almost as if they'd been abducted, despoiled, and done away with—but by what unknown agency?"

"Odd. Reminds me of one of my patients at the Academy, an extremely handsome, bright young detective sergeant. 'Do you believe in male rape? You should, you're dealing with it big time around here, admitted or not. Know how many cops, male and female, were molested as kids? A lot. Funny, you're kind of a perp yourself, in a way. Think of the word *therapist*. Could be broken into two words, *the rapist*.' "

"And now we resemble the cops at the precinct, unearthing at the sudden behest of an ambitious district attorney a cold case—or perhaps to be somewhat more exact, those cadets of yours at the Academy, recruits learning their lessons before being sent out onto the streets.

"Not that one is up to doing any of it, the age one is and stiff in the tenets—not up to fielding clever, informed, and worldly cynical tales of arrogance, obsession, and tragedy elsewhere than on the operatic stage. Not up to roaring off down original paths, identifying all operative personnel, scrutinizing all background details, including birth, rearing, race, creed, protean colorings of skin, hair, and eyes. Also positions taken on specific issues of paramount importance. Not up to creeping around corners, steaming open envelopes, defragging hard drives—no, none of it. The role of duty scripter was never one's remit, and I've got my alibi ready, just in case, for the mess left on the floor. One of the big boys did it, then ran away. I hid under the bed until he was gone."

"Is this alibi calculated to misdirect agents of the attorney general?"

"The attorney general is a dismal fool, a pathological misanthrope extracted from Ulster Presbyterians. As to the agents, one gathers they pretty much follow suit, whatever their several extractions. No, the alibi is designed to thwart the machinations of the common snoop. Anyway, you'll find it all in there, chapter and verse, hyle and fabric, *Cav* and *Pag*. And all along the story tells the storyteller, *this is it*, the dance there can only be when there is something to be danced sets about dancing the dancers, the song sings the singer *sur n'import quel pretexte*, and the ends justify everything.

"This must be where I ask, What are we looking for; you answer, The point; I ask, Which one; and you answer, The one we've been missing all along."

"Our premise—however it be characterized—certainly has a great hook. And hooks are like corners of the world, none of which, despite our arrogance, can be called either lost or little—unless they all are. In addition we are all-out for the head-on post-ironic, the torque in the switchback, some definite resolution."

"Or another."

"Let's not ask for the moon—the tides are yet in need of it. Therefore, should we wish to do such a thing by lamplight in these darkened hours as talk the whole of the tale into a machine possessed of a function known as Voice Recognition, to bring to the generation of this dispensation whatever it is we do bring, then the machine would see to it that our version of, if not the whole of it, then at any rate the more markworthy details of our storied lives, was *keyboarded*—turned into a telegram in the proper sense of that word—one sent across what must by now seem to be the ages, from a time time out of mind—*Fado, fado, Depuis longtemps, Es war, Ci-fu*—to an era in its own estimation all *at sea*."

"We said the same—all at sea. Whatever did we have to complain of?"

"It never seemed to me *you* had anything at all to complain of, but I seem to remember *our* complaining we hadn't enough spare time. Everybody was saying it was an unprecedented time, the corrected version of *Der Zeit Ohne Beispiel*. It was a time of nylon stockings with scrupulously straightened seams, of pressed trousers with severe, knife-edge creases in them. We'd hit the beaches, dropped the bomb, won the war. Things were happening, and we all wanted them to happen with us, to us, and on our account. It was all very well for the likes of yourself, the world's ultimate diva, artistic bombshell, and rumored double agent, but what of us out there in the darkened auditorium? What of *our* lives?"

She took a brief moment to think about that.

"Obviously it's up to you to tell them."

"If what you say is true, then

> *'Me, all to meane, the sacred Muse areeds*
> *To blazon broad emongst her learned throng.'* "

"Nonsense, you're well able for them—however, can you deal with yourself in the third person?"

"Do you mean the Holy Spirit?"

"Perhaps metaphorically. Can you do it?"

"As long as it's not on a first-name basis."

"I can see that."

"But were we," he continued, "any of us driven mad by chivalric romances—even when they were all about us thinly disguised? Did we cast off from Red Hook or from Coenties Slip for the mysterious and seductive South Seas in search of a great white whale? Did we do any of those things at all?"

"Perhaps in a way—perhaps in search of a great whale of a tale."

"How then to begin the telling of such a story, of the search for—the concoction of—the biggest whale of a tale that—"

"Ever emerged? A sort of *Moby-Diva*? How about *It was the best of times, it was—*"

"No—in truth it was the best of times, full stop."

"*Plaisir d'amour*, full stop. Only no one ever did—never so much as paused."

"It was, indeed, for us full throttle, in both our cities."

"Indeed. Indeed, I suppose we could recognize the main feature as a tale of two cities, of New York and Dublin, with newsreels and cartoons of London and Milan, swerving from the solemn, thrown in. In fact *thrown-in* might best define a great many of the formal procedures employed. *Voulez-vous troublez la salade, Madame?*

"However, there are two great threats, two gaping pitfalls in the undertaking to hand, the first of which is succumbing to the seductive notion that the lot of us, so engulfed in the mystical thrall of the woman unto herself you were back then so as to—"

"And none so engulfed as she unto herself."

"Yes, perhaps. In any case, so engulfed as to believe ourselves ordained to operate as a kind of come-again contingent of the Elohim mixing it up in no end of improvisational ways with the sons and daughters of mankind, somehow succeeding in those immediate postwar decades in creating and living in a miraculous and nightly renewable world all our own, dispensing with the promulgations of historical authority and all its many pomps.

"Such as: its arrogation of the relative degrees of truth, its obsessive-compulsive fetish for the demarcation of centuries, millennia, eras, epochs, and such like devices proper to the writing of epic and its successor forms, all wantonly misappropriated with no thought to the consequences of such rapacious larceny by historical investigation, secretly terrified adepts, and also with the forensic methodologies of archaeology, paleontology, and, indeed, geology and cosmography themselves—all similarly stressed into carving out regulation-contour pigeonholes in which no such thing as a pigeon now or ever did put up, we must resolutely and unequivocally declare with Wilfred Owen that the world is the world, and not the slain nor the slayer, Amen.

"For there are indeed no such worlds and never were as the Homeric, the Virgilian, the Dantesque, the Genjian, the Spenserian, the Shakespearean, the Cervantesque, the Miltonic, the Racinian, the Molieresque, the Goethean, Schilleresque, Romantic, Dickensian, Baudelarean, Symbolic, Melvillian, Whitmanian, Dickinsonian, Jamesian, Eliotic, Kafkaesque, Joycean, Beckettian, Faulknerian, modern, postmodern, postcontemporary, or even Czgowchwzian. The world entire may well be correctly enough characterized ontologically either by the concepts of Will and Representation and simply by

Maya, TzimTzum, or the third part of that trinity also inhabited by the flesh and the devil. The Big Bang we cannot possibly allow—people are either shocked by the idea, which is vulgar, or laugh, which is worse. But German ideas such as *Vergangenheitsbewaltigung* and *Lebensweiheitspielerei* sound thoroughly respectable and, indeed, I believe, are so.

"The mirror held up to nature is not nature, it is what Hamlet says it is, a mirror—a rearview one. One moreover that may without apparent cause and at any time, in any place, without warning, crack from side to side, for in such a mirror things do appear closer than they actually are."

"And the second great treat, should it be just at present conveniently to hand?"

"Conveniently, yes. It is of course succumbing unguardedly to the witless journalistic rubric of *covering the story*. Journalists are dispatched like slippered gumshoes to cover the story, and that they do, down to the last hoarse whisper of the last would-be witness to the unfolding mystery—unheeding of the obvious fact that so covered, the story inevitably smothers under its own wrappings, suffocates on its own breath expelled into the zippered body bag.

"Enter to the rescue, metaphoric discourse, a strong dose of the oul *Dinnseachas*—that seductive poetry of time, place, and situation by which our forebears sought to gain control of the unseen forces that could cure them of their ills or curse them out of their health.

"Our forebears, who by their own accounts never had enough hours in the day nor days in the year either to settle down to the further task of affixing their every piece of present to the adhesive past—they were streets ahead of Nietzsche in formal understanding—that no matter which way you looked at it still loomed, or to get the spells down right in all particulars. They got the potions down all right, but never the spells—probable cause, the weather. Far too many dark and stormy nights, *mar dhea*.

"For example, listen to this. 'In the collective atmosphere of a newsroom, you learnt to write with people chatting to you at the same time, or barking into phones.' "

"*Learnt*. English or Irish? Nobody we know at the *New Yorker*."

"Irish—*An Irishman's Diary*, no less. And whom do we now know at the *New Yorker*?"

"A careless reference to more gracious time—do go on."

" 'A writer who needed peace and quiet would be better off looking for another job, away from the news editor occasionally reading your work over your shoulder, or maybe even tearing it out of the typewriter, screwing it up into a ball and throwing it away. Those of us who have been hardened beyond self-consciousness by such experience pride ourselves—blah-blah-blah-blah.' You can imagine the rest. And they *believe* it! No wonder they can't see that what they're doing in writing up their covering fables, their unwitting and unaware pronouncements of a metaphysic in which any type of ambiguity, uncertainty principle, or double bluff is surplus to requirements, is simply romancing a template, like a crossword puzzle, following a few standard clues set in a subliterary dialect, and filling in the blanks."

"Absent the subliterary dialect, much the same might be said of the sonnet—but perhaps just this evening, in honor of the date that was, you have silence—"

"Exile and cunning on the brain? No, but quietude will promote the recollection of emotion in tranquility."

They had opened the French windows, preferring the cooling night air to central air-conditioning. The woman who had been Mawrdew Czgowchwz looked across Gramercy Park past the statue of Edwin Booth to the still-burning gas lamps of The Players club and the National Arts Club, closed for the night, and to the old Sonnenberg mansion and Sam Barlow's brownstone town house, both darkened now, former venues both of stellar fetes given on what had seemed a nearly continual basis for such high-stakes types whose counterparts in Dublin society were known with the subtle yet pointed irony of that renowned floating world as 'the great and the good.'

"One hesitates to delve so into the memory trunk, should the best of them be lying doggo at the bottom of it."

"The answer to that of course is simple: simply upend the trunk, like an hourglass."

"They'll want to know where the bodies are buried."

"Don't speak of it—haven't we only lately lost Ralph and Carmen in the same week."

"Ralph and the tapes, Carmen and her knitted leg warmers, gone—which may be after all why we're doing this just now. We must not underestimate the dead—we know far too well the tricks they can play, with our memories, with all the paraphernalia of testimony.

"In addition, the stories of the outsiders, they who make us the insiders their subject, may admit of a plethora of conceivable ranges and styles, from oral histories to adventure tales, from the fantastical exploits of comic-book heroes to the routine, sluggish pulsations of domestic melodrama, in a capacious and broadly expressive entertainment medium, capable of capturing both the hairsbreadth movements of individual human consciousness and the colossal crosscurrents of global society."

"They told us pictures would accomplish all that."

"So you made one."

"I was in it."

"I'd say you were. So did the Academy."

"Yes. What else would you say, were it up to you?"

"For posterity, you mean. *Give me your arm, old toad; Help me down Cemetery Road.* Not my words, Larkin's, but they'd do better than anything I've so far written."

"Wasn't it you once asked, 'What's posterity ever done for me?' "

"The motion picture was said at the time to be able to continue, to greater effect, the bardic work of book and poem, play and opera, and then some."

"Yes, 'and then some' was ever the inducement."

"Able to attend to the multiplied demands on humanity and benevolence."

"Orphrey, quoting Griffith, said something like that."

"Within another framework altogether."

"Oh, well, *frameworks.*"

"Ralph said, 'I love the movies the same as everybody else, but if you're talking about multiplied demands, opera—'

"Besides, what sense does that overbearing fictive jive known as narration, in its rapturous enthrallment with the sound of its own voice, make at the end of the day, when in real life there's no telling what may happen next and the best that can be hoped for is the opportunity for serene reminiscence in a long twilight. You know, if you really are doing a line up the Avenue in *victim empathy response* and other state-of-the-art recovery ministrations, take heed—you may soon find yourself called to duty as close to home as right around this table.

"Plus which they're all now babbling on about nonfiction fiction—as if they're asking for *corroboration* from a reality they view as somehow stable. Not to mention their deluded sense of what they're calling the *transgressive*. They imagine themselves Promethean when all they've got clenched in their fists are books of unreliable matches, pun intended.

"However, quizzical asperity is one thing and withering scorn quite another. Restraint of pen and tongue is in order in order to clear a space for the vaunted undertaking."

"Young Tristan said, 'You've got a great story to tell, Grandmother, a better story even than Bianca Castafiore, her voice of doom and the theft of her adored emeralds, and you're quite wrong, it has not gone past its sell-by date, not by a long shot.'

"In any case, if what's wanted is something more than Old Bag Talks Back to Life and Love, there is surely at least one truckload of letters and diaries and sound-recorded exclamations extempore of various and sundry deponents of consequence that might be consulted, no?"

"You know what Hunt Stromberg wanted for *Maytime*? Undisputed evidence of a love great enough to endure through eternity—"

"As Mae West once said of men, What, only *one*?"

"—while keeping the story free of consummation or remembrance of ecstasy."

"What drivel—when ecstasy is itself all consummation, with neither memory nor notion of endurance involved in the dance. What interests me more is random memory, the tapes of the Other Voices. Like sitting at a play, or opera outdoors in summer, and hearing everywhere the voices from others' lives. Eliot was a *naif*—there is no liberation, either in memory or in desire, from the past, the pluperfect or the future perfect explosion their fusion effects. And nothing, but absolutely nothing, speaks out of its own silence."

"If the topos is the premise and the premise—or, since this is apt to be a long one, not exactly high concept, the premises—may be typified as a precinct, and if at the precinct station one or more of the big boys made the mess on the floor, traces of which still pester us, then the next move is to give the premises—we're back to them—a quick recce. That's forensics."

"Is this a procedural?"

"Open and shut case; television wrecked motion pictures, although not before you garnered the gold-plated statuette."

"*Pilgrim Soul* is only part of the story."

"So it is, and we're not going in for metonymy either. The story that writes itself has been given the whole ball of wax to grapple with and not just some highlights discs. It itself partakes as well of the need to know."

"Which my late lamented husband—he of the metaphoric English longbow—said we ought to get over, the better to allow the secret knowledge buried in our needs themselves."

"Your late lamented husband had his reasons."

"Like many another secret heart. Shall we go on—the dangers involved, for example?"

"I realize that. It's going to have to be your choice."

"After all these years you still say 'real-*ize*.' It's your charm."

She took up the telegram a second time, and read on.

FOR NERI WAS A DEAD CENTER SCORPIO THE GREAT WORLDS RAW CONCERNS WERE FLATLY IGNORED CONTROVERTED BY ENDLESS GRIMY SABBATICAL RITUALS STOP THE ROLLING ELECTRIC ITAL TIMES SIGN MIGHT PROCLAIM IN ITS CAREER THE END OF THE MODERN

WORLD STOP ITAL I MORITURI RAPT UNBOTHERED WOULD RANT ON OVER THE LATEST MORI TRIUMPH AT THE HOUSE ON RECORD IN PARAMUS AT THE STADIUM STOP MORIS DICTA ON EVERYTHING AND EVERYONE IN MUSIC WERE LOUDLY RECITED BY ACOLYTES IN ANTIPHON OVER TABLES LITTERED WITH CLIPPINGS REVIEWS VILE COFFEE AND AUTOGRAPHED DIVA GLOSSIES IN BLACK AND WHITE AND SEPIA NONE OF A LATER PROVENANCE THAN THE LAST YEAR BEFORE THE WAR STOP NIRVANA MORI WAS CONSIDERED AGELESS HER VOICE DEEMED IMMUTABLE STOP ELDERS WHO COULD ACTUALLY SPEAK OF THE MORI DEBUT WERE HAILED AS ITAL I MORITURI AS THEY PASSED THEIR WIRE RECORDINGS OF MORI BROADCASTS LIKE HOLY TRANSCRIPTS FROM FOOL TO FOOL

"Then to resume, in any event it was the time—it was the season."

"A restless one."

"Terribly. Its sudden-updraft events convergent with rifts in the whole of the culture."

"Events that took place a half century ago."

"Forty-seven years to be exact—an interval of definite duration. But if we start it, start in retelling the story of it all—relating how the Mawrdew Czgowchwz that was you, a creature both corporeal and imagined, who in spite of her potential for vagueness ranks among the great lady loves—"

"Vagueness."

"—of civilized lore, along with Savitri, Helen, Dido, Lesbia, Clodia, Messalina; The Magdalen, Heloise, Laura, Beatrice, Emer, Aoife, Deirdre, Grainne and Iseult; the Dark Lady of the Sonnets, Dulcinea del Toboso, Swift's Vanessa, his Stella; Keats's Madeline, Lady Caroline Lamb, Lotte von Weimar, Marguerite Gautier, Ayesha—She-Who-Must-Be-Obeyed, Cynara, Odette de Crécy and Molly Bloom."

"Crecy. The Battle of Crécy. The French crossbow archers overwhelmed by the English longbows. Allegory. Yes, that season haunts the mind—as well it might . . . as well it—"

"The season of the getaway."

"Some getaway. Shall we talk about motives, opportunities, means? Turn the parlor into the situation room?"

"Such an investigation would require more space—a lot more space, for witnesses alone. We'd have to hire a hall—or give a garden party over in the park, a thought both felicitous and poetical, scholarly and glamorous, open to ingenious interpretations and absolutely closed to fools.

"*In aula ingenti memoriae*, Augustine says. *I come out of the fields and into the spacious palace, to the great hall of memory where there are innumerable treasures. There are stored up whatever forgetfulness has not swallowed up and buried. When I enter, things rush out in troop formation, each crying out 'I'm what you want!'* "

"Autograph hounds—nobody's fans."

"Never indoors long enough. Assailant or assailants unknown, in troop formation, no less. '*These*,' he continues, '*I wave away with my heart's hand and from memory's face, until what I wish for be unveiled, and appear in sight out of its secret place*.' The ancients, who knew much—admittedly a quantity numerically at any rate less than our own stocked store, knew how to train the memory—so that Proust's madeleine dunked in his *tisane*, together with the uneven pavement connected to the uneven stone in the baptistry of San Marco, are, like so much else in Western Civilization, anticipated by Augustine.

"They may even have known, although I have never found it so recorded, something of what is called *The Anticipation of Memory*, whereby in recollecting the affect—elation, appetite, etcetera, associated in youth with a robust confidence in the shape of things to come—feeling on top of the world—one can talk oneself into a state in which the affect attached to remembering seems identical to that so long ago attached to foresight."

"And write beyond the ending," she said. "*Wish for*. He doesn't say what actually happened, but only what he wishes had."

"No, he means what he wishes to remember—he trusts that what he recalls happening—having happened—as dictated to him by what the prophets called *Bat Qol*, the daughter of the Voice of God—what the Greeks called *Thea*, as in '*Menin aeide Thea Peleiadeo Achileos oulomenen* etcetera,' in fact, did, in every delineated particular."

"Did happen. *Here is how it must have been.* Wisdom literature."

"Let's call it that. And let's invoke Dante. '*Che qui per quei di la molto s'avanza.*' And by the way, speaking of *Salammbo*, were you the first to program Benny Hermann's *Salammbo* aria in recital? The tape is running."

"So far as I know I was—at the Hollywood Bowl. Rudi Friml put me up to it. Benny was there, and Rudi, and Erich Korngold, and their families, and Bette Davis, who came alone. Eileen Farrell programmed it subsequently, and really was much better—the *volume*!

" 'Sang the shit out of that piece of music.' "

"And so she did. I always got a kick out of Eileen's sailor mouth."

"What I remember are the bewildered looks when the orchestra played the first crashing chords, the dawning recognition and the giggles when you started singing, followed by the gasps of shock and awe when you opened up, went full throttle and—well, as Ralph used to say—"

"Peed."

"One is divided between a strong normative remnant within the self and the ego's passion for gnosis, abandoning the official historians for the schizoid cabalists time and again, seeking to transcend the most debilitating confines of the epic, to wit the shackles of narrator-text and embedded focalization."

"That does seem a little—well, even for you—"

"Hyperattenuated, yes. Actually I've just been remembering something Scotty Reston told me at Magwyck all those years ago—that when reporters from the dailies used to interview the big shots coming down the gangplanks on the North River, they'd jot down a few loose quips, roll up the pages off the notepads and fasten them to the legs of carrier pigeons that would then fly to coops on top of the newspaper buildings. Leads an extra poignance to your poor lost pal's performance in *On the Waterfront* years later. Ain't free association grand: pages from one's own notepad *pile up* on the table until a stiff wind blows them to the floor. One soon gives up the table and soon the floor is littered ... of course all this is metaphor, isn't it, because one's notebook is an IBM laptop, and nothing ever falls to the floor, or for that matter into the Recycle Bin ... well, hardly ever, and a good thing, too, when one looks out the long window at all the fat gray pigeons in the park across the street, who couldn't fly to the top of a hiding-place tree much less to a pigeon coop atop the Times Building were there any left."

"Your poor friend Reston was a dupe finally."

"He was Scottish; all Scots are dupes. All Swedes are marching toward a strange destiny, all Scots are dupes, and the world is too much with us, late and—"

"You and those Swedes!"

"Perhaps because in Ireland a Swede is a kind of turnip and you know yours truly and turnips—a grand passion still. Still, it's not so much the Swedes as such as the statement, which has to be the most compellingly spurious oracular pronouncement that old hag Dianetica Freelunch ever made in her long years hung up in a sack on the wall in that Chinese red bedroom. I shall never forgive that harridan for ruining denim for me. After she started drooling all over it, I threw every last pair of dungarees I'd ever owned away. Of course it was time, one was over forty.

"But, to take just the pivotal season fifty-six—fifty-seven, it did seem to have a life of its own entirely independent of the events that led up to it, something not true of seasons precedent or subsequent. Altogether though, if you accept the proposition that for the years from forty-seven to seventy-four inclusive, with some spillover in both directions—because in those years things really did follow the New York *season*, that kicked off in October and was run down by May—in which virtually nothing went unsaid and very little unrecorded by increasingly efficient devices—nothing of small consequence was brought under discussion at New York parties . . . if you accept *that*—"

"The place to seek Mawrdew Czgowchwz is *on line*."

"Everybody back on line!"

"As it was in the beginning, is now, and—"

"Now, don't blaspheme—you know it's terrible luck."

"A *pishogue*. Well, think of the ways then that the old line that formed at night in the freezing cold of a New York November was exactly like the new electronic Web of pathways crossing every barrier there used to be—and think of who inhabited the web—no more flies trapped the forces of a superior main force technology, but all spiders out to snare pieces of the undisclosed as never in recorded history since the hegemonies of the priesthoods of Nineveh, Babylon, Memphis, and Thebes, the Pythia, the Sibyl at Cumae, and the entire legions of Druids from Gaul to Galway. A great stable of sects and an industrious mint of schism such as never before has threatened to trumpet down the last of the crumbling curtain walls of Christendom until not a stone shall be left upon a stone—no opinion too strange but found credit and exchange.

"And I invoke it, the Web, I suppose, because the first four years of the twenty-first century have produced enough strange and unsettling development to haunt a far longer period, and I look to nostalgia for relief, back as if toward a time which produced a similar concentration, but of a measurelessly more benevolent nature."

"There was one Strange—a priest, as I remember."

"Yes, but not to be found on that line, only—"

"Elsewhere."

"Quite so—and speaking of lines, he certainly did have one. In the dance to the music of time he certainly could can-can. The story told from his point of view would have been to say the least of it skewed to the most preposterous angles. Were he alive still, he'd be a great one indeed for the online performance, likely would have engendered a cult following, perhaps even founded a church.

"But the Old Met Line—our line—what was it but the ultimate elsewhere? And out back along Seventh Avenue the sets stacked up against the wall, in all weathers, to be hauled back to the warehouse in New Jersey—did they not indeed provide all the materials necessary for a kind of fantasy shantytown or a Potemkin village of a fabled phantom realm?"

"Was that our world? I suppose it was, by and large. It was certainly one that I, having had my fill of the self-styled real world, would have been glad enough to inhabit for all my remaining days, had not—what, by the by, is the *by* of *by and large*? I've never known, really."

"It's a sailing term—you either sail by or sail large, and so the command, 'make voyages, attempt them; there's nothing else.' *El Camino Real.* We no longer sail. How we used to, though, by and large and otherwise, and all continually dreaming the Night Sea Journey, and waking to trade seafaring tales. Now we stay home, looking forward to a better time—the past—keeping within our precinct—as in Old New York. *In new precincts like Gramercy Park, a newly flush bourgeoisie fashioned one enclave after another dedicated to varieties of gregarious amusements: men's clubs, opera houses, pleasure gardens . . . each one as much a sanctum as a playpen.*"

"By and large. Where did you read that?"

"In the *New Yorker*—the Horace Greeley one."

"Horace Greeley. '*Go west, young man!*' "

"Actually, it was John Babsone Lane Soule."

"Is it antiquity we were in?"

"Seems so to me."

"Perhaps the Mahatma was right back then, and we were all there—wearing our ornamental epithets, and our chic hats—learning lessons of one kind or another, making judgments over hazards and conflicts—"

"And the Other Voices. We might even bring back old Moriarty."

"It seems to me you spent a lot of time and money getting rid of Moriarty."

"Yes, and Job Gennaio might not be thrilled at his return. He's never really cared for alter egos, and he didn't care for Moriarty at all. But I've been listening to the rebroadcasts on the radio on Sunday nights, and there he is again, all voice—and what a voice—Lamont Cranston, The Shadow, busy knowing what secrets lie in the hearts of men, chuckling at destiny, and plotting his courses of invisible intervention with Margo Lane. And had there been no Shadow in nineteen forty-three when I first came to New York, there could have been no Moriarty.

"And so, the other voices in the other rooms as they are severally heard. Try that one on for the Mind of God or the Omniscient Narrator. Or this. If we write 'Let the saga unfold,' enclosed in quotation marks, one impression is created, whereas if *Let the saga unfold* appears on its own . . . and so forth, rather like, *he caught a glimpse of himself in the long window, posing that night as the mirror as it were held up to nature, talking a blue streak, and wondered what after all was going on.* Are we ourselves? Do we exist? Is the divan oriented in an east-west alignment? Etcetera.

"Whatever else, they'll not be getting some condescendingly welcoming get-to-know session, but a real old-time in-at-the-deep-end read—which reminds me of almost my favorite line in the schoolboys' effort, the part where, banging out one of her dreadful columns on the old Corona, Kilgallen is swilling down the Rock and Rye and snaps 'Let 'em print *that!*' and the narrator lets us know in parenthesis 'They didn't.'

"And resonant on the Broadway Rialto, of which the Metropolitan was one attraction among the dozens, its peculiar patois adapting to the occasion of the Diamond Horseshoe, so you'd hear touts look in the paper and say, 'Hey, get a load of this broad singin' Carmen!' Which could only mean that Rise Stevens was for one reason or another other off it that night, and the picture was of either Jean Maderia or Belen Amparan."

"And speaking of the old days and the West, you went west in nineteen fifty-seven, at the end of that season."

"Yes, the season that was a lifetime—or seemed so."

"Your aunt Madge would've said the time got away from us."

"Just was. The *Just Was* chronicles. You know, 'Just was, my dear, I cut through Shubert Alley . . . etcetera.' What is wanted is what modern mathematics came up with: new methods for rapidly convergent iterations. The *seanachai* knew how. The old-told tale. As for narrative continuity beyond the certainty of syntax building space-time and revealing mastery of an existential judgment over hazards and conflicts."

"What of it?"

"Therefore, to such as complain to us of unconventional means, we reply, '*Us*, Sir Madam, what has it to do with *us*? We have a number of serious-minded acquaintances with children, one of whom comes to mind, Gwendolyn by name. No one with the least sympathy for the exquisite can possibly expect Gwendolyn, a girl raised with every advantage to enter into a compromising relationship with yet another best-selling mendacious female memoir, or to form an alliance with a thriller!' Of course you were, under the guise of State Department cultural envoy, giving stylish recitals in embassies and continuing to sing in code, a spy."

"Destinn bewitched me with tales of her daring exploits in espionage. My exploits weren't all that daring. Besides, I'd have done anything for Harry Truman, who was an absolute brick, as was Bess—and Margaret did have a voice, only the old nerves got to her *fiatto*."

"Dinner with Stalin wasn't all that daring?"

"Certainly not. He was terribly superstitious, and knew all about *Tosca*, and nobody ever told him I'd never gone near the part."

"So that was that."

"Yes, and so, thanks to Harry, and Carlton Smith, my control, I traveled the world, lived in luxurious embassy residences in some of the world's most beautiful cities, staffed with servants—nearly all local operatives in love with the idea of rising above their station to the dizzy height of postwar international intrigue, and consequently easily duped—picked up odd languages and idioms, always useful for singing fake lyrics not a soul in those audiences ever twigged to ... all very jolly, indeed, even if they wouldn't have me stopping at the Imperial when I went back to Vienna for Octavian—absolutely convinced I'd be taken into the cloak-and-dagger room and murdered by one or another of the defectors from either side incessantly criss-crossing the lobby. Espionage Grand Central Terminal the place was, absolutely.

*

Enter Moriarty (What The Shadow Knows).

That they there this night do not methodically etch, and unroll for display on the Sheraton oval table, in transparently schematic allegorical fashion, for their own lexical satisfaction or for the edification of others sorely in need of instruction in the refinements of close reading, their blueprints for a figment-sustainable biosphere. Rather they allow these to *appear*, self-drawn as if by a trick of animation, according to the designs of the latest and most erotic epistemological rage in the history of thought, self-similarity. Up to the second are they two, despite age, despite infirmity of any kind. Yes.

Thus do they begin to examine the labels on the many tapes turned in by those who originally made them—in an importantly true and poignant sense both the tapes and they themselves the engineers, for the sword cuts two ways or the weapon has a kickback, whichever way you care to look at the forensic details of the evidence so painstakingly assembled. Absolutely.

Our quondam protagonists review these tapes in the early hours of the morning, reacting strongly to the statement, *Had Mawrdew Czgowchwz not existed, it would have been necessary to—*

It vexes them, which slows things down. It begins to seem they might, neither of them, at the rate they're now going, last the night to tell of the end of the season alluded to, or of the birth of the twins Tristan and Jacob Beltane either. Their tale might well turn into *Tristram Shandy* unraveling on Jacob's ladder. They might not let it go until it blesses them, and it just might not.

Not, let it be hoped, that insufficient nights lie in the offing to come to the conclusion of things, but only time will tell, which of course is its own difficulty, for time can tell nothing that will not need to be revised, thus prolonging even further—

For in spite of the fact that she is, since the death of Margaret Hamilton, Gramercy Park's most celebrated resident, the fact is that Mawrdew Czgowchwz as a construct has all but ceased to exist. The person—thus represented heretofore as caught up in all those hieratic postures and aureoles of vague distress, how-are-ye, as presented in MNOPQR *STUVWXYZ*, regnant in a postwar New York of epochal opera nights, concerts, plays, art exhibitions, and literary dinner parties, in which love affairs and a mix of sensuous and intellectual attraction in general, whose brilliance, obscured by its redaction in newspapers and magazine gossip columns, early television coverage, and potboiler fiction brought into collision old-money aristocrats, writers, bankers, industrial magnates, theatricals, cabaret singers, opera stars, high-priced courtesans of all genders . . . all activities fertile ground for literary exploitation—was now determinedly present in the world merely as Maev Cohalen, the psychoanalyst known in the neighborhood of Gramercy Park for stopping and chatting up the mad in the streets.

Presenting some few quick notes on the dictates of form of which determined readers might wish to avail themselves.

CHRONICLE (the past)
APOCRYPHA (the *psst*)
GAZETTE (*modus vivendi*)
JOURNAL (*modus operandi*)
RECORDS (and tapes: particular of Saturday afternoon Met broadcasts and the intermission features: *Opera News on the Air, Opera Quiz*)
PROTOCOLS:
 dithyramb
 conversation
 epistle
 narration (manifesto)
SITES OF CONTESTATION (*loci*)
REGISTER (The Grammar of Motive)
PRINCIPALS
CHARACTER MEN
CHARACTER WOMEN
JUVENILES (*jeunes premiers*, ingenues, soubrettes)
COMPRIMARII
CHORUS
SUPERNUMERARIES
DANCERS
CHOREOGRAPHERS
ORCHESTRA

MAESTRI

PROMPTERS

STAGEHANDS

PASSING TRAMPS & THE CIGARETTES (passim) who sing in chorus the Ellington song: "Love is Like a Cigarette"

FURTHERMORE AND AT ISSUE:

Sense memory. For the woman who was Mawrdew Czgowchwz, the sea, the air, the Atlantic storms, the summer meadows, the flora and fauna, the incomparable skies and mythical vistas of Connemara. The environment of the Convent on the Rock and the associative sensations of communal life among women.

The concomitant elements of the landscape and environment of southern Bohemia, the convent in Prague and for The O'Maurigan, in place of the fabled madeleines, Attracta's barm brack & milk tea, at Poulaphouca in the County Mayo, Dugan's doughnuts, delivered fresh daily in wartime New York, Brown's Mixture/Stokes' Expectorant in the sickroom. On the radio: Hitler, Roosevelt, Pearl Harbor, Churchill, Big Ben, Edward R. Murrow, live from London (short wave), H. V. Kaltenborn, Gabriel Heater, Éamon de Valera's notorious and farcical "Comely Maidens" speech to the *Dail* in Dublin (short wave), Hiroshima.

EMOTIONAL RECALL (The Window of Opportunity)

STARTERS ORDERS: The Objective (the condition of music)

RELATED DOCUMENTS:

"Documents" is used herein in the broadest sense and includes all written, printed, graphic, or otherwise recorded matter, however produced or reproduced, including nonidentical copies, preliminary, intermediate, and final drafts, writings, records, and recordings of every kind and description, whether inscribed by hand or by mechanical, electronic, photographic, or other means, as well as phonic (such as tape recordings) or visual reproductions of all statements, conversations, or events, and including without limitation, abstracts, address books, advertising material; agreements; analyses of any kind; appointment books, desk calendars, diagrams, diaries, directories, discs; drawings of any type; estimates, evaluations, financial statements or calculations; graphs, guidelines; house organs or publications (e.g., fanzines); instructions, interoffice communications; invoices; job descriptions; ledgers; letters; licenses; lists (including *The List*); manuals; maps; memoranda of any type (no matter how ambiguous, one through seven); microfilm; minutes; motion pictures; notebooks; opinions; organization charts; pamphlets; permits; photographs; pictures; plans; projections; promotional materials; publications; purchase orders; schedules; specifications; standards; statistical analyses; stenographers' notebooks; studies of any kind; summaries; tabulations; tapes; telegrams: teletype messages; videotapes; vouchers; working drawings, papers and files.

Also crossword puzzles, encryption by musical notation, Scrabble and, as already indicated, TzimTzum—and why not, since the poet has already brought him up, hoary old Aristotle's grammar of poetical composition.

As, to take an example, in the citing of the names of certain lunar *maria*—which the poet, unable to continue with the recitation of an early poem, cannot this night, due to age and disremembering summon up—to the, as it were, authentication of the features of the face of the man in the moon.

We, of course, can easily summon them—technology to the fore. It takes a remarkably short time to call up the very map of the moon that's in it, and to discover that the *maria*, the "seas" in question are: the Mare Serenetatis, the Mare Tranquilitatis, the Mare Imbrium, the Mare Vaporum, the Mare Cognitum, the Mare Nubium, and the Mare Humorum. As to the elaboration of the conceit of the voyages across these seas of the moon, they constitute the weaker part of the original poem, later revised, and need not concern the reader perhaps already disposed to look at our poet and his efforts in a kindly light.

In any case everything had shattered and new things had to be made out of fragments. Sense memory, emotional recall, the rear window of opportunity, predesignated alibis, epitomized by the prevalence in those days of both exquisite matte and awkward stock footage back projection. Receding silhouettes clambering out of the way of agents in hot pursuit, their capture leading to debriefings highlighted by frank and unforced exchanges of views —of which there are a great many in a free society.

An unstable mix of elements drawn from a time of unprecedented terror turned into one of unprecedented triumph and made to conform to formulas that varied greatly according to the inventors, from the firebrand mother and the metaphysical father to Kathleen Ni Houlihan, to the Blue Nuns and Madame Destinnova, to the Prague Linguistic Circle, to Hitler, Stalin, Churchill, Roosevelt, Truman, Masaryk, and the Dulleses, to Reynaldo Hahn and the Paris Opera, to Edward Johnson, Rudolph Bing, and the Metropolitan, to La Scala, Covent Garden, Carnegie Hall, and its studios, to Orphrey Whither and to the very contingencies of invention itself.

Moreover the difficulty greatly increases when we attempt the fuller view of transparency, a view that recognizes the decreasing visibility of what we look through as an inevitable function of our increasing clarity of vision through it, acknowledging the paradox of dialogical knowledge . . . and much else besides.

Therefore? Reduce everything to binaries, the better to analyze the double-edged conception of transparency, at once enabling and thwarting, emblematic of the dialectical motion of the need to know.

They will sit up through the night, as the tale unfolds, and what they will discuss is the problem of being as it were characters in a book and then setting out to find the authors of that book and finding them. The question of Other Voices, Other Rooms arises, and yet there's only ever one room, the one one's in. People build multiroomed, labyrinthine castles on the ground and inhabit them vainly—the only place to build a castle is in the air—if one is sitting in a room reading, one is in other rooms, too—one has achieved the long-promised bilocality of the glorified body.

The O'Maurigan himself is much taken up and ever was with the classical theme of *nostoi*, composed of those ballads of The Return that have for millennia in all language systems gone into the making of the epic, and consequently with the enervating phenomenon of the echo. The echo is not the effect of the voice nor is the voice the cause of the echo. The echo is *made evident* through the *medium* of the resonator; it must be *accommodated*. Which brings the delvers into the question of precedents and suspected causes to the immemorial Greek and Irish topos of hospitality—to the absolute obligation of welcoming, sheltering, and protecting the stranger, with no understanding of the stranger's intentions.

To investigate so far as they could tell, everything that was the case: the world: that world. (The past another country, undiscovered as of now, and. They become again now voyagers.)

The O'Maurigan's conversation was ever characterized by the cross section, by his of a sudden cutting into and across the matter of a conversation with startling, eccentric commentary, and this from nearly the first instance of speech.

In later years, while others engaged in horizontal conversation on given subjects in the Hibernian manner, he would quite suddenly *list points* in rapid succession, all on the vertical. These would cut through the often tangled matter like Alexander's sword through the Gordian knot, on foot of which he quickly acquired the reputation of being difficult—with the upshot that he began to remark quite insistently on his not being listened to (but then would you?), said condition leading quite naturally to feelings of isolation and the curious habit of never taking off the watch his father had given him, the one with two separate dials, one set for Ireland and the other for his birth place, New York.

As they have said, everybody smoked back then. Everybody smoked and drank and sang and danced, and so it was only inevitable that when seeking to characterize his chorus of Other Voices, he would name them The Cigarettes, and assign them by way of the strophic ode, the song most suited, one popular at the time, from the collective pen of Duke Ellington and company, "Love is Like a Cigarette."

"If they weren't lighting cigarettes," she remarked, "they were lighting candles."

"Yes," the once-young lord replied, "to the Infant of Prague."

There's no question—they live in mourning for a greater time. They are increasingly beset by the sense of anxiety at the mere thought of opening the book of evidence and inching along through the endless store accumulated in the course—of the years. Anxiety of confluence. And of the crossword puzzle.

Sad that—*aber was man nicht erfliegen kann, muss man erhinken.*

To illustrate: the idea of a Crossword Puzzle Explication Language Event, inconclusive at best, for language bends not happily to man's will.

THERE	WAS	A	TIME	TIME	OUT	OF MIND
WHEN	THE	CULT		WAS	OF	THE
OPERATIVE						
IN		THE	SHADOW	OF		TIMES
BUILDING			ACROSS			
OF	IN					
THE	SHADOW	OF	FELL	EVENTS	THAT	CASES
THAT			ON			
PRIOR	OF		AND			
OF	AND	ALSO		TO		WERE
CONCLUSIONS	RECORDED					
	KEN			EVERYTHING		
	THE	FOR		OVER TO		IN
THROUGH	AGES					
	WHYEVER		THEM	THE	IT	WHICH
TIME						

AND OF THE WORLD
TELEGRAM OF
DESTINY OUT
WITH ALL AND
MERRY OF
INTENT SOULS SUN
PRANKSTER MIND
JOURNAL
AMERICAN
NEWS
MIRROR
POST
AND
BROOKLYN EAGLE

Or to take the example of the plan stated in dialogue.

"SO TO BEGIN AT THE BEGINNING ALIKE
OF THE STORY
TO BEGIN WITH WHICH IDEA AT FIRST TIME
UPON
BEGIN AND END TOGETHER THAT IN
THEIR STORY
END OF THEIR POINT THEIR
TIME WHEN
IT STORIES IN QUEST
WAS ALL ALL CONTRACT TIME
TIME A
INTO
OFF STORY
ONE
OUT DOES

STORY

OF IS

THE POINT

TO

THE

CONCLUSION

THAT

IS

NO

CONCLUSION

AT

ALL

AND ITS SOLEMN TELLING."

FURTHER

ALONG

THE

SORROW

OF

LOST

LOVE

In sum, therefore, it goes like this. *No circumstance of importance from beginning to end of the disclosure shall be relayed on hearsay evidence. When the writer of these introductory lines*—perforce thrust upon us—*happens to be more closely connected than others*—and therefore must perforce declare an interest—*with the incidents to be recorded, he will retire from the position of narrator; and his task will be continued, from the point at which he has left it off, by other persons who can speak of the circumstances under notice*—accidental and deliberately contrived—*from their own knowledge, just as clearly and positively as it has been spoken before them,* period.

*

"We cannot assume that same cavalier dispensation in the pursuit of the essential truth, not if we are to be archived and sent to dwell in marble halls, the Library of Congress for example, where both documentation and the dictates of form are held in high esteem."

"The dictates of form, the man said. The dictates of form, I'm afraid, are going to have to suffer, as we did. If lives fall apart, and they do, there is no reason stories based on them and written down should not do likewise. The elements out of which the so-called Mawrdew Czgowchwz Saga was engendered were by any fair measure an unstable mix, and she herself a phantom, a ghost in her own story."

"And you yourself were once the woman in white, though not in moonlight on Hampstead Heath.

"Nor was I ever what you might call a bride."

"Only of Bluebeard. No, in recollection, one sees winter white, at a Metropolitan Opera press conference. And although the sophisticated modern reader has no time whatever for the Victorian novelist's habit of describing in minute detail the costumes characters wear, that outfit was a knockout and sticks in the mind like an apparition. White satin suit, white silk turban, white fox stole—a knockout.

"The entire structure of the languages we use—the syntactical arrangement of the parts of speech, punctuation, the subjunctive—the familiar grammatical constructions—it now appears are nothing, alas, but taxonomic artifacts, useful for informal description perhaps, but so far as theoretical standing goes null and void."

"And singing isn't in such great shape either. This place does look like a room of the Archives in the Karmelitska—like everything else in Prague, absolutely outside time."

Let the saga unfold.

II

As the H.M.S. *Queen Mary*, having sailed at noon from Pier 44 North River, at the foot of Forty-second Street (in the wake of such exuberant and strenuous festivities as characterized embarkations in those last years of transatlantic passenger traffic), had continued her stately progress downriver through the Narrows and out into the North Atlantic, Ralph, Alice, and the remaining Secret Seven had headed over to Fortieth Street and Seventh Avenue to the Burger Ranch to compose themselves, only to be met with news of the startling events under way just then down the block and around the corner on Broadway, where, stacked under the marquee up against the closed front doors of the Metropolitan Opera House's main marquee entrance, cord-bound reams of some sort of publication were being scissored open, under no apparent supervision, by local office workers on their lunch hours. Right then and there, from under the counter, the stalwart waitress Rhoe, mainstay of backstage information gathering and supervision, handed the newcomers on the scene copies of the document in question, something called MNOPQR *STUVWXYZ*. They had all experienced the self-same reaction: none.

"Irving is climbing up the stairs of the BMT at seven as usual to come open the place up and notices these two kids, maybe sixteen or seventeen, but they would not, says he, get served at Bill's, unloading bundles from the rumble seat of he thinks about a ten-year-old or so Ford jalopy. 'You know,' says he, 'like the one in the Archie comics?' End of story, apparently, only not exactly."

"Complications, Rhoe?" The O'Maurigan asked.

"You could say that—here, go sit down and read this."

THERE WAS A TIME TIME OUT OF MIND IN THE SEMPITERNAL PROGRESS OF ITAL DIVADIENST AT THAT SUSPENSORY PAUSE JUST PRIOR TO THE ADVENT OF WHAT CAME TO BE KNOWN AS MNOPQR-

DOLATRY OR IN CERTAIN QUARTERS ITAL STUVWXYZCHINA WHEN THE CULT OF NIRVANA MORI FLOURISHED IN THE HOTHOUSE AMBIENCE OF THE CROSSROADS CAFE ON 42ND STREET ACROSS BROADWAY FROM THE VERY HOTEL WHERE IN THE GREAT DAYS CARUSO HAD IN SOMETHING LIKE THE SACRAMENTAL SENSE RECEIVED DESTINN WHOSE PALMY LOBBY ONCE ORMOLU MARBLE AND VELVET HAD BEEN TRANSFORMED INTO A VAST DRUGSTORE AND WHERE LATELY IN CARUSOS SUITE A PODIATRIST INSTALLED STOP THERE AT THE CROSSROADS CAFE IN THE SHADOW OF THE TIMES BUILDING NOVEMBER TO NOVEMBER FOR MORI WAS A DEAD CENTER SCORPIO THE GREAT WORLDS RAW CONCERNS WERE FLATLY IGNORED

In next to no time, while the others continued silently scrutinizing the brazen text, The O'Maurigan had risen without a word and, as Rhoe later remarked, seemingly floated out the door, bound for the Western Union office a block away on Broadway to order its entire contents telegraphed shore-to-ship to the outbound vessel. This, whatever it was or might turn out to be, must Mawrdew Czgowchwz and Jacob Beltane be made aware of before the *Mary* had cleared the channel between the islands of Nantucket and Manitoy, passing over the grave of the *Andrea Doria*, for having read only pages one and two he had gone into the state it is said editors share with fishermen and lovers, one in this instance, however, more than just tinged with that particular sense of the uncanny he had only ever experienced at home, at Poulaphouca, in the Barony of Tirawly, on the north Mayo coast, when out walking he would ever as instructed give decent berth to the whitethorn trees—the *scriabh*—and to the many ancient and mysterious mounds called fairy forts no farmer in his senses would disturb for tillage or sheep or cattle either for idle grazing, for the beasts had sense as well as their keepers, for the Other Crowd, the Good People had their ways of taunting mortals: the wild sounds of their piping and their singing and the ghostly lights seen time and again in the dead of night by walkers along the boreens, but never so far as ever he'd heard by leaving haunted scripture on the doorstop to be read of an early morning.

*

THERE WAS A TIME TIME OUT OF MIND IN THE SEMPITERNAL PROGRESS OF ITAL DIVADIENST AT THAT SUSPENSORY PAUSE JUST PRIOR TO THE ADVENT OF WHAT CAME TO BE KNOWN AS MNOPQR-DOLATRY OR IN CERTAIN QUARTERS ITAL STUVWXYZCHINA WHEN THE CULT OF NIRVANA MORI FLOURISHED IN THE HOTHOUSE AMBIENCE OF THE CROSSROADS CAFE ON 42ND STREET ACROSS BROADWAY FROM THE VERY HOTEL WHERE IN THE GREAT DAYS CARUSO HAD IN SOME-THING LIKE THE SACRAMENTAL SENSE RECEIVED DESTINN WHOSE PALMY LOBBY ONCE ORMOLU MARBLE AND VELVET HAD BEEN TRANS-FORMED INTO A VAST DRUGSTORE AND WHERE LATELY IN CARUSOS SUITE A PODIATRIST INSTALLED STOP THERE AT THE CROSSROADS CAFE IN THE SHADOW OF THE TIMES BUILDING NOVEMBER TO NO-VEMBER FOR MORI WAS A DEAD CENTER SCORPIO THE GREAT WORLDS RAW CONCERNS WERE FLATLY IGNORED

As the strange dispatch from shore came up word by word and line by line on the ship's teletype, its plot thickened like toiling muscle in corded loops, rendering more and more vivid the characters of the real-life melodrama asleep above deck. (The ship's operator thought, yes, it, too, has the look of epic poetry, appearing as it emerges to be writing itself—giving rise in his mind [just then distracted from his absorbing game of solitaire, his long night's reading of *The Search for Bridey Murphy*, and his work in progress, a new translation of the *Aeneid* into Morse code and cast, as it were, on the high seas alongside the H.M.S. *Queen Mary*] to the old word *marconigram*, and the romance it—)

The Watchman would read it through the night (the first night out) and only in the morning—or whenever they awakened—see it delivered to Mawrdew Czgowchwz and her consort, Jacob Beltane, the matter of whose unfolding legend it discoursed upon (a legend that—owing not merely to the quality of its chief protagonists' vocal endowment and musical art, but quite as much, the radio operator opined, to their genius for relating to the press, for being photographed beyond exceptionally well, and for embodying something very dear to the hearts of Americans, residence in a great hotel: the dream emblem of a rich, carefree high bohemian life—becomes the stuff of tabloid journalism in New York on a scale fairly eclipsing the bewildering saga of the courtship and wedding of the millionaire Philadelphia bricklayer's beautiful blonde Oscar-winning daughter by the runty crowned-head croupier from the French Riviera, the detonation by the triumphalist archons of the imperial American republic of the first hydrogen bomb in the South Pacific, the Egyptian seizure of the Suez Canal, and the sinking by collision with the *Stockholm* of the *Andrea Doria* in that notorious corridor—a graveyard of lost ships—between the islands of Manitoy and Nantucket).

Sempiternal progress of Divadienst. The radio operator found the phrase evocative and deserving of commitment to memory.

Politics the contest between what is right and who is charming.

Immutable. The last year before the war—and the onset of events, the Watchman thought, hallmarked by catastrophes of a magnitude theretofore depicted only in demonology and in the Book of Revelation, catastrophes that changed the world forever, events whose terror may have rendered finally insupportable the very idea of salvific legends, of the stringent precepts of the Religion of Aesthetics, of philosophy, and of all enterprise but the immediate. All good things must come to an end, including, presumably Western Civilization, pack up all its care and woe there it goes moanin' low blackbird bye-bye.

And in order to get all that in, as well as tell a coherent story, he thought it would certainly help to give a more direct and exact account of the relationships among the characters in what had, indeed, become The Mawrdew Czgowchwz Saga, and the circumstances in which they were all found at the beginning of what had become their story . . . but he had other things to do in the world, in fact on board the very ship in question, and the first of them was to get the dispatch together and have it delivered to those he knew to be the principal players, lolling now in their flowered bower.

Funny that. When the cabin boy, summoned to deliver the cablegram, had returned all agog at the quantity of the blooms, the radio operator had told an old Sophie Tucker joke ("Ernie sent me a dozen roses again tonight. Y' know what that means, don't-cha: I'll have my legs up in the air till morning." "What, ya ain't got a *vase*?") The lad had blushed to the roots of his golden hair. Who did he think they were in there then, St. Mary the Virgin and John the Divine?

*

FROM FOOL TO FOOL STOP THE NIRVANA PRINCIPLE IF NOT SO WHAT NOW HELD SWAY STOP MORI DISCS OUTSOLD THOSE OF HER EVERY RIVAL AT MACYS AT THE GRAMOPHONE SHOP ON MULBERRY AND MOTT AND WITH SOME DEGREE OF EXACTITUDE COULD THE PARTISAN CRITIC FRANCOBOLLI SPEAK OF THE SEEMINGLY ENDLESS MORI ERA STOP IT ENDED STOP TIME TOLD ON NIRVANA MORI WHENCE ITAL THE MORIAD TOOK TURN FOR THE TRAGIC THOUGHT BETTER OF THE ROUTE AND DEVOLVED INTO NEAR FARCE STOP A CONTRETEMPS ABSOLUTE IN ITS DICTATORIAL SEVERITY BESET ITAL I MORIBUNDI STOP THE WALLS FELL FROM THE FANTASY TEMPLE OF ITAL NIRVANA LULTIMA STOP MNOPQR STUVWXYZ HAD COME TO TOWN STOP MNOPQR STUVWXYZ BECAME THE DIVA OF THE MOMENT AND THE MOMENT WENT ON STOP SHE GAVE A NEW MEANING TO PRESENCE BECOMING AS HALCYON PARANOY DECREED QUOTE OF THE MOMENT ITS LIFE ITS PERSONA EMBLEMATICA ITSELF STOP

Events nevertheless that had brought to New York, and finally to the attention of the Congress (which had awarded her by proclamation American citizenship), the politically and artistically controversial Mawrdew Czgowchwz, there to become the nucleus of a certain group of stylish, talented, and driven refugees.

MNOPQR *STUVWXYZ*: rather a tired sight gag. Everybody—at least everybody who read any one of the seven major dailies—knew that Mawrdew Czgowchwz was pronounced "Mardu Gorgeous" even if Winchell said the name in print looked like "a Polish eye-chart" (showing himself up as slipping, for everybody knew she'd come in highly dramatic circumstances from Prague, and that there was a Cold War aura about her that made her story more interesting than rivalry at the opera. *Nirvana Mori*, however, for Morgana Neri, he thought wasn't bad. The dispatch must be some sort of elaborate (unimaginably costly) shivaree contrived by the diva's more worldly intimates in New York—modern equivalent of the old custom of rattling pots and pans, whistling, coon shouting, and jumping up and down beneath newlyweds' bedroom windows—like in *Oklahoma!* After all, Mawrdew Czgowchwz was not only Czech, but Irish, so between the customs of Central Europe and those of the Emerald Isle (as for example pictured in John Ford's *The Quiet Man*) . . . but the diva and her companion, were at the moment perhaps the world's most glamorous adulterers. The dispatch therefore must be the sophisticated New Yorkers' notion of a shivaree for glamorous adulterers—and most probably contained not only a concise and ribald account of the primary narrative—the meeting and mating of Mawrdew Czgowchwz and Jacob Beltane—but also other layers of expanded versions of different aspects, historigraphic, political, aesthetic, religious: of all different aspects of the controversial argument—self-contained units feeding into the top-line narrative. And beneath *those*, as intricately woven a set of marginalia, footnotes, and splices off the cutting-room floor culled for their pedagogic value for the coming generations world without end amen.

SHE WEDDED MUSIC TO MIMICRY TO CREATE MUSICRY STOP SHE WAS THE DEFINITIVE DIVA STOP SHE STILL IS STOP HER PICTURE WAS ON EVERY FRONT PAGE THAT WEEK JUST PRIOR TO THE VERNAL EQUINOX THE FULL MOON AND THE EARLIEST EASTER THERE COULD BE STOP THE ITAL TIMES SPREAD FOUR COLUMNS ACROSS FEATURED HER AS OCTAVIAN BEARING THE SILVER ROSE STOP PARAGRAPH NEW YORK MARCH 17TH QUOTE THE RENOWNED CZECH FALCON CONTRALTO MNOPQR STUVWXYZ LANDED AT MIDNIGHT FROM ROME AT IDLEWILD AIRPORT TO BE MET BY A CROWD OF SOME FOUR THOUSAND PERSONS A SCANT DAY PRIOR TO HER FIRST APPEARANCE OF THE SEASON AT THE METROPOLITAN TONIGHT STOP MISS STUVWXYZS PUBLIC FEUD WITH THE MET MANAGEMENT WAS SETTLED AMICABLY LAST WEEKEND IN THE WAKE OF A HUNGER STRIKE IN WHICH MANY HUNDREDS TOOK

PART AND WHICH RESULTED IN A TWO WEEK SIT DOWN DEMONSTRATION ALONG

(Knew, too, that at that epochal airport press conference, Mawrdew Czgowchwz—a famously temperamental mezzo-soprano, returned to the Metropolitan Opera to sing Verdi's Violetta—told the world what *oltrano* signified: a singing voice beyond existing categories, quantum companion to a temperament beyond tendency.)

BROADWAY STOP THE SETTLEMENT EFFECTED MISS STUVWXYZ HAS DECREED THAT QUOTE ALL IS FORGIVEN STOP ADDITION THE DIVA HAS MADE THE STARTLING ANNOUNCEMENT THAT SHE NOW FEELS READY TO MOVE INTO A NEW VOCAL CATEGORY THAT OF DRAMATIC SOPRANO DAGILTA.

(Tired of singing, as the saying went, witches, bitches, and boys.)

MISS STUVWXYZ HAS COINED A NEW VOCAL CATEGORY WHICH SHE CALLS THE OLTRANO STOP EXPLAINING THE MOVE IN HER PRESS CONFERENCE EARLY TODAY SHE ANNOUNCED QUOTE I AM NEARING MY 40TH YEAR STOP I WILL THIS YEAR COMMENCING TONIGHT WITH VIOLETTA SING 40 ROLES HERE AND THERE STOP THE REMAINING ROLES ARE

As the teletype dispatch lengthened far beyond any previous such communication in his experience, narrating in what the Watchman considered a somewhat frenzied way the events leading up to Mawrdew Czgowchwz's singing Violetta at the Metropolitan, he returned to his reading of *The Search for Bridey Murphy*, keeping one eye, like a crocodile napping in the Nilotic mud, on the progress of the amazing tale. But how reliable could the account really be, he wondered (having always longed for knowledge of the truth). Hadn't a woman writer herself declared women impossible to write about because their lives were full of secrets?

Wasn't Literature clarifying enough—and who, for instance, could Mawrdew Czgowchwz have been in a previous appearance—except perhaps one of the truly historical characters she's portrayed. Dido—but was Dido truly historical? Was the *hysterical* Pharaonic princess Amneris? Or, considering the big splash she made at the Metropolitan, the historical Iseult? Or another Irish legend—but no, she probably could not have been her own mother, the role she's on her way to Ireland to play on the screen. Unless that when a body's mother dies in childhood, as this Mawrdew Czgowchwz–Maev Cohalen's mother, Great Flaming Maev Cohalen did, would there be time to . . . clearly a metaphysical question. No relation to the fact of life as we . . . oh, here comes more.

IT HAD ALL BEGUN AT AND IN A CERTAIN PLACE AND TIME AS PARANOY WAS TO REVEAL IN ITAL THE STUVWXYZ MOMENT BUT WAITING FOR STUVWXYZ WAS QUITE OUTSIDE HISTORY THE THIRTY FIFTH DAY OF THE THIRTEENTH MONTH OF THE SEVENTH SEASON STOP LATER SEASONS THEY WOULD COME TO CHRONICLE SEASONS INFORMED BY EACH AND EVERY TIME THAT SHE HERSELF ITAL STESSA WOULD MOUNT THE BOARDS MADE UP FROM DIVERSE PAINT POTS AT A MAKEUP TABLE MIRROR RINGED IN MERCILESS BULBS ABLAZE AND HEAP ON MUSIC A VARIETY OF DISGUISES NONE OF WHICH COULD HOPE TO EQUAL OR OBSCURE WHAT SHE WAS IN HER IMMUTABLE SELF STOP SO MANY TIMES STUVWXYZ THE SQUARE AND OR THE CUBE ROOT OF STUVWXYZ OR STUVWXYZ TO THIS POWER OR THAT WAS STILL STUVWXYZ AS IS THE NUMBER ONE AND STUVWXYZ OVER STUVWXYZ FIGURED TO SHAZAAM IN A TUNNEL OF ELECTRIC STUVWXYZ MIRRORS WAS BUT STUVWXYZ STOP

More metaphysics. However, for the Catholics the soul is already in the child alive in the womb—however it is they'd know, what with the pope a man. Course they do say one time and one time only the pope was a woman—cause of the hole cut now in the chair they carry the old wop around in. Not just so he can take a crap on St. Peter's bones whenever he feels the urge, but so if it should have to be proven to the likes of say another Mussolini that he's an anatomical man, some official could reach up through the hole and palm His Holiness's low hangers. Probably also why he's always got to be Italian come to think of it. Interesting question: who is canonically entitled to grope the pope? His confessor Coglioni? His housekeeper, the German nun? Or some angel, likely some archangel? The archangel Gabriel, or Raphael perhaps: he's the doctor. Except angels are metaphysical—hence the head of the pin that's their dance floor, and the question of its capacity. But if the pope was even once in history a woman, then of course that's who Mawrdew Czgowchwz must have been.

What do the Hindus say? Could maybe be that swami who came on board two feet off the gangplank giggling at everybody like Liberace . . . or one of his retinue—their luggage through-checked to Benares. They're all booked on the train to London, the out east of Suez—but not through the canal—the Egyptians have seized it—via Cape Town on the P&O.

Ah, here comes more.

IN THE LATE SUMMER OF 1947 ALPHA HAD RETURNED FROM A LOFT PARTY ON LOWER SEVENTH AVENUE FED UP LOOKING IN ONE OF HIS NOW INCREASINGLY SHARP MOODS IF NOT FOR TROUBLE IF NOT FOR FURTHER TUTELAGE IN THE HARD WAY THEN AT LEAST FOR DOT DOT DOT STOP FLIPPING ON HIS PREWAR BAKELITE PHILCO TO SEEK SWEET SOLACE FROM THE PREDAWN FM AIRWAVES HE CAUGHT A CLEAR TRANSCRIPTION OF THE PRAGUE FESTIVAL GALA PERFORMANCE FROM MIDSUMMER NIGHT STOP LESS THAN AN HOUR LATER HE CAME RANTING THROUGH THE HEAT UNDER THE DOG STAR TO THE DOOR OF A CERTAIN BROWNSTONE KIBBUTZ ON ST MARKS PLACE CARRYING A PAPERBASED TAPE IN BOTH HANDS AS IF IT WERE A LIVING THING STOP SITTING DOWN HE LIT TWO CIGARETTES STOP NONE WHO RECEIVED HIM HAD BEEN PREPARED FOR THE SUBLIME ALL BEING TOGETHER IN BED STOP IT HAD TO BE HEARD STOP

Alpha at his radio. He was like me: it had to be heard, he told them all—in bed together on St. Marks Place. The voice of this Mnopqr Stuvwxyz had to be heard—as if he were insisting that unless and until it was heard by them, the Secret Seven, it wouldn't be heard by the world and its mother, in bed together, asleep. The world as if unborn to this Mnopqr Stuvwxyz.

They would hear it and so give birth to her legend, as she would give birth to them, rearing them *presto* to be the *Stuvwzyzski Strelsi*—urban agitprop militants, packing rods. Alpha, their capo, as both gunman and angel—maybe the angel Raphael, physician to their ills. After all . . . all in bed together; must all have had a bad flu—*la grippe* . . . something dire. Even if it was all allegory or what have you.

And since one is the first on board to be reading this, one, too, is a kind of—only there had best be no plan to burst in on them together in bed, whether they are ready for the sublime, not ready, or have long since got used to it. I shall send a cabin boy—that angelic-looking Billy Budd type.

At all events, that *Traviata* televised—and the onstage party following were better than Literature—temporarily. She-Who-Must-Be-Obeyed dancing with everybody and being overheard, then disappearing to the dressing room whilst the party roared on. By that time all of New York had crashed the thing and the third-stream crowd had taken over the band—and what else could one expect with Gunther Schuller playing oboe in the Met orchestra. They brought the morning papers to her in her loge. She stayed sequestered for the longest time, presumably reading—but who knew? At any rate, she stayed, surely aware of them.

THE LATE CITY FRONT PAGE RAVE REVIEWS STOP MUSING ON THE INSTANT AND RELENTLESS TRANSMUTATION OF GESTURE INTO REPORT SHE GATHERED HERSELF TO HERSELF AND TAKING A NOSEGAY OF SLIPPER ORCHIDS FROM A BOX AMONG THE DOZENS STREWN ABOUT THE ROOM WALKED DREAMILY TO THE STAGE STOP THEN ORDERING THE HUGE BACK WALL SCENE DOORS OPENED TO THE DAWN SHE TURNED TO THE ENCHANTED THRONG AS THE RIVERDAMP DRAFT SWEPT IN AND THE FIRST FULL SILENCE SINCE JUST BEFORE MIDNIGHT FELL OVER THE AUDITORIUM STOP SINGING QUOTE ITAL LALBA SEPARA DALLA LUCE LOMBRA WITH QUOTE BILITIS AT THE PIANO SHE CALLED THE EVENING OVER STOP THEN WRAPPED IN GRAY CHINCHILLA SHE WALKED WITHOUT FURTHER CEREMONY OUT THE GREAT WIDE GAP IN THE OPERA HOUSE WALL AND UP SEVENTH AVENUE

THROUGH THE ALL BUT DESERTED RIALTO ALONE FOLLOWED AT A DISTANCE BY HER RETAINERS LIKE A STAR STOP

"Bilitis." Dame Sibyl Farewell-Tarnysh of course. Bold. Followed by her retainers. Like the swami, but not two feet off the gangplank, but on the level. If the retainers were two feet off the sidewalk, she was not. Of course she's a Taurus and she hit her peak that night. Some said she angered the gods—that what befell, the reversal of good fortune, was a foregone conclusion—not that anything has been concluded. On the contrary it seems the story's just getting off the ground—or at any rate out of ship's berth. Now voyagers sail thou forth to seek and find.

NINE MONTHS LATER IN THE SAME YEAR OF THE QUOTE OLTRANO ITAL TRAVIATA TRIUMPH SOME FEW .WEEKS AFTER WHAT BECAME SO WELL RECALLED AS MORIS LAST NOVEMBER MNOPQR STUVWXYZ HAVING SUNG THOSE 40 ROLES RETURNED TO HER NEW YORK TO DO HER SEASON OPENING IN YET ANOTHER FIRST ATTEMPT ISOLDE STOP THE WHEEL HAD COME ANOTHER FULL CIRCLE STOP ALL OVER GOTHAM PREPARATIONS FOR THE SOLSTICE FOR THE NEW PRODUCTION OF ITAL TRISTAN UND ISOLDE FOR SMART SOCIETY FETES YULETIDE SHOWBIZ COCKTAIL BASHES AND FOR ANOTHER YEAR OF THE CENTURY OF TOTAL WAR TOOK ON THE STUDIED HIERATIC TONE CHARACTERISTIC OF ELEGANT SECULAR PAGEANTRY STOP AS THE TOWN HIBERNAL WAKE COMMENCED TO END IN THE FALL AT THE NEW YEAR OF THE GREAT WHITE BALL ON THE GREAT WHITE WAY MNOPQR STUVWXYZ REMAINED CLOISTERED AT THE PLAZA SECURE IN HER TOWER SUITE STOP

But not secure enough after all for the Neriacs or for their confederates at the opera house not to impinge, and more. Mawrdew Czgowchwz had neglected to take into account the obvious fact that the linked chain of gala events her life had become in New York must contain that standard social-column extra, the crasher. Had she known her metaphors as well as her operas, she'd have realized there's always a witch on the waterfront to fuck up the gradient masked ball. And had she not thought of it, her protectors ought to have known the possible outcomes of making old Neri an object of ridicule—freely passing out their cracks on the Met Standing Room Line the way vegetarians, Trotskyites, and Jehovah's Witnesses did their tracts and screeds—but nobody did, and thereby hung the treacherous tale.

In sum, when the Neriacs decided that the heinous calumny known as the *Nericon*, made up over the telephone by that or those one or ones lately revealed as the author or authors of this MNOPQR STUVWXYZ thing, had embarrassed their goddess into premature retirement, and therefore in vengeance set out to do voodoo on Mawrdew Czgowchwz, the Czogowchwzians should have been aware, but, like the benighted captain and crew of the *Andrea Doria* ... well, it hadn't come to that, but hell hath no fury like demented Italian priestesses of a diva scorned, and, mind you, more may yet be revealed.

Odd that—*Un Ballo in Maschera* takes place in Stockholm and the *Andrea Doria* was sunk by the *Stockholm*. Or it takes place in Boston, and the ship was sunk off the coast near Boston. So what—anybody who thought about it would know, too, that Mawrdew Czgowchwz, who always wore her own hair onstage, would be particularly vulnerable—but nobody thought about it except paranoid schizophrenics in regression getting messages from the control tower at Idlewild or the Empire State Building television antenna—and they were too busy hearing Trotsky was still alive, working as a janitor in the opera house in Mexico City, or Jesus Christ was coming back to earth, born again of a virgin but this time instead of in Bethlehem, a suburb of Jerusalem, in Scarsdale, a suburb of New York City. Especially since Mawrdew Czgowchwz was singing Isolde, a witch, and so they, The Neriacs got some hag stooge to sneak onstage while Mawrdew Czgowchwz was being positioned on deck for the first act of *Tristan*, clip a lock of her flaming red hair, and bring it downtown to Hester Street, near enough to the East River waterfront, while the performance was in progress.

My word, I do hope she's safe on board with us. She must be, really, to the extent any of us is. Been a nervous time this, in the North Atlantic, what with hysterical Italians piloting liners like dodge-ems on the Autostrada. Give anyone the jitters.

OLD MALA CENERE SAT AT HER VERY OLD MOTHERS IMMENSE KITCHEN TABLE RAGING IN OBSCENE SICILIAN AND DRESSING A SMALL HEADLESS POPPET IN SOILED REMNANTS OF RAG CLOTH BUNTING STRIPPED OFF STALLS AT THE PREVIOUS SUMMERS SAN GENNARO STREET FAIR STOP A FACELESS HEAD FASHIONED FROM A DIRTY OLD NYLON STOCKING STUFFED WITH URINE SOAKED SHREDS OF THE SAME DAYS ITAL DAILY MIRROR FEATURING PICTURES AND COMMENTARY ON THE NEW ITAL TRISTAN ON MNOPQR STUVWXYZ AND THE MET STANDING ROOM LINE SAT GROTESQUELY DISPROPORTIONATE ATOP THE TIN BREADBOX NEARLY COVERING THE FOUR MEDALLION PORTRAITS OF MUSSOLINI THE SACRED HEART THE MADONNA AND POPE PIUS XI PAINTED ON THE SLIDING LID STOP THE GRIM CURSE OF THE CENERE QUOTE A TE DALL ABISSO LA MALA SANTANATALE QUOTE ERUPTED HEADING A LITANY OF VILE INVERSIONS STOP

"Wittgenstein said what we must do is lifelong battle against the bewitchment of language."

"You know this thing about my being typically English, is really—"

"Absolute rubbish?"

"Crap."

"Better yet—American style."

"The Mars-Beltanes certainly spoke the language—and sang it, too—"

"But were never English—even by marriage."

"Not even by—are you bringing up marriage?"

"No, for fear my dinner decides to come right behind it."

"Feeling seasick?"

"No, not at all."

*

The sun had set. The waves broke upon the sands of the beach at Coney Island, deserted in the late September twilight but for a few lonely walkers each a world unto himself, none paired with a companion.

In the Main Reading Room of the New York Public Library at Forty-second

Street, the while the gray stone lions crouched sentinel on either side of the grand staircase on Fifth Avenue, The O'Maurigan put down the manuscript of MNOPQR *STUVWXYZ*, having just read the section in which

They lay together laughing. He had just returned to the loft on Twenty-eighth Street with an array of late-edition newspapers (he wished to learn the town's ways), and together they'd discovered Dolores's *column speculating on questions dizzily relative to all the various libidinal quests and successive findings of one* Mnopqr *Stuvwxyz, oltrano, its multiple penumbral references to* Stuvwxyz *meetings, matings, partings, and reunions becoming under* Stuvwxyz's *close scrutiny so transparently legible—had she not in fact become herself adept at decodage—so easily traceable to the movie-mad reporter's obvious lust for* Middle-European *espionage melodrama, for* Midwest *roadhouse film noir, for the trials and tribulations of love goddesses, and for epics of the* Egyptian, Graeco-Roman, *and* Byzantine *world that one recumbent oltrano spent . . .*

He pictured them recumbent, as they likely were in that moment. Then, looking down again at the manuscript, neatly typed in case-sensitive Courier, considered the difference in effect between reading a text as composed and reading it as telegraphed—all in upper case and with such insertions as STOP, ITAL, QUOTE and whatnot else—putting him in mind directly Greek epic poetry. MENIN AEIDA THEA ETCETERA, indeed. And of the *sous-texte*: telling not of the fury of The O'Maurigan, but as must be admitted then, there, and definitely, of the forlorn dread of the ultimate abandonment: the certain knowledge that his idols, for so they were, would be from then on doing things and saying things in which he could have no part.

Which had the unwelcome effect of making him almost morbidly cognizant of the perils of attempting serious work there in the reading room, shoulder to shoulder with the regiments of comely graduate students oblivious to all but their subjects, and with the many seasoned scholars, some undoubtedly illustrious, poring over the great writings of Eastern and Western Civilization, and ever more with the "outcast state" crowd, the paranoiacs who came in to keep warm and habitually had called up the *Tertium Organum* of Ouspensky and Paracelsus's writings on the Iliaster, the Aquaster, gems and longevity, one of whom he now observed sleeping the restless sleep of the would-be-justified. These, too, were, he thought, if less apparently so in the enforced silence, his anonymous choristers, more Cigarettes who knew what, when they lit up, they might indeed contribute?

He realized "they two" were out on the Atlantic, asleep, and if New York is like a great ocean liner on the Sea of Time, then from time to time—in fact rather incessantly—the *radio room* will be *getting messages*. There will be other voices, too, in other rooms, that if we were to hear them, we *really would go crazy*: schizophrenic.

As he passed out into the hall, heading toward the staircase down to the Fifth Avenue entrance, he overheard two men of a certain telling age in earnest conversation.

"I could tell you—"

"I'm sure you could, darling, many others have."

*

The exertion of recalling accounts of the collapse of Mawrdew Czgowchwz (particularly the part detailing the matter of the infamous Cedrioli curse, which had backfired) had given the Watchman a turn. "Mala Cenere" he knew was Old Mary Cedrioli, the already half-crazed perpetrator sucked into the vortex of madness itself from which as a consequence, she, a patient at Creedmoor State Hospital, asylum for the insane poor somewhere in Queens, may never be extricated. Such a turn that, like the hapless passenger in a recklessly speeding automobile on a narrow, winding road at night, who turns narcoleptic rather than endure the terror of prompt extinction, he had fallen asleep at his station. The cabin boy, entering, found him there.

The cabin boy entered the radio room to take the dispatch.

Something again was stirring in the radio operator. The ship's clock struck eight bells. Just as suddenly as he had gone under, he revived, poured another cup of coffee, made note of the presence of the cabin boy—looking terrified (afraid it appeared of throwing up on somebody or falling off the ship and over the edge of the world—surely not of the dispatch, which he couldn't possibly) and returned to his examination of the dispatch from shore reading of the entrance of Mawrdew Czgowchwz onstage at the Metropolitan Opera, after two acts of perilously oracular dramatic soprano vocalism, in the last moments of *Tristan und Isolde*, lurching, seeming to forget her music, and then in a voice nearly double the size (reckoned loud enough normally to be heard in the borough of Queens if not necessarily through the walls of institutions), commencing to sing in a language nobody could understand, Isolde's "love death."

ALPHA SAW THE COUNTESS OMEGA GAUTIER BEGIN TO STAND AT THE VERY BEGINNING OF THE ECSTATIC FINALE STOP SHE STOOD SUPPORTED A SECOND OR TWO AND THEN FELL BACK INTO HER CHAIR AGAIN FAINTING AWAY AT ONCE STOP ALPHA WHO HAD BEEN AT HER SAME SIDE AT THE ITAL TRAVIATA SHOOK HER GENTLY STOP REVIVED SHE COULD ONLY MURMUR STOP ALPHA LISTENED VERY CLOSELY HIS EARS SO FULL MEANWHILE OF MNOPQR STUVWXYZS VOICE HE FEARED PARALYSIS STOP THE COUNTESS GASPED QUOTE MY ITAL LIFE SHES SINGIN IN THE ITAL IRISH EXCLAMATION POINT STOP IT WAS TRUE STOP MNOPQR STUVWXYZ SANG THE ITAL LIEBESTOD THAT NIGHT IN THAT SAME TONGUE THE IRISH ONCE SANG IN OF LOVE AND DEATH IN THE WEST STOP IT WAS OVER STOP IT BEGAN STOP THE NOISE THEY HEARD BACKSTAGE SOUNDED LIKE ONLY ONE THING STOP REVOLUTION IN THE STREETS STOP THE CURTAIN HAD GONE UP AND DOWN ON THE SAME LOVE DEATH TABLEAU THREE TIMES BEFORE WHAT HAD BEFALLEN MNOPQR STUVWXYZ SANK IN

The Watchman, caffeine energized, more avid now than when the news was first published, read anew the account of the collapse, descent into hell, and return to life of Mawrdew Czgowchwz.

It had begun with the announcement made the morning after the *Tristan* by the Countess Madge O'Meagher Gautier (*O'Mega*, he thought: not bad) and then continued through weeks of anguished waiting—weeks in which, he well remembered, as his vessel sailed back and forth at its record speed across the wintry Atlantic—that neither on ship nor on shore was anyone talking about anything so much as they were talking about what had befallen Mawrdew Czgowchwz. Not about the alarming new hillbilly singer whose appearances on television, commencing with the Dorsey Brothers *Stage Show* on CBS, seemed to presage a more unleashed period in the entertainment business than many could contemplate with equanimity.

Not either about Nikita Khrushchev's denunciation of Joseph Stalin in front of the Twentieth Congress of the Soviet Communist Party in Moscow (an event which, given merely her known history, all reckoned would have given the Czech diva the utmost satisfaction).

MNOPQR STUVWXYZ ENTIRELY PHYSICALLY WELL WOKE EARLY THIS MORNING IN A STATE OF COMPLETE AMNESIA STOP SHE KNOWS NOTHING OF HERSELF HER PAST NOR RECOGNIZES ANYONE AT ALL STOP SHE WILL SPEAK ONLY IN THE IRISH TONGUE, AND ONLY THEN AGAIN AND AGAIN OF WHAT APPEARS TO BE A VERY DISTANT MEMORY STOP SINCE IT IS ONLY WITH MYSELF MY NEPHEW SHEM OMEGA AND MY NIECE ANNA LIVIA OMEGA THAT ANY WORDS AT ALL MAY BE EXCHANGED WITH THE PATIENT IT HAS BEEN DECIDED THAT SHE SHALL BE TAKEN TO MY OWN HOME MEGALO MANOR FOR REST AND TREATMENT UNTIL THE DRASTIC CAUSE OF HER CRISE BE FATHOMED AND DEALT WITH AT ALL STOP I KNOW THAT MNOPQR STUVWXYZ WHEN SHE SHALL BE HERSELF AGAIN WILL THANK YOU ALL EACH ONE FOR WAITING THROUGH THIS DARKLING TERM OF WINTER TRIAL WITH HER STOP IT WILL I KNOW BE THROUGH OUR LOVE AND OUR

Not the Dow Jones crashing the 500-point ceiling.

Her immutable self again. What crap. Well, in real life, though, they did get smart. Instead of getting some metaphysician in to foul things up, they got the shrink.

AFTER SPENDING SOMETHING LIKE TEN MINUTES ALONE WITH THE PATIENT JANSENIUS LEAVING THE DIVA SLEEPING QUITE AS SOUNDLY AS SHE HAD SO LONG SINCE SLEPT IN CONNEMARA STOP CAME DOWN INTO THE PARLOR TO MEET THE ANGUISHED VIGILANTS STOP QUOTE WE HAVE MADE A BEGINNING STOP WE TRUST STOP WHEN HE SAID IT THEY MURMURED STOP THEY ALL ASKED EVERY QUESTION STOP QUOTE IS MNOPQR STUVWXYZ INSANE STOP QUOTE

MNOPQR STUVWXYZ IS NOT INSANE STOP QUOTE WHY DOES SHE SPEAK IN IRISH QUESTION MARK STOP QUOTE BECAUSE QUOTE JANSENIUS DECLARED FLATLY IN A DEAD HUSH OF PETRIFIED ATTENTION QUOTE MNOPQR STUVWXYZ ITAL IS IRISH STOP THE COUNTESS OMEGA PASSED RIGHT OUT STOP ALPHA SAT DOWN ON THE FLOOR AND WEPT STOP WHAT HAD HAPPENED WAS STOP JANSENIUS AN ANALYST OF GENIUS HAD PLUMBED THOSE FATHOMS OF THE STUVWXYZ MIND WHERE LAY LOCKED THOSE SAME SECRETS THAT ALL THE WHILE IN THE LIBRARY SHEM READING IN QUOTE THE FENIAN PANTHEON THE STORY OF GREAT FLAMING MAEV COHALEN STOP

The Fenian Pantheon. The story was published on St. Patrick's Day, after the nun had come over from Dublin to break her vows of silence and tell everybody who Mawrdew Czgowchwz was—the daughter of Flaming Maev Cohalen.

THEN ON THE HOLY EASTER SUNDAY WHEN THE NATION ROSE SHE WHO HAD AWAKENED THEM WAS NOT TO BE FOUND AMONG THEIR NUMBER STOP NOR WAS SHE EVER SEEN OR HEARD OF AGAIN IN IRELAND OR IN THE WESTERN WORLD STOP NO BRITISH IRISH OR AMERICAN INTELLIGENCE EFFORTS HAVE EVER BEEN SUCCESSFUL IN TRACKING HER DOWN STOP THE ONE FORLORN CLUE TO THE ENIGMA FOUND ON EASTER MONDAY 24 APRIL 1916 IN THE LEFT BREAST POCKET OF THE TUNIC OF ONE JAN VACLAV MOTIVYK CZECH PHILOSOPHER POET

Yes, yes, reputedly Wittgenstein's lover at Cambridge.

A RESIDENT IN THAT LENTEN TERM AT MAGDALEN COLLEGE CAMBRIDGE STOP RIDDLED WITH BULLETS IN SACKVILLE STREET BY BRITISH FUSILIERS ON CASED IN A FRAME STOP A PORTRAIT OF HERSELF GREAT FLAMING MAEV COHALEN TOGETHER WITH A LOCK OF HER IMMORTAL HAIR DEFACED ITSELF WITH SHOT THAT HAD CUT THROUGH

Violated flaming hair again—or first: it's a motif, clearly, a revolving one: the daughter of the mother dead in childbirth, a bastard given mother's name necessarily omitting the "great and the "flaming," which then the nuns judiciously remedy, naming her again, after the saint once as famous as their Bridget and their Attracta, she whose name means Great One, and so found again—like the woman claiming to be the czarevna Anastasia Romanov. Mawrdew Czgowchwz, love child fathered as it were on Ireland herself, Kathleen Ni Houlihan, by the Czech poet-philosopher and raised in anonymous seclusion at Convent-on-the-Rock, in Connemara in the far west of Ireland, is then bundled in a panic out of the country during their Civil War and sent to Czechoslovakia where, because the father had written a sonnet sequence honoring the Czech diva Emmy Destinn, depicting her in her many celebrated roles, the diva takes the orphan in at her castle at Strážˇ, in southern Bohemia.

Destinn, a legend every bit as famous in her day as Mawrdew Czgowchwz is today, who at the Metropolitan Opera in nineteen ten, opposite Caruso and Scotti, under Toscanini, created the role of Minnie in what musicians regard as Puccini's finest work, *La Fanciulla Del West*, dies. The girl is brought to a convent in Prague, but one June night soon thereafter, she leaps over the wall into a life of music and metropolitan adventure.

What a story, including the bloodhounds of the Church nipping at her rear end.

Plus which, the sentinel told himself, whimsically, in consequence of so much else, the philosopher-poet father's name was not Motivyk, as given in the long dispatch, but Moravec, whose great bombshell hermeneutic work, in the form of numbered aphoria collated after his death by his former lover Ludwig Wittgenstein (who authoritative rumor had it was crazier about Moravec than Brahms had even been about Feurbach) was called not *Were It But So* (cute little title nevertheless) but at Wittgenstein's insistence *Vecs Moravecs*. Wittgenstein had pleaded with his beloved to let him be "a reedy flute that you will fill with music" and was so wrecked when, after dragging him off to the luxurious rooms of the Haus Wittgenstein, the rustications of Schloss Neuwaldegg, the purlieus of the Staatsoper, the Prater, and the fleshpots of Vienna and finally the chastening icy fjords of Norway to that little cabin near Troldhaugen to live out their naturals in conjoined bliss, the maverick had returned to Cambridge, became embroiled with a Fenian *woman* firebrand, and was thus brought to a premature death at the hands of the British forces occupying Ireland, that he, poor Wittgenstein had left Norway and joined the Austrian army) had (nevertheless) sometimes become so overwrought at Moravec's erotic combination of beauty, brains, talent, and betrayal, he would chase him around the common room of the Moral Science Club at Cambridge (and perhaps again around that cabin up that fjord) brandishing a poker. And who to the sentinel's certain knowledge (got from culling the passenger lists of the Cunard company, idly perused on many a winter crossing in stormy seas) had twice sailed on this very ship, the *Mary*, to New York, once in nineteen thirty-nine to consult with his pianist brother Paul (the one-armed commissioner of the Ravel Concerto for Left Hand) in the matter legally freeing (for, they said, a shitload of Wittgenstein gold) his sisters from the grip of Hitler's racial purity laws (during which visit he had taken a fancy to an Italian shoeshine boy in Central Park, likely one with a comely bearing and an insider's knowledge of opera) and again ten years later on his way to a rendezvous with his former student Norman Malcolm, in Ithaca, New York, from whence no tales of any extreme poker-wielding high jinks had leaked.

Furthermore it was said that Wittgenstein's later work *Philisophical Investigations* was so indebted to *Vecs Moravec* that the anxiety of its influence led Wittgenstein to the edge of metaphysical doom. (Had this double-dome never gone nightclubbing—or seen a stage show?)

SHE HAD SLIPPED OVER THE CLOISTERS HIGH STONE WALL INTO THE SHADOWS OF DEMIMONDAINE PRAGUE STOP AT FIRST SHE HAD TAKEN UP WITH THE MUSICIANS IN ART NOUVEAU DANCE HALLS AND THE NEW ART DECO BARS IN NAMESTI REPUBLIKY STOP NEXT WITH THE RADICAL AVANT GARDE IN PARIZKA SINGING DODECAPHONICALLY AND IN HOMMAGE BLACK AMERICAN JAZZ IN SPARSELY FURNISHED ATTICS AND SHABBY GENTEEL PARLORS STOP AFTER HER DEBUT AT THE GERMAN THEATRE DESTINNS OLD GANG HAVING AS THE AVANT GARDE PUT IT TRACKED HER DOWN SUBORNED HER AS CHERUBINO IN ITAL LE NOZZE DI FIGARO IN 1933 SHE HAD LED TWO LIVES ONE ON

THE STAGE ANOTHER IN CELENTA IN COMMON LAW WEDLOCK WITH AN OBSCURE COMPOSER CALLED NMLKJIHG STUVWXYZ BEARING HIS CHILD STOP STUVWXYZ NONE OF WHOSE SCORES SURVIVE WAS SHOT BY THE NAZIS OUTSIDE TYN CHURCH IN OLD TOWN STOP

In reprisal for his part in the assassination of Hitler's madman, Rudolph Heydrich, at Lidice.

FROM THENCE HER PERILOUS JOURNEY ACROSS THE HORTABAGY PLAIN TO THE DANUBE IN THAT TERRITORY ALONG THE BLACK SEA KNOWN TO THE ANCIENTS AS COLCHIS WHERE JASON FOUND THE GOLDEN FLEECE AND THE WITCH MEDEA FOUND HIM STOP WHERE IN LATER ROMAN OVID WAS EXILED FOR OFFENDING THE EMPEROR AUGUSTUS AND WHERE AFTER THE GREAT SCHISM THE OLD BELIEVERS

And then the wanderings through significant time and space of Mawrdew Czgowchwz—under the encoded moniker MNOPQR STUVWXYZ—only just now ending. (If a beginning, time out of mind can ever for convenience sake be called an ending. Better to say *stopping*—at the start of the new great love.) More interesting—compelling really—all of it than anything she ever did in the opera. Going to Town Hall only to find *him* singing in *her* register. Then their singing together, only last week, on the island of Manitoy, cast as twins in a new work. Two halves of the one, exactly like those Egyptian twin-brother-sister gods. Compelling.

A stage show such as a musical—*South Pacific? Call Me Madam?* Wonder if Wittgenstein caught either? Poor bastard. Imagine him sitting there listening to Pinza sing "This Nearly Was Mine." He'd've gone up to Ithaca and thrown himself right down that gorge. Unlikely. More likely something at the Metropolitan. Czgowchwz in *Der Rosenkavalier?* What irony! Was Nabokov in Ithaca that year? They might have got on or not have done at that. Wittgenstein, ambivalent about Freud, called psychoanalysis *Dunkelzauber*. Still, considering his sister's analysis and the fact that all homosexuals with sisters dream of turning them into boys and sodomizing them—sounds right up the Russian's chocolate tunnel, wot? Also whether he admitted it or no Wittgenstein must have known Freud was on to *something* new and different for pudding with that libido lark, whereas Nabokov, having fathered the singer son has seemed nearly as much a career eunuch as Henry James, always called both Dostoyevsky and Freud absolute frauds.

THEY LAY TOGETHER LAUGHING STOP HE HAD JUST RETURNED TO THE LOFT FROM HERALD SQUARE WITH AN ARRAY OF LATE EDITION NEWSPAPERS STOP HE WISHED TO LEARN THE TOWNS WAYS STOP AND TOGETHER THEY DISCOVERED DOLORES COLUMN SPECULATING ON QUESTIONS DIZZILY RELATIVE TO ALL THE VARIOUS LIBIDINAL QUESTS AND SUCCESSIVE FINDINGS OF ONE MNOPQR STUVWXYZ ITAL OLTRANO STOP ITS MULTIPLE PENUMBRAL REFERENCES TO STUVWXYZ MEETINGS MATINGS PARTINGS AND REUNIONS BECOMING UNDER STUVWXYZ SCRUTINY SO TRANSPARENTLY LEGIBLE SO EASILY TRACEABLE TO THE MOVIEMAD REPORTERS OBVIOUS LUST FOR MIDDLE EUROPEAN ESPIONAGE MELODRAMA FOR MIDWEST ROADHOUSE ITAL FILM NOIR FOR THE TRIALS AND TRIBULATIONS OF LOVE GODDESSES AND FOR EPICS OF THE EGYPTIAN GRAECO ROMAN AND BYZANTINE WORLD THAT THE ONE RECUMBENT OLTRANO SPENT

Still recumbent, on the voyage out—to Ireland, to make a film on the mother's life. How more Byzantine can it get? *What is the world? The world is everything that is the case.* What is a world of one's own? What does it mean to be speaking to oneself? (the very question deliberated at Wittgenstein's Cambridge lecture, given on the cold, wet afternoon of October twenty-fifth, nineteen forty-six, nearly ten years ago).

THE SUN HAD SET STOP MNOPQR STUVWXYZ SITTING DREAMILY ALONE AT THE LONG HIGH WINDOW OF HER TOWER SUITE LOOKING DOWN AT CENTRAL PARK THOUGHT QUOTE ITAL ENFIN CLOSE QUOTE THIS TIME TOMORROW QUOTE THEN SHE STOPPED REMEMBERING STOP HERE CAN ITAL BE NO THIS TIME TOMORROW STOP HER FATHER IN QUOTE WERE IT BUT SO QUOTE HAD INSISTED THAT STOP SHE REFLECTED NEVERTHELESS STOP IN THE NEXT BRILLIANT SUNSET OLTRANO FOR OLTRANO THEY WOULD BE ALONE TOGETHER OUT ON THE ATLANTIC MAKING FOR IRELAND INTENDING A PERFECT LIFE

STOP THE NEW YORK NEAPORT IDYLL TRULY AN ENCHANTED PATCH MUST NOW GIVE WAY SHE REASONED TO SOME CALMER WHISPERING STRETCH STOP A MUTE EVOLVING CONSTANCY MUST OPERATE BINDING THEM TOGETHER IN GENTLE PRIVACY STOP THEY MUST SCHEME TO SHUT OUT GLARE STOP SOON THEY WERE TOGETHER AT THE WINDOW STOP THE CONSORT STOOD DEVOURING AT ONCE THE VIEW AND A PINT OF CHERRY VANILLA ICE CREAM STOP

Means they're getting ready to fuck. He's ga-ga over American ice cream—the columns were full of it, Winchell in particular. Hilarious. They ordered a couple of dishes of it sent in earlier. He favors chocolate, pistachio, cherry vanilla, and butterscotch. Hilarious, canoodling over bowls of garish ice cream. They're certainly more interesting, of inestimably greater value, than the god-awful Windsors, and no mistake.

MOMENTS LATER WALKING OVER THE BRIDGE ACROSS THE POND HE GOT UP IN PALE GREEN AND BLACK SHE INVOLVED IN GRAY AND GAMBOGE BOTH COSTUMES DIAPHANOUS BOTH FIGURES REGAL IF UNREAL SEEMING THEY HALTED TURNED AND LOOKING BACK UP AT THE TOWER WINDOW THEY HAD SO LATELY STOOD IN EXCHANGING VOWS STOP THE SKYLINE VAULTING IN SILHOUETTE AGAINST A RED SKY TO THE WEST PIERCING A BLUE BLACK EASTERN SKY WITH STONE SLAB SHAFTS RANDOMLY ILLUMINATED LYING BANKED TO THE SOUTH BENEATH AN EXPANSE MIDWAY INDIGO BETWEEN THE DUSK AND THE DARK EMBRACED THE PARK STOP TO THE NORTH AS THEY TURNED MASSES OF AMORPHOUS TREES AND LOWSLUNG OPAQUE CLOUDS REFLECTING SPLASHINGS OF LIGHT BECKONED THEM THE GUESTS OF HONOR STOP A BRILLIANT ORANGE MOON ROSE OVER THE TOWN STOP THE NEARER THEY CAME TO THE GREAT MEADOW THE LOUDER THE MUSIC AND MERRIMENT GREW UNTIL BEFORE THEY

So, the music and merriment of embarkation have ebbed into calm. The sun has set serenely—tomorrow the traditional revels of second night out, when more will be revealed.

THEY STOOD TOGETHER AT THE STERN WATCHING THE CITY RE-

CEDE ON THE DISTANT HORIZON UNTIL IT SANK LIKE THE KINGDOM OF YS STOP THE ATLANTIC BEARING THEM AFLOAT AS IF ALOFT SPREAD OUT ON ALL SIDES STOP THE DAY HAD DRIFTED ALONG IN DREAM TIME STOP AT SUNSET THEY WERE SEEN TOGETHER STILL LEANING ON THE OVOID TAFFRAIL OF THE ITAL ARCADIA SIPPING CHAMPAGNE AND STOUT FROM THE SAME PINT JAR STOP FEELING APOTHOESIZED LOOKING BACK WESTWARD STOP THE FLAMBANT SUN SLIPPED INTO THE ATLANTIC SEEMINGLY BENIGNLY LEAVING THEM IN THE STILL AND SPLENDOR OF A PURPLE TWILIGHT AWAITING THE SHADOWS THE STARS THE MOON AND THE NIGHT STOP SHE WAS NOT MNOPQR STU-VWXYZ SHE WAS HIS ONLY DESIRE STOP HE WAS HER LONG KNOWN LOVE STOP THEY SPOKE FROM EXPERIENCE AS IF FOR THE FIRST TIME STOP THEY SAILED AWAY TOGETHER STOP THEIR TIME WAS TIME OUT OF MIND STOP

No, there's no sunset topside on any vessel called the *Arcadia*. There's about to be a sunrise aboard the *Queen Mary*, and we are, on board, in fact almost as far ahead of the writer, bound for Cobh and Southampton at top-knot nautical Cunard speed, and the only question left to ask is, will they have the captain marry them before Cobh, or not?

In former times paths were not cut through and laid down to provide the simplest, most direct route from here to there, wherever they were. There were any number of cultural and religious considerations determining the routes of paths across the landscapes.

Enough. What does Aristotle say? *The unity of plot does not consist in its having one woman as its subject. An infinity of things befall that one woman, some of which it is impossible to reduce to unity; and in like manner there are many actions of one woman that cannot be made to form one action.* Something of the sort, anyway—not that anybody gives a toss about Aristotle these days. Shocking, really.

*

Sometime later the cabin boy was on his way to the notorious adulterers' stateroom, glancing with virtually no comprehension at the missive. New to

Atlantic crossings, he had never anywhere seen a cable of such length—perhaps, he thought, they'd had them in the war, emanating (a favorite word) out of Bletchley Park (top-secret, highest-security book-length transcriptions of the lately broken Enigma code). Those were the days—they must have been.

The ship went into a roll; his legs turned to rubber. Good job the hairdresser had earlier in the evening made him swallow all that Dramamine, and for a booster a couple of those red capsules called *Quinalbarbitone*. He sat down on the gangway floor for a while to read a little more of the dispatch, feeling oddly estranged from all motive, care, and press of duty. Sod it, he'd sit there on the gangway floor, feeling internal, until they'd sighted land if it came to that—the southwest coast of Ireland. Else some passing steward would find him there, relieve him of the thing, and take it in, until such time—call it a bit of a bunk, one of a different sort than that in which he'd agreed in the spirit of adventure born of pluck to meet the hairdresser, and happen others later on. And if they missed him in the melee and came to find him sitting there on the gangway floor, well there it was, wasn't it then.

*

"*Their time was time out of mind.*"

"Stop."

"Yes, stop."

"So it says there, right there, in bold teletype block print. Slow curtain, the end. Cut, print it. It's a wrap, and we who are about to die salute—"

"Who, reader? Reader, they married?" "It gets even better. The fuller view of transparency, a view that recognizes the decreasing visibility of what we look through."

"Always with a banquet—which we've already had."

They lay together in their stateroom propped up in bed by a mound of white pillows, frowsty amid a profusion of floral arrangements, cellophaned Bon Voyage hamper delicacies, body scents, and limerance, and talked, about themselves and about the others represented in the text they'd been delivered

—it now lay atop a pile of vocal scores—in the form of the longest telegram the frazzled ship's radio operator had ever sent topside.

"It does take you right up to now, doesn't it," her bed partner Jacob Beltane remarked, with equanamity. "I mean if one were to die this minute—however life goes on, does it not, in the two hundred and first year of the sempiternal existence of Mozart, for such as are not—merely anyway—dramatis personae in operatic fables."

"It distracted me from what I woke thinking—awoke singing actually."

"Did you awaken singing? I didn't hear."

"Silently. '*Wie du hast, wie du bist, Nieman—*' "

"I recognize that lyric—two women in bed together, right?"

"One is meant to be a man—oh well, a boy—which is the part, to add to the confusion, if confusion there be, that I was singing."

" 'Men vent great passion by breaking into song,' said Giambatista Vico."

"Women have been known to contribute also. Of course it was my debut role, Octavian, which had always been Destinn's idea, although she dies before it happened. She dies so young, only forty-four. That's why the part about Destinn's lobby being turned into a vast drugstore—"

"Caruso's lobby, wasn't it?"

"Not the way it's worded, that's what's rather charming. In any event, lobby or not, she traveled with a virtual pharmacopoeia, yet died anyway at forty-four, played out."

"There were no passionate woman singers, as such, in Vico's time—and now there are those who think of me as one."

"Nobody in this bed, I can assure you—unless, like in Zola, there is some imaginary creature lying in between the principals."

"Such as the composer, or the librettist, or—anyway, I dislike the opus, I always have."

"It's weak in sum, I agree, but women are weak, and will sing it."

"You made a sensation out of singing it."

"Odd that. I always used to beg them in Vienna to let me sing Hansel instead. I adore the work—as apparently Mahler did, too: he took the prayer for his first string quartet, composed when he was sixteen. They used to play it in Prague, the men I—"

"Yes."

"And then last year when I gave them the Marschallin, and for the trio high C instead of emitting some sound of exalted womanly resolution I let out a wrenching wail of pain—also incidentally became the first since Frieda Hempel to do both the Marschallin and the Queen of the Night in a single season.

"Strauss once, at a dinner party, claimed he could indicate in music whether a character first picks up the knife or the fork. I seem to have picked up the knife, and done something with it more like Floria Tosca than '*Marie Therese wie gut sie ist.*' "

"Noel Coward is right to point out the extraordinary potency of cheap music. *Rosenkavalier* is that, *Salome*, too—in fact *Salome* really is crap, although Welitsch made everybody crazy when she did it. Laverne will do likewise in the spring in Fitz's new translation. And where's the harm?

"Hans von Bülow said, when it comes to Richard I prefer Wagner and when it comes to Strauss I prefer Johann."

"Many call *Parsifal* kitsch crap."

"Not Debussy."

"No."

"I almost did though—and I was in it, in that dreadful Bavarian *dorf*, up to my neck in all that male adolescent regression, and all I could think of was Merman's great good fortune, to be doing *Call Me Madam* night after night in New York."

"Do they get married at the end of *Call Me Madam*?"

"Who?"

"No matter. Perhaps I was dreaming—of the main chance of things, as yet not come to life, which in their seeds, and weak beginnings lie in treasured—"

"Have we such a weak beginning?"

"I was brooding—I know it's trashy to brood."

"Such things become the hatch and brood of time—the wide world's prophetic soul dreaming insistent on things to come. Like Marfa in *Khovanschina*, my favorite part for many years; I longed to play it, but never could at the Bolshoi; Stalin hated it—feared it, he as much as admitted to me. How she sees the boyar's future in the dish of water and then self-immolates, taking all the Old Believers with her."

"I don't reckon the Secret Seven's any too devoted to *Khovanschina* either."

"Of course, I could never match Doulkhanova."

"No, nor could I."

"Really? And you know there that other thing, too, about *Khovanschina*—the thing about the scribe. They none of them can write, so he has to write all the dispatches out for them, and at one point in the melee, he comes right downstage and announces his imminent departure from the scene, and indeed we never see him again. He's a bit like the holy fool in *Boris* and evidently as important to Mussorgsky."

"The writer having written all that is to happen then absconds."

"Exactly, and rather like the present case."

"Oh, dear, are we not likely to continue?"

"Then there was a thing that premiered at the German Theater in Prague, just when I first ran away from—*Verlobung in Traum*. I'd quite forgotten all about it."

"Betrothal in a dream."

"Yes. A Russian story. Dostoyevsky—or Dostoyevsky is in it, or he's offstage . . . I don't really remember. I do remember there was a funny line in the libretto about Madeira—about going off to Madeira and watching all the Spanish dancers—"

" '*Have* some Madeira, m'dear—' "

"Which the poets all picked up on and howled over, because, of course, Madeira is Portuguese."

" 'I've a whole great big cask of it here.' "

"What?"

"Madeira—a whole great big cask of it here."

"I shouldn't be surprised, with all the rest—"

"It's a *song*! From Flanders and Swann."

"I was just thinking now of Jean Madeira. She called me up—it was just after I'd given a radio interview about roles—and said, 'You know, Mawrdew, I'm grateful to you for leaving your Carmen, Delilah, your Orfeo and your Octavian in Europe—and I know Risë is, too, and if Blanche isn't, she ought to be God knows—but do you think you could put together a band, get into a dress, and go sing it at Carnegie? I can't get to London so easily what with Belen Amparan and I covering every goddam low role in the house, and I sure could use some pointers in the French diction department—and so could they, but I really long to hear your chest voice in the *mon coeur*.'

"Actually, I'd heard Risë in the old Prague days, in Wolff's *Corregidor* at the Deutsches Theater. She was the first American I ever met; she'd been told at Juilliard to go to Europe and so she did—to Salzburg, then to us, although I was the only one in the crowd who'd go into the German Theater to hear a Jewish American. Czgowchwz was furious with me. They'd wanted her to do her Oktavian, but either she herself demurred, or her people did out of—well, it doesn't really matter, because Risë is a brick, really, and a hell of a good Carmen. She was good back then in Prague, although she says now she didn't get it at all.

"In any case I didn't know then that Madeira was Portuguese. Anyway I sang Carmen, and much else—but at that time I do think my best role, after Cherubino was Ježibaba, the red-haired witch in *Rusalka*. Talking though of *Verlobung in Traum*, the music was a bit like Korngold's *Das Wunder der Heliane* and a bit of Weill, and the soprano line was tremendously exciting—a little like *Die Frau ohne Schatten*."

"Nice."

"It was, very. He went to the gas chambers."

"Who?"

"Krasa. The composer. A Jew. They got him. They got Viktor Ullmann, too, for his *Kaiser von Atlantis*. Not Strauss—they got *him* in quite another sense. As he got them, and what they . . . Drive you . . . Of course *Frau* is . . . well, there's something to it; there isn't all that much to the others—as Miro was so frantically pointing out to me when I decided to have a go at the Marschallin. It drove him mad that there are people who live in the twentieth century and pretend to understand it, who will not listen twice to the *Gurre-Lieder*, but who will go to hear any old tart with a line in sentimental self-betrayal and calculating self-interest sing the Marschallin."

"Marriage put all that in your mind."

"No, I was thinking how the world is evenly divided—as on any number of questions—as, for instance, whether the pathos of an aging woman is a matter for serious consideration—"

"Or?"

"A crock of shit, as the younger generation like to say. I was also thinking of *Vecs Makropoulos* and of the fact that Miro so loathes the Four Last Songs that in fifty-two he actually conceived a plan to take the Guild Theater—that newsreel place just opposite Radio City Music Hall—run the footage of the liberation of Auschwitz, and play the Schwarzkopf recording over it. The State Department dissuaded him, reminding him that it was the Russians who were the liberators."

"I see. They murdered Gypsies in Auschwitz, too, you realize that?"

"I do—Gypsies, Jews, and the men who love men. He had it all worked out, and talked about it for some months. '*Und die Seele unbewagt*,' he'd say, '*that* we play over the smoke pouring out of crematoria stacks!' Nobody could seem to make him understand that, apart from everything else, it seemed a little—"

"Tasteless?"

"Nobody could find the word. As to *Vecs Makropoulos*, this stateroom looks a whole lot like the opening of the second act of same, with flowers strewn all over the place."

"I heard it once. She falls asleep in the second act, doesn't she, while the suitor is rattling on?"

"She's terribly tired—and immensely old."

"You thought of that?"

"And much else, such as *matrimonio riparatorio,* the Italian custom after a woman has been, shall we say, *taken.* We're neither of us Sicilian, but we are each of us more than a little Gypsy, and somehow it amounts to . . . my mind wanders, looking at this thing."

She picked up the telegram and shook it a little.

"*Taken's* just the way you feel—the way I feel."

"You mean as in for a ride?"

"Something—something like *That's all there is, there isn't any more.* A legendary line in the annals of American theater, spoken by Ethel Barrymore, reading a letter. As you may know that voice has by now become the almost official voice of the Sibyl, as sort of contemporary Modjeska, who they said could move an audience to tears by reading the telephone directory. She can say anything at all and people are moved. At the end of *Portrait of Jenny* she appears out of nowhere to address a young girl who's just said something like 'What does it matter if she was real, she was real to him.' 'How very wise you are, my dear,' she says, her eyes gleaming with what looks for all the world like the light of the wisdom of the Ages. It seems that when, as a young star ingenue, she came to the end of the reading of that letter and said, 'That's all there is, there isn't any more'—in that lovely way you hear Mrs. Belmont speak the word: *enna*—audiences were absolutely mesmerized by the music, and a little tagline became an oft-repeated statement. Something of the same sort happened with Katharine Hepburn's recitation of 'The calla lilies are in bloom again—such a strange flower.' She actually seems to be saying *flah.*"

"I see."

"How do *you* feel? You look a bit *shagged.* I mean, here we lie, going on about aging and fatigue, which hardly seems what we ought to be going on about just when, as it says in this imaginative little opus, we've sailed away together into a purple twilight, for a life together time out of mind. Dante calls this the hour out at sea, in which longing and sadness spring up in the absence of dear friends to whom one has bid farewell. Also that love's new pilgrim will hear a bell ringing in the distance. I thought I just heard such a bell a minute ago."

"The bell for dinner, ringing in the gangways."

"Ah—well, we shall have that sent in."

"Yes," he said, taking the document from her, "and as to this, I suppose either the thing is of no consequence whatever, and ought to be tossed overboard and not spoken of further, or that what it *is* is only the prooemium to a much longer work being composed even as we speak."

"Yes, one that addresses the question of whether we force an audience into submission—and Simone Weill called force that very thing which turns those subject to it into what Fitz would call reified objects of duress—or seduce it, like whores, which perforce lets our subjects stay customers. This is a question, by the way, that never occurred to Merman, *the* American vocal genius."

"And," he continued (a little warily, for in the complicated set rules and forfeits undertaken by virtue of one's so entering into the life of Mawrdew Czgowchwz, Jacob had not yet come to the point of automatic determination in respect of when she was actually through speaking as opposed to only drawing breath), "I suppose I feel that it's true what they say—what is generally said, that is: it's well for the betrothed of a rich woman."

"*What?*"

"With the High Queen of Ireland for her mother, albeit deceased."

"An idea more fanciful than anything in that romance you've been perusing, including the flamboyant sun, the stars, the moon, and the night, or than anything likely to be composed by forces still at work of whom we have less than imperfect knowledge, even as we speak."

"Too fortunate a woman not to be superstitious."

"Actually, I'm still having trouble, being so connected to Ireland after all those years of being catalogued as sumptuously Slavic—consequence of course of having onstage reincarnated, though I say it as shouldn't, the great prophetess Libuse, founding genius of Bohemia. Many predicted as a consequence I'd live to reincarnate, onstage in a new work, presumably of Creplaczx's, the ferocious warrior queen Sharka. Oh well, as Masaryk rather quaintly insisted, *pravda zvitezi.*"

"Sounds like men walked the plank and were fed to Sharka."

"Actually more the case of Sharka walking—or riding men's planks, wearing them down to thinnish reeds."

"Gracious!"

"Oh, she could be that, too, when it served her book—which brings us back to—"

"I'd have killed to hear your Libuse. Actually, *flambent*—the sun. Got something against romance, have you?"

"I do."

"*I do*. How I long to hear you speak those words—at me."

"I might—one of these days."

"As they say, not for our sake, darling; for the children's."

"What they don't *say*! What they *don't* say is what that sake *is*. I've done all right for a bastard, haven't I?"

"Notoriously well, I'd say."

"Anybody ever tell you how *British*—"

"*You* have; you *have*."

"For a Gypsy—"

"I was brought up in East Anglia, so I am English. Whatever befell me befell me there—there and on the Isle of Man. And all-in-all I rather like the Queen. I'm not however very British. I dislike nearly everything about them and their Britannia."

"I stand corrected ... lying down. Oddly enough, the poet Auden said nearly the same thing to me, at the Metropolitan, at a rehearsal, when I took over Baba the Turk from Blanche Thebom. Odd fellow. Did you know that as a child he sang the *Liebesnacht* with his mother—taking the *Isolde* part? He was there the night I did the part—or did it in, as some remarked. Of course, it's also said that when she was ten, Flagstad, given the score of *Tristan*, memorized Tristan. It's supposed to mean something, but I don't remember what."

"Tristan is the better part."

"It is, isn't it. Perhaps I should've essayed it—like Hansel."

"There's always next year, as they say in baseball."

"I will say you do sound—in the damn thing—like a human being—a mortal man. They make me sound like some sort of enchanted—or perhaps rather hexed—Stradivari cello . . . you know, fashioned in Cremona by the devil, with a will of its own, but well, not exactly *animate* for all that. For the first time in my life I understand that thing about if so-and-so didn't exist, it would be necessary to invent so-and-so—and I don't think I like it. It reminds me of that Nazi Heisenberg who demonstrated uncertainty—as if we hadn't known enough about *that.* They don't get that *flambent* angle right either do they, whoever they are, Who *are* they, anyway?"

"Whoever they are, they've clearly got your goat."

"I'm happy to say I've never kept a goat. It's *unnerving*—shall I tell you why? It's only just come to me. They've got us doing as we like—as we do—but *saying* the things *they* imagine!"

"Rather the reverse of God, wouldn't you say?"

"No, I would not. I wasn't raised Protestant."

"Nor have you read a lot of Schopenhauer."

"They tell me my father read Schopenhauer."

"Which they—this they?"

"No, *they*, my coadjutors, my informants. So they tell me."

"My informants once told me you read the contents of Molotov's diplomatic pouch whilst Stalin lay dead stinking drunk at your feet. It seemed to me, if true, something The O'Maurigan ought to write up and Creplaczx compose. The authors of this dispatch—they're not he, then?"

"Oh, no, never—it simply *isn't* Fitz's style—either the thing itself, or to undertake the thing at all—and it's *while*, not *whilst.*"

"Not even when drunk?"

"Who, you? You don't seem the least bit drunk to me."

"No, him."

"I want to say I hope not, but no. Even supposing for a minute he'd—his approach, his way of saying things, drunk or sober, is far more subtle. The names for instance. The one for me isn't too bad, Alpha and O'Mega are really rather good—and Shem is a teaser—one of the things he read as I was convalescing last winter was Shem's opera house charade from *Finnegans Wake*, a thing that got around, so anybody might have picked up on it—but to call Neri Nirvana Mori is a little too close to *nervy* for him to flirt with, what with his sense of decorum—although I must say the substitution for the title of my father's book is a thing he'd be pleased enough to have thought up—*Were It But So*. Although he'd be more likely at that to have called it *If Not, So What?*"

"Nervy. Well, you'd really need to be hellishly nervy to do the thing in the first place. What is it the Irish say—you'd want to have the neck."

"Indeed, but, you see, 'Helluva Nervy' is what they all used to call Herva Nelli, when Toscanini forced her on the Met and R.C.A., and the coinage was attributed to *me*, so that I lost out on the Toscanini *Aida* to Eva Gustafson—or so Valdengo and Ruby Tucker assured me. It's just too—"

"Contextual."

"Only just. And Pelerin for example is not from Mozambique, nor Madagascar, but from Mayotte, between the two."

"I know it—or of it. Said to be the remnant of Lemuria, just as Ireland is said to be the remnant of Atlantis."

"Fitz couldn't resist being accurate about such—and for instance he was one of the few who knew I was never any such thing as fired from the Metropolitan. It was merely that Bing wouldn't give me the Violetta or the Isolde; thought I'd lost my mind entirely. Fitz would've made quite a thing out of what was really going on behind the *sciopere della fame* and the sedan chair and all the rest of it and still told nothing but the truth. The 'Hollenius' reference does suggest him—it *was* his fiction: a *real* Hollenius—from *Deception*—to taunt Miro about his jealousy, but the fiction became a common reference on the line. He also routinely refers to the Mr. and Mrs. Merrill as Margo Channing Sampson and her Bill. And there is one direct quote from *Under Nephin*, a few short lines from one of the parts parodying Yeats, reconstructed into a sentence."

"You've picked that out."

"Because in the hearing it jumps out at you.

'That circle whose center is nowhere and whose Circumference is everywhere
Both was and was not described.'

"But there are infelicities and inaccuracies abounding of which Fitz—who would never, I think call himself such a thing as Seamusin O'Mega—is simply not capable, not even to blow a smokescreen. The Countess getting in a coarse horse laugh on one of my *Carmen* broadcasts, indeed! I've never sung Carmen in New York, over the radio, or at parties even. Carmen is Risë's role there, and when Risë takes ill, then it's either Blanche Thebom's or Jean Madeira's. Ditto Oktavian. I've always been perfectly content to keep both for Vienna and London. In fact, the whole tone of the friendship—the Madge and me—is oddly off."

"A little too *Lena Geyer.*"

"Perhaps—or to nail it, a little too Olive Fremstaed and Mary Watkins Cushing."

"And Miro doing *Visions de l'Amen* alone, for instance, when it is a four-hand piece. What he likes to do actually is play it at home against a tape of himself. In public he does it with Sybil."

"As it were."

"Although talking of them, I liked the part where Miro orders Sibyl to stop playing Scriabin for fear of calling the Russians in. But it might have been even funnier to have him playing—as he really does like doing—Leo Ornstein's *Suicide in an Airplane.*

"Anyway Fitz doesn't really go in for smokescreens ... more smoke-*rings.* You know his routine on 'The Cigarettes.' But calling Mary Cedrioli *Mala Cenere* while actually the best onomastic gesture in the thing is a thing he wouldn't have done at *all,* because of the still undetermined true nature of whatever it was that attacked one—from *within*—that won't be revealed easily even after years of analytic work with Gennaio ... excavating one's own Troy."

"Ours rather—or is one to represent the Trojan Horse?"

"You do lay siege—and you are devilishly—"

"Wrought."

"You and your way—the Way of Wyrd. Yes, you are to excavate with me—*dig*, as the Secret Seven say. And finding Troy, Freud said, was the closest to human happiness one could get. Groovy."

"As the Secret Seven also like saying—of us, for example. Yes, we shall find our—in Connemara . . . where the Trojans went."

"After Carthage."

"And after Rome."

"Good, because having sung both Cassandra and Dido, I know neither they nor Ariadne either are the way to human happiness . . .

"But back to those initials. Those of 'Mala Cenere' match not only those of Mary Cedrioli but also my own . . . and of course Maria's, before she threw in the extra M."

"You forgot Margo Channing."

"I thought of it, but really, apart from the fact that the whole thing takes place in a single season there's not much of a match. Laverne is hardly an Eve Harrington, Madge is hardly a Birdie Coonan *or* a Karen Richards, Miro is a bachelor and the only director in sight is poor Valerio. What's he called in there?"

"*Valentino Virgolo.*"

"A smutty pun. Virgo-*la* is the comma—a *bent* mark, and Giorgio Vigolo is the critic who said Callas had four voices—a self-evaluation attributed entirely falsely by our author to me. In any case, Valerio is hardly a Bill Sampsom type—in fact, in Italy, as we shall discover when he arrives in Milan in April, he's regarded by the begrudgers as Visconti's Eve Harrington. No, there's no parallel, unless the attempt to suggest somebody in the family circle—rather than just somebody in the Family Circle, if you know what I mean, personally emptied the gas tank."

"There is that about it which suggests inside—"

"Undoubtedly. The servants are amusing, but so cardboard. Ivy Grudget is made up out of whole cloth, but the Wedgwood thing is a little unnerving. There never was a Wedgwood at Magwyck, of course, but poor Cousin Willy up there in the second-floor back parlor does particularly like to wash up the

Wedgwood cups and saucers and cake plates. Of course, he's never had enough to do, so when Fitz was at Regis the Jesuit Strange got him put on as some sort of assistant sacristan at St. Ignatius.

"The whole recasting of the supposed *curse* at Christmas in terms of Santuzza is a clear reference to Lina Bruna-Rasa, who used to be let out of the crazy house only to sing Santuzza for Mascagni. Very inside that, because of course the rumors were that sometimes she would break out and go to the opera house and skulk around under the stage—exactly what this *Mala Cenere* is represented as doing. That and snipping off a lock of my hair and sticking my cutout face on a poppet—which whether it happened or not still gives me turns to think about. And Bruna-Rasa, like Maria, and like Yours Truly, had a large and somewhat unwieldy voice. Oh, there are wheels within wheels."

"Gyres ... *gyres*, now that you're being Irish."

"Yes—and talking of that—being Irish—or not—the *real* kicker is Anna Livia for Lavinia."

"Again from *Finnegans Wake*."

"Yes, but you see, Anna Livia is Lavinia's proper name."

"Is it?"

"It is. She hated it and adopted Lavinia when she first learned Latin and read the *Aeneid*, and simultaneously discovered Lavinia was Emily Dickinson's sister's name. It's not a thing that's known at all outside the family—and in this case is more than likely a coincidental stab on the clever meddling authors' part ... but Fitz would never have done it—no more than he ever has, to my knowledge, or ever would have, I think, called her *Vanilla*!"

"No, I see that."

"And then there are the reverse of infelicities. In the *Aroldo-Stiffelio* gag for instance, the author apparently knows that in the *Stiffelio* version of the overture there appears the first unmistakable foretaste of *Aida*—hence, the Amneris debut looms. Mirroring effects. He knows, too, that we call Jim Kilgallen's daughter *Dolores* and that the Countess won't let her into Magwyck, even as Mrs. Kohlmer, as often as her squibs jab for an invite. And in that connection, I do rather like the WCZG gag. One's own radio station! A woman could *do* things with one of those."

"If one were you."

"But other strange red herrings . . . what can it mean when poor Grainne de Paor is demoted to 'Grace Jackson-Haight?' There is a neighborhood in Queens called Jackson Heights; perhaps there's a clue in that. And that finale! Us standing all day long at the taffrail drinking Black Velvets! And the *Arcadia*! No, Fitz would have had the sense—the *poise*—to place us right where we've been since our ship sailed through The Narrows two days ago: in bed. Not very romantic let's allow, but the truth nonetheless."

"Not very romantic? Well, I've been having a very good time. A riot, if the truth—"

"Don't be a lout, you know what I mean—exactly what. And by the way, did you ever jump up on the stage at the Wigmore Hall and embrace me?"

"Certainly not! A very good time—with all these flowers lying about the—Ralph?"

"What do—oh, no, no, *no*. Ralph wouldn't take the liberty. None of the stalwarts would; they're too protective. Probity is their—of course, they trumpet things. *Too much*! the Secret Seven will say when they hear what's—and Paranoy will go on the air. Madge will summon Arpenik to Magwyck to discuss midwifery. They'll get Gennaio to invoke Demeter, among others. Fitz will write something—privately, to us. They'll all raise a great cry, and all New York will hear and know—but no; not this romance. This is the work of an interloper, perhaps a committee of interlopers."

"A parliament."

"Yes, I'd say so."

"It looks a bit like a parliament in here, with the mirrors on both walls speaking of mirroring effects and the inclusion of same in the dispatch. You I mean, at the dressing table: I like that—but, look, we are all the members, both the whips and both the leaders as well. I expect I'm in opposition."

"That's as it may be—but put away the whip."

"You know what I am in your life? A national complication—perhaps after all a bit of a Joe Soap, choose how. Anyway, a parliament of schoolboys was what you let in, I suppose: schoolboys and their masters?"

"In the heel of the hunt. Yes, wishful—no—*willful* schoolboys. The give-away is the aphorism that pops up toward the end. *Reality does not occur, it is enforced.* And calling *Izvetsia, Iznayou.* Very undergraduate that. Yes, it's a thoroughly undergraduate statement wedded to the neon night, desperate to hold back the dawn of working day."

"Well! Well, of course, you let them in. In fact, it occurs to me in my current state of distraction that there is that about it which suggests you could have written it yourself—to razz me."

"I let them in, I know I did. I like schoolboys—and especially brilliant ones—always have. My father was one, remember? They got that right, which makes me wonder. What's true, what's not—all that. Gennaio did tell me that the Changeling Fantasy is a commonplace, especially among girls. I did *not*, however, write this document—unless, that is, I did so in my sleep, dictating it, infelicities and inaccuracies abounding, to the archangel Gabriel, who then relayed it to the ship. Moreover, you ought to know I couldn't have, since we've spent every waking moment since May 4th together."

III

Looking across the park again, she lit a cigarette, a gesture he had not seen her make in decades, and which he realized, almost in shock, had the immediate effect of wiping those decades away. She inhaled deeply then blew blue smoke out into the night air.

"By then of course, the Company was leaning heavily on my case, as the kids say, playing the congressional proclamation citizenship card, insisting it was my duty as an American to go back to work for them. 'Look,' I said, 'I've already told you Horowitz's piano tuner is a Russian operative; take the money and run.' Do you know, they actually said that whether or not I married Jacob or simply opted to live in sin, I'd never be allowed to tell him about the work? I said, 'You and I have very different ideas about the meaning of *the work*. The truth is, yes, the English and Scottish witches did repulse the German general's plan for the invasion on Britain; if you can't take that in, then refresh yourselves by having a read of *The Scarlet Pimpernel*.'

"Of course I didn't know the Mahatma was one of theirs—British Intelligence. You never did either, did you?"

"That I did not. I'd read Narayan, of course, and really should have known an awful lot more than I did about the mahatma mafia, especially since as Gypsies my mother's line went all the way back to the Punjab, but what with British and Intelligence being at that time for us all, in the light of the Cambridge spies and Suez and so much else on which so much seemed to our benighted minds to depend, something of a contradiction in terms. I mean, Good God, to be known as 'Sis.' Any road, all I knew about the worthy oriental gentleman, until the cover story was rather airily blown to me by your worshipful sometime control—"

"Carlton only ever loved three sopranos in his lifetime, Mary Garden, Victoria, and me. Then you came along, and he took me aside and said very seriously, 'Oh dear! Well, as it turns out now, I've only ever loved *two* sopranos—two sopranos and two *oltrani*."

"—was an heiress had found him in Benares, under a baobab tree, shanghaied him stateside, then on his watch went rather too speedily home to God, and that at a party for the Windsors at Jimmy Donahue's he met Swithin, throwing the net over him and several other neurasthenic crazies in thrall to Fulton Sheen, getting them to ship out on the *Mary* to Southampton and from London to Goa on the P&O, final destination Benares. But then one never knew one way or the other. Swithin tried on the voyage out to tell Kit Pickersgill *he* was *CIA* out to bugger MI5 *and* the *Securite*, which in those mad days might even have been—"

"*Ah, chi ha si possuto credere!*"

"Exactly."

*

The rapt votaries of the Mahatma Chandragupta Bhairava-Bhaktivedanta —having carted their gongs and prayer rugs and graven images of Kali, Great Mother/Great Destroyer, up the gangplanks and through the wide-avenue Edwardian-Georgian gangways and imperial crystal-chandeliered public rooms, bound east in a *bhikku* exaltation, lending a certain "Uranian" luster to the atmosphere aboard the *Queen Mary*, purposed, indeed, to portion their days at sea according to strict precepts of *brahmacharya* and *vanaprastha*, to avoid the reckless indulgences of wayward aporias and impulsive tea-time chats, sipping instead in blissful silence their brew decocted of the leaves of the *Rauwolfia serpentina*, and sharing among their various genders little personal tokens such as neckties, hair ribbons, leather watchbands, lipsticks, compacts, Maybelline mascara boxes, Mennen aftershave lotion to engender the stage of *sannyasa* and the beginnings of disincarnate *ardhanarishvara* chief among their spiritual goals.

Now, having finished their reading and discussion of another scene from Rabindranath Tagore's *The King of the Dark Chamber*, they had settled into a round of canasta in the card lounge (for *dhavana*, the Mahatma knew, and the playing of canasta in little groups of four—the perfect number—scorched spiritual avarice. For to sneak a peek is not to see—"tee-hee." Also that fostered *dharana* and the sea fostered *dijana*, thus forestalling the advent of ambitions toward the attainment of *samadhi* until the long march from Goa to Benares.).

Nevertheless, fretful, constitutionally unable to establish or maintain custody either of the eyes, the ears, the nose, or the throat (consequence of which they'd consigned themselves into to the swami's keeping), the votaries had been keeping close watch on the many notables on the passenger list (in First), most particularly the stellar couple, household words to such as commonly had no household to speak of, who had yet to make an appearance on deck.

"They hold to the Inner Chamber still. I meld."

"Canasta is more a symbol of life, really, than a game of cards. They are undergoing an enchanted patch: gay for them."

"Yes, let them be . . .

"Wouldn't you just love to know, though, what—"

The Mahatma Chandragupta Bhairava-Bhaktivedanta, having utterly proscribed "any outward attempt at the achievement of" the merest kenning of, much less the "skylark" ambition of pursuing "an interim prophylactic perfection"—having disallowed for the duration of the ship's voyage any further yearning toward Upper Access, *samadhi* and the boarding of the Greater Vehicle—spoke cautious counsel out loud to his charges.

"Eet ees ahs it wahs weeth Varuna and Vasistha who sailed across thee eemeense oh-se-ahn een a ship weethout sails, weethout sailors, weethout bahlahst, ond Varuna revealed to Vasistha thee secrets Vasistha came too onderstahdnd everything!"

"But Sri, master," a voice interrupted, "were not both Varuna and Vasistha both men—in fact father and son?"

The Mahatma grew severe. "Eeet ees Wajnavalkya heemself who says, 'Onlehs one ees willing to become een fuhl knowledge like the thoht dot ees thoht, thinking ees dongerous.' Soh—more and more of less and less. Send not to know. *Tat tvam asi*! Cards, cards!"

"Swithin can play cards and contemplate the *atman-brahman* simultaneously. And that's to say the least of it—the very least."

"Then let's."

"Pray, no hortatory dos, no minatory don'ts."

"Not wanted on the voyage."

"I think," said Swithin (given to thinking in flashes), "I must just absolutely give in—the way *they* have. Their story has the essential qualities of a true romance: fantasy, ayurveda, escape, consolation—rather like *The King of the Dark Chamber*. And after all, is not the *Visshuddha* chakra the place of ether and dreaming?"

"Yahs," the Mahatma agreed suspiciously.

"And wouldn't they be *lovely* in an opera? They say *his* mother told fortunes on the pier at Yarmouth, and as for *hers*, well, I expect we shall have to wait for the completion and release of *Pilgrim Soul*—and even then, it will be required that we grapple with the allegory, but the Gypsies come into it too; that much one knows for certain. And do not the Gypsies derive from India?"

*

Mawrdew Czgowchwz looked around. "Time to clear these flowers, isn't it—if there was a microphone stuck in them, they ought to have had their fill of us, anyway."

"You're *such* an evolved creature of intrigue—a spy at heart. You were a spy in the war."

"All Central Europeans are spies. Destinn was a spy, Mata Hari, Lya de Putti, and more recently Heddy Lamarr—in fact she broke a code—or so they say—with George Antheil at the piano. So, too, were Leslie Howard, and, although not Central European, rather dedicated to certain Ruritanian fantasies, Noel Coward. Also Merle Oberon and a whole regiment of Commanches."

"Imagine."

"Indeed—and spies have no hearts; I found that out."

"I have a heart. You actually once had supper with Stalin?"

"Yes I did—once. Are you a spy?"

"No—and who on earth was Lya de Putti?"

"One of the greats of the European silent screen. Hungarian, spied for Romania against Bela Kun. Translated from Budapest to Bucharest one dark, wet and windy night just as the Romanian army was crossing the border the other way. Later the hated rival of Marie of Romania."

"You actually had dinner with Stalin."

"Unless it was his double, yes—but he was beastly, stinking drunk enough to convince me."

"No wonder you disdain the part of Tosca, it would be nothing but anticlimactic. I'm not a spy—or as Attracta tells Assumpta in The O'Maurigan's virginity joke, not *yet*. I'm one of intrigue's developing embryos. A plot element, more close-thrown than far-fetched—for the time being, any road."

"The time being *time out of mind*—so it says here. *Time Out of Mind* is a picture by Robert Siodmak. He directed Stanwyck in *The File on Thelma Jordon*."

"What did I tell you? A plot element in a picture by—"

"You'll catch up soon—hatch something of your own; something sensational."

"The way you lead a bloke on. Promising to tell stories of love and luck worthy of Acrasia—then threatening to toss out the blooms from the bower before a petal has dropped to the floor."

"Oh? Let me give you a tip. If you ever go into the spy racket, *don't* try posing as a schoolboy soprano. Insouciance is not your forte; you're too tall for the gestures—even lying down."

"Not soprano, ma'am, treble. And no intention of transforming. That's one thing you told me they left out—the true story of the transformation. You told me nobody but Jameson and Madge know it, and now me. So we are the Secret Three—as Madge put it, a new Trinity: an unlikely new version of the Three Gay Fellas. No, I'd pose as what you posed as—a nun. We'd be two nuns in fugue—with babies. What an exciting upbringing for the twins."

"Which reminds me—nun does—that there's one more living soul I must tell what happened, because in all the excitement of her coming to me in New

York from Prague and waving her wand and all the rest that followed until you, I never told her how I ended up on that stage singing Violetta. I have that to tell and you besides, and this—how can you be so sure it's twins?"

"My sources; my voices. Confess me to her?"

"If you like. I can't argue with your voices—not one of them. They are what got me to you. Besides, the cailleach in Ballywhither said the same thing, only for some reason I didn't like to tell you just then. Yes, confess you to her. What do we do now—that's to say *just* now?"

"*Patience good lady: wizards know their times.*
Deep night, dark night, the silent of the night . . ."

"Until such time?"

"Let's play cards."

"Patience—you propose that?"

"Not patience, and not solitaire; Wyrd pontoon."

"Some day you'll show me your Tarot—you said you would, but you said you'd tell me when first. Pontoon, eh? That pontoon pack of yours—uncanny—like all your devices, like Gypsy ways, like your voices."

"They're what got me—to you. One day I shall be permitted to show you my Tarot—in the mean time, pontoon."

"Pontoon, I believe is complicated. I'm used to Hearts, where you only have to keep track of two things: has the Queen of Spades been played—"

"The Queen of Spades generally signifies death."

"Generally. And has the hearts suit been broken. Did you ever see *The Lady Eve*?"

"I don't believe so—why?"

"Well, they meet on a ship, and she's a card sharp and—well, she marries him in Connecticut, only she's pretending to be English, and they have a scrap on the train—she's planned it—over all the men who—"

"We didn't meet on a ship."

"Well, no, but somehow I feel we've met *up* . . . with—anyway he jumps off the train into the mud."

"Messy. You're no card sharp—are you?"

"Well, I *was* thinking of Minnie—and of Miro's *Lola Montez*, to help scare up a production—ideally at the Garden; Bing would never countenance it at the Met."

"And I certainly have never seen you pretend to be English."

"No. Lola Montez was Irish—but I imagine you knew that."

"No, I only knew she's buried in Brooklyn—now let's play pontoon, shall we?"

Each card in Jacob Beltane's deck bore a number, a value, a picture, and a legend. Thus, before calling up another card in a given deal, the player must reckon the pictures and the legends in conjunctive calculation with the values and the numbers.

He shuffled; she cut; whereupon he, drawing back, smoothing the bed linen to clear a space between them, dealt.

To Czgowchwz: ten of hearts up / six of clubs face down.

To himself: nine of diamonds up / deuce of spades face down.

The numbers, pictures, and legends operating were:

Ten of hearts, card #7: Bouquet of Flowers—an absolute indication of a long and happy life. If children are nearby, extraordinary honors and fame.

Six of clubs, card #43: Lightning—denotes surprise, disagreeable in accordance to distance.

Nine of diamonds, card #39: The Human Heart—signifies great joy when near.

Deuce of spades, card #34: The Star—insures success in all enterprises when near. When very distant some unlucky events.

Jacob, holding the nine and the deuce, must play for increase toward twenty-one. Mawrdew Czgowchwz, with ten and six might hold, although—

"I do like your ten of hearts, flowers, and the number seven; but what might you be holding," he sniffed, "facedown?"

"My deep dark past."

Jacob ran his quicksilver mind over the pack's four aces, so.

Spades rapiers warning according to distance hearts the fox proximity distrust of acquaintances distant less danger clubs the crossroads shadows and sunlight misadventure or miscarriage of events hovering diamonds the birds dire misfortune when near.

(She's got the ace of spades down. As distant from the ten as whether she play it as one or as eleven. Is she playing eleven? She's empowered to demur, moment-counter-moment.)

He frowned and drummed his fingers.

She drummed her fingers, signaling the measure.

"Come, show, or draw."

"Another. You fluster me."

He drew the ten of spades faceup. The legend: The Rod; near: predict family quarrels; distant, pecuniary losses.

Mawrdew Czgowchwz surveyed her adversary's progress. On the board nineteen and contradictory legends. Perhaps a civilized scrap. Signaling for a card, she was dealt the ace of spades. Drawing breath in sharply, Jacob Beltane hissed, "Irish. Bohemian."

"I shall have one more for four."

"Four cards in Wyrd pontoon is beyond the pale—reckless, unheard-of."

"You're after hearing it only this minute."

He dealt up the four of clubs. The legend: The Key; if near a certain augury of success; if surrounded by unlucky cards, the prognostic is a turn for the worse.

"Rapiers, flowers, the key. Fox in hiding?"

"The heart, the rod—what *not* hiding, watching, waiting—spy."

"You've got it—twenty-one."

" 'It? Hell, she has *those*.' What have you got instead?"

"I've got it, too; exactly so—*unheard-of*."

"Synchronicity. A lot of it going around lately; charged atmospheres. People calling one another unbidden on the telephone. Insiders blame nuclear testing in the South Pacific. What next?"

"In a tie one reads high cards."

They read her ten of hearts against his ten of spades—flowers against the quarrelsome rod.

"*L'arcana parola*—difficult to determine," he announced, with executive finesse. "The rod, ten, close to the nine, heart, is far from the unlucky deuce. Briefly, either pecuniary loss or wrangling. Your ten of hearts, abundance, and your pretty flowers conquer all. Four cards in Wyrd pontoon—beyond outrageous!"

"I can, briefly, explain your pecuniary loss. We're discontinuing Wyrd pontoon, switching to poker, with a fresh deck. All straight ace-through-king, no jokers, no legends. You avoid the quarrel you seem to fear, and I take your shirt in seven card stud."

"*Tre aci e un paio*, eh? That's sounding a domineering note. I've been given to understand poker is a game of chance."

"As W. C. Fields said, not the way I play it. And safer than number games—where one might always, having done a gypsy *bajour* on the Old Countess, win time and again with three-seven-ace, only to come a cropper one cold windy night, when the Queen of Spades bats an evil eye. It is now time to perambulate on the deck, then eat."

"There's a mercy. Cards away! Ordering in?"

"We can't. It's second night out; we must join the captain."

"Talking of joins—the captain could marry us."

"Not at dinner. One outrageous trick per diem is my limit."

"And tomorrow?"

"Tomorrow, after I take your shirt in dimes—"

"I shall find ways to go on living—in sin."

"You know, there's an old Irish song that goes 'The people were saying no two were e'er wed, but one had a sorrow that never was said.' Also, I should tell you, in the Czech resistance, as a double agent I had to go and sing at any number of awful civil-ceremony Reich weddings."

"Never a triple agent then?"

"Never—but then as Fitz's former confessor, the Jesuit Strange, once put it to me, the only triple agent is in truth the Trinity. In any case, at the weddings, the spouses held *Mein Kampf* instead of the Bible, and instead of vows the commandant proclaimed of the woman, '*Wie die ewige Mutter des Volkes ist.*' Put me off the whole shenanigans, I'm afraid."

*

Lavina O'Maurigan Papers and her husband, David, also abed, were also deep in conversation.

"And in the second place, I do *not* call him, *Jamie*, and he does *not* call me *Vanilla*—good God at night!"

"I've remarked upon that not being the case."

"And *who* is this Jonathan Stein, for instance, I'm supposed to be married to?"

"Oh, that's quite clear. David covers Jonathan and paper covers—"

"What?"

"Rock . . . *Stein*."

"But what is it—where does the rubric come from?"

"A New York street game."

"Oh, is Park Avenue a street?"

"Not in that sense—we played it in Central Park."

*

"Futhermore," Swithin crooned, stacking hearts, "*a propos* figuration, *voila comme ils ont alisses a travers la salle de jeux, l'une a cote l'autre comme deux figures allegoriques!*

"They are hierogamous," he declared. "Although they have clearly only just risen from the nuptial bed, it cannot really be said of them that they have known ordinary gratification, being themselves so clearly the express gratification of Nature itself.

> *'Their lives did shrink to one desire, and soon*
> *They rose fire-eyed to follow in the wake*
> *Of one eternal thought.'*

C'est ca!"

"Swithin is *angelic*, this way," a votary declared. "Sanitary, sane. His calm surpasses understanding—or skips it anyway. Merely to hear him employ the word *shrink* properly is a benediction." Swithin, quivering, demurred. "Like Whitman, darlings, I shrivel at dark thoughts. Of course, *originally*, the rituals of hierogamy prescribed double suicide as consummation—but we have come into the modern world. Even the Master said as much when he delivered me from the devil's chains . . . from—" and looking into the middle distance, he shivered, "acci-*dental* cirr-*cum*-stances!"

The Mahatma, stacking clubs, nodded. Quite so. Swithin's deliverance from out of the bondage of the witchcraft known as psychoanalysis was—speaking, in the present case allegorically—a feather in the guru's cap.

For Prosper Swithin had only very recently come through a difficult time—quite a more difficult time, indeed, than his accustomed attacks of the vapors from things that he read in the papers' gossip columns—and the helicoidal graph of his decline—his substance wasted on fairs and fiestas, jigs and reels, reckless alliances and rodomontades—was the talk of more than a few closed groups on each side of the Atlantic. Booked to sail out from New York that July lately past, on the *Ile de France*, he'd started out early celebrating his own send-off sousing up at the Oak Room bar, even prior to Rotten Rodney's movable marathon bon voyage bash—a stingers-and-Dexadrine vaudeville turn that, gathering momentum and recruits as the night wore on and the stingers evolved into diamond fizzes, opiated hashish and arak, had played whistle stops at Le Cupidon, the Iridium Room, the Byline Room, The Copacabana, The Latin Quarter, The Mais Oui, The Cherry Lane, Lenny's Hideaway, Dick's Hat Band, and Chez Mae, then segued into the Everard Baths on West Twenty-eighth Street off Broadway for steambaths, swims, shenanigans, and barbituate cavorts (during which Swithin, groping the towel boy Freddie, and cooing lewdly had chastised him with "Oh, *dear*—and there it says in Deuteronomy, in the sissy King's own English '*Thou shall not have in thy bag divers weights, the one greater and the other smaller.*' I shall report you to the Better Business Bureau, that's what!").

All this and more before winding up at a sidecars-eggs Benedict and café Armagnac breakfast at Reuben's. It had continued on board ship, with Swithin, a dithyrambic chorus of one, romping through the deck, bridge, pool, and *Grand Salon*, until, tiring of his audience of international drifter lounge lizard hecklers, the cynosure of all eyes had collapsed in the back row of the cinema, self-consumed, sick, and withered in a diseased superfoetation, during the climax of John Huston's *Moby Dick*. There he had slept like the submerged dead, a child in the womb, as insensate as driftwood, during the dramatic hours during which the *Ile de France*, reversing course and cutting her engines in the treacherous corridor between the islands of Nantucket and Manitoy, assisted in the rescue of passengers off the stricken *Andrea Doria*.

Then, waking in a damp shudder, a lone left thing in a dark room, Swithin had staggered in hideous distress up flights of stairs and out onto the Boat Deck only in time to see the Statue of Liberty pass in dawn's early light *from right to left*.

The noise! The hordes! Evidently he had been evaporated for weeks, months, the while something hideous had happened to Europe, again. What wild howl . . . what triumphant ravage . . . who *were* these people, huddled in clumps and heaving to and fro, like Sargasso? Victims of a torpedoed vessel, an act of war—history had run amok once more: these were the last days in time! And what had been said of Jonah fleeing Joppa was all too true of Prosper Swithin, even if he had come aboard in New York with a hat box and more than one valise, led to the wharf by such shades as passed for friends. How plainly fugitive he was, too, as marked as any of the murderers of Sodom. Oh, most contemptible and worthy of scorn; with slouched hat and guilty eye, shy of his God: skulking among the shipping like a vile burglar hastening to cross the seas—to Tarshish and beyond—and now Leviathan had spat him back upon the shore, and terrors upon terrors.

O dedi
O dada orzouza

O dou zoura
O dada skizi.

Acci-dental circum-*stances*! ran braying through his soul!

Prosper Swithin, formerly known in Church of England musical circles as Piers Shuttlethwaite, had been born Nigel Noakes, in Aldershot (as he liked to point out "right in the gay proximity, dear, of the Eleventh Hussars"). The boy had been, as a child of an age to know the paving of the roads of sorrow, a delicate instance much plagued by croup, and worse. Found by agents of philanthropic and celibate bent in a pub, singing a bold rendition of Arthur Askey's popular ditty, "I'm a little fairy flower, growing wilder by the hour," he was immediately removed from this den of detrimentals and (not for the last time) re-christened (thus saved then and there from a East End life of oisting, nipping, lifting and shaving, and almost certain incarceration either in the workhouse prisons or, considering his prettiness and his seeming-ingrained predilections, in Colney Hatch, for the length of his natural days), and made over in due course and expense into the bijou boy treble at the Westminster Choir School a prize adept, singing both at the Abbey and at St. Paul's Thomas Tallis, Bartlett, the celestial Ash Wednesday vespers and similar anthems of the just.

During the first weeks of the "Phony War" in the fall of 1939, he'd climbed into the dome, to test the echo and heard a voice in the silence. *Know all things to be like an echo that derives from music, sounds and weeping, yet in that echo there is no melody.*

Fainting, he'd been transported to a nursing home in Kent. After Dunkirk the bombs began to fall in earnest, he'd been evacuated to New York. There, commencing with scarlet fever and strep throat as a consequence of the ardors of deracination and the voyage, he woke one morning, orphaned—out of Aldershot in the nick of time, but without his people—with a what seemed broken voice and a full-blown case of measles. Shrieking in horror at his face in the mirror, he'd further damaged the delicate chordal transition, winding up compromised by a laryngeal scrape that earned him the soubriquet "the frog prince."

Following his first performance in New York, with the Gramercy Chamber Trio for which occasion, Benjamin Britten and Peter Pears and Wystan Auden, in a war-morale mood, had him rechristened Prosper Swithin and adopted by the Episcopal Church in America's Diocese of New York, and trained into a prize alto at St. Paul's Choir School on West Fifty-eighth Street, and in the Episcopal Savoyards (Dead Eye Dick in *H.M.S. Pinafore*, his star turn), he nonetheless developed a vexing attraction to jazz, finding ways (blood will out, they said) to sneak off to Harlem, to hear "low down nigger noises and wails in the night, fit to make a boy's ears burn and fill his young brain full of frisks!"

Mesalliances with Episcopal vicars had followed, begun in the mottled glows of late afternoon sun coming through late nineteenth-century stained-glass windows, and continued in their studies (invariably decorated with pictures by Flandrin, Henry Scott Tuke, Glyn Philpot, Ludwig von Hoffmann, and illustrated duotone monographs of the works of Praxiteles, Canova, and Arno Breker), their penchant for humming *Jesu Joy of Man's Desiring* and *Hail, Gladdening Light* at odd times both exacerbated his already fraught nerves and "alto" tendencies. "So I smoke a little too much . . . and I drink a little too much . . . but what else do you do at the end of a love affair?"

Years passed. Finally, as he put it, "free, white and twenty-one" (although actually some years older) and at the behest of a Sullivanian analyst he'd met at the Byline Room to go back home and *pick up the pieces, he'd booked passage* on the *Ile de France.*

Running amok (*O Dedi, O dada orzouza!*) in response to all that—and more: in sum the exhaustion resultant from his lifelong quest for meaning, control, and recognition in the context not just of society but in the arena of his own paradoxical self and its manifest of warring impulses (*and* convinced he had been spared digestion by Leviathan expressly to return and preach The Word of God to Nineveh: New York), the vociferant (his mind an unhinged door swinging and banging in every wind) had been apprehended in a state of certified public madness. (The police report read: "Having run naked out onto the deck, the subject lay down under a lifeboat. Retrieved and covered in a deckchair blanket, he stammered out gibberish: '*O dedi! O dada! O dou zouza! O dada skizi*—acci-*dental* circum-*stances!*' and proceeded unshod down the gangplank, dragging his right foot behind in a broad, uncertain descent to the pier deck. He acknowledges no one. His jaw is slack, his eyes glassy.")

And from police custody and the Observation Room at Bellevue, bound away, signed-sealed-and-delivered to a certain Dr. Zwischen's House of Balm in the Berkshires ("reposing in the midst of the most beautiful scenery in Western Massachusetts, within sight of Melville's beloved Great Tom, the hump-backed whale of a mountain he had looked out on while composing his masterful and preternaturally prescient allegory of the American Republic, portrait of the daemonic Lincoln and all, and combining all the influences which human art and skill can command to soothe and restore the wandering minds gathered to its precincts"). Rival institution to McLean's and Chestnut Lodge, and successor to Zahler's New Thought Sanitarium ("Henceforth the name of the game is *force*.")

Zwischen (called *Schadenfreude* in MNOPQR STUVWXYZ) having adapted the theories of Weir Mitchell concerning female neurasthenia to the fagged-out tremors of thoroughbred mental cases, to the rehabilitation of "delicate" men of Anglo-Saxon origins (exclusively, for this *was* the "restricted" and refined New England of the Transcendentalists, and the very name Zwischen had, initially, caused tremors on its own). To live (he, Swithin later averred) like Dostoyevsky in Siberia, in perpetual fear of being flogged with the knout, restrained in the *fluchtige hingemacht* tradition by the *Geradehalter*, the sacrificial *yupa* of the Zwischen regime—said to have been successful with Otto Klemperer over a decade earlier overdosed with Thorazine, subjected to the *noyade*, the proof by water, overdosed with insulin and/or plugged into the wall, clapped with earphones, and made to listen to the orchestral compositions of Furtwangler, and forbidden, alternatively to view, on the new television set in the solarium, so much as a single episode of *In This Our Life*.

"*Mensch, er ist ein Erbkranker!*" was the initial verdict, but the scandal that threatened to set off was met with the revision, in English: "The patient is strenuously insane; nevertheless, there are veridical signals at the root of the display: claustrophic unease, torpidity and stagnation, lethargic fatalism and a meticulous, calculated submission to absolute masochism. What we intend effecting is the abrogation of the *Trennung*—odious separation fostered by the Romantic Age. At the conclusion of the *milieu therapy* the patient will be reintroduced to society in celebration and that absolute peace between interiority and exteriority that recognizes their joint victory over romantic illusion of all kinds and rescues perceptible appearance from the contempt in which it was held by the dystonic ego. What you see is what you've got."

From which snake pit he, Swithin, was in mercifully short order extricated by the Sullivanians—but not before rumors of surgical skullduggery, psychic gralloching, and electrode cranial remolding of the cognitive dissonance with which the fact of abuse confronts our wish to live in a benign universe were heard spread ("Wigged *out*, poor darling—no exchange, no refund. Not since the memoirs of Schreber!), had done their work. Wigged out, I tell you; his entire *Archiv des Gedachtnisses—geblitzt*! It now seems he's convinced that what's happened to him is he's been translated by karma *back* into an earlier life—preincarnated, if you will, as poor Starr Faithfull aboard the *Ile de France*, and that *they* were attempting to toss him—now her—*overboard*, like the dismembered body of Prajapati—"

"Who?"

"Prajapati, darling—at the Manitoy lighthouse and make it look like *suicide*, when he—now she—"

"Whosis-Patty, you mean?"

"*Prajapati*."

"Is that a he or a she?"

"I don't know, darling. Anyway not him—or her—but Swithin. Torn, darling, from their fast clutches by a valiant French *marin*. That, of course, means to her that this is the year 1931 and that she has to get *out of that place* because, of course, she has *things to tell us*—such as *everything* that is going to happen unless we *intervene*, unless we change our ways. Y'know—Hitler and Pearl Harbor and television and the atomic bomb. *How* the restored Miss Faithfull rationalizes the current contours of her anatomy is not reported, but you can bet your bugle beads Zwischen has a kicky explanation to hand as he slaps on the serrated gold crown and warbles his little imprecations in German about the merciful atrophy of painful recollections. Something about the fallacy of misplaced concreteness—depends on it—agents and forces fashioned out of generalities. Rich Jews flock to him in their droves—which is *insane*, darling, because he's a second *Mengele*!"

The Sullivanians put Prosper Swithin into a colony on the Upper West Side, but he would migrate across town, and, finally, falling into Jimmy Donohue's clutches, he became party to the doings at the Penn Post, nearly got involved in the Billy Woodward murder case, filled Fulton Sheen's ears full of his degrading Episcopal Church experience, and was very nearly baptized at St. Agnes's. He was present at the party at which J. D. threw the Puerto Rican hustler out the window, which pushed him near again to the edge, until finally, the Mahatma . . ."

The Mahatma's regimen, raw eggs, canasta, and forbearance ("Dohn't let thot *dukkha* get you down!"), together with reliance upon the healing energies of the seven chakras and the Life Force (*not* those dubious quiverings generated by orgone boxes and the electrode, for the Godsend was not minded to squander his teachings upon the autistic) had made of Prosper Swithin that which months of Sullivanian immersion (both Sir Arthur and Harry Stack) had not availed: a new human specimen, and a vibrant presence among the sect (who had begun to suspect, with some asperity and many mixed feelings brewed of both ambition and late capitalist consumer angst, that the last would, indeed, be first, and this newest recruit, lapping *lassi* like a stray cat, was indeed spinning on the final cycle in this *kalpa*.

Yet, that said, many among the Bahktivedanta elect, Swithin paramount among them, we're more anxious to attract the famous couple as ever they might be to osmose the imports of the more paradoxical sutras they had pledged themselves to master with a view to inviting ecstasy in the New Dawn —for they had read too of the concept of *darshan*, which allows that merely getting next to persons of celebrity or importance casts a *nimbus* upon the spectator. ("Lohd love a duck, they are but tots," the swami mused. His clear, washed, indulgent mystic's eye trained eastward as the buoyant main bore witness to All's Oneness. Time yet for tempests, rigors, trials. ("Tee-hee-hee-hee-hee-hee-hee!")

*

They were out on the veranda deck, settling into deck chairs.

"That was," she said, "Mahatma and company."

"Across the crowded room—where they looked happy."

Tilting deck chairs back, they surveyed the spangled night sky roofing the Atlantic.

> " '*In the rapture ocean's billowing kiss,*
> *In the fragrance wave's ringing sound,*
> *In the world-breath's wafting whole—to drown,*
> *To sink unconscious—highest bliss!*'

"Slow curtain, the end. Only I sang not those words in German, or in English or in any other tongue. I sang *The Lament of the Hag of Beare*, and somehow made it fit the notes. I wonder how Wagner would have taken it? Probably not in his stride."

"Dressing gown billowing furiously behind him. Shouting, roaring. Would you like," Jacob inquired, "to know the stars? Who they are when they're giving a party at home? Their influence?"

"Of course you know them, you studied them at Cambridge; you were an astronomer, and a physicist, and a mathematician, and dare I say so, an operative at Bletchley Park."

"I was some of those things, but as to Bletchley Park, the official record states one was brought down from Ely, where one had been ordained in secondary orders as the deacon choirmaster, to offer choral evensong in the Quonset huts. What was made of one's mathematical skills on the one hand and of one's suspected or inferred associations at Cambridge in nineteen thirty-nine..."

"*Nuff sed*, as they say in Gotham. There might be a microphone in any one of these extravagant floral pieces—the peonies, for instance. Where did they find peonies in September? California, one supposes. At any rate, the stars. In their naked indifference one feels they are at best disdainful."

"Naked perhaps, indifferent, never. There's Venus, for example."

"*O vagabonda stlessa d'Oriente.*"

"See, you know her."

"It's just something I used to sing."

"Yet another life ago?"

"In Verona in summer. I was the villainess, don't-you-know."

"Praying to the vagabond."

"Wanton, wretched, desperate, doomed; open chest contralto scorned—outdoors, floodlit for the multitudes; all in fun. They used to say in Prague I was born to play those roles—redheads, and wicked, and I got a reputation for being *like* them. Isolde-like, they'd say, and then 'a mercy she hasn't the role in her voice.' And another would say 'She may, one day' and they'd argue about the voice and about me as if I weren't present."

"What was your wickedest role then—if you care to say."

"Oh, Amneris, without question—especially when I sang it with Welitsch. We had it worked out so she was hot and driven for Aida—Radames was nothing but a beard, and I went into orgasm on top of the tomb as the last spotlight dies. It made people *crazy*."

"Under these stars," he continued, "all the marine dead since the voyages of Brendan slept in peace—until the advent of engine a century ago. They have been stirring the spirits ever since, to no one's benefit."

"As they say where we're bound, 'Ye could sing all that, if ye had the *chune*.' Isn't that Andromeda?"

"It is.

Now Time's Andromeda on this rock rude,
With not her either beauty's equal or
Her injury's looks off by both horns of shore,

Her flower, her piece of being, doomed dragon food.
Time past she has been attempted and pursued
By many blows and banes; but now hears roar
A wilder beast from West than all were, more
Rife in her wrongs, more lawless, and more lewd.
Her Perseus linger and leave her to her extremes?
Pillowy air he treads a time and hangs
His thoughts on her, forsaken that she seems,
All while her patience, morselled into pangs,
Mounts; then to alight disarming, no one dreams,
With Gorgon's gear and barebill thongs and fangs."

"Czgowchwz had a great liking for the phrase *mazel-tov*—said it meant 'under a benevolent star.' "

"Do you mock my science, ma'am?"

"Not well, and don't call me *mahm*—it makes the flesh crawl right off my bones. Please go on; I'll keep still."

"A cloud came over you when you were speaking of Czgowchwz. I do realize—"

"I never wanted to sing Marfa again."

"Oh?"

"She prophesies doom—she carries it in her."

"You can't think you—"

"Oh, can't I though? I often think of very litle else."

*

"They must come in at some hour."

"I could play on through the night."

"The Om hum of the ship is so—"

"The sheen of the full moon at sea!"

“ ‘They live enamored of the lovely moon
Then dawn and twilight on their gentle lake.
Then Passion marvelously born doth shake
Their breasts and drive them into mid-noon.’ ”

“Would it be importunate to amble out, only to observe them—*figures glissantes, l’une a cote l’autre*—”

“Cards! Cards! Noh she-non-ee-gons. Meestah Swithin, parhops ahs on exercise in deetochment you wud care to releyht to those parsons uv oah pahrty who are not soh familiah as we weeth the story of the garjus diva?”

Swithin did so, in garbled fashion, ending with, “So you see, she was saved right in the nick of time.”

The satisfaction seemed general, at any rate until one votary was heard to enquire anxiously of another,

“Dear, what *is* the nick of time?”

IV

They had driven from Symphony Space down Broadway to Columbus Circle, then down to Fifty-seventh Street and across town past Carnegie Hall and site of the old Russian Tea Room to the comfort of Fifth Avenue, stopping at a red light just across from Tiffany and Company, then down Fifth Avenue, snubbing in silence the transformed precincts of their old Rialto.

"The worst of it," he declared, as they sped past the New York Public Library, "as I've discovered in forays of late isn't the new neon, as enervating by night as the old neon was on top of a bright noon sun as experienced after a night on Dexamyl—epitomized, I've decided by the NASDAQ sign taking up the whole facade of the building it clads that's turned the place not so much into a lesser Kufürstendamm as into a lesser Ginza—*who* won that War? In truth it's probably more in line aesthetically with the juggernaut progress of Mammon in the new century than, say, Gehry's mooted designs for a new Brooklyn skyline. After all just as surely as culture follows money, do all rubrics pertinent to life itself's essential mystery dog the tracks of Mammon.

"No, none of it—not the obliteration of Birdland, or the Taft, the Latin Quarter, the Astor, the old Times Building or worst of all of our gorgeous once gold-brick Florentine brewery where you yourself season upon season—how did they put it, the schoolboys? It was well put—heaped upon music a variety of disguises none of which could hope to obscure her own . . . whatever that was."

"Immutable self, I'm afraid."

"Yes, well, as a certain other mesmeric enchanter of our sometime acquaintance—one revealed at the end of it all as indeed as genuinely American a phenomenon as both the Confidence Man on his Mississippi steamboat and the Wizard of Oz, refugee from the Omaha State Fair there behind his curtain in the inner precincts of the Emerald City, one declared of his charges, they were but tots. And yet, to write 'But like Stuvwxyz over Stuvwxyz or Stuvwxyz to this or that root or power was still Stuvwxyz, as in the number one, and Stuvwxyz reflected by Stuvwxyz in an endless hall of Stuvwxyz mirrors was but Stuvwxyz' was simple thing. They were gifted boys, and slyboots both.

"And there in that auditorium you did weave night upon night, performance after performance for seven seasons of the greatest abundance in the history of the Metropolitan Opera—I could go on, you know, without—"

"The word of a lie. You could, unopposed. Then again you could get to the verb."

"—performance after performance with unprecedented and unforgettable auditory vehemence ecstasy we . . . but wait, do the ecstatic wear garments—or do they cast them off?"

"Nice ones wear them—but generally of light rather than sound."

"Indeed so, darling Blake. He never did hear you, and well on top of everything else, you were *son et lumière before* the French came up with it for Bastille Day. No, it's much worse than any of that. I can't for a fact tell you—I don't know and I haven't even *heard*—does Rosa Ponselle still stand in cut stone facing southwest in her immortal Norma pose up there on the second-story pediment of the old I. Miller shoe building where you first said hello to Andy Warhol dropping off sketches later collected as *A la recherché de shoe perdu* and he nearly fainted—"

"Actually that happened up on Fifty-seventh Street where I. Miller had moved. He'd come backstage so many times, never asked for an autograph, never spoke a word, I was that curious. We talked about the old country that afternoon—of course he'd never been. He told me they called his people Bohunks in Pittsburgh, which he obviously hated. I thought him bright and intelligent, no sides to him whatever and altogether delightful. Not in the least diffident either—but there is no such thing I think, or ever was as a diffident Slavic—only very purposedly silent."

"He was indeed both for a time. Or Marilyn Miller as Sunny, La Barrymore as Ophelia, and Thalia Bridgewood as Peter Pan? Do you realize that one has been reprimanded in Old Hollywood for seeming not to know that Norma Jeane Mortensen was named after Norma Talmadge and Jeanne Eagels, and later renamed Marilyn Monroe after Marilyn Miller—which of course, irony being the invincible force it is, she later in fact became?"

"I loved that girl. Her like will absolutely never come again."

At Twentieth-eighth Street and Fifth Avenue he had looked out the taxicab window a block and a half west, past Broadway to the street that had been in the 1890s in the era of Tammany Hall the main thoroughfare of the notorious Tenderloin and, later, from 1910 on for a generation, called Tin Pan Alley, the street on which from that time until the dawn of the Age of AIDS the best-known address was number 28, the former Everard Baths, the walls of which had withstood the conflagration that had signaled the death knell of postwar (lately called pre-Stonewall) Queer culture, the reconstructed premises now housing a thriving Korean retail mall, and toward another building, on the north side of the same block in which he had for many years kept a loft apartment.

He suddenly found the innumerable shades of that horde of stylish, seedy, eminently successful and utterly broken men, his own phantom self, poet, pederast, lover, and *seautontimoremenos* out of the mind of Baudelaire among them, present and accounted for regularly at roll call, passing in file across his worn mind's eye, climbing into Checker cabs to barrel down Broadway from Carnegie Hall, the New York City Center, innumerable Broadway theaters (the early, hungry crowd), and any number of after-theater supper parties in restaurants and in apartments ranging from bohemian walkups on Second Avenue to the opulent duplex and triplex residences of the starched-white-collar moneyed on Park and Fifth avenues and across Central Park in the somewhat more Continental abodes of the West Side intellectuals in the Hotel des Artistes, the Dakota Apartments, the Beresford, and the Osborne down on Fifty-seventh Street diagonally across from Carnegie Hall (the more seasoned, relaxed, and reliable clientele), the cabs turning a sharp right on Twenty-eighth Street to drop their passengers off in front of the white marble facade flanked by that pair of green-orbed entryway lanterns identical to those marking New York's police precinct houses (for the entire operation had, indeed, been owned and run, like clockwork, by the New York Policemen's Benevolent Association. God, what a time! God, what a town! How good God had been for a time).

He then saw the street on one of those nights, years along in his career, the smoke and flames pouring out of the windows and bodies dropping onto the sidewalk, and in the early dawn, ambulances and fire trucks, and then in a subsequent, stiller dawn a boarded-up door with a painted sign NEVER AGAIN!

They had passed Madison Square and the Flatiron Building, turned across Twenty-second Street to Lexington Avenue, then right again to Gramercy Park, left, left, and left again to stop in front of number 47 Gramercy Park North—when he realized that of course there were no manuscripts in cupboards, no tapes, nothing but his own sojourn *in aula ingentium memoriae* to account for those night journeys, surely as memorable and unquestionably as formative of the man he'd come to be, as any journey elsewhere on earth, as any play, poem, book, or stele inscription ever read, as any event in any theater ever attended.

"You've been thinking the voices," she said, "about the Cigarettes."

"Indeed, how they must file out in chorus into the telling."

"Sing for the suppers just like the rest of us—one particular song."

"I'd rehearse them in it now, but I'm sung out, entirely."

"And to enthusiastic personal notices—the *M'appari* was really just lovely."

"Ah, well, couldn't let old Dedalus down and the drink heavy on him—sure 'tis a good man's failing, so it is."

*

Now that was lovely, so it was. Nonetheless, forby and forthwith for an interval at the very least, a new description of the telling is called for, and that on the heels of the dying notes of the aria only just alluded to by Herself that at the end of the day the whole shebang (if y'll pardon the liberty of a familiarity, and a ribald one at that, but sure wasn't she ever a robust woman?) is about—and what's it about, the aria? (Paris by the sound of it, or is it an *apparition* that's in it, or both together). The aria the once-young lord has only just delivered to plaudits we've been told, the dying notes finding welcome again in the consoling pages of that book, the one this one that surely isn't.

Yes, it is indeed oneself, Himself, The Other, no *violer d'amores* by the way, or oil painting either, no resuscitator of the poem of force, that's certain, for who was it decreed, *no forcing, it's fatal*? A Dublin man of some description, that's plain enough. But sufficient unto the day that's in it, though he says it as shouldn't maybe but sure isn't it just as false t' shove yr own horn up yr bloomin' arse as ever it is t' try blowin' down the walls of Derry with a tin whistle? Save it for the *seisiun*, recommends yer man in charge.

The collective voices, indistinct, distorted by such gale-force winds as regularly sweep through the canyons of Manhattan from river to river (often accompanied by the very thunder, lightning, and torrential rain of which these two, the protagonists so far are sitting at the open French windows waiting to welcome in), suffice not. Therefore 'twas the poet's conundrum (and he'd not sheathed his manhood in one of them affairs in decades). Dare he summon this one, oneself, Moriarty, so seldom heard from lately? And as the unprotected thought is father to the deed, enter yr servant to lay out somewhat the strategy (don't *talk* to me now, ye must have one or shut yr cake hole right up this instant) for the working out of the (subliminal) "down" solutions of the imaginary puzzle, to wit, the saga itself.

It is the great misfortune of the necessarily incorporeal life that nobody will leave you be. They will recklessly invest you with *attributes*, with qualities, with *nature* (of which I personally have none—no qualities, *kein Eigenschaften, kein Eulenspiegelen, nichts*. No more than did the Confidence Man on his Mississippi riverboat or that old spalpeen out of the Omaha State Fair, the Wizard of Oz, behind that curtain in the inner chamber of the palace of the Emerald City at the end of that yellow brick road. Him with his levers and switches, his smoke and mirrors and *television* fifty years before the fact—och, I'm tellin' ye now there was a touch of the oul' Ariosto in that twister, an a bit of the oul' John Dee on top of him, *mar dhea*.

So that, in consideration of these expecting returns, explicit and detailed, from their investments let it be known there are times when the heart grows faint, and the mind, like any other mind that tells itself it knows itself (and these allowances are made under no prompting of idle self-contemplation) rather than give out, gives in. Would not ye do, were ye the incorporeal whim of a melancholy boy (that was, but there's another thing: time does not register in the mind of a figment: it's always the same day, the day he thought you up). Let one's position be defined.

Nevertheless, passages in this narrative are soon to come that will set the minds of many in judgment of one's forensic conduct: they who either from fear of the world as it is, of things as they are, or from sterner motives of self-concealment, self-delusion, self-loathing, and self-service, are capable neither of arranging their ideas nor of admitting of the necessity by way of the plainest of narratives of going back far enough in the proceedings and lifting every veil that billows in distracting zephyrs in impediment to their course. They are ever with us. Fuck 'em, and all their steeds.

The substance of the information thus obtained is as immediately follows in the living, breathing, sighing, moaning, shrieking, howling transcript of uncommon events. One might have liked to relate the narrative not in the words—often interrupted, inevitably confused—of the speakers themselves, but rather in the words of the brief, plain, studiously simple abstract committed to writing for one's own guidance and for the guidance of one's legal advisers—

(Your *what?*)

A pleasantry. One realizes one holds no claim on the estate. Therefore let the tangled be most speedily woven and let the flashlight held up in the darkened hallway discover it in its corner—for without the tangled web there can be trapped no flies.

Let the lot of them talk blue streaks out of hell, even if the effect upon the reader, poor devil, of so much random dialogue from anonymous mouths must be the equivalent either of sifting through absolute reams of vexing gibberish or of hearing recited yet again the elements of a story they know only too well—in either case rather like sitting through *Siegfried* or plowing through the cetology chapters of *Moby-Dick*.

Which *might* be justified by the fact that so many beached queer white whales of men do sag the steel springs of the dormitory's beds . . . none of them fighters like Melville's leviathan, although they all seem to have been in the War, many in the Pacific, where, to hear them tell it, they made their own gay beaches in deserted coves on the far sides of the islands they took one by one from the Japanese. So that there is after all in the collective tale indeed a quality of genuine heroism connected to sailing in the South Pacific and coupled with the image of Manhattan itself as both a ship and a right whale. Grab it.

Additionally, does not the wise old Fenichel insist that *most people are other people*? Then, too, as in modern psychoanalysis, where the narration of the past is seen as a kind of double-blind, placebo-emetic process, the progressive experiencing of the narration of the present, in session, the only real enactment–re-enactment: a theatrical magic show featuring legerdemain, forgeries, labyrinths twisting and turning like great sewer systems beneath social services, both servicing and exploiting subterranean anxieties, etcetera. Mirrors opposite mirrors—but we've been treated to the felicities of that particular simile once already, although it might be worth remarking that none of the endless mirror images of the woman who in performing life was Mawrdew Czgowchwz, ever represented anybody else.

So that if I, Moriarty, looking into that mirror, tell ye the story of the young lord's coming down Broadway on the very evening after the sailing of the *Mary* (Oh, he'd gone up to Magwyck and fed the cat, thinking of an early night, but what an engine is manly lust in an Irish bravo: there's more horsepower in it than what's under the hood of any Checker cab—*vide supra*—and that ye can tell the Cardinal himself if it suits yr book—yr *bouk* if ye happen to be of the Coombe in dirty darlin' Dublin born) it's going to be in the nature of a complicated business, so it is, *mar dhea*.

Plus which and hereupon, given that the fact that all epic language is a mixture of dialects, we shall be busy marking the continuous parallel between contemporaneity and antiquity. *Nous avons retrouves bien d'autres choses contenues dans le bagage mythique de l'Humanite depuis la nuit de temps.*

(So to speak, yes.)

Yet still and all, no one knows better than I myself, and by myself alone may tell, the tale. In that I am a little like Orestes—we both are, The O'Maurigan and I, and how not, so. *One like me is here; there is no one like me but Orestes; he, therefore must be here.* Tell *that* to Fenichel. Of course, Fenichel does say "most people" and we are surely not most people.

Why not come along, so, for the *craic*. Moriarty's Tale, brisk and efficient, no neurotic pauses, copybooks blotted like the face of the moon *Eh, bien, a nos oignons.*

As night descends on the moonlit Atlantic, the young lord goes out from Magwyck, his official daylight home on East Seventh-fourth Street, on one of what he affects to call his nights *errant*, to the ocean-liner city's lower decks, stopping for intervals of varying lengths, none exceeding twenty minutes, at certain New York City Transit System subway gents' toilets, finishing in the one in the Fifty-seventh Street station, terminus of the BMT Brighton Beach Line.

Then, coming up onto Fifty-fifth Street and Seventh Avenue, he proceeds directly one block west to Broadway, then turns left to wander downtown through the neon Floating World of Gotham (in the wide space of the world night) past the Paramount Theatre and the Astor Bar, the Museum of Oddities and Wonders, and the United States Armed Forces Recruiting Station, to Forty-second Street (naughty, bawdy, gaudy, sporty, where the underground meets the elite), thinking all the while of the wise words of Apuleius: *media nocte vidi solem coruscantem*, finally coming to a halt at the Crossroads Café across from the Times Tower.

A white preacher man with long white hair and beard is standing on the sidewalk next to a sandwich-board placard which reads: ATTENDANCE ON PUBLIC STAGES INTOXICATES A POPULACE AND DIVERTS THEIR MINDS FROM WHAT OUGHT TO BE THE GRAND OBJECT OF THEIR STUDY, THE PUBLIC GOOD. THE END IS NEAR. A turned-out black man in a zoot suit stops and reads the preacher out.

"We's *awl* duh woid made flesh, Bartho-le-*mew*, an' duh woid we's made flesh *uv* is *fuck, dig*? Now why don' you go gettin' jus' a little bit *real!*"

From there, a swerve, avoiding the locus of that morning's melodrama, avoiding the Western Union office and the opera house, the Central Coffee Shop, Bill's Bar, and the Burger Ranch, proceeding instead west again, down Forty-second Street, past Hector's, cafeteria (hooker's roost), the F*A*S*C*I*N*A*T*I*O*N arcade, the eccentric almost-skyscraper Times Tower, and the Strand, Victory, Apollo, and Alden theaters to the far corner of Forty-second Street and Eighth Avenue, south portal of Hell's Kitchen, where stood a black preacher of more orthodox stripe, impeccably turned out, standing alongside another placard, reading: HE IS THE WORD MADE FLESH, and exhorting the crowd.

"And they that did feed delicately are desolate in the streets!"

And what, thinks the wanderer, seeking both the way in and the way out in words, of the flesh made word? Definition of fiction or galling fatuity, *tout court?*

Pressing on: down Eighth Avenue to the Dixie Bus Terminal on Thirty-fourth Street, from the interior of which, day and night twenty-four-seven-three-sixty-five, the agrarian and proletarian hordes of the great Republic, unceremoniously disgorged, fan out, having come to town as if buffeted by any of the four winds or all of them at once, from somewhere, anywhere elsewhere, to find their dreams walking the streets on stilts, determined to be hoofers, winding up for intervals of indeterminable length as hookers. Press on.

Turning east, he proceeds at a quickened pace down dark and lonely Thirty-second Street, passing the notorious Penn post, averting his gaze (for there are forms of debauchery in the aftermath of which the whiplash of remorse can cut so deep into the enfeebled soul that there comes about the helpless commission of the one sin said, in the light of syllogistic logic, to be unpardonable, that against the mercy of the Holy Spirit).

Crossing Seventh Avenue, looking back over his shoulder at the great colonnaded facade of the United States General Post Office directly across from the Caracallan hulk of Pennsylvania Station, to read the famous frieze inscription: NEITHER SNOW NOR RAIN NOR HEAT NOR GLOOM OF NIGHT STAYS THESE COURIERS FROM THE SWIFT COMPLETION OF THEIR APPOINTED ROUNDS and to ponder the history of his kind and the accomplished if not often swift completion of the self-appointed rounds of the compulsive sexualist—the Rake's Progress—carrying gonorrhea and syphilis as relentlessly as any postman (and ringing many more times than twice), so on, so forth, *sic transit* systems.

Images now assail him of the *petit bleu* and the *pneumatique in Paris* (he having both sent them and received cordial replies, one time from the Ritz to Mawrdew Czgowchwz, on the occasion of her triumphant debut at the Salle Favart singing Massenet's Charlotte, another time from the Irish Embassy residence to Gertrude Stein and Alice B. Toklas on the rue Fleurus) colliding in his tremulous mind with memories of Rake Street, the little crossroads hamlet near his ancestral home, and since the tragic wartime death of both parents (it was they, he thought, were careless, not he), as The O'Maurigan, hereditary Earl of Tirawly his country seat, Poulaphouca, in the shadow of Nephin Mountain in North County Mayo.

And finally, to bring our young lord to that unconscionably long day's journey's end, the shortcut through Pennsylvania Station, temple of alluring destinations, so many of them—Miami, New Orleans, Chicago-and-on-to-The Coast—so very beguiling in prospect, continuing east past Macy's, Gimbels, and Herald Square, then to the right down Sixth Avenue to the corner of Twenty-eighth Street, turning east again to number 28, to pass through the doors and climb the white marble steps of the Everard Baths, nexus of all routes in from Europa, Africus, Meridies and Septentrio to the Mandala City of the New Beginning.

And all along the way "Faces blanched by regret, sunned by crime, beaming with sin, rusted by vain virtue," a Central Casting cattle call for the heretics out of the Sixth Circle of Dante's *Inferno* (odd that, the telephone exchange for the very district is Circle Six).

Press on toward home-from-home, the Everard, noting certain formal aspects of the surround. The flatness of Sixth Avenue (officially the Avenue of the Americas since who remembers when) with its all-night coffee shops immortalized by Edward Hopper in his *Nighthawks* and of hundreds of long flat-roofed railroad-flat rooming houses, lately being converted one by one into "efficiencies" and housing painters, sculptors, photographers, and on the street floors wholesale flower businesses, *passementerie* and *parure* emporia (adjuncts all to the immense Seventh Avenue garment industry), photographic supply shops, and much else, including those roosts called home by the small army of character men and women essential to the theater and armed with résumés, eight-by-ten head shots, and meticulously culled personal notices (often dating back decades) always on call, as on Broadway, and increasingly downtown as well, play after play opened and more often than not closed within a matter of weeks, for life upon the wicked stage is, indeed, if not quite so zealously dedicated as the preacher man did hold to the intoxication of the populace with a view to diverting their minds from the contemplation of the public weal, nevertheless nothing like what a girl supposes (the boys, in our young lord's opinion being more in line with the delightful narcissistic vacancy of Dickens's Nicholas Nickleby, supposing next to nothing all the while more than casually disposed to seeing some quantity of their wildest dreams come true—and he'd get back to them later).

For as it was, famously Puckish as a child, that merry wanderer of the night, up late at adult parties, turfing his little sister out of bed to get up the cleverest little theatrical charades, sing songs old and new in the sweetest voice delighting all and sundry, had changed. What child after all, those who loved him troubled themselves in wondering, was that after all to father such an increasingly rueful, somber man?

For, Irish as they were in the main, they would not stick it that what they considered one of the worst excesses of the French Revolution, the assumed malaise of the Romantic poet, even if it had fostered the gorgeous poetry of James Clarence Mangan, but come on now, shift it, should cloud the life and work of their own attested genius. There were by centuries-long established tradition four poetic genres upon which the Irish bards had founded their reputations, and only one, the aisling was of a keening, dreamy nature, mourning the loss of something precious, seeing it come again in a dream. It was intimately associated with the immortal music of the fili as heard on the uileann pipes (the ones that called from glen to glen to beautiful errant beloved Donal Og, or Danny Boy as he'd come to be known by the Irish diaspora). Were you a poet of contemporary Ireland, however, having composed your aisling, you rolled up your sleeves, tucked in the flowing open collar of your work shirt, and put the shoulder to the wheel to turn out work in each of the other three.

Indeed, they said to themselves, his sad and lonely verse was without the word of a lie, even the so-called lie of art proclaimed by the likes of the immortal Oscar Wilde, the most absolutely beautiful such-like expression to spring from the Irish soil since the first poems of the revered poet of the people, Paddy Kavanagh, going on twenty years now since. It was a conundrum, to be sure, but as the Countess Madge O'Meaghre herself, the poet's remarkable aunt, had declared, "Conundrum is all very well—the shadow of Dundrum isn't," and that was of that tune name.

This is thy hour, O Soul, thy free flight into the wordless,
Away from books, away from art, the day erased, the lesson . . . done,
Thee fully forth emerging, silent, gazing, pondering the themes thou lovest best.
Night, sleep, and the stars.

And who's he kidding, now, on his late lunch hour? The boy can't wait to shut out the stars, banish sleep, get into that sodomitic fuck hutch and start acting like something in a banned book—to *underline* the goddamn day, to write its traces on the walls, to once again be flayed by art, the art of art on art, of post-mortem, of the opera no soap would dare to sponsor. The one thing holds—no two: the night, and death, for every time he walks in there he strips off surely to dance an audition for Death.

And so of larger—Darkness—
Those Evenings of the Brain—
When not a Moon disclose a Sign
Or Star—come out—within—

and finally, from Hart Crane:

I, turning, turning on smoked forking spires,
The city's stubborn lives, dreams, desires,

Is this opus a romance? An allegory? What are the moon and stars: astronomical or astrological? And what of the ciphers he was on about back there? If he has the one and yr servant has the other, then that's a *kiss* in cryptography—the coincidence of two disparate cryptograms transmitted in different ciphers, each containing the original plaintext, the solution to one thereby leading to the solution of the other. Of course that's double-talk; if you've solved one and uncovered the plaintext, what's the point of looking at the other? Unless my logic is faulty—it would be, I suppose, a sort of *deformation professionelle* caused by exposure to the incessant maddening drumming hum of non sequiturs and desperate pleas.

Notwithstanding, if one cipher—his or by proxy his spanking new narrator's—can be represented by the transcription of everything these ones get up to confabulating in the daytime and earlier evening, and them in their good stitches: the cipher depicting the imitators as though they were actually performing the societally approved, in whole or part, rites encoded, and the other—Yours Truly's—made to represent the transcription of the gushing font of their unleashed discourse when naked, or nearly, then—a *kiss*? Sure yer man would take a kiss off a lot else, *mar dhea* before he'd take one off me, I'll tell y' that in plaintext, free, gratis and fer nuthin'.

Or as he would put it, not a second time—

But where were we? Right, here. Every evening at Broadway-White-Way lighting-up o'clock sharp and until the Crack of Doom at Sodom-and-Catamites Lost Battalion Hall, watch yr step ascending the marble staircase, as it can be slippery bytimes. And lest we neglect, in setting up the Everard, the essential All-Walks-of-Life trope, let's get down to it directly, along with the hobbles and the crawls, the continuing drama of life at Sodom Central. The Camp names, the assumption of an estranging patois and an exaggerated accent, so that many sound the same, but if you care to listen you can begin to distinguish differences. The various garments hung up on hangers in the rooms, and rolled up in stand-in lockers. The valuables stashed away in safe-deposit boxes (and if there was ever a haul . . . but the PBA owns and runs the place with efficiency and to an enormous profit, otherwise what might night court look like after a real sweep-out). Nighttown isn't in it: sure they'd be slittin' their throats altogether.

Therefore let us liken the little scenes that follow to sections in a strophic song in the Dionysian dithyramb. Live theater, gentlemen (for alas, we cannot be held responsible for the likely emetic effects upon so many of the ladies or we'd lose our insurance, surely, therefore *at your own risk* madams), anonymous principals and chorus moving up and down the halls, around and around in the steam room, and at the inverted altar of the plunge pool. See the chorus move across the stage, then back in the other direction, then stand still for the epode; these are The Cigarettes.

In the Dionysian dithyramb man is aroused to the highest intensity of all his symbolic capabilities. Something never felt before forces itself into expression—the destruction of the Veil of Maja, the sense of oneness as the presiding genius of form, of nature itself. Now the essence of nature must express itself symbolically; a new world of symbols is necessary, the entire symbolism of the body, not just the symbolism of mouth, face, and words, but the full gestures of the dance—all the limbs moving to the rhythm. And then the other symbolic powers grow, those of music, rhythm, dynamics, and harmony—all with sudden spontaneity.

Plus you could take an enema and get a good massage.

As the ould particle said, here goes nuthin'.

Entering the Everard, across the street and down the block from the loft he keeps adjacent to Bill's Wholesale Flower Market, The O'Maurigan tells himself with a certain wonder that this block was once the epicenter of the Tenderloin and later on was Tin Pan Alley itself. He whispers upon ascending the stairs to his assigned cubicle on the top floor (always recalling the same distinguished thing: two blocks from here as the crow—and not the raven—flies, in a row house on the north side of Twenty-sixth Street between Lexington and Third avenues, Melville lived with his family and climbed out onto the roof to watch the fires burning at Astor Place in the terrible draft riots of 1863, and in which his beloved son Malcolm, in his own room on the top floor, put a pistol to his temple and killed himself, breaking his father's heart forever) and whispering "*Gott es dunkel hier!*" Until adjusting to the gloom, you're well on to blind, so the effect is that of walking through a radio show, one like *Duffy's Tavern*. "Hullo, Everard Baths, the Colonel ain't here."

Whereupon, taking over from all of us, separately and together, who might have benightedly thought ourselves charged with the telling hereabouts, the Other Voices of the Night, in remarks of a generally analytical and for the most part approbatory nature on the hardly unexpected appearance of our hero.

"Enter His Nibs."

"Is that a pun? If it is, say, 'His *Bent* Nibs.' "

"They do say he has a mind like—"

"A steel trap? No, I'd say it's more like a weir."

"A what?"

"A *weir*, dear—it's a kind of mesh trap in streams."

"Well, he is *weird*, there's just no denying it."

"He is like Bulldog Drummond, dear—out of the night, and into his American adventures. True it is that the miscellaneous scraps of evidence on his case that have so far come our way amount to little more than a stationery alibi—like a dry stone wall. He comes from a part of the world famous for them, you know, and—well, a dry stone wall is held together by nothing more—or less—"

"Than the artful arrangement of its constituent parts that is so, dear, but then so come to think of it is a house of cards. He is alarmingly distant as he walks through the wilderness of the world—"

"He rests not. His multifarious desires propel him relentlessly from the Lyceum to the pleading place."

"Oh, *brother!*"

"Can you not find something to do in the *bathroom*, Birdie?"

"Fer instance? Waitin' for you to get normal could take forever."

"To me, despite his bearing, which is impressive, he is not, as the French say, *bien de son peau*. I see him as a Heathcliff, wild on the vine. I hear a voice calling him—*Heathcliff! Heathcliff!* in the mist on the moors. He seems unheeding, unaware, as if listening to other voices . . . it's *too* enveloping!"

"Thank you Miss Oberon."

"A heart in love with sighs himself doth smother."

"Oh, *brother!*"

" 'A man that is born of a woman is of short continuance and full of trouble. While his flesh is upon him it shall be sorrowful, while his soul is in him it shall mourn.' That's *Job*, dear."

"But suppose he was born by Cesarean section—from his mother's womb untimely ripped? That's *Macbeth*."

"Your husband?"

"Actually, dear, that's not Macbeth, it's Macduff."

"What with so many—"

"*Can it!*"

"Well, I just *cannot* picture him at forty."

"I see him from time to time walking around in circles in the mist in the *steam room*. It is *too* enveloping. His face when it looms up at you fairly *erupts* with drama. The gaze is grave—comminatory even—yet absolutely radiant. Who was it said, dear, the poet's mind has windows of its own from which to gaze at secret views. Somebody divine."

"Secret views of steam-room walls? Far out, darling—very Zen."

"It is perhaps because he spends so much time in there, all but concealed within the soothing, exfoliating vapors, that whatever sufferings he has been put through have not by so much as a *trace* left their profaning mark upon the freshness and beauty of his face."

"Well, just now he looks like he missed the boat and it's too far to swim."

"I endorse him—I support his caustic dexterity and melodious eloquence. Sensitive natures such as his will always, it would so seem, be at a loss to know quite how to behave in the world, beyond maintaining their personal dignity and erect posture—for much it grieves their hearts to think what man has made of man, and all the more so in places like this."

"I like him—or would, if he'd let me. For all his dark preoccupations, that whiff of the illicit always on him, he's possessed of a subtle wit and an exhilarating sense of the high comedy of infatuation."

"Of that, yes, and of the hollow burn of attraction, too, and the tireless workings of sexual expression. I'd like to pump him, thoughtwise, on a subject—wouldn't you?"

"And how! *Sur n'importe quelle pretexte*, Solange, *sur n'importe* quelle *pretexte*."

"He has the poet's eyes
—Sing to him sleeping . . ."

"There are shadows shifting in those soft gray eyes, disturbing ones whose form remains a mystery to all who see them and who would like to see them dispelled—and don't give me any crap about a desperation born out of secret longings the nature of which he cannot admit even to himself, because nobody who comes in here has—unless of course he longs to fuck a gorilla."

"Sweet grace of low replies,
—Why are we weeping?"

"Because, dear, those low replies are not to us."

"And the assembly dropped to its collective knees, crying out with one impassioned voice, 'Fortunate indeed are they who draw from the inexhaustible mine of the young lord's virtues! We would stand by him, through thick and thin—we would clutch at his straws!' "

"A cat may look at a king—or a prince, dear—and a pawn may move to the far side of the board and get to be a queen."

"*Get* to be? Give it to us horizontal."

"Well I don't get him at all. The way you all put it, he's got everything—heart, soul, silver, gold. The world's his fucking oyster, but he's choking to death on a pearl."

"Like on a piece of *hard candy*?"

"That's his heart in his throat, maybe."

"I don't know about that; the way he sometimes, when he is drunk, throws himself around in this den of felonious intent, he seems a boy with nothing to lose, especially not a heart. He has an imagination, yes, that cannot be denied, focused entirely on himself."

"Le poete conserve une conscience claire dans son psychose, et aucun obstacle ne s'oppose a la concentration de son attention. Il epreuve le besoin de faire de l'introspection. Un certain syncretisme s'est opere dans ses croyances—il a l'impression de depersonalisation ou du dedoublement de son *moi*."

"Et voila s' accomplice!"

"That is wickedly untrue. The poet is, despite appearances, never focused on himself, but always on the world, and on the world within the world, following the secret protocols of the maculate voluptuous. And as to his heart, he must inevitably find a way in all this—"

"All what?"

"All—*this*!"

"Careful of the sweeping gestures, Rose, when you're smoking a cigarette."

"Sorry—to let his heart loose again, as it must once have been—loose from the cold cruelty of restraint which some necessity forced him to inflict upon it before he bade farewell to those scenes associated with the all-too-brief dream time of his happiness."

"That was a mouthful, darling—come up for air!"

"When things were fine in Glocca-Morra, you mean."

"A sensitive, vehement, passionate soul, one in a thousand in these vain, grasping times. Plus which, when he has finished a poem, he must feel heroic, fully realized, and of course, paradoxically, *spent*—the inevitable fallout from such a shredding experience, easily mistaken by many as aloof."

"Sends bolts of lightning, does he darling, through your tired bones?"

"Perhaps the odd shiver."

"To me it's simple—he eschews complicated melodramatic affairs and concentrates on his poetry."

"And he's far too refined to eschew with his mouth open."

"Ha-ha-ha—big-city funny."

"Excuse me, what you are all trying to say may be summed up by the following: the fusion of ideal self, ideal object, and actual self-image as a defense against an intolerable reality in the interpersonal realm."

"Reason which, all playwrights should be dead for three hundred years."

"You may think you're being flippant, but you touch on something."

"Yes, dear, I know."

"Nevertheless, he remains unresponsive."

"Only in here, dear, only in here. Neither in his poetry nor in his social intercourse does he bottle up his fluency."

"I want to be a line of his poetry!"

"And I, darling, his psychoanalyst's couch."

"Yes, pychoanalysis is *such* a wonderful thing, isn't it—it's really all about *words*. In that, of course, it closely resembles—and for some replaces—poetry. It employs all eight of Aristotle's descriptions of words—ordinary words, strange words, metaphors, ornamental words, coined words—such as *cathexis*, for example—words lengthened, in the German manner, or curtailed in the American, and most importantly words altered in form—screen words! I know he has a psychoanalyst—who doesn't in that set—I wonder how all that time on the couch affects his poetry?"

"Screens reminds me, it's getting to be time to put up the storm windows."

!@#$%^&*

"My god, did you hear all that? What's going on in here tonight, anyway?"

"I've been checking around myself—seems its like some kind of impromptu symposium: the liberal arts faculty fags from Columbia, NYU, City College, and Fordham making up a kind of coven under the not-so-full moon. Sure is interesting—not that I understand all that much."

!@#$%^&*

Moriarty, so, to resume, in the suspensory caesura. Thickening the haunted plot, enter Fred, the towel boy, a former Police Athletic League welterweight boxer and cutman, whose job it was to stanch the flow of blood from wounds sustained in the ring. A saintly figure currently employed days at Bill's Wholsesale Flower Market down the block (*vide supra*). A voice from the corner taunts him in a friendly way. He feigns complete inattention.

"Hey, Freddles, come on, whip it out! The word is you can get eleven dimes layin' flat out in a row on it stiffed up. That's a dollar ten!"

"You put a frame around it, Fred, I get you a one-man show in a major uptown gallery—for no commission."

"I dunno about you, but I'll buy that for a dollar!"

"A dollar *ten*, cheapskate."

"C'mon, Freddie, batter up! It's the top of the ninth here and these homos need a homer soon and bad, or the game is lost—and we ain't talkin' about the poet who went blind from jerkin' off on account of he had no luck at the baths in Sparta neither. You got here three of the hundred neediest cases, so come on, you big bad boy, throw a hard-on, have a heart!"

"C'*mon*, you guys!"

"C'mon, yourself, Fred—in the beginning was the word. Show us what ya got. I heard it's in *Deuteronomy*!"

"C'mon, Fred we're *boys*—we're at that *stage, y' know?*"

"*Gedaddaheah*."

"Okay, we're no boys, we're old degenerates, but we still suffer. Some people say size doesn't matter, or shouldn't matter—something—but we say little things please little minds. *Tu non sai quanto sofrir i tuoi vecchii genitori*. We wouldn't care if it was a mercy flash."

“Can the dramatics, willya! Anyway, I got front-page news, you’re no Leonard Warren.”

“This boy does never cease to amaze me. He is the Obedentiary Precentor of this sacred grove.”

“Indeed so, dear. Would that he were infirmarian, sacristan, and pittancer as well—distributor of charitable doles of a particular carnal nature.”

“Why amazed? Maybe I don’t get to *go* to the opera and mingle with the in crowd, but they got a radio in the office where I work days. I can listen to the broadcast on Sa’dd’y afternoons.”

“Dear Fred, you’ll be a danger in paradise.”

“Awww.”

The O’Maurigan sharply intervenes.

“Ignore them, Fred.”

“Pisses me off, how they think we’re ignorant.”

Fred walks away in a huff, calling, “*Towels!*”

“You love that boy don’t you, dear.”

“He is a man on the side of the angels.”

“I think so, too—and I’d say is far from stupid.”

“Freddy’s intelligence is global, unfettered, and directed to the deep experience of human need. As a consequence he never resorts to the cold and wiley strategies of oblique discourse—which, of course, leaves fools deciding he wears the cheerful and practical air of one insensitive to atmosphere.”

“I know, dear, and I know just how sensitive to atmosphere he actually is—and that johnson, a great miracle of nature! I’ve come across him standing in the showers head titled back in the spray as the rod of his own empire swings metronome-like below. Unhappily, however, his sweetly straightforward discourse does seem to invite the jibe. Perhaps after all the job fit is a little—well, dear, in a homosexual bathhouse . . .”

“You see, that remark about the frame reminds me that he lost the job you got him in that downtown paint shop, and that the day job you’ve now fixed up down the block at the flower market seems more, I don’t know, appropriate, wouldn’t you say?”

"Not lost, it was time to give it up. He enjoyed the deliveries to Guston and Franz Kline and especially all those tubes of Alizarin orange to Lee Krasner, who never stopped talking to him about Jackson, but never about a meeting. Fred is much more happily engaged over at Bill's doing up fancy arrangements for weddings and funerals and orchid corsages for senior proms."

"And don't forget *sailings*! You see Parsifal among the flower maidens?"

"That is a very nice idea—and very much more to the point than the frame remark."

!@#$%^&*

Moriarty again, clocking further, for was it not wisely, if to be sure rhetorically, demanded by the Stygarite, *what, indeed, would be the good of the speaker, if things appeared in the required light even apart from anything he says*? Because, as ought to be evident from earlier remarks, there is little enough light in this dispensary as it is, and that, of course, by request of the clientele, so stung by ruthless glare.

For many of them have spent time in brightly lit rooms being interrogated—and worse. How much time have they spent since, sitting in one small room after another, listening to life's victims, life's witnesses, and life's criminals—listening intently to lies and excuses, pleas and rage. The last thing they want the rooms to be is well lighted—although clean would be an improvement.

With which observation we withdraw behind the arras, or its equivalent, or disappear in a cloud of steam (never smoke, not in a firetrap such as this), to return it cannot be predicted when. Don't touch that dial.

"He can not be called *sans gene*, that is a fact."

"He's young, strong, and fortified by potent chemicals—and as you have just observed, far from heartless."

"Well . . . maybe so, but his dead father's hand is stuck so far up his ass it's got his heart fast in its grip and is *squeezing* the blood right out of it—and *that* is the gay meow on *that*!"

"It would perhaps be much kinder and more accurate to say that in matters of the heart he is badly self-advised."

"Well, he went to a Jesuit school, and you know about them and their famous training in the ability to defer gratification."

"He is burdened by his solitude stretched too thin to bear."

"He does say interesting things about *Hamlet*."

"He misses his father and his mother both. Likely mother more than father. Indeed, I understand the Catholics terribly well when I hear them singing 'Mother dear, O pray for me, as far from heaven and thee, I wander in a fragile bark o'er life's tempestuous sea.' "

"Wrong again, Miss Agnes. If he is a homosexual—and if he isn't, I give up—then he can take his mother, his primary erotic rival, or leave her, in memory as in life. If he is a homosexual, he longs to be held in his father's arms, aloft like a monstrance, for all to see."

"The mother, you know, was a very beautiful and very famous actress of the Irish stage, on tour here in New York with many film offers when he was born. And the father was a great beauty, they say, who wore genuine emerald studs and cufflinks with his evening wear, which he bequeathed to the son—but the son's afraid to wear them, for fear of being likened to Clifton Webb, which is a great pity, for they would go so well with his gay green eyes."

"His eyes are gray, like woodsmoke."

"Oh no, dear, they're green, like a cat's. You have to see them in the light."

"Indeed, it is extremely difficult for one of his class to broadcast himself in any way. Apart from anything else, the legal sanctions against doing so can be, even in deliciously corrupt Gotham, formidably stern, a grim fact to which anyone who has ever spent a night in the Tombs can attest."

"Well he's a poet, isn't he? Who was it said art is born of humiliation?"

"Yes, a poet and an orphan, yet he seems happy enough with his rich auntie and all her friends—ladies of fashion, ladies domestic, ladies professional, literary ladies, of birth and culture. And to that degree he is stepping out on his relations by coming in here."

"I'm glad he does, he's in divine shape—and *hung*, too. Maybe not in the Fred category, but it's a well-known fact you can have a feel in the steam room if you go about it politely."

"I believe all hurlers are hung."

"All what?"

"Hurlers, dear, he was a hurler in school back in Ireland."

"But what is a—"

"Hurler, dear. It's a sport—something like lacrosse. You can watch it up in the Bronx—in a stadium adjacent to Van Cortlandt Park on Sunday afternoons."

"I'm generally booked on Sunday afternoons."

"Well, if you'd go a little easier on the the tea rooms—still it's a funny thing, I've always heard the boys in blue tend to be more *lenient* on Sunday. Where were you nabbed, my dear, Grand Central?"

"*Booked* means *invited*, Mae—to a matinee."

"Oh? And what shows play on Sundays, darling?"

"A *matinee* is a reception in the afternoon—a chic one!"

"Oh yeah—pink tea."

"Not just pink tea, as you're so ready to call it, but discussions—serious discussions about art and music, theater and politics."

"Her extraordinary exertions have made Bea highly successful in her profession."

"Politics, huh. I never thought of you as political, dear, but I'm real glad to hear it—maybe you can answer a question that's been bothering me for years. What do you think Trotsky intended by saying it was the duty of the Party's every *member* to *penetrate* the *backward parts* of the working class?"

"I wouldn't know, I'm not a Communist, and we're actually not working-class people."

"I agree your subject cannot be called heartless—despite the instinctual suspicions he harbors of the motives of men—entertaining as he does in his sumptuous loft apartment—a last remnant of the legendary Tenderloin, just down the street. Did you know that in the Gay Nineties, Twenty-eighth Street was known familiarly as the Pleasance? And later of course as Tin Pan Alley. Oh, yes, we cavort with legendary shades . . . where was I?"

"Just down the street in His Nibs's fuck hutch."

"Yes, yes, next door to the flower market, where he entertains visitors from other cities, from the provinces, and from distant shores, sometimes in uniform, sometimes out of it."

"Indeed, years of repression and inhibition occasioned by the change in his upbringing, following his parents' death on an espionage flight from Lisbon to London . . . all that and then the more important sorrow, that which—since after all we quickly reach a limit in our patience for the poet's recording of his own peculiar vexations, the sorrow it is every important poet's business to record, the sorrow over the incurable anguish of the world."

"Must get you down."

"All these, steadfastly unavoided in his accounts, would nevertheless not seem to have tamed the ebullient Irish *beau geste* leanings in him. It is said that even as he manifests a solitude inaccessible to praise or blame he gives his visitors breakfast, and more, offering a kind of scopic as well as a type of wholesome fraternal support. I find that immensely honorable and touching."

"Yes, his generous trust in others does seem to grow innocently out of his sense of his own truth—and anyway, dear, hospitality is the Irish way of life."

"Well one fine morning it may turn out to be that Irish boy's way of *death*. Every hand he has been dealt so far seems flush with love and luck and luxury. One dark night he may be dealt the Queen of Spades!"

"Oh, don't *say* that!"

"Ignore yourself, woman—you are overwrought!"

"I am *not* overwrought! It is high time somebody told him *gay knock* is *not* a shrine in County Mayo where bent schizophrenics make novenas to the Virgin Mary! I can't help noticing, the little I know of him, that as fame seems to be fast approaching, he becomes still more hesitant. Most chancers at the fame game envision the happy outcome as something like being wrapped in sable; from him the distinct impression one gets is that he regards it as being slowly encased in a winding-sheet. Also he drinks like a fish, which nobody needs to be told, do they, is always a feature at the inquest."

"The cup is the shield of Dionysius, darling—or perhaps he is merely keen on emptying bottles that they may be made receptacles of *notes* dropped into the river. Lonely rivers run to the sea, sings the song, perhaps carrying his missives *zu neuen Ufern*, to other shores—happen to some poor lonely heart in Fiji."

"There is an *aura* surrounding him. He's seldom in the columns. Winchell in his pursuit of prime sinuendo avoids him, which is—"

"Unusual."

"Highly."

"He is above all that—his life is circumscribed by work."

"Circumscribed by work or vice-versa."

"Excuse me, no, I simply cannot abide the reversal of natural relations of the elements of a proposition. It makes me crazy."

"Really. And are *you* a homosexual?"

"But, in fact, he *isn't* circumcised—I've peeked."

"You've peaked all right, Whoressa, it must be twenty years since."

!@#$%^&*

"That charades room in back of the lockers is a glittering charnel where lamps shed no warmth, no matter it is steamier in there than the steam room, hotter than the hot room. There they come and go, like the stranger mutations of Hieronymus Bosch's *Garden of Earthly Delights*, to play such old gay games as 'What Do I Hope to Harvest?' Harvest, indeed—from all that seed spilled onto the floor. 'These we old what portion that remains is ours?' is more to the point—or to get classical about it '*Non est inquirendum unde venit venison.*' "

"I wouldn't know anything about the entrees in the coffee shop, but I do know that as a result of a kind donation by a certain sympathetic Armenian restauranteur in the neighborhood, they have this very night put down a new Isfahan rug in the back office!"

"The beastly beast is in there now, tryin' t' crawl up a number's ass, tongue first."

"Queen *Jane*—how *ribald* you have lately become!"

"*Must* you call me that *silly* name?"

"No, dear, but *The Fabulous Seymour Fishbein* just seems a mite too *formal* under the circumstances. Anyway, the main attraction is downstairs, and I don't mean that three-ring circus going on among the old marrieds in the steam room. There's this crackpot sitting at poolside, deep end, talking to himself in a slow, mournful tone, enumerating any number of scientific principles concerning the immersion of the body in fluids. It is a Camp."

"We call her Weeping Mary, for her tears are copious—indeed, she weeps enough for all three Marys present at the Crucifixion. She comes in weeping drunk—you know how they get, first jocose, then bellicose, then lachrymose, then comatose. She must get bellicose elsewhere—likely she arrives having been tossed out of some low-dive flat on her ass to spend her hours lying in the dormitory weeping. She says she weeps for the sins of men, that the Lord may hear her and grant mercy."

"Mercy!"

We now attend to signs in the coffee shop.

THE WORDING IS EVERYTHING

Love Leaves Its Stains

RESPONSABILICE DE SUS PERTINENCIAS

Blanchisserie er Repassage a Facon

Les Rix Doivent Se Poursuivre a 'L'Exterieure—Attempts To Raise Tumults Will On No Account Be Tolerated. We Reserve The Right To Issue Admonitions And To Levy Fines Directly. We have been in business a long time. We have been cussed and discussed, boycotted, talked about, lied about, lied to, hung up, held up, and robbed, and the only reason we are staying in business is to see What the Fuck is going to happen next.

—The Management

I am lookin' for a big fat daddy with meat shakin' on his bones. Consult reception.

HE WRESTLED WITH HIM UNTIL THE BREAK OF DAY.

Res contr'Amor non esquirens, lai on sos poders s'autra.

—*Raymond de Mirval*

*

"Why are we called *musical*? Well, did not Plato say that music brings a charm to sadness? Now if that ain't us in a nutshell, why are there nutcrackers?"

"*Pillow talk*? Not in here, Mary. Shitload of *pill talk*, though."

"Through the labyrinthine passage of our unintelligible world the trivial and the terrible walk hand in hand."

"I *know* darling, I've just seen them upstairs in the hallway."

"*Double-entry*?"

"That's what I said, bub, and she's not even an accountant."

"Excuse me, we were discussing Aristotle and the requirements of tragedy."

"Plato, Aristotle—"

"The Greeks invented us, darling, it's as well to pay attention."

"Duly noted. The tragedy of homosexuality. What further requirements are there—to be ugly? And don't I remember something about not being able to decide whose fault it is—that it's all Fate? That I could go for. One war where only they were at fault was enough for me—it seemed to *solve* things. Weren't we all young and foolish to fall for *that*."

" 'Crying in the sunshine, laughing in the rain—' "

"It served its purpose—taught those of us who came home in one piece and sane that in order to be alive we don't always have to have an opinion as to whose fault it all is now."

"*Tragedy, therefore, is an imitation*—"

"—*of Life*. Fannie Hurst. Claudette Colbert and Louise Beavers. I cried so hard I—"

"—*not only of a complete action, but of incidents arousing pity*—"

"Look around you, darling—just look around you."

"—*and fear. Such incidents have the very greatest effect on the mind when they occur unexpectedly*—"

"That's for sure—incidents such as fire and sudden police raids."

"Plots are either simple or complex, since the actions they represent are naturally of this twofold description."

"I'm sure it's terribly important, dear, but it's a little *dry*."

"There's a rumor you know that Universal is going to remake it—for Lana."

"The action proceeding in the way defined as one continuous whole, I call simple, when the change in the hero's fortunes takes place without Peripety*—"*

"Without *what?*"

"Peripety. Walking back and forth—hush now."

"*—or* Discovery*, and complex when it involves one or another or both.*"

"Well, that's us—walking back and forth—but as to discovery—"

"Excuse me, Peripety means something entirely different—it means a switchback."

"Is that anything like a backshoe? I was thinking of Concha—"

"You are both ignoramuses. The word is *Peripeteia*, and it means a decisive reversal of fortune."

"These should each of them arise out of the structure of the plot itself, so as to be the consequence, necessary or probable, of the antecedents—"

"I don't think the existentialists believe any of that; in fact—"

"Hush up, now—*behave!*"

"There is a great difference between a thing happening post hoc *and* propter hoc."

"That Aristotle, what a guy—I didn't know he spoke Latin."

"You mustn't ridicule Aristotle, Algernon, he is essential to the theater."

!@#$%^&*

"Ya argue well, dear—they hadda oughta groomed you for *Augmentations*. Excuse me, what do you want?"

"Oh, sorry, the guidebook said *vaut le detour*. Interesting, isn't it, about rooms. Even an eye as accustomed as mine—I'm in the trade—to taking in swiftly and without apparent curiosity what a room betrays about its occupant, is at something of a loss when the message is as ambiguous as it is here, in a room inherited rather than personally arranged, and for only eight hours at that—and how time flies."

!@#$%^&*

"Stessa whispers her secrets in no known tongue."

"Well, in my opinion, although she may consider herself Dame World in baloney curls, she is in truth a coarse, vulgar woman, one book of Green Stamps short of a Mixmaster, and I am *finished* with her. I believe in the rigorous subordination of *panache* to *tenue*."

"Very strange—what's Augmentations anyway?"

"I think it's one of the orders of angels."

"Oh, yeah, sure—let's see now, there's the Augmentations, the Ministrations, the Consternations, the Vexations, the—"

"That is not true!"

"Well, then?"

"The truth is y'wouldn't know, dear, that one's so *referency*. Could be it's a religious order—there's the *Presentations*, and there's the *Premontratensians*, maybe there's also the *Augmentations*."

"I think it has something to do with the law."

"As in the profession? Could be—Stessa picks up a lotta information cruisin' the terlets at the N.Y.U. Law School. Last week it was something to do with *Assizes*. You couldn't get her to shut up about whatever it was for love or money. *Assizes* . . . *Assizes*. Finally Duessa just read her out raw. 'We got *all sizes* in here, woman—if ya can't find one that fits ya, go to Lane Bryant!' "

"Well, Duessa is a big strong girl, and she can get away with that kind of squelch, but I don't advise others to try in on, dear because Stessa has been known to turn real hysterical and *claw people*! Only last week we heard her screamin' 'Your *fist*! I wouldn't let your fucking *pinky* in so far as the *proximate interphalangeal joint*! Now get out, *before I kill you*!' She sounded *exactly* like Rock Hudson bellowing at Bob Stack in the great climactic scene in *Written on the Wind*. 'Get out! Get out before I *kill you*!' Have you seen it? It's *divine*! All we could think of was how we'd all have to show up at the inquest wearing black straw picture hats. Best to pretend you're stoned—she's terrified of drugs, poor girl: thinks they're part of a Communist plot to enslave the populace."

"Well, I find her rather pretty—certainly, the complexion is remarkable. In former times I suppose she'd have been called whey-faced, but pallor is very *in* nowadays, so—"

"*Whey*, huh? Little Miss Muffet. Well I can tell you what happened. To the curds—they're inside her *skull* passing for brains. Cottage cheese soaked in urine is what—"

"That is so vulgar. The fact that she is a principled and dedicated *undinist* . . ."

"Yeah, singin' in the rain—the golden shower."

"Pardon the interruption, but did you know that in Tudor England sweet curds and honey, heated, were a dessert dish at the best tables. *Warm suckets* they were called."

"Yeah, I did know that. I think Bette Davis and Errol Flynn ate them in *The Private Lives of Elizabeth and Essex*."

!@#$%^&*

"Faith gave way to faithlessness hard upon the fall of Montségur. The valedictory was enacted in earnest and without pity. *Peine foret et dure*, darling, *peine forte et dure*."

"Oh!"

"But much has improved in the succeeding centuries, so that we devout communicants of various organizations of the caring agnostic—atheists we shun: they are uniformly loud and overbearing—no longer fear the lash of the whip or the flames of the stake, or the rack, or—"

"Oh, that's a coincidence. At Tad's up on Forty-fourth Street and Broadway you can get a flaming steak with baked potato and salad for a dollar ninety-eight."

!@#$%^&*

"And now come on, relax, willya. You missed the last train and you don't want to wake the baby—she's bound to understand. Get some sleep and we'll call her in the morning. You were up all night playing pinochle with the boys from the office. You know, they can smell another woman on you like *that*, but not a man. No harm done anyway, nobody misses a slice off a cut loaf."

"Well . . ."

"Used to be was Yolanda Veranda could turn on a *dime*—no more. She has changed that dime for two nickels with *holes* in them to wear on a string around her neck. She has assumed the perpetual aspect of one who eats dried roots and has contemplated perdition one time too many. *C'est tragi-que!*"

"This is too true. Moreover she dotes on her tragic role—that of Queen Clytemnestra—and has played it to the hilt on any number of occasions. Happily for the human race, however, she is a Clytemnestra without offspring, for imagine the consequences! 'I coulda been decent,' she once told me, with a terrible sneer on her face, 'for an income of fifty thousand a year.' And who knows? Like many another scheming woman come undone, who knows but she was correct in her assessment—that it was only a question of money and fortune between her and an honest woman?"

"Oh my, you are *so* Victorian, Velma."

"Well, so was Oscar Wilde—so there!"

"Indeed, and to tell the God's-honest truth I have ever found you to be a fundamentally forbearing woman, regularly inclined to forgive, on the Christian terms of repentance."

"I suppose I am at that—anyway, *I play the play*."

!@#$%^&*

"Departing youngling—callipygian, no?"

"Very definitely—comestibly so."

"Eat in or take out?"

"Take your pick. As Dorothy declared, 'I always say, take me or leave me—or in the usual order of things both.' "

"Yes, darling, the *Bath Story* is one he finds exemplary on account of the mode of discovery. *A discovery using signs as a means of assurance is less artistic, as indeed are all such as imply reflection; whereas one that brings them all in at once, as in the* Bath Story, *is of a better order*."

"Well, I guess I get the point—*all in at once . . .*"

"Hier kommt alles zu allen."

"Ganz richtig!"

"There is so much reckoning, so much counting—it becomes oppressive."

"The world is too much with us, late, soon and next."

"May I quote you on that?"

"To anybody but Winchell, darling. *Nobody* wants to be in Winchell any more, not soon, not late, *never*. He is too *over*."

" 'Miss Picayune,' Ah sed ta huh, 'Ah am too *through* with your bein' so *argumentative*! You say all this English law is based on *precedent*, and when Ah ask a simple question like well then, how did it get itself *started*, you look like you're *gonna slit mah throat*! Ah do *not* like to be threatened."

"I have had similar experiences with the bitch."

"You want to be careful with that one—Stessa. It's a habit of mine always to give in to her; I find by experience that it saves big noise."

"This is quite true—many more than Stessa knows know Stessa."

"For what she is."

"She came down wrapped all right, so it seemed at first—then turns out somebody up there forgot to put *This End Up* on the fuckin' box. Ever since those guys threw her out of that pool hall, she's been unhinged. Darling, she still thinks thirty-eight atomic bombs dropped on retardation targets in Manchuria was a *fabulous* idea. What can you say to *that*?"

"Pool hall—she shoots pool? Now, that is too-far-*out*."

"Why? Mozart shot pool after all."

"And Stessa is like Mozart? Give it to me—"

"Easy? Okay, easy. Mozart had a foul mouth; he particularly loved to tell shit jokes. In that regard he is like Stessa—or the other way around, I suppose."

"She never racked a line in her life—she went to the pool hall to watch the player's asses do their dance while they were lining up a shot. She had a run for her money, but finally they read her beads—presto change-o, the *heave*-ho!"

"*Too far out*—wheels within wheels, preacher *declare*."

"Yeah, well they'll be carryin' her out of here on wheels one day, singin' her same old song, 'Time was I offered a bosom and a presence and *orchids*!' "

!@#$%^&*

"The sleepy eye speakin' the soul—the one with that much more white around the iris than other people's—turned out to be old Concha skunked on horse. We got her to St. Vincent's in time, but they were goin' t'press charges until Uncle Carmine pointed out certain facts relative to contributions—and retributions—etcetera—and Concha was sent home to rest up. Since that time she has become more wary of entering into chemically induced states of recreational bewilderment and has taken to making an honest living into the bargain."

"I hear she runs a backhoe in a salvage yard somewhere over in Brooklyn."

"That's right, she does—on Bushwick Avenue, near the Rheingold Brewery."

"She has some story, y'know—going back to the late thirties when, as a result of an unhappy altercation between her father and a certain *capo* of note, she, her recently widowed mother, and the rest of the family found themselves out in the street, looking up at the smoldering shell of what had lately been their modest home in Bensonhurst. Concha herself, reduced by misfortune to the necessity of accepting a situation, became *chauffeuse* to a person of a certain distinction in what is crudely called the Underworld. Then, finding herself adrift after Luciano skipped town, and perilously compromised, she cut a deal with the Dewey Commission and turned states' evidence—after which in typical fashion the nefarious hypocritical, lying sons of bitches pulled a double cross and threw poor Concha to the fucking wolves."

"The way she looks, hadda oughta been her dream come true."

"Yeah, well she'd fucked them over anyway. There was not a scrap of information she'd given them that was not destitute of the smallest fragment of foundation in truth. Every name on her list was already a stiff on the losing side of the big game, sent to the bottom of the East River in a new pair of concrete shoes. The wolves had a big, fat raucous laugh with her on that one."

"Don't y' just love Italian broads, man? Fuckin' balls of brass on 'em—especially of course when they're guys to start out with, although not only, by no means."

"Well, she sure is on the make for men tonight."

A face, a figure, entering.

"Here I sit—I make men in my
own image, a race like me, to
suffer to weep, to enjoy life
and rejoice, and then to pay no
attention, none at all—like me."

Sitting down on the narrow bed.

"Hey Mister Swan, you're pretty restless tonight, huh? Stickin' your head in through half-open doors."

"Yes, well, you see, my mind misgives me; my mind misgives me sadly. I have premonitions."

"That's O.K., whatever's gotta happen's gotta happen."

"I fear savage reprisals."

"Savage reprisals—who from?"

"Youth, young man, youth. For it is none other than callow youth, fearful of and repelled by age—age that after all holds all its markers—that counsels rage against what is for us the palliative comfort of beautiful twilights. Proud youth that revels in its attribution to us of morbid feuds and blazing hatreds played out against the background of an age they cannot fathom, as it passed before the advent of television."

"Don't be afraid, Mr. Swan, we're here looking after you."

"I fear I shall soon die and no one will remember me."

"Me either, Mister Swan—but why should you or I care if anybody remembers us; we won't be remembering them, will we?"

"Oh, why *thank* you—you've given me something to think about. Still, my memorabilia—"

Rising, leaving.

"Who was that, dear?"

"That was Mr. Swan—Matthew Swan—he who witnessed the Creation."

"He is very paranoid—and very old."

"Well, he has a strange and terrible story."

"Yeah? Like *What is your name? Magda Sorel. Age? Thirty-three?*"

"Better—it would definitely make a better opera. He was the most beautiful boy on the Bowery—the most beautiful boy in New York. And then he met Tchaikovsky."

"*Who?*"

"Tchaikovsky, dear, Pyotr Ilich Tchaikovsky. When he came to the historic gala opening of Carnegie Hall. Matthew Swan had been a hod carrier on the site during the construction, and he went back to hear what the music sounded like. Somehow the penny press got a line on the story and ran with it—human interest, don't-cha know, and somebody else persuaded 'Pete' as he was being called to meet with the boy. Of course one thing led to another, which provided some major titillation, darling, in the Tenderloin, as Pete's shall we say *extramusical* reputation had preceded him."

"*And?*"

"Swan Lake."

"Oh!"

"And a broken heart among his souvenirs."

"Ah sed ta huh, 'Miss Mary, Ah weep for that you are so *naive*. When an *offisuh* of the *loah* says he *likes* you, he ain't talkin' 'bout either yoah soft feelins foah people or yoah baby-blue *ayes*, he is sayin' you make a *dandy suspect* in sump'n or othuh, what is *felonious*. Dig?' "

"Man, rising up into something titanic, is victorious over his own culture and compels the gods to unite with him. In his self-controlled wisdom he holds their existence and the limits of their authority in his hand."

"What an interesting way to think of masturbation, dear—so *affirmative!*"

"Life is many days, darling, and many nights."

"Not so many as all that, if you ask me."

"*Stasimon*, darling, a song of the chorus."

"That's us."

"Without anapests or trochees."

"I should hope not—talk of religion in here ain't fittin'."

!@#$%^&*

Moriarty reporting.

Whereupon our hero meets his pal Delancey. Together they notice significant numbers of the drunken repressed—"Man. I got so fuckin' drunk I don't remember a thing!"—spoiling for a fight: some in the process of being ejected. Veterans fear a raid on the premises.

Freddy comes out from reception carring more clean towels.

"*Towels!*—oh, hey, how are ya? How's tricks?"

"Few and far between, Freddy; few and far be—"

"*Towels!!*"

"The half of it ain't ever been rightly told. But *Fred*, while I *have* you—there *is* something I've been wanting to ask you."

"*Shoot.*"

"Ah—yes, well, actually it's about the *robes*."

"Reception supervises the robes—I'm towels."

"Yes, dear, but I thought, as you're always so *solicitous*."

"*Yeah?*"

"Yes, you are—you are, if I may put it in a homely way, exactly the sort of young man one turns to when the jelly jar gets stuck. In fact your solicitude—*bene agendo nunquam defessus*—is one of the saving graces of this . . . but what I was wondering was, if there couldn't be a little *starch* put into the robes? It would boost morale in my opinion. I mean so many come in here feeling, well, *played-out*, frankly, and just a *bit* of starch in the robes might make—"

"You would have to take that up with management."

"Oh, I see. Ah, well, dear, 'twas was but a fleeting thought. I'd not for the world become so *louche* as to put you in anything like a compromising position. It's only that you *have* been seen entering through the Sacrist's Gate with the *obedentiaries*, and have doubtless been admitted into the secret archives—the Hall of Parchments, the Room of Inventories and Indexes, the *Riserva*—and you see, I care very much for the robes. Whoever it was said it said rightly that the uniform's great virtue is that it tends to minimize irregular characteristics, and I did feel, dear, that in the light of such I might prevail upon you to press one's concerns upon their worships' notice."

"Those guys were Security."

"Freddy, darling, let's call a spade a spade, and hope it has a heart underneath, eh? Those boys were the Policemen's Benevolent Association, Stud Beefcake Patrol on the hoof. A little modeling on the side—perhaps an audition. It's hard to know the man behind the badge—but never mind—take no notice of a meddler."

"*Towels*! Oh, hiya—howya doin?"

"Without, Freddy, without—and not loving it."

"Oh, sorry t' hear that—well, keep your chin up."

"Thank you, dear, I think I will. You know, Freddy, I do really love you—sometimes it amounts to something like *veneration*, and in those moments I swear to you if I knew where you lived I'd go there and kiss the knob on your front door."

"Yeah, yeah, yeah—just don't rank me out, okay, man?"

"Rank you *out*? Freddie in my platoon you are first lieutenant. You are the *seal of dharma transmission*—you are the *man*! For many who come in here, when you cry out '*Towels!*' hear only a modest young man on his rounds of the night crying out '*Towels!*' But there are those among us for whom your voice is as the voice of the *muhjadin* atop the minaret, calling to prayer the Saracen faithful."

"Yeah, yeah."

"I *mean* it, Fred, I do. I think you're beautiful—but then there are times when I think *I'm* beautiful—generally around closing time. Everybody's beautiful at closing time."

"We never close."

"This too is true—like the Windmill Theatre during the war."

"*Towels!*"

" 'Took a group—for onion soup—at *Gare de Lyons*. It never shuts.' 'Like Chock full o'Nuts.' Isn't that *divine*—it's from *Bells Are Ringing*."

"Isn't she just *divine* in it—the word is Julie Stein is going to do the music for a life of Fanny Brice, and she'll star. I can't *wait*."

"The only bells that are ever gonna ring in here are fire alarms . . . maybe."

"Oh, what a horrid thought at the beginning of the season!"

"*Season*, the woman says—who the hell does she think she is, Thalia Bridgewood? This is an all-year-round amateur hour, Mona, only there ain't no contracts offered."

"*Towels!*"

"I've heard Fred does very interesting things with wood."

"Would he would do very clever things with me!"

"We've learned so little about him since he's come among us."

"True, all we know really is that he has beautiful genital component parts and a beautiful soul to boot, which seems unfair."

"Well, as the Bard says, 'Look whom she best endowed she gave the more.' Or to put it in words of our own low time, them as has gets."

!@#$%^&*

"Et *sangloter d'extase les jets d'eau*, Jane!"

"*Quelle joie*."

!@#$%^&*

"Lady Luck does have a Christian name, darling, she's called Grace."

"Oh."

"So is Fanny Spellbound—actually—*Your Grace*."

"Poor soul."

"*What?*"

"I see you don't know . . . well, few do."

"Are you mad, everybody—"

"Knows what she does, yes dear, and that she doesn't wait for the full moon, either—but not *why* she does it."

"For the same reason we *all* do it, Mary."

"Not quite. The fact is Her Grace—Gracie—is a blackout drinker. Hits the Scotch every night after dinner before retiring. Usually she passes out, but now and again she keeps going—into blackout, on which occasion the M.O. is always the same. She goes in mufti—in itself ridiculous, since it's based on the collegiate look. The poor thing's actually been sighted in button-down Brooks Brothers shirt, pressed chino pants, and dirty white buckskin shoes trolling Eighth Avenue. In Gilhooley's she's usually seen tanking up some more—on which occasions she is absolutely *a bottomless well*—before hitting the stage doors of the musicals across the Avenue. On those occasions when she doesn't score—and they predominate—she returns to Gilhooley's. She always closes the joint, after which they pour her into a cab, say, 'Fiftieth and Madison, Johnny' and the job's done.

"When she *does* score—usually in winter, when it's coldest and loneliest in a chorus boy's humble flat—it's back to the Chancery for a *loud* carouse. Then sometimes, if they can't get the pony out of the place before the first morning mass, Gracie will wake, and start *screaming the place down* that an intruder has broken in through the window.

"Oh, it's a sad situation—said to have started years ago after she started up an affair, cold sober, with a leggy blonde from *One Touch of Venus*. She'd just become an archbishop, but wasn't yet a cardinal, but someone ratted on her to Pius XII and they came down heavy on her. It's all too sad."

"What a story—everything but—"

"The bloodhounds? No, dear, *including* the bloodhounds—much with. I know one of them. He was on the night shift, waiting up for the old trollop, but fell asleep. Woke to the sound of *grunts*. Went to knock on the bedroom door, but found it *open wide* . . . and there she was, the Cardinal Archbishop of New York, darling, with the stevedore's legs thrown so far back, his cock was dangling against his fucking *nose*, going at that asshole like a *truffle pig*. Story is, when it's all over, she goes and gargles with Listerine and holy water. Do you love it?"

!@#$%^&*

"What wild ecstasy? What struggle to escape?"

"I don't know, dear—I've never known; I've never dared inquire. If this life is a custodial sentence and not a suspended one, I for one will not fall prey to the fantasies engendered by Hollywood prison-break pictures. Whenever I even think of it, I see me gunned down in the gutter in the rain."

"Very Warner Brothers, dear."

"Isn't it—and I'm never fool enough to imagine myself as Miss Davis daring to go to the Olympus Ball in a red dress. And that's to my credit."

!@#$%^&*

"What's Stinky doin' sittin' all by huh lonesome in the corridor?"

"Poor ole Stinky's got it bad, and that ain't good."

"What *love? Stinky?*"

"In a way, yes—consequences of, at least."

"*Chagrin d'amour*—Stinky? I can't believe it."

"Oh, don't sing that song at huh. She's got the *clap*, front and back simultain'ously tagethuh. Huh candle burns at both ends until she can see Dr. Brown in the morning—and if she thought it would last huh whole life long, she'd take a pink bath."

"Say not the struggle naught availeth, darling."

"Say it isn't so, say it isn't so—everyone is sayin' Stinky's finished, say it isn't so!"

!@#$%^&*

"Yes, you could say that as I had no brothers, I had my druthers."

"*Could I.*"

"Yes, but of course since I came out, I have both."

"*Fornix*—the vaulted arch of a brother. The origin of *fornixation.*"

"My brother despises me—it breaks my heart!"

"I've joined the Mattachines, a band of loving activist gay brothers, all linked together—"

"Like a chain gang."

"That is unlikely—we are not in Georgia."

"We're not in Kansas no more either, Toto."

"Over the rainbow—a divine idea."

"Ain't it though—just. Y'know, dear, up at Niagara Falls they got a permanent rainbow—leastways when the sun's shining. Y' could go over it in a barrel."

"Well, all this brotherhood and affirmation and *expansion* talk makes me terribly nervous. It seems to me we must take a leaf from the Shakers' book and *cut back.*"

"Cut back, dear—how?"

"Most of us, fortunately, do not reproduce, but we must take a serious overview and stop indiscriminately encouraging young males to embrace our ways. Are you familiar with Malthus? Well, you ought to become so forthwith, particularly with his ideas concerning *the constant tendency in all animated life to increase beyond the nourishment prepared for it.*"

"That's ridiculous. Unless and until wives learn to give decent head—don't hold your breath—those penile spigots will not run dry."

"You've got to have a dream; if you don't have a—"

"—dream, then how you gonna have a dream come true. Yes, dear, it's a Barnum and Bailey world, just as phoney as it can be, but it wouldn't be make-believe if he believed in theė. Want to know something, dear? Your sincerity just melts my cold, cold heart. And not just my heart, dear—*all of me* seems to be melting. What a *world* what a world! Who would've thought that a good little girl like you, in a place like this, could destroy all my beautiful wickedness. What a *camp!*"

!@#$%^&*

"Oh, my dear, the discernment of paradox is not to be confused with hypocrisy."

"No kiddin'. Gee, I'd like ta stay with ya, Spinoza, and hear more on the subject, but I got somethin' soakin' downstairs."

!@#$%^&*

"Una is vertiginously glamorous, and realizes that to survive in this world as a glamorous woman you have to dramatize every moment."

"That may be, but she is quite directionless."

"That's not true—she simply prefers a goalie to a goal."

"It's just no use telling you anything; you know it all."

!@#$%^&*

"Yes, his first time—he's just come to town, he's gorgeous, positively *effervescent*, and a *higher mathematician.*"

"Really, darling, the wild complexities of the young are *too* shredding!"

"I found him cruising the halls—well, walking, talking out loud—saying how terrible it is about Hungary and all the rest. I thought I should calm him down, so I brought him in here for a cup of coffee. He seemed a little woozy, so I asked him was he all right, and he said his brainstorms sometimes create problems with his semicircular canals, which he charmingly referred to as his gyroscope. He said often when he comes rushing into his office at the University with one going, and throws himself down on his chair, he misses. I got him settled in the banquette, up against the wall, and the coffee really got him going—full bore."

"In two words, dear."

"Oh, it was *fascinating*! He told me all about the primes. The primes are spread so thinly among the natural numbers that the probability that a randomly chosen number is prime is vanishingly small. Most numbers are not prime."

"Sister, you've been comin' in here how long, and you just learned *that*? And to think they told me you were *educated*!"

"Very funny. You never learn unless you listen. For instance there is a well-known formula for generating perfect numbers from primes. A perfect number is one whose factors add up to the number itself. The smallest perfect number is six—one plus two plus three, see?"

"Six is my downward limit, no question—and I mean *soft*."

"Then we got into a discussion—or he did—about the continuum description of general fluid flow."

"In here? How appropriate! I'd check the boy out myself, dear, but you know, I don't think he quite fits my portfolio."

!@#$%^&*

"Sophronia doesn't come in here for the sex—not to hear her tell it, anyway. No, the rough-and-tumble that interests her is the *verbal*. She comes in here to get an *education*—and, as she puts it to then go—*ceteris paribus*—and get a rub-down by a really good *massagynist*."

"What is *certeris paribus*?"

"It's Latin, dear."

"I got that part—what does it mean?"

"Except Sundays and holidays."

"It does *not*! It means other things being equal."

"Oh, yeah—t'what?"

"To Freddy's *dick—Jesus*!"

!@#$%^&*

"She is living, I fear, in a sunken capsule of illusion, referring to her *delicate prowess* in the fine art of seduction."

"All art aspires to the condition of music."

"Yes, I know, dear, and that broad is in there now bangin' out 'Chopsticks.' "

"John Cage is forever banging out 'Chopsticks.' "

!@#$%^&*

Moriarty at your side—a word or two in your ear.

We are now entering the steam room, where our young lord is about to come upon the dim outline of two older Mott Street *mafiosi* masturbating together with gusto, while the PBA boys, wrapped in long towels sit together on a tile ledge, averting their solemn gaze.

"Si, e buono. Spogliarsi insieme—si, insieme, nudi nella doccia. Schizzarsi l'acqua addosse, insaponaesi, lasciar correr l'acqua e le mani per i corpi, piegarsi indietro in modo che l'acqua cadedanso ci solletichi il torace, il ventre, la stomaca, il cazzo. Prima l'acqua fresca e poi la bocca calda di un bel ragazzo. Ma chi potra resistare in questi luoghi tristi?"

(Hssssssss)

"Should you have stayed home, dear, and thought of here?"

"Oh, you who drip with scorn, someday *you'll* be old—mark my words, and *terribly ashamed*!"

(Hssssssss)

Two old priests in conversation:

"Da ver. Chi e buono con l'ali e coi remi quantunque puo, chiascun pinger sua barca!"

(Hssssssss)

In the coffee shop, styled the *event room* as in crime fiction.

"Whatever her allure, whatever her determination, I do not think she will ever prove a homemaker. I had to tell her just the other day that just because you *can* use Crisco for *that*, does *not* mean you can use K-Y to make *pie crust!*"

"I don't believe nice people use Crisco for that, do you?"

"I seem not to have made my point."

"It's rude to point, darling, but we are tolerant in here."

"Amplius lava me ab iniquitate mea."

"We'll have to see what can be done about that, Sophronia—maybe Freddie can send you out with the robes and towels."

"Concerning the workings of pleasure and pain, pleasure is the lowering of energetic cathexis, pain is a heightening of same. The ego, which at its inception is still far from robust, becomes aware of the object cathexes, and either acquiesces in them, thereby with stark determination crossing the boundary of terror into the realm of voluntary subjugation and unmitigated narcissistic delight, or else attempts to defend itself against them by the process of repression—"

"Nobody we know, darling."

"—or by oral mastery of the object—"

"Yum-yum."

"Come on, will you—I've got a midterm in this shit on Monday."

"Betcha can't wait for graduate school, hon, where y'get t'do *your* orals."

"What are culture and intellect compared to a really hot fuck?"

"Accompaniments."

"Really? I sing *a cappella*."

"It's a *card trick*, see? You take the four jacks, the four aces, the four kings, and the four queens. Now here's the story. . . ."

"What'cha writin' there, Mrs. Metalious, yer memoirs?"

"No, a novel, a scorchingly real novel. Here listen to this. 'He lay back as the woman mounted him. Up, up into her body slithered the tree of life.' "

"She fucks a *tree*?"

"It's called poetic license."

"Oh yeah? She fucks a tree, I call it *splinters*."

"And it's there walking in the high woods
That I could wish to be—"

"Hey wait a minute, wasn't there a girl she fucked a god she turned into a tree? Maybe this is the reverse—maybe she fucks a tree she turns into a goddess, huh?"

"Apollo and Daphne. Those Greeks were far-out. All those fabulous gods fucking mortals—they laid the foundation of all our dreams."

"I must lead the sympathetic and attentive friend to an elevated position of lonely contemplation, where he will have few companions, and I whisper encouragingly to him that we must hold fast to our luminous guides, the Greeks."

"And the men that were boys when I was a boy
Walking along with me."

"She fucks a tree—and nine months later what, a big apple falls out?"

"That would be very symbolic. I saw this avant-garde play? A girl gave birth to a lightbulb—that was symbolic."

"She fucks a tree."

"It's a wonder t' me y'can concentrate—"

"Oh, I've always written in public places."

"So have a lotta people, dear—the tea room stall-wall scribes fer instance. I wish those two schoolboy fairies would come in here to do their busywork instead of shuttin' themselves up in their double room. Of course, it's probably just their homework they're doing in there—I mean what else could it be?"

"What else? The Dialogues of the Catamites."

"I think they're dear."

"Really? I fear neither one of them quite lights my fire."

"Not even as *kindlin'*, darling?"

"Well . . ."

"Well, the mouthy one sure is a ringer for Oscar Wilde."

!@#$%^&*

We climb the stairs now, to the dormitory.

"So she heaves into view coming out of a room and I ask her how was it, and she says back, 'The food was okay, nothing special; the service friendly if distant. I read somewhere that when you go trolling you should always bring salt along to liven up what you catch and eat.' "

"Drugs."

"Probably so."

"Absolutely."

"Abide with me, will you darling, all through the eventide?"

"I'll stick around—I'm workin' swing watch, and that means sob-sister detail—but whatever you are *on*, Doll, I'd like a gay dose of it, here and now."

"Actually, my darling, I'm on laughing gas—it's a long story, I won't bore you with the details, but on it I reach out with my mind to other dimensions and feel the blossoming of my senses as they open to behold the essence of the world."

"Yeah? Well as long as it ain't silly syrup—I skeeve on needles bad. Also it ain't eventide, it's fuckin' one in the morning, and that mouth organ playin' down the hall is startin' t'get on my fuckin' nerves—awful sad soundin', like a baby cryin'."

"That is Monica Harmonica—an older person who's been coming in here since the days of the wagon trains, where she learned to play the instrument. Actually she is a Harms—from the music publishing family—and Monica is the camp name somebody gave her—Monica Harms, harmonica, get it? She knows only three or four tunes, '*Plaisir d'amour*' which you are hearing now, 'The Streets of Laredo,' the 'Meditation' from *Thais*, 'Songs My Mother Taught Me'—a real tearjerker—and a couple more. And in true fact she does no harm, no harm at all, and may even heal a little—bringing consolation to the desolate. Of which of an evening we have a goodly number—another fact."

"The song my mother taught me was 'Pistol packin' momma, lay that pistol down!' Made me a star turn at children's parties."

!@#$%^&*

"That sure is a fine stand of corn you've got there."

"You can have all you want, so long as you pick it."

"Action precedes attitude, Cunnegunde!"

"Get out of here, Duessa—this is a private party."

"So to speak. He is *all yours*, Miss Ventricle, but take my advice, don't strain yerself."

"She is rotten, that one, rotten to the core."

!@#$%^&*

"Mr. Lincoln had a male lover, called Joshua Speed, and with Mrs. Lincoln away during the Civil War, clearing out the merchandise at H.H. Walker's in New York, they had a great deal of time to spend together with young Todd in the White House, talking about *opera*, which Mr. Lincoln dearly loved—especially *Norma*. Now you tell *me*, darling, just what that indicates. Had Mr. Lincoln lived he would have issued another Emancipation Proclamation for the fairies—and lock-and-sin hospitals for incurables such as this would have become unnecessary!"

"Did you ever in your life hear such a tale?"

"*Quod volimus credimus libentem*, dear."

"Huh?"

"We believe what we want to believe."

"I wouldn't have seen it if I hadn't believed it, dear?"

"Yes, if you like."

"I don't necessarily want to believe *anything*—not anything I can pin down anyway."

"Would you willingly be deceived, then, by a beautiful lying man?"

"I suppose so—the beautiful part would certainly make a change."

!@#$%^&*

"Look, darling, let's start with a basic definition, all right? A beginning is that which is not itself after anything else, and which has naturally something else after it."

"Oh yeah? *Find* one."

!@#$%^&*

"The poor dear is a refugee from Sioux City, where she was vice president of the coiffure guild, so she's given up a lot to be with us, but things were getting out of hand out there, what with that poor old cocksucker being convicted of killing that eleven-year-old boy, and one of the jurors said a man like that who listens to Liberace on the radio is capable of anything, and them cooking up a new law that declares all faggots entrapped by cute undercover cops automatically demented and put in the state asylum and given prefrontal lobotomies like poor Miss Rose."

"Was she guilty as charged of the transgression?"

"That I don't know—why do you ask?"

"A competent defense attorney will advise the accused of the weight of evidence and, if guilt exists, of the substantial mitigation advantages of so pleading at the earliest opportunity."

"So will a priest, darling, on any late Saturday afternoon, anxious to get out of that stifling box and back to the rectory for a long hot soak, a languorous, voluptuous jerk-off, and his roast beef dinner."

"You know what Dorothy Parker said, don't you, about frontal lobotomies?"

"Yes, dear, I do."

"I'd rather have a bottle in front of me—"

!@#$%^&*

"One soaking wet evening, there came to the tavern four workmen, who demanded lodgings for the night. So you put the four jacks down on the table, one in each corner."

"Sneeze on Monday, sneeze for danger
Sneeze on Tuesday, kiss a stranger."

!@#$%^&*

" . . . peas, beans, lentils and chick peas complement the grains, largely meeting protein needs and restoring nitrogen."

"Really? I've heard the same said of three male loads and a green vegetable."

!@#$%^&*

"It's a common error; the past imperfect and the gerundive are quite often confused. Always identify the construction before you go further."

"*And* the construction worker."

"Excuse me, this is a private discussion."

"On a *riveting* topic."

"And how did *you* do on the Latin Regents, my dear, or were you dispatched to a *trade* school?"

"We were tutored at home—Father didn't want us mixing with ruffians."

"And you did not—you were groomed for executive status, primed to take on globular responsibilities. Then along came Bill, an ordinary guy; you met him on the street and might hardly have noticed anything else ever again, except as luck would have it along came Bob . . ."

!@#$%^&*

"Know how young male long-tailed monkeys signal one another to come and play? With *open mouths* and *raised eyebrows*. Sound familiar?"

"That's what I like about coming in here, y' get yerself an education in the finer distinctions. I tell ya, *high brows, low loins* could be this terlet's motto!"

"I think in here our kind comes into its own."

"Yeah, it's own *fist*, baby, nine times out of ten."

!@#$%^&*

"We call her Lily Lumbago. We mean no harm, dear, and neither, of course, does she, but comes a time the endless recitation of ailments just gets you down."

"Well, she seems to have finally connected to a sympathetic ear—there she is right over there refreshing her fagged old gums on Mediterranean delicatessen. Where there's a will there's—"

"A greedy, receptive ear, yes indeed—usually but not always that of a relative. Well, I suppose stranger things have happened than that a tired old queen should leave her platform shoe collection to an anonymous Italian sailor."

!@#$%^&*

"Wheat grew best in lowland valleys and highland plains, while barley tolerated the drier semideserts and hills—am I boring you?"

"Oh, *no*!"

"Civilization, you know, doesn't come from—"

"Gristede's—I know, and I am interested in intellectual subjects, *honestly*."

!@#$%^&*

"Self-actualization, dear, in a time of increased meaninglessness and confusion."

"You *pay* for that?"

"You might try it."

"I'm actual enough already—and I often believe I'm the only thing that is."

!@#$%^&*

"You want to know about doctors? I'll tell you about doctors. They lie, we die. *Ge-sundheit!*"

"I was recommending Doctor Brown—a saint."

"So recommend—but don't sentimentalize a clap mill."

"You're a hard woman, Agnes."

!@#$%^&*

"Is it true the rich are different?"

"In point of fact the rich, unhappily, are all the same—acting out in some delusional melodrama of destiny their robber baron ancestors cooked up to exonerate themselves. Vicious, petty, relentless, doing sickening things time and again, regardless of the consequences, regardless of the pain it might cause them or anyone who gets in their way."

!@#$%^&*

"The workmen had scarcely got settled in their rooms, when four policemen came to the tavern and desired accommodation for the night. The landlord at once introduced the four policemen, all one each, into the rooms. You put an ace over each jack."

"Sneeze on Wednesday, sneeze for a letter,
Sneeze on Thursday, something better."

"No, darling, Francis Poulenc did *not* write a ballet score for Margot Fonteyn, he wrote a ballet score from the fables of *La Fontaine*; it was called *Les animaux modeles*."

"Well, I was close."

"So were the Windsors."

!@#$%^&*

"Come in, darling—sit down, and tell me we belong alive."

"Do not despair. The noblest deeds, the sympathetic emotions, self-sacrifice, and that calmness in the soul, which the Greeks called *sophrosyne*, all are attainable. For the belief that we can discover the true nature of all things—"

"Spare me."

"I sympathize, darling. The circumference of the circle of knowledge has an infinity of points, and the noble and talented man inevitably comes up against some border point on that circumference where he stares at something that simply cannot be illuminated. For instance when Popper said he held the belief that reality could be *established*, Wittgenstein said in effect, 'Take your beliefs to the synagogue,' which was met, of course, with shock, but Wittgenstein seemed unaware of it and continued. In the end he took up a poker from the fireplace and brandished it as Popper fled the chamber in wild terror.

"In any event at this point the above-mentioned sees to his horror how logic suddenly turns on itself—often viciously, in a convulsive, unstoppable arc—and bites its own—"

"Foot?"

"Tail, darling. Then a new form of knowledge breaks through—the acknowledgment of the tragic, which in order merely to be endured requires art as a healer and protector. Then he can cheerfully say to life *I want you, you are worth knowing*—and so grasp it."

"Have you any idea—can you even *guess* how many men I've said those very words—"

"Not to men, dear, it is to life itself one—"

"And what is life itself to the likes of us but a man?"

"I'll leave you now."

"That might be best."

"Excuse me, did I hear somebody in this room mention *poppers?*"

"Wretch! Do not seek unclean things in a sanctuary of learning."

"And *you* can go to *hell* with your *gasoline panties* on!"

!@#$%^&*

"Edwidge prefers married men—exclusively."

"Because of what their wives won't give them, I suppose."

"Exactly."

"That is becoming corny; educated women everywhere suck cock—I read it in Kinsey."

"That may be so, dear, but Edwidge does the other thing—attributed to depraved monks in medieval times and to the Knights Templar of the Order of the Red Cross of the Hospital of St. John of Jerusalem, later the Knights of Malta, and that in our own time only dedicated fairies, Chinese whores, and the Duchess of Windsor do. I think you must know of the practice to which I am obliquely referring."

"Yes, I do, and I do not approve of it."

"It disgusts you, darling. *Si vil non sei.*"

"Nothing human disgusts me—"

"Say it again, Saxon—hush—only to *me!*"

"—but the practice is too dangerous—it can result in lockjaw."

"Well, Edwidge digs husbands of other women, these Bronxville Galahads gone AWOL, for the most part a quite respectable assortment, though by no means stilted in their manners. Of course, she's as fickle as seed thrown to the winds, but in that she's scarcely unique, is she."

!@#$%^&*

"And the dead shall arise and walk among us."

"Peace, Garance is not dead, she does not sleep—venerate her."

"The evidence is *this* is her *residence*. She certainly must think so herself, because she once left her room key in the coffee shop—Oh, it was ages ago—and with it a little small-print card from the Policemen's Benevolent Association that read, '1. Always use deadbolt. 2. Secure valuables. 3. Report suspicious persons or acts. 4. Never open door prior to verifying ID.' "

"*Deadbolt?*"

"Yeah—why is it that everything that happens in this dump, and everything that's talked about, is so fucking *metaphorical*? It's really startin' t' get on my gay nerves."

"I can't help you, dear, I did not write the script."

"Garance has found a way to live cheaply, and without tears. She takes her meals with Dorothy Day's people and helps them out in small ways, plays a little bridge, a penny a point, at her club in the afternoon, claques at the opera, and enjoys her repose with us."

"Her *club*?"

"Yes, dear, the Century. She comes from the most distinguished people."

"Can ya beat that!"

"Afraid not, darling—you can't join it either."

"When he returned to the parlor, he found waiting four gentlemen."

"Sneeze on Friday, sneeze for sorrow,
Sneeze on Saturday, see your beau tomorrow."

"You put down the four kings, one each, on top of the jacks and the aces."

"Sneeze on Sunday, hell all the week."

!@#$%^&*

" . . . 'and I swear I didn't know whether to shit or go blind.' 'A brain-taxing choice, dear,' said I, 'for certain temperaments. I'd advise a trip to the Penn Post; there you could do both and be the main attraction for nights on end.' A silence fell.

"Then she called me a *trade-last*! I slapped her face. 'You call me that?' I said. 'You with that tired, worn old kooze of yours, plowed to a dried-up rut and belched on by how many infected bronchia the Board of Health could not imagine!' *Nobody* talks to your mother in that way without there be consequences, sometimes worse than can be allocated by a blistering tongue."

"Well, in my opinion, the Penn Post is, except for the likes of Lincoln Kirstein, who *is* interesting, in every conceivable way beyond the pale—the sulfurous realm of dragons, of *golem*, of unspeakable creatures from the sea's bottom—"

"Deep calleth unto deep in the noise of their water sports."

"Of heinous wart hogs whose lives though lingering long are lodged in lairs of loathsome ways. A dread manifestation in four dimensions of the heresy of Nathan of Gaza."

"I hear it's haunted by the ghost of Billy Woodward."

"Tell that to Pollyanna, upstairs, singin' over and over, 'To hold a man in your arms is wonderful, wonderful.' "

"Poor dear, the closest she ever comes to *that* is holding a dick in her fist—and only for a split second, when some poor sucker comes around the corner too fast and his gown has not been properly fastened."

"Just worn out, huh?"

"Worn *out? Mira, Lupe,* how about she looks like the Trojan passed around at the mob's last gang bang—the old one that sprang a *leak*! She is the gray sunken cunt of the world, if you want the truth. She's *through,* she is remaindered historical romance!"

"Soon after there came into the same room the *four ladies*."

"It is bad luck to bring a hoe into the house."

"Darling, as the French ambassador finally said to the whirling dervish, '*Ca suffit!*' I mean, is there a *payoff* in this card game or is there not? Because if there is not, I am giving my seat here to the biggest lady. Call me old-fashioned and *vieux jeux* into the bargain, but I like a payoff—or at least a *story*—like the three cards in *Pique Dame* and the havoc they create."

!@#$%^&*

"I am ergophilic, darling—I'm an ergophile. I never plan ahead—I never even buy green bananas."

"He clutched me with fat naked paws. Really, my dear, if the old wart hogs are going to insist on taking such liberties, they might at least wear rings!"

"So this one night I asked him, look, *is* there a—"

"*Incompertum adhuc,* Whoressa, as yet we know not."

"Hush, you—you don't even know what it was I asked him if there was such."

"Which hardly matters—as yet we know nothing."

"No, the ego *cannot* organize the drives!"

". . . and if you don't know that there are more *fabulous men* at *every level* doing *the most important things* here in New York than ever were in Paris, London, or Rome, you have not been paying attention to world events since the war—and I do not mean only Abstract Expressionism and the GI Bill."

"Excuse me, darling, wasn't that G.I. JOE?"

"Actually, if you must know, it was Kilroy. I got it off a toilet wall. He forgot to leave a number. I concluded he was making a general statement."

" 'For who can fail to recognize the optimistic element in the heart or dialectic, which celebrates a jubilee with every conclusion and can breathe only in cool, conscious brightness, that optimistic element which, once pushed into tragedy, gradually overruns its Dionysian regions and necessarily drives them to self-destruction, right to their death trap in middle class drama.' Nietzsche, dear—and so very relevant to our own time—all these terrible, stultifying *talky* plays!"

!@#$%^&*

"Being taken by a man makes me feel *alive*—you understand?"

"Of course, Millicent—but then plugging your vibrator into the wall socket will do the same thing for a lot less trouble."

"I require more—I require wilfull *abraision*."

"You put the four queens, one each, on top of—"

"Don't tell me, darling, the workmen, the policemen, *and* the gentlemen."

"It is bad luck to count the stairs."

"Now, did you hear that, chile—*willful abraision*. Whut Ah say is to each her own, but that sort of thing has seytin' *repercussions*. Why do you know that in the latest catalogue of supposed depravities that these teh'ble Freudian monstuhs ahr puttin' out, the progression is *cross-dressing, water sports—including the high colonic—leather, rubber, an element of pain, loss of control, and a bit of rough*? Which attempts to flat out *de-clare*, chile, that drag is the start of the downhill slide as surely as maryjane leads in about a month's time to a major *her-o-wyne* jones! Now you just try tellin' Miz Sapphire that thing—that the splendor of her bearing, her gowns, her jewels, betokens her losing control and having ugly men shit all over her face—you jus' *try* it!"

!@#$%^&*

"Although generally speaking, it's the orifices, sometimes it's merely the crevices."

"Bathsheba, you could slap that up on the signboard of the Little Church Around the Corner, and they'd come all the way in from Bay Ridge on the BMT t'hear ya hold forth on it!"

"Speaking of which—orifices, crevices—there goes that Melusine—half girl, half snake . . . *clock* huh!"

"Yes, one among many who come in here with the weight of the world on their shoulders seeking to forget the old love in the triumph of new fortune."

"Unlucky in love, lucky at cards—that it?"

"That, too."

"Well, I wouldn't know about her shoulders, but I can tell you what I see written on her tombstone. *Western Civilization Sat on My Face*. And her taste in *men*—I despair of it. No wonder she slithers along the ground so, she is in her element."

"I have charged her with that. She replied '*Video meliora proboque, deteriora sequor*. It's true, but remember it was true of the Redeemer, who sought out the company of lepers, thieves, and prostitutes.' I felt *chastened*—I did."

!@#$%^&*

"You never wear perfume with pearls, grandmother said; the pearls become discolored."

"Oh, I don't know about that. I mean if the meaning of the concept is entirely exhausted by a description of the relations on which it is based, is it a rule of life? I *like* my pearls off-white—thanking you and granny all the same."

"We do argue so, don't we, over the propriety of the various applications we make concerning the *appareil* of the opposite sex."

"I am afraid I don't understand you at all—for the third sex there can be no such thing as an opposite."

!@#$%^&*

"That cock won't fight."

"Mercy, I never want a cock to fight—I just want it to relax itself and *stretch*."

"Well, quit gawpin' at that one, he's not for you."

"A bruiser—and trouble?"

"Mad, bad, and dangerous to blow—make one little slip of a single tooth and you'll be spittin' it out along with half of the rest in yer head."

"*Mercy!*"

"None whatsoever."

". . . and the black arms of tall ships that stand against the moon, their tales of distant nations, darling."

"To each his own. The black arms I desire are standing right there in that open doorway."

"You cover not the waterfront, I take it."

"You take it straight."

"I do when I can get him to miss that train."

"The night draws on."

"She hovers . . . she hovers."

"Poor thing. Shall we call her Miss Near—or near miss? In any case, should she snag anybody, whatever they go lookin' for up that old ass is *mined out*."

"I ran my fingers down his wet, white flank and—"

"Darling, you make the boy sound like a horse!"

"Only in one particular."

"How *pert*."

!@#$%^&*

"You want some Numi silks for misses' wear, darling, you want some hosiery maybe, or maybe some elegant cashmere long shawls, you trot yourself right over to Lord and Taylor. You want some hot gay sex fun, get your ass in here and hunker down right now!"

"People around here must think my asshole is a revolving door."

"You come sit by me, pet, and I'll teach you manners enough to turn that revolving door into a lucrative paying turnstile."

"I do like it when people show some respect. I do not seek their gratitude or their approval even, although they might perhaps feel a certain sense or *privilege.*"

"As Jung has written, darling, everything wants to live, including filth!"

"Who's Jung?"

"An eminent psychiatrist, pet, who also thinks life is a dream."

!@#$%^&*

On their way to the coffee shop, the young lord and Delancey espy through the glass front doors the red and white flashing lights of an idling police patrol car flashing outside in the street. A voice shrieks, "You and that fuckin' card game—here comes Lilly Law, and she ain't the Ace of Hearts!"

"It is bad luck for one to comb his hair after dark."

"*Red alert,* you fornicators! The precinct chariot has just this minute pulled up outside the front door. Find that Miss Delphine who mopped that bracelet and hide her in the cellar. Let the woman marinate in her own gay guilt, for she is indeed a bad example!"

"We think she has sought gay sanctuary in the steam room."

"Oh, my God—the paste diamonds will *melt!*"

"Unlikely in the extreme. That girl is *Nosferatu.* She can turn the steam room frigid as a meat locker down on Eleventh Street—where you go, Mona, on hot summer nights to shop for your wholesale *veal chops,* right?"

"*Fresh!*"

"That's what I hear."

!@#$%^&*

Moriarty, m'dears, fresh from slumber, from a sojourn with Oisín himself in the Land of Tír Na nóg, brought back to life, such as it is, among the living mortal living *hier mit die Schuldigern* as the empress daughter of Keikobad a sort of high-price-ticket Mikado in that opera he took me to in his head a year ago in London town to hear herself, the oltrano diva of the twentieth century, do the part. *Die Frau ohne Schatten.* Funny business life in a woman's career. Yer woman Mawrdew Czgowchwz cannot be said to have a life without shadows, but in the clear and blazing light of art . . . nothing to do with the moment, alas. What's this Himself was muttering to himself as he came in Before . . . *Gott, es dunkel hier!*

Brought back by the piercing hue and cry, the clamorous hubhub of frantic fairies. It would seem a patrol car from the local precinct up on Thirty-first Street has in the past few moments arrived at the front door of the place (and I on horseback, riding the wind in the company of that manliest of heroes, Oisín the Wanderer, all that incalculable force field beyond light-years distance away, think of it!), its emergency lights flashing. There seems, mind, to have been no siren heard, which really, after all and *c'mon* now, girls, one would have thought sufficient to allay dread fears, being a rather clear indication of the lack of aggressive (or might one say *cathectic*) design involved in the business if you ask the likes of me who negotiates so freely between men and their motives.

Notwithstanding which, did the halls the shrieks of shrill women giving tormented stillbirth to their delusions of a more endurable tomorrow—but I've just this minute been told knew that. Would you ever care to have this job? Arrangements can be made this very night at the front desk. Full benefits, Blue Cross, Blue Shield.

In any case, back—well, in a place like this, one does not casually declare oneself "back in harness" for fear of creating an erroneous impression as to one's availability for *things*. For although no Other can normally attach himself to a stranger, oddly, should but *listen!* Do you hear it? The young lord and his bosom pal Delancey, in the coffee shop, unaffected by the surround, discussing the world and its ways, beginning with Freddy.

!@#$%^&*

"Fred says they were going operational full tilt at Bill's making up the bouquets and baskets."

"Can I whisper a secret? I'm glad they've gone. I must commence doing something with my life."

"You mean besides getting ready to make a debut that will—"

"Knock them all flat, dear? Sure thing—me and the Greek."

"You're far too modest, you know you are—and besides, your voice doesn't wobble."

"Don't talk of it. I have a repeating dream; in it I'm singing Pollione and I have my choice of three Normas, Anita Cerquetti, the Meneghini, and Gina Cigna. I ask, 'What about Mawrdew Czgowchwz?' and am told 'Mawrdew Czgowchwz has retired from singing to make a home and have children.' 'But what about *Pilgrim Soul*?' I plead. 'The role has been recast and rewritten for Siobhán McKenna.' I wake in a cold sweat."

"*Actus reus. Mens rea.*"

"*Mirabile dictu.*"

"*Omnes Gallia est divisa in partes tres.*"

"Right, Cerquetti, the Meneghini, and Gina Cigna."

"*In vitam venturi saeculi, Amen.*"

Soterius at the chessboard. The Deconstruction of the Everard as the hidden apotheosis of the *grand salon*—with all the expensive clothes in the lockers and all the jewelry in the safe-deposit boxes—and what a *haul* it would all make. "Why do you suppose it has nevuh happened? Darling, is any more proof required of thuh benevolence of thuh Policemen's Benevolent Association? Ah give whenever Ah can—and generously."

"Remember, chile, though a pawn may be queened—thuh symbolic reenactment of a phenomenon in European courts of thuh time, such as thuh court of England's Edward thuh Second, whereby thuh king transfers his trust and affections to a *minion*—thuh queen may *nevuh* be pawned."

"A *minyan*? A minyan is ten Jewish men—"

"As you were, girls—come out from under your desks. Lilly Law is only here to complete transactions with the front desk."

"In *uniform*?"

"Bastards! Acting like they own the fucking place."

"What can you mean, Stiletta? They *do* own the fucking place."

"It is bad luck to burn the cob when popping corn."

"He calleth all his children by theah name, and *mah* name, not that you are entitled the way He is either to know it or to use it, is Soterius—*alias dicitis vulgariter* 'Sapphire.' Ah wuz *created* of mah name, like *Semiramide*; thuh *woid* in each case bein' that of which thuh nominated is the *personage*."

"It is said that in *Don Quixote*, Part Two, Cervantes, in envisioning Dulcinea del Toboso *en travestie* brings his creation to the very limits of representation, but I say Sapphire goes further still: I say Sapphire goes beyond—above and beyond—the limits of representation heretofore *tolerated only* in fiction and up there at Phil Black's, into something like the astral plane come down to earth—for Sapphire is nothing if not star-begat, yet very terrestrial, indeed, and consequentially in a position to negotiate between realms with the utmost cordiality, ever keeping a Sibyl tongue in her head."

"Excuse me, everybody, for interrupting, but I've just heard you mention *positions*, and speaking of them, I'm in a rather awkward one. Has anybody in here found a key on a bracelet? I seem to have locked myself *out of my locker*, if you can believe it!"

"This is the coffee shop, Miss Two-Shoes; the fuckin' Lost and Found is at the desk. Lost key, indeed—lost *cause*!"

"You come sit down here for a minute, chile, and let me donate some essential info'mation to yoah stoah. This dump's *name* is *Lost Illusions Found Out*. But they do say that the blackest hour comes just befoah the dawn. If that be so, then I am thuh angel of that very hour, and 'though I may on the face of it be of that race Mr. Rudyard Kipling, an ugly old pederast, called the sullen new-caught people of the earth, half demon, half child, I may not have possession over Judgment Day, Oh, yes, sweet yes I will have mah say!

"I am not yoah fairy godmother, chile; I cannot change things into othuh things, but neither am I some dumb smoke-ass coon in a caracul coat down on a guest pass from the Mount Morris Baths, but rather a woman motivated, incentivized, and metabolized to pursue a cultivated life, educated in N'Awlins by exiled Belgian Beguines, in thuh *foyer* of whose motherhouse hung on opposite walls reproductions of Mister Annibale Carracci's *Rape of thuh Sabine Women* and Mister Breugel's *Slaughter of thuh Innocents*, both of which made a great and lasting impression on me in my younger, carefree, salad days.

"From them I learned my prayers, thuh catechism, thuh French language, and some groovy arithmetic, and therefore, though not an unduly severe woman myself, I can and will if necessary read you out to *whale shit* foah yoah own bettuhment, and that I do assure you is an invaluable *seyvuss* in this vale of tears, Life.

"Take mah own vunnuhble case. When you are told by thuh white folks th' Almighty put in charge of you that you are thuh same shade as your excrement, such information may *smart* some, but it does without doubt put you in touch with a sehyt'n reality. And keeps you on yoah *toes*, too, for a careeyuh such as mahn depended to a very great degree, chile, on urgent summuhnses to scheduled meetin's wit' unspecifahed pehysuns at inconvenient tahms—jes like whut goes on in heah ev'ry naht, which mus be whut *attracts* me so to thuh place—*nostalgia*, chile.

"And don't you be worryin' none 'bout yoah key, cawse thuh men at the desk got *pass keys*, which is neccess'ay foah when sad queens lock themselves in they rooms and swallow all they sleepin' pills at once."

!@#$%^&*

"Who is *that* one?"

"Soterius? A great diva, dear, very well aware of her own consequence, toast of the musical dance halls, Bowery resorts, long-gone good-time bars and oyster cellars of old deviate New York, when our kind and our loyal sisters were characterized by the tabloid gutter press as *dainty elves* and *stern women*.

"Many—a prime example, Joey de Sweat—will tell how they started from scratch; well, Soterius started from itch, and did not arrive in New York by bus or train or hitchhike, as have so many, but from *by sea* from Savannah itself—*il y a terriblement d'annes*. The old Savannah of juke joints and barrel houses and cathouse parlors, fully informed with the old and bitter knowledge of the morning—debarking at Pier 36 North River and charging down the gangplank to reclaim from that ship's hold some mighty fine pieces of steamer trunk luggage—always the mark of a headliner traveling show-woman, a person of consequence, a force to be reckoned with. When Miz Sapphire comes down hon, heaven comes down with huh—you unnuh-*stand*?"

"Of course, if the right *monsieur* were to come along, I would turn the Schiaparelli and every other stich I own, *ransack* Bergdorf Goodman, take a gay canter through Saks, and start out for Paris, France, Chile, with a completely new wardrobe, like a woman without a past."

"Hear that? That girl works in overtime until she fries. Anyway, she became known in the Life as Margy LaMont. Discovered by Carlo Van V., the Ward McAllister of his gay day, without whom the various cotillion suppers and dancing assemblies of the arriviste set would have had no tone at *all*. He brought many gentlemen of color, including Soterius, both to the Mechanics Library on West Forty-fourth Street, which then as now contained many thousands of well-selected and instructive books, and after a time of further exposure to learning, to places such as Scheffel Hall on Third Avenue and to the Fifth Avenue salon of Mrs. Mabel Dodge Luhan, at which socialists and anarchists, Freudians and free-lovers, artists and activists, and all manner of horticultural gentlemen, including the famous painters Charles Demuth and Marsden Hartley, debated the issues of the day."

"And that one—Soterius—was a star turn?"

"Oh, my *yes*! As she pointed out, under the camp name Sapphire. You might say she flourished with many a flourish of her own, and as Dostoyevsky points out, dear, a flourish can be a most dangerous thing—requiring as it does enormous taste—but if it is successful... now, you may have heard tell, dear, of the Windmill Theatre, in London. Well Eldress Sapphire was right out of our version of it—tilting at 'em night after night; she *never closed* in *any* war; she was overt *tous les jours*, darling, twenty-four hours, a floor show all on her own, and that did not mean *sauf dimanches et fetes* either, it meant *dimanches et fetes inclus*.

"Oh my, yes, *elle versait sans interruption*, becoming one the reigning queens of the Village, roped in extraordinary length of lambent pearls, gleaming like you-know-what against her blue-black skin—for she is what they call in the

South a blue-gum nigger. They are *terrified* of persons her hue—they tell their children that if they get bit by a blue-gum nigger, they *die*.

"Holding sway over a generation at places like Dolly Judge's Flower Pot, The Jungle, Club Onyx, and Trilby's. She headlined often at Jackie Law's Studio Club, child, on Fifteenth and Fifth . . . a stone's throw from Mabel Dodge Luhan's, only by then Mabel was hosting fairies such as D. H. Lawrence down there in the desert of New Mexico and the closest thing New York had to a celebrity hag was Texas Guinan. Plus which, she, Sapphire was a healer-woman; she had a concoction for the crabs she would douse a body with, intoning '*Crabs begone!*' and by next morning they wuz be-*went*.

"Then later at the parties of Alelia Walker, herself the toast of the Harlem Renaissance and the daughter of Madame C. J. Walker, the former slave child of the Breedlove clan wiped out by General Grant who became the greatest black entrepreneur of her day, purveyin' hair straightnin' products.

"Then voted—Soterius-Sapphire, child, not Mabel Dodge Luhan, not Texas Guinan, who was an undependable woman, a terrible liar, and vulgar as a sewer—y'know what they say, dear, there's a use for every part of the pig except the squeak, well, Texas was all squeak. Voted, Sapphire was, as Margy LaMont, Miss Bye-and-Large of, I believe, nineteen thirty-three.

"By that time she had starred in Mae West's *The Drag*, in Bridgeport, Connecticut, Bayonne, New Jersey, and for one night only, Sunday, February eighth, nineteen twenty-seven at midnight, at Daly's Theater on East Sixty-third Street—'Wilhelmina, *bar* the *door!*'—and had become the long-reigning and absolutely socially omnipotent diva of the Rubaiyat, the Club Pansy, and Harlem's very own Rockland Palace ballroom. 'Come on up, see me—I'll bake yuh a pan of biscuits.'"

!@#$%^&*

"The diva"—Soterius was heard announcing in serious tones to an audience augmented by men from the desk—"doesn't sit on no couch, sofa, or davenport neither; No, darlin', the diva stretches huh body out on the *divan* and yet, withal, chile, the diva is *adroit* in huh *maneuvers*, in othuh words *actively in-*

centified, you dig? And the whole time *arranged* long on the horizontal. As the French say, *Elle peut toujours s'en tirer. Elle a tout écoutée elle a tout entendue, elle a tout comprise, l'obvie et l'obtu—tu comprends, cheri?*"

"*Oui, madame, je comprend.*"

"It is bad luck to meet a left-handed person on Tuesday."

"But perhaps her greatest moment came right after the war when, having sung with the likes of the great Noble Sissle and *not been read out*, she sailed on a big float out from Sayville on the Feast of the Assumption, costumed as the Empress Theodosia, dear—and that in spite of the fact that, as you may know, the Byzantine Church doesn't *hold* with the Assumption, preferring to speak of the *Dormition* of Miss Mary Mother of God. But Soterius, darling, could never be anything *dormant*—and speaking of things both secret and Russian, as everybody *is* these days, I can't tell you how she did it, because it is *too* fantastic, but the fact is that what she wore as *parure* on that triumphal occasion was absolutely nothing but the *crown jewels of White Russia*—that's Minsk, y'know, after which Minsky's *Gaiety Theatre* on Forty-sixth Street—later transferred courtesy of Mayor La Guardia to Jersey City—was named. No, I can't tell you how, but those jewels, darling, live here in New York, property of whom they belong to be property of, and kept in the *vault* at Morgan Guaranty, but on that Feast of the Assumption, they were worn out to Cherry Grove by our Soterius, as the Empress Theodosia."

!@#$%^&*

"The life of a diva, chile, is the subject of legend from the very stah-ut. As sehycumstances change, new int'rests do reshape the pehcepshun of thuh past—as in thuh po-trayal of them dumb nigguhs in *Gone Wit' thuh Wind*. In the hay-unds of sehytun pehrsuns posin' as *authuhs*, the life of the diva may be used to sehyve ends quite unknown or irreluhvent to the diva huhself, and so it goes, you dig?"

"Oh, *yes*!"

"It is bad luck to break a bird egg."

"So, you see, it is always an honor indeed to have Sapphire here with us still, for she is a girl after our own heart, like the great thirteenth-century Burmese queen, See-Saw, the heroine of *The Glass Palace Chronicles*, who reigned beside two kings, encountered oracle-eating tigers, murderous intrigue, Tartars, and groveling courtiers, happily surviving all: her two husbands *and* the Mongol invasion, the darkest possible deeds done in the brightest possible sunlight, and participating all the time in calm and enlightened metaphysical discussions. And all the time, she Soterius was herself the most lavender thing there ever was, and you can see the traces of it still, although she is weathered under the electric lights.

"I mean *lavender*, child, for Sapphire is one of those wonders of the earth a man creature *colored mauve*, which allowed her to pass out of whatever world her forebears inhabited into the World of Cosmopolitan Attraction and by concentratin' huh *mahnd*, to gain admittance to he-whore places such as this, from which until we went and fought side by side with white boys in the war against the Krauts and the Japs we dinge were politely but firmly excluded. Isn't color prejudice a funny thing, though? You know, in Rio de Janerio there is no such of a thing."

!@#$%^&*

"To dig I am not able, darling, and to beg I am ashamed, but I am courteously willing to be as dependent as ever on the kindness of strangers."

"It is bad luck to sit on a pair of scissors."

!@#$%^&*

"Henry the Eighth was a *scumbag—period!*"

"Absolute power corrupts absolutely."

"Mawrdew Czgowchwz isn't corrupt."

"Mawrdew Czgowchwz has sung Giovanna Seymour—it has made her compassionate."

!@#$%^&*

"Soterius is the fierce, proud survivor of himself. In a microcosm where all movement is strictly regulated, the diva defies the narrow constraints of race, creed, religion, and custom that bind the overwhelming majority of her subject people. There is no room at the apex for weakness."

"It is bad luck for a black hen to come into the house."

"Will you *shut up!*"

"If someone sneezes while something is being said, it is a sign that it is the truth."

"The woman is crazed and worn and not to be trusted on sensitive subjects. The allegations she confidently puts out far, far exceed the plausible reach of her access."

"Oh, *baby*, now isn't that *just* the *purpose!* No doubt can darken such a truth. Yes, you are in no uncertain terms a benefactor of the *race. Bless* you!"

"All my pretty tonights, yes, and not a tomorrow amongst them!"

"Simple Simon didn't me no pie man, chile, on his way to Vanity Fair, oh my, no. He met a man with the attire of a harlot and subtle of heart, and he went with that man all the way to this house right here, in the twilight, in the evening, in the black and blue of night. I s'pose it took that long 'cause he was comin' down from the Bronx or in from Jersey or somethin'."

!@#$%^&*

"You see, dear, Orfamay was there that night, in the street outside that house on Laverne Terrace."

"No!"

"Yes."

"*Caramba!*"

"They're in there *doing one another's nails.* I call it incestuous!"

"It is bad luck to watch a person out of sight."

!@#$%^&*

The young lord, while descending two flights to the coffee shop, hears echoes of many voices.

"Nobody seems to get it that *camp* is the short form of *campaign*—and this dump is campaign headquarters. All the cubicles, d'y'see, are our *campaign tents.*"

"How *wonderful!*"

"She gets fifty scoots a hoot, no exceptions."

"Not even for servicemen?"

"She was asked that. 'I volunteer once a week at the USO in Times Square. Satisfied?' "

"You can't take issue with that."

"For the want of a nail the shoe was lost, for the want of a shoe the horse was lost, for the—"

"West led a diamond to East's ace, and East returned a heart jack. West won with the ace and returned the queen."

"Yes, but in what condition?"

"*What?*"

"Mildred, get out of here now—mind your own wicked business."

"A queen's business *is* diamonds. Answer me."

"*Mildred,* you may be *excused* from the *table!*"

"Go fuck yourself in Macy's Christmas window."

"I can't bear it."

"I know, dear, there's no privacy in the place—never was. Mildred, you *know* it's nowhere near Christmas. Oh, she is an unhappy child. It runs in the family."

"All unhappy families are—"

"Yes, dear, I know, but you see, if she throws herself in front of a BMT train at Twenty-eighth Street, the police will come in here and *make all of us* get down there on the tracks in *our robes* to identify the poor, hideous, broken remains—the head on the uptown track, the rest of her where she took the plunge on the downtown side. Now I don't know if you've ever witnessed—"

"I have *got* to go get a Bromo-Seltzer."

"Now, Mildred, see what you've done—I hope you're proud of yourself!"

"Very."

"—want of a horse the rider was lost, for the want—"

"Welding links of heavy chain for his *thresher?*"

"That's what she said, dear—verbatim; I didn't like to pry."

"I wish you had."

"He wanted to go bowling. I said 'I can't go bowling—bowling is a *violent* sport!' "

"It is bad luck to spin a chair around on one leg."

"—the battle was lost, for the want of a battle the—"

"And as for life, dear, wake me when it's over."

!@#$%^&*

"But for that they'd called my time up, I would have stayed with the starveling creature—leastwise until she had drifted off. No girl in that condition should have had to cry herself to sleep alone. 'When thou goest through the waters, I will go with thee.' Isaiah, darling, forty-two, three. But there was nothing—"

" 'Forty-two, three' sounds like a football scrimmage."

"You're *such* a man!"

"Well, I have been."

"—kingdom was lost, and all for the want of a nail!"

"Yes, dear, Nietzsche fears, unsurprisingly. 'The breeding of an animal allowed to make promises: is this not the paradoxical task nature has set itself with respect to man?' "

"He certainly knew everything about paradoxical promises, particularly from misdemeanant men."

"Is that your philosophy? If so, there are more things—"

"I don't *have* a philosophy, my darling, I have a *warbrobe*—much of it from Schiaparelli, in particular this one black strapless. I do love Elsa—did you know she refers to Coco Chanel as *La petite couseuse*? Of course she comes from real quality, does Elsa. Did you know her uncle discovered the canals of Mars, which is *too* fabulous, even if it turns out they're not canals after all. Any further questions?"

"Can't think of one—that makes it pie."

"Thank you, it is a rare comfort to be understood."

"Oh, my God, at *last*—I'm *coming*. . . . I'm *coming*!"

"Oooh—don't you *love* it when the guests make breakfast!"

"The violent bear the kingdom away—one of the hard sayings."

!@#$%^&*

". . . they'll come to my room and take away all my things and throw them in one of those—what do you call those things they have in the street?"

"I suppose you mean a Dumpster, Mr. Swan."

"Yes, that's it, a Dumpster—and take all my memorabilia away to the dump and leave it there to rot away and nobody will remember it or me either."

"We know where you live, Mr. Swan—we'll make sure none of that happens."

"You *will*?"

"Of course we will—we'll look after everything. You have the respect of everybody here, being a man of wise countenance, light-stepping, and with an air of understanding."

"And I don't even know your names."

"You don't have to know our names—we're all your friends."

!@#$%^&*

"She radiates the dreams of youth and the life force of the very eternal—but you listen to me now, you know what your problem is? It is just this: you are not lavender *enough*. I don't mean *swish*, either. Lavender works for freshness and cleanliness—that's how come I wear it in here—and has magical properties, both as herb and as flower. Positively miraculous when used in cases of unresolved guilt, or when you find in your emotional connection a feeling of things being awry, when no matter what confirmations of love you receive from people and situations as you *trampouze* the halls, you always feel...

"No, you must go up to Max Schling and buy lavender—*fresh* lavender, we are *not* talking sachet, which is what old ladies stick in their dresser drawers to make them forget the smell of stale twat. *Fresh* lavender. And bring it home and strew it, child, in your bed and in your bureau drawers, that each and every morning—afternoon, as I believe you much prefer—you may wake up pure, and simple. Then go uptown and rip the pants off another Roxy usher!"

"It's *etta*-mology here and *eeta*-mology over there."

"I would have thought it was both."

"What do you mean?"

"Over there. I would have thought the first the past tense of the second."

"I don't... *Oh, I see!* That's very clever. Gastronomy."

"Gastronomy or perhaps anthropology."

"Anthro... Oh, *dear me!*"

"... and at the hour of the wolf, as in the great religious houses, comes the Great Silence."

"In here?"

"In this same place, for many of our number are ardent adherents of humanism—a philosophy, darling of the caring, committed agnostic."

"Far out."

"*Suadentque cadentia sidera somnum.*"

"It is bad luck for a girl to be in church when she is asked to marry."

"All the same, there's an alarming social reality behind all of this, isn't there?"

"Yes, it's called balance of probabilities burden of proof, and it nails us to the cross."

!@#$%^&*

"But who *is* everyone? Tell me that—and why is it always so *dark*?"

V

"Here is the dawn. Anything but the above. Martial, overbearing, lewd."

"The sea is glass, reflecting the Chimera."

Mawrdew Czgowchwz, serene vessel, wondered idly whether she, like the *Andrea Doria*, might perish of complications, of collisions, were not precautions taken—and what precautions now considering the essential ones taken on her part (for she had not fornicated in a fog: she remembered that surely) had somehow availed nothing (but that was not the way to put it, if the births were so desired by the wizard consort). The man will prevail.

Cut in two in the event in a fog by a prow and sunk—on behalf of a pair of monozygotic tyrants—but *how* can such a thing be known?—who, having done to her what she had done to Maev Cohalen, would make their way in the world—and probably into show business. An idle fantasy (unlike the contorted reveries typical of afternoons before performance nights, afternoons spent contending with warring contraries, scheming ahead, negotiating with chimerical contenders: quizzing the outcome of this evening's show, that broadcast, those retakes in studio, some interview ("Madame Czgowchwz, a question about your almost preposterously nervy, quite unprecedented *Fach*") it came and went without a trace of that other fear—the one she felt might well capsize her—attendant upon the very thought of *filming*.

After all, was not to be the *exponent* of so many roles not in essence a condition of number—that selfsame by which one is oneself so multiplied?

What *had* she been persuaded to get up to—like some new Naughty Marietta on the high seas. "Ah, sweet mystery of Life could I but find thee / Ah, could I but know the secret of it all." The secret, too, of the *oceanic feeling* Freud had sympathetically described, largely as a result of listening to his female patients, and not, unlike Jung, who fucked all his regular as a Swiss cuckoo clock, trying to quiet them down, but more like Leopold Bloom, becoming one of them himself.

Could she postpone, even for a—no, the picture must be made: to do a thing, one does it. As for birth and death and evening, it would be evening when they woke, to go to town.

"You know, I've been meaning to ask you—at what age did Moravec die?"

"He was thirty-three. Why?"

"And Czgowchwz when the Nazis shot him—how old?"

"Odd—he was thirty-three. But why—"

"I'm thirty-three."

"Oh, *really*—I'd no idea!"

"I can't think why, as I was born in twenty-three."

"Twenty-three. Quite a year. De los Angeles, Callas, and you. You first, I believe—that true?"

"You know very well it is—and as for comparisons, who was that Bohemian born in the same year as Beethoven?"

"Anton Reicha, as it happens a superior composer—not to Beethoven naturally: there's apparently no such thing, but in the general sense. I don't find the comparison apt."

"I suppose it's not; I'm not very likely to sing either Norma or Madame Butterfly—not even at after-theater supper parties. Still and all. . ."

"Still and all, what?"

"Thirty-three is three-three, is six. And triple six is the Number of the Beast in *Revelation*."

"Don't be—"

"I'm not. I'm not having any part of it. But certain precautions want to be taken."

"If you say so. On the other hand, Rachmaninoff composed his Second Symphony at the age of thirty-three—instead of dying."

"And very beautiful it is. It *does*, now you mention it, have that instead-of-dying appeal."

"That is called the depressive-surrender stance."

"If you say so."

"Also, thirty-three is the number of the daevas."

"Oh? I'm only interested in one of those."

"Shall we go in?" she proposed, yawning awake.

"Could we stay out here a while more?"

"I suppose so. What's the coming attraction? Your nostril's slanting again."

"Fact is, we're watched."

"I was aware of that much earlier—from the gaminq saloon. It's why Madge so wanted us to fly. 'Especially on that boat, dear, all they all do the livelong day is slope around the public saloons hoping to get a good gawp at The Windsors.'"

"Just behind the bulkhead there—see—two small dark fox eyes darting out."

"A spy—in the dread Kilgallen woman's pay."

"No, this is different, unpracticed and sudden. I believe a child—definitely female."

Mawrdew Czgowchwz swung around. "Come out!" she called. Silence prevailed.

"You've frightened her—you would me—but not away I think."

"I'm tellin' the nun. You stole a bun. Ran around the corner and gave me none! Come out, come out, whoever you are—it's too late now for hide-and-seek!"

There was some respiration, followed by the sound of scuffing shoes. Then, turning the bulkhead's corner, a small girl edged toward the couple in the deck chairs, seeming to stand no taller than one of them in the upright position. (Manners, anyway, Mawrdew Czgowchwz marked.) She appeared to weigh very little, and her frank, exophthalmic gaze alarmed Jacob. (The diva seemed delighted; she whispered from chair to chair, "She has the look of a *wren*!" They later agreed that at eleven she already looked the way she would probably look at forty, but they did hope she would grow.)

"I'm very small—may possibly never grow."

"Oh, come on now."

"It's true, you know. It causes anguish; I overhear the parents."

"Well, now you're found out, come here, size that you are."

The girl came abreast the two in their deck chairs.

"I do apologize for spying on you both. I really do not wish to be seen to be seen lurking behind things, pestering the immortals. It's such bad form."

"Really?"

"No—I mean yes. Lord, you must both think me an awful little *stookawn*."

"Not in the least," the diva replied, while Jacob, adrift in language difficulties, looked on patiently.

"It's because the parents were talking on and on about you, as they have been doing since the moment we sailed—and that's only today's discussion, mind. We three are disembarking along with you, from this galleon into the same tender for Cobh: we're going home, too."

"Lovely," Mawrdew Czgowchwz declared (a little tentatively, her consort felt, and why not), "and who's this you are when you're at home?"

"I'm Miranda Mae Manahan. Only I've decided from now on it's Miranda *Maev*. Would you mind? I'd be grateful if you didn't—and needless to say, if you *approved* I'd be. . ."

"What would you be?"

"Likely, in Manahan's view, off the edge—quite."

"Well, I don't know really would I want to be remarked on, now, for instigating a thing like that. We've met, you know, your parents, my companion and I, last yesterday evening in the Grand Saloon. Excuses were made for a missing Manahan, said to be seasick."

"I wasn't seasick and you wouldn't be. Manahan himself instigated my nerves long ago—and admits it. You would at most be declared an accessory after the fact."

"How very interesting. I don't believe I've ever been an accessory. I've played second fiddle—"

The child shot her gaze back and forth between the couple.

"You *never*—you either. Manahan calls you twin monarchs of musicry."

"Oh, but I *have*," Mawrdew Czgowchwz assured her.

"She's played small parts," declared Jacob Beltane. "She's played Lady Macbeth."

"Well, I've never heard you in that one. *They've* heard you in *everything*, didn't they tell you? They were up on Manitoy at that shivery thing you sang in the hurricane. I got the whole story all over again night before last when we sailed past the place—Manahan was going on and on about the *Andrea Doria* and ships' graveyards—perhaps you see what I mean about his instigations—and mother asked him to stop, he might frighten me.

"I decided to give out to them. 'Not nearly so much as having been abandoned all summer did, thank you both very much,' I replied, 'with you having the times of your lives with not a bother on you.' They were at the big party for you in Central Park. *I've* been nowhere all summer but this dreary music camp uncounted miles from nowhere in the middle of some woods, doing nothing but solfège, but now that's over. Now we're bound for Ireland, home, and perhaps they'll turn over a new leaf. I mean, first he proclaims you *life-enhancing* and then forbids his child to disturb you. I consider that unsound, don't you? I call it muddleheaded, but for all that I wasn't going to get into a right barney with him over it—and to be fair that would never happen anyway, as he is a pet, if not a pushover. 'Well, all right,' I said to him, 'I *shan't* disturb them—I shan't go *near* them; I shall spend the whole rest of the voyage in the cinema, looking at *The Lady Eve*. I go every day—tomorrow they're showing *Moby Dick* and *Bus Stop*. I *was on* my way there, when—well, I've obviously gone back on my word.' "

"Aren't you being a little—well—*severe*," Mawrdew Czgowchwz cut in, "both on your poor father and on yourself? In any case, do sit down."

"I will so, thanks. The fact is Manahan puts little enough pass on my word anyway—not that I'm a patch on that little fiend in *The Bad Seed*."

Jacob Beltane reached out and pulled over another open deck chair, forming a triangle.

"Oh, thank you. Perhaps I am severe on Manahan, but he does jumble his indications—outrageously."

"Poor man," Mawrdew Czgowchwz tutted, nodding commiseratively, and then yawning again.

"Nevertheless," the child declared, easing into the deck chair, "he is a pet. The world and its wife says so. He's even let me put a little money into the ship's pool and guess the daily mileage; you know what the Irish are—inveterate chancers all."

"Well, you may let him know on both our parts that you have been delightful company, and any question of disturbance is—"

"He'll collapse, you realize—then directly put me on the rack."

"The *what*?"

"He's wildly nosey—Irish."

The child had sat, arms folded across her chest, embodied in that singular *thuswise* manner in which the women of Ireland dispose themselves whenever they are seriously launched on the business of gossip: indicating God's evident and absolute truth in its no uncertain figures and terms.

"Whereas mother is an American, or more exactly a New Yorker."

Jacob felt absent, awash, footless, at sea. His experience of children was scanty. Raised by his paternal grandmother in the wake of both parents' death by misadventure, he had had little peer intercourse, and by the time the Hitler war broke out and he was already well advanced in music and in wyrd, had been forced to conclude that childhood was an illusory concept, a name for an interval that, if it could be said to happen at all, had befallen him one gray wet afternoon on the Norfolk broads. It had happened at some length, perhaps to others. Here now was this—diminutive item, talking an outrageous blue streak. Not an adult, surely, more an aerial, or other-planetary—the fact, the concept, of paternity loomed, gravely. He thinks of Lolita. MC has told him of her meeting Nabokov when she sang *Il Barbiere di Siviglia* with his son Dmitri.

Maev and the runt, he observed, gabbing like two biddies, had formed a fast attachment like *that*.

"And so of course they brought me. I knew I'd love it, from the radio you know. The very idea of *singing out loud* about all that, especially before one is suspected of having a notion of what it all—all *that—is*. And they decided, well, if she demands to go then she must know—something, and she must go to at one and the same time the best and most accessible. Manahan's precise directions—adorable. So it was *Aida* on Christmas night four years ago, and then *Carmen* at the New Year's matinee. I don't remember much from those years—school, endless, pointless school, and summers in Ireland to restore ones sanity, but I remember *you*, I can tell you. I thought the way you twirled that vast orange cape up and down the stairs and all over the place in *Aida* was just absolutely bewitching—far more aware of what a cape *means*—than the way that great lump of a toreador diddled his scarlet one around in *Carmen*. Was *he* a card! And then of course on top of—there was that *sound*. Yours."

("How she makes her noise," Mawrdew Czgowchwz recalled.)

Jacob took a handkerchief from his pocket and wiped his forehead.

"But I'd known all about *that*, it seemed, since the *womb*, because Manahan is and always has been thoroughly cracked on the subject of your singing, and mother always listens—to him, to you. It's contagious: all our friends, and all the people who come in—including, for instance Miss Margaret Burke-Sheridan, even—must listen—to him, to you. You're a Manahan household word, I can tell you. I talk too much."

"Nonsense."

Miranda Mae Manahan nodded and sighed. "So Manahan says—jabber, wocky, and gibber—"

"No, dear," said Mawrdew Czgowchwz, "I mean the allegation. The notion that you talk too much."

"Oh? *Oh!*"

"You are merely inquisitive."

"That is a fact."

"Tell me this though, how is it that you aren't in school now, in late September?"

"That is a labyrinthine subject indeed—but I can give you a small hint. You come into it—or rather you're in it already, the labyrinth, as vital projections. Sufficient to say that one's perceptions concerning the proposed educational institution, which shall be nameless, and the running of it by a particular order of hooded women, happily destined to remain so as well, made one shudder at the mere thought of being enrolled there. There was something horrible in itself, too, in the blind, unreasoning distrust of the future which the mere passage of it through one's mind seemed to imply."

"Really?"

"Well, *yes*!" But more importantly just now there is the question of *his voice*. Do you know they're saying on board—or one of them? That the ambition in the voice is the ambition of an ecstatic. The overtone surround unearthly—calculated to disturb, to disorient."

"All that is true; but whisper it, or he'll awaken, suddenly."

"I'm awake suddenly; all ears, all calculating ambition."

"Oh!"

"It's all right, dear," Mawrdew Czgowchwz assured Miranda. "We were discussing," she informed Jacob, "some of the commentary the Manahans overheard in the hurricane on Manitoy. Interesting the things people say."

"Sure, where's the harm, says you, and a bit of *style*. In a hurricane, yes. Like a shipwreck, isn't a hurricane is always a dead giveaway, a transparent metaphor for what is really on their minds: such calculations like of 'and how *does* he make his noise?' "

"It seems these people, none of them identified, *were* talking about singing—or thought they were."

"Of all things—just darting about the premises battening down hatches and talking about singing—nobody we know?"

"Well, as it happens, yours in particular."

"Imagine! Little enough people have to talk about, isn't it, during hurricanes, since the war and the forties ended."

"Have the forties ended? Has the war?"

"Perhaps not. Perhaps things don't; perhaps they merely stop. Start, stop—

the way music, hurricanes, and conversations such as this one." Jacob, smiling contentedly, stood and walked away down the deck toward the stairway to the staterooms.

"Oh, dear," Miranda asked Mawrdew Czgowchwz, "did I do that?"

"No, dear, he did. We talk, they stalk; we weave, they cleave—or so we're told."

"Nevertheless I fear he is like Manahan, who would never admit to the sentiment, but who sadly wants a reform in the construction of children. I don't entirely disagree. I was really getting to him yesterday, writing things down in my journal, then tearing out the pages, crumpling them into some class of polyhedrons, and tossing them overboard into the calm Atlantic—leaving a trail of very small paper icebergs all swept under the ship's wake in a minute of course."

*

Mawrdew Czgowchwz and Jacob Beltane were thought to be sound asleep. Elsewhere on board, the Mahatma's squadron, their ambitions toward autarky checked, gathered for afternoon canasta. From the bridge the first mate scanned the blue horizon for indications. In the lounges and bars, fore and aft and at poolside, smart talk turned to futures. In the library, serious readers scanned contemporary affairs ("Now here's *another* one. Do you realize in the last seven years, there have been over a *hundred* cartoons in the *New Yorker* having to do with shipwreck survivors?"), illustrated travel literature, inspirational self-improvement manuals (*More Ways Than One*, *The Rest of It*, and *What Would Life Be?*) and here and there, contraband "travelers companion" fiction published in France. ("This one, dear, the testimony of a pedophile lepidopterist; absolutely electrifying—have a look.")

In the darkened cinema, a screening of two decades of newsreels ("That Day To This") passed the afternoon. One soul sat with his journal open, writing over and over "the ocean, the ocean, the ocean, the ocean," and nodding.

Jacob woke abruptly to the treble clang of topside bells sounding melodic-thematic over the ship's engines' bourdon and seemingly continuing the themes of his dream music until the hypnogogic state dissolved and he sat up. Mawrdew Czgowchwz lay sleeping. Her name, her other name (folded within), her body, her children . . . She shifted. He took up a book and read: "In the days and weeks immediately succeeding conception. . . ."

Twins: one for each tit. Embryos as "microliths" (standing stones, ogham stones, Newgrange). "We do not have children, rather they pass through our tissue uncognized and unalterable. The embryo can become only the thing its parents are, or perish. It is one of nature's mysteries that this law, which cannot be broken from generation to generation, is somehow broken cumulatively over many generations; otherwise how would new species arise?"

Mawrdew Czgowchwz stirred awake. Outside the open porthole she heard a voice reading aloud a series of numbers. Jacob, leaving his studies, had turned to the silver-tasseled program for the Atlantic crossing. Far too much was advertised. She tried to reassure him.

"That's not a contract, you realize, not a role you've signed to sing for tall hats."

"Do you suppose we could play cards the whole time?"

"Creating stark connubial impressions. Cards suddenly remind me of Destinn and *Pique Dame*. 'You will learn the role of Lise,' she commanded, 'which I created for America at the Metropolitan in the same year I created Puccini's Minnie for the world.' I replied I'd rather sing the Countess, and was given to understand that when I sang Lise at the Národní, she, Destinn, would be singing the Countess. Of course, it never happened; Destinn died."

"What's shuffleboard?"

"Shuffleboard? Something like dancing."

"Talking of dancing, here's a Peabody marathon. And Macramé—they're teaching that this afternoon, along with origami and fondues. In the cinema they're showing *The Lady Eve*. If we go, will it help me understand you better?"

"What a question."

"While you slept, I read about Stradivari. His instruments were all made according to Pythagorean numbers."

"Isaac Stern prefers his Guarnieri to any Stradivarius; he told me."

"I was reading about the cellos in particular."

"Do tell."

"The author says that in the nineteenth century Stradivarius cellos seemed to mimic the roles of the great divas of melodramatic fiction: desired but never truly possessed by rich men who, for the sake of art, had to surrender them to their poor but honest lovers."

"Really? I never can picture rich men with lovers like that."

"Not the rich men's lovers, the diva cello's lovers."

"Do tell. For the sake of art?"

"Yes, and one of them, owned by a poor but honest French cellist, was so coveted by a Russian nobleman he wrote a blank check for it—but the cellist refused him."

"I have never known a Russian nobleman."

"No, I suppose not—Stalin was hardly that."

"Rostropovitch owns a Stradivarius cello—he comes close. The Library of Congress does, too—there's allegory in that."

"What the world needs—another allegory. Anyway, Stradivari worked with strips of maple as thin as one millimeter, using a hot iron and humidity to shape the ribs around the hourglass curves of the instrument. You have hourglass curves."

"Not for long more."

"The wood may have been mysteriously seasoned. He got his wood from the Veneto, and when stored in Venetian canals, it encountered microbes that altered the acoustic properties."

"Sounds like Pinocchio singing through a congested nose."

"Allegory. But there's more. The varnish contained resins collected by the bees of Lombardy from the blossoms of poplar trees, mixed with oil of spike lavender. . ."

"Lavender, eh? I wonder—here, lend a hand."

*

H.M.S. *Queen Mary* at sea

Dearest Rotten (Darling) You (My Own) Divining Rod, Light (at the end of the tunnel?) of My Life,

> *Breaking, at long last, the September silence....*
> *Yours simply wildly truly,*
> *Star Faithfull*
> *(a.k.a. "The Magdalen")*

Foundering vessel that one is, drawn from tempestuous seas and stashed secure aboard the monumental *Mary*—it's not for naught I've gone about as I have (*omnium bipedium nequissimus*) cowering like a stowaway in the ship's hatch, in some lightless corner of the bilges—and this from one once used to pleasing not only men—and women—but *crowds*. Haunted, dear, by that spirit which the natural malignity of solitude raises within the circle of every heart, forcing us, from the terrible economy of misery, to feed upon the vitals of others that we spare our own. Consequence of me bringin' up, dear. "O, luckless child of London born / Too early of her breast forlorn." Not to mention: "He touched the hem of Nature's shift. Felt faint—and never dared uplift," etc. What tell you him of Job, the daft old bugger.

For true it is, dear, that the shadow of misery did so envelope one's infant days—frankly put, the bitch all but dropped me in a ditch and took a burton. Picture of me, she was, so people said, or the other way 'round, I suppose is how you'd put it properly. Thus dampening the diapason of one's nature as to give a lasting and ineffaceable *tinge* to the pursuits, the feelings, and the very character of one's entire subsequent existence. Fostered alike by beauty and by fear, dear, just like bloody Wordsworth! Indeed, the contracted habits of one's early life—nerves and brain created entirely for sensitive perception—had the effect of exalting one's imagination even as they pitifully impaired every other faculty, until in one's own mind one became as beautiful and dangerous as Helen, who cut the legs from under troops of men.

Which is not to say gran did not do her best.

That said, to the body of the letter—can I bring it off: can I *imagine*, can I *conceive of* such a thing (as) a body of any kind: of a letter, or of work; of a living creature, man- or (shudder) womankind. Yet I must try, I who have believed (talking of daring uplift) and must again that men, important men, desire me, for myself. (No, I have not rebounded; no cocktails, no Dexadrine. No more the me that ruffled out in his silks in the habit of malcontent, the horns of Elfland none too faintly blowing, that no place would please him to abide in long, to shock the normals rigid. Or to put it another way, *cunctat fui, conducat nil.*)

I stay put, I sleep—but I sleep in a quivering palsy of nerves. I dream of great white things that will sink the ship—of the whale... of the iceberg... of the great white cleaver prow of the *Stockholm* (and sometimes of Garbo as its what is that word, maidenhead?). Or I did first day out.

To report on the second day, I must admit... but now, dear, I fear my mind, in defiance of the boundless evenness, of this Sargasso-like expanse of overfed complacency, and, I'm afraid, be it repeated, in despairing contemplation of the sour residue of an empty life, has come to resemble a mountain pass in winter, shagged with frosted hanging woods, obscured in cloud and tumbling through fragments, rocks, with sheets of cascades, dear, forcing their silver speed (and how I miss *my* silver speed!) down channeled precipices. *Miseram me omnia terent, et maris sonitus, et scopuli, et solitudo.*

I do ramble, dear, but then at school I always did greatly prefer Silius Italicus to Livy on the Punic Wars... and was shunned for it, too, dear—not that I, like some ... but then I suppose I was a right berk in those days and not at all what you'd call a boy with spine and mettle, but the fucking truth of it is we were *all bombed*, except for the Royal Family.

And the awful thing about it all is, dear, I simply *adored* the Krauts—in the pictures, anyway. I mean *Triumpf des Willens* and all those costume melodramas—tunics, sashes, soutache braid, flashing swords with gleaming pommels... you know. In another life and time I have surely been, with my precocious appreciation of flowers and sunsets and my very real, attested gift for china painting, the Belle of Berlin—and loved it: the androgyny, the exoticism, the enslavement. I used to hope and pray they'd invade England and I'd end up their prisoner, a delicate and impassioned being who shuddered in their arms, dear, and fell into half-dead swoons at their frowning behests and taught them English ways—treasure hunts and cocktail drinking and the pursuit of shrieks.

Oh, darling, the terrible consequences of weakness!

And they're smart, too. Do you know the German proverb, dear, of the *Eulenspiegel*—the owl's mirror? It says that if you give the owl a mirror, it still doesn't know its ugly. Now the English would never think of that—owls that they are who think they're rather gorgeous. They are so stupid when it comes down to it they really should have been invaded and lost the war proper.

Do you know why they didn't—the *only* reason? The witches. Can you credit it? It's true, dear, they all got together in the New Forest, at Epping (imagine it as I do, all gnarly, as drawn by Arthur Rackham) and danced naked, dear, tail up, the way they do, in the clearing in the wood and Hitler never invaded England. The C of E tried to say such a thing never happened, letting on in that smarmy way they have that witchcraft is nothing these days but poltergeists and parlour tricks. Well, fuck that, says I, for a game of bloody cowboys and Indians. *That's all you know*—it was the witches saved us all from the massive, cruel, blond Aryan jackbooted Hun . . . meddling old sods that they were, thank you very much indeed!

I ought to have been a witch, dear; I had the spirit for it, but they dance around naked, and that means men and *women* dear, and that I just couldn't imagine—my dreams being of parading in high splendor through London with fourscore retainers in liveries of Reading tawny and chains of gold around the neck. All the same, they kept Hitler out of England, did the witches, and Napoléon before him, dear. And it isn't true either that they traffic with the devil. Not English witches, dear, who are all white. French witches do, they say—as do Scottish witches (as Shakespeare knew). And Italian witches are, I believe very wicked, indeed, but then so are Italian Catholics, from whom the witches learned all their devilment—just ask Mawrdew Czgowchwz.

Yes, I must admit rather like witches. If they'd first sent me—Westminster—to a warlock instead of to that sozzled old hack in Cavendish Square, he had prevented the invasion of my own self's sceptered isle by—yet all the same I sometimes—often—wish the Krauts had invaded England after all, instead of the Yanks. I didn't—still don't—fancy Yanks, dear. Everybody in London was falling all over them, and one did see the appeal. They're so *there*, aren't they, taking up so much *room*. But I'm afraid they do tend to be rather *coarse*—even the Episcopals, with all their bijou versicles and responses, their psalms and canticles at bloody choral Evensong, and don't I know *it* and *them* well-all-too-well! Never talk to me, dear, of musical offerings—I've *been* one. Mutton dressed up as lamb, no question, past masters of chicane, yet coldly misted, too, in grey mad sorrow.

Nevertheless, consequence of the pipes, one was invited—no, *beseeched*—to rejoice in the lamb by no less than Benji the Bent himself, who went in for lamb pie in a big way, dear—whole racks of it, pink, and positively *drenched* in *red currant sauce*—never mint. Took me down to that house in Brooklyn, dear, with that smelly old ear Auden and the cute Kraut Golo Mann, whose own daddy, and I don't mean sugar, couldn't keep his hands off him. I didn't get much out of listening to anything anybody said—certainly not to Auden. I know a little bit about English poetry, dear, though you may not think so, and so far as I can make out all that woman has ever done is rewrite Kipling's "If" for bolshy nellies. Or out of the Bowleses or that Carson McCullers either, but Miss Gypsy Rose Lee was another article. Her mother was a *murderess*, dear—did you know that?

Benji was and is a terrible old queer—I liked Mrs. Tippett ever so much better: used to call her Mistress Tidbit, sometimes Mistress Tipple, and she's much the better composer. Of course I was prejudiced, I *was* a child of our time. But Benji was resilient. And witty in a rather old cod way. I remember once hearing him in conversation with a young musical person who'd just discovered that Da Ponte had been among other things a unfrocked priest. Under the impression (the young person was) that that meant something like exile from Italy or excommunication from the Church for trafficking with evil spirits—something along those lines. "Oh, I don't think so, dear" said Benji. "I rather think all that happened was he was hauled up before the bishop and told he must stop wearing *frocks*." Sweet, isn't it—anyway you know, in Benji's mind, I believe, Peter Grimes doesn't die at sea at all, but is picked up by pirates just like Hamlet and makes it to London, where he goes to work in a boy brothel in Belgravia, which, of course, he eventually ends up *owning*.

I was having this lunch in town with him and the Missus—the Companion of Honor, dear—this some time after my voice had broken and I was trying to retrain with Alfred Deller, a great singer, dear, just like the Missus—and don't mistake me, dear, both great singers and both great big *women*. Although not in the Missus's case onstage—I'd have given a lot to be manhandled by him in *Peter Grimes*. But this one time Benji was going on about Henry James and *The Turn of the Screw*, and Miles and Flora, and how he was so taken with the material, with its ultimate *mystery*, and I said to him straight out, I said "*Mystery*? Pull the other one, darling, it's got bells on. I reckon there's something very real at the *bottom* of that story. I reckon that housekeeper missus looked out the upstairs window one day—the window with the view into the garden and saw her angelic little Miles sucking the gardener's cock—or the gardener's son's—or both together." Well, I thought the Missus was going to lose her Welsh rabbit, that I did. But Benji only smiled that *enigmatic* smile and told me I was a very naughty boy for one who'd had such a gorgeous voice.—*who'd had*! How those words have haunted me since.

Have you any notion, dear, how absolutely gorgeous my voice was—

how fucking bloody ravishingly pure? For instance, in Benji's lovely *Ceremony of Carols*. (And it never really broke, you see, it only darkened to alto when I was fourteen—but for seven years, I *reigned supreme* in the boy soprano world.) People said Ernest Lough sounded like a tin whistle in comparison, and at Westminster I was complimented by nobody less than the Duke of Kent—who was a divine and dashing man and so, of course, was killed in that dreadful air smashup—and in New York even Mabel Mercer said so; she came to Saint Thomas just to hear me, and afterwards at the reception in the residence I did my little music hall turn—spirited renditions of "Up in a Balloon, Boys" followed by "*C'est pas Paris, c'est sa banlieu.*" I had very good French, dear, that I did—got it by osmosis, really, because I never had a lesson, or a pen pal either for that matter.

No, the fact is French letters weren't part of the lives of boy tarts, if you take my meaning; weren't thought necessary in our grooming (grooming, dear, is what they called it, 'zif if we were bloody 'orses 'stead of bloody whores) as we couldn't trick them in the way they all feared—although who on earth, boy, girl, dog, or cat, would want to go and have a bundle of joy off one of them is quite beyond me—and not much is.

(Call it the steep perspective of the staircase.)

I had a special friend there—not the Paris suburb, darling, I'm sorry to say, for I'd have liked a bit of that lark, Gitane cigarettes, soiled knickers, pong, and all—but at Saint Thomas. Oh, yes, it happens, even to the likes of us, dear little sacrificial black sheep that we are in their game of pass the parcel—*oblates* being the technically correct bijou term. It was glad, confident morning then, and when we sang the psalms. Well, dear, the psalms sung in choir sometimes breathe a certain *language*, and our voices directed to one another could scarcely have been misunderstood. They weren't—my little friend was sent away: made a *domestic* in St. Andrew's, Southampton—the Dune Church. How is it the old song goes, dear, "He's listed away for a soldier—my own!" I met him years later in that place that name of which always gives me such a laugh, the Millstone. Risen in the world had he, on the arm of some old stoat, filthy rich of course, from the other side of Mecox Bay. "You know, of course," he said to me, "I shall never forget you in the *Pie Jesu* from the Fauré *Requiem*. You know what Proust said about Fauré: buggery and choirboys. Well, we lived through it and came out the other end, so to speak. Now let's go outside and do in the bushes what we never did at school. It might be a one-off, but so what?" And, of course, it was—one never was one for romancing out of doors, especially in so much company: it was like trying to do it in the subway, except it didn't get one anywhere.

I was a wild thing, y'see, that raged through all their lives, singin' like a bloody angel and battin' me bluet peeps at all the lovely toggies and them only too keen to snap-flash away to their hearts' content, but increasingly argy-bargy offstage and off camera—until they couldn't bear it longer, and so they put the snatch on me, dear, to employ the American idiom, which one ought do.

Of course, following right along in the same vein, they needn't have bothered. I mean to say I'd nowhere to go, really, and to make something of a pun, that snatch was part of the boy all along. Then, too, I don't know how you feel about it, dear, but I'd so much rather have been Catholic and had them buggering me to the tune of Palestrina, Mercadante, and Fauré—and down in Little Italy it might even have been Mascagni—than have to suffer the indignity *and* warble all that bland, astringent crap we did at Evensong. Too right.

You're not, of course—crude, dear—but take the so-called Duchess of Windsor. Duchess, my arse—Margaret, Duchess of Argyll *there's* a peeress of the realm and, of course, the lovely duchesses of Norfolk and Kent. No, Wallis Warfield Simpson is nothing but a common tart—and like all tarts drawn to wealth and power like dung flies to putrescence. Yes, a common whore dreaming a whore's dream of orb and sceptre, however much that awful Lucius Beebe and his like sucked up to her in the war years—the war *she* brought on. She besotted him—got a good strong whore's hold of both his orbs and his pretty sceptre, too (what there is of it: not so much in the event, rumor hath it) and squeezed the lot until he fairly swooned! And *he* could have made it up with the Krauts, everybody knows that, and been a lovely king and everything and let the filthy French go to hell.

Oh, how can war be seen as anything but a camp, dear—although with Benji and the Missus I couldn't possibly have said and I suppose it's true that I should've followed their example and turned pious pacifist. But there's something in it all dear that at first almost makes me want to kneel in reverence at the Cenotaph—until I've got a few gins in me, and then it makes me shriek with laughter. The Hundred Years' War, the Wars of the Roses, the Civil Wars, Monmouth's Rebellion; that idiot's cotillion you call your Revolution, the Peninsula War, Trafalgar, Waterloo, the Crimea, Your own Oh *so gorgeous* and *inspiring* Civil War, starring *two of our* loveliest women, dear, Vivien Leigh and Leslie Howard. The Boer War, the bloody Kaiser War—the flower of English manhood rotting away *in portions of bodies*, darling, in the stinking trenches or cut down like summer hay at the Somme, the Hitler War—all those gorgeous Aryan Siegfrieds with all those lovely pips on their collars face down dead in the Russian mud.

The Battle of Britain, all the church bells in the kingdom gone dead silent, to be rung only in the event of an invasion. Death raining down from the skies—I know me history, dear, from bloody *experience*—and now the very Hun scientists whose V-2 rockets dropped the rain of death on us all are one and all, even as I write, being fed caviare and truffles—or herring rollmops—and swilling great steins of *Löwenbräu*—schnapps on the side, *bitte*—by the American *établissement*, all in aid of our *glorious* future, in which one fine day some splendid Yank will get to take a crap on the moon!

And they're still at it, dear, with Aden and Suez and God knows what next, and spying and counterspying on and against the bloody Russians—and all of it a bag of shit.

(Thwarted, she hunched down sulkily in her chair.)

Oh, I know I shouldn't hate, dear. Hatred rebounds on the hater, etching wrinkles into the countenance, and rendering one in the end a wailing, creased-up old misery. And as a child I was merry, dear, merry as a grig. But, oh, it's *awful*—I tell you. I never was a bloke that made the going, fair enough, fair innings—gibbering lips confess. Who was it said thus you may see that whilst some triumph with olive branches, others follow the chariot with willow garland—but there are times when I just cannot *bear* being me! If only I was someone else, like Bridey Murphy or the Grand Duchess Anastasia . . . just *anybody else*! Even Little Lord Fauntleroy immured in vaguely medieval fancy dress and holding a bunch of white Parma violets—the way the vicar used to like to kit me up, dear, in all those press-ganged pageants at Saint Thomas.

Ah, Saint Thomas, where ministration was heaped upon ministration and, in spite of pious phrases, all would-be chancers at beneficent exhalation and plainchant did nightly tremble with fear and abhorrence as the fucked-out demons of boredom and fatigue, their pious paws muddied to the bloody hocks in fetid lust no number of hypocritic dips into the sacred font they made, played spinster whist.

"We have this treasure in earthen vessels," some vile old scroat, quivering in a palsy, withers all in a turmoil, breathing all over you the stale breath of desperation, would moan in your ear whilst holding up to his needle nose your soiled smalls—you were issued two sets only and laundry was done just once a week—inhaling the frankincense of your sweaty crotch and shitty bum, like as not visualizing some strapping Victorian pantry-boy, until the watery spunk poured out all over the back of your little pink arse.

That's if you were lucky, and they'd believed you, and cared, when you said, "It *pains*, sir!" Which meant exactly what it fucking bloody well *said* and not, "Please sir, I'd like some more," as in bloody fucking *Oliver Twist*—a well-named book if ever there was one. But not a lot of them did—believe you. Why should they after all when all their belief bones had been shot through to the marrow with some arsehole Christian *credo* or another, and when they weren't grovelling in pursuit of that perfection they were as caught up as any fucking ecstatic on the books with, speaking of arseholes, turning little boys with little pink slits into bloody slurry-twat tarts like yours truly.

"There, there, now, good strong boys don't bottle out." *Tantum religio potuit suadare malorum*. Dear. *Sed animan non saptare posse* (for what it's worth).

And what is the price, dear, of a young boy's soul? I have sat at High Table and dined off turbot Mornay. ("Turbot is ambitious brill," says the song, and that was me, as ambitious a little piece of brill as ever was fished from the sea.) If you increase the pressure, you raise the temperature—physics, dear—and one has never in life seemed to be warm enough.

One is but flesh. Neither does one mind so terribly the thought of growing old—after all, one seems to have been born that way—and of living in the past in deliberate exploration of the time of one's happiness (Rachmaninoff's Second Piano Concerto here). It's merely that one lives in absolutely sickening terror of the possibility of *there never having been such a time*.

Mitred heads with forked tongues in 'em: wicked, if symbolically apt. And familiarity will dull reverence—especially a certain *kind* of familiarity—arisen, they like to tell themselves, out of esoteric pressures and rare idiosyncracy, throbbing with violent rhythms of passion and surrender—to what, ask I, when it was always them givin' us a length and never the other way around—but which we, the underlings (and some of them ogres was *heavy*) thought of purely in terms of barter for treats. And when reverence goes, mockery replaces it—it must do, otherwise the child goes barking mad, or caves in and joins ranks with the bastards. So for a start it's "Meet me at the cottage door for a bit o' ten-bob upright," and so the way is laid, dear, the way is laid.

Come to think of it, it's pretty funny, really: *bottle out*—and humor serves to stem the fury. Actually, truth to tell, dear, one was treated rather better than the general run, I suppose, because one was more *prized*, you might say (which has its own double meaning). Yes, dear, one was the prize at the bloody church fete's *tombola*—at the church bazaar as you Yanks like to call it. Caw. And as a consequence one never did feel quite safe, except later on, when darkness fell, in the embrace of a gin bottle. Yes, gin was mother's milk to me, and father's milk (unpasteurized) as well.

Take the case of the final trill in the *Panis Angelicus*. Sounds like a murder mystery, and in point of fact murder was in their hearts when I pulled it off for the bishop (if y' take my meaning, which is in this instance chaste as ice). What it was, I'd thrown it in at rehearsal—you know the part, right at the end, in the reprise, and the old wanker choirmaster—and like my Old Flame I can't even remember his name—blew a fucking *gasket* at the temerity of it.

You see, I did have *the* most divine trill in the boy soprano world—learned it off Bidu Sayão when she sang Manon at the Metropolitan. In the gavotte in the *Cours de Reine* scene, and ooh, she looked divine, all in silks and satins and laces, and I suppose it was only natural for me in my little red cassock and lace-trimmed surplice...

Anyway, I threw it in, and the old wanker *rounded* on me, dear. "Shuttlethwaite"—as I was then—"let us leave the vulgar touches in the *Panis Angelicus* to *French* choirboys, shall we—along with the more *lascivious* pronunciations of Latin texts favored by our Teverine brethren." (Catholics, dear.) Did I say wanker? I should in conscience recant a calumny, as the bloody old sod had by that stage likely succumbed to *wanker's block*.

Well, I said to meself, the thing was *written* by a bleedin' Frenchmen, but I bided me time—too many tiltyard accidents had already befallen *yer sarvant* in his brash youth (ages seven to eleven, dear, when I'd butt me head unwisely against anything, wearin' no colors but me own crimson cassock) until the bishop arrived. And really just to annoy him I think (for he weren't spikey at all, and didn't at all like smells and bells) they programmed the *Panis Angelicus*. And I thought to meself, well, in for a penny, in for a pound, and in the moment I let go with the Bidu Sayão *Manon* trill from the *Cours de Reine* scene. The effect was fucking electric—I mean to say, dear, heads *swivelled*.

Well, the bleedin' bishop, she comes right up to me at the end and says, "And who or what inspired the *trill*, Master Shuttlethwaite?" And says I right back, bright as a new penny (and giving it the real Limey-pullin'-the-forelock intonation—nice bit of chum, dear, for the feeding shark) "The Lord, Your Grace." "The Lord?" "Oh, yes, Your Grace, in a mystical vision, like. I saw Him standing there in a pool of golden light, with the angel Gabriel and Palestrina." Shut him up, it did, *and* the rest of them. Last thing they wanted *just then* was havin' me pulled in for mystical visions and *normalized* at bleedin' Doctors Hospital (in the electrical closet).

'Course hadn't I faced the nellie old cunt already once before, not that he'd've remembered, at my confirmation, when I'd answered such questions as are put to a young cadet in Christ's army, and received the sweet little slap on the cheek that goes with the sacrament. And lo and behold, dear, the wanker was smiling down at me. "A privilege indeed, Mr. Swithin. *Quis audat vincit*." Rather classy that, I thought, from a bleedin' bishop to a lowly choirboy. Only think of it, dear—one was quids in with the *hierarchy*! Visions of preferments and great wodges of lolly all down the road paved with the very best intentions.

And from that out, one wanted certain things acknowledged, however tacitly on the way to the general public's being made aware of one's existence and remit, via recordings and appearances at major halls—principally that it *was down to oneself* that the bloody choir of Saint Thomas was drawing crowds for Choral Evensong like treacle tarts left out on the sideboard, dear, draw bloody flies.

You had to hear me to believe me, dear, in the *Nunc Dimittis* of Josquin des Prez—brought me whole awful experience of the war to it I did. *Lord now lettest thy servant depart in peace*. . ." Tear your bloody heart out. Therefore, should I feel like recreating meself at Sunday matinees by singing the songs of the Parisian working class, or the haunting bitter laments of the sidewalk cafes of the Argentine—none of that lot had ever even *heard* of Carlos Gardel—*then I would do*. Plus which, dear, as you like to say in New York, my whole life was in fact the very *opposite* of *nunc dimittis*—I was longing desperately *to be let in*.

How I hated them, hate them still, alive or rotted dead. Put them adjacent to anything in a tiara and they positively shat frankincense. (Always excepting the Antichrist in the Vatican, whom they actually did seem to despise—she'd been too palsy-walsy with Munich and Berlin—*Unter den Linden, jawohl*, for them to tolerate. She with her positively *Babylonian* three-tiered gold tiara thing with all the bloody *bijoux*—thirty-five rubies, dear, thirteen emeralds, eleven sapphires, and eleven brilliants on top.)

Hated them one and all with their fucking fluting High Church tone and their awful, *awful* attempts at whispering sweet nothings into a boy's ear, such as, "Slender as a willow branch, quick as a colt, you are the living finial on the gatepost of my heart" and "You are the bail laid across the stumps of my destiny." That's cricket, dear—sticky bloody wickets and golden fucking ducks, starched whites and upright stances, the *whoosh* of the bowl, the guard at the crease and the crack of bats hitting cherry red balls, sending them soaring high over the bloody boundary . . . all too complicated to go into, like playing for the ashes . . . the ashes of a young boy's dreams.

Anyway it'd all make you want to puke up your bleedin' guts right then and there, on the bleedin' kingfisher-blue carpet.

And imagine thinking that belief in the devil is illogical. *Illogical*? There's a devil all right, dear, let me assure you, and he's mad keen to take the hindmost.

I remember this one in particular. Doing his bloody memoirs he was, calling them *Attendant, Lord*, until one dark and stormy winter evening, whilst idly fingering his prized collection of cairngorms and moonstones, he dropped off the hooks—just like that, dear, keelin' over sideways over his port and walnuts whilst the addled verger who'd been *his* bum boy—whose once young and promising life and lovely dream of honor bright and fortune fair the bastard had left a smoldering ruin—was just then out next door, in the very act of winding the venerable vestry clock. *Sic transit* Gloria's mondo.

At the funeral they played and we sang "The day thou gavest Lord is ended," and as it was being announced—you know, "Turn, please to page such-and-such in your hymnal," when loud and clear—we heard it in the choir, dear, came the catamite verger's emendation, "And none too soon!" Cast a bit of an extra pall on things for some, but, of course, for others—many others—it made, not marred, the occasion.

I shall tell you this much, dear, by way of sisterly counsel: if you're ever tempted to set your cap for a proper English toff—and frankly, I can see you going at just that very lark hammer and tongs, ending up in the Visitors Gallery of the Upper Chamber—*The Other Place*—*riveted* by the goings-on—all those heavily whipped and roster-driven peers of the realm all robed and mantled, with their two, two and a half, three, three and a half, and four rows of shitty spotted rabbit fur (though again, knowing you, you'd likely reel in one of the better hereditaries still sporting ermine) putting down starred questions and going on and on into the night about bloody fuck all—or maybe for you, dear, in your honor, the endless ramifications of the Wolfenden Committee. And I can just picture you, dear, staring enrapt at the Dyce frescoes in the Robing Room (you'd have got the geezer to sneak you in, pretext of being a nephew or something bloodlined). They're of virtues, although I can't myself remember which ones. Why I shouldn't wonder you'd find a way to have a sit-down on the steps of the throne—reserved, dear, for eldest sons. You'd be a kind of *eldritch* son.

In any event, should you do—and I'm bound to say, dear, it would make a lot more sense to yours truly that this prison-visitor lark you're on about now. I mean I do understand how you feel about not becoming a *surplus woman* of no use in the world, but a sensible woman, brisk and practical, who *visits prisons*? Really, dear, is that really you? Apart from anything else, what do you *talk* about up there at Sing-Sing—what *do* you *talk* about? And what do you *wear*, apart from a cloche hat?

Come to think of it, though, I did know a woman who used to do it—visit prisons—and she said to me this one time, "There is something terribly satisfying about looking at a convicted felon *behind glass*, and in that same glass, when the light gets lower in the afternoon, one sees one's own reflection, superimposed on the prisoner's, and there's no getting away from it, one's features are somehow *transformed*." Of course, as she was a true woman, she visited women prisoners. I remember her telling me about one born without a vagina—rare, but not unknown. What a world. I sometimes wonder what my role in it is—something fulfilling, or a bloody walk-on?

Any rate should you do—I have a vision of you now before me, all veiled, dear, and crowned round with pink rosebuds and mignonette—do make bloody well sure it's one who sits on the *temporal* side of the House, and not the spiritual. Or better yet in your case perhaps one of the rakish crossbenchers. You'll be particularly glad when the House rises for Easter and you're off on the wing down to Taormina or Marrakesh and not bound for terrible Switzerland because the clot you've taken up with has himself taken up the study of Romansch, and is quite certain he can find his holy God in Nature whilst tramping the mountain paths of the Hinterrhein. Or worse yet, dear, there's you, styled a *secretary* or perhaps even an *amanuensis*, on the bloody train in the company of His Grace, the wifey, and their ghastly twin daughters down to some sodden little minster on the Welsh border, the whole boiling simply *keen agog* with great plans for long day trips to Snowdonia, the Lakes, the Cotswolds, and the lower slopes of the Cumbrian Fells—or else to the Fen Country 'round Ely—lovely old hole, dear—to splodge around in the marram grasses of the Great Soak.

It's generally the married ones who enlist the more obvious catamites; the bachelors haven't the neck.

Full voice I cried for madder music and for stronger wine. Brave, intelligent, and vivid I was—just ask them—and have since childhood, since the eruption of language, accepted the inevitability of lying, a thing as comes natural to an orphan child who must make his way in the world or else fall back into the realm of tarts, dossers, and filthy old slags.

Yet even a heart as dark as mine caged, in a body so useless—deep sunk in sin and agony at Evensong (for many were the bitter kisses on this bought red mouth) the tragic star sank deeper still and did wage war against itself—is stalked by dread of vengeance. Vindictive lust can do you worse than wrinkles.

They said I had a cradle-on grudge against circumstance. I said to them, I told them, "I was never *in* no cradle." (Slipped into the common vernacular, as I often do for effect.) "I was put into an open dresser drawer." (Not that I was never rocked, dear, for the whole of that awful flat they lived in before she scarpered rattled like something you rode on in the fairground every time the boat train from Dover tore across the nearby viaduct bound for Victoria Station—and as it happened, forecast-wise, the line was *not* immaterial.)

And of course all that plays right into the hands of these bloody headshrinkers—mad keen the lot of them to make you out half a dozen people, all out of their flamin' box, all utterly without hope and entirely without promise but for their—the shrinkers'—esoteric ministrations. I expect it's how the bastards justify their fees. I mean to say, if each of us is to work out to be half a dozen cases, it stands to reason we're going to pay six times the fee. At least the Mahatma keeps it simple. "Everyone has a second, innermost soul." You can buy that—it's value for money. Not that I ever gave the shrinkers a *brass farthing*, dear—not a *dime* of the money I earned the hard way—done up as the Scarlet Beast, the Whore of Babylon, golden cup in hand, filled with abominable things and the filth of me bleedin' adulteries—but my former warders did, lest I tip the old wink to the bloody police as to how one had been been diddled, in serial fashion—slap in the withers time and again, one's slanting eyes defiantly averted—by the lot of them, panting like spent hounds as last lights glimmered in the vestry windows.

It was white slavery what they did—they *despoiled* me, dear, leaving me a damaged thing, a bob-a-job canary with a broken wing, so I shall never be a bride and walk stately in white past the tearful assembly whilst the bloody organ plays "O Promise Me!" Glad confident morning will n'er come again.

Oh, get me riled enough, dear, dreary little Estuary upstart that I am, and I shall take it to the Archbishop of Canterbury herself—and I shan't put a tooth in it neither. I shall turn Queen's evidence at the Old Bailey—sort 'em out good and proper, the whole rotten, stinking lot of 'em. *Giuro!*

Such as the time the vicar, sack of old frightened bones that he was, dressed himself up as Cardinal Pirelli and me as the little dago acolyte Angelo (not that I knew what the lark was at the time, as I'd precious little time for reading anything but situations), and off the two of us trotted to the Episcopal book tea with a lot of old rotted talking doorposts on Morningside Heights. I also found out at a later date that the caper nearly got into Winchell, because Fanny Spellman got wind of it—thought she was being sent up, dear, vis-à-vis that spurious book, *The Foundling* what Bennett Cerf published that she never wrote a single bloody fucking line of. It was only Fulton Sheen and that hag of a "duchess" calmed the waters. Yes, that and many other tales, too, concerning *Americae sive quartae orbis partis, nova et exactissima descriptio*, to which I was sent as a war orphan—some sort of payback for Lend-Lease. The war may be long over, dear, won by lovers of freedom everywhere, don't make me laugh, but loose lips still may sink a ship—and how I would adore to see that particular bark, the Episcopal Church in the United States of America, together with the whole boiling of its odds, sods, and pervies go down. I'll give them their parish-pump polemics—I'll give them *piles!* I've no qualms, dear *di vengarmi di prezza di moneta*. The Episcopal Church in the United States of America is rich, dear, *filthy* rich.

I shall revenge myself on men; this will be. I shall campaign with every means at my disposal, dear, in order that one day the truth may be told. I shall give them all notice of the question—spill cans of beans all over their teatime toast points. Read them the official caution, or whatever it is you lot call it—*rehearse* them as 'twere for their charming interviews with the bailiffs—have you got bailiffs, dear, in the New York police? No matter—putting the lot of them into raging mucksweats, then climb up onto the bloody rooftops and shout it down into the bloody canyon streets of Manhattan. How, to quote Walter Pater, they did delight themselves delerious in all the fell charms of the ungirdling of the loins of youth. I shall bring them into ridicule, contempt, and scorn. I shall have them dragged crop and neck to the stocks and pillories, I shall—I *will* do all this and more! The only question (quite an absorbing one, in fact, worthy of contemplation, which is what one is meant to be learning all about on the voyage out) is *how*. A series of quick knockdowns, like going at flies with a flit-gun (just one's sort of gun, that) would suit me right down to the ground—and yet there is the enormous attraction of slow, meticulous, ruthless plotting (a category of contemplation). It's been my life's work, really, watching, listening, writing all of it down. It's second nature to me now, like breathing out and breathing in . . . *gorged on cock*. (Just at present one's in the activity-displacement stage.) And I'm bloody good at it, too, good enough I shouldn't wonder to gain both an international reputation and a settled place on the best-seller lists.

One thing I've never had is match temperament—worse luck, dear. (We didn't have bloody tennis in the East End, only darts—plus which nobody there had the figure for tennis. All the men were built like jockeys and all the women had enormous jugs. Funny that.)

On the other hand, I must not be rash: candor and rashness, were ever my besetting sins—and a tendency to be sarky. There were certain advantages to it all—and they, the warders, did willingly admit me into a community of taste, especially for things like landscape, jade, and orchids, not to mention such ceremonies of a, shall we say, biblical bent, such as the laying on of hands. I really ought to concentrate on these—and on forbearance. Sarky forbearance. (Who was it, dear, said of the British they can take an awful pounding and still go on planting lobelias?) Because it must be said the Episcopal Church in the United States of America is bloody powerful, too, especially when faced with the threat of compromise. So I said to meself, right, I shall not betray my true feelings, which in any case are unworthy of me (fat lot of good *that* insight did: gave me a fit of the choir-loft giggles was all). Let them remain unaware of same; let the ghosts of them lie.

But ghosts don't lie, do they—not in an English story, and so me feelings *festered*. I began to have *symptoms*, dear, and that gave them exactly what they wanted (for I'd not deceived them after all, only in true British fashion meself). They had me sectioned, dear, put me into that place, tried to have me stitched up for a lunatic, a bloody nutter, *shanghaied*, I was, *kidnapped* into a system of séance, hypnotism, and the darker aspects of voodoo—and you do remember, dear, I'm sure you do, what Bela Lugosi said in that picture about voodoo. "Superstitious baloney!" the fool taunted him, but he remained composed. "Superstitious perhaps . . . *baloney*, perhaps not."

And I was never one to go mad, dear, no, never. I'd go *spare*, it's true, and it didn't take much to make me snap me rag, but I'd not go mad—not *until they incarcerated me*, like Nijunsky—when they yoiked me out of me own life, *only then* I truly (*horresco referens*) went off me fuckin' head for actual.

You know Nijinsky said, "I will not be put into a lunatic asylum; I dance very well and give money to anybody who asks me for it." Well with me, admittedly, it's been otherwise in the second instance—I've taken money from anybody who cared to offer—but I *feel*! I'm a *feeler*, as was Nijinsky, and for that they had me hauled before the beak and stashed me in a pesthouse, dear. Swore I'd threatened to top meself, as if

I'd ever be so vulgar, *or* contribute any more so-called *evidence* of the congenital maladjustment of the homosexual.

Carrion birds only ever and always have a single, steely purpose behind their hovering.

But you know, dear, bad as it was whilst I was there, I was told by an old veteran that had I been twenty years older and put in before the war, they'd've done colonic irrigations every morning and induced fevers in me with strains of malaria and typhoid. I said, "I don't know as I'd've minded the high colonics." I mean to say, Mae West insists they're what give her that complexion—but, really, darling, *malaria*! All that quinine water you'd've had to take, and not so much as a *fingernail* of gin in it either, you can bet your auntie's frilly knickers.

Well, anyway, dear, I've done me bunk and am out of there now—and out of America, too. I never did belong there; it's a country where a man is esteemed by the success he makes of his life, whereas in England, where much amusing weather is made of the sufferings of others, we are so very fond of failures. Therefore, I shall either find God and a purpose in Benares or, like as not, go back for good to dear, dirty England and be what I was always meant to be, a trollop in the Cinqe Ports.

But first, this being second night out, I'm going to *dress for dinner*—just let them try and stop me!

(A woman's desire for revenge outlasts all her other emotions. Cyril Connolly said that. Takes one to know one doesn't it, dear, especially one of the male lesbian variety.)

There was a garden in the asylum I was sent to, dear, with a long winding lane trimmed with those frightful delphinium borders in bijou blue, cream, yellow, and white. A suggestion was made that as I was English (however did they know?) I might like, by way of Occupational Therapy, to take part in looking after them. "I'm English all right, and fair enough," I said to them, "but as it happens I am not a horny-handed son of toil, nor do I tip my cap at betters, but as you seem to think these things, that, frankly, make me want to spew black bile, might need a watering . . ." and then and there, dear, I flipped out the lizard and drained him all over the bloody things. They seemed, I must say, ever so grateful for the attention—the delphiniums, that is. I dare say the nurse attendant would have been, too, had it been another willy in action—one of the willies of his dreams, don't y' know. Not like in *Giselle*, dear, more like on Twenty-eighth Street.

Anyway, wasn't that the last of the little invalid's strolls down the garden path, I should say it was. For the duration of the voyage, that is—until we come to the floating gardens of Kashmir, dear, where I can't imagine there is a single bloody fucking delphinium—and there better hadn't be either, or this time they'll be shat on, I promise you!

Let me tell you, dear, about Aldershot during the war—the rough training ground for thousands of raw recruits. You can't imagine the tension in the barracks. All those boys from every little village in England, primed in all those little village lusts and no outlet but the regulation regimented *feu de joie* at lights-out, dear, that got to be more chore than satisfaction—in the time-honored British way. Once in a way they'd get off down to a nightclub in Hastings, built into one of the eighteenth-century smugglers' caves. Fuck the women standing up they did, or said they did.

There was a corporal in the cookhouse, culled from some chalky corner of the Kentish plow, as most of them were. Camber Sands he was called—only liked Sandy better. A bit of a stranger, one felt, to the cursive hand, but knew everything there was to know about the caves and all the stories of the orgies held in them. Loved to sing "We'll Gather Lilacs in the Spring Again" whilst rolling out the dough for the Cornish pasties. Hated all women, or nearly. "There's but two women in the kingdom that's worth the price of admission and that's the Queen Mother and the Dame of Sark." He was speaking, of course, in those days of May of Teck, after whom this tub we're on coursing over the bloody bounding main is named.

I'd sidle up to him, once I got the way of it, which wasn't long. We were sitting there one evening in the kitchen playing a game of snap, when I asked him, "Corporal Sands, what were you before the war, a cook?"

"Indeed, not, squire, I had a proper trade, I did. A saggar-maker's bottom knocker, I was, and may be one again when we've finally flattened Berlin and this filthy war is over. Not that I ever let on, no. I preferred they not know all that. Much prefer they see me as was some dozy bugger off the mill floor I did—and so they did, so everybody was happy as fucking, Larry, cannon fodder and cannon fodderer alike. I got that good at mumbling and dissembling; needs must when the devil drives."

"Golly!" I said, fairly awash in what you might call the eloquence of expressions of the soil.

"In a word, squire." And he went on then, dear, straight to the job of flattening yours truly. "You know," he said to me, "you're a pretty little red-cheeked muggins, a regular little bluebell in the patch of spleenwort England is these days, and I know another kind of snap—would you fancy a go?"

"Yes, please." There was a war on, dear, and you didn't just lie back and think of England, you got on the stick.

And on foot of that one audition, I'd got the part. "Called to the colors, are we Mugs?" Thus he'd tease me. "Up for a little chew of the Spotted Dick? Aye, but you're a teasing little brasser at that. Come here to your mate, conniving imp."

But in point of fact, dear, what I'd longed for and soon got, front and back, was anything but spotty—talking of the larger questions of life. A tusk shaft of ivory it was, and curved that way a little, too. Up, that is, dear, curved up; it was ever so exciting to look at in the lamplight. And *the* most gorgeous ballocks—like pigeon's eggs. I couldn't keep meself calm near him, not for a minute. "What's to pay, lad?" he'd tease. "You're all of a tremble. Back for a second stab at the rasher, are we then? Hold on a tick, whilst I finish off these pasties, and we'll go a ride at the amusement park—that suit you?" He had a way with the euphemisms, did Corporal Sands—"Sandy" he let me call him—and I was bloody good, too, at what I did, as good as ever I was at singing—and in a rather similar way, come to think of it, with the additional skill of *palpating* the pigeon's eggs, which drove him quite mad. (Let's just say that if I turned a bit hysterical about things in those fraught days, the legendary British stiff upper lip would have been a real *impediment* in the work I'd taken on.) A sweaty mass of seething lust is what we were, Sandy and I. He called me his little arse bandit—the filth call us that, you know, especially when one of us gets bumped off as happens and they have to look into it not very hard. We call them the filth, dear; you call them the fuzz. Peculiar.

In any event I took old Sandy away from his pasties and his lilacs in the spring, to another realm, one not at war, leaving him time and again a sated heap there on the bloody cookhouse floor.

"For he on honey-dew had fed
And drunk the milk of Paradise."

Or as near to it anyway as comes of scarfing down the spunk of an angelic East End choirboy. And then it was my turn—one given me aforementioned throaty talents I managed to stretch, dear, into a whole bloody pantomime. As easy as letting the air out of a balloon, dear, too right it was, and after a time, I'm afraid, about as exciting—again more chore than satisfaction. I'd become blasé, don't you see—a lot of that happened in the war; it was, they said, a kind of shell shock. All the same and all in all, dear, I'd have to say I had a good war—a lovely war, actually in many ways.

Once in a way, you know, for a laugh, he'd take off his apron, fold it neatly over a chair, undo his flies and haul the tosser out—and who was it, dear, said, "Amazed the gaping rustics rang'd around?" That was about a parson, wasn't it, and not about an army cook havin' a wank in front of a gaggle of the inch-and-a-wish cadet brigade. You'd be had up for that lark now, and put away the way I was, but not back then, not in the war. You might be reprimanded, lightly, but you wouldn't be put up on any sort of charge over it.

Yes, about a parson, and Corporal Sands was no parson, only that the folding of the apron was like something you'd see in a vestry (as later, indeed, one so often did, in a telling way, when piety and reverence for frilly lace and silken raiment in the service of the Almighty would turn so quickly, the service done, into ardor for the server, and two servants of the Almighty, priest and acolyte would end up writhing naked and wanton, there on the vestry floor). "And still they gazed and still the wonder grew." To quite a length, dear, be assured—egged on you might say by the mesmerized appreciation, until, as the poet has it, "and forth did the particulars of rapture come." (To which add *in fat splats on the flag-stone floor*, Florrie, and know from this out that your correspondent, abject wanker that he is, is no slouch at versicle composition, and glad of it, too, if only as it gives his left hand something else to do.)

Did I ever tell you, dear they tried to break me of that, too—sinis-whateveredness? They did, of course. Tied me left hand behind me back and made me write right-handed, but after all those years, once I was alone (so alone) I took back the right to write left—freeing myself to do all sorts of other things ever so dexterously, such as waving from carriages driving down Piccadilly, fingering fine silks at Turnbull Asser and playing Ravel's Piano Concerto for the Left Hand upside down and backwards.

I might say I got my first lessons in that barracks kitchen in Aldershot along the lines of "what was thought but ne'er so well expressed." Yes, lessons that determined me, for good and all, to be, whatever else, *expressive*. What was the alternative—to blush unseen and waste one's sweetness on the desert air? Not bloody likely, Mister Jones! Then the odd time we'd get out into the air, climb a hillock, and let the wind run through our hair, our eyes watering all up, and once in a way walk out under the stars before moonrise—you could see the stars in wartime, with the blackouts, and only the moonlight was dangerous. We'd go together down the lanes, hand in hand. There'd be no sound but a dog's howl from some distant farm, and the small country noises of ditch and field, dear, that always gave me the sudden dreads, and he'd hold me close and whisper words of comfort until finally I couldn't stand it longer, nor could he, and I'd pull at his trousers 'til he opened them and dropped them to his ankles, and I'd go down on that monster he kept bound up in there like the howling, hungry mongrel I was.

"You've got a grubstake in life, Mugs—don't let the bastards snatch it from you. You jib at nothing, or at very little—pluck's what you've got, darling, and a dab hand at charms. With that pretty girly voice you've got and the right charms, you could land yourself a right good screw, I reckon." That's what he said to me. Feeling that hectic, I laughed; he just smiled—he was a rough-hewn darling himself. "That's to say if we both get through this filthy war, what nobody at the end of it will get anythin' but fuck-all out of, saving the bloody armaments manufacturers, the ordnance suppliers, that lot. They'll be quids in, make no mistake. And if you still fancy old Sandy come then, I reckon we might yomp it down to The Weald on a fine summer's day. We'll have fires in the evening and drink possets"—that's what he said, bub—"and you can give me a song or two and I'll teach you a little wider *repetoire*. Well be deserving of larks, if only for coming through . . . if there's a God. Of course the world's changed for good—and for the worse—that as plain as naked daylight. Why even before the War there was hardly a single reliable umbrella mender left in London."

I could decipher early on, dear, the handwriting on the wall. I saw very clearly what history would record of yours truly. "Removed to Chepstow, he thrived in the Forest of Dean." A bloody sodding life of growing orchids in the potting shed. Well, knickers to that, as the downstairs maid advised the butler; I broke that code, make no mistake, and sheared off clear of that direction. Oh, I tell you, dear, them snouts up in Bletchley Park could've used yours truly for drills unusual to little

Margarets of his type. Afford me the pleasure of their company to the tune of a couple of wets and a matey exchange of giggles. Value for money I'd've been, frightfully good at bridge, and a credit to bloody King and Country as well! And while they were at it they could have had me trained in *sapper work*. . . .

Suit them if I'd yielded to an overdose, or been murdered—which thought gives one pause, for although much as when in a mood one wouldn't mind being murdered, one *would* mind *terribly* knowing that the investigation into one's murder would likely go on unaccompanied by numerous queries from the press, followed by headlines, at least in the tabloids, and remarks in the social columns.

I was saying as much to that big bruiser who's just come off being Arthur Gold's inamorato, and is himself having strange seizures and being administered all sorts of tablets—and I don't mean like Moses on Zion, dear, I mean what you lot there call pills—all sorts of them. He's a poet, so I was told. We didn't talk about poetry much, in fact not at all, as he kept going on about Bidu Sayão and Maggie Teyte and Povla Frisch and of course Mawrdew Czgowchwz—he'd first heard her in Naples; went over from Ischia with Auden and Chester Kallman, if you please, when they were out there being a ménage à trois of some description. I thought he was dreamy myself, although they all say he can be a nightmare—all except O'Maurigan, who apparently dotes on him, says he's a real American genius and only needs time, which from what I hear if he's not careful he could end up doing in that accommodation up on the Hudson.

One's a weak thing, dear, one confesses it, and is moved by the smallest soup spoon of violence in an exquisite temperament.

My original people were from Welling, in Kent—true men of the soil, dear. Yeomen of the Plantagenets they'd been devolved sommat into gamekeepers, both sides. On the old Victorian estates. Many gothic tales recited of the gentry: suicides, incest, miscegenation in form of dalliances with visiting wog potentates, which often would add to the general population of the demesne some swarthy little stableboy or scullery maid. Buggery, of course, bugger after bugger creepin' up and down the richly Axminstered stairs into this or that poorly heated cave of a bedroom. It was as popular as lawn croquet, they said.

My old geezer was a fairground boxer, among other things, who sported a billycock bowler hat to go with his name and reputation. Cut a fair dash, Dad did, and a fair old twister, never in a scrape he couldn't dodge out of *presto*. You might've thought from that and from the fact that *she'd* run off to Scunthorpe with a garage mechanic he'd take against me, but the fact is it was quite the opposite: he was mad gone on me. Saved me life, too. I'd a lethal case of diphtheria at a year old. Visiting his mum—Gran—of a Sunday, and it was him rushed me to hospital and stood by me through the night after the tracheotomy. (Interesting that, I used to think in later years, had the tracheotomy to do with giving me my gorgeous voice? Or my progious ability *to take a cock as long and thick as Freddie the Everard towel boy's in one gulp*? You wouldn't think so, but I used to wonder.) Anyway the story was ever after told me, by Gran and all the others—neighbors who'd heard the sirens and seen the ambulance arrive. And so, of course, he was ever after my one and only hero—and the sad truth is, dear, heroes' sons are notoriously prone to dissipation. The shrinkers tried explaining it all to me, but I said to them that unless and until they could bring dad back, or furnish a decent equivalent, they were only tormenting me the more with their interpretations. Bastards.

Yes, he was mad gone on me, Dad was—not that he ever touched me improper. He did, of course, show me how to have a lovely time in the bath—*to be cautionary with the dandy bits*, was his expression, and *intensity of bodily joy*. (Always wondered where he'd picked that one up; it was a bit *posh-sounding* for him, and surely didn't issue out of the mouth of any vicar—or anybody Sally Army either: they were always hangin' about.)

He'd started coming round Saturday nights, you see, as well as for Sunday lunch—but never to supervise me, not as such. He'd have his bath first—of course, I'd peek in at him lolling in the tub, pipe in his mouth, the dark hair on his body flattened like an otter's pelt. Then he'd pop out and run me a fresh tub and, after a decent interval, pop his head in or call over the transom, "Getting on, are we, old fruit?"

"Yes, Dad, thanks ever so much."

And I'd hear him laugh and go away saying something like "Too right! No point to all the waitin' and all the worritin'—anyway, you're off, and Bob's your uncle!" Which I never understood for ages, as Dad had no brothers and Mum only one, and he was called Trevor. And he'd go away, Dad would, whistling some George Formby song. Mad keen he was on George Formby—you know, the wanker with the ukelele.

Yes, he was a bit of a wag was Dad in his billycock bowler, and unlike his progeny prized by his peers—I've no illusions on that score, darling, nor do I seek pity, a thing that revolts me to my core. Popular all the way up to South London and the East End, something more's the pity he never could show me the knack of, like he did the bath lark. And consoling, too. Sometimes, if he found me desolate, he'd sit me in his lap and say, "Now, now, squire, needn't be all that glum; worse things happen at sea." Well, I never saw how that could be so—I'd always imagined sea a romantic place with everybody up to hornpipes and that—and in a way I was right, only I'd never imagined I'd be so *excluded*, which is so much worse at sea for there's no long dark alley to run down to toward the shady waterfront, is there. (And there I've gone again getting metaphorical and metaphysical, a thing I do, dear, to render the universe less hideous and the moments something lighter—to paraphrase a famous French nellie of the century that was before our own, a poet by no coincidence whatever, gone absolutely out of his (married) nellie mind for a little *tranche* of provincial tart like me; it never works.)

Quite the lad, yes, quite in spite of being of a sickly little nance progenitive. Done any number of favors for this one and that one and the other, too, while he was at it. Many were the faces what he could lean on in Gipsy Hill, as he himself put it to me, should he ever need a favor back, although he never did, it seemed. At least not one from mortal man, if you take my drift. The favor he and them could best have used they didn't get, most of them. Blown to bits, Dad was, with all the others that time in the first Blitz, in forty, the one in late December when the Guildhall and eight Wren churches—one of which yours truly was nearly gone to choir at—when the Gog and Magog took a direct hit. You want to talk about "Hurry up, ladies and gentlemen!" Havin' a roarin' laugh, I was always sure, in spite of what was came raining from skies. Took no more notice of Jerry's bombs, dear, than of hailstones. Drove poor Gran quite literally mad, his demise did. Suited him all the same—to be blown to bits into squelching oblivion, with no recoverable trace—far more than rotting back into the earth in one of the municipal cemeteries—for he was no religionist, withal he doted on my singing and taught me lovely naughty songs in rhyming lingo and pretty ditties once sung by Marie Lloyd.

"Mind you," Gran said, "he mightn't've lasted in any event—he'd awful dodgy bellows."

(No point, see, to all the waitin' and all the worriton'.)

Whereupon back foxtrots the trollop from Scunthorpe, all motherly concern, wreathed in Ashes of Roses by Bourjois, garage mechanic in tow—turned out it was all at his insistence. Well, Gran sent the trollop packing, although I dimly recall she was very warm with the handsome mechanic, explaining as she told me some time later how she'd put it to him, resulting in him promising never to punish me—which of course was the wrong tack to take with Gran. Either she flat out didn't believe anybody who'd say such a thing as wasn't natural, imputing *motives*, or if she did believe him, she reasoned he'd spoil me rottener than Dad had already. "I've no prosecution against chastisement," said she, "for as the twig is bent, so grows the tree, and children want *righting*, but I'd not have the child corrected by another man's rod than his own father's, or failing that, as needs must, by blood kindred, as I'm sure you'll understand, sir."

Well, I can tell you, dear, the report of *that* little peroration set me dreamin'. I'd only ever glimpsed at Dad's cock the odd time we'd stop in the lane for him to have a piss, and up to that moment I'd never so much as *glimpsed* at another man's, but at her words all the heroism of me dad came rushing up at me in the form of two things, his grinning mug and his lovely fat cock with the blue vein in it plainly visible in the yellow streetlamp in the lane, and what do they say, dear, *the rest is history*. Except that what happened to Ashes of Roses and the garage mechanic I've never known—those were turbulent times, and much was lost.

In any event, Gran sent me to a cousin in Basingstoke, and from there I was posted back to the metropolis—to Streatham, to a cheery vicar to warble in the choir loft. War work it was, dear, *uplifting* people, and there was nothing could stop me, not damp, catarrhs, not even the evil sulfur fogs, all yellow and thick as pea soup and lethal to many. To me and to my voice they were nothing worse than Dad's pipe—that's the one he'd stick in his mouth, dear, not the one I used to wish so he'd stuck in mine.

Yes, Streatham. It was actually Stockwell, but they let on as how it was Streatham, which was meant to be bloody posh in comparison, although with everything likely to be reduced to rubble at a moment's notice, you'd wonder why they'd bother lying like that—that is until you come to the realization that the whole of British life is a bloody lie. And then in that period when the air war went quiet, to Pimlico, and it was there I was discovered in the choir—singing, that is. I did a stint at Westminster, lived through the Battle of Britain and then presto changeo, it was off to America, right into the bosoms of Benji and the Missus.

I can't say the rest is history because it was all history, wasn't it. A riot of history, and I was right smack at the center of it all.

I have a very short backstop to boredom, dear; I don't belong in this boring 1950s world at all. I belong, I'm that sure, back in the late forties West End, if not quite opposite Anna Neagle in *Maytime in Mayfair*, then certainly adjacent... somewhere in the vicinity. Lunching at Rules with some old male auntie who spent his entire working life wearing a bloody scarlet robe and sitting under the Lutine Bell at bloody Lloyd's until a bloody ship foundered at sea, and listening to his stories of life between the wars at the Café Royale, to his quips about Binkie and Ivor and Noël —they all had twats like open trenches, that lot, and mouths to match.

Then later in the long summer afternoon lollopin' down Piccadilly with old Rag, Tag, and Bobtail, me mates, to take high cream tea at the Ritz, eavesdroppin' on the bloody toffs who used go on and on about heraldic murrey, and which of the two Hermiones was more divine in *Rise Above It*, and the larks they've had with the nancy boys in the Sadler's Wells corps de ballet.

They'd splash out, ordering lashings of everything and put on the posh, like it was all bloody marvelous and they didn't give a toss or a tupenny fuck about anything and life was a flippin doddle. Thought they were so bloody naff, dear, because they disdain umbrellas—"So Neville Chamberlain, really, so terribly reminiscent of *appeasements*!" They'd let the rain rain down on their silly faces until the flippin' mascara ran down their silly cheeks in sooty streaks, and switch inauthentic into Polari slang, as if they'd known the gutter, as if they'd come up from struggle or knew anything of Limepit Vale or Ladywell Road. We'd have a laugh!

So you see I *will not* down-pedal my legitimate ambitions for a better life, not when time and again I've been so very *close*!

Oh, I'd bloody well have taught them a thing or two about the gutter, darling, hard cheese and all, given the chance, and lashings, even if it was nearly 1950 and they'd never been nearer the navy than Portsmouth—mutton chops with it, and I don't mean bloody whiskers either. And every chic girl in London knows the Berkeley is more divine than the Ritz for tea, but not yer bloody poof morrisin' down Piccadilly, dear, like it was Coronation Day.

I would let them have the lashing of my tongue—but when it comes right down to it, frankly, I couldn't be arsed, I really couldn't.

My soul longs to weigh anchor and throw itself into the unbounded bosom of some immaculate friend. Or jump ship—which I could almost do, dear—we come within sight of the Channel Islands, and I did once sing for one of Sandy's two darlings, the Dame of Sark. She complimented me something gorgeous. She'd take me in, could I get there on a trawler. Course I'd prefer the Queen Mum, dear—the present one, now the Dowager's dead and gone, as who wouldn't? The Scotch Bar Maid we call her, lovingly—but she was never a great one for choral Evensong. Could I've wangled meself into *Variety*...

We are sinners: these devilish passions tear down the edifice of a holy life.

I dreamed I was a nun, dear, and not just any nun, mind you, but the nun picking penises from the phallus tree in the illuminated manuscript of the *Roman de la Rose* at the Bibliothèque nationale. Was I born to be Camp? Would that it were so.

I tried reading *The Anatomy of Melancholy*, dear, to see could I work out why I was always going off in a growler, but it's that dense, that I never did. *The Anatomy of Melancholy*! Well, I know enough about the melancholy of anatomy, anyway—reason enough to take up this celibate spiritual lark—leastways for an interval; for a season, wot? Oh, and the artists among them one was obliged to assist in the pursuit of their plastic ideas—whisper who dares. Sitting there in the bloody nude being reconfigured time and again by some ponce who thought of himself as the reincarnation of M. A. Bone-a-rotti himself, in attitudes he'd made himself familiar with through attendance at the Ballets Russes de Monte Carlo. Talk of uttering obscene advertisements—I could bloody sing of it! You try it sometime, darling, posing as a young Assyrian warrior in some biblical tableau, got up in a revolting tunic of white butter muslin clasped with a black patent leather belt, standing legs apart at twenty-five past seven on, thanking you, the balls of your feet. Had I any sense, I'd've given the bastard a foot in the balls, but until I started drinking, dear, I had no spunk at all.

I mean bloody hell, darling, if Coral Browne can play Bathsheba, I can fucking play Salome. Do you think there's any chance at all, dear, that in the end I shall be delivered over to good intentions? That my life may become even the slightest bit the way I'd once envisioned it: bleak moors and a wasted castle providing the elements for a tale of forbidden love and expiation, the violent elements rending the airy landscape and beating in time with the turbulent swellings of the heart arrayed in full fig? Apparitions haunting the dense shadows whilst urgent horsemen thunder across the backdrop of a pale sky, cloaks billowing and nostrils flaring? And in the end, dear, great bursts of sunlight and salvation Any chance at *all*?

Likely not. Caw, will you ever forget that piss-elegant soiree you took me to at Carlo Van Vechten's, when I was going on about some caper of me youth in London, and how the coppers nicked me out of a bunch of young things, though I'd not any real part in whatever caper it was, and I said, "No matter, guess who *it was they fisted*?" And there came this deathly silence, and I was ever so confused, 'til you pulled me aside and told me *what the word meant* in America. And I remember I *shrieked*—I absolutely shrieked, "What *are* you *saying*—they put a *hand* up there—and *close* it into a *fist*—and *proceed*?"

I near fainted dead away, and had dreams for absolute *weeks*. I mean the gutter's the gutter, dear, and a brawly shunt is a brawly shunt, but even today, with all that's happened, it shocks me rigid to think there are men who actually *shove their fists and forearms to the elbow* up one one another's arses.

You know whose music I love, dear? Wilhelm Friedemann Bach. They say he was a drifter, that he died in poverty in Berlin, but I say so what. It's a known fact that his da loved him the best out of—what was it, twenty-two? Well, that must stand for *something*.

I've got so *introspective*. Perhaps because I was an alto, and in Kraut theology, dear, the alto was said to be the very voice of the Holy Ghost. And that woman, that Mawrdew Czgowchwz woman, talking of altos (I shall always think of her as one no matter what she goes about calling herself). *Vera incessu impatuit dea*, dear. She's enough to—oh, what's the use!

You want to know something really funny? In that place they tried to call me a schizophrenic—tried to say I manifested a breakdown in selective attention. I'd love to hear the vicars' response to that. I *can* hear it: "Breakdown in selective attention? Why, a more calculating little—"

Rotter, darling, I do feel in my artichoke heart of hearts that I've given the old three-sheeted wog a fair free trial. Let me then unstick my mits from the (folded-napkin) prayer position long enough to take pen in them, before I forget how and, talking of Life Lessons, have to be told again *here's how*. I used always to say of a situation—almost as if it were an entity, and one under the gravest suspicion at that—that I was determined to get in bang to rights—emphasis always on the bang.

Oh, what one would not dispense from one's store—could one but arrange oneself into a semblance and sally forth—after an hour of the duress of his holiness's protracted drone, for a minute (let's not ask for the moon) of Miss Mabel and Teddy Wilson. After all, dear, a boy does like to get his leg over now and again.

All day looking out to sea, at sea, wondering whence, whither, whether, whatnot. Brooding on it, so pregnant with possibilities, teeming with life. Thought of you on the beach at Fire Island, refusing to get your feet wet, cautioning, *The Lord alone knows where that water's been*. Funny the things you remember, and...

Helpless when confronted with his assertions, I am bound to question my warder's motives, although bound to assent to the diagnosis done on me (consistent with the evidence and with too many assured eventualities). Yet, when I am kept away from—she's in there now, with him, the warlock. They're *all* in there, less like a group of passengers, more like some tactical expeditionary force, doing whatever, saying whatever—for you know exactly what I mean by *in there*. What we've always meant—our kind—by *in there*, though I'm not supposed to say so, to talk like that, because it sounds as though I think my nose is pressed against the glass again and I'm *imagining being kept out*, and soon I'll be *imagining I'm shut in*. Milerapa says it's poison to crave.

Yes, here I am, on the voyage out, with that woman. Where she is—*ou se devine la presence*—there is Life: that's one thing I know. And yet *I hear the trained soprano. She convulses me like the climax of my love grip.* (Wanker, *wanker*, nasty spanker!) *Steeped and honeyed morphine... my windpipe squeezed in the fakes of death.* Bloody fool should have felt what I felt with the diphtheria... not that I remember, though *I do believe my throat does.*

Plus which, darling, the *complexion*! Shouldn't wonder she positively *swims* in fabulous creams and body unguents made of melted pearls.

Small wonder poor O'Maurigan is so cracked on her and thinks she hung the fucking moon—under the rising of which, his donkey cart makes its way home, filled to overflowing with creels of scented turf—ever seen any of it, dear, it looks like great *turds* dropped by one of their hero giants, like Finn Mac Cool. In any event God help us all, the witch is devastating—and getting it regular from the warlock. Because they weren't *vocalizing*, darling, in that stateroom, and neither of them has been *near* the piano in the music room, and they weren't involved in any bloody *sacra conversazione* either. Nor naked Christian witness before the Lord. No, I can tell you, somebody's love bubbles were bursting, so that soon the first of a possible brood of little warlockets—

I say *weren't*, for the news buzzing aboard this hour is how suddenly after ages and ages the two have emerged from the bower of bliss, had all their lovely floral arrangements moved out into the public recreation areas, and taken on acquaintance with this one, that one, and the other one—the way it only happens on a ship. You know how the story goes (I wouldn't, my voyages have been torments all), including a little family of three Irish: the father, the mother, and the child, a girl, who looks and looks at Czgowchwz like—well, dear, y'd have t'see it: it'd put you in mind of Nina Novak's Giselle gawping at the royals out on their hunting party. Sweet child, if you like the type—Irish, that is: precocious, and with an edge of steel, no mistake, when she wants something.

Then there's a mother-countryman of mine, the camp-as-ten-tents poet Pickersgill, who with his great friend Cholmondeley, of the Norfolk Cholmondeleys, dear—the warlock is Norfolk, too, y' see. They're all in there now, dear, doing that camp contradance they call the Madison—everybody lined up in two rows like at some cowpokes' ball, and I, like the clinging lips of famine—

Oh, rotter, I know I am pressing my runny guttersnipe's nose against the windowpane—it's dawned on me, all late and wrong—but what to *do?* I shall re-go *barmy!* All the bloody *woo-choos* across the room, directed at others! How shall I clap a seizing on the main stay. How get them *to let me in.* (And meanwhile, has *she* sung the soprano part in the Sea Symphony? I have! I am whimpering now, that I am, in *gemissements de desespoir.*)

'Tis dangerous, darling, when the wanker comes between the pass and fell incensed points of mighty opposites, and piteous when the whip hand suddenly turns into the wanker's fist.

Not that one expects sympathy; in the end one expects nothing.

It was terribly very foolish of me not to take out citizenship papers and study for the test, with a view towards going into the peacetime navy. Only minutes ago I heard a man's voice reading out loud, "The Bay State fleet was manned by successive waves of adventure-seeking boys." Now isn't that *me?* Then "high wages and the ocean's lore pulled the Yankee boys to sea, but only promotion—or rum—could keep them there." I'd settle for promotion, dear, I swear it—but from *whom*, and for *what?*

How does she *do* it to them all? I think the same way offstage as on—putting the vocal jazz aside dear, because it's not that. (It's tits-and-a-wink, dear. Lot to be said for it; sure beats fits and a wank, although sometimes I think it's not so innocent as all that: indeed, sometimes I wake up screaming, seeing her not as Juno in all her thousand wild and graceful attitudes and surrounded by all her preening peacocks, but as the black goddess Kali, fed fat on human hearts, dear, and sporting her collar of human skulls.)

And as for *him*—well, dear, I started out the same way he did, with a voice. I sang in great cathedrals—and at popular entertainments, where I sometimes would don a frock and take off Marie Tempest in *The Geisha*—not that I'd ever *seen* the old bird, dear, but it was a turn an old party from Aldershot taught me, and it went down a bomb every time, I can tell you. It was the war, that's what it was. The war and masturbation, at which I was, as they say, a dab hand, that left me thus, a suffering sod stranded in the social frost, through whose rags the winds of winter blow. And yet I hope to get it back, or some of it, through prayer and meditation in Benares . . . if the earthquake doesn't hit first.

The music of the spheres is what—for isn't music the alchemy, dear, by which the gross body is made subtle. (Was this not the wherefore of the Meneghini's swallowing a tapeworm—so as to look like Audrey Hepburn, though she may sound like Tarzan? I mean the reports indicate the sound these days is total jungle.)

Masturbation reminds me: the Mahatma wants all us boys to practice conserving our spunk, dear, instead of piping off the things that are in ferment—sending it up some flu in the center of us to the—talking of subtle—subtle chamber located somewhere in the vicinity of the Third Eye . . . at any rate no panky into the hanky or anywhere else. Don't quite know what he wants the girls to do to *damp* the fire. Moreover he does *word games* on it—leastwise I think that's what they are—a bit like that free associating the shrinkers got us to do. *Free association*—there's a laugh, I used to tell them, for every time we associated it cost somebody (though never Yours Truly) a bloody packet. Because if it's not word games, he really is a nutter. It goes something like this, only you have to *hear him say it* to get the full effect. "Whereas reproduction also called propagation is the planting of seed in arable ground, the dissipation of same, since it does *abate reproduction* we call *reprobation*, and for this there is no *manumission.*" Well they all sat silent as little white lambs with their tongues cut out, and I said to them all, "*Arable* land—and him a Hindu. Too strange." Of course they didn't get it, not one of them—not remotely linguistic, dear.

Well, anyway, perking up, I then gave him back a bit of your American dreamboat Wanker Whitman—as we were all sitting around in a circle and as I said completely lost for words the whole boiling of them, I outright declared, "I dote on myself; there is that lot of me, and all so luscious / Each moment and whatever happens thrills me with joy." Well, the old bastard starts in *glaring at* me—but in a hot second switched expression—it was almost magical how he did—to that very gaze of the beatitudes it used to take those Episcopal Church queens two stiff gins minimum to bring off.

Anyway, it's a lie. Each moment, whatever happens, fills me with such *dread* these days I'm too exhausted to even *think of* working it up, but I can't for the life of me imagine this as a way of life. Swami should only know, as they say on Seventh Avenue, that one long ago developed one's own strenuously satisfying method of conveying said stuff of all Homo sapiens propagation to said area of the head. At Westminster during the war just before being deported. We were, after all, meant to be saving on linen washing. It was *mimesis,* dear, wasn't it, a gesture identical to that notorious *uroborean* technique taught by the fakirs of Marrakesh to Richard Burton (the English writer, dear, translator of the *Arabian Nights,* not the Welsh ponce currently larkin' about Broadway and the West End and playing Alexander the Great in the cinema like he was bloody Rupert Brooke). Somehow one also managed to equate it in one's widening mind with *The child is father of the man.*

At any rate, one was caught at it. "You are the *nastiest* little boy there ever was in England—a filthy little *sponge* of iniquity!" And, of course, thanks to the will of He Who Rules the World, report of one's agility reached over the pond to Saint Thomas Church sooner than one's mortal coil was dropped at Pier 33, North River. I can't say it was part of my audition at the school, dear, but they were ever so curious—in fact one of the proctors took me into the library there and showed me an account of the very stunt, in a book on the Egyptian gods by some Edwardian geezer called E. A. Wallis Budge. It was the specialty of somebody called Khepera, and it's how he became the father-mother of the twins Shu and Tefnut. The proctor assured one that from that Egyptian myth—by, y'might say, a curious set of chances—the more enduring legend of the birth of Athena from Zeus's head came about—and from that the Trinity. In such wise, dear, bowling on, was one brought closer to God (which was, of course, what Wordsworth was getting at in a roundabout way, wasn't it. Do you suppose *he* . . .). The one unpardonable sin, in Egypt, was doing it in the temple.

And therein lay the rub, dear, because your servant was found doing it just there—well, in the choir loft, actually, into an open hymnal (as it happened, all over one of Byrd's vespers). I'd gone up there for a little rest and and a bit of hush, but as you yourself well know there is not rest for the wicked and no hush that can, as it were, *muffle* the summoning voices of carnal desire, and I thought to myself, well, I can't spill it out onto the ground, can I? That's what Onan did and God struck him dead—and it was then I saw the hymnal open on kneeler, And. . .

Did you know, heart, that the Indian cobra has *two* penises? And that a *scruple* was worth thruppence and that there were twenty-four, scruples of silver to the ounce? It does, it was, there were: just ask the sons of bitches born with silver spoons in their mouths (who grow up to learn how to charm the world's snakes and to take two or more penises at once, et cetera).

And yet sometimes I sit down and scratch me 'ead and say t'meself, *what are you doing*? The Mahatma, who can be coarse, refers to India as the *open cunt* of Western Civilization. If so, what am I *doing*, darling, drifting inexorably towards an *open cunt*?

I feel as though, having conveyed these tidings, I may just drop dead, torch in hand. (Should I do, dear, have the little boys sing the Barber "Agnus Dei" will you?) I know I was saved from the Blitz to live a life (more or less like you on hire purchase) not merely to get and hold a job (I never schemed, was never ambitious; my only desire was to be an *adornment* in someone's lovely home . . . and cream it good and proper—after all, darling, just what do these marks think they inspire in us, *religious awe*?) And anyway I can't kill myself; I have aspirations, firm plans to attend certain types of events with certain kinds of people. One was not fitted out, dear, for the rough end of the market. I mean to say, one *was there* at the New York opening of *The Cocktail Party*, which is more than can be said for the likes of that bitch Dennis Pratt (calls himself Quentin Crisp, if you please—isn't that *hilarious*?) and his Piccadilly rent boys who only *talk* about going abroad and get no farther than Brighton. I desperately need to travel to certain key places. I can't drop dead. The orchestra's playing *Invitation to the Dance*. Might as well live and make connections.

Circumstances are guiding me, dear, to serious issues—vast perspectives of success unroll themselves before my eyes, *E strano. Cessano i spasimi del dolore, In me renasce, renasce—m'agita!*

I think I shall slip down to third, now, for a bit of a think—there's nothing like mixing with the thirds, I find, to stimulate the creative mind. Then I shall reascend *and dress for dinner*. Tomorrow yet another day may be, but starry tonight comes first.

*

Mawrdew Czgowchwz, having closed the score of Messiaen's *Poèmes pour Mi*, lay sunning on the top deck while Jacob Beltane lounged directly below in conversation with the poet Christopher Pickersgill and his reticular companion Cholmondeley. The diva, idling, surrendered to what underlying—

Life is one term . . . curving, now-then . . . I keep yawning—it's the afternoon sun . . . forbearing. Jacob is so loquacious . . . a comfort it, like the plump quail in Neap Wood who calls his name. Like the doves in the wainscoting each morning. Like those demanding gulls swooping in the ferry's wake off Manitoy. Like his telepathic screech owls. . . . *Jacob's more than musical*, Sibyl divined.

Particulars of male conversation drifted up.

" 'Let them be *sea captains*,' she said, meaning women, of course. Ironically, she died with husband and child in a shipwreck off Fire Island, within sight of the shore."

"Yes, well, when all's said and done. . . ."

"There's not much else."

"*No help for it*, we used to say."

"In the war? Dear Kit, don't neglect there it is."

"Yes, yes, the language, protean, is unwieldy. In case you think it's easy, as *Paranoius Arbiter* informs the world."

"I wouldn't have thought you'd own that."

"No help for it—*there it is*. There."

Time out—no time but now. The past parts, is lost from now—from his out all said and—

"Blissful day."

"A day for life."

"Songlike."

"Fair as new coin."

I surround another now; the man, as such, becomes dispensable.

Unsay that, nun. No, reverie is whatsoever—luck of the draw.

That sun. Like in those lazy afternoons on Manitoy.

Then that fiendish tempest—then NOIA. I dreamed that day—he did, too—of someplace ours. Then we went at that music. Sang the shit out of it, as Eileen would have said.

In case you think it's easy. . .

"It has become increasingly necessary to feign."

"But one cannot simultaneously feign and underscore *feign*."

"One can in conversation."

"The era of the written word is clearly—"

"In any event, pretend."

"Absolutely. Otherwise—"

"The untold want by life and land ne'er granted,
Now, voyager sail forth to seek and find."

"Whitman."

"And Mrs. Prouty—and Bette Davis and Paul Henreid with Claude Rains in the background. Ilka Chase hovering. John Loder passing through . . . and you and *La Divina Oltrano*, the way we picture you sometimes. Without the cigarettes, of course, but looking up at the evening sky and saying things like, 'Let's not ask for the moon—or the stars either; we are the stars.' "

"Wittgenstein was dead right when he said only Hollywood films are the real thing."

"I don't think we—"

"No, not you, I'm sure, but us—it's how we think."

"Because of the doctor in the story you—"

"We are foolish, aren't we—but there it is."

Singing:

"We deny them, we depart, borne away
One another we become
Voyager and voyager
Sail we forth to seek and find."

(Then that convulsive stretto, the tormented passage work. Suffocating—but for his breathing alongside—even if he does happen to have the most intimidating lung capacity I've ever encountered.)

She began humming softly the rising melodic line of "*Che puro ciel.*"

"Listen to that."

"Lately she's forever humming that, I don't know why."

"Why ask—the *sound!*"

"I imagine it in forty roles—like the forty pipes of Wulstan's great organ at Winchester . . . in the tenth century."

Jacob looked out at the still calm Atlantic, knowing that in it was the image of the dark sea or origins, the limitless, immeasurable, formless *arnava* of the Vedic seers, the *rsi*, forever threatening to swallow all (as literally as it had the *Titanic*, the *Lusitania*, the *Andrea Doria* and all the galleons of the Armada his forebears had summoned God's Breath to dispatch. One of which, Maev had told him, the *Califia*, laden with gold and broken apart on the rocks of Mayo's northern coastline at a place called Downpatrick Head, had provided the O'Morachains, S.D.'s forebears with all they would ever need in the world, or want, except perhaps for immortality: he'd never been too sure, not even singing their hymns in cathedral choir school in Norwich, what Christians, even apostate Christians really wanted.) Forebears . . . Progeny . . .

Leaving the memory of the last of the *Poèmes pour Mi* while humming the opening bars of '*Che puro ciel*' had ushered Mawrdew Czgowchwz into dream time, into the dream theater, where freaked clusters of memory, of performance—of her forty roles, as it were, pasted on her face like so many cutouts from scores, librettos, program kiosks, and newspapers.

"*Figlia di Faraoni . . . io stessa l'ho gettai!*"

"*Que pourrai-t-il que dans ces lieux l'amour a perdue sa puissance.*"

"*Wer wagt mich zu* HOHNEN?"

"Oh, living I, come tell me why. . ."

Twisted, gawking fancies, forming, paraded in, minding nothing. Murmurs fleshed peopled schemes, weaving, winding, wearing searching, stalking, sniffing, sighting, snatching, savaging.

"*Di miei passati giorni. . .*"

"*Mais ils ne sont pas a mon gré.*"

"*In mio man' alfin' tu sei!*"

"*Dalle due alle tre.*"

The procession continued—self after self in role upon role: forty, like the organ pipes, like Johnny Forty Coats, the Dublin "character" The Countess Madge had evoked in that connection. She in forty coats—and tales—observed by colleagues, benefactors, promoters, and enemies, drifting through the dream arena while painted flats ascended, descended, slid sideways on tracks.

Manon *en gavotte* at the Cours la Reine (with the Parisian critic Gavoty), the panniers of her silk-brocaded costume filled with bonbons from Fouquet's, past Mary Magdalen, the Marschallin, Frau Langsam, Mother St. Mawrdew, Masaryk, and Prince Orlovsky, sitting together chin wagging in the formal gardens of the Belvedere Palace. Amneris and Norma playing dominoes on the floor of the immense Temple of Ptah at Memphis. Salome at Maxim's, dressing Oktavian as Mariandel in her cast-off veils. Melisande alone, waiting, in the Forest of Fontainebleu. Carmen telling fortunes at the Crossroads Café for Dido, Isolde, and Katisha.

Whereupon all the dress extras, part singing in ragged chorus,

Beautiful dreamer wake unto you—you've seen you in your dream you dwelt in the Music Hall.

Dream lover put your arms around you...

Then Mother St. Mawrdew announced with summary severity,

> *"When you say to the Self Self—*
> *The hollow echo parries*
> *Just the way they say—the way*
> *Yourself your self remembers....* Et ego in Arcadia."

The ship's horn of H.M.S. *Queen Mary* blasted in salutation to the *Ile de France*, crossing east to west, waking her.

A voice intoned, *And before the throne was a sea of glass, and round about the throne four beasts full of eyes...*

It's not the Arcadia—it's the *Queen Mary*. Whew, that's one for the books. Must be the pull of the fathomless deep—the atmospheric pressure, the calm. The *Arcadia*. Ought to go jot that one down. It was the men, she thought, their gabble... unquestionably, the men.

The buoyant Atlantic became for her the inquisitive host whose patience may be running out, and the reverie some propitious turn, as if dropping tokens of information, of recall overboard in whispers would assure the ship safe passage (as if, indeed, she *were* called the *Arcadia*, and some sortilege *were* needed to safely speed her crossing) from island kingdom to island kingdom, Manhattan to Erin, life to life—a ridiculous suspicion on such an afternoon.

The men had gone. Mawrdew Czgowchwz kept thinking. To be abundant: to be teeming with life—to be the crucible; to compose—or else to act in motion pictures, ones like *The Lady Eve*. Card sharps, shipboard glamour, racy banter, all that. "Snakes are my life." "What a life." Also "I've been English." But if she married an Englishman, she would be English. Mae West, in *Goin' to Town*, after she sang Delilah, married an earl, and she didn't turn English, or if she did, she did it offscreen. An earl's wife is a countess. Funny to think of Mae West as the Countess.

How might she, she wondered, by right pretend to be or even plan on becoming a serious motion picture actress like the dame in *The Lady Eve*, with all that equipoise, all that élan, that snood, those shoes all overnight—no matter what Orphrey Whither or this handsome, ardent Manahan propose?

In the beginning was the word—and the word was *proposition*.

The *word was preposterous*—a gaffe. Why had she—why hadn't she—grumble, worry, woe betide.

*

The Mahatma had decided to leave his charges temporarily to their own devices (singing songs from Broadway musicals under the supervision of Prosper Swithin's companion) and walk the decks. Mawrdew Czgowchwz, stretched out in repose behind dark glasses, was watching the equinoctial North Atlantic sunset and humming the Catalan strophic song *El Marinar*. Something glided into view.

"Thee wurd *ver-an*—dah is of Hindi origin. Thees ees yur porch, yur croh's nest, garjous deeva. *Mah-du* also a wurd een Sonskreet meaning *swit. Swit* theengs veddy impoh-tant in India."

Be asleep, be *comatose*; breathe evenly—*evenly*.

"*Ras malai*, etceter-*a*. You were humming in thee throht. Thee throht chakra, *Visshuda*, is thee plehce of ether and of dreemming."

(And *vagal* is both throat and vagina. Strangulation, strangulated tone and locking in intercourse are all versions of the same thing. Next?)

"Thee bridge between thee bohdee ond thee mind; thee gehtway uv reepressed knohledge uv dee pohmegranate tree uv weesdom. Thee weh to thee prohpheteek *green* longuage uv thee hohly weemen. *Yoga ... citts ... vritti ... nirdha*. Thees ees 'Yoga ees thee sopprehshuns uv thee oscee-leh-shun uv thee mentahl sobstahnce.' "

(Yes, no more tears.)

"Yahs, you hov the look ahlmust of *apanga*, uv thee golden glow of Radha. *Gat-e... gate-e... paragat-e*. I pahs on now—bye-bye."

Nuts. "Oh, hello there, your—forgive me, what are you called?"

"Pray not *warship*. Tee-hee-hee-hee-hee-hee-hee."

Pray what not all. "How does one address you, then?"

"Oh," the swami declared, then joining his palm together in the *namaste*, he said, "Mahatma Bhairava-Baktivedanta. *Maatma, Sri*, ur, een *intee-mott* seizures *Ma-ha-ba-ji*. Dot I tehl you for you weel here eet wis-pahd."

"Ma-ha-*ba*-ji?"

"Tee-hee-hee-hee."

"You're, a jolly swami, at that, are you not, Ma-ha-*ba*-ji. And is it so that you used to work for the railway?"

"Yahs—ahl dee livelong day. Tee-hee-hee-hee! Ahl ees bot *saff-ron*: veil of Maya, web of seeming."

"All of it—nothing but saffron?"

"Monnereesum uv speeking. De Sufi Mostah Rumi sehs:

Aut bee-ohnd ahdeahs uv doing raht ond doing rahgn
Dere ees un field. I meet you dehr

(In a field of poppies—where have I heard that?)

Wenn de sohl lies down een dot ghras.
Thee world ees to fool to tulk abaht...

(It's a lazy afternoon...)

"Een hees surch fahr ree-ahl-ee-tee, mon he uncover nuthing bot ee-looshun ond boom-boom. Der ees nuthing. Nuthing but tat tvam asi—dot you ahr! De rest ees sutra, bandhu. *Pratityasa-mutapada* ees all."

(And the beetle bugs are jumpin'...)

"Imagine! I don't mean to pry, but the reason I ask that about the railroad is that in my long-gone youth—*nei miei passati giorni* is the way it's put in my religion—I used to sing a song about a boy called Johnny, who claimed to work on the railroad, but was really a minion of the sea. An enchanter, but a killer, too. A boy Lorelei if you like."

"Ah, dees Lora-lye, I knoh. Eeen dee reever Ryne. Eees bee-yu-tee-ful, lak dee goddess Lakshmi."

(Lakshmi. Hmm. "*Ou va la jeune Hindoue. . . .*")

"The girl in the song says he has no heart. I'm sure that is not true of you. The rest of what?"

"*Btrahma, Vishnu, Siva*, dey are dee *gohds*—beeger dan dee goddesses; dey are dee *tree-morty*."

(The three dead? The three Murphys. The three dead trees?)

"Same ees you cahl dee tree-neety."

"Ah—the three gay fellas."

"Dees ees a joke?"

(Tee-hee.)

"Something of a—yes."

"Mmm. Ahlso dere ees *Shahkti, Purusha, Prakriti*; ahlso *Devi, Kali, Krishna, Rahda, Lalitha*—all monnereesum of speeking. Ahl dee nooses uf *Varuna*."

"*Nooses*—for *hanging*, you mean?"

"Tee-hee-hee-hee."

"I've escaped more than one of those in my time."

I shouldn't about this one's heart; these ones can always put one of those chakras where their hearts ought to be.

"*Ahspects* says your Bodhisatva Jung, a veddy clevvuh fehloh, heem, deevoted to Lalitha, dee Player ond li; a, dee play."

(Wonder how many chakras make a dollar these days; must check.)

"As in *Turangalila*. So I believe—and rampant in the company of rich women. It is not recorded that he devours widows' whatsoevers . . . but then why wait?"

"Eh?"

("Has them telling all the world," Orphrey spat out that night, in his cups, "they're dreaming of archetypes, how-are-ye, when all they're dreaming of is his stiff Swiss prick!" No patience at all for him. Now Michelet, there's a connoisseur of the archetype, if you like. Says the greatness of the whale is that it encompasses the natures of both fish and woman. That's an idea!")

"Eh?"

"Skip it. There used to be saffron fields in England, and a place called Saffron Walden. Pretty name; town's still there; I believe the saffron's all gone—to Spain.

"However, *all* mannerism of speaking? I didn't realize—one doesn't of course. And according to one myth I *have* heard, Brahma was the offspring of Shiva's seed deposited—somewhere—in Lord Vishnu. That's a very cosy myth; it reminds me of the fact that the Irish call members of the Holy Trinity *The Three Gay Fellas*."

"Dot meeth is veddy—opehque—veddy *muddied. Ahspects* is bettah holiness. *Avatar* ahlso *vaa-tari*: hee crohsses down. On beefore dere wehre dee gohds there wuz ohnly the suspicions of Prajapati—wheech ees duh nameless progenitor."

(He crosses down, she crosses up—but never behind the furniture. Dress stage. "Don't just *do* something. Miss Bridgewood, *stand* there! Your *justification*? We'll work work on it, darling—*promise*!" Men.)

"So dee proximitee uv *manipura* ond *anahata*, fahr exomple, een Kundalini yoga—so dot dee wiley *day-mohn anahata* eenheebits de compuhlsive seempleecities of de dense ond smokey *manipura*, ond beecohms de *dee-totched ahspect* uv de emohshunal *chahge—aerated*, oz de light plehys thru de *fy-ah*."

"Mmm—*stride la vampa*. Aspects merely—no deposits. Perhaps aspects of varying *value*, if not of varying hue? Perhaps it may be said after all that although it is all of it saffron, some of it is more saffron than the rest—if you take my meaning?"

"Thees ees eet. Ahl ahspects, thee gods, and ahl thee aneemals een train.

You cannot see them, bot they are here on thee boht—like on thee ark of Noah. Weeth Brahma ees thee goose, weeth Vishnu ees thee eagul, weeth Shiva thee bull, on hees sohn Ganesh the—

(Ballocks.)

"Elee-font. Weeth Eendra ees thee elephant ahlso; weeth Kali ees thee tigah, weeth Rama ees thee buffaloh, weeth Ganeesha ees thee raht, weeth Agni ees thee ram, weeth Kama ees thee parroht, for Kama ees thee god uv Luv! Ond thee torns and torments uv luv—dey ahr thee greht sum uv thee deeseepleen dot ees *Bahkti*!

"Remember *tat tva asi*—dhot you *ahr*. Thee rest? Ma-*feesh*, ma-*feesh*. Pointing fingahs."

(*L'arcana parola*. What a pitch . . . but why? This is as too true a fool as I've seen in the world in some—meet me in the field behind the ha-ha, tee-hee-hee-hee. Dot you *ahr*. Ralph says, "See how you are?" I prefer Ralph.)

"That reminds me of some questions I've heard put—perhaps you know the answers to them. What is the point of one finger pointing? When there is more than one finger pointing, can they be said to be pointing at the same thing? If two go in search of a thing—say in the field out beyond the question of doing right and doing wrong—the one always finds it; does this not prove the other need not have gone looking? Or not? I expect these are Buddhist questions though, and you're not Buddhist."

"Ah, no—dee Buddhist is dee *prohtrstohnt* uv dee Brahman. Bot, garjuous diva, deese ahr cleerly bot *metuhfizzicle* qwasshuns, and as soch con hov *noh* ree-leh-shun to the focts of life os we knoh thehm—*tee-hee-hee-hee-hee-hee*! Dey are like dee noise ons stahtik frum Rahdio Mommon—Dobble-yoo-Gee-Haitch-Ell . . . Dots fohr *wohnt, geht, hahv, luhze*. Ninetey-seex pint tharee on the dial, A.M. ond P.M. Dee noise dot droewns out dee musik uv dee doncce uv Shiva. For I hov seen mayself the dahnce of Shiva een the West—at Meester Bolonsheen's Noo Yark Ceetee Centah—ond I hov seen Kali warshipped in the parson of Mees Martha Gray-ham. Yahs. *Bot*, eef you would knoh wot hoppens wen two go in search of a ting, ond eef you wud knoh thee weh uv thee stopping uv deesiah *ond* thee weh uv thee stopping uv thee deesiah to stop deesiahring, you muz study thee *Mah-hah-bah-rah-tah*, paying pahticular ahtenshun to Kunti."

"Oh?"

"Yahs. Kunti is your role. Veddy, veddy lohng. Bot veddy strung—fohr shee ees doing wot Kreeshna command: shee eees ovahcohmning dee dahrk *eye-or-sha*. Two of Kunti's prayuhs, ah uv pahticulah int'rest. Dee furst:

Bhave 'smin klisyamananam
avidya-kama-kasmabhih
sravava-smaranarhani
karisyann iti kecana

"Wheech ees: 'Ond yett uthers seh dor you oppear'd to rejuvuhnet dee devohshun sarvice uv hearing, rehmembahring, warshipping, ond so on, een urder dot dee cohn ditionned sols soffering frum mahteereeahl pongs maht tek oddvahntage ond gehn leebahrehshun.' Ond dee sehcund:

Ke vayayam nama-rupahyam
yadubhih saha pandavah
bhavato'darsanam yarhi
hrsikanam ivesituh

(*Izvestia?*)

"Wheech ees: 'Os dee nehm ond fehm uv a pahteekulah bodeh ees feeneeshed weeth dee dees-oppeah-runce of dee leeving speerut, seemahlahlee, eef you do not look upuhn os, ahl ouh fehm ond octeeveetees, dee Pandavas ond Yadus, weel ehnd ot wahnce!'

"Ond de bee-yu-tiful gentleman, yoah con-*soht*, he muz pay ahtenshun to the role uv Yudhishthira, orid dee gehm of dice against Sakuni, and mohr theengs."

"I see. I wonder can you tell me, Ma-ha-baji, why it is I think that all the while you are saying what you are saying, you are saying something you are not—so to speak—saying?"

"Tee-hee-hee-hee-hee-hee-hee. *Tat, tva, asi*."

("*Ah sir ben mio*" is a song I prefer.)

"Have I caught you out at something?"

"I cahnfess to you garjus deeva, ond I tell you a theeng I cahn not tell thee uthuhs, for they ah but tots."

"Oh?"

"Yahs. Eet ees thees. *Saffron*, eet ees old, old, old, *old* Hindi wurd means *ah-tumies*."

"Excuse me, what sort of tummies?"

"*Ahtumies*—leetle, leetle, thee *most* little—"

"Oh, *atomies*."

"Yahs."

"So everything is atomies. So it *is*."

"Yahs. *Pye*-thagoras, veddy fahnaus uld Greek?"

"Yes?"

"Geometry—uhreegeenahl seen—all dot. Ahl prefeegured in Vedanta."

"I knew about geometry—*pi* R squared."

"Yahs."

"But original sin—did he invent *that*?"

"Uhreegeenahl seen ees een dee Mahabarata. *Pye*-thagoras kehm to India. Lahrned dee seecrets uv dee ages, gee-ometry; Uhrigeenal seen. Dee *Dukkha uv luv*."

"Is that something like *Plaisir d'Armour*?"

"Eet ees dee soffering."

"Ah, then it's *chagrin d'amour*—the other half—the completion of the song."

"Wheech ees?"

"Joy of love is but a moment long; the pain of love endures your whole life long. An old French song."

"Ah, French."

"You thought it was Pythagoras?"

"Jolly diva. Also dot dere is no abaht-to-bee; eet is always ahlready. So een dee *Mah-bah-bah-rah-ta chaturanga*—dee ureegeenul gem uv chass—weech, eef plehyd *to*-deh wud eeleemeen-*ate* ahl wahr."

"All war?"

"Ahl wurh—*evehn between divas*. Tee-hee-hee. Ond *Pye*-thagoras toht everytheeng ees *numbah*. Nunbah ees *ahtumies—*ees *saffron*! See?"

"Ah—that's lovely. So *that's* what you've been saying."

"Tee-hee-hee-hee-hee-hee-hee. *Dunt* bee-*tray* me!"

"*Betray*? Not for the world. I'm an old humbug myself."

"Tee-hee-hee-hee-hee-hee-hee."

*

They sat together at supper in the Veranda Grill exchanging glances, and relaxed, as if the day had been a workday.

"All the while he was talking I kept thinking of Destinn—she was interested in all that—and of one of the very few threatening things she ever said. 'I was the greatest Aida there has even been, and you will be the greatest Amneris, and if you ever try to sing Aida, I will raise up out of the trap door and kill you.' "

"And then?"

"He showed me a few positions—of the hands."

"Yes?"

"*Mudras*. The Vitarka mudra reminded me of some of Milanov's more exquisite hand movements in *Forza*. Whereas the Abhaya and Anjali mudras were more like Victoria's in *Butterfly*—"

"Really?"

"Yes, when she sings about going to the mission chapel. "*Io sequ'il mio destino, e piena l'umilta*."

"I heard her at the Garden. I don't remember much of the movement; it was the most beautiful singing I'd ever heard."

"Or ever will either."

The Manahans waved from across the room.

"The Manahans are interesting. Tall, dark, handsome him."

"He."

"*Tee*—he. Over against her lesser disposition—tawny, diminutive, slender—"

"*Meow.*"

"Not in the—*fruit de mer* and ortolans, or—"

"The land doth will, the sea doth wish—spare sometime flesh and feed of fish."

"Is that something from the Vedas?"

"I don't think so—from some enthusiast of vegetables and salads. In any event, no ortolans. They roast them alive—that's happened too often to me I may say."

"Hm. Well, in any case *ortolan* is an anagram of *oltrano.*"

"So it is—moreover the correct way to eat them is to throw the dinner napkin over the head—which reminds me of Herod's gesture in *Salome*. It's said to facilitate inhaling the perfume of the creatures, but Janet Flanner thinks it's a probably a ritual meant to indicate the desire to mask shame. Pouilly? Sorbets?"

"Vouvray. Always. Neither of us knows anything whatever of family life. Although you have often enough been addressed as *Pia Mater. Sic te diva potens carminae sacrae...*"

"Go on."

"How to finish? Transform our little lives for now, for always..."

"Well, the Mahatma is more interested in what he calls *Swadhyaya.*"

"*Swad*—as in *swaddling*? As in psychic diapers?"

"Of a type: it means 'self-investigation.' Oh, and 'there is nothing to expect. Nothing is about to be—it all already is, or is all always-already.' "

"*Ja-ja*?"

"Are you having role anxiety again?"

"If I am, I had better not admit it, or you won't—"

"Won't what?"

"Oh, take the plunge."

"Rather an unfortunate expression, in the circumstance—like *walk the plank*. Reminds me of 'wander in a fragile bark o'er life's tempestuous seas' from 'Mother Dear, O Pray for Me.' "

"Your mother might well be doing just that as we . . . there's rather a lot of talk of danger on the premises lately—or have you noticed?"

"The always-already, or already is. And now the *Mahabarata*, which is apparently as old as Genesis and goes on forever. The Dusky Answer to the Untold Want was going on about it—it and much else in the strangest accent. I must say I found him more entertaining at any rate than Gurdjieff, who was nothing but a horse's ass. Anyway, it seems I'm to get busy obeying Krishna, and overcoming the dark inertia. . ."

"It is peculiar, that."

"It is *beyond* peculiar. Who *is* he . . . where does he *come* from? I mean, I've heard Hindus speaking. I *met* Gandhi. This number, talking of dusky answers, looks to me like some kind of a dusked-up *muzhik* in a Lilly Dache turban and sounds like Milanov trying to imitate Louis Armstrong. Anyway, the *Mahabarata*. There was no copy of it in the ship's library, but there was a sort of dictionary of Hindu terms, and I looked up *apanga*. His Awareness the swami was getting pretty personal. I remember Peter Brook telling me, when we were rehearsing the *Faust* at the Metropolitan—I don't like the work, and there was nothing in it for me really, but it was a big new production slated for opening night, and Bjoerling and Victoria were in it, and Rossi-Lemeni. I did a turn as Marthe for two performances. In any case, Peter told me that his great ambition in life is to stage the *Mahabarata*—said it might take him thirty years, but he was determined to do so. Presumably with many actors awash in *apanga*, if not *samadhi* Me as Kunti."

"Kunti. She any relation to Kundry?"

"I rather imagine a forerunner. Anyway, I suppose, with no singing voice left by then. I really should call him up and tell him Pythagoras got original sin from the thing."

"Really?"

"According to His Readiness. Got the whole thing from the *Mahabarata*—

and maybe geometry, too. Funny that Kunti begins with K. All my K. roles have been a source of pointed comment in estoeric circles. Kundry, Klytaemnestra, die Konigen der Nacht, die Kaiserin, Kostelnicka, Kabanisha, Katisha.

"Advanced ambition, public and private, seems to be entering a new dimension in our time. Small wonder Consuelo so relies upon her *sfumage*, her *ecremage*, her *decalcomania*, her powdering."

"Not to mention her Veronal."

"This afternoon I remembered what Gennaio said, when I told him I thought I might get pregnant, since we weren't—he said, 'Somewhere in evolution the idea came in that the only way a woman could be prevented from bleeding to death was to have babies.' 'What about nuns?' I asked him. 'Oh, nuns are men.' '*What?*' 'Yes,' he said, 'according to Saint Jerome and Saint John Chrysostom both. "*Once a woman prefers Jesus Christ to a husband and babies,*" says Jerome, "*she will cease to be a woman and be called a man.*" ' 'And what if she prefers singing to husbands, babies *and* Christ?' 'Then she is a martyr. And Chrysostom said of the female martyrs that they were *virile and full of manly spirit.*' "

"*Soprano* is grammatically masculine."

"The *Fanciulla* recording is a good idea, I think, but I really have to set about rejecting Destinn, after a fashion, because the next thing I remembered this afternoon was that playing with dolls was forbidden at Strasz, and how often I was let know that I had come from the nuns for a purpose both higher and other than the normal run of women. 'I have never been interested in bearing children,' she told me. 'Participation, in the propagation of the species is, artistically, an abdication.' There was however one little doll that she kept hidden away in a safe place—an Egyptian image of the black Isis, with her veil thrown back. If a man came into the house, the veil was put down over the doll's face, and it was displayed that way next to a statuette of Isis's ibis. Sometimes, during a vocal lesson, the doll would be put on the piano, the veil thrown back, and in response to my asking, 'But how do you *get* the voice out into the bubble in front of the face?' she would say 'Don't be always trying to *take* the secrets of things from me. Don't be so anxious to know if I even *possess* the knowledge you want. Only ask yourself if I am possessed of the knowledge of the nature of the Egyptian darkness. Then, when you look at the ibis, think of a parrot—and for now, become that parrot.' All *that* came back to me because talking of sacred animals, the sacred animal of Kama, the god of Love is the parrot. Well, perhaps that parrot talk of danger you're hearing on the premises, warning—a man come prowling about the house—is me, still trying for dear life to figure out what Destinn meant. Of course, if Kama is one's role—another K., notice."

He took her hand. "I've not come prowling about the house. I came to be of use to you . . . to help occasion—"

"You have—you do."

"Not enough—not readily. My existence has been too ruggedly tribal—too preoccupied with sport, with climbing, with—"

"I feel better suddenly—let's eat this food."

"It's off your chest?"

"Mannerism of speaking. You have happened by, fresh from your sport, scissored me from the saffron web of seeming, and rescued me from Kali's tiger, from Shiva's bull. Perhaps you, too, know the secret of the Egyptian darkness. Will you look at all this fish!"

"Spoken like a—Ma-ha-ba-ti. Funny how his worship's every utterance seems a ready book title. *Pointing Fingers*, for example, would do admirably for 'Dolores's' collected, or Winchell's, really—and *Kali's Tiger* is something I can imagine Gloria Gotham issuing. *Shiva's Bull*, now, is perhaps a more Paranoy title."

"Life as a commotion of titles. You know, after we'd gotten up I found myself wishing after all that Magdalen were aboard."

"Talking of pointing fingers—the two of you."

"I do miss that—it's the sole thing, but I do."

"You and Noah's wife. 'I will have my gossips!' "

"No, only the Madge, who never, so long as we've known one another, has let me go to the ladies' lounge alone."

"You have a point."

"It's just so strange—our moods . . . our moods. . ."

"You, a jolly diva lady, prey to moods?"

"I don't know. Life can't really be a matter of saffron and tee-hee-hee-hee-hee-hee-hee, now can it?"

" 'What is laughter but the cabaletta to grief?' "

"I, of course, never said any such thing—but it's not bad."

"What do you think of *Now, Voyager*?"

"It was a swell picture—in the singular."

"Well, in the plural—do you like it that way—in the plural and sans comma?"

"What for?"

"I don't know—a song cycle . . . something like that."

"Well, yes, I suppose—it's from Whitman you know."

"One could begin with Whitman."

"And then?"

"I don't know. Various things that get slipped under the door."

"I suppose you *could* sing it if y'had the tune. But it's funny, really, because last spring, you know, after the Melisande, a long cruise somewhere was suggested—the Madge and I, splashing out, cutting loose—but Sibyl said, 'I do wish you'd stay home—there's somebody coming to Town Hall.' And it was you."

"Yes, wasn't it."

"But that's not all. The mention of the cruise gave Fitz the idea for *Now, Voyager* as an opera. He thought we might be able to get Miro to compose the first act in treacherous dodecaphonic, and then switch to his own vaulting post-Janacek for the transformation—which would of course also be from alto to soprano. Then the question of the little girl in the story arose."

"John Oak and little girls?"

"He was afraid writing her would bring on a nervous breakdown, and on that note, *Now, Voyager* sank."

"So he accepted *Salome*?"

"I believe he looks on Salome as a decadent boy-girl."

"Like Shiva. *A propos*—"

"Yes?"

"Ma-a-ha-ba-ti *and* the *Mahabarata*, perhaps we ought to remember where Gypsies came from. If we're at all susceptible to tee-hee-hee-hee, we neither of us licked it off the grass, as your Countess puts it. I do love you."

"He said to her, fork in hand."

"What do I know of the *Mahabarata*, or love? Wait till I've lived, at least though the birth of the boys." The boys—or perhaps the decadent boy-girls."

VI

H.M.S. *Queen Mary*
The North Atlantic

Dearest S.D.J. (The) O' Mine,

The Guy Chum and I, your duplex-but-never-duplicitous *sissy-rones* send this (in somewhat haphazard fashion, our cursives and unicals, magiscules and miniscules of sensation all mixed up in two whirling brains) the word on our floating world the Big Mary (and all its personnel, whom I call by name—they're tagged, y'see—but whom the Guy Chum, that Homeric homo, has taken to calling, when they go about as they do coaching passengers at shuffleboard and darts, "Topside" and "Riptide" and "Row-hard" and "Stern-man" and when they're being quite fetchingly bossy at lifeboat drill, "Stroke-Oar" and "Breaker" and "Bowsprit").

For openers, let's put it this way, shall we, slightly modified, from Whitman (whom I have lately come upon the awful Prosper Swithin, former thrush, reading in the library).

The teeming lady comes
The lustrous orb
Venus oltrano
The blooming mother
Sister of the loftiest gods

More sister to you, mother more likely to all the rest but to *him*, of course, the husband, the wife (to him by whom she may bear—for to scope them is in truth to feel you twig their turn of mind) although she seems now lover, now sister, now mother—and thus resplendent in thrice-Czgowchwz ceremony. Consequence of Irishry, yes? The triple-headed goddess. Or try it this way, as copied down from the typescript of Master FROH:

and while I spend my
time listening to a foreign soprano
sing the truth
the earth is everywhere
brown and aching

We, of course, are seaborne, blue-skied, and pain free. For she's enough, the woman, with her charms and ways, her sinuous, bewitching alembic *ethyr*, to make you wish (in Uncle Virgil's immortal longing expression) you were (or to pray to God to wake tomorrow) a lesbian. (That's to say *you* do so: God's already a lesbian.)

Therefore, as she makes one feel chivalric to the point of Albigensian heresy, why not admit *The heavens on high divinely heighten her divinity with the stars and make the deserving of her deserts* (in particular, the ice cream) *her greatness deserves* and be done with it.

Without being unseemly cruel, she is at the one and the same storied time the Theban Sphinx and the *Principessa* Turandot. ("*Circa regna tonat.*") "What being," she demands, "possessed of a single instrument, has sometimes two voices, sometimes three, and sometimes four?" The answer: Mawrdew Czgowchwz—but who can say it? As Casanova remarked of the Roman castrato Giovanni Osti (called Di Borghese): "One looks (he ought to have added, one listens), the spell acts—*ubi vult spirat*; one must either fall in love or be the most stolid of Germans." Which, of course, is entirely unfair for the Bosch pay her worship as none since Frau Minne. (*Minne-Minnie*—is the *Fanciulla* rumor at all true?)

For example, what other singer of one's acquaintance could conceivably come up with the following? "Why doesn't it seem to have occurred to commentators that in *Pelleas*, Yniold, clearly a boy whose birth resulted in his mother's death, and who despises his stepmother for taking his father away from him, is *lying* to his father about what he sees through the window, thus inflaming his rage and bringing about Melisande's destruction? This is, I suppose why they so often cut the scene with the shepherd, which is the pivot of the plot. When the little monster walks away saying "*Je vais dire quelque chose a quelq'un*," you realize in a second, if you know what's going on, what it seems to have taken the author of *The Bad Seed* an entire evening to demonstrate. It makes you wonder. It certainly made Mildred Allen wonder when I brought it up in rehearsals."

It occurs to *me* that Swithin, the child, could have sung Yniold. *Potestne esse femina quae dicitur heroina materia Epopoeia?* Is it true, really, that her Oktavian debut in Vienna, when they proposed taking her along to the Sacher, she said, "I'm fucking a Czech Jew—that's him over there arguing with Karl Popper; gorgeous, isn't he? Better than a Schubert song. Is that going to make any kind of difference? It's not a question of the menu, he'll eat anything on it." Apparently, drawled it in the Viennese manner, the key operative word being *schtuppen*. You would know, no?

And finally:

> *". . .there never was a world for her*
> *Except the one she sang, and singing made."*

And yet, and yet—chiefly and yet one gets the distinct impression that she would rather *not* accept an idolatrous discourse that insists on exalting the woman (or the diva either) as a disembodied object of male praise. (Has Walter Benjamin got to her?) Especially now she's got her man (who calls you John Oak, one hears). Thus Czgowchwz, like Gorgias, teaches the relativity of meaning. Meanwhile, she and the mate drift '*over the surface of time like two swells upon the sea, one so close upon the other that neither can reach a peak and break, until both, unrealized, come to shatter coincidentally upon the shore.* ("And even as they clinked glasses did the thirsty wasps surround.")

Talking of mates, we are at something of an advantage, the moon and

I, the Chum and Beltane, the Manahans, and perhaps even poor schizo-ceramic Swithin and his male *duenna*, a creature himself out of the pantomime (absent the elaborate Dame drag, but formidable enough in mufti) on whose horns I must say the little Cockney sparrow does seem *impaled* (given to employing two words in particular, *chronic* and *killing*) whilst the pair sit together playing cards with that glassy-gaze gang of bowwows over whom the slippered swami, the *Badhralok* Bahadur holds sway. (I wholeheartedly agree with your assessment delivered dockside as they all clambered aboard, and suspect him of being an alumnus of that same University of Calculation, a shill, or verger at most, of the Self-Promotion Church of Absolute Moneyism, threading the needle to effect his karmic sutures, and I foresee the wretched Swithin—really a mad thing, a sort of lesser, gabardine Heber-Percy, a job-lot Ganymede out of what Dickens called the *frowning districts*, who rode the backs of vultures rather than of eagles, through clouds of incense rather than of glory—currently obsessed it would seem by otherwise-named Maitreyas, Koot Hoomis, and Moryas, trammeled and worn, devoured by strange Himalayan beasts, should he insist on pushing on—and up—from Benares, through Kashmir to Shangri-La, to be made lunch of like Horace Walpole's lapdog by the Alpine wolf, or the little black man who sat next to the queen of Tonga in the Coronation parade . . . but let me not commence rehashing dear old Noël's most effervescent *mots, esquises,* and *boutades.*)

I do wish one could think of the Mahatma as a harmless old wank merely, as dubious and finally as inconsequential to the general pleasure of the wicked world as the swami who hooked Willie Yeats, thus blunting even further the fine point of his infrequent pleasure, and of his little vaudeville as no more sinister or slapstick than the spectacle of the Lowells and Clare Booth Luce nosing up to the baptismal fonts and fingering the lace trim on scarlet Romish chasubles, hijinks all hardly central to the main movement of the Mind of the Age. But what if not? One wishes then to embody Lady Caution and *warn.*

Emanations, departing from their dreaming Original, go on about their business.

Pending which, let me tell you the funniest thing I've so far heard—from a rich crazy, daft as a bush, of the type still convinced that the senator from Wisconsin had the right idea, only went a bit too far. Some particle in the lounge was gassing on about India having been fascinating to America since the first transoceanic news dispatch on the Atlantic cable, which, if you please, read something like "all China open to trade . . . Christian religion allowed . . . Mutiny quelled . . . all India becoming tranquil." Whereupon the crazy, on the Mahatma: "Is that so? Well, own my feeling is this swami and his whole gang should've been subjected to Coast Guard screening. It seems obvious that their presence aboard ship is, if not so obviously conducive to outright mutiny, certainly inimical to the security of the United States of America. These are the very sorts of people who used to go around in public inciting strikes, work slowdowns, and civil disobedience."

So, you see, in certain quarters the fear is this holy wog with the glint adrift in the fabled third eye is spearheading a *movement*. He is certainly sparking a controversy, for another passenger, a liberal, of course, rounded on the accuser thus: "Is this system of secret informers, whisperers, and talebearers of such vital importance to the public welfare that it must be preserved at the cost of denying to the citizen even a modicum of the protection associated with due process?"

"Who says any of them are citizens?" was the reply. "I'd like to know more about them."

A rather more informed comparison I think might be made between Mahtama and Melville's Confidence Man on the Mississippi, together with the observation that today's Atlantic is like that Mississippi in a number of ways: its great liners like the old paddle steamers, showboats crawling with every kind of mountebank. But more than that, whisperers, talebearers, and hull-down informers do remind one of our New York, of Roman Catholic clergy, of the FBI at the Stork Club, of Hearst journalists, of I *Neriani*, of rampant gossip, the will to power, and the cult of television celebrity, et cetera, don't'cha think?

As to the coagulated votaries, whispered-tale bearers certainly, particularly the ubiquitous Swithin, from whom the more sensitive avert their gaze, as if he really were barking mad or, as my Guy puts it of the gormless, couldn't tell silly mid-off from dee leg—a mistake, I could, of course, assure the lot of them in your name, but I shan't—for he cares for two paramount things in life, orchids and extortion.

(You of course well know how he, Swithin, one night long ago, by trailing the deacon on foot all the way down Sixth Avenue to 28 West Twenty-eighth Street, found Fort Sin, taking to it like a duck to water, in spite of the fact so many men there said "so what?" to him, he concluded it was the fashion. How, holding his piece, so to speak, he lay there in the dark: the same vulgar little *coureur d'alcoves*, the same shitty little *allumeuse* in dingy robe he'd been in red cassock and white surplice or nasty little Episcopal Church–sale suit, playing at pallors and tremors, alternating languid gazes with bouts of filthy temper along the lines of the female shark so wantonly fucked by Maldoror. For to understand him, before he turned himself into a roving anecdote, like one of those ribald tales heard along the roads in days of old, making stopping at inns the pleasure it was, as you tracked them over a continent, we must go back to younger if not happier days, when the question first arose. What besides induced sleep was there to iron out the sadness and the puling petulance from that pointed little face and replace it with something more innocently open? Prezzies? Only up to a point. Beyond that point one thing and one thing only: rapacious sex.)

And *overhearing* things, like telephone numbers, and *jotting them all down*—he soon felt himself in a position with a significant remit to translate insubstantial dreaming into sorry purpose and *call in the chips*—to get the fools, so he imagined, to stump up for fear he'd cough it . . . until he picked one or two *wrong numbers*—such as that of the Chief Inspector. His recompense came in exactly two words: *skip town* (or *stumps* would end up being all that was left of his once-lissome little girlie legs: they'd have to put him on casters).

But hope springs eternal, and he may yet evade the righteous fury of the law—although the Noxious Weeds Act must surely remain the occasion of some worry.

But you know all this. I got the whole story quite free of charge from Gray Foy at the *kermasse* in Central Park, so it ought to be accurate, at least in outline and essential particulars, and anyway I could listen to that boy all night.

He would have it (Swithin) that he is an *ambiguous* creature, but the close reader sees at once that whatever ambiguity might seem to exist lasts only a moment and that few if any of the initially possible alternate meanings can be sustained. In sum: the dismal little pawn that madly thought itself the wiley rook.

No, poor Swithin's lines have not lain in pleasant places. I see him lying there on the tremble of detection: sad child upon the darkened stair; poor flaxen foundling of the upper air, an illustrated plate from *The Anathemata of Kew*, his complexion pallid as a maggot's, dreaming of black-currant lardy cakes and jam and of living in eroticized intimacy on a houseboat in the Thames. (Rinsed, but never laundered—not even naff, sergeant, simply, deluded—usually into the belief that his life would one day inevitably reach a pitch of dramatic intensity sufficient to occasion a murder.) Remembering the singing and the elocution tuition, and most of all the terrors of being flung forward and bent over black wartime radiators that gave off no heat at all while greasy hot things were rammed up his otherwise. That's his memorial legacy—of which the entail can only be a lifetime dedicated to revenge. (It must follow as the night the day.)

He is not, significantly, without resources in terms of referential pluck. It's said that once at the Everard an attaché at the German Embassy, waking to find him rifling the pockets of his overcoat, remonstrated, "*Aber was bist du?*" Swithin purred, "*Ein Tier, mein Herr, ein Tier!*"

Then, too, there are things said of him that if true are rather engaging, such as that he once held a Sunday afternoon audience of blue-rinse New York Society women and (ditto) mixed clergy spellbound when, after singing a few lovely Schubert songs he launched into "*Aber der Richtige*." (This did I hear myself from a raddled old operatic Annie at the Met *Arabella*.) Seems nobody at all knew what he was singing exactly. Imagine! And if he'd sung "Some Day My Prince Will Come," he'd have been silenced and put out on the street. Life is a . . . fill in the blank and we shall write a hit song, maybe compose a Broadway–West End musical. Two things we know it's not: a dream or a tale told by an idiot full of sound and fury signifying nothing (in itself, mind you, an example of the kind of incendiary talk that, well, gets theaters burned down. God doesn't like it, finds it a disturbance of the peace—rather, one supposes in the same way the rich American deplores loose talk of the utterly illusive falsity of it all.)

Poor dear, it really seems that a secure billet in some benevolent order of quiescent depressives ("Admit Bearer") sustained on brown rice, vegetables, and root teas is one of the only two ways likely to prevent his reverting to late-night cocktails of twisted regret, tenebrous hopes, gothic imaginings of espionage—of secret inks and letter drops and midnight assignations in curtained wagons-lits—and long, bitter denunciations. Callings out of all who've done him down, tried to drop him in, or fillet him like the day's catch. How the bloody vicar's warden would give two-and-six for the kindness, and it was bloody hard-earned, et cetera—then going out from his drum with the ferocity of a werewolf to disturb the general peace, bent of doing them a mischief as he's been done a mischief by.

The other, of course, being the lockup at Dun Ravin' somewhere beyond Ilfracombe in the farthest reaches of Cornwall, and him sustained on heavy veterinary tranquilizers or wolfsbane.

And how he watches people—watches us all, wondering do we buy his line? And loving every minute, as we for our part wonder, can the Mahatma, indeed, have assisted a victim of the most horrible of all false imprisonments to escape, or has he contrived to cast loose upon the world such an unfortunate creature whose actions it is now his duty, as it is every man's duty, mercifully to control. Which?

And yet the odd time he can be clever and winsome. "They used *berate* me in Streatham for givin' meself *airs*—said I was trying to get them to put me up on a pedestal, I said, 'A pedestal? Not really—perhaps just up on two wooden *planks* t'keep me *arse off the damp!*' "

Dharakaya, darling, Suchness, Nirvana Sunyata . . . and canasta, darling, canasta, canasta, canasta.

On board, re Swithin:

"I must say to me he seems a guileless little sprog."

"To go naked, darling, is the best disguise."

"He's certainly very sis—do you suppose there's any *boom-bah*—or does that bear thinking about?"

"Doesn't look to be, not any more. Talk has it he was once a stroppy little particle, but to look at him now—pretty *knackered*—it's hard to get a purchase on the idea. Something has befallen him."

"Yes, it has. It seems certain acquaintances threatened to do his legs for him, and they didn't mean shave and wax, you may be sure—so I don't know how guileless he can rightly be said to be."

"He seems *aerated*, and trembles like jelly."

"He is cajoled and chivvied along with a degree of difficulty."

"But must not the wind be tempered to the shorn lamb?"

"Perhaps not, dear, to the wolf in sheep's raddle. One intuits torrential rages—moorland rills in full spate. Do you know what he said to Lady Peel? '*Darling*, can you *possibly* have *any notion* in how many Windsor chairs a boy like me's been hard done by?' "

"The *crust!*"

Beltane was rather more sympathetic, offering a prospectus geared to understanding. "I feel for him," he said. "I suppose, because in some essentials we were formed alike. You're ten and eleven years of age. You wake up in the morning in the society of your own sad thoughts, and get dressed and go and sing Matins and Lauds. Then you have breakfast, go and sing Prime and Terce, and then you have singing lessons all morning. You sing most of the afternoon—Sext, Nones, with a little desultory scrum kickball or whatever you like, until the prefect comes and puts the boot in, and then you're scrubbed down in cold water, given your tea, and dispatched to sing Evensong. And then you're put to bed. Nevertheless, one feels one can read the sign across his forehead, that says *Dentem fulmnium cave*. Living in another time, and referred to sardonically as 'the good time that was had by all,' but in his own estimation a specimen of early thinnings, soon dropped from the tree to make room for the good fruit to come, and left then to shrivel on the ground.' "

(To which an emendation. This Camus cult strikes me as ridiculous, and the idea that the first and last philosophical question is the same: shall we commit suicide. Rubbish. The first and last philosophical question is surely, as Goethe put it, May others live whilst I do? The specter at the feast, though he dared not tell himself *that* dismal truth, in light of all the publicity.)

As to the others, there they sit, as hapless a lot of grounded coryphées as ever was, folding sheet upon sheet of construction paper into shapes meant to suggest the variegated silhouettes of Diva (not Deva) in a number of her most celebrated roles—and *that* ought to keep said congregation occupied the remainder of the voyage) knowing that we who know of the four voices of Mawrdew Czgowchwz are apt in consequence thereof to seem little smug, perhaps—they as a consequence feeling somewhat *comme des etres extratessesses* in relation to the oglers and the whisperers (what I remember they so charmingly called in Dublin "the "pass-remarkables") here aboard the semiofficial *Narrenschiff* of the Lost Empire. (A trifle long-winded, but we've just come, the Chum and

I, in from the music room where we've been spending an agreeable hour at Schubert's Fantasy in F Minor for (our very own) four hands—and the piano isn't in such bad nick at that.

Let us then, shall we, whilst we're in four consider these—the four Czgowchwz voices—in relation to the four voices of Woman Herself: nun's plainchant, the Siren's Song, the lullaby, and the Crone's cackle. We'd heard, I reckon, two of these sufficiently well: the Siren's Song for lo these years, and then only last spring, in the Tower Scene of *Pelleas*, the plainchant (has anything been replayed on tape so often in recorded time?). You, I suspect, may already be possessed as well of that knowledge the rest of us (always excepting the consort) have only lately been vouchsafed: she does the corncrake crone-cackle terribly well. Here's how we've come to hear it.

Following a group reading—Manahan's idea—of Chapter 40 of *Moby-Dick* ("They left it out of the picture"), the book having passed hand to hand and some of the women allowed to be sailors (indeed, I myself was the Long Island one), an almost spontaneous discussion of English masochism, sparked by the peripheral vision of the hapless Swithin—who would have been very good, indeed, as Pip, I thought—I proposed a little meditation that might well suit the Bahadur elect: on the catalogue of sails on sailing ships.

You will see straightaway how I was pirating myself and my little lyric *tragedie* of the misadventures at sea of that seasick-boy-soprano-from-Bristol-impressed-into-the-Royal-Navy, one *Buddy Bilious*: the scene in which Buddy, seeking to ascend from the body wrack of *mal de mer* toward the crystalline, aerial, sonoric Mind of Mu, attempts somewhat in the vein of Mircea Eliade's *Bengal Nights*, and vainly in the upshot—or, as I recall, what you termed the up*chuck*—attempts a meditation on the sails of the great clipper ships he's been having Coleridgian visions of, until, interrupted by Nemesis/Clapboard, happening by, is mocked, verbally scourged, and spat upon, and loses his sea biscuits, poor devil, all over his vile tormentor's shoes, and for consequence is forced by the twisted but undeniably handsome and compelling officer to undertake repressive measures.

That led to a discussion of part-singing peer humiliation in English public schools, and suddenly, rather wildly to the story of Wittgenstein's famous 1931 Confession, in which he was driven nearly to suicide by the memory of becoming violent as a schoolmaster in the Austrian Tyrol, taking the pointer to his pupils and bloodying more than a few. Then someone—a stranger to me, later identified as the ship's radio operator—said that after returning from Austria to Cambridge in 1929, he (Wittgenstein) would routinely confess to coshing those to whom he felt most drawn—"*mit der Faust oder dem Stock zu drohen—es eine Art de Liebkosung*"—together with his propensity for becoming attracted to the wounded and disabled. He also offered the following, which led to the following following it:

"To understand Wittgenstein's philosophy, or at any rate its *provenance* apart from the deep debt to Russell, its reaction to the sentimentality of Moore, its mathematical leanings, and its profound debt to Moravec, it is necessary I believe to understand the utter musicality of the brain that charged it forth, the musicality of the Second Viennese School. The *Tractatus* is really deeply indebted to Schönbergian theory, while the *Philosophical Investigations* begin by being Bergian and end by becoming a reflection in words of Webern. The music is the key, and the key is the lock is the door is the room."

"And the way out is the way in."

"Yes."

"And, of course, the room is empty."

"The beautiful room. Yes, empty. Kafka, yes. Which in Wittgetstein's case—a big *Fall* of his *Welt*—must have been the condition of eminence and the absence of fame—which of course he'd have tried to give away, the way he'd already given away all his money."

All of which led quite naturally under the circumstances of time, place, wind, and weather to a discussion of flogging in the English navy, and some speculation about whether they still—well, certainly not aboard the *Mary*, not at any rate *en plein vue*."

M.C. suddenly, reacting to all this carrying-on and to Beltane's voiced suspicions (in-lieu-of-any-spontaneous-offering-of-his-own-experiences on the Norfolk Broads) concerning the chichi swami's secret disciplines ("Tired of a life of words without meaning? Try our turkey trot of meaning without words") declared,

"It is not, in fact, up to philosophy to fill the beautiful room—which is empty because the fat lady is still in the vestibule with everybody else, enjoying a cocktail, when perhaps she really ought to be in the kitchen warming up to sing. Any minute now, as Wittgenstein well knew from his bringing up, they will all pile into the beautiful room and the *soiree musicale* will finally get off the ground."

Then, avowing the only other Gilbert and Sullivan role besides Katisha she was ever interested in was *Yeomen's* Dame Carruthers, M.C. commenced singing:

"Oh the screw may twist and the wrack may turn, and men may bleed and men may burn—" and *that* led to my emboldening the proceedings further with my "Furling Rime" M.C., never to be outdone in the pivoting of turns, decided to bolster my farrago—and you remember the tune: from the *Yeomen's* yeomen's chorus to bolster the Carruthers broadside. (More than a passing nod here to the great tradition of the English glee. You remember the glee: that form by which from the death of Handel to the rise of Mendelssohn secular part singing was carried on in England—and not only there: I believe at Harvard and Yale. Are there not still things called glee *clubs*? Simultaneity (somewhat in the manner of Tibetan monks singing whole chords individually). M.C., then dilating on the vertiginous soprano rhapsody "Ah, Sweet Mystery of Life" (something else, as it turns out, she learned from the nuns), let us know for our edification in the meanwhile that "Victor Herbert was Irish." The whole thing sounded something very like the following looks.

PICKERSGILL

Sorting, mending
All depending
Delving, welding
Quite intending
To be seriously weary
Languid and yet chanticleery
And all its horde
Whilst conceiving
Faintly grieving
O'er some bygone Summer's evening. . . .
To the stories
Of old glories
All for love
And all for Allegory—Oh,
Flying jib jib foretopmost staysail
Foresail lower foretopsail
Upperforetopsail foretopgallantsail
Foreroyal foreskysail lower topgallant staysail
Foreroyal studdingsail foretopgallant studdingsail
Foreroyal studdingsail maintopgallant staysail
Mainroyal staysail mainsail
Lowermain topsail uppermain topsail
Maintopmost studingsail maintopgallant studingsail
Mainroyal studdingsail mizzen staysail
Mizzenroyal staysail mizzensail
Lowewrmizzen topsail uppermizzen topsail
Mizzenroyal mizzenskysail . . . spanker

MAWRDEW CZGOWCHWZ

Oh, the screw may twist
And the rack may turn
And men may bleed
And men may burn
O'er London Tower

I keep my silent
Watch and ward. . . .
O'er London Tower
And all its horde
I keep, I keep my
Silent watch and ward—
Ah, sweet
Mystery of Life could
I but find you. . .
Ah, could I
But know the
Meaning of
It all.
All the
Yearning etc.

"Spank 'er *again!*" a voice, not one of ours, cool as paint, barked from somewhere updeck, followed on the same downwind, aftershock by the offended, panicked (female) ejaculation.

"*Mister Swithin!*"

"Bags. I get to Jolly Roger 'fore the mast!"

"Mister *Swithin—really!*"

"Oh, sod off, you silly bitch, can't you see *it's all a lark!*"

Murmuring became general. So much, I thought to myself, for the enantiodromia of that soul on the tremble of detection. (Never attempt to combat wickedness as if it were something sprung up outside the self: Augustine of Hippo). I felt sorry for Swithin; indeed, I almost liked him, poor little chaffinch. All his life he's been desperate to make people laugh, and there's not the least mystery as to why: that awful, annihilating terror of being ridiculed: the very worst and most characteristic English fear. (Fear itself you might say.) The desperate fear that uses overrefined diction to mask (therefore surely betraying) a fatal native coarseness. The very one, of course, that has been all along his trump card—his only passport, talking of cards, out of the Vedic haze, out of a twilight life of bridge, bad novels, and social fatuity, of the antiques shop and the semidetached in the better part of Wimbledon. I could suddenly believe that his Fréhel and Lys Gauty impersonations had become legendary in the *Little Revue* at the Cherry Grove Playhouse and that there was some justification for his adopting the attitude of the undaunted and irrepressible Peggy Hopkins Joyce (and is it true—for you must know—as Winchell asserts, that she met her latest heartthrob, the young Brooklyn stripling, in the men's room at the Stork Club?) that "a girl should always be a little superior, and especially when she has a speaking part."

Another voice, from somewhere above us admonished severely, "Delight—top-gallant delight is to him who acknowledges no lord or law but the Lord his God, and is only patriot to heaven!"

"Ah," said I out loud into the breach, once more glad of the opportunity, to prescribe. "Allegory. She the figurative warbler who speaking otherwise speaks to one and all in a sublime confusion and, schemer that she ever was and is, lurking in our intention, would have us own that one thing signify another, or might so, or might as well, just in case."

"Metaphor's all right," the cynic advanced, "as far as it goes; I prefer men, myself."

I cannot let such a slur pass without rejoinder. Give me ten metaphors that are stouthearted metaphors that will fight for what metaphors adore. Give me ten metaphors that are—and I'll soon give you et cetera.

Sniffers at tiffin on the old veranda. Gadabout tongues the equal of any to be found in Lyons Corner House or the Ritz legendary lofty-chattery cafe.

All said and done, a word in your ear. Do be wary of your venerable director's young Irish cousin. Naiose O'Heither, known to you and bound for New York. "Naoise O' *here*, Naoise O *there*, O chancers beware, Naoise O *everywhere*!" is one you hear, and of course "*Amnesia O' Whore.*" And they will say, won't they, that where there's smoke there's tobacco and small boys—and they who go on saying it are, of course, your Irish Cigarettes—in this case dear, *Cork-tipped*. (Just so you know.)

Ten thousand metamorphoses, *darlinghino*, could I detail you before the sunset, but the one I hope you'll like best is that because we all missed you so, My Guy the Chum doing a not at all bad imitation of your dreamy Broadway drawl, broke out into "I hear singing, and there's no-one there" to which Czgowchwz immediately responded, "Y' don't need analyzing; it is not so surprising," whereupon I chirped in with the reprise of "Sorting, mending," and this Manahan person (who seems to have been sent along by either Fate or Orphrey Whither to stand in for you) broke out into the first chorus of the *Libiamo*. The bijou quartet effect, therefore (*et cantare pares et respondere parati*), dear, rather in the manner of the stanzas of your *Under Nephin*, which, though I say it as shouldn't, ought to have been taped, was as follows.

CHOLMONDELEY MANAHAN	CZGOWCHWZ	PICKERSGILL
I hear singing	Y'don't need ana-	Sorting, mending
Libiamo nell'		
And there's no	Lysing, it is not	All depending
lieti calici		
One there	So surprising	Delving, welding etc.
etc.		
I smell blossoms	That you feel very	Quite intending
And the trees are	Strange but nice	To be seriously weary
Bare. All day long	Your heart goes	Languid and yet
I seem to walk on	Pitter-patter. I	Chanticleery
Air. I wonder why	Know just what's	Whilst conceiving
I wonder why	The matter because	Faintly grieving
I've been there	O'er some bygone	
Once or twice....	Summer evening	
I keep tossing in	Put your head on	To the stories
My sleep at	My shoulder	Of old glories
Night and what's	You need someone	All for love
More I've lost	Who's older	And all for
My appetite....	A rubdown with	Allegory
Stars that used	A velvet glove	
To twinkle in	There is nothing you	
The skies are	Can take to relieve	
Twinkling in	That pleasant ache	
My eyes	You're not sick	
I wonder why	You're just in love	

Ship's bells rang salutation; th'Atlantic hove. Enough for now for you from me, I think. Left to my own devices I know I could go on with the aim of entertaining your fancies the more—for here in my cave of the heart *I see lots of things you blazing beauties make invisible by the light of your own glory.*

But something too much of this—protestations of affection bordering on mash notes, and me a married geezer. In spite of the fact that I should not like to think of our relationship as consisting entirely of dissections of motive, and allowing for the fact that as Augustine said to God—complaining of the seductive power of music—in your eyes I have become a question to myself, and that is my infirmity. (The Guy asked me did I ever think along the lines of forging the uncreated conscience of the race? I said, in the first instance the race I presume held in question is only about seventy years old, so what's the rush, and in the second instance as things stand they have you up both for forgery and for in certain instances, even around Halloween, Christmas, and Mardi Gras and absent three articles of male clothing, ascribing in the public street to the conscience of said race out loud.)

Oh, well, Classical Moderations, *Literae Humaniores*, congratulatory viva, and still a sentimental lad, though not, withal from Shropshire, from Streatham. With the odd desire to quite retire and with one's friend make life entire a thing removed from the muck and mire of a world ruled over by fools and liars, and live next sites of bare ruin'd choirs, in a houseboat buttressed with old spare tyres on the Oxford Canal, hard by Aubrey's Bridge, at Thrupp.

But one was beginning to talk about you.

I do believe that no matter what—whether it turns out by Thanksgiving and after the *Under Nephin* launch (which, as you well know, only the fucking Michelmas term—*et penitos toto divisos orbe Britannos*—would, and will, make us miss, but only, haply, this last time) that you've gone straight as Cuchulainn's spear, or at Epiphany that you're queer as Dick's hatband, or even that after a Shrovetide of prayer and meditation and another season free of operatic commitments and every-nighting at the ballet (where as you pointed out to me, you can sometimes hear the Irish dancing below stairs), you're still poised in that wildly provocative attitude, hair in the wind, at whatever station of the Via Dolorosa between the True Blue and the Lavender, the last thing you, a druidic Irish Dissenter, desire or require is an adoring English Catholic complication, especially one so *hung up*, as your new expression goes, on such a work as the *Incendium Amoris* of Rolle (which work I have kept by me lo these many years, the way you once told me you kept the *De imitatio Christi* of Thomas à Kempis). Ah my soul's beau ideal, Richard Hermit, of whom it is written *he studied at Oxford until he was 19 and left without a degree. Back in Yorkshire, he ran away from home after making a rough and ready hermit's habit out of his father's rain hood and two of his sister's frocks.* If that ain't English Catholicism in a (rough-and-ready) nutshell. *Two* of his sister's frocks! Well, he was obviously a big-broad Yorkshire boy. And in drag he'd have been a *big broad, period*, so you see it's just as well.

What we, my Guy and I, shall cherish 'til Fortune flings us stateside next, is the kindness your great Irish heart has shown us in Manhattan. And your utmost savvy. You may not as you have insisted be among those who wholeheartedly embrace Whitman as Progenitor, but I do see in you par excellence his stance:

> *Looking with side-curved head curious what will come next,*
> *Both in and out of the game and watching and wondering at it.*

So, when the tennis gets a little too rough, should it do, send for us. We shall behave as little like the Sassanach as ever we've learnt how. We shall live at the Sloane House; we shall work in a box office (City Center perhaps, as we, too, could be quite as happy as you are evening after evening looking in at the company in their glory) or a bookstore, in the checkroom at the Museum of Modern Art, or as fact-checkers on Forty-third Street—anything but char at that piggery down on St. Marks Place.

As to the career, although both of us went to school to him (and like him in the company of the burly sons of burly centurions), neither of us is, alas, fated to be a Horace (not even a Horace Walpole). Nonetheless, we shall continue straight scout as one man with *primus and forever a full heart—brimfull, bubbling, sparkling, and running over like the flagon in your hand, my lord.* (And for pity sake, *don't* be *sensitive* about being rich . . . it gives *such* a bad example. Your coeval Merrill isn't, and although his money is so new it squeals, you both, as I understand it got your fortunes from pirates.)

And *secundo, the necessity of bestirring himself to procure his yams.* Just remember, "whosoever studieth in the universities, who professeth the liberall sciences and to be short who can live idly and without manual labor and will beare the port, charge and countenance of a gentleman, he shall be called *master.*"

Talking of cabaret (and of certain port charges consequent upon immigration), my dream *is* to do cabaret (not the charabanc cabaret of the Sitwell-Graveses, thought in social circles to be literary and seen in literary circles as mainly socialite), but like your quirky friend Lehrer. First off, I know you must always call the place "the room" and learn how "to work the room" so the first thing I'd do is say, "What a nice room! (*Room,* not *ruhm,* as you've told me—the more not to sound the likes of that appalling little blond shit walking around New York wearing my Christian name assisting that rather grim Singhalese and the even grimmer rich poetess at River House with *Poetry London–New York.* When he sits there cross-legged, babbling things like "I name thee, O Shakuntala, and all at once is said," it's all one can do not to round on him declaring, in so many words, "And I *read,* you, O smarmy little cunt, and all at once is read!")

Then I'd open with a number that was the rage of England just after the Great War, "I've Never Seen a Straight Banana." Then a medley. The Chum to tickle the ivories, interjecting points. I'd tell jokes going back to Archy, Charles the First's famous jester who so tormented the appalling Laud. But I would—I shall—endeavor, stage by stage, to assimilate. A kind old hand recently advised me that *it is imperative, if Britons are not to misunderstand their fellow-speaking democrats in the United States, which lacks, due to its traditional definition in terms of nothing but the atomic Cartesian, Lockean and Humean* laissez-faire *assumptions of modern political and economic theory and non-conformist Protestantism, without any compromise with medieval, hierarchal, religious and political forms being set against a background of nothing but nature, a past.*

(Bet you didn't know Descartes, with a little help from Locke and Hume, thought up the atomic bomb. Think I can get all that into a song? Lehrer does.)

Against a background of nothing but nature. It does seems to be too true that for the artist: the poet, the choreographer—vide Mr. B.—to succeed to the very heights, he must forsake the society of the men-y and go along alone towards Parnassian precincts to hang out with the girls, stern task mistresses they be, who if crossed will assuredly all of them line up in a *planche* phalanx against the betrayer—like the Willis behind Myrtha, and in one single mute nullifying voice twist the poor bastard into herniated, braided licorice. Therefore, surely is yours the wiser course towards home—from home towards home, one might well say, but one seems to remember having already heard those selfsame words said by you—and why you spend so much time on that strange and wonderful island surrounded by the wrecks of nineteenth-century ships.

Kierkegaard says, don't he, that Life can only be understood backward, but must be lived forward. The Chum meanwhile insists, "You must alert the O'Maurigan to the ululations of this Baba Ga-ga, who seems like certain animals to have a real aptitude for the infinite plasticity of superficial characteristics." (We have dubbed him the Mahatma Bahadur-Baksheesh Sing-Sing.) "The last thing alive Mawrdew Czgowchwz must be encouraged to become is *Shahnti* Irish!" (You could call Chum a skeptic, perhaps a little too under the influence of Hume.) I told him you'd had advance word about the old wank and was on the case even as we spoke at sea.

Live forward, *darlinghino*—making your way to the rostrum of the Gotham Book Mart and intoning there the very words cried out by Amhairghin as he sailed into Kenmare Harbour calling the rivers and mountains, the animals and the spirits in stones: *Ailiu Iath n-hErend!* Take a note now and then in mirror writing . . . and in the meantime, don't worry about the woman of your soul's charge: *Elle est bien entourée, et c'est la mer ainsi qui ordonne a travers elle. C'est ca.*

Yours in all chores,
Christabel

P.S. Did you know many once believed female singers did not menstruate because the neck and the throat had a deep connection with womb's door—and blood flow would so deplete vital heat as to prevent the necessary combustion . . . or something like that? It's occurred to me that in some sense, we think of goddesses like Mawrdew Czgowchwz in this vein—as if, for example, they (in this instance She) are thought of as perennially pregnant—by us, with us . . . or something like that. What do you think?

P.P.S. Strange gnomic words overheard this evening on the Promenade Deck: "Sad isn't it, that when Hart Crane jumped off the stern of that boat nobody so much as threw him a life saver?" Soft laughter in the seaborne twilight. People can be very cruel.

*

A sudden squall came up from nowhere in the late afternoon. As the *Queen Mary* began to pitch and roll and tables slid from port to starboard, voyagers took to their cabins. Canasta became impossible for the Bahadur secession. A careless passerby spilled gin and bitters all over Prosper Swithin, who began to cry, softly, rallying his coreligionists to his side and removing the others entirely from the veranda lounge to the cinema and the revivifying glamor of Marilyn Monroe in *Bus Stop.*

Jacob went out and walked the deck. The vessel's slippery, shifting ground became as if alive: the floor that breathes gained a kind of topographical reality. Peril, real or imagined, he thought, keeps knights and knaves alike alert.

("This is almost Homeric!" a passenger exulted. "Oh, I hope not," his companion demurred. "Homer's tempests are overlong, sea-technical, and tortuous.") Jacob climbed to top deck, unfurling a fantasy of crow's nests, flying jibs, foreskysails, topgallants billowing spankers and flaming corposants from Hakluyt. How truly, he marked, do storms at sea betoken the agitated life of man.

*

"Have you seen *Bus Stop*?" Kit Pickersgill asked Mawrdew Czgowchwz, in the music room, as he played through Chopin's ballades and the storm raged outside.

"Yes, in New York. She's sensational in it."

"Do you know her—or have you met?"

"Never. Orphrey Whither's promised to introduce us. Somehow I can't believe she's really corporeal; she's so overwhelming on the screen; it's as though she could only possibly exist in those dimensions, as a kind of abstract of loveliness."

"Yes, she's a bit like Moby-Dick."

"She *is*?"

"Do you know it?"

"I do not, neither the film nor the book. We'd thought of going to it last night, but thought it might be, well, cheating. And, frankly, Gregory Peck? Someone said there had been an earlier version, with Barrymore."

"Yes there was—with a woman put into it."

"For good measure."

"For good box office, I should have thought. But I've been told it was that—the picture itself, not the woman—that was responsible for the re-issue of the book after seventy years."

"I've seen it sitting there in the library—not the kind of thing, one imagines, for a voyage like this. One hears it said all the time, everywhere, that it is the great American epic. Is it that, do you think?"

"Oh, *yes*, without question," Pickersgill affirmed, looking out the streaked windows at the rough sea. "Nothing else at all compares to it."

"I do remember *Wonderful Town*, with Rosalind Russell, and the line that got the biggest laugh of the evening—I think it was Dody Goodman's—'I was reading *Moby-Dick* last night. . . . It's about this *whale*.' I'm afraid the only other thing whales ever make me think of is Nelson Eddie's voice."

"Oh?"

"Yes, he's the voice of Willy the Operatic Whale—a cartoon. They say whales actually do sing, don't they?"

"Anyway, to learn how to have that affect on people Monroe has—but then you do!"

"I don't think so. No. Not *that* effect."

"But you will—when *Pilgrim Soul* plays theaters. They'll be going mad in their droves. You'll see—you'll hear from them."

"If and when it—who was it said, 'What one can do, another can do again.' "

"What?"

"What—oh, sorry, an expression I've remembered hearing—don't remember where. 'What one can do, another can do again.' Sounds—I don't know—fishy, somehow."

"I agree with Mr. Pickersgill," a voice declared, and there once again stood Miranda Maev Manahan. "And he plays beautifully as well."

"Oh . . . well, thank you—on both counts."

"I'm awfully sorry, I don't mean to interrupt, truly I don't."

"You aren't interrupting, dear."

"Sometimes I so badly want to be forty."

"I'm that and more—that's one thing another can—but don't be wishing your life away so: it's unsettling—alarming."

"I'm that and more. Manahan agrees with me that the boy who cried wolf was only clairvoyant, and so got his, the way they do, but that the boy who said the emperor had no clothes on was a dangerous sociopath. I think this tub has stopped rocking."

"Would you like to take a walk on the Promenade Deck? I think Mr. Pickersgill will excuse us, at least as women."

"I shall do more than that, I shall absent myself directly. *A tout a l'heure Mesdames.*"

"I wonder if it would help me get up the courage to ask you *the* question," the girl said all at once.

"Uh-oh. Well, look, perhaps you'd better ask *that* question in here, just in case you don't get the answer you're looking for."

"Or, I could ask a question without looking for an answer."

"Just warming up—a few simple scales: that kind of thing?"

"Oh—you've cried wolf! You're *clairvoyant*—you are!"

"*You* are histrionic—you realize that."

"Warming up . . . simple scales—you know *exactly* what *the* question is."

"Oh? Terrific. Now tell me this: Do-I-know-that-you-know-that-I-know what *the* question is?"

"I can't bear it. The question is, of course, Would you ever give me a lesson? There, I've said it, and only this morning I *knew* for sure that I didn't, and never would have the neck to!"

"A lesson? A lesson in what?"

"Singing! It was *her*, that's what it was—I've just realized. Her singing 'That Old Black Magic' made me just bold enough—funny, though, that I haven't fainted away. Manahan's right: I have no shame."

"I've never had a lot of it myself. A woman who took me out of a convent when I was a lot younger than you are now told me—on the way to the castle I was to live in with her—not to bother with it."

"Gosh."

"You may well add."

"A castle—in Bohemia?"

Suddenly Mawrdew Czgowchwz heard nuns chanting, children wailing, a man laughing, a woman singing—from Smetana's *Libuse.*

"In Bohemia, yes: in a lovely place called Strážˇ. All right," she continued, sitting herself down at the Bechstein, "how do you want to begin—with something familiar?"

"I can manage the whole of the '*Libiamo.*' "

"Don't you dare—you're much too . . . young."

"You mean small. I realize I shall have to step into some very tall heels before we ever see eye to eye."

"Do you know '*O cessate*' "?

"Yes, and '*Caro mio ben*'—and, for the matter of that, '*A-vous dirai-je, Maman?*' I can sing more insipid music than I—Uh-oh. Look, I'll sing anything you like."

"It must be something sensible—not like the '*Libiamo.*' "

" '*Voi lo sapete*'?"

"Only kidding—what about '*Voi che sapete*'?"

"Well—all right, yes."

"Cherubino was your debut, wasn't, it?"

"Yes—yes, it was."

> *"Voi che sapete che cosa e l'amor,*
> *Donne vedete s'io l'ho nel cuor. . ."*

"That was quite good," the diva assured the devotee. "Quite grasped. You clearly haven't been wasting your time in the distant woods, no matter how many parties you may have missed. I put it that way because if this is the kind of thing you want to do—"

"I'd kill to sing. Didn't you absolutely always want to sing?"

"I was meant to be a nun—to sing that way."

"You and Norma—you showed them. *You* showed them all it wasn't necessary to jump into any fire, either, simply because you'd decided to go out and live life, didn't you—*voi che sapevate che cosa e l'amor.*

"Now I want to sing something just for fun, though it's serious, too; shows the way I feel about things."

"Yes, go ahead. Serious things done in fun are that important."

Miranda Maev, standing hand on hip, belted:

> *"You ask I got to be the star I am,*
> *The very brightest of the stars that I am.*

I'll try to tell you how it came to be
And, and if you like you may quite me.
When I was only seven I learned to walk
But I developed a kind of shake.
I was embarrassed, but everyone said
A walk like that just goes to make...
Talent,
Bee-doup-dee-doop-dee-doup-dee-doup dee.
Talent,
Bee-doup-dee-doop-dee-doup-dee-doup-dee.
In school my grades were not so hot,
But you should see the marks I got for
Talent.
When I was only eleven I learned to talk,
But the words seldom came out right.
I was embarrassed, but everyone said
Why that's so original and you're so bright, you've got
Talent,
Bee-doup-dee-doop-dee-doup-dee-doup-dee,
Talent,
Bee-doup-dee-doop-dee-doo-doup-dee-dee.
Now you may doubt that this is so,
But they said at Actors Studio it's
Talent.
To all you aspiring young boys and girls
Who desire success.
I say 'Work hard and study hard and lead clean lives!'
But that's only a guess.
And when I'm twenty-nine I hope to have
The Oscar they say I'll earn,
Because they're doing a version of War and Peace
And Mr. Tolstoy said I'd be just wonderful as Peace—

I wonder who's playing War.
Talent.
Bee-doup-dee-doup-dee-doup-dee-doup-dee.
I must leave, it's getting late
For Forty-twenty-thirty-eight, that's me!
Talent! Dee-doup-dee-doup-dee-doup-dee-doup-dee!"

Mawrdew Czgowchwz, that nonplussed, wondered whether...

"That was lovely, too, dear, in it's way, although I didn't—"

"Get the ending, with the digits? Manahan explained it to me."

"He *did?*"

"Yes—did you see the show?"

"Well, yes, we did; Jacob has a friend in it."

"The funny English lady? Oh, she's *very* good. Yes, Manahan says the business with the digits is typical American humor; they all do it with their Social Security numbers."

"Oh, is that it?"

"Silly, no? But it brought down the house; that and the man in the frocks taking off Bette Davis and Tallulah Bankhead. I thought it might be a good audition piece for Zerbinetta—I already have all the top notes, I thought it would show the *zing*."

"It is a thought."

"I hope Miranda hasn't—"

"She most certainly hasn't. Anyway she must continue—singing that is."

"Oh, yes, well, we did think that—she does, does she?"

"I'm afraid so; I'm afraid, too, that I was having something of a déjà vue. You see, I was a *very* difficult girl."

"We can't do a thing with her, and I'm afraid I'm losing faith in convent schools."

"There's this to be said for them: one meets one's match, in temperament, in singularity, particularly in Ireland—and we are Irish: bound away, as they say, on some strange course."

"I was hoping we were on due course for home."

"I've given her a song to work on—a lovely Catalan song about a girl who's kidnapped and taken aboard a ship."

"Oh."

"It's the right thing for her voice just now."

"I don't know why," Manahan declared, "but I find that comforting. Lately she's developed a passion for strange recitations, such as 'The Lament of the Hag of Beare.' A lovely Catalan song about a kidnapped girl is more than likely just the thing right now, after all."

The Manahans left the pupil and the teacher to their work.

"About those exercises you gave me to look at."

"Yes?"

"Mother says you told her every morning and every afternoon for a *year!*"

"Not a day less."

"They're not very interesting."

"I'll tell Madame Marchesi so, next time I get her on the astral plane. They're the drill—take it or leave it. At year's end, there may be a voice that's forgotten '*singing, la voce in gallata.*' "

"What happens then?"

"As I recall, one turns the book upside down and starts again, front to back."

"I can hear Manahan now. 'Miranda, would you like to go sit on a tuffet someplace and practice solfège?' Actually, it would give him the greatest parental satisfaction to know I was bound and articled and gainfully employed. His greatest thrill—greater than any thrill of first-nighting—was always the first day of the autumn term."

"You know you exaggerate."

"When I was born—in the Mater hospital—the nuns may have neglected to carry me upstairs first, thereby inclining me to downward ways. He's been heard to—perhaps if I were permitted to practice only *ascending* scales?"

"Those are clearly metaphysical speculations. My father was a metaphysician—or was he *anti*-metaphysician? In any case, the voice must neither incline nor decline so much as *recline*, stretch, and *attend*, like a cat."

*

They were nearing Cobh harbor and could see clearly the lighter awaiting their arrival.

"Back there," said Miranda, "we passed it earlier this morning, is the Beare Peninsula."

"Where the hag comes from," remarked Mawrdew Czhowchwz.

"'My body seeks to make its way
to the House of Judgment;
when the Son of God thinks it time,
let him come and claim his loan.
My arms when they are seen
are bony and thin;
dear was the craft they practiced,
they would be around glorious kings.
My arms when they are seen
are bony and thin;
they are not, I trow, worth raising
around handsome youth. . . .
I speak no honied words,
no wethers are killed for my wedding;
my hair is scant and grey,
it is no loss to have a miserable veil over it.
Little do I care
that there is a white veil on my head;
I had a covering of every good color on my head
as we drank good ale.
I envy nothing that is old; except the Plain of Femhen;
though I have donned the thatch of age,
Femhen's crown is still yellow.
The Stone of the Kings in Femhen,

Ronan's fort in Breghon,
It is long since storms first reached them,
But their cheeks are not old and withered.
I have had my day with kings,
drinking mead and wine; today I drink whey and water
Among shriveled old hags. . .
The flood-wave and the swift ebb;
What the flood brings you the ebb carries from your hand.
Happy is the island of the great sea,
For the flood comes to it after the ebb;
As for me, I do not expect flood after ebb to come to me.' "

"But of course, you sang it in the Irish, didn't you—at the end of *Tristan und Isolde*."

"So they, tell me."

"Oh, I *love* that song! *To hold a man in your arms is wonderful, wonderful, in every way, so they say.*' "

*

Voices (English) yelling down the gangplank to disembarking passengers
"We're in the book, give us a bell—say you will!"
"Been, a *hoot*—give us a toot!"
"We shall never forget you, any of you."
"You've stolen our hearts away—absolute *robbery* on the high *seas!*"
"No, darlings, really—*jamais de la* vie, promise you, honor bright!"

VII

Whither Park
Co. Limerick
Michelmas

I flatter myself, dear sister, that I give you pleasure in letting you know I have safely passed the sea.

(So to speak.)

Dearest,

Pursuant to wobbling in the lighter in Cobh harbour, a night at the Metropole, and many interrogations (entirely too many, and entirely too many of the *Duirt bean liom go duirt bean lei* variety) and a most engrossing parlour with Miss Joan Denise Moriatry, high priestess of dance in Ireland, but of course you knew that. Strange woman. Redhead. Born in 1916, or thereabouts. Gallant crusader against the Republic's ban on the second position. (That's one you never told me—no wonder Ninette de Valois got out and never looked back.) Is obsessed with notions of a ballet on *Pilgrim Soul*, but also dreams of one on *Riders to the Sea* and one on Edel Quinn' s progress from the company of the Dublin whores to that of the consumptives in the Congo. Feels it's timely. I said it seems to me what's timely is the murder trial of Mamie Cadden. I told her if she were to do one on that woman, she'd be the Martha Graham of Ireland, even if she had to go to London to get it done.

Then, later, at a little supper in the hotel, a proposition in earnest: would one care at all to have a little demonstration by one of Miss Moriarty's avowed disciples of what he called "the renowned Denise method." One fell flat for it, of course, whereupon the lissome little card stood there in first position, solemnly intoning, while dipping into demi-plié, "De knees *out*, de knees *in*, de knees *out*, de knees in..."

And so finally, after rattling in the Armstrong Siddeley up the narrow roads of County Cork into those of County Limerick, into the long, curving gravel-lined drive past great clumps of the most amazing beeches, their trunks like alabaster columns and he we all are, safe as big houses within the gates at Whither Park, due to stop the goods of a month, while shadows on hillsides do lengthening fall. And I must say right off Destinn's incredible gabled, turreted, groin-ceilinged, crocketed, and finialed *Schloss* at Strážˇ thirty-three years ago was no match for it (even with the strange luster imparted by the legends that Schubert had stayed there, and played there, and encountered the undines there).

Your tireless description of Orphrey's demesne's crenellated stones aforesaid sentinel beeches, coppiced ash, avenue of larches, its acacia *berceau* and palm-treed winter garden, its monkey-puzzle trees (and what *are* they? They're a mite unnerving) was no exaggeration: something the lackadaisical Bord Fáilte ought, should they ever decide, in the proprietor's own formulation, to actually admit of Ireland rather than only hint at it, emulate.

Although it occurs to me as I say it that the place *was* occupied by Fenians in the Civil War—much the same as Bowen's Court below, in Cork, but the difference, according to O.W. is rather telling. Here, as there, all the good stuff was stashed away before the lads came calling —here down below in the adjacent caves, accessible from the kitchen. Which, of course, they, the Regulars, hardly ever left, being good boys attached to the hearth at heart except to go up to the library to be read to. Now, at Bowen's Court it is reported they liked to be read *Kipling*, if you please—whereas here, Orphrey insists, they spent the whole of their stay engrossed in *Melmoth the Wanderer*, reveling in the reported cruelties of the Spanish Inquisition.

In any event, what a pile, and what a misted season for sitting housed in it, sheltered, recollecting, tilting the repercussive ambivalence, and trying to rearrange and press before they wilt away entirely the blooms spring's awakening, of summer's carouse—and now your pal is knocked up.

It is the truth: the village biddy midwife confirms it. ("Tis in the eyes, Missus, and faith I wouldn't like t' be affrightin' ye, but I'd stake me gift on there's two little chislers comin' t'ye—but sure let there not be a bother on ye fer it, with them paps. Be God, some of these girleens today—well, it'd put you in mind of the knobs on turbots, so it would, not that they give shite fer it what with the bottles and the *formulas* and that.") Yerwoman is said to be *piseogai*, so it's as well to listen—although the persistent rumor that she may while you're looking at her turn into a hare and go off and clean what milk and butter there be in the parish is a fairy tale.

(*So?*)

And in the cook's tea leaves as well ("Sure I get a feelin' in me *wather!*"), and so the good Limerick household staff start in with the prayers to St. Munchin (patron of the county, did you know?) with whom as a Galwegian one is not acquainted.

Plus which, the cures (is it an ailment, really? I suppose so, what with original sin and everything). Anyway for the cleansing of the blood, breakfasts of young nettles, culled each spring and stored in the press, it seems, against the servant girls' confinements—all of which are by the way in this district jollily managed with nary a whist to the *priesht* (who, in any event, we're told is so pious he always forgets: what I say is he's a *day-sint* little one who's got the goods as some few of them do). For the chills, dry mustard in hot water (English, of course, but no bother on it for that, so) to soak the feet and calves and never go above the very bottom of the knee), carrageen, of course, for the rheum, and what's this else—oh, yes, porter ale and an egg in it once at the noonday meal (called dinner, as well you know).

"And don't be lettin' them lay you out flat, Missus, and swing a *pen-*

ju-lem over you fer t' know are ye carrying forward. That was tried here once, and the poor one lay hypno-*tized* in a stupor for weeks and, when she came to, had no memory at all of bein' *married*—which didn't sit so well with Himself that'd married her."

Orphrey in the meanwhile—storming all over the place in his bespoke three-piece dark green heather-fleck thornproof tweed, his sturdy brogues, and his black priest's hat, wielding some ancient ashplant stick, acting the *fear an teach* as if auditioning for MacLiammoir—demands a thorough examination of the premises—mine. Your woman here refers all seekers to the father. He is a very winsome fellow as you know and keeps a pilot's log, entirely in neumes, he is pleased to call *Voyagenesis*.

Whereas, I woke up this morning singing (remember Bebe Daniels: "Sing Something in the Morning") or rather waking from a dream of singing "*Nous n'avons pas toujours vingt ans.*" "Vingt *ans? Nou n'aurons pas encore quarante!*" As they all say on the Line: "She carries on, regardless." (Although of two minds. The romping of sturdy children may be just the thing for Ireland's fields and villages, but for the singer's diaphragm? Of course, at this stage I don't believe they quite romp.)

Jacob's other journal (the one in prose): all affective fluctuation dutifully recorded, and those, too, in the weather—abounding in the hyle and fabric of our lives. The weather without/within: the drops in barometric pressure aligned with the hormonal soughs occasioned in *Mopy-Diva* by the invasion upon life's ground by them we speak of in guarded voices, not yet prepared, apparently to address them, except perhaps by general assent (hope they like it) eyes turned up, down, or sideways.

Jacob himself: all elation. Much preoccupied, he fidgets, he neglects to vocalize—and then, like now this minute, one hears him in another room, humming first the cello part of Bloch's *Schlomo*—he has a *thing* about it—then Saint-Saëns's clarinet sonata, and then at the piano, going through that long and languorous introduction to "Morgen" and then again the voice—the *voice!* Well, they can go on about mine all they want: when I hear his it's like hearing Victoria's—as even, as strong, as crystalline: no break at all on D–F-flat–E, none. I don't care if I ever make another sound—and then he'll stop, and then the silence and the suspense is something almost like another kind of song. Then he's like to rip through *Comfort Ye* or *Every Valley* . . . and the descending trills are the very equal of the Callas coloration in "Qui la voce" and if that isn't, as they say, a new thrill in Handel . . . until at length either he breaks into Idabelle Firestone's "If I could tell you/Of my devotion etc." for which, I can't say exactly why, he has developed a real affection, or pokes his head in here, saying he's off for a little, riding the roan palfrey Tantivy to Sui Finn and the old sun priests' Hill of Aine at Knockainy-by-Hospital. (These are but grand names to me, still as I sit, remembering that Pegasus, a pet of his in the night sky, was a monster sprung from the neck of the slain Medusa. Not that we have to hold a brief for every female in the old earth, but as one of the names Ralph uses for Neri in the *Nericon* was "Medusa Niente.") He goes into the pub here and samples gillars and pickled eels. He gathers pertinent information the way he gathers rampion, in fistfuls. He says if he cannot (yet) have samphire, he will have rampion. He almost appears to have forgotten the theater . . . but I tell you, he is the very ditty Marie Lloyd used to sing come real: everything he does *is so* artistic. Then, as now, he and Orphrey speed off in sputters in the Delage into Limerick City.

"And the azurous hung hills are his world-wielding shoulder
Majestic—as a stallion stalwart, very-violet-sweet!—
These things, these things were here and but the beholder
Wanting; which two when they once meet,
The heart rears wings bold and bolder
And hurls for him, O half hurls earth for him off under his feet."

Io l'amo come il fulgor del creato. Si.

Orphrey privately counsels me not to let him out at night or he'll hook up with the Other Crowd and come back with fierce tales of jumping the Shannon.

It's a bit thick anyway that according to the new Apocrypha, this is all supposed to have happened once already, which is to besmirch what truly happened. What we did by killing Heydrich, what happened at Lidice, how we got the boy to Palestine.

The boy comes to me in dreams, as the burning boy sometimes and again to instruct me as the Messiah, able to sing whole chords (although never the Devil's). It's a good thing after all he doesn't know the *Czeska* went out into the world—to seek and find—after turning him over at the Danube.

How we got ourselves and the boy out of Ruthenia (necessitating, of course, another demythification—of one's supposed travails in wartime Russia. "You spent the whole of the war as the guest of this Hungarian baron whose American wife and child had gone back to the States?" "In a word, yes."), out of Mindszenty's palace in Budapest, to Rome disguised as a seminarian and thence to the Dominicans at the Biblical Institute in Jerusalem where he was immediately introduced and received by the chief rabbi.

Remember muddles? I am increasingly melting into them . . . Such as the now-famous "The way out is the way in." Or is that not more of a paradox, actually—and incidentally, you realize, very nearly exactly signposted as such in Czech: "entrance" is *vchod* and "exit," *vychod*—used to be a staple gag item in avant-garde cabaret monologues in the early 1930s.

Speaking of which—monologues . . . but can starting a long letter be called launching into a monologue? Surely not if the interrogatives in the letter are not after all rhetorical.

Anyway, you'll recall the one that starts out, "Me forst husband was shot in the Dardanelles—now that's a turrible *painful* part of the body ta be shot in." Now I do recall in sorrow that both my father and my first (figurative) husband were shot in more parts than the Dardanelles, but it follows not in consequence that, as is blithely proclaimed by amateurs of empathy, sacral metaphor and female destiny, that the propagatrix-designate becomes in a stroke, as in the Annunciation, the Pia Mater, increasingly invested in the mysteries of the Cosmos or the continuum of love and sacrifice said to be her specialty. No soap. If anything his (or their) story bewilders her the more—*what* is all the negotiating among men of action worth to end up being shot in the Dardanelles?

I do wish I could be talking to you out loud—well in point of fact I am, into the Dictaphone, but the Dictaphone has not your expression and offers no riposte. In the meantime, outside the windows dark knolls and screens of trees, the network of hedges, abrupt stony ridges, slate glints from roofs give the landscape a featured look—but the prevailing impression is emptiness—one perhaps imposed upon the situation by the viewer to contrast it to the hurly-burly of a voyage the likes of which no memory serves to—

Let me tell you a bit about the voyage. Jacob, the man you proclaimed in no uncertain *for me*, out on the qui vive, made one of those big shipboard hits the columns still delight in telling stay-at-homes and been-nowheres about so they can believe in motion pictures, feeling happier about civilization. One of those indelible "Who's that?" "You mean you don't *know*?" impressions even among seasoned veterans of Atlantic crossings ("real bilge rats," one of them said, which brought me up a bit short). He, Jacob, was sparked I think by a happily renewed and augmented acquaintance with Fitz's poet friend Pickersgill, and P.'s companion Timbrel (who is, I gather, something of a tourist in this life, looking into the delirious professions, trying to decide something or other, "neither ambitious nor not," according to P. *Very* handsome), whose combined passion for the *opra* is something you could chew on. (Really, dear, what the "hi-fi L. P." record hath wrought!)

I had a good time, too. There was aboard, of course, that Mahatma Fitz had met at a New York conclave of esotericists and tipped us the wink on. ("All is but saffron: web of seeming: tee-hee-hee-hee-hee-hee-

hee." You heard it transatlantic.) Assorted fakers: no Windsors. Happily, instead, there were the Manahans. Last night out was given over to a rather hectic, but genial symposium—talking blue streaks about Life and Art, and wind and rain. You'd have triumphed easily. Pickersgill is trying to write a comedy that is "all denouement." I should like to paint his face (he's got the mouth on a slant) while he tells me all about Cambridge and the reputation my father still enjoys there, and then what happened at between father and Wittgenstein that, they say, sent that strange man to Ireland years later, looking for—

Because if he found it, then—well: did he draw a map of where, I suppose, or was it merely at the end of a rainbow in Mayo—somewhere on that plain between Croagh Patrick and Nephin as Fitz believes; or in Connemara after all: near Convent-on-the-Rock; or in the cave along the strand at Glassilaun where Grace O'Malley left it on her way back to Clew Bay. (It or the crucial clew or the true map of where to find it. . .)

I expect you're aware of Fitz's gesture on *Pilgrim Soul*: flinging the finished script in segments down at the one end of the Atlantic cable that it might, as it did, surface entire on this the other end in just the time it took the *Mary* to slip over the waves, and then flying storyboards to match: storyboards! Mind you, they won't let me look at any of it, a turn I don't think I like. I ask you, would Grace Moore have put up with it? Would Gerry Farrar, who played Joan of Arc, for DeMille, a job not unlike playing Maev Cohalen for Orphrey Whither (though could he hear me say so, he might well fire me on the spot and go and make a picture about Kitty O'Shea)? Would Novotná? Destinn? Likely not, but if not, then what? As you once declared in another connection: there's more horses arses than horses around the place.

Destinn. Of course, the whole Miranda Manahan situation brought back with full force, and in ever greater detail, the entire Stráž idyll as Phoebe to the divine Emma. The feasting, the excess, the enchantment, the talk of espionage, and the odd fact (Orphrey declares proves entirely what a true Sybarite she was) that she kept no roosters in the barnyard so that her morning sleep was never disturbed. (I'd been wondering if Orphrey would go for the idea around here, and brought it up. Likely not, he said, for the populace, hearing of such a scheme would surely know to lay it at the odd one's bedroom door, and I doubt my condition could be used as a reason, either, for they're fussed enough already to think I'm making a *fillim*, so indisposed and at my age.)

Odds, ends & random remarks, some overheard:

From Orphrey, last night, the following dictum:

"It'll be a great oul' picture all right, if only to show that whatever of her, the rest of them were all madmen. All of them. Most of them were mad with the notion of a republic, which nobody really wanted, but at the head of it all was Pearse, who was mad *as such*, antecedent to his notions. And the dago as well, *ab origine, exuding* dago lust for murder and betrayal."

Miro has agreed to do the PS score. (Although you can hear him hearing himself scorned—*Hollywood*—as if by Theodor Adorno, from Hollywood, like Louella Parsons, from Hollywood.) Hard to realize, though it's true, that all the while we're actually here in Ireland, we'll be thought, spiritually to be "doing something in Hollywood" simply because the process shooting is rendered at the Hyperion Studio on Formosa and Santa Monica.

Remember when I told you what the Czechs had said—in Mala Strana, even after the war: that I'd been called "the guttersnipe Erato of the Czgowchwz." I remember the response: "Glory be t' God that we got you away from that clowder of catatonics!"

Yes, we may be here, in Ireland, but Jacob's still there on the island Manhattan—ever more so. Of course, there was never any question from the outset of where we would—but he's not even a little excited about being back in London in a fortnight—whereas being back in New York (and then traveling overland to Los Angeles!). Which means real estate. It would no longer do to camp out at the Plaza (and anyway, just before we sailed, in fact, the morning of the fete in Central Park, Consuelo called, all urgency, announcing, "Have your final fling—apotheosis from a window, or whatever, because you're going to have to check out of that place for *good.* I see vile things happening to the premises in the coming decade. (What letter from Wherever has she opened preemptively, I wondered.) In any case, it's true: one requires a foyer of one's own, evocative Aubusson, Azerbaijan, Cavan, and Dun Emer carpets, mudguards; a new door, and old hearth; a new electric kitchen, a nursery, a music room, a Steinway, *meubles, tchotchkes* (would *love* to be known as Mawrdew Tchotchkes), a little theater, and a house blessing in multiple rubrics.

Jacob has set his sights on Gramercy Park and means to have something there by hook or crooked knife. I must say, 'twixt thee and me, that for one whose mysterious mother told fortunes on the pier at Yarmouth, and who was brought up on a barge on the Norfolk Broads, he has formidable metropolitan preferences. "The most important point is, you have Gramercy Park in your past," he announced. "Indeed, I do," I replied. "I've been to the Sonnenbergs more than once, to dinner." "More so." "Don't you mean *moreover*? As in 'Moreover, it's a good place to raise children, with the park out front?' " Question: do you think one can bring children up self-sufficient and spoiled rotten into the bargain?

The reflected glow of life through the medium of remembrance . . . but, as with Augustine's beatitude, and as with Attracta's virginity, *not yet!*

The nights draw in. We leave in the week for Galway and Convent-on-the-Rock. Connemara! We two are booked for a parlour with the Lady Abbess herself. Beltane and the prioress: another wheel turn. Then out to the very rocks for a shoot. Meanwhile, Orphrey's familiars are said to be covering *Divil's Inn* from Parnell Square to St. Stephen's Green twice daily, working the pass-remarkables over: stopping in at Jackie Farrell's in the holy hour for summaries, lounging around in Davy Byrnes, The Bailey, McDaid's, Mooney's, infiltrating the discreet circles dining of a

Tuesday at Jammets, canvassing at the Hibernian, the Russell, the Shelbourne, the Gresham, and after hours at Groome's: hobnobbing there with the roustabout TDs and gassing universally of nothing but the *fillims* and this one in particular—and of the locations and the commotions and the casting: open house to idle metropolis's entire histrionic population, as extras and featured players in the swirling monumental epic of the Nation-in-Arms. The entry of Maev Cohalen into Dublin (in Whitherama, no less). Maev coming out of the West (soundtrack: "The West's Awake!") in closeups, freeze-frames, and lap dissolves—and here at last is the point. Would y'ever come over yourself? *An feidir thu mheaddladh as an teach aon oische?* If you can take a minute's time out, that is, from the composition of *All I May Own*—or bring it along, why not? Or is that only *another* made-up thing the wag—or wags—put into M-N-O-P-Q-R S-T-U-V-W-X-Y-Z? Orphrey says to tell you he happens to *know* it was James Jeffrey Roche and not yourself who taught Teddy Roosevelt the Irish language.

Your representative the errant thrush never desired your sustaining company more. Never mind, get on with you to another of your incomparable First Fridays—and give them all my love

'Til the whence, the snow-white swans of Whither Park (Fingin, Aed, Fiacra, Conn) report: you'll be a godmother, so.

This from your own,
M.

P.S. Curious detail: the little window shades that depend at a pull from the family portraits, giving lengthy particulars of the lineage: the most interesting besides those called Whither (from O'Heither) those called Wayfaring (from O'Fheiring). And who was that Italian the Borgia pope rewarded with a high office for proving the family descended from Isis and Osiris? Anyway the pope's son poisoned him. "*Iside placata, si schiude al ciel.*")

P.P.S. Do you suppose Fitz is completely serious about coming over and himself playing the Pearse role, small as it is, *that way*?

Whither Park
Co. Limerick
Michelmas

Dearest Haly,

No, I am not a seagull; I am a charged particle. As charged as any felon, and charge it, please. We'll pay when the ship comes in. Is this any way to feel? Still at sea? "I *gave* that performance!" "Yes, darling, you gave it—and I heard it, in the same way you gave it, over the phone." O Temperance, O More-aches—and O *mio babbino card*!

The four great evils of civilization, according to the parish doctor, a druidic piping seer, are the telephone; "this thing called telly—vision—it tells ye *nuthin'* y'd want t'know—and all of it, *mar dhea*, from England and *A-merry-ca*"; chemical fertilizers; and antibiotics. So there. (The oracular you would be *revered* in these parts, but you'd've come a long way from New York, as you put it, "merely to experience all this weather.")

I thought a propos the several oracles flying in and out the windows, I might do well (in between earnest stabs at *A Treatise Concerning the Principles of Human Knowledge*, in a lovely, sturdy, and autographed first edition, not much thumbed since acquired) to read something historically documented about the Whither presence here, because for all one knew the current satrap might have won the whole pile in a card game at boarding school in Kildare, built a Potemkin village with the cheap labor available during the Emergency, hired the oracles from Bard-I-Con, acquired at sales in Eastcheap and Auteil the various Renaissance "wonder cabinets" about the place, loaded with nautilis shells and ostrich eggs, fossils, stuffed crocodiles, oddly wrought bones, and what-was-that under glass on the landing that looked like a unicorn's unicorn, and had this dame at the P.O. imported from The Liberties, Dublin 1, to incarnate the local rune keeper—so I asked Jacob would he on one of his excursions drop into a reputable library in another town, to which request he responded by going into Limerick City and retrieving an appropriately dusty tome with, as he put it, *virgin-uncut* pages, from which I proffer the following extract:

> In dealing with the influences and the processes inside the estate system which shaped Irish town development up til mid-nineteenth century, it may be noted first of all that telling contributions came from landlords or their representatives when they took it upon themselves to preside over and to invest in town development. Landlord-induced change in all cases grew out of deep rooted association which normally entailed a residential link between a family and a particular settlement. Newcastle, Adare, Glyn and Ballywhither provide the outstanding examples from County Limerick of towns that derived strength and character as a result of forthright landlord involvement. The motif of castle, mansion, demesne and town was best exemplified in the last mentioned core estate, which had developed its present lineaments well before the Act of Union, and where landlord influence has continued to make a more sustained impact than in any other town in Limerick with the exception of the larger (albeit rather less integral) Newcastle.

Your correspondent returned therefore with chastened glance and sharpened attention to our local historian, the postmistress who lets us know this further:

"The Whithers were in all times, good and bad, *resident* to their native demesne and transacted their own business without either attorney, money-broker, agent, keeper, driver, or pound-keeper; they seldom visited London, and even more rarely Paris, and though repeatedly *lucky* were scarcely ever known to frequent the gaming tables or the race meetings, but lived as their resident *file* Deiseal Mac Tuathal so eloquently wrote in the early 19th century, *in peace and quietness at home, in the ould ancient habitations of the counthry.*" (Obviously our specimen Whither is making up for lost times out.) "*Riding by night up and down the moonbeams, quaffing the Maydew from the gossamer threads of the early morning, and living a merry social life, singing, dancing and playing with wild Aeolian music.*"

(You do feel so hear hereabouts vibrations and echoes remnant of all that *craic.*) "And though (perhaps because) they never canted nor dispossessed, never took nor demanded *male or malt*, head-rent, quit-rent, crown-rent, dues or duties, county-cess, parish-cess, tithes, priests' dues, poor rates, rates in aid, driverage, poundage, nor murder money, or heavily taxed to support the murderer, or pay his passage to America —employed not sheriffs, magistrates, barony constables, bailiffs, keepers, drivers, auctioneers, tax-collectors, process-servers, gaugers, spies, poteen-hussars, police, nor standing army; passed no promissory notes, and served neither notices to quit, ejectments, nor civil bills, they exacted from the people a reverence and a respect such as few potentates, civil, military or ecclesiastical could ever boast of, and from Providence—who will gainsay it—a gorgeous return in the earlier years of present century not only in the present Whither's progenitors fabulous success on the New York Stock Exchange and the Chicago Merchantile Exchange, but in the discovery within the revered demesne of not only the Whither Chalice but of the Ballywhither Caves as well.

"The Ballywhither caves were discovered on 4th May, 1888, when a local laborer, quarrying limestone, accidentally dropped his crowbar into a crevasse, and hit the head the *sideheog Iubhdan* sleeping off the *poitin* of the night before, the better to rise, lick the restorative May dew off the gossamer threads of the early morning, and thus refreshed, set about his thirsty work that day, the fourth and last of the Immortal Feast: spreading in the ears of all the local parishioners the Evangel of the 4th of May." But you've *realized* the Evangel of the 4th of May, so no need to—and anyway you're right about there being certain things (unlike, for example, Mrs. Woolf's sausage and haddock) upon which one is rather more likely to *lose* than to gain one's hold by writing them down.

Anyway, re Orphrey. I do believe I've come to understand matters a little better as a result of these studies in forbearance. O.W. evidently feels himself to be on life's long roll, and inclined to be thereby from time to time beside himself (taking up thereby half the county Limerick), given to raving as an exercise and impersonating a thing demented. Last night, in the dungeon room he calls *The Keep* (I thought of the catacomb where Jack Benny kept all his money on the radio), he screened *Ominous* (in two dimensions: thank God). And I believe for certain that cavorting to be heard, swooping in and out through the great cave-hearth from reaches unspecified, were the ghosts of at least seven generations of Whithers and Thithers and FitzYons—together will all their Whither, Hither, Thither and Yonigal cousins, german and collateral—until I tell you I was wishing after a quid's worth of the Tullamore in my mouth to keep my heart up and it from attacking me, as I was quite suddenly feeling not at all too well in my overall health. (*Ominous*, of course, will ever promote sensations.) The light came up, and at once did the rumpled *Wunderkind* O.W. with the D.W. ambitions (and mastery) commence calling out (from the slide-tray appendage his brain came bursting out of Creation's vortex into his cranium equipped with) his new picture, *Pilgrim Soul*, shot-for-shot (all shuffled, fanned, and catalogued, according to some undecipherable code he has developed to outwit sabotage in the Industry, in the Irish, natch, and taken down by his secretary, an unperturbable woman of middle years called Eithne Grimley, she who has kindly and without fuss offered to transcribe this which you will be receiving through the mail slot before the week is out and the October First Friday is upon you.)

As for Fitz's storyboards—but that's another story: you are a grave of secrets, are you not? Anyway, I don't get it: how pictures are generated out of the words—I wouldn't want to testify (at the murder trial I mean, except for wearing the big black picture hat). The point for me is that I now imagine I won't be required to do too much of anything at all of what's known as the *histrionic*. The way it *sounds*, she's really something of a ghost in her own story—something, indeed, that seems able and moreover disposed to come and go up and down chimneys, like the banshee. Events surround her, and conspire, with and against her. She lives and loves, triumphs and dies rather purposely, giving birth to—oneself. But in the end we're not to know who, really, she might have been. That at any rate is the immediate impression. (I mean *was* she born at Knock on August 21, 1871, in a tinker's encampment, or was she not?) Perhaps when the O'Heither and The O'Maurigan have slugged it out further—wasn't it three minutes a round when we went with Toots Schor to Madison Square Garden?

In any event, main or otherwise, yesterday I was terrified of playing her; today I'm nearly resigned. (I seem to have lost my wits. It's a matter of "come along now, woman, we're bound to find them somewhere along the way by the the side of the road.")

Apparently, she is Ireland. Therefore, I'm to look monumental (Mae West platform shoes under broadcloth shirts and man-tailored tweeds?) I fully expect to be handed a *punt* note and ordered, "There—play that." Where *do* I go to find her "living I"?

I needn't perhaps go too far into the personal, or whatever residue one might have discovered toward a woman who, apart from anything else—historical-political, tragicomic, epic-romantic, was one's own mother. Let me not get too inwrought.

Had this dream: all dressed up in empire as Tosca, but the music was the *Hoffmann* "Barcarolle." Determined to board some ship I couldn't see, and just down the wharf, something called *Arcadia* with everybody on it (knew them all) waving wildly in my direction and beckoning me to board it and not the other. Great blasts of horns (in Ab and G). I was making for the phantom ship—from which the invisible helmsman's voice shouted down, "You go along wit' your friends, lady; you can't come on heah, dis is a tramp steamer." Undeterred, I sashayed up the gangplank, flinging on the deck a purse that directly burst, sending silver dollars spilling over the deck. "Show me to my cabin, sailor!" Where in the world?

What is the talk of New York? Give out! Give out!

Love broadcast (live)
M.C.

Whither Park
Co. Limerick
Michelmas

Sybillacarissima,

You will have heard: it's on the cards. ('Twas ever said, at serious hat lunches, in committee, in camera, abroad in the coffee houses of the Rialto: you always could, woman, by and large, when the chips were down, take the measure of a standing man.)

Goings On: in this instance no such thing as proper precaution, leading to natural outcome: more becoming than prevention in this instance. Anyway, there it is, the upshot and the sequel we've started reading now into one another (forecasting snowy nights in front of fires? Probably).

Here is part of a little description of the place we've come to, done by the capable local postmistress, that's stacked in a neat little pile next to the window of her cage, goes for sixpence, and is at that price very good value for the money (as one is always so glad to find said, in your United Kingdom's better critical journals, of one's recordings in the shops) and that folk pick up on their way here for the *cuaird*, or visiting.

"Ballywhither is a farmers' town: the workfolk for miles round come in for fairs and shopping." (There will be such a fair there at *Samhain*, at which time many and various manifestations will occur.) "The shops other than chemists—of which there are a great many—smell of porter, boot leather, bacon, sausage, *drisheen* (*boudin noir*), and shag. The people of Ballywhither feel at the outpost of a country they know. Roads out of the town go under the mountains or up through passes over into Tipperary and Cork, but these two counties are each of them another world."

Another, and another again! Are there not, dear, worlds within worlds—notwithstanding the proposition that all is but saffron. (Or, putting it again in the postmistress's elegant grammatical terms "from this reach of shadow the road emerges into the open heart of the region I spoke of at first.") And then from another reach of shadow, I remember how in my convalescence last winter Fitz and I tried looking at *Another World* in the afternoons, and found it wanting in seriousness, and how darling Rhoe from the Burger Ranch came through, insisting, "Look, I know Mawrdew Czgowchwz, and I can tell you she'll respond to *In This Our Life* right off the bat the way I did." And did she not!

I ought perhaps to have studied that television screen more carefully—even if, or perhaps especially if, television is nothing but auditions—but who alive knew *this* was going to happen? (Not the buns in the oven, the film—or, come to think of it, either, both). Or that these (shall we go ahead and call both outcomes issues) would be the nowaday worries, with no time out? I put it to you all written out to implore you—mistress of the fugue, and so much else—put it back to me in whatsoever fashion you find becomes creation.

Apart from anything else, and in point of fact, it is too late to renege: there you are, and there it is. I have only yesterday committed to the post a letter to Her Busyness the Madge (the which I let you know for form's sake, hoping by the time you receive this same that you will have heard its contents entire over the telephone, and) which as I think on it is nothing other than an admission of terror coupled with a hasty, fitful attempt at self-absolution. (Do you not find we are best at that particular ministry in the late afternoon, in thrall to *l'heure bleu, l'heure exquise*—to all the fumes and vapors, to the failing light a woman of a certain age?)

When is it you fly to London? Should we do something there together to attract crowds? (Nothing threatening: some simple songs in the middle of an autumn afternoon. At the Wigmore, in the lashing rain—moody, *grisaille* things, many by Reynaldo Hahn, and us gowned in Charles James indigo satin? Hard to sing in, his carapaces; Dietrich does, if you want to call that singing, and as for sitting at the piano . . . Mainbocher? Merman likes him—and she certainly does sing. Vionnet-inspired Ceil Chapman? Anyway, as t'were fitly greaved and gauntleted, to benefit some gentlefolk. Or to "seed" a scholarship fund (presuming we have by then agreed to allow "them" to start coming up from their callow twenties; for if we do—you know it's true—they'll come up in their droves, as they say here in my—other—country).

Or shall we do in on a stage set—a model say of O. W.'s folly here (looks like the one from the Met's *Cosi* you laughed at when Eleanor and I were in it together) with the inscription over the portal, *Liberty, Learning and Select Amusement.*

What am I saying? I've left *him* out; that will not do. The three of us then. What about *La bonne chanson* Fauré's own version: we three plus string quartet? (What was she saying about "simple songs?" *Dis donc!*)

The crossing was, I think, just your stuff, or would have been, had you on impulse swept aboard. Your partner on vocals here spent most of the voyage lolling, dreaming, eating, and being made party to varieties of male ambition. (Very much including that of these gluttonous motes of souls installed in a suite within, within the distance of a swallow, and gaining, according to science, strength by the hour in the aftermath of the meals mum's fed, the no-longer-necessary-but-nevertheless-increasingly-agreeable attentions she's paid in bed. And I may say breakfast doesn't either begin the day's intake of information or *begin* to describe these particular same. These are scraps of conversation she almost unthinkingly gathers (for it's said they "hear" from the first, that the very wall they first appear to be but the archaic scripture on has ears, well before theirs ever are configured, and, like dear Ralph's tapes, stores stories for them that they can if they are taught to try, retrieve). And in fact the very air she breathes, the air she makes her noise with. Cheeky buggers.

And in the macrocosm, numbered on the passenger list of the *Mary*: some swell collection of original prints, select vintages, dead-cert turns and drip-dry shirts, for example, the poet Christopher ("Kit") Pickersgill, whom you may know: he is the one, ain't he, who dispatched that ode to Eva Turner, and thus has been known to or by in some fashion one "Bucky" Beltane, just now absent without official leave-taking, out galloping again today, one supposes, astride a gorgeous roan called Tantivy (but I digress) and quite an up-and-coming attraction. Fancies himself, Kit does, in his cups, a buccaneer foretopman lashed to the rigging like Ulysses, sailing the straits of Reputation, determined not to be had in to supper by either the Scylla monster he calls Mrs. Oughtn't or the Charybdis he calls Mrs. Ifshewould. (I confess, dear, I've never read *The Odyssey*; nor *Ulysses* nor *Pilgrim's Progress*; nor *Moby-Dick*, although I am assigned the third and the last chapter of *Ulysses*—in preparation for *Pilgrim Soul*.)

Boldly, with the flaming zeal of the newly converted, I put it to him, that psychoanalytically speaking these two fairly transparently *naughty* screen-personae were none other than the masks of his introjects: his sublime or God/parent component, which becomes his necessarily tyrannical judge, and his subject component, which demeans him, and of which he desires to rid himself. Not interested—your countrymen aren't as a rule. (So odd, considering Strachey—or is it? He *did* invent that hideous word *cathexis*. I always think of Miss Caswell. "Well, I can't say *cathexix*, can I? Cathexis may be somebody's *name*.") It angers me very greatly about Virginia Woolf. (Equanimity, indeed!)

Anyway, I liked the poet Pickersgill, and he and the aforementioned equestrian, along with the rhymer's boon companion, called Guy (as in rope) Timbrel, fell in together quickly and easily. Then there were the Manahans, a Dublin alliance featuring a somewhat troubling little offspring who will not stay in school (not even, they avow, among the Quakers), a she who's in possession of the most oddly poignant freshet of a voice, along with utterly congested notions—at majestic eleven years: what was I saying about the ones in their *twenties*?—of what to do about the ripples its vehemence effects. I'd love you, Dame, to have been present when she sang 'Voi che sapete.' Talk of maternal instinct!

I'd rather (much) digress, and gossip the more. A propos, why is it that, even here in fabled Ireland, where they'll talk the hind legs off the donkeys, London gossip is unquestionably the utmost in delicatessen? I don't mean Liberace, dear, although I ought to tell you that that special train they laid on for him has given O. W. fresh inspiration for the management of his new fillim's star's great launch in the Hibernian capital. "I'll ride from out of the awakened West on the railroad into Dublin," I told him outright, "in any nicely appointed carriage, but if you *dare* call out of the pubs and audition rooms of the metropolis a gaggle of ostentatiously weeping creatures of any sex whatsoever claiming to have themselves been, or to have had deceased relations in bold evidence on the premises or in the environs of the G. P. O. on Easter Sunday 1916, I might find it necessary, in order to oblige audiences with Something Called a Temperament, to devise for publication in the press statements for which I promise you, you are *not* prepared."

I mean, of course, the riveting accounts of that female Russian discus thrower charged with shoplifting hats from the C&A in Oxford Street—all that publicity fanning the coals under the testy ribbon clerk's *mot*: "Well, I mean to say, it's what the Russians *are*, isn't it—a nation of shoplifters."

What I ought to have said to him was, "And that'll be only for starters. Fancy the civic reaction when your protegee, chancing her histrionic arm tries walking out of Clery's front door *in character*—for isn't it known to all and sundry that Great Flaming Maev herself, in the confusion and the shooting, the marauding and the looting, slipped in to the very same emporium with the rest of the looting shawlies ("Would yiz look at them breakin' all them lovely windas!") and picked up out of the linen stores a lovely lace tablecloth and out of lingerie a few smalls, before heading into the broad daylight of O'Connell Street then back to Connemara to give birth? So the living I, A sporting free, gratis, and for nothing the latest local Lilly Dache knockoff, and under it one of those turban affairs that came in and were quite suddenly all the rage among devout women at the time of the Eucharistic Congress in 1932 (and which they and their daughters still will wear to the Pro-Cathedral for Forty Hours Exposition and Solemn Benediction").

But I could not—say all that. I can write it, but I can't—yet—spin it off the tongue in its entirety in great long loops the way they can. But tell me, you who must be in the know, is it so that the Bolshoi won't go to London unless the charge against Comrade Ponomareva is withdrawn? And more importantly, what were the sizes, shapes, and colors of the hats purloined? Particularly the shapes, I think. (It occurred to me, you see, that if they were *discoid*—know what I mean? I feel you must.) And, of course, since Garbo is said to be on her way to London to attend the Bolshoi and meet Ulanova, how may the situation be resolved—unless of course the Sphinx, herself an inveterate shopper (though so far as we know not shoplifter, but then who would prosecute?) playing Portia, stands clemency advocate for the frailty of Universal Womankind. Mind you, Garbo never worked for Universal—probably never even heard of it. Still and all, do I take you with me?

I've been looking at a sheaf of Miro's sketches for the scoring and can tell immediately from the clustered density of the notation that what necessity obtains will surely reveal itself to invention in the form of a piano concerto, for a virtuoso: to counterpoint with vehemence in the scenes in which first she stalks the world, then rides wild, the easy, pieces she played with her fingers when sitting down in public.

(You get the picture: the Field, the Chopin, the Schumann, and the Liszt represent and underscore her manners—what she learned after she was translated from the Gypsies in the glen into great house—

generic Irish Big House, early to middle Georgian, with subsequent improvements: scenes to be shot in the Spring at the Manahan's place in Kildare—the Creplaczx concerto will serve to portray her racked soul—and Ireland likewise. But this is not merely scene painting, happily, or there'd be little left of Ireland. I'm thinking of Mahler, to Bruno Walter, about the Third Symphony. "Don't bother looking at those mountains; I've composed them all away." Well, I should be almost frightened to return to Galway—for fear of missing the Twelve Bens of my childhood.)

So, waiting, wanting, Ireland. . . . Herself . . . until—and Miro seems determined to in the first place provide something both complicated and so implicatory (to mince to wormlike hash those wicked tongues who have already put it out that since the life itself is nothing more than a flashy remake of *Dangerous Moonlight*, what is required is a flashier-yet replay of the Warsaw Concerto, itself everybody's favorite Rachmaninoff knockoff, and you know how Miro feels about Rachmaninoff) *and* to outdo Liszt and thus silence for all time, or the time being, whichever lasts longer, all chatter as to his being the Gounoud to my Pauline Viardot (and you *know* how he feels about Gounoud), as if Liszt had actually composed "Un sospiro" for Max Ophüls to soundtrack *Letter from an Unknown Woman* with.

(And of course Orphrey's not for a minute going to allow her to fall apart to a Liszt tune, is he, the way Ophüls let poor Joan Fontaine?) I already detect something: *le petit phrase* agon: her theme, his theme, their theme . . . The Nation, The Oppressor, The Warrior, The Nun. Sometimes I think he's getting back at me for what happened at the *Tristan* last year—as if I were some kind of Zdenka Fassbender and he poor Felix Mottl (whereas, instead of giving him cardiac arrest, marrying him on his deathbed, I went under and let him live without me).

In any case virtuoso: this means you. Do say you will. There wouldn't be any infra-dignation in a Dame of the British Empire consenting to perform an original cinemusical composition created for a film concerning the Dublin Easter Rising of 1916? The young Queen's a good sport, ain't she? (And I did dream—what did it mean—that you played Max Reger's *Inferno Fantasy and Fugue* on the *ondes martineau* to a packed-out Albert Hall. The *armwork*—how you did, dear, sling that ring along that rod!)

O.W. is off tomorrow in his own person to review locations. ("If Connemara doesn't look like Connemara, we'll transfer to Big Sur!" "I'll *not* be shunted off to California!" I complained to Jacob. "It might give you all sorts of interesting ideas about Minnie." "Destinn, I told you, gave me all my ideas about Minnie." "The illusion is the thing they go for; you know that." "I had the illusion I was being presented, not some landscape!" These men molders, these Olympians and their obiter dicta. You feel like Giacometti's wife when he tried to get her to shave bald, consequence of his conviction that hair is a lie.) Orphrey can, I suppose, say anything he likes to me, and if he concocts an ice flow in the Shannon, I suppose that'll be all right, too, but I do hope he doesn't, like Griffith did with Gish, *sing* to me! Griffith was after all a baritone, trained for the lyric stage, but Orphrey—well, I suppose you'd call him a *basso buffo*, but the idea of hearing him rattle on the *catologo*, a tone flat does not fill one with feelings of unmixed delight.

And so it goes, the rolling pictures motion: do come see.

As ever in Musicry,
And the Life
M.

Whither Park
Co. Limerick
Michelmas

My dear Doctor Gennaio,

"In this Munster county so often fought over there has been cruelty even to the stones; military fury or welling-up human bitterness has vented itself on unknowing walls."

Installed here behind walls I cannot agree to think of as unknowing (over which enormous beeches whelm), in a room giving out on the open courtyard, your patient is enlivened and instructed each day by the music of the Perpetual Past. (For accompaniment, an old yardman plays "My Thousand Times Beloved" on the uileann pipes, and jackdaws respond. I presume a jackdaw: for all I know it might be a singing duck—or the kitchen maid, Noranna, taking one off: she does the fairest imitation of a rabbit eating lettuce anybody's ever heard in the world.)

May I tell you that the entire demesne has, time out of mind, or at least since Marco Polo was a houseguest, been organized according to the best principles of feng shui (which I have only just found out, though it will be no news to you I daresay, means "wind and water." Perfect for Ireland in all seasons).

Cashel Orphrey—or Schloss Whither, a Norman pile augmented by successive Elizabethan, Jacobean (now enclosed in), Georgian, and Regency amendments—is situated facing one hill above the others to the southeast: a true dragon: the knolls along the ridge are its backbone (as the Milky Way is called, in the antipodes, the Backbone of the Night) and the stream is the salivation of its mouth: gold (in sunlight) and silver (in moonlight). Quoth Kuo Hsi, a landscape painter of the Song dynasty. "Watercourses are the arteries of a mountain, grass and trees its hair; mist and haze its complexion."

In the eighteenth and nineteenth centuries, Whither Park was called, whimsically *Kowloon* or the Nine Dragons (although there are only eight ridges: the ninth, dragon was said to be the Whither heir). Under this name the whole boiling—house, outbuildings, pagoda—was then carved in ivory miniature in a great arc out of a single enormous elephant tusk: an *objet* on display today in the library, under glass. The name went out in the mid-nineteenth century, scored as British imperial, colonial and wicked, when the heir Fergus O'Heither, reverting to the original of the family name, joined T. F. Meagher ("of the sword") in opposition to Daniel O'Connell and appeasement. This same O'Heither then went off with Meagher in the great gallivant to the American Civil War, thence to Montana, Colorado, and California, never to return to Ireland, leaving the castle to be run by and to pass in inheritance to collateral Whithers, of whom Orphrey seems to be the lone grandson, although some years into the century a creature appeared, claiming to be the son this other, this Fergus O'Heither: and here was his story.

His mother was standing on a porch at Antietam, watching a backyard skirmish at the scrake of dawn—for the war did spill over into your-man Everyman's backyard—much as the war did in Bohemia, Slovakia, Moravia, and Ruthenia—when a Union soldier wearing a green shamrock on his blue coat was shot through the—as they say hereabouts—baloobas. (Two "shawlies" on a bus last year passing the Rotunda Hospital in Dublin where lay in state six of the unfortunate Irish solider volunteers caught in the horrifically bloody Congo war: "Och, God have mercy on the poor fellas, isn't it a shockin' terrible thing!" "It's them Baloobas—they's ahl the same, y'll never change 'em.")

In any event, this bullet then flew straight through one or the other of said Fergus O'Heither's baloobas—also known, from another story, as the Dardenelles—then proceeding in its career, without so much as a by-your-leave, with neither further tarry nor ado, straight into the, as if it were, waiting womb, of Antietam's Miss Fauquier—*and this nearly immaculate conception is recorded in American medical history.*

Now about this article claiming to be the offspring of the bullet that had swum the balooba-Dardanelles of Fergus O'Heither: it's said he ended his days happily enough. O.W. is quick to point out that he was given a position in the household here considerably higher than that afforded Lambert Simnel, the Pretender crowned at Christ Church, Dublin on Whitsunday, May 24, 1487, who ended up the scullion in Henry VII's kitchens at Whitehall.

The story of the bullet in the baloobas is still told—transposed to The Troubles of 1923–26 and attached to variegated scenarios, all to do with this that or the other deed or title—in the Ballywither public house, called, though owned and run for generations by a family called O'Sullivan, O'Heither's. They don't mince words about the place. When the old biddy in said she knew I was carrying twins, it was in the Irish, and translates "sure there was two thoughts and not just the one slithering around in that fella's knapsack—and the wonder is it doesn't happen more in the world than it does for doesn't a man have two ballocks on him!"

And who was it described music as "sex, organized in precise metrical intervals?" We'd real-*ized* it wasn't stray bullets. Still, I can't help thinking that when Wagner said that a good performance of *Tristan* would drive an audience crazy, he forgot to mention what might happen to the Isolde. And before I forget (or suppress) it: we have found the Cornelia/Sesto duet from *Giulio Cesare* the perfect thing to warm up on together. Calling Herr Doktor Freud!

The Pagoda has seven storys and is widely regarded in the neighborhood as a colossal and uniquely shaped *rath* for the fairies. On the night of the fire at O'Heither's, it was reported that a great commotion of the good people were seen swarming out of it to assist in the dousing of the flames—for the O'Sullivans have never stinted in their tithes of drink to these themselves—the Other Crowd—in and out of the boon times.

Leibniz says it's a long way from the intellect to the heart. You told me that. Without even citing the local geographers. I can tell you that it's a long way to Tipperary, too, even from hereabouts. (In which connection Jacob says that when I lose my fear of horses, it'll be no long way whatever to Minnie. From Minne to Minnie: a chapter in *In This Our Life*.)

I remember the white mimosa on Manitoy (and Emily Dickinson's drawings of herbs). There were swinging shelves of it veiling the entrance to an oak tunnel.

Indoors, dreaming, reluctant yet to think of proceeding to wild Connemara—where one may find at Convent-on-the-Rock not the solace and the reassurance (and the *Pilgrim Soul* locations so dearly) sought, not the kindly dancing Beguine women of the Ordo Ancellae Oblatiae Hiberniae (whom Jacob cannot help but thinking of, and plotting to apprehend, as the "Sisterhood of Medieval Marys" from *Bleak House*—a work I've not read). Not these, but instead, nodding upon a bleached log by the shore of the freezing sea, beneath the ringed chalk-white Samhain moon, his *Wyrd* furies, the "they" who've sworn to track him down: the Graeae. (To dream of driftwood is in my opinion to entertain miscarriage; I'll get to that maneuver in the course of this confession.) Also, he calls Connemara my Troy—which puts me in mind of both Cassandra and Helen. He says I'm a bit of both—says I was born there, and must as it were return as a captive there to see it destroyed.

"Connemara, destroyed?"

"In a way, yes."

"And what's the horse, then, the film unit? Sure I've heard Fitz refer often enough to Orphrey as the horse's arse."

"It is, yes—as was *The Quiet Man* unit, for surely you see that they are the very machines of the outside world that will, emitting from their bellies as do the jets that put down at Shannon every morning, whole contingents of confederates who once inside the gates will oversee the demise of the Ireland you were born into."

"Not a bad thing in compare," I said, "if they demise altogether poverty and tuberculosis and the rule of the wet priests."

An aside, on *Pilgrim Soul*, the motion picture: what *is* it? They talk of mood swings in pregnant women; what of them in pregnant, scheming film producer/directors? One day The Creator is on as if it were (and ought to be to me) a great lark; another as if (it were, ought, etc.) a sacred mission: a Magnificent Obsession. (Oh, to suddenly awaken starred in something like *that*!)

When he is not going on in the one way or the other like that Orphrey (having resumed the former ancestral habits of stately regularity and decorous grandeur such as become a magnificent and well-ordered household of which a cultivated Irish gentleman is head and president) will sit agreeably of an evening playing the recorder, while Jacob plucks the psaltery. But there's no Countess Madge to sing the Song of the Vagabond (Let-Back-Pending-Investigation-And-Accounting-of-Her-Circuit-of-the-Hemispheres-and-her-Forty-Years-And-Then-some-of-Bearing-Mute-Witness-Uttering-Nothing-To-The-Purpose-In-Spite-Of-Her-Heralded-Much-Vaunted-and-Accomplished-Noisings: Turbulent-Unaware).

Therefore, here, as if back on the veranda deck, at sea, lolling as if abandoned, the wild goose grounded but mind-winging in her fondest, fiercest, most fabulous (ferocious) thoughts: yet you have your way with her. You laid'such emphasis on the voyage as return ("Origins are clamorous; be patient hearing them in their say."), and, oh, I won't tell you about this now, but there was such another on board the *Mary* who'd been sent in such a way on such a voyage back, who nearly died on the account. I will only tell you that a certain Sullivanian put him out to sea earlier in the year, and that this time out he was sailing under the colors of one Mahatma Bahadur Bakshish. The rest is, as they say, as it shall appear (likely in certain "columns"). The itinerant is one Swithin, and if you could get your—for the smallest fraction of the shortest hour—but I know: yours is a program of attraction. I was reminded being with him of the moment when, in collusion with M. St. M., you prepared the Waterford crystal bowl, filled with holy water and, according to the instructions given to the Cathars of Mount Segur by the archangel Raphael, covered with scorched parchment and bade your patient look deep therein. (*Let* them rant that analysis is witchcraft: as Rhea Esther Zuckerman is wont to say, they should only know.) Wherein I did, indeed, see my reflection upside down: the proof of the efficacy of the Cedrioli curse. I was reminded because I felt being with poor Swithin that yet a worse curse, the product of an even more intricate, perfected, and diabolical praxis than the Neriacs, one possibly even worse than Malicious Animal Magnetism at its most, well, *magnetic*, had been put upon him—a some hex if that treated by you yourself working in tandem with an anointed cunning woman in a blue veil, would yield only to the shock of his beholding his addled head, instead of lying inverted at the bottom of the bowl, bobbing sideways on the water's surface...

I wanted to—I don't know, save him, or something; I don't know why. (Why not?)

Also there were the Manahans, old neighbors of the Countess. He is a Dubliner, of course, and the heir to something bulky, like flour, oats, or barley, and she's a New Yorker. (She's from the diocese, and the madams, but she leapt over them. Clever girl; has a good head on her shoulders.) They've spawned a startling original called Miranda, who now wants to call herself Maev, aged eleven. (More of Miranda/Maev anon, but she's a clever thing, and won a pot of money in the ship's mileage pool two days running.)

But now back to the goose: she's got to try the embarkation promise, and no perhaps. It is arduous and thirsty work keeping the line held fast between the past and the present, but work is life. (All the while aboard ship the Atlantic undertow: the submarine activity: all forces forced reminders. Jacob points out that in science, waves are said to *propogate*. You heard it transatlantic.)

"Now fer the cause of yer bewilderment, Missus" offers the genial, silver-tongued and lore-loaded gatekeeper at his station under the great oaks, when I walk out and stop to him for a talking interval, "y'd be wantin' to know the words of that darlin' sad poem from Ulster counthry—where all the long sorrows of the world do originate..."

Fa d'ean beag a b'aille gaire ar imeallna gcraobh
Chan ceist duit a bhas go brach is e nite le haol. Which is to say something like

> *"Your surpassing-lovely little*
> *laughing bird: look-you fret for him*
> *no longer For his dying that*
> *he got in the wash of lime."*

Many things are only to be reckoned in the old tongue.

Margaret Burke-Sheridan writes advising I wear pearls "for the duration." Obviously, says Orphrey, she's had the goods from MacLíammóir the town crier. But why pearls? One of the women here says its for Saint Margaret—*Margaret* means "pearl". Why Saint Margaret? Didn't I know Saint Margaret is the patron saint of childbirth (this in a whisper, as if to remind me the whole thing is very hush-hush), as she herself escaped from the body of a monster—the devil, apparently, disguised as a dragon. In Antioch.

You might recall how Ralph will point to Alice, or another, inaugurating his remarks with the phrase, "This one...." Well, this one dreamed last night, drifting along in a bed the size of a *curach*, of two-other voyagers. "You surround two-others now, insisting on becoming all they may be," said the voice in the dream—that way: "two-others"—as we walked (was I with you) through...was it the cave at Tintagel with the tides hauling the driftwood and the bladderwrack in as if to furnish the place....Or was it the tunnel in the Ramble in Central Park that echoes as we took shelter (was I with you or with him, of with Fitz perhaps) in late May from an electric storm.

The cave's walls, or the tunnel's, were, apart from damp with running tears—was this, I heard myself ask, the fourth labor of Psyche: was I to gather a vial of such black water from the hidden vent in the mountain rock guarded by four dragons? (one would so much rather not)—scored with figurations—and now I'm suddenly reminded that only yesterday I wrote to Sybil F-T metaphorically, of archaic scripture on the uterine wall (in the manner of that Pompeian fresco in which the reveler, pictured semirecumbent, is yelping, "Enjoy yourself, I'm singing!"). Or were the graffiti merely the names of courting city couples and rambunctious, determined kids (much like this one) marking their lives' vivid moments, saying they were there, and what the hell? All over the place as well, inscribed in various curvilinear positions, is the number 9, and Jacob rattling on saying, if I've got it correctly, "Not only are all multiples of nine numerologically nine, but one may take almost any number over ten, reverse the digits, subtract the smaller number from the larger and the answer would be a multiple of nine." Did you know that?

Why would I want to do such a thing, I wondered.

Had I dreamed I was a great cow sitting down on a milk float...

The feeling in the dream, or perhaps the screen-feeling clouding the rest, the restive undercurrent was that of touring at leisure through one's own life via chartered itinerary, wearing sensible footwear (and dangling participles: I'll get this thing out of me yet). Echo, silence, then another voice, official-sounding, recorded, hollow, uninflected, disinterested (*disinterred?*) THIS WAY, THREE FATES, NO WAITING! (Imagine if there were nine: would *anybody* be able to sit through the first scene of *Gotterdämmerung*? I've just remembered, Ralph also absolutely always says, summing up an argument, "*This* way...) Then I heard Jacob singing "Beautiful Dreamer." (He has fallen absolutely in love with Stephen Foster, *the* American song writer as he insists, born on the Fourth of July... like Fitz.) "Beautiful dreamer, wake unto me..." Then an argumentative voice—Paranoy/Percase? "What I want to know is, did Stephen Foster hear Brahms's Second, or did *Brahms* listen to Stephen *Foster*?" And then the lilting voice of Maire Dymphna, O.A.O.H.

"Whenever you're near,
All my fears disappear
Dear, it's plain as can be..."

Were the markings the familiar names and faces? Were we in the Tunnel of Love at Steeplechase Park, with the stalwarts drifting alongside in a great regatta such as the one of Galway hookers with red sails that comes across Galway Bay from Spiddal to Kinvarra every August—sporting like nutsy Fagin—or were they, in another living tale, each name a new name the New Line: all the available earthly names and faces to choose from in fashioning two more forms for light to fall on. To create life stories, start with names, toss, then stir. (Or as the waiter said at Fouquet's on the *Quatorze Juillet*, 1948, as I sat looking out the window at the army loading the aircraft we'd just put down in the middle of the road onto a *camion*, '*Vous etes venue parmi nous comme Alecto—caeli convecta per aura. Voulez-vous troublez la salade, Madame*?" *Would* I—although isn't Alecto, in Virgil anyway, terribly *old*?)

What in creation *are* these bonded others I surround?

And if they were figures, rounded figures without names, were they the phantom offspring we engender merely by admitting thought? I heard teenage voices, all trebles chanting the way they do in the streets of New York: "Find 'em! Feel 'em! Fuck 'em! Forget 'em!" I turned to the names and faces in the audience and declaimed, thunderously: *Scostami, profani—Melpomene, son io. Ciao, Ralph!*

Now I *ask* you!

Regards from your patient
M.C.

P.S. A propos caves. It has just come into me through the secret hearing tunnel (as I was on my way to drop this on the hall table for the post) that Orphrey plans a long elaborate sequence to be shot in the famed Ballywhither Caves. Apparently to conflate some sort of Neolithic imagery and supposed ritual with the Fenian secret meeting: typically held, of course, in the snug, or in the cellar beneath, of the pub. Was I dreaming *ahead*?

P.S. 2: There may be a spot of trouble brewing in the misted glen. Overheard as well on the aforementioned foray: Boss Whither, giving out on Fitz's storyboards for *Pilgrim Soul*. "*Storyboards*. How-are-ye? One does *not* view these offerings with feelings of unmixed delight. *Storyboards* obtain in the lavender purlieus of Universal Pictures; let him diddle the Hunters and their Hudsons and all that *male-order* company thriving under the benign gaze of Detlef Sierck with varieties of *storyboards* and leave off thinking he can teach Grampa how to suck eggs! We are for *story hieroglyphics* at Hyperion." Therefore, as some "theys" say, *bolt* and *gird*—for they are suspicious, these men who walk the earth!

P.S. 3: I suppose the reason driftwood = miscarriage is that it tends to wash in, then right out again in the next tide, ending up none knows where. Also, if you look at driftwood, the faces you make out are most like the faces of embalmed fetuses you see in those pornographic medical treatises on abortion the diocese favors as evidence of its contention abortion is foul murder.

It is being said that dirt from the graves of Black Hand killers removed from the neighboring P. J. La Vecchia mortuary and interred there in unmarked graves in the old St. Patrick's Cathedral graveyard was used by old Mary Cedrioli in the working of the curse.

Must close now, as am commencing to hallucinate.

Whither Park
Co. Limerick
Michelmas

My dearest Tangent,

I know the way you despise being nicknamed, and I never have, have I, but only today I noticed for the first time ever that there is an *ange* concealed in your *prenom*, and that when it's extracted, what's left is T-N-T. . .

I come to think that's what's happened this morning—in lieu of a craving for bizarre comestibles such as gillars and pickled eels—is, I've been onomastically galvanized: by last evening's impromptu here at Cashel Orphrey. Sometimes referred to by the diehard Republican begrudgers in the neighborhood as *Castle Rackrent*—which *is* a calumny: we may not be given any great dressy-gentry example, tending, as Virginia Woolf once said of her gang's preference, when weekending at Monk's House, to "just skip about in old clothes," and there may not be quite nearly enough limewash regularly prepared by the upkeep staff, nor may what there is be regularly enough applied to the facade of the Regency wing (that in any event does seem to have rather too abruptly inserted, like a platinum incisor set in a mouth of ecru molars and canines, into what was once the west battlement: blown to smithereens by the English only in history's mind *minutes* ago).

However, the premises (Norman-fortified keep dependent to the main dwellings, consisting of portions of Jacobean galleries once gabled and half-timbered, all encased not in curtain walls but in a small Regency palace, half again the size, we're told, of the Aras an Uachtarain in the Phoenix Park, a great house in the tradition of the Royal Pavilion at Brighton) are in no manner, means, or description tumbling down. And "Otranto" may for all I know get somewhere near to the spirit of place, but I've not read the book and can offer no remarks. Apparently the Georgian period came and went unnoticed.

Indeed, the number of books I have not read is startling, and starting to get to me—and to think that in Pařížská we thought we'd read everything important. We were children who were never really properly educated (albeit clever ones, who understood Kabbalah and became expert at sabotage and the assassination of front-rank Nazis).

Which fact seems to be underneath the following, categorically announced last evening by Orphrey that Czgowchwz was an obvious-descendant, direct or collateral (W and L being in the language interchangeable) of the Leon Czolgosz who shot McKinley. I thought to myself, is this man trying to drive me back out of my mind? I don't need the aggravation; I'm not so entirely well myself that I can afford it, and that's another fact.

At any rate, nobody has (as yet) tried to decipher Creplaczx, or to turn Miro into a Pole: he wouldn't like it if they did. As you know he is wont to hold up the record of the Czechs against that of the Poles in respect of the Jews . . . and he's dead right.

And then I remembered discussing it with you at some serious length, at the time of the M. St. Mawrdew visit to New York, in the aftermath of the prioress's startling disclosures, when I said to you, "Well, if they've discovered I'm actually called Maev, why can't I be called Maev from now on?" "In addition, or instead?" you pressed. "I don't know," I waffled, "either—both. After all, Anne McKnight of the City Opera is called Anna de Cavalieri in Italy." "Maev-Mawrdew Cohalen-Czgowchwz?" you asked? "Well, why not?" I remember countering, edgily. There were precedents, weren't there, and coincidents as well? There was Whosiewhatsis Schróder-Devrient—the one who drove Wagner so wild by going hoarse and barking out "*Tod!*" in *Fidelio* that he wrote Senta for her. And that one whose diary you adore, that Lillie de Hegermann-Lindencrone. Then in our own time, Nanny Larsen-Todsen, Iris Adami Corradetti, Lina Bruna-Rasa, Gertrud Grob-Prändl, Åase Nordmo-Lovberg, Mary Curtis-Verna, Maria Meneghini Callas, and Ralph's two favorite Camp divas, Aida Versanoi-Savanca and Violetta De Pensatici."

"Yes, indeed," you admitted, taking a deep breath, so I knew something *echt* Percase was on the way, "and there was at one time, for a single night, on the billboard of the Teatro Victoria in Barcelona, one Victoria de los Angeles Lopez y Garcia, announced in the role of Mimi (whose real name, you may care to recall is Lucia. The answer to Lucia *What?* has happily disappeared in history's mists, time out of mind), but she (the very young Miss Lopez y Garcia, not the not-long-for-this-world Miss Mimi, or Lucia, *Qualcosa*), in the warm afterglow of her triumph at the Victoria, thought better of her billing—perhaps even thinking ahead, as I suggest you do right this minute, to the aftermaths of future triumphs, and the vexations of autographing—with the charming result that she wears, properly speaking, no professional surname whatever—but then neither, after all, did Arletty, and neither does Hildegarde—lending a slightly irregular, somewhat raffish tone to her *radiant Spanish thrush* publicity, in that she is addressed here as *The Fabulous* Victoria de los Angeles or as Miss de los Angeles merely, and in England, howlingly, merely as Miss Los Angeles, as if she were the winner of a Southern California bathing beauty contest rather than the radio contest that put her onstage at her namesake theater, and had been sent as a finalist, rather than to the Metropolitan Opera in New York, to the Convention Center in Atlantic City, New Jersey, and there directed to parade, wearing spike heels and a Jantzen bathing-suit, under glaring white lights, down a ramp, then shortly next, under rose pink, dressed in a white organza evening gown liberally decorated with fresh gardenias, to sing *Un bel di vedremo* followed by the extempore offering of an uplifting message derived from life experience.

"Similarly, in spite of the fact that she has decided to demonstrate—or at any rate put on exhibition—a singularly touching fealty to that rather unnervingly, self-effacing little Bolognese *maritino* (or *sposetto*) of hers—something similar may have occurred to Madame Maria Callas (nee Kalegeroupoulos), when, selecting orts and particulars from the rich, not to say *loaded* store of *her* natal nomenclature: Anna, Maria, Sophia—"

Remember the time, years ago, Ralph was minding his own business on the line, reading *Variety* and holding down two or three dozen places, and the young man strolled up to the performance billboard—I think it was my first Met Ortrud—looked at it quizzically for several minutes, looked to Ralph and said, "What's that name—Polish?" "Czech." "Thought so—looks Polish. Looks like a Polish eye chart. Thanks." Exit. He was neither seen nor heard from again. Do you suppose *he's* the author of MNOPQR *STUVWXYZ*?

And then, when we were aboard the ship, as we kissed *au revoir*, the very last words from you in my ear, were "Maev-Mawrdew Czgowchwz Cohalen-Beltane?" And anyway, didn't you—hadn't you already by then—let me know that Mawrdew means simply (Celticly) the equivalent of *high type*—or, as Arpenik once interjected (I remember now: we were *a trois* in the restaurant kitchen, standing around the venerable cast-iron eight-burner coal stove from the original Shanley's: Arpen was perfecting the *imam bayeldi* for the evening meal) *big shot*? That's the way I'm telling it, just so you know.

Jacob means the Supplanter. (But you knew that.)

Therefore in the spirit of all that, I offer you, the Yankee settler-proprietor and scion of people responsible, on Manitoy, for the creation of an entire community, the following.

"The Whither family (erstwhile O'Heither, in which form the name appears in ecclesiastical records of the reign of Elizabeth, unearthed, as the result of tunneling undertaken in Ballywhither early on in The Emergency, from the ruins of the Cistercian abbey pillaged by the Welsh agents of Henry the Eighth, preserved in sixteen vellum sheets serving as the protective wrapping of the now world-renowned Whither Chalice, and as well in a letter from Edmund Spenser to his friend and fellow court poet, Sir Walter Raleigh) has suffered to a degree on account of the caves, as some of the family became active members of the Column during the War of Independence. Because the caves served as an occasional hiding place, a portion of Whither Castle, as well as the fourteenth-century Tor Ballywhither were blown up as a reprisal."

Well, dear, we're to go down into them tomorrow, "on location"—no cameras, only old us, "skipping about etc."—and I'm to be introduced to the formations, the more significant of which indeed have names —Finn Mac Cool, Diarmuid and Grainne, Iseult, Granuaile, Sheela-na-Geeg (a pet, they say, if a bit of a show-off), Cúchulainn, of course, and —I give you—Margaret Burke-Sheridan, cast as whom, I can't wait to see: Butterfly? Magdalena de Coigny? The Lily of Killarney? Herself, as she appears today? But then there would have to be a grouping, like at Madame Tussaud's—for she's never ever been seen out of doors in merely her own stellar company—of herself on the arm of *Meehawl*, Hilton, or flanked by the redoubtable Longfords—immense he/ diminutive she—or by Gwladys McCabe and any of her set, or indeed, by The Whither himself—by the way giving *Eamonn de Longfort* these days increasingly, a money run both in his prodigious avoirdupois ("I want more potato!") and in his reputation for prodigal outlays in the pursuit of Art. (Orphrey himself on the subject of the comparison: "Will y' not *talk* to me of that deluded *earleen's* expenditures, or of his much-ballyhooed beneficences either! Metaphorically speaking, I've spilled more than he's pissed!") There's nothing like metaphor, is there.

Whereby I'm suddenly reminded of Daphne. Must drop a sponsorial note to Miss Zuckerman, whom I left working on the Transformation Scene, in preparation for her appointment with Langsam in Vienna. A little transformation goes a long way.

Speaking of all that, of metaphysics and *Metamorphosen:* an inventory on certain transactions in which one has become involved in the round thirties Deco mirror affixed to the dressing table in the bath. In the first place, I feel stranger in the bathroom than in any other apartment in the castle. It is *such* an obvious theatrical set that what I feel most like is Mae West's maid, giddily luxuriating in quite unaccustomed style after the finest woman who ever walked the streets has instructed her in the matter of the freshly drawn and scented bath, "Take it yerself, I'm *indisposed.*"

And secondly, when, sitting, soaking, the bather (Beaulah), growing drowsy from the heat and the soothing scent of lilac, peers through the steam, she notices that as the mirror has misted over, a perfect floating globe has formed, centered in the glass and taking up a little over three-quarters its total area, a perfect floating soap-bubble-like globe stained in an amorphosed interpenetrating areas: blue, rust, white, and bottle green, giving the impression of looking down at earth from some vantage rather higher than a high-flying secret reconnaissance plane, not to mention the one she is supposed to have flown from Prague to Paris. She feels that she has become like Tsuki-jumi-no—? the goddess of the moon, imagines herself in a delirious moment singing that exquisite phrase of Cio-Cio-San's in the incomparably lovely voice of a previously mentioned singer,

Somiglio la dea del la luna,
La piccola dea della luna
Chi scende al mare
Dal ponte del cielo.

She imagines her vantage allowing her to make out, to ascertain, for the first time places time out of mind renowned, for example, Beaulahland, Allemonde, Tir Na nÓg and the Seacoast of Bohemia.

The experience made this one (Beaulah), soaking supine in the salt-scented pool and prone to taking on parts, to giving impressions of women more regal and executive than she, think (if thought was what...) of two things at once. (Handy, isn't it, the way we've been trained to read the mind's arrangement of our organized intervals simultaneously on two staves?) Of Armida's magic mirror, and that sorceress's imprisonment of the itinerant Orlando; and of my fantasy of late Spring, of *my* Technicolor television in wide-angle Cinemascope with stereophonic sound (the tenacity of which so alarmed Arpenik, and I can well see why, acquainted as she was and is with the refugee desperate who walk about mad in the streets of New York, receiving instructions from the antenna on top of the Empire State Building).

And then to wonder if Jacob, who sings Vivaldi's *Orlando Furioso* music so stunningly...

To whom (the aforementioned stunning singer) I mentioned (a propos Technicolor, and the tinted stains in the mist on the mirror in the bath), having heard another of the gatekeeper's County Limerick sayings. "Colors are the deeds and sufferings of light and the longest-suffering of them is green." ("*Wie kommt es*," a voice, not singing, suddenly demanded, of *me*, "*Dass etwas durchsichtiges grun aber nicht weiss sei kann?*") "Perhaps" (and not *Vielleicht*), the singer offered, apparently not in reply to the hectoring voice, but rather to the gatekeeper "because being bang in the middle of the visible light spectrum, green *gets* it from both ends—and not only from both ends, but from all the multiple-of-seven octave frequencies of electromagnetic radiation on either side—if that's what the spectrum properly has, sides." "You're becoming *very Irish*, so you are!" was all I could say back; I concluded, however, it was enough (because you know the old saw about the strangers. They came and stayed, becoming more Irish than the Irish themselves.).

... and not only the Seacoast of Bohemia, but, as on that certain epochal *vol de nuit a Paris*, the Matterhorn in moonlight I remember, I said, "Oh, look, *there*—it's the Matterhorn in the moonlight!" Oh, *dear*! One was supposed to have been alone, wasn't one? Isn't that what it says in the anonymous romance? Well, one wasn't alone, nor at the controls. One said "Oh, look!" to the pilot.

This with love from the pen of your palavering.

M.

P.S. Jacob has the twins named: The one in (the key of) F is called Tristan the one in B, Jacob.

P.S. 2: And would you ever mind telling me, if you know how Miro's idea for an opera on the life of Louis Eilshemius got itself turned, as recorded in MNOPQR *STUVWXYZ*, into a libretto by "Rotten" Rodney Bergamot for Maestro Creplaczx, on "the life, art and hierophantic genius of Puvis de Chavannes?" Someone is baiting others to someone's own peril: Herself the Madge, for example, would not be disinclined to slap smartly the limp wrist responsible for the aforesaid stab at camp, for she is a great champion.

P.S. 3: Of course, Lina Bruna-Rasa went insane. (Which by the way Anita Cerquetti most emphatically has not—only she seems, poor woman, to have had some kind of stroke. High blood pressure, excess weight. Awful, because vocally she's titanic. Oh, *dear*!)

*

Whither Park
Co. Limerick
Michelmas

My dearly Secret Seven,

It is perfectly true (as reported in the document you have undoubtedly had occasion to examine, entitled MNOPQR *STUVWXYZ*, now making its way up, down and across town, and undoubtedly to Brooklyn, Queens, The Bronx, and Staten Island, too, not to mention such far-flung locales as Paramus, Yaphank, Greenwich, and Philadelphia on Tuesday nights), that Ralph did once ask, a propos yours truly, "could she *be*?" So I wonder: the same now, ever again?

The relentless goings-on of the past two weeks supposedly committed to repose (and here called a fortnight) would make you wonder, too, out loud. (Is there any other way in our frankly metropolitan racket?) So many thoughts, so much polyphony, such carousal, all in the mind! And into the bargain, you realize, your woman is pregnant.

You, my original friends in New York, who "sent for" me from farthest Eastern Europe ("Whoever you are, we think you're *fabulous!*") must rejoice with your protégée, now dealt a whole new deal in life. ("Now get this: you're going in there a star, and coming out a mother." High time she donated something to the world and its worth besides high-art vaudeville sensation.) I hope I can hear you all saying, as if in one voice "flawless"—for if, indeed, I gave you, as you did put it, "what to live for," I seem to require of a sudden a little something in the way of the reciprocals.

Does this sound terribly arch, coy, or—I confess it does sometimes seem to me that I have stretched to indecent and/or illegal lengths in the matter of seeking support. As (spies, relay) one anonymous detractor at EMI has put it, "to have gone in, in a manner and to a pietistic, geopolitical and emotionally exploitive extent quite unrivaled since the convergence of the musical-aesthetic and the histrionic life of Richard

Wagner, for the extreme of *appoggiatura* . . ." (Sybil insists this is their response to my continued disinclination / repeated stalling—for reasons we are all perfectly well aware of and definitely need not publicize—to record there, for them. I've come to hold with Messrs. Paranoy and Percase in the severe view taken by both that the pun, no matter how extravagantly festooned, is still the lowest form of wit.) And now I hear you all in your original summons, counseling, "Whatever happens—and we believe, with the force of the first hearers of either the Four Gospels or the first Emmy Destinn records, take your pick, that if and when you bring your Art and Passion to New York you'll first stand them on their heads and then be in for it, the full ride. We can assure you the reaction here to you will be anything *but* lukewarm."

Since when, "anything but" has proved itself my very handiest expression.

Lukewarm. I've just remembered that time summer before last: Ralph telling me (over the phone to Buenos Aires) about the heretic Neriacs—branded by *La Serena. Stessa*, in one of her more delirious pouts, *I Tiepidi*—violently opposed to her undertaking Lady Macbeth at the Cincinnati Zoo. They were too right, remember? She went demented in rehearsal (first time she'd ever heard baboons and macaws responding to her singular art—although as dear Alice did immediately point out, the difference was entirely academic between the sound of *them* sounding the way God designed them to sound, and the sound, of a Saturday night at season's midpoint, of the "Morganimals" bleating from the other side of the footlights at their deluded high priestess.) Whereupon our pal Mary C-V stepped in, and enjoyed a much-deserved triumph.

We've been in cahoots, haven't we, for nearly a decade now, and I have so greatly valued you. (As one kindly backstage prelate put it to me, "Really, if you put those seven together with their angels, they're the new version of the *Vierzehn Heiligen*, the Fourteen Holy Helpers.") We've seen the forties end, yet refuse to do so. Much has "gone down"—much more is on the way. My own feeling is jocular, airborne, reflective. (I've been looking at things reflected in quite gay new ways in Hibernian transforming mirrors.)

The misty air in these environs does not, however, conduce to firmly precise locution; rather otherwise. I may say—as the English put it—that neither would it seem have I ever permitted myself the airs that do so (which in the end may have been a bit of as mistake: to decide to be so down-to-earth as to cut off certain frequencies of oracular transmission. And yet one would not willingly be Mary Garden, so ethereal as to seem never to have quit the precincts of Allemonde. . .)

Meanwhile, many strange dreams of role-playing and much with listening to Memory (sounds like a wire recording of a band of Viennese *comprimarii*, in collision with Met supers, singing *Carmina Burana* at a *Silvestersnacht* gala at the Liederkranz Hall in Yorkville, in about the year 1939), and of course wondering while wandering what I shall be missing this season in New York. Victoria's on sabbatical in Australia, so that's that, but the main thing is: *do not one of you miss opening night*, I charge you in "musicry." (See MNOPQR STUVWXYZ, page 2: not bad: I've about adopted it.) This is the Norma of history, in fact life itself. Alice, do not lose your whole mind and unwittingly initiate some rivalry. Ralph, keep those tapes spinning, reeling in events unfolding in the Great Maze bordered by Thirty-ninth and Fortieth streets, Broadway and Seventh Avenue: in the pit and in the aisles, in the auditorium and in Sherry's, in every bustling *camerino*, everywhere indoors and beyond the walls and windows on the fabulous line as it hugs the temple, disdaining the curbside *and* the gutter: let's get it whole, shall we?

Perhaps I need not (but distance disorients perspective) especially pray you support Laverne all the way in "the transition." Salome may seem risky but it's her willing risk, and finally (ahem) her head (and her head voice). She is to meet with Frau Langsam—the woman who gave me my tops—in November. Salome is *not* suicide; if you don't chest it, everything's negotiable. After Inge Borkh, and especially in the wake (Ooops, sorry!) of Welitsch, it's no Broadway lullaby, but then Laverne is no pan-flash doxy. She's an evolving diva, and the same kind of credit to Bensonhurst and to the New York City school system that the season's principal debutante is to the same system and to Washington Heights —not to mention the credit each woman is to Mediterranean Civilization (in general).

Clacking absolutely *verboten*, as is our custom. If and when usher George suggests it, because he almost certainly will, it will only be to fatten his already Neriac-fattened coffers, and we simply cannot allow Laverne to be grouped in that boiling. Cheerleading encouraged. This is the Word of the Lord as revealed to your correspondent in a gleaming Technicolor vision of Margaret Burke-Sheridan as *La Damoiselle Elue*, had this very morning "on location" in a grotto of the Ballywither Caves. (You are there, or will have been, as I, alas, shall not, in your gay, and come what may, young hearts.)

The Irish have an expression: "Don't *talk* to me." It indicates, roughly, the direct opposite of what it demands, but not exactly, in that the intent is more like "Tell me not in so many words, but anyway." Such as: "Did y' *tell* him?" "*Tell* him? Don't *talk* to me." "Well, did he say anything to you as a result?" "*Say* anything? Come here till I tell you, he nearly ate the face off me!" I think of this I sometimes in relation to my—he isn't my husband: but not exactly. "Did y' tell him?" No answer. Next. Stupid, but there—as the English say—it is.

I wonder if you know the answers to the following questions?

How did your original cable get through the Iron Curtain without censoring? How did my return letter manage same—and meanwhile why have you never told me that an English translation of the entire text of that document is (since *when*?) carved into the wall of a toilet stall in the ladies' shall-we-say-*lounge* at Lodovico's Pizzeria on Forty-sixth Street (only a few doors down from the building frieze featuring Marilyn Miller as Sunny, Ethel Barrymore as Ophelia, Thalia Bridgewood as Peter Pan, and Rosa Ponselle as New York's last—before now—great Norma), right next to "Connie died in here waiting for an order of baked ziti."

(This I had to hear, in a general catalogue of "hidden glories" of the Gotham Rialto, from a marked card called Swithin, a fellow passenger on the *Mary*. (What more, I torment myself asking, to no avail, upon waking each morning, has likely been kept from me?)

Many more—occasioned by casual perusal of the above-cited MMNOPQR *STUVWXYZ*, a fetching enough farrago, but there are an *awful* lot of apocrypha and lacunae therein, not to mention the glitz and the *chazerai*. Example: it is pure Murine, good for a giggle, but really, Ruby, that its *protagonista tore* poor Neri's wig off "in an excess of violent fury apposite to her conception of the overwrought Amneris." It was the merest buff, but the ditz had forgot her *glue* (in so many ways) and be-that-as-it-may have, what with, and forsaking all others, I distinctly recall the silly old transformation, which looked like a cluster of bias-cut Brillo pads, sliding *sideways* all the while she knelt, gesturing like an scalded hysteric toward her foot soldiers in the Family Circle, who, in order to avenge diva's honor would have had either to parachute into the orchestra or run down the seven flights, out into Fortieth Street and around to the side doors, allowing plenty of time for the management to bolt the doors.

And I never—*giammai*—threw the fool thing in the prompter's face (Neri's cousin, Baldassare Buscemi, on special danger-money duty that night, as on all *Morgana-notti*), all agape as said face by then sure was. One merely let the article drop, like the proverbial charred potato. I dwell somewhat at length on this one example, because, as is said hereabouts, one feels the author(s) of MNOPQR *STUVWXYZ* "didn't lick it off the grass." In fact, I seem to remember this very supposed incident having become something of an opera party turn. (One I grant that enacts a more scented and colorific version of the unfortunate and fairly dreary mishap, and subsequent lapse in stage deportment—although what was she to do, poor girl, with her curiously shaped head swathed in underwig tape and her chin straps snapping all over theatrical creation—but, nevertheless, one that, unless we are all to begin believing our publicity identical to, rather than coincident with, the stark reality of our situation and the conduct of our lives' ways . . . you get the gist.

What *is* the name of that loquacious and extremely savvy male negress on The Line, the high priest of Gloria Davy's sect? ("She's *in* and she's warmin' up on 'Sh-boom!') Sports the black mouton car coat, and immaculate white gloves in the afternoon? "Hank" comes to mind, as does "Pauline". S(he) has that terribly funny, veristic take on Paulette Goddard that goes something like, "Paulette likes to be given *jewels*, you know. She'll say to her many gentleman admirers, 'Now, darling, don't you bring me candy, and don't you send me flowers; you just give me *jewels*—any size; big ones, little ones; I don't mind.' She has invested her money wisely, and is a rich woman today!"

It was you, Alice, who pointed out how I will go on about gems. I remember it perfectly well; it was the night of Victoria's Metropolitan debut, and I told Milly Miller after the performance, just before she introduced us, that what with those fabulously liquid flashing black eyes, and the fabulous indigo luster of her Andalusian middle voice on "*de me voir si belle dans le miroir*", I'd finally *got* the Faustian point of the Jewel Song. Whereupon Percase (or was it Paranoy) announced that gem lust is an evolved method of balancing the four humors, each of which (I can't now remember quite how apart from the sanguine ruby) is represented in geomancy by its talisman gemstone.

What do you think then of a pregnant woman, having lately emerged from a labyrinthine limestone cave (located here in the manner of some cellar stairs, right under the backyard: as strange and yet familiar as if its entrance were say, at Magwyck, just a few paces in a girls' game out into the world off East Seventy-fourth Street—directly under the O'Meaghre dolmen), through the walls of which, seen illuminated in circles of electric torchlight, run veins of what looks like merely frozen, rather than calcified gem blood: cardinal, royal blue, emerald green, crystalline). A pregnant woman who imagines returning after midnight, in the company of the gatekeeper's wife, the two carrying each in the one hand a torch of burning flint-struck flame (in the manner of the catechumen Cathars) with which both to find the way to the source (of the Matter) and to melt out of the walls the precious ichor (or Corporeal Substance), and in both other, deep milk pails or wide sod pans to contain the lettings? There is a Rilke poem that contains this:

Das wer der Seelen wunderliches Bergwerk
Wie stille Silberze gingen sie
Als Andern durch sein Dunkel Zwischen Wurzeln
entsprang das Blut, das fortgeht zu den Menschen
und schwer wie die Porphyr sah es aus im Dunkel. . . .

I sang it once, in the Creplaczx setting. I really don't like Rilke much; our gang in Prague didn't take to him. He always reminds me of a woman who wears jewelry in the morning—a womanly version of Hermann Göring. Or really more like one who, gorgeous enough under lamplight the night before and the veteran of any number of encounters in alcoves, had sat up into the morning drinking coffee, hasn't changed, hasn't had a bath before breakfast, is still wearing the whole of yesterday, and still considers herself *alluring*—which, except to those with very special tastes, she simply isn't.

(Perhaps had he been psychoanalyzed after all, and was purged the effluvium of all that impeded his genius rather than as he feared, of the genius itself, he'd have learned to make do with a single strand of the very best pearls, apart from the sanguine ruby Right for any time of the day or night; you can even sleep in them. Perhaps the living poet The O'Maurigan most admires said it best, "Rilke was a jerk." Therefore, although I have made something of the Berg/Rilke *Traumsgekromnt* in recital, I'd as soon have Miro set Paul Celan (I even have a title for him, *Die Antschellieder.*)

Where are the experts (Mrs. Gotrocks hooked arm-in-arm with Mrs. Belmont) only out visiting the sick somewhere. (Nice women, who "get took care of" really don't work, do they?) There being no special virtue in ever saying as I have, "Thanks, but no thanks," you'd wonder why I had never a thought of such a thing as a rainy day. Literally, a rainy day in Holy Ireland, and me in it, *mar dhea*, chancing the one arm on me in a game of mirrors and pictures moving within, the while the other's hooked into the bargain with that of another vagabond vaudevillian, another Gypsy (but a real one) in which we undertake to arrange decoratively weighty quantities of precious stones as talismans, or candies (to go with the Ogham oatmeal cakes Noranna bakes on Tuesdays. Noranna being one of the women who keep house here: not to be called servants merely, although they are obviously, by custom *glebae adscripti*. Orphrey refers to them categorically as "yer *wans* about the place." And so they are.)

Emeralds, of course, the imperial gem: ones the approximate contour, dimension, and weight of the seven goose eggs in the Imperial Russian Tuesday evening coronet. (Would they say "boo" to a goose?) And then mauve diamonds—confections designating the practices of the demimonde in, the same way as did Alphonsine du Plessis's wearing of the red camellia on certain evenings of the month . . . and from that simile to rubies the color of blood, and star sapphires like the eyes of purblind Fate drawn open and bathed in belladonna (many curious visions of late of these in particular).

Yes, since I've been sleeping the voyage off here at Whither Park, I dream and dream of caskets and caskets of gems. Betimes the caskets tip and spill great showers of them, while I laugh (the trill needs work: it's commencing to sound like gargling: no competition for Miss de los Angeles there—though she's told me she's through with Marguerite on the stage, which is swell: I never have to go hear another goddamn *Faust* again in my life). Whither advises Jacob to purchase a sack of marbles; the notion leaves me cold. (Why do I tell you this? Your own affinity for gems: your many-faceted compassion.) I'd settle for pastrami: *they'd* fly some over, but *really*!

Do you negotiate with the sacred polyhedrons? Jacob's elaborate descriptions of the inhering values of certain stones cut significantly is, as his exacting valuations of sensory data do tend to be, beguiling (especially when one is apt, in the drizzle, to turn sullen, and especially, sullen drizzle or no, in the evening, after dinner), when he sits, one leg wrapped around the other, both hands articulating space in a small fire-lit room. (There is just one such here at The Whithery, a sort of apse off the library.) When he quizzes me about the dreams, delving into structure and emission, all I can dredge up is being heaped with gems, radiant hunks of them—bright, cool, opaque, translucent—and sometimes it's more like being *pelted*, like the woman taken *imprevue* in her *loge* by the bearded onanists. In fact, I can almost hear the remonstrance: she offers it herself, disdaining to throw herself on the mercy of any of the many wayside interveners of her acquaintance. "Listen, let him who is without sin cast the first stones—and make them precious specimens, or you're wasting your pitching arm!"

I imagined somehow that with your cast of mind you might decipher something encoded.

Mirrors and motion pictures. Earth turning for *Pilgrim Soul* runs apace. (We were down in the cave doing just that, and so I thought of you, and yours: the planet itself and the gorgeous and evocative script. Evocative that is of the Maev Cohalen that was and is to be she who was ever displayed, never obeyed—but did she ever wish in her heart's heart to be either? So far as scene goals go, what are hers? What *did* she want? Where *was* she going? And God love Stella Adler for teaching me to ask, and for teaching me to *aim*. I shall never forget meeting her that afternoon "by chance" chez Consuelo, and being told right out, "Your vehemence is divine, but your *schlepping* it about the stage that way is *boring*, darling, *boring!*")

The main thing I have to learn to do is to *sit tight*. All well and good, but not if it's after all a version of go-sit-on-a-tuffet. (A patronizing remark from Orphrey about filmmaking such as "Pet, there's nothing you have to *know!*" is all I have to hear to get my Irish up—and my Czech Jewess-by-proxy with it, if you don't mind.) Carmen was a snap compared to this: I haven't the smallest idea what I'm about—her either, though I believe she was born to Irish tinkers, who are today miscalled "Gyppos" but are in fact nothing other than the descendants of the dispossessed in the Great Hunger, which renders them archetypal.

Meanwhile the Dominations, Virtues, Powers, and Thrones have not as yet cast a leading man, so that of all things one need know nothing of the most bewildering is (or isn't, depending upon your point of view) portraying one's mother in intimate collision with one's father, yoked in the mind to a cipher (I hinted shamelessly about you-know-*who*, but Orphrey got very testy. Said Universal's got him under contract; he costs the earth to get on loan-out, and although he, O. grudgingly admits, is the camera's current true beloved, he can act apparently only under Sirk. "We'll find somebody cast in the same mold who looks as if he might have written philosophy." Certain fancies are more than merely calmative, *non e vero?*)

In any event we depart almost immediately for Connemara ("The West's Awake") back where it all began for yours truly. Pray that when the interior geography has been remapped in relief one may find some accommodation in the wilds. I do mean that, because as soon as it's so and all that follows from it is realized, it's up and back to New York to discover a house and refashion it a permanent home.

My love to Consuelo. She requested I not trouble to write, but took instead the loan of my little gold compact. Said she'd consult the mirror within once a day, and figure, out what was what with me perfectly well (and who may doubt it? Not I.).

Meanwhile, I rely upon you to champion both Laverne and the Meneghini, and to continue fighting for standards ("You know the drill," as Orphrey is continually informing the mob here—who, of course, don't). We must always remember that there is rot at the core—that the General Manager of the Metropolitan Opera is the man who, in 1951, when Jeritza ill-advisedly came back and sang Rosalinda with Ormandy, taking the Czardas down a third and still going to pieces, stood in the wings indulging himself for all to see and hear in a fit of hysterical laughter, and chomping on his usual banana like a deranged baboon.

In the mean time, I shall hang out in the Mother Hemisphere, making a picture (good *shkelt* the gardener says, who's mad keen on the fillims, especially since *The Quiet Man* of the ones in Technicolor with Ireland in them), then deliver a pair of boys. (I asked the gatekeeper's wife who's read my tea leaves if she thought, since there is apparently no chance of either of the boys being a girl, I was missing out in this life, lacking ever a born daughter. "Och," she replied, *Byes, gurls*, sure I've had both and there ought t' be somethin' betther!")

Some day next year we must go over all Ralph's tapes just once more. I really must get the story straight myself, for when those boys get to listen and make some sense out of their mother's time and place, out of the words and the music.

Bookoos of assorted charms,

Your pal,
M. Czgowchwz

P.S. I realize, Ralph, you never, in fact, wrote anything called *The Moricon*, which, therefore, could not have been the motivation for *I Neriani* molesting me backstage. It is the method of the anonymous author of MNOPQR *STUVWXYZ* to mix the real and the made-up (and I agree that "Ralph" isn't really you—not the you I know. But then who—when, as they say, she's at home—is the heroine?) And, as the English say, there it is. I agree that reading the thing is skeevy, but I'm told by everyone here that nobody thought there was semblance of himself either in *Ulysses*. And I do think in all fairness that "the deviated septum" is not at all bad.

Yr
MC

Whither Park
Co. Limerick
Michelmas

A *stor mo chroi galora*, Daracushla or Acushla Fitz,

(Should mood with you so have it.)

As I have just put down (first read) *Under Nephin*, I shall find it impossible to speak to you the adequate speech, but then we have never, we two, gone in for the precise, have we, all told? Nevertheless, since this letter surely will not write itself, I must try my best to chart the swell.

Let me therefore begin by referring to *Pilgrim Soul*. As I may not to read it, "until such time as we can realize it into moments," and am forced to eavesdrop (not hard in this place, when out of any old hole in any odd wall down any winding corridor or stair you might likely hear some snatch of anything, and be listening to it coming either from another room, another passage, another season, or another century) and am rewarded by hearing the following (which I do believe was being dictated over the phone in the library, because much of it would be repeated over, and *spelled*, into an ear at the *Irish Times* in D'Olier Street, in the Hibernian metropolis wherein each of us was conceived, although, as luck or mischance would have it, neither born).

"An astonishing achievement, full of the boy's own vision and song!" (Tell me, who may this "boy" be? I know the man: S. D. J. The O'Maurigan Himself.) "Full as well of the accomplished truth of another, greater time—in the past that is the ground of the telling." (I liked that bit: it reminded me of philosophy, of aesthetics, all those things we so uproariously did mock all last winter.) "The devices for conveying the historical information are done as if informed by an eye stationed at perfect vantage—"

(I wrote it all down in the Speedwriting you and Trixie Gilhooley taught me last winter for to transcribe my dreams, having happened along—talking of perfect vantage—as I did—not last winter, yesterday with pen and notepaper in hand, meaning to drop on the hall table for the afternoon post a letter to your auntie I'd just completed. "And the utterances put into the mouths of the forbears, of their private tragedy, are precisely enfolded with verisimilatudinous accuracy the great historical sweep." In any event, so declare Lock, Stock, and Barrel, appraisers, in the person of O. Whither, comptroller. (If it's any news to you, of sooth or balm, I do believe he cares a *graydle* for you—as for us all to be sure—after his fashion: the Gargantuan.)

I ask myself therefore, in response to hearsay, what can you have done and how can you have done it, when so little is known of her, my progenitor, that is (that was)? You know, Tsvetaeva said her own mother's rebellion and longing had grown into her child *to the level of a scream*. (Poor Tsvetaeva, of course, betrayed by her own daughter, hanged herself.) Talk of the mystery of character, destiny, and worth—now, how is one to play her? How to join in those mysterious activities you picturists connote—or, as has been said by a woman in the know we know, revere and talk about: how to do one's level best to prevent oneself looking like a sixty-by-forty-foot horse's arse up there on the wide Technicolor screen. As to the bewildering wizardry with which you would seem to have completed the work and sailed it overseas like a folded-paper airplane (not even stopping to refuel in Newfoundland) over the heads of a schoolroomful of earnest drones—or like some guided missile fashioned timelessly—I think I've got your number: that is surely called *sprezzatura*, but will you not have mercy on their wits? (That they may love you this side idolatry, awed, not annihilated.) So insinuates one wily Gypsy to another, with a view to demanding, as the corollary—

For how shall we embody it with true conviction without you? (And now you've got *my* number: MANipulative 1-2345: if *he* answers, pretend you've called to order Chinese food.) Orphrey is severely frothed: he murmurs various imprecations. Yet, I imagine you'll stay put (as indeed you should).

You will do as you like, won't you, as we promised one another we each would do? And if you should convince Miro to do a *Double Indemnity* for you, and if you think Jacob really would be right for the fall guy, I do indeed see the possibilities, vocally and dramatically. (Only perhaps not *so soon* as I've found him ought I play the broad he fills full of lead at the end.)

Tell me this: do I tend somewhat to jumble my indications? It may be because I am confused by what extremes you men are apt to go to in dreaming up roles for a woman to sing. Seems it was only a year or so ago Miro was trying to sell *you* on an opera about Therese Neumann, telling anybody who would listen that it was the only direction to go in after *Lulu*. (And Paranoy said, "What, back to *Maria Egieziaca*?") A fascinating idea to me at the time; nowadays I'd be reluctant to catch anybody's *sniffles*, never mind accepting the stigmata every Friday night—why I'm also glad in a way I became too indisposed last year to consider taking on Poulenc's Mother Superior's death throes. Bliss it is indeed to be preparing a no more spiritually complicated vexing role than a girl who cheats at poker to save the man she loves (for God knows the vocal line is hard enough, but worth it without question). Destinn was absolutely bang on about the opera, it is his masterpiece, and my assuming Minnie is both joy and mitzvah.

You will know our tidings either by telephone from Magwyck, or if you are, indeed, keeping yourself there by the great whoop up the stair. Will you be glad? "Another form for light to fall on" is what Jacob says.

Everything is coming true. Are you glad? I hope so. To say "I know you are" seems the height of impertinence. (What *did* we decide that height was—wasn't it exactly four feet?)

I carry with me always and reread often, for the good of my heart and soul (and not merely to be edified by perfect written English, even if it is true as you insist that there's nothing better for either than it), your consummate letter of the *Pelleas* afternoon. It bears in every line the clear and authoritative mark of the guardian, taskmaster, instructor, friend: all that you are—all that and more.

Do you remember when you were at Trinity, and over for a holiday, you would stalk backstage after some *Aida* or other and ask me *in just that way* why whatever? concerning Amneris. Why thus-and-such (and your auntie would cry out "My life, it's The Grand Inquisitor, Dom Thusandsuch, O. P.! That's the Order of Prosecutors.") And we'd laugh, but you'd only smile to humor us, and then persist. Like the clerk from Probity, Eaves, Dropping and Snoop, our trustworthy solicitors. (Wasn't it Probity sported the truss—or was it Snoop?) Or like the canny scout from Mordant, Trenchant, Telling and Trew, producers on the rialto, who smoked those panatellas, the gimlet-eyed fitter from Fitz and Startz, haberdashers, who like Jack Spratt ate no fat, or like the package tour vendor from Huffing, Puffing and Mufti—and I've forgotten the rest in our onomasticon—save for Florence Fels-Naptha, wasn't she to do with hygiene promotion? Only that you started the game from your revered Browning's Hobbs, Nobbs, Stokes and Doakes, who combined to paint the future from the past, wasn't it, like a press of agents, or a congress of *repetiteurs*. And I remember when you first told me you didn't much care for Rilke and I said I didn't either, and we agreed that a rose, pure unfolding, pure thrust, is *anything but* a contradiction.

Because as Neruda writes, *la rosa, sin porque florisce, porque florisce.*

And as we're talking of naming names, the following little anecdote. Your delightful English friend Pickersgill asked me on board the *Mary* could I think of one for his revue. "What's in it?" "Oh, dear—well, lots of high comedy, intercut with vignettes to do with the ignition of flaming desire—desperate consequences of—that kind of thing. I have convinced myself it is time to revive the much-maligned Lyceum melodrama."

"Well, what about *Close Cover Before Striking*?"

"What?" he cried, throwing his head back, as if something had just flown overhead—as indeed gulls had been doing for some time as we were within sight of landfall off Mizen Head and some very old passengers were talking about the *Lusitania*, and about Schull, where in the local pub (the Bunratty Arms, I heard it called) one can sit in front of the fire in deck chairs off the catastrophied vessel. (And as Garbo calmly replied, when they asked her to come back to the screen as Lola Montez, "*Vy wud I want to do dhot?*") I said, what about *Close Cover Before Striking*?" "My God, that's it—that's *it*! You're a genius, a *genius*!"

Forgive me, but I hadn't the heart in me to tell him it was right out of our second drawer rear compartment. Did we intend it for anything serious, such as either of the first volumes of either of our intimate memoirs? I do hope not; he seem so pleased, so genuinely grateful. (Some old who-the-hells were actually pointing fingers.) He himself I thought rather quick, for instance this, right off the cuff, or so it seemed, on motion pictures: "Oh, now that you're American, you must invoke your national poet: he foresaw them, the spell they would cast." "Did he really?" "Oh, yes, and wrote a poem about it.

> *'The Untold Want by life and land n'er granted*
> *Now voyeurist sail thou forth to peek and mind.'* "

(I thought it rather clever. I wonder do you?)

He's certainly charry about Auden. I avowed I'd always found Mr. A. delightful, especially when he'd come around backstage with Chester K and the redoubtable Parson T.—"Nunc" as you call him—in my Waltraute days, and say things to me like "I do love the way you get her *age* across. None of the Valkyries is a young woman. They are all of them as old as God, and much heavier."

Then, too, his venomous stance against the Sitwells is perhaps a little overdone, but then he does seem truly pained, rather than merely jealous of their réclame. "I like Sacheverell all right," he said, "but those other two are Sin and Death combined, the author of *Notable Excrescences* worse even, as sin is said to precede death, and to preordain it, than his sibling." I pointed out that Edith, in fact, precedes Osbert by birth, to which he replied, "Not from the point of view of Literature or of Infamy."

He then tells of attending during the war (as a Westminster boy scholar) the royal poetry reading at the Aeolian Hall. Avows it the world's worst experience for an adolescent aflame with poetic ardor, going so far as to say had Beatrice Lillie not been handing out programs, he's certain he'd've fled, begged for a transfer to Bletchley, to apprentice the decription men or mop floors, and never opened a book of verse again.

He calls Edith the Morgana Neri of poetry—a serious calumny, no? Intends to put them into *Close Cover* as Sir Bogus Drivel, Bart., sister Elspeth and brother Fleance. Bogus a great admirer of Kitty Piccadilly (the Pickersgill alter ego, I understand) but she suspects him of getting more than the cleaned up dictation back from the secretary, Dodo Trumpet. Everybody sitting around a broken-down Italianate country seat called *Montebuffone* in chairs shaped like oyster shells, reading the witches scenes from *Macbeth*, sniping at one another, the world of the philistines and the awful (stoic, unperturbed) servants in ghastly French.

Fleance has a wife called Crimea and a son called Clerestory, who bicker incessantly, and a fey composer of skeletal tunes called Brocas Clump, a regular visitor. Dodo and Bogus sally forth to do battle with Cuckoo Weir, M. P., a philistine, but Dodo's slingshot backfires, wounding Bogus, who takes to a great Jacobean closet bed. Very backstage.

Talking of which, the overheard commentary on the fate of the *Lusitania* led in our corner to the cautionary tale of Granados and the gold specie he insisted the Metropolitan pay him in for the *Goyescas* premiere, which ill-charmed horde lies sewn in Senora G.'s hems at the seas's bottom. (Or did their spectral selves find a use for it—installing themselves perhaps in sumptuous apartments on the *Gran Via* adjacent to the palace, in the Kingdom of Ys?) Don't the British, in particular, *love* pointing fingers at quirky historical figures.

Talking of pointing fingers, I did (and I don't, not frequently). The swami you forewarned us of (and really you are the *best* spy). Jacob said later, "You are sought after by a retired Indian railway worker, and I am plagued with the unwelcome attentions of a retired British civil servant. What is there about us?" He refers to the man called Gerald Gardner, sometime friend of Margaret Murray, who seems, especially since the rescinding of the archaic English laws against The Craft (an event Jacob likes to refer to as "Repeal" saying, "Things were better, you realize, in many ways before Repeal," which makes *him* sound like an old retired American bootlegger) to have cornered the market in explication of Wyrd ways, and set himself up on the Isle of Man as a kind of antipope.

But no, more of this in letters. One of the disciples of the former railway worker, your creature Swithin, sufferer of *angosia paurosa* put down variously to The War, the Career, Society a terrible withdrawn entity whose poached cod face one did somewhat recall, does seem to be on some sort of mend, but will look toward us in such a longing way that I said out loud, "*Who's* that?" (Did I find out!)

And then again, having engaged him in conversation. ("Get to talk about himself." *Why?*) did I find out more than is strictly necessary—more than ever sufficient unto the day—about this one, that one, and the other one. (A obvious consequence, one imagines, of the narrator's having lived entirely through others—perhaps, it occurred to me from having been taken at a frightfully impressionable age to see *Craig's Wife* on the stage. I can still hear your voice in the tag line: "People who live for themselves are generally left to themselves." It's almost my favorite of your character women impersonations, coming after Barrymore's "How very wise you are, my dear," from *Portrait of Jennie*.)

Anyway, I've tried to forget everything the poor vindictive stretcher case let me in on, but some of it has not been at all easily expunged. (You know how it is: you tell yourself, "Oh, I could use *that*.") A lot of it reminded one of nothing so much as the classic Milanov rejoinder to the old geezer who one night backstage hit Madame with "Zinka, do you know what some of these boys you welcome into this dressing room after your performances are *doing* on the outside?" "*Zo . . . vot?* In Za-*greb* dey've bin doing all *dhot for years!*"

And to be sure, Swithin found his own particular "why just that way?" to put to me. "Madame, why did you land in Paris in just that way?" Imagine! Shook me nerves, I tell you. "State secret," I replied, surrounding it with as much air as I thought I could manage believably, without tipping—and then had the idea to add, "of course many observers declared subsequently it ought to have been done on a *broomstick*." It's this manuscript that's circulating isn't it, recharging the quidnuncs' batteries—and, of course, I'm taking a chance even writing things to you this way in a letter—albeit from a "neutral" country, and let's not get into *that*—that might compromise the Fourth Republic. De Gaulle of course would love that, as so would De Valera.

I ramble. Indeed, I have been going in these days almost entirely for rambles . . . rambles and and muddles. (Rambles and Muddles—advertising? Landscaping? Mumbles and Murk—undertakers?) Which reminds me of Swithin on the Mahatma's ("tee-hee-hee") metaphysic. "A transit system, really." Cute.

Looking after something new, assuming custodial duties. Jacob is listening for the sounds they make, and life becomes in the strangest way yet a matter of finding ways of saying things—as if we shall, not this day or the next or the next, but soon enough be by the occupying forces held to account, and what if be caught without details—of same, or some, or any. (*"Ah, chi si credera?"*)

I have an idea you know what I mean. Here one is, after years and years of saying, singing, hooting, tooting, and as they say enlivening every role without ever wanting to do much more. Imagine had the capacity to do it given out, leaving one leftover, with no more idea than the prompter in the little hooded trench has of how the noise is made, of how to make a simple declarative statement of one's own, much less the interrogatives and imperatives. What *do* I mean: must I still fear? The past, the inchoate, the unraveled, the vertiginous—but all that passed, and one woke in a room.

I remember a house where all were good
to me, God knows, deserving no such thing:
Comforting smell breathed at every entering,
Fetched fresh, as I suppose, off some sweet wood.
The cordial air made those kind people a hood
All over, as a bevy of eggs the mothering wing
Will, or mild nights the new morsels of Spring.
Why it seemed of course, seemed of right it should.

I shall think of you with love on the night of your debut at the Gotham. *Under Nephin* is a very beautiful poem, and I'm happy you've retained in the collection the poem you sent me with your first offering of flowers backstage—white roses in a yellow-blue vase. In the mean time, just now I hear uproarious commotion in the house: evidently something has been caught, or let get loose. (It couldn't be the cured ham, could it, that was last seen—and smelled—smoking over juniper branches?)

Meanwhile, the old yardman here plays the *uileann* pipes, and the young groom the *bodhran*. Things are a lot calmer than they were a century ago, at the time of the following letter, found (undated) in a volume of Sheridan le Fanu novels in the library.

"Several murders have been committed in the neighborhood. We habitually take our arms with us to the dining-room, and eat our meals with our loaded pistols on the table, guns leaning against the chimney piece. It is surprising, when one gets accustomed to it, how little this circumstance affects the appetite or weighs on the mind."

I remember a time when we all did exactly the same—but that was long ago, in another country, before one woke to the call of your voice.

All love,
Your collaborating
M

P.S. Hours later, it seems strange to be sitting here dictating into a machine, in the dead of night in a castle in Galway, knowing that by the time this reaches you another First Friday will have taken place, with your auntie having presided over same in her great wing chair, and all the Cigarettes, as you call them, having filled the ears in the walls of Magwyck with yet another loquacious installment of the ongoing Gotham carnival. Do any of them know anything at all about the listening vents or that Maywyck was a particularly shady consulate before the War? What I say is, good job if they don't.

I've been glad being away from it—off the midway, anyway—at all times until now—when there's still time to fly back, in Gypsy disguise and—would I get away with it? Probably not—but I'd love to hear the new tapes, except of course there won't be any . . . unless the FBI have taken a notion that the place is wired to the Russian Embassy.

VIII

Moriarity with you again, darlings, sans preamble this time. This one you figure out on your own, and if you can't, you really have picked from the wrong pile.

"So how was the reading—is he any good?"

"That I couldn't tell, I don't get poetry, but he looked so good I'd say he got them by the balls—the women included—and, of course, he had the fags all in big time tears."

"They make a tape?"

"And break the seal of confession? Not that crowd."

"Well, we're set up—think we'll get anything good?"

"Whatever we get they'll pay the money—they'll cop to anything. Sure beats working for that Kilgallen bitch. Peanuts to monkeys is what she tosses—you're supposed to think it's some fuckin' *honor*. Only for Chrissakes don't let the Armenian clock us. He may know it was done last month at Ceil Chapman's, but when it comes to anything to do with the Countess Madge or Mawrdew Czgowchwz he gets—well, like an Armenian."

"Mawrdew Czgowchwz isn't here."

"Yeah, and Duffy ain't at Duffy's tavern. Take my word, huh."

Two other waiters assigned to the First Friday were whispering.

"Say nothing about this to anyone, right?"

"Trap shut, man, and bolted down. What's it that French pastry chef at the place says."

"*Bouche cousu.*"

Yeah, booch-cooze-oo Thing is, we worked the tape deck before, but what's with the fuckin' *body wires*? How'd those two afford fuckin' FBI instrumentation? They're only goddamn *school kids*!

"They got ins with the cops is what I was told. From the Everard Baths. The cops own the Everard Baths, and they're helpin' the kids with their homework."

"Now I've heard everything."

"Not yet—not by a long shot; the night is young."

!@#$%^&*

"Will you just look at that thing on La Gilligan's head? We *know* how the *hatters* went mad . . . but what's *her* excuse?"

"That, dear, is a *Tania, a* one-of-a-kind creation."

"Really? They must both be using the same nail polish remover."

"Ah, *crudele!*"

!@#$%^&*

"*Not* another American opera by Douglas Moore! Maybe Lenny Bernstein, or another of Carlysle Floyd's parables. You won't get Sam Barber, he's gone to ground, skipped town, won't answer the phone, prisoner of art on the Met commission, which I don't think is even American. What's it called?"

"*Vanessa*. A prettier name than Mildred, isn't it—or even Susannah. So evocative—and it is American, the opera, although it takes place in a nameless country far to the north, and has a cantankerous baroness in if who won't say a word to anybody."

"Well, that sounds just like Vermont, and the Baroness von Trapp, with the difference of course that nobody can get her to *shut up*. Not content with hauling that family of unctuous rebarbative warblers around, *she* can't stop telling the world what a lovely evening in the lyric theater could be made of her life—the nuns, the escape from the Nazis, tutoring the Baron's children, a la Anna and the King of Siam—all of it, set to lovely lyrical music. An evening I am most anxious to miss."

"Hmm, nuns . . . escape from the Nazis . . . the baron."

"Evocative?"

"*Evocative*—that *word!*"

"Douglas Moore is said to be evocative."

"Czgowchwz likes Douglas Moore."

"I was *about to point out* that La Trapp's story would seem to run along parallel lines to the story of Czgowchwz—of course crowded with richer incident."

"I've never heard of any baron in that—"

"*Really*? Then you have never read Eleanor Perenyi's *More Was Lost*."

"Well, no, I haven't. I know Eleanor is the Baroness Perenyi and is friendly with Czgowchwz, but I've never been apprised of, or heard tell of a pertinent connection."

"It's all between the lines, dear, in *More Was Lost*."

!@#$%^&*

"Who's that over there pouring conversational gin into Marya Mannes's ear?"

"*That's* the legendary Glenway Wescott, dear. He was at the reading and thinks our young host is *the* up-and-coming man. Lately he's been doing volunteer work for Kinsey, and the word is he'd just love to enlist the debutant to help out in important ways."

"Gore Vidal was at the reading, too. Glenway had tried to find out was he on the list, and they lied, making him bilious. He really hates the guy."

"Gloria Vitriol can be a low-down woman—I've witnessed it."

"Who is that dark, striking woman over there?"

"That is Doctor Evelyn Gentry Hooker, a great friend of O'Maurigan's analyst Gennaio—and talking of moments of love and insane asylums, she has embarked on a study for the National Institute of Mental Health aimed at keeping men who are, well, *musical*, or *so*, and say they are in love, *out* of insane asylums."

"Really?"

"Yes, well, that's it in a nutshell anyway."

"How you say—such as that Prosper Swithin person, for example, who to hear the talk of the town has fled our shores for the holy city of Benares and from there into the high Himalayas, apparently trying for a fifties remake of *The Razor's Edge*."

"There's simply no telling where some of these people come from."

"Oh, there's *plenty of telling*, darling, much of it quite amusing; what's wanting is hard proof."

"Well, I suppose, after all, we are the little nucleus, as—"

"A word in your *ear*, dear. In the first place there are no more nucleii, there are only spinning particles, impossible to pin down, and in the second place to compare the Countess to that harridan in Proust ... I suppose the next thing you'll bring up is the little train. There were in fact model trains, put down at Christmas for a few years during the war, but not—"

"In point of fact, when Hans goes down to Princeton on the Pennsy, he gets off at Princeton Junction and gets on a little put-put that goes—"

!@#$%^&*

"All great ideas are simple, dear. Their too-tangled ramifications have most to do, necessarily, with *staffing*."

"You aren't religious at all, are you, dear."

"Oh, I don't know. I like what the Jesuit over there was saying as I came in—about individualism and its decline in our time reflected in religious matters. He said the problem with morals in America today is everybody trying to keep up with the Niebuhrs. I liked that, it showed a certain wit."

"Really? Well, my dear, I wonder how you would like hearing him from the pulpit. I did once—dropped on impulse into that place on Park Avenue where he edifies his flock—and do you know what I heard him declare? The following: 'The lofty concept the Church has forever held relative to the vocation of the Jewish people... does not blind her to the spiritual dangers to which contact with Jews can expose Christian souls, or make her unaware of the need to safeguard her children against spiritual contagion.... As long as the unbelief of the Jewish people persists,... so long must the Church use every effort to see that the effects of this hostility do not redound to the ruin of the faith and morals of her own members.' I found that appalling."

"Ah, well, inevitably in any society one finds conflicting denominational sensibilities and ethnic allegiances that divide the most seemingly cozy little patriciates into competing factions. But as has been observed, if one goes in for roulette, both the red and the black are necessarily encountered. Plus which, he's a clever weasel is F. X. Strange, S.J.—you would never hear him whisper a breath of anti-Semitic innuendo in here. He knows on which side his bread is buttered."

"And he undoubtedly gets that tired of munching on dry communion hosts."

"Listen, all must steer a cautious course. Dorothy Day is present."

"I understand the gaming table metaphor, but tell me this—why is there a *billiard table* in the music room?"

"You don't know, do you—shame on you."

"To me it's clear enough. '*Eux uno disce omnes.*' "

!@#$%^&*

"He who has politics merely has no life."

"I cannot agree. *Felix qui potuit rerum cognoscere causas.*"

"*Tout comprendre, c'est tout pardonner?*"

"Yes, exactly."

"Politics has nothing to do with causes. Politics is epiphenomenal. And your friend Felix, if he is responsive to anything at all, is of necessity entirely responsive to phenomena."

"My God, talking of phenomena, look over there at the Baroness von Trapp! Speak of the devil and quicker than a wink . . . Who let *her* in?"

"Nobody did. That's *not* the baroness, my dear, that's Dorothy Day."

"*That's* Dorothy *Dean*?"

"No, no, dear, that's Dorothy *Day*—the lustrous braids of Ate coiling tightly 'round her scheming head."

"They do look rather like the cables on the Brooylyn Bridge."

"Whoever she is, you don't like her very much, do you?"

"I don't like the likes of her—nor she of me. Whatever of that, the little black woman over there, looking the place over like she's never seen furniture before? She seems to be tormenting Frank O'Hara while his two friends look on with what, satisfaction?"

"*That's* Dorothy Dean—a phenomenon of the Age."

"Possibly. Of the two friends of O'Hara, one is called Jimmy—he was Auden's amanuensis on Ischia just after the war and now works at MoMA with Frank—and the other's called John, connected to the Cambridge Poets' Theater and that strange Bunny Lang crowd at Harvard just when The O'Maurigan was up there teaching the Irish language and expounding on the remnant of Irish prosody to be detected in Romantic English poetry. He's just back from Paris for a spell. They are all homosexual and write *outré* poetry about New York. They, too, are interested in recruiting our host."

"I see—and those two beautiful girls over there—dark hair, dark eyes, brimming with intelligence?"

"The two black-eyed Susans, yes. They both came east from Los Angeles a few years back. The one over there is Orin O'Brien's best friend—you know Orin, she is George O'Brien and Marguerite Churchill's daughter and plays double bass for the NYCB. She's always bringing musical people down to Arpenik's. Her friend—that Susan—is an actress. The other one acted, too, at university—Chicago. Played Ismene, walking off with all the personal notices, but then she startled the academic world by marrying Philip Rieff, whereupon people joked Rieff had brought home an Indian squaw. The word on her generally is that she is quite seriously brilliant and goes about smouldering a great deal."

"Would you say she's smoldering now? True, she's smoking Balkan Sobranies, but that in itself, in the absence of sustainable corroboration, cannot be said to constitute a smoldering woman."

"Is Rieff here, too?"

"Oh, *no*. In the first place he stays up in Cambridge, and in the second place, he's more than a bit *too* doctrinaire. They try to keep it *fluid* here, even if sometimes you might be forgiven for thinking you'd crashed an editorial meeting of *The Reporter*. And you know what Stendhal said—"

"A lot, it seems."

"He said the art of conversation grinds to a halt when *husbands* are around. No, she came in with her small son—Rieff's child—who's upstairs having a nap—unless he's reading Schopenhauer by flashlight under the covers. I believe they're planning to divorce."

"Divorce? Mother and child?"

"No, not the *child*, the *husband*. *Honestly*, dear!"

"Well . . ."

"Anyway, she comes down regularly to New York to work as a brain; writes for *Partisan Review*. Sontag's her name."

"Sontag. Nice name. Gal Sunday, is she from a mining town in the West?"

"Yes, in a way—she's from Los Angeles, by way of Arizona, I believe, and then Chicago, and now from Cambridge—although just before I thought I heard her say she was a New York native, but what that means I can't quite make out."

"Well, if she is a squaw, then perhaps she's a *Manahatta*?"

"And the other dark-haired, dark-eyed girl from Los Angeles?"

"Orin O'Brien. As I said, daughter of Marguerite Churchill—the actress, no relation to that wet brain with the cigar who sails around the Mediterranean on yachts shouting battle orders—and George O'Brien the beauteous star you may recall opposite Janet Gaynor in Murnau's *Sunrise*."

"Who could forget him? The good big boy in the big bad city—they didn't need voices, they had faces. He became a cowboy actor, and she divorced him."

"She must have been quite mad; he was the most beautiful man in Hollywood."

"In any event, three graces or three dark norns or three beautiful witches even, if and when they come back for Halloween. *Comme vous voulez*. Orin usually talks to the poets and musicians; the first Susan, the actress, to political correspondents; and the Sontag woman to the more abstract brains. You see, she's over there now, talking to Doctor Evelyn Gentry Hooker, Glenway Wescott, Louise Bogan, and Alfred Chester. Looks to be some confab."

"Who is Alfred Chester?"

"*Look*, call me tomorrow *morning*, will you? We'll do a postmortem."

!@#$%^&*

"Czgowchwz? Yes, of course I know what the name means, there's no mystery whatsoever. It's the Czech word for anybody who comes from Człuchów, a town in Poland."

"It isn't at all, it's merely the Czech equivalent of Korjus."

"Well, in either case, she would not actually not be a not Bohemian at all, but a Pole—perhaps Miliza Korjus's long-lost sister? That would be interesting."

"Well, then, is she the North Pole or the South Pole?"

"Mawrdew Czgowchwz, Maev Cohalen ... this unpronounceable thing circulating. What *is* her name?"

"What's in a name?"

"That is not true—moreover, Shakespeare the Rosarian *knew* it wasn't. Juliet dies because it isn't. The rose name was an ambiguity—one title of the Virgin Mother of God the Virgin Queen arrogated unto herself was *Rosa Mystica*. The Tudor rose was red and white. So when Juliet says that, the audience hears their monarch's epithet and agrees that by any other name, yes ... but at the same time no. Shakespeare the botanist knew that when you are cultivating roses you must not only *never* say 'come along, lilies of the valley,' even in jest, but then why *would* you? Moreover, you must always address the rose by her proper name. You must say, "Come along, 'Madame Alfred Carrière', and you Rosa Mutabilis and 'Rose de Rescht', 'Mabel Morrison', 'Prince Camille de Rohan', 'Gloire de Dijon', 'Zéphirine Drouhin', 'Reine des Violettes', Rose de Meaux ... come along, come one come all. It is the only way to get them to thrive, for they are touchy.

"As to Czgowchwz, it is *not* the Czech word for anybody from any town in Poland, *or* the Czech version of the Polish historian of philosophy August Cieszkowski. It is etymologically and homophonically related to *Grzywacz*, and, though not strictly linguistically—since Hungarian is at root no known tongue—to Boczov. It is a way of saying Jew, which, if you want to know the truth, is all you have to know."

"Or, you could read the *Cratylus*—a name essential, decorative, evocative—"

"I'm reading the *Gorgias*."

"Let's read them together out loud. Like, you sing the *Libiamo* and I'll sing *Giovanezza, giovanezza, primavera di bellezza!* Let's try it."

!@#$%^&*

"Ozenfant and Dunoyer de Segonzac, overdue for reappraisal? Well, well."

"Christ—in the flaming asshole department, that one is the fucking *Hindenburg!*"

"Existentialism, fevered metaphysic of the Europe's demise, has declined from the putatively metaphysical through the aesthetic, the moral, and the political in record time, according to the entropic quotient and its functions on view in the second law of metaphysical thermodynamics, reaching its conclusion and undergoing its thanatic paroxysms in a fittingly degraded terminus, the magazine world of New York and in the quotidian dispatches of Winchell, Kilgallen, Cassini, and Company. Logical positivism, a cool metaphysic native to the Eastern Seaboard, has, according to the same second law, rather a longer life expectancy: indeed, it may be the last metaphysic of all, if we accept the proposition of the eternal cybernetic, which is its most distinguished and erotic brainchild."

!@#$%^&*

"Well, dear, now you know, no bird ever flew on one wing, and that includes the eagle of the Republic. The problem *is*, when the right wing gets as strong as its gotten in the face of this Russian paranoia, the Republic might, like the dodo bird of Scholastic philosophy, succeed, by flying in ever-decreasing concentric circles, in flying up its own asshole and vanishing!"

The strains of the two-piano version of the *Hansel and Gretel* Overture by Charles Tomlinson Griffes, played by Tangent Percase and Dame Sybil Farewell-Tarnysh, drifted in as the door to the music room opened and closed.

"The end result of German Idealism is Nazism; the end result of French Romanticism, Symbolism, and decadence is existentialism. Heidegger, unsurprisingly, is the same as the end result of German Idealism: Aryan Nazism. The end results of English materialistic pragmatism are logical positivism and the Church of England. The end result of American Deistic mercantilism is television. Television and cybernetics will subsume all the above categories and all so-called politics derived from them into the New World Order, which, as the Virgin of Fatima announced, must coincide with the conversion of Russia."

"What will become of Socialism and of socialists?"

"They will continue to grudgingly accept the grim reality of materialistic pragmatism by shopping in thrift shops run by the Episcopal Church in America, which still confesses with Canterbury."

"The Letter . . . in nineteen sixty."

"I'd say more likely nineteen ninety or thereabouts."

"*What* is he talking about?"

"Cybernetics—artificial intelligence—like in *Desk Set*. There's been a big conference on the subject up in Cambridge—rumors are just now starting to trickle down to our level. It's apparently going to utterly transform our world with the force of a second Creation."

"Why does that make me think about the Tower of Babel?"

"Such a Phrontisterion it is in here!"

"Well, it is *some* kind of front, I've *always* said so. It's probably not the I.R.A., but *something's* fermenting in here that's not white lightning—not literally, anyway."

"Excuse me, it's wine that ferments; white lightning is distilled."

"Oh."

"What I say is there are too many Phrontisterion monsters being let loose. It's more like a Halloween party, plugs in the ears and all: *nobody* listening, everybody waiting and it isn't even Halloween. It's rather more like Dr. Johnson's strange household of vanities and charitable cases: Mrs. Williams, Mrs. Desmoulins, Miss Carmichael, Dr. Levett. There's even the cat, not called Hodge, or Podge, but Rosencrantz, if you please, which does tell you something."

"New York, New York! All these *dexiatatoi*, all these *aristoi* vying, vying."

"Yes, I often think of the Marschallin's levee when I come here, even though it's always in the evening, never in the morning—of the Countess as the Marschallin hearing the petitions of the distressed children of the aristocracy—all these chic European refugees remind me of the distressed children of some aristocracy made defunct by the war. And then, too, inevitably, a tenor sings something sentimental, or some like entertainment is offered."

"*Dexiatatoi? Dexa-myl-atoi* is more like it!"

"You're *in* a beehive, pal—the one written up by Maeterlinck."

"Now where have I just heard that name?"

"The Congress of Vienna."

"Oh—yes . . . I see. Well it is like that in here."

"The Congress of Vienna. Maeterlinck. You are too cruel—admit it."

"Maybe you're right—go fetch me that priest, will you?"

!@#$%^&*

"Louis Budenz does not do evening parties—only chic communion breakfasts."

"I don't think that can be true."

!@#$%^&*

"Venice is very strange. The stage set for a vast number of anonymous melodramas over the centuries—lately a motion picture set, for charades like Katharine Hepburn refusing to simper over Rosanno Brazzi, bottling it all up and falling instead into the Grand Canal, and Alida Valli falling hook, line, and sinker for, I give you, Farley Granger as an Austrian captain during the Risorgimento. And today? The home of that extraordinarily ugly American woman—as an Italian put it to me, *ricca, bruta, spaventosa*—Peggy Guggenheim, who goes to Caffè Florian at three in the morning and listens to Viennese waltzes, quite unaware, as is very nearly everyone else in the place, that Saint Florian is the patron saint of Austria, the nation that owned Venice at the time Alida Valli—"

"Was falling hook, line, and sinker for Farley Granger, yes, yes. Actually Farley Granger is a lovely man."

"You do understand, *Tristan* could only have been composed in Venice."

!@#$%^&*

"The ensorcelling rooms of Magwyck—full of immigrants from blackhole kitchens sitting side by each with émigrés from crystal-chandeliered drawing rooms on curule chairs in the parlor—perhaps it *is* a beehive all said and done."

"Part beehive, part hen hutch, *n'est-ce pas*?"

"There's Hiram Hayden, darling—teaches writing down at the New School. Responsible for Sigrid de Lima, among others. Let's sidle over, shall we, and inveigle? It passes the time."

"*Carnival by the Sea*, you mean? I love that!"

"Prizewinning American female writers. Clare Booth Luce . . . Pearl S. Buck . . . Lillian Hellman . . . permission to continue this catalogue of human folly?"

"You're much too severe. What about Carson McCullers, Katherine Anne Porter . . ."

"Cocktail waitresses!"

"Gertrude Stein, Jane Bowles."

"Concierges."

"Flannery O'Connor . . . Dawn Powell?"

"Be quiet—Dawn Powell is standing over there."

"Well, then what about—oh, Zora Neale Hurston."

"Who?"

"There is simply no talking to you. You at the very least ought to realize, if you do realize anything at all, that America's greatest poet is a woman."

"Laura open parenthesis Riding close parenthesis Jackson?"

"Emily Dickinson!"

"I see. Not Amy Lowell, Ella Wheeler Wilcox, Emma Lazarus or Edna Millay."

"No, Emily Dickinson."

"Then you mean *was*. No dead anybody is either a man *or* a woman."

"You're all ignoring a *very* important woman writer who happens to be right over *there*, opposite Dawn Powell. Hortense Calisher. *She* is the up-and-coming Woman of Letters."

"All I know is, all these divas, of whatever provenance, of whatever persuasion, resemble most the several wives of Zeus—contesting their shenanigans is *always* an uphill fight."

!@#$%^&*

"Lehrer? Yes, a terribly bright boy—so much happier in show business than he was in academic life, I believe, and an absolute knockout at *Le Bon Soir*."

"A wizard mathematician, isn't he?"

"Yes, dear, but he realized how utterly constraining mathematics can be."

"You mean his Gödel was killing him?"

"Ha-*ha*. He came to understand that any discipline that attempts to tell the truth by relying on the proposition *if . . . then* inevitably leads to unavailing grief."

"But surely his songs do that—all songs do that."

"That may well be true, dear, but as you may have noticed if you can *sing* a thing, almost nobody minds in the least *what* it's saying or doing."

!@#$%^&*

"*Every* political opinion is a compensatory reaction to an untenable situation."

"I think Emma Lazarus must be the patron saint of this crowd. 'Give me your tired, your poor . . . The wretched refuse of your teeming shore. Send these, the homeless, tempest-test to me.' I lift my skirts beside an open door. You know, like that."

" 'The wretched refuse of your teeming shore.' "

"There's no stopping the creature. Look, this is supposed to be a *salon*, not a settlement house! Anyway the greatest living writer as it happens *is* a woman, and she's right down on Patchin Place. 'Just being miserable isn't enough,' she wrote, 'you've got to know how.' "

"Oh—Djuna Barnes. Everybody thinks she's dead."

"Well, she isn't—she lives in the village, near Dawn Powell. The noise from down there is she's making the rounds of all the writer bars, cadging drinks and accusing The O'Maurigan of stealing her nearly completed play, on which she has been working for something like forty years, and which O'Neill is supposed to have called far greater than his thing—"

"His *what*?"

"His thing with Fredric March and that lackluster wife of his."

"*Long Day's Journey into Night*."

"Is that what it's called? I never go to the theater. Anyway he stole it—her thing—or so she claims, besotted by Mawrdew Czgowchwz, got Creplaczx to compose a score and put it on in the theater Percase built up there on that godforsaken atoll off—"

"Excuse me, there are no *atolls* on the Eastern Seaboard—only in the South Pacific."

"Oh, she probably thinks they stole that, too—they say she's been drinking since the turn of the century. Off Massachusetts. Anyway that thing NOIA, wasn't it called?"

!@#$%^&*

"It's always a little nineteen ten around here—bright young things leaning against the Connemara marble columns in foyer, smoking. You expect to see Mabel Dodge Luhan slinging hash."

"True, but it's really that like in all great Irish houses, then and now and evermore; Tír Na nÓg and the Twilight Zone. The Countess set the tone as soon as she arrived, just before the war. She seems to make time go in circles, and do you know how? In her domain, she's a kind of Penelope contradicting Ulysses. Weaving and unweaving with the utmost dexterity the tapestry of time, place, and situation."

"Setting and resetting clocks, agendas, and timetables. If you would miss your train to Connecticut, come here. You may have noticed they never lightly shake the parting guest's hand but with open arms, as if he would fly away, embrace him. Many have observed that the door greeting is always perfunctory. 'How are you' indistinguishable from '*Who* are *you?*' It puts many of the more self-regarding off their game for the night. But as suggested, do notice and be instructed that the parting guest is invariably grasped and held. It has often been remarked that it can take an hour to get out of the place. All that is very Irish, dear, very Irish. Time is neither money nor measurement here.

"In an odd way, thronged as it is, Magwyck sparks a certain nostalgia—memories of lovely evenings by the fire, couched in front of the wireless, listening to the likes of Sydney Torch, Albert Sandler, and Olive Groves. The

'Meditation' from *Thais* . . . Volkova's lullaby from *Sadko*. No callers . . . bliss. Most odd."

!@#$%^&*

"Mahler's Third, my dear, is the apotheosis of *Hansel und Gretel*."

"Hold it *right there!*"

"Oh, I don't know, I rather like Copland's music—or used to. I remember his 'Ode to Pharmeceuticals' or whatever it was called, at the World's Fair in thirty-nine. What I *don't* like—it's heresy, I know—is people stomping all over the stage barefoot in time to it. People ought to wear shoes when they dance is my feeling. In fact, they ought to wear shoes everywhere outside the bathroom."

"Birdie."

"Excuse me?"

"Skip it."

!@#$%^&*

"In pictures, dear, just before bad things happen, a saxophone plays."

"Pollock at his best depicted orgasms."

"There are plenty of *parfumé* French operas, the majority by Massenet, that Czgowchwz can indulge herself by appearing in, but I do not think *Werther* is one of them. The fact is, it is necessary for Czgowchwz to be dominant, and Charlotte after all is merely prominent."

"Interesting about this concept of decades. Is it all really going to change in nineteen sixty?"

"Oh, absolutely—with or without a Democratic victory. When the pope opens the Fatima letter."

"I find this twentieth-century mania for decennial demarcation and distinction questionable. *What* happened in nineteen ten to change everything so absolutely? In nineteen twenty? In nineteen thirty? In nineteen forty? In nineteen fifty?"

"You have a point, but the dates are close. It was nineteen eleven, the coronation of George the Fifth, first cousin to both the kaiser of Germany and the czar of Russia, all of them look-alikes. Three years later, war. It was nineteen

nineteen, the Treaty of Versailles and the abandonment by Britain of the gold standard. Within a decade, world financial chaos. It was nineteen twenty-nine, the market crashed on Wall Street. A pattern seems evident."

"I couldn't agree more. It was nineteen forty, the fall of France. I forget what happened in nineteen fifty. The Holy Year . . . Oh, yes, but of course—Korea."

"Moving right along, I don't go in that much for politics, but I certainly don't envy whoever is elected to the presidency in nineteen sixty, that I can tell you."

"Whyever not, dear—is there something awful about *that* in the Fatima letter?"

"That I wouldn't know. I'm referring to the Indian curse of the seven generations."

"*What?*"

"Absolutely. After the Great Displacement, when they saw how The Great White Father's word had been broken, they reacted. Every president elected every twenty years—a generation—since eighteen forty has died in office. Nineteen sixty is the seventh generation. Consuelo was told it all when she was struck clairvoyant by a Shoshone woman in forty-seven."

"Imagine!"

"You needn't . . . you need only anticipate."

!@#$%^&*

"*Hysterion-proteron.* What did he mean by—"

"Physics, dear—or chemistry; you take one hysteron and one proteron, and—"

"I heard that—it's not true. It's to do with *thought.*"

"I prefer gin and vermouth myself—only not one-to-one; I prefer one-to-seven."

"There's too much smoking and *far too much drinking* in New York."

"Did you know that smoking and drinking were the two main causes of World War Two?"

"Smoking and drinking? But Hitler did neither."

"Exactly."

!@#$%^&*

"I think it very likely Masaryk committed suicide—by defenestrating himself. It may be insulting to his memory to suggest otherwise. Those who came into his apartment and tossed things around, to make it look like the Russians had murdered him did the Czech cause no good. What was he to do else—flee with Marcia Davenport? As somebody has said, if *you* had the choice of throwing yourself out the bathroom window or running away with Marcia Davenport—impersonating Ingrid Bergman in the last reel of *Casablanca*—you would throw yourself out the bathroom window. We don't know if Mawrdew Czgowchwz was with him earlier in the day—but we think she was."

"Will somebody please keep an eye on Miss Dean? That's a very good Peck and Peck blouse she's wearing, and I just hate to think of what might become of it if she goes much further down the path she seems to have so deliberately taken tonight."

"*Tonight?*"

"Is she actually ever *invited* anywhere?"

"That much is uncertain. People don't take responsibility. What we know is that she is sometimes heard to murmur, 'to the feasts of the good, unbidden go the good.'"

"Yes, she was invited. The O'Maurigan is quite fond of her—has been since Cambridge days."

"Well, the way she looks at you, says nothing, and then walks away completely unnerves me, I don't mind admitting it. I think of the social secretary in that Dawn Powell novel who went into an adjoining room and transcribed in shorthand everything everybody said at parties."

"*A Time to Be Born.*"

"Yes, it unnerves me—completely. Somebody—"

"Yes, dear, at this very moment, right under our twitching noses."

"Dawn Powell—she writes for women, doesn't she?"

"Women and certain sensitive men."

!@#$%^&*

"This is the American opera decade."

"What say—could we not save all party talk about America for the Fourth of July?"

"Nobody's ever in New York on the Fourth of July."

"They will be this year—The O'Maurigan's new play is opening."

"Blitzstein is setting *The Little Foxes*. What a perfect role for Czgowchwz! 'Ah hope you die—Ah hope you die soon. Ah'll be *waitin'* for you to die!' "

"*Anatema su voi!* I have the feeling she's through with roles of that stripe—that Isis is placated once and for all. Hence the plans to record *Fanciulla*."

"Well, I heard that Lenny has been toying with the idea—for City Opera—of an opera about Mabel Dodge Luhan. A kind of American *La Rondine*."

"*La Rondine*? I find that hard to swallow."

"Hah-hah-hah-*hah*!"

"Blanche."

"Odd you should bring up Hellmann's *The Little Foxes*, I mean."

"Well, the last truly talented women writer I know of—pace Djuna Barnes—was V. R. Lang. Did you see *Fire Exit*? I thought it was something extraordinary."

"I saw it in Cambridge, and I saw it here. It was *death* here; Johnny Meyers produced it. Walter Whosie was supposed to supervise the rehearsals, but after all, he's an investment banker—and something of a theatrical angel. Anyway the opening nearly killed poor Bunny. People were *running* toward the *fire exits*, no kidding."

"Yes. She did die—but so did I."

"Yes, but then she went and died *dead*."

"Well, Bunny was willful and very thorough. She could've done with somebody to clean her clock. As it was she lived only long enough to teach Dorothy Dean revenge."

"They say The O's new play is driving him completely nuts."

"Well, let us hope Evelyn Gentry Hooker will keep him out of the bins."

"I've heard it's all about the world."

"More likely the universe—together with what Mabel Dodge Luhan called

La grande vie interieure. Much with crowds enforcing the moral economy. He likes to mix and match."

"Crowds enforcing the moral economy! What has he done, turned *Communist?*"

"I believe he intends, like Miss La Trobe in *Between the Acts,* to show us ourselves as we are, with the means at his disposal—a noble ambition."

"He is so multifarious: poems, screenplays, theater!"

"Multifarious fairies are now in the ascendant."

"This is true. You know, they used to take cover; now they take umbrage."

"And our little life is rounded with a *schlepp?*"

"A little profane perhaps, but so meaningful for our time, no?"

!@#$%^&*

*

Moriarty again. Cut to: the Everard. I shall lead on, you may read on and discuss amongst yourselves the innumerable issues raised.

The rumor is a new game has been started, replacing "What May I Hope to Harvest?" called "What Do You Like to Do?" The old queen who always takes the "suite" at the back of the lockers on the first floor is said to be running it.

"Lawd *today,* chile, there's more faggots squoze inta that room tuhnight than such which you would find in thuh Dress Circle standing room at thuh Metro-*politan* Op-*ruh* on the Metropolitan Opruh's openin' night of *Norma* wit' Maria Meneghini Callas! Only you must call it the *Undress* Circle, as they are awl in costume as *Naked Truth,* and *restless,* chile—restless like a bunch a crazy ole ring-shoutin' darkies up t' the Abyssinian Baptist Chuych, no *foolin'!*"

"Not all naked, dear: some are veiled in colored silks, like houris, and many are as richly caparisoned as medieval *imagines agentes,* active and striking, richly dressed and crowned."

"How one longs to be a woman in a kimono, bustling through an exquisite forest! One's entire thrust in life *is,* after all, aesthetic rather than, well—"

"Carnal?"

"You understand."

"I understand, darling, but for all that I believe you, I wouldn't in your shoes get that close to the mains—not unless you're wearing rubber boots, anyway."

"Excuse me, did you say *houris*?"

"I did."

"Oh, chile, they'z all old *huaz*, thas a plain, true fac'. So many men and boys in each othuh's awhms, one and awl with lewdness in theyah very loins—but they must be of a sudden inclinin' toward bein' of a mind to better theyselves, 'zif they wuz locked in at some all-night *tarry sehyvice* up on Lenox Avenue, becawze last I passed they'd done broke ranks summat and was all spillin' out inta the *hawl* and sittin right down on the dirty *floah* recitin' *pomes* tagethuh. 'When the Frost is on the Punkin' and 'Up at Old Aunt Mary's.' "

"Excuse me, but that's '*Out to* Old Aunt Mary's.' "

"Oh—well, excuse me, but, of caws, you would know."

"It is the truth, I can second it—about the charades room and the spillover. They are lined up down the length of the hall. I don't know what goes on once you get *in* there, for I am by temperament neither joiner nor spy, but I will tell you this, the lineup is comprised entirely of lithe and lissome numbers holding on to all the doorknobs to steady themselves, as if against the force of all-powerful nature and the indefatigable protocols of life herself—as at the *barre*, all of them practicing glissade, entrechat, assemblé, relevé—jeté, God be thanked—yet I would not be surprised if once *inside* more than auditions—"

"But is it art?"

"I don't hold with it. I realize that there is always the hope that greater numbers mean greater efficiency, but in my experience it is almost never the case."

"What is she *saying*?"

"Nobody ever knows, dear, but she's always that sure of herself."

The O'Maurigan passes, occasioning remarks.

"He is called Sinue. He Who Is Alone. The fever of Thebes is in his veins. He knows he was born to live in the twilight of the world."

"He is alone because he is an artist. It is precisely the artist's more intimate and habitual acquaintance with isolation that gives him his greatest advantage—the inverse of expertise in manipulating the tawdry social politics of this cruel and desolate town, and world. Isolation is the natural condition of art in America today. Isolation is our artistic truth—isolation, alienation, naked and revealed unto themselves—for the artist has foresight, cold comfort that it is—such are the conditions under which the true reality of our tragic age is mirrored in modern art—so there."

"True prophetic foresight is explained by its relation to the archetypes."

"Oh, *God*, not *Jung*!"

"Why not? He's hot."

"The negative manifestation of the type you invoke—the intuitive introvert—is the crank and the dreamer, unable to combine intuition with his objective and external perceptions."

"Such as they are. Yon prophetic soul doesn't score when drunk."

"I cannot *bear* claptrap Jungian jargon."

"Oh, can you not. Well, let me inform you, dear, that it is Jung and the Jungians who have afforded our kind with as much dignity as we have been able to assume in this day and age, whereas the Freudians attach electrodes to our private parts and turn on the juice while showing us pictures of beautiful naked men. It is the Jungians who take us on wonderful mythic journeys through the world of the archetypes, of which none is more thrilling than the Night-Sea Journey, So go to your dreadful Freudians, to your Fenchels and your Berglers and your other patriarchs, but leave the rest of us to our great adventure. You're not wanted on our voyage."

"Beautiful naked men: he is one of them. If you look closely you will see that there is nothing wild, nothing immodest in his manner when sober—it is quiet and self-controlled, a little melancholy and a little touched by suspicion, his gait and actions quite free from the slightest approach to extravagance. When sober."

"Well, at long last he's dropped the I don't like to be touched routine.

Abadessa cured him of it. Cornered him in the coffee shop and read him his gay beads, and as I happened to be seated at the next table, with my back to them, alone, I heard every word; it was an earful.

" 'It doesn't play, dear—not when in actual fact you're like Molly Bloom, just dying for a touch. It's just not you, and for a very good reason—you're Irish. That *Noli me tangere* shit is the bane of rich white American Protestant boys, and is very easy to psychoanalyze. Every time they think of being touched, they think of their fathers warning them against spongers and freeloaders and all who would take advantage of them and so the very worst thing they can be is a soft touch.' "

"That is a sweet, but utterly naive interpretation of the phenomenon, which if you can for a moment park the Jungian archetype palaver—put a gay dime in the meter—and listen to reason, I believe I can diagnose succinctly as arising in your darling poet's case from the commonplace but in certain particular cases unbearable trauma of losing one's baby teeth."

"*What?*"

"It is a hapless vicissitude far more wounding in the hyperactive male child given to frenetic masturbatory behavior who immediately and catastrophically fantasizes he is being unmanned—"

"Wouldn't that be un-*boyed*, darling?"

"A semantic detail, merely. And it's no joke, particularly if he is a homosexual child who has on the morning after the traumatic event awakened to find money under his pillow, supposedly left there by a supernatural being."

"Uh-oh!"

"Well, I don't buy it—fairies are strongly credited in Ireland."

"Yes, and they can be malevolent, can actually snatch young boys away from their families. It's not much of a stretch to envision him lying there, a terrified four-year old, alone in the dark in a big house at the back of beyond, imagining himself—"

"Mutilated and scornfully recompensed."

"Exactly. Thus, as Freud points out in *Beyond the Pleasure Principle*—and I di-late upon the original text in the interests of specific application—on the one hand the mechanical violence of the trauma of the lost tooth—read the detached penis—"

"Yeah, I've heard that."

"—would liberate a quantity of sexual excitation which, owing to the lack of preparation for the unbinding—and worse yet of the suspension of masturbatory activity necessarily occasioned by the phantom horror of their being nothing there with which to masturbate would—"

"This is incredibly fascinating!"

"I can't bear it—and *We're* accused of *jargon*?"

"—prove defenseless against the onrush of anxiety, producing a traumatic effect of some severity. On the other hand, the simultaneously perceived physical injury to the tooth-penis, by calling for a hypercathexis of the injured organ would bind the excess of excitation, producing an overdetermined quiescent cathexis, which easily becomes a regular and debilitating habit."

"That's what the priests are always saying, darling—in plain words."

"I could just *spit*!"

"Speaking of which—priests, dear, not spit—the fact is he isn't always so alone as that. I've seen him in here in Strange company, as you must have, too. They seem quite a close couple. Could it be your boy is a secret seminarian?"

"Oh, honey, the priest? She is an ugly old hulk. They came in together tonight!"

"Was he in priest drag? I wonder would he let me try on his biretta? It's a hat, don't-cha know, that's just absolutely *perfect* for my shape of face."

"I wouldn't were I you bring up the shape your face is in, dear. Not tonight."

"I shall hold that remark under my tongue until I can spit it out."

"Well, why shouldn't priests come in here? They are after all in the last analysis the only women in town one can absolutely rely on not to squawk, no more on the lilies of the valley than on the roughhouse boys. Besides, is not the very sight of the moral and pious a check to the wicked? We could all use the services of a priest, if you ask me, hapless as we are, souls darkened to pitch by the marled crepe of deadly sin. Kneel to anneal, darling, kneel to anneal!"

"Oh, Sissy, how *retrograde*—to so rigorously match black crepe to sin. You know perfectly well that since the war the little black dress has become *de rigueur!*"

"Go on, mock, since you do it so well, but I understand what an Irish boy needs, even in a place like this. The rapture of self-sacrifice, the quality of mercy, the joy of reconciliation, the relief of forgiveness, and I say let him be so accommodated."

"For a nice accommodation, call Regent—"

"The quality of mercy, my ass. He looks more like a cop than a priest to me. Looks like he's thrown a lot of little people against a lot of hard brick walls."

" 'For the longest while there was only Ireland
Spread out like nothing else—there being nothing
Else in the world—to the north south east and west
Of Nephin Mountain, one thousand two hundred—' "

"Excuse me, what is that you are reciting?"

"I am reciting words that are more than words, that are the written symbols of the languid lights that flash across the poet's beautiful soul. I am reciting the absolutely gorgeous opening lines of *Under Nephin*, which is the new book-length poem written by the person you have been so without any feeling dishing, that's what."

"The Jesuit writes *poetry?*"

"Not the Jesuit, the poet—he who disdains us, never giving us the time of day."

"And you're not so sure you're not sorry he doesn't, darling."

"I could hate you."

"You read it nicely anyway—not British."

"Thank you—after all, it's a poem written by an Irishman."

"That wouldn't stop some. I swear to God every time Margaret Leighton comes to Broadway, half the queens in town start in with '*Railly*, dahling? How *awful*-faw yew!' and 'I couldn't be *ahss'd*—I simply couldn't be bloody *ahss'd*.' Happened again at dinner tonight, at the Finale. Finally I had enough, I said to the queen, 'Either get it right or *can it*, Griselda—your post-alveolar frictionless continuant, quite frankly, *sucks!*'"

"There's more in it, the poem, about a little boy, early on in the war—called *The Emergency* in Ireland—sitting in a grassy field high up in the driving seat of a newly purchased gleaming green and bright red tractor, that is absolutely *elevated!*"

"My trains of thought used to be elevated, 'til they took down the El."

"Yes, he comes from someplace deeply rural, there's that to consider."

"Maybe—although he's not much like a Nebraska farm boy."

"Oh, well dear, neither was Virgil, as a matter of fact."

"You could say he has not been enveloped in the prophylactic film of exclusively postwar culture. Of course, as you so accurately point out, there was no war in Ireland, because they were all too poor and De Valera was more than half in love with Hitler."

"Who?"

"*Hitler*, dear—surely you have *heard* of *Hitler*?"

"Not him, the lover—Della who?"

"De Valera. He was an Irish version of Franco. Still is. In Ireland they called the War the *Emergency* and everybody rode their bicycles over cityscape and countryside. Nevertheless, many Irishmen took the part of the Allies, fought alongside the British, including the parents who went down in that plane—as a consequence of which, it is said, there's more that's deviated in your poet, than the septum—whatever the septum is."

"Well, it is my fervent wish he finds a beautiful boy."

"As well he may, yet the danger in such cases is that the new find will always be part of a love triangle—there's simply no avoiding it."

"Yes, but there's always the hope that the triangle will prove to be isosceles, in which case the sum of the square of the hypotenuse is equal to the sum of the squares of the other two sides."

"My dear, if one only had a brain like yours!"

!@#$%^&*

This is Moriarty, eavesdropping at a door.

"You got the transcription?"

"Yes. It's getting dangerous. He came in with the priest only minutes after me. He didn't see me, but we can't risk staying. The way he clocks—"

"Every beautiful male face, yeah. Next time, we'll wear Halloween masks. But what's to connect us? That's why he hires the heavies. So, give me the pages, will you. I'm not checking out of here tonight—too much to miss. Anyway, he was well on his way to getting shitfaced, and if you just put on lipstick and mascara and walk swish, he'll pass you right by. He can't handle swish at all."

"Remind me again please why we're doing this."

"We're doing this so that when the voices on this tape read themselves transmogrified into the characters we're creating, they'll be forced to alter their worldview dramatically, to wash the scales out of their eyes and open up their self-regarding minds to things beyond their imaginings."

"*She* gets it, don't you think? I mean she basically *has* to get it."

"She gets it. She doesn't absolutely completely *get* it that she gets it, but on the level of tribute, she gets it. Also that the credit redounds on us."

And all the while, wait till I tell you, next to me (happen I were corporeal) at the door stands pal Delancey, the best of good eggs. My God, says he to himself, they're the ones, and they're not finished. They're out trawling for more. (He'd be beside himself, so he would, but for yours truly, phantom I nevertheless be.) What to do now? Storm in and . . . no, it's too bizarre, and they'd only deny it boldface, the whole thing. Give them more rope? Get hold of Vartanessian: talk to him. See can he put names to them.

!@#$%^&*

"Read your Bible, dear. Had the girl kept her face resolutely turned away from the Cities on the Plain as ordered to . . . but nothing would do but she had to turn to have one last good look at Syphilis and Gonorrhea—and for that was she turned into a pillar of saltpeter."

"The breathless whisper of love, the wild danger of locked doors—in Hindi. Simply *electrifying*."

"I'm sure, dear. Just remember, don't try it at home alone."

"Put that kiss where you found it—on my ass!"

"Because, you see, Aristotle says *a verb is a composite significant sound involving the idea of time, with parts which, just as in the noun, have no significance by themselves. Whereas the word 'man' or 'white' does not imply time, 'walks' and 'has walked' involve in addition to the idea of walking that of time present or time past.* Funny, he says nothing at all about future time—but the Greeks were pessimistic."

" 'Scuse me, chile, foah inneruptin' yoah grammar lesson heah, but can you possibleh tell an innerested pawhty jus' whut yoah ole Greek philosophuh, bein' so precise about the white man's qualities gots t' say about *black women,* huh?"

"Well, I don't think—"

"You bet yoah ass. You go 'round liss'nen to them Greeks. Why, don't you know they kept *slaves, Nubian woman slaves?*" They were a *disgrace,* chile, a *moahtul disgrace!*"

"And the noise inside is so like gulls swarming!"

!@#$%^&*

"I tell you man, priests are all fuckin' *crazy.* My kid brother still goes to confession. I asked him why, and he says to me he likes giving the new young priest a hard-on. He's like me, my brother, he swings both ways, and man, he is so fuckin' horny he's got me doin' it with him—I fuck his ass, which he goes apeshit over, moanin' and laughin' and he tells me about this Chinese broad over on East Broadway when he fucks her she shoves these *steel balls on a fuckin' string* up his ass and pulls them out one by one while he shoots in her cunt—and this is my fuckin' *kid* brother!

"Anyway he goes to confession and all he tells the priest who is anyway by now half asleep because my brother waits until like ten o'clock on Sadd'y night when the priest has been at it all day is how he jerks off and the fantasies he has—whereas he never jerks off no more, unless after gym class maybe, I don't know, and these fantasies are like not fantasies, but *shit he has done,* or so he claims. And this is what the fuckin' priest tells him. That Jesus Christ as a growing boy had nocturnal emissions—wet dreams—just like every other healthy young man, only his guardian angel *like cleaned him up* after every one, and also that Saint Aloysius Gonzaga, patron saint of adolescent boys, had these same dreams—I don't know did he mean the same dreams as the boy Jesus or what shit, but anyway that if my kid brother would keep his hands off his private parts and pray to Saint Aloysius every night, Saint Aloysius would ask the boy Jesus to send him wet dreams! Is that the limit?"

"Man, that is so fuckin' crazy I gotta jerk off immediately."

"That's cool, I'll do it with ya. Fuckin' priests, man!"

!@#$%^&*

"My ambition is musical. I want to connect my lips and my tongue to that whistle-clean asshole of his and make him go *toot*! When I see him just lying there, like an enchanted pool of still water, all I want to be, for life, is *engloutie*."

"Do tell. Like maybe with six slugs in your back in the bottom of the river?"

"*Un unica raggio di bene—da ver.*"

"A melting pot. Where else find all the races of the earth, free from exclusivity, subject entirely to Gotham's most genial hospitality and hybrid vigor, its extended view of men and things. And you know what Homer says? The gods themselves, disguised as strangers often drop in from abroad. Heretofore remote figures at distant podia, they become our sudden intimates. Not to mention the fact that hundreds—thousands—of musical boys, enchanted boys—"

" 'There was a boy, a very strange and gentle—' "

"Boys who have discovered in high school they are *so*, who arrive in their droves at New York's bars and bathhouses and stay on in very much the same way as did the Civil War deserters—they who had fled their own encounters with the wanton waste of life for the *anonyme* possibilities of the big city, braving the incessant surge of the blank-eyed multitude rather than return to their small and terrible hometowns where certain arrest awaited them—a scant century ago. Excuse me, am I *boring* you?"

"Oh, no, please go *on*—I love men on the run!"

"Where else may such boys, with due deference in their manners and calluses on their hands, experience the easy interchange of courtesies under the writ of gentility, and that closer view aiding the candidacy of acquaintance? Where else may the underwhelming and the taciturn, in their workaday lives cashiered from affective fraternity, rub elbows—"

"*Elbows!*"

"—so to speak—with the articulate and the intellectually fermented, to have intercourse with persons capable of conversing about Shakespeare and Beethoven in an intimate, dynamic relationship of mutual exchange fostering the continual manifestation and interplay of their energies, all in aid of their own moral uplift? Hardly at the Saint Marks, the Beacon, or the Penn Post—the proceedings in such establishments being hardly of a nature to bear investigation by respectable strangers."

"Where else? Well, let's see, there's the men's room in the Grand Tier of the Metropolitan Opera House, the tea room at Fifty-seventh Street on the BMT, downtown side. That's in winter; in summer there the Ramble, there's—"

"That's right, make fun—but ramifications ripple outward."

"Meaning?"

"Meaning that as a result of the cultivation in here of such intense masculine sympathy and deportment—the nourishing of free love, in itself more exacting than wagework, and also such things as cultivation of dress sense and attention to matters of personal hygiene, numerous embassies, consulates, banks, investment houses, and other businesses vital to the health of the nation have been enabled to regularly dispatch their drummers to European—and lately even South American, African, and Asian—tycoons, lords, barons, and magnates of industry; men of wealth, power, and prestige in the United Nations—real men, darling, who like expensive clothes, hard liquor, fast cars, and dirty jokes, and just *happen* to be *of*, or beset *by*, depending upon your point of view, our common *persuasion*, and bring them here for as good a time as they are likely to get in the metropolis?"

"*Deportment*? You tell those embassy numbers *deported* is more what they'll get if this dump, this bolt-hole for the sex-starved dispossessed ever gets anything like the renown you seem to be suggesting it has already won. Orgies as character-building calisthenics! Last night's impenetrable meaningless boy as *physician*? You think we should advertise, like the Rotarians and the Elks? Fashion shows, *pedicure's*, maybe?"

"I was just thinking—"

"Oh, God, not tonight!"

"Bitch. I was just thinking it's a pity Jane Austen never got to come in here—or the equivalent establishment in Bath, because there must have been one; she might've learned how to portray men outside the company of women. As it was she had no idea."

!@#$%^&*

"You ever fuck a woman, man? Tell the truth."

"You wouldn't call her a woman. My kid brother, he fucks—"

"You said—Chink chicks who shove steel balls up his ass."

"Yeah."

"Yeah, I was lookin' at some of this new pornography they got out in color? You know, when a woman shaves her cunt and it swells up, the cunt lips look exactly like lips—face lips? Of course, she has to lay on her *side*, so they look—"

("What are those two queens yammering about next door—face-lifts?"

"I heard face, *lips*.")

"Yeah, that's true, I was readin' that myself in *Sexology* magazine, man—and there's this guy now says some of those women's cunts actually have *teeth* in them, so that makes it even more true?"

"*Teeth* in their *cunt*?"

"No shit, man—but only certain women—women that are pissed off at men."

"That's every fuckin' woman I ever knew man, starting with my mother, my sister . . ."

"Listen, there's a new attraction in the party room tonight. That Ship Card Desk queen from the *Journal of Commerce* has brought in the cabin boy off the *Queen Mary*, Mary, full of *firsthand impressions* of Mawrdew Czgowchwz and the paramour on the voyage—they are filling up so fast down there, it's like a Basie jam session at the Famous Door!"

"Sounds more like amateur night at the old Blowhole Theater—later Tilyou's Insanitarium—in Coney Island."

!@#$%^&*

"Haven't you heard—in hell there's no retention!"

"There is no hell—but I believe in abolishing retention, all right. I am becoming a Zen Buddhist. The Supreme Way is not difficult, it simply precludes picking and choosing."

"So, you never say no to anybody."

"That's right."

Strange holding forth to The O'Mauriganon, usurping my position; I don't like it.

"The security guard in the dormitory, entirely more conversant with the buttocks of the night than with the forehead of the morning, is as blind, as mute and as sexless as the triply-mutilated eunuch musicians of the baths at Granada—they carried no tales of assignations between the great and their—the great don't seem to be bothered who sees them with whom here, do they? Perhaps looking at him sitting there—a kind of totem to the old practice—deludes them. He is guarding the right place, at any rate."

But let us hasten to our closet melodrama, vigorously getting under way.

THE O'MAURIGAN. I wasn't going to end up, so I was not, another Jesuit wreck, merely to satisfy Ignatius Loyola's demented notions all bound in briars and crucified on the main mast, a life dedicated to the *flagellato ad nocte* and the gaudious miseries of the Holy Rosary.

STRANGE. Oh, *that*. At Dunwoodie we used to beat our pillows.

THE O'MAURIGAN. Of course it was my own fault with you, I let you see me—

STRANGE. The all of you, and never to my disappointment. There were never any rough, crude boys at Regis, there were only those who, though never brighter than you, were as New York youngsters, more sophisticated. They would refer to your pudenda as 'Aaron's rod recumbent in the burning bush.' You came to me for counselling —you loved me then, and sent me mash notes I still keep in my breviary for hard moments.

THE O'MAURIGAN. You're fabricating—I never—

STRANGE. Oh, but you did—you called me counter, original, spare Strange.

THE O'MAURIGAN. You must have misheard me. I may have asked on one of our walks in Central Park, had you any spare change. My allowance in those days was pitiful.

STRANGE. You wrote to me, I tell you; I've saved the scraps, all of them. Then there was the little calumny about you at Regis, that you spent exactly as many hours a day masturbating as Loyala set aside for the direct contemplation of God, moreover that your utility manual, your book of one hand, was not Frank Harris's *My Secret Life* or the unexpurgated *Fanny Hill*, but the collected poems of Gerard Manley Hopkins.

And whatever else I may or may not be, I am not just another Jesuit wreck. It was I who took you in hand and cured you of your Docetist heretical tendencies. You didn't think Jesus Christ either pissed or shat or had an orgasm before—

THE O'MAURIGAN. Before what, the jewels? You wanted them. I can hear you talking to yourself, in Latin. "*Fovit prius pro peccato inter anum cum duobus del Regis, qui laetificat juventutem meam.*"

STRANGE. I remember you came to us, talking of the *Spiritual Exercises*, already primed, already convinced you were a kind of felon before God. A touching, but densely heretical boy, suffused with encratite enthusiasm, subelite in temperament and polemical against contrary positions. Fording the Tiber would be more difficult for you, we saw, than any long day's Liffey swim. You wouldn't believe me when I told you that the same Ignatius who prescribed all that took delight in dancing for all the young postulants to the Order and who came to your defense with Father Superior when you blasphemed Loyola, declaring out loud that if a vision of the Trinity could not be described in words, then the Trinity would be a false doctrine, whereas what it is is really a sort of sublime crossword puzzle? I remember, too, your accent—on *mind* and *life* when you recited your great passion, Hopkins:

The vault and scope and schooling
And mastery in the mind,
In silk-ash kept from cooling,
And riper under rind—
What life half lifts the latch of,
What hell stalks towards the snatch of,
Your offering with dispatch, of!

THE O'MAURIGAN. The lines still hold—hell, snatch and lifted latch—even though the coarser boys had their sport with them. I so prefer Gerard's manly chastity to Crashaw's slobbering over the named body of Christ. I remember the first one you taught me:

With witness I speak this. But where I say
Hours I mean years, mean life. And my lament
Is cries countless, cries like dead letters sent
To dearest Him who live, alas, away.

STRANGE. Yes, well, they got theirs—the coarser boys, that is. The cunt, as Horace says, was a great provoker of fear long before Helen made her fatal entrance. Long before and ever after. Christ was so afraid of it, he chose crucifixion.

THE O'MAURIGAN. *Jesuit!* You and your kind, blending in inherited hysterical Spanish fashion the barracks mentality with that of the sacristy, sitting in your *studiolo* like love locked out, like unholy Furor personified, hunkered down on terrible weapons, made me a wreck! That idiotic Loyala and his examination of the beginning, the middle, and the end of the thought process—the thought process is ceaseless from all ages, and can no more be anatomized than can time, or, if your God has a part in it, from eternity itself.

STRANGE. For to thy sensual fault I brought in sense.

THE O'MAURIGAN. Lascivious sense, in whom all ill will flows.

STRANGE. Perhaps. In any case, those Protestant preparatory schools with their naive faith in the cold charities of the world would not have suited you. Good Tory manners and the watered-down English version of Western Civilization as curriculum. Reading crap like Ruskin, who disparaged the ecstatic saints, claiming that "with their cloudy outlines, or with their impossible virtue" they "deaden human response." Refusing to acknowledge the very real presence of the very devil himself, Son of this World, who with the reluctant permission of God and Saint Ignatius Loyola we ourselves . . . etcetera.

God, thank *God* John Henry Newman, the greatest English prose stylist of the century, found Rome, and that you were so thoroughly immersed in him preparatory to Trinity and later your sojourn at Harvard, its air reeking with the teachings of the foulmouthed William James—calumniator of Teresa of Ávila and Aloysius Gonzaga both.

THE O'MAURIGAN. How you hate William James—I well remember.

STRANGE. Not hate, despise. You hate the brother; I would hate the quack psychologist were there hatred in me. As it is, I rue his influence on the American mind.

THE O'MAURIGAN. Such as it is. I don't hate the brother, I pity his hopelessness. Who could hate the boy in that portrait in the library at the Century Club? Nobody with a heart, surely. The liquid, mournful, gaze, seductive as any little piece of street trade Whitman ever took home—of course, with finer haberdashery—which reminds me of Leontyne Price's latest *mot*. "I reckon Tosca and Bess are a lot alike, only Tosca's got better clothes."

STRANGE. I think you began at Regis to masturbate over that portrait—

or was it over the portrait of Hawthorne in the House of the Seven Gables in Salem?

THE O'MAURIGAN. My father's ghilly in Mayo taught me how to masturbate diligently; he considered it essential information. When I asked him why the Catholic priests and the Church of Ireland ones and the Presbyterian crowd all gave out so against it, was it not an awful sin? He said, "Are ye *serious*? Lad, sure it's no more than blowin' yer *nose*! Now go up to yer room, strip off, get up on the bed, take yer Willy in yer fisht and get on with it—and don't be talkin' about the prieshts, sure aren't they're all after doin' the same themselves?"

STRANGE. And did he give you a demonstration, do it with you?

THE O'MAURIGAN. Only the once, and without touching me, but the truth is I never did get very far along with it. A bit of froth that looked like starling spit. I was shut down. How could I do anything at all when all I could picture was him lying at the bottom of the Bay of Biscay? Her, too, of course, but I never really thought of her as dead, just away somewhere, on tour.

STRANGE. Ah, the Protestant Irish.

THE O'MAURIGAN. We are *not* Protestant Irish, we are Irish. And as for God and his very existence . . .

STRANGE. It is the final proof of God's omnipotence that he not exist in order to be.

THE O'MAURIGAN. Sweet. Yes, I confess it, there are times when I pray to God to wake and find all these years since Regis and my exposure to the most liberal Catholic education available in the world—*Ad Maiourum Deam Gloriam*—administered by thugs whose sacred vow it was to impose the hegemony of the written over the oral, to stamp out all forms of circus, carnival, conjuring, and chiromancy in Europe, to bring to country village and city slum alike that same battleship gray, waxed mahogany religion with its superabundance of consuming agonies. And to infiltrate the paranoiac middle clashes, there to give the most exquisitely sensitive counseling to troubled spirits while provoking Catholic mobs to massacre Protestants . . . to find it all to have been all a bad dream—like history itself.

STRANGE. You spent your adolescence being educated in the equivalent of the *Ecole Normale Superieure*, reading the *Agudeza y arte de ingenio*, *El héroe* and the *Oráculo manual y arte de prudencia* of Baltasar Gracián y Morales—a thinker who makes Teilhard de Chardin sound like a mountebank from Greenwich Village. You were going to make the *El criticón* into a piece of epic theater, staging it in Carl Schurz Park in front of Gracie Mansion in protest against the excesses of the Walker regime. I could, in view of your present theatrical ambitions, and were I a vulgarian of the Fulton Sheen type, leak that reminiscence to the mandarins of "Talk of the Town" at your precious *New Yorker*.

Catholic education in America is equal to any on the primary and secondary level, but unhappily loses its nerve on the collegiate level—mirroring the condition of Europe, where what was once the cardinal sin of *delectatio morosa* is since the Enlightenment not only defended, but has been raised to the level of instructive method.

For it is Protestantism's central dogma that it has taken Western Man out of the childhood and adolescence that Roman Catholicism had kept him in. Which is why Protestant Europe goes mad in and on Italy. The truth, of course, is that Roman Catholicism is the genius religion of the aeons, its only serious rivals Hinduism and Zoroastrianism, which begam to be played out about two thousand years ago, and needed to be replaced.

And when the repressed childhood and adolescence of Catholic Europe erupts in Protestant Europe, the inevitable result is nothing less than the brutal ideology and savage methodology of Nazism.

THE O'MAURIGAN. You seem to have left out the Jews in all this.

STRANGE. What is it Lady Bracknell says to Jack Worthing concerning the Liberal Unionists? "They count as Tories; they dine with us, or come in the evening at any rate." Naturally you wish to embrace your beleagured Hebraic cousins. Are not the Irish the lost tribe of Israel?

THE O'MAURIGAN. What a life you let me in for, you casuists. *Perpetuum vestigiam*, all right.

STRANGE. In the accusative case?

THE O'MAURIGAN. You bet your old fat smelly arse in the accusative case. I sometimes wonder what if early on that fatal morning in Merrion, the sun just up through the autumn mist off Dublin Bay, Boland's bread van idling peacefully in the lane below, the car had arrived to take me off to the Silesian Aspirinate at Abbeyleix—the joke was they made you swallow aspirin for every complaint—instead of all the way down to Limerick, to Fownes, whence soon airborne, with the holy terror on me of knowing *they both* had so lately been shot down on the flight from Lisbon to London on me, and the American flight crew insisting the skies were safe in the otherwise the treacherous Atlantic—to New York, directly into your so finely manicured hands. What then?

STRANGE. They'd not have sent you to the Christian Brothers?

THE O'MAURIGAN. Will ye ever shut up yer gob for the once! There's two things in Ireland about which *you* know *fuck all*, and that's the Christian Brothers and The Pioneers.

Fade-out.

Moriatry. In that case let me tell you all what would have happened had he in the early years of the Emergency been taken up to the venerable Saint Columba's—there in the Dublin Mountains, looking out to Wales on a clear October day, from whence Saint Patrick came to Ireland and later the magpies. Sitting shivering by a grate of burning sticks and turf, hearing frightful rumors drifting in from the *wans* in the kitchen of the incipient invasion of the island by Germans from a U-boat off the shore of the Beare Peninsula (but sure might it not be all fer the best at that, wasn't England's trouble Ireland's gain?)

while Yeats's blue *igni fatuii* rose from the fire, preening like the sacrilegious, lascivious slut, Sal-*omee,* preparing to manifest themselves on the village below.

Languishing, the damp invading him, being immodestly touch-taste-and-handled, and called *bijou,* by that raptor known as the Head Beak—and likely by his smarmy cadets as well, and, despite his faultless Greek, his Latin, and his Irish, inevitably, and with dire horripilation, assaulted by some vile Church of Ireland headmaster, with the directive 'Boy, let down your small clothes!' And left there, with no strategy of solace such as that afforded by the sacrament of Penance in the offing—for though there was a kind of confessor, a pardoner there at St. Columba's, there was no sacrament of penance.

That said, let us return to the business of the moment in the *studiolo.*

Fade-in.

THE O'MAURIGAN. You ruined my life. You're—you belong in the Vatican, so you do.

STRANGE. Park Avenue suits me more, as do these environs, which in point of fact are in certain particulars very like the Vatican. This place holds as many fell secrets, there are replications of the Room of Tears, and one of the Door of Death. We walk through it, every morning, noon, or night we enter or leave the place. Think about it some time.

Also, considering the number and variety of academic scholars who come down from Columbia or up from NYU or in from wherever else to let their inhibitions have a whack at getting lost, and the number and variety of the important texts of the ages, in reproduction, they've brought in with them, we have a kind of virtual *Archivio Segreto,* too. It is virtually certain that at least one, and more likely many readers have sat down in these dim cubicles to read through the depositions of the trial of Galileo or the petition of the Eighth in the matter of his divorce from Catherine of Aragon, depositions tracking the courses of Marian apparition, and such things I know not what they are, but many in their own time and place the terrors of the earth.

THE O'MAURIGAN. And the cash register, what is that in disguise, some class of a multigeared rotor encoder?

STRANGE. Would you put it past the FBI? I wouldn't myself, not in the least—year after year of bugs and wiretaps and what not else...

And as for your life, darling—as for the lives of all of us, the *Anthropophagi*, there is no longer any such thing as *life*, not in any acceptable sense, only a protracted, enervated and delerious physiology. Then —*alleluia!*—death and transfiguration. *Perche la bonta infinita ha si gran braccia*...

In any event, the thing I remember best from those fleeting years is your no longer wanting to be called Jameson, but Fitzjames, and so we dubbed you Fitz.

THE O'MAURIGAN. You should remember. It was on a walk in Central Park with you we came across the statue of Fitz-Greene Halleck, there in a row with Shakespeare and Goethe. I thought he must have been somebody important, but you said he'd only been some mayor's press boy in the last century whose reputation in the same literary circles that had first coddled and then frozen out your great hero Melville had gotten itself ridiculously inflated—and yet the name, and the attitude, turned my head. And Fitz-Greene Halleck led to Fitzjames O'Brien and to the birth of Fitzjames O'Maurigan. I'd never much enjoyed one of my names being that of a brand of whiskey.

Then later that same day, back in your office, you gave me *Billy Budd* to read. I was fourteen years of age. I suppose I ought to thank you—but it *was* cruel in a way I think. I have never suffered more over a story.

STRANGE. You wanted to understand America. What was I to give to read, Parson Weems on George Washington and the cherry tree, or, God save the mark, *Huckleberry Finn*?

THE O'MAURIGAN. Cherries did come into it though, didn't they, or at least one did, mine. I should have run away from you there and then, shouting the fucking halls down. I should have rung up the archdiocese, denounced you to them, and had them summon the Superior General.

STRANGE. Who'd have calmed you down and given us both conditional absolution. I did think you might do something like that, but you see you loved me then. No longer.

THE O'MAURIGAN. I do not in my heart hold you in a place reserved. A priest is not meant to be a bender and a shaper of wills, yet I respect you. The sex was, I must admit, delightful. You were without question a most subtle and masterful instructor.

STRANGE. Better than your father's ghilly in Mayo?

THE O'MAURIGAN. Yes, well the truth of the matter was his tutelage was somewhat premature. It was you first got me to ejaculatory orgasm. Also the sense of privilege suited me

STRANGE. Ah, my diligence! I could almost desire you, again—I do desire you again, worse luck, just as I desired you back then. Desire you in religion again.

Fade-out.

!@#$%^&*

"Nietzsche makes a terribly important point about orgies. According to him, the purpose of the orgy in ancient Greece was not to send the personality into ecstasy, but to give sudden release to the ferocity of the divine, intending *to calm it down* so that it would leave the participants in peace for a time afterward."

"Success may not come with rushing speed, darling, but, Dexamyl can make a difference for sure."

!@#$%^&*

"And scientists, too, such as not only biologists, which you might expect, but physicists and mathematicians as well, and particularly game theorists, darling, working out the many fabulous implications of Von Neumann's numi theory of parlor games."

"Parlor games!"

"Yes, published nearly thirty years ago in Budapest."

"Oh, we have Hungarians *pouring* in now. Why, there are two of them in here tonight who, if they continue as they are, will surely prove the *campiest* duo to come out of the land of the Magyars since the Dolly Sisters! They take a double—very grand—and open this scrapbook they bring with them, lay it on the little table in there and *light a candle*, darling, to some rather gorgeous dark creature draped all in black silk, turban and everything, slinking across the floor like Garbo in *Mata Hari*—and they draw *quite a crowd*."

"Not only Hungarians, refugees of many countries, particularly the unpronounceable ones, fleeing the wider violence of the world, sparked by the love of change and the dread of home, and among them exquisite sensibilities, in eerie communion with the dead and dying victims of unspeakable political barbarities."

"Excuse me, that gorgeous creature to whom you refer is none other than the fabulously legendary Lya de Putti—a divinity of stage and screen *entre deux guerres*."

"When I was at Princeton playing games—we were always *fair*, exactly as the popular story concerning the popularity of that act that photographs so much more convincingly than... but then if we don't make sacrifices for art, who will? Anyway, there was a beautiful mathematician on campus famous for insisting game theory could be expanded, from two-man zero-sum head-on collisions with fixed payoffs to open-ended veritable *gang bang* proportions."

"Fixed payoffs keep this place in operation."

"Well, speaking of hybrid vigor, I heard a German diplomat of no inferior rank exclaim only last week—in fact he was singing it, '*Ist wunderbar! So wunderbar!*'"

"A very popular song, dear, in Germany, always sung by the legendary Zarah Leander."

"Who's that?"

"That, dear, you must ask your German diplomat next time he comes in singing."

"Yes, my dear, I shall. 'Now must the city swell and fill with a multitude of callings which are not required by any natural want; such as a whole tribe of whom one large class will have to do with forms and colors; another will consist of the votaries of music—poets and their attendant rhapsodists, players, dancers, contractors; also makers of divers articles, including women's dresses.' That's Plato, darling, from *The Republic.*"

"He went on to M.I.T."

"Plato—*did* he really!"

"No, you fool, the gorgeous mathematician."

"M.I.T. Darling, they're all *Communists* there!"

"Oh, not this one. This one wore Brooks Brothers button-down collars, you know, that *poof-up* around the tie. Well, *last week*, you could have knocked me over—"

"Unlikely, with those round heels."

"I saw him walking up and down the halls, *here—not* in the shirt and tie: they were where they belong, hung up neatly on the door of his cubicle. You can always tell a gentleman, even in places like this and overnight on a train."

"True it is, my dear, as Propertius noted, '*sunt apud infernos tot milia formosorum.*' "

"Oooh, *Latin!*"

"You bet your ass, dear, she passed the Regents. And when she barks like the three-headed dog in the Underworld, all you need to do is throw her a box of Cracker Jacks and she calms right down—as if you shot her up with heroin."

"Anyway, wearing the same off-white gown we all wear, and wailing in what seemed like genuine pain about how terrible it is what with Suez and Hungary and everything."

"Plato is the beautiful, doomed boy in love with James Dean Sal Mineo plays in *Rebel Without A Cause.* Funny about coincidences . . . and a little sad."

"That's funny, I heard about somebody at M.I.T.—this was quite a few years ago now—who used to pedal up and down the halls on a *unicycle*, smoking cigars and eating peanuts—like something out of a circus! Quite a turn, they said."

"Oh, *darling*, can we possibly get him to come down here?"

"I say it's crowded enough in here already. *Entia non sunt multiplicanda praeter necessitatem.*"

"You're being beastly, both of you, but it's my own fault. Who was it said, 'Do not render to dogs that which is sacred, nor cast your pearls before swine, for if you do they may trample them underfoot and then turn and tear you to pieces'?"

"I do believe it was Dorothy Parker to Clare Booth Luce."

"It was no such body in clothing, it was Matthew Swan."

"Who?"

"Matthew Swan, the Ancient of Days, in those very words—all of them."

"That daft old bird? *Never* believe a Russian. Consider Alger Hiss."

"Matthew Swan's not Russian, not really. In his dream, but not . . ."

"Well, *my* particular genius is nothing like that. Naked, exposed, his hair the very color of midnight, of remarkable depth and shine. I felt his searching dark-eyed gaze on me: his large, grave, wistfully attentive eyes, and met it with all the fervent longing there was in me. His nervous uncertain lips . . ."

"Oh, get a *grip!*"

"*Werweile doch—du bist schon!*"

"Oooh, *German*! It's so fucking *cosmopolitan* in here!"

"Nothing promulgates faith and obedience more than a sense of wonder."

"He's so beautiful, it makes no difference he's slow at conversation."

"I always say when a man is beautiful, that in itself is his half of the conversation—the rest is up to the woman. I really believe that."

"Later he explained to me the history and everything about the invention of zero; the Indians did it—the sari ones, not the feather ones—and it was as important to mathematics and thus to life itself, as was the invention of *why* to philosophy."

"I love philosophy—especially when mixed in with science. The two traditions. For instance, as an example of the cross-fertilization of biology and metaphysics, I have always been interested in the question is the semiflaccid, the detumescing penis, after ejaculation half full or half empty?"

"The whole thing is just *divine*, darling—little you. Big him."

"I tell you there was something in him as new and hungry and unspoiled as Adam, something unkillable that must have been in the first man who walked erect, something incorruptible that made him seem wrought of marble. One could—did—imagine him living on and on, so that when old age shall this generation waste, he must remain, in the midst of other woe than ours, a friend to man after man after man. And oh, darlings, the flash of his big white teeth! I would follow him to hell if he asked me to—I *would!*"

The speaker fell silent. Others took up the discourse in earnest.

"And who are you suddenly, my dear, the See Manhattan By Night tour guide?"

"*Cosi diceva Abadessa—e s'en andava!*"

"Everybody ought to have an ideal man."

"Who walks erect. Yes. Mine is reticent in his self-expression, but honest in what he says; strong and essentially aggressive, but fair and protective; independent in his thoughts and feelings, but cautious and on whole polite. He is self-confident, but modest—and eager to perfect himself. He mistrusts women, but is not intimidated by them."

"And he likes the way, when he sits down after a long hard day walking erect, you go right down on your knees and suck his big white cock."

"What if he does? Anyway, I've been looking for him lately, but he hasn't come in. Last month when I was so sick with the flu and couldn't even go to hear Maria Callas sing Norma, I felt I might actually die, and I had a strange fantasy of him coming to my funeral—an unreasonable fantasy, I realized, for it would hardly be characteristic of him to join a crowd to look at anything, but I imagined he did come and see me laid to rest. I imagined him at the grave, standing apart. . ."

" '*Alors, dans l'amour il y a toujours l'un qui baise et l'autre qui tend la joue.*' "

"Ooh, *French!*"

!@#$%^&*

"I never minded being a working boy, but I was born with tastes, you see, tastes nourished in those days by life on the Bowery, and he believed in me and gratified them. He admired me and gave me lovely presents, including a beautiful china Easter egg, which when looked into portrayed a beautiful winter scene, with a troika in it and three lovely little men in greatcoats and sable hats and three little horses, of course. He said was inspired by his own divine First Symphony, called [in Russian] that's Winter Dreams, you see. Yes, think of it, *me*, admired by a great and beautiful man. No boy can resist admiration and presents, but from a great and—"

"Yes, Mister Swan, and he sure was beautiful."

"I speak not for the present moment of his immortal genius, but, I suppose considering where we are, of the beauty of his naked body. He is bones in a box now, in a hallowed grave in the city they all call Leningrad, but, oh, what he was! Photographs don't do him justice—he was a god of a man!"

("Can it be true?"

"Well, they say it was carved on stone walls for years—or scratched, anyway.")

!@#$%^&*

". . . all fifty-six partitions of the number eleven—and he can prove that there are no zeros as far east as the border through one! I could listen to him all day, all night!"

"Until the end of time—yes, dear we know, you are that smitten."

"Well, I suppose the real problem is, once you decide in your mind just what the ideal ought to be, you can't really be expected to at one and the same time hold on to that thought *and* put up with *anybody* the way they really *are*."

"Who said it is madder never to abandon oneself than often to be infatuated, better to live a wounded captive and a slave than always to walk in armor."

"I dunno—Oscar Wilde?"

"Oscar Wilde's family was originally Dutch, like Erasmus. Erasmus did not care for the Middle Ages."

"We get Dutchmen here, too; the crew of the *Nieu Amsterdam*."

"Well, dear, old New York was once New Amsterdam."

"Really? Well, it's New York now, and it's going to be New York forever."

" '*Vedeva Troia in cenere e in caverne!*' "

IX

The Galway Express, *An Domain Thair*, with Hyperion Productions' elaborate nineteen thirties Pullman parlor car caboosed-on the rear, slowed as it approached the Hibernian capital. A fine, light drizzle continued falling. Looking out on the left side through the half-draped smoke-glass window, Jacob Beltane saw (floating in the space composed as a compound of the outdoor landscape and the reflected interior) the obelisk in the Phoenix Park, pointing resolutely toward the occluded sun.

"It is representative of the myths of solar ascension and of light as the lancing spirit."

"What is?"

"The obelisk, all obelisks are. For example the one in Central Park that came from Alexandria, as so did the one on the Thames Embankment, behind the Savoy, where we'll be stopping in December. According to Tangent Percase. All obelisks, are so representative, due to their upright position and the pyramidial point at which they terminate."

"Speaking of which—if ever this train does likewise, does terminate ... How *do* you ever retain all that information, all those uncountable Percases-closed? I appreciate the man's erudition, but the *velocity* of it, sometimes it'd give you a real pain in your face."

"But they're so *perceptive*! The perceptions. Everything is something else. Thomas Browne says pyramids, arches, and obelisks were but the irregularity of vainglory and wild enormities of ancient magnanimity."

"When they were all mighty, and before everyone was someone and noone was anybody. That obelisk there is less than a century old, had originally to do with Wellington, then subsequently with Fenian aspiration and with the Phoenix Park Murders. As does Kilmainham Gaol out the window over there.

And one might not credit the builders of either with magnanimity. Vainglory, yes—all that lancing vainglory. Met by the cup. Lances, *athanes* . . . witch symbols. The Blue Nuns of Saint Vitus, Saint Dymphna, Saint Dervla, etcetera, all other secret witches—cunning women from the time of the Cathar persecution who flew through the night as the belief would have it to the West of Ireland. Also, as Sybil Farewell-Tarnysh pointed out, you an *Athling of Wyrd* and I, the diva, the supposed center of attention."

"Percase says 'True goddess worship disappeared in sixth-century Egypt with the Coptic Christians' suppression of the cult of Isis and did not really reappear until the Metropolitan Opera debut of Mawrdew Czgowchwz impersonating Isis's high priestess.' I rather like the sound of that."

"More eyewash. Lancing spirit?"

"Like a drop of that *potin*—can go right through you. Sounds too like something akin to *Pilgrim Soul*. I do love it when you say things like 'I won't say what I could say.' And 'any more' and it doesn't mean 'that's all there is.' "

"Odd, isn't it, how we were ever capable of understanding one another at all, despite the so called commonality of the English language? Nice that we had music anyway."

"Were? Had? Forebodings? Do we not now, even as we speak?"

"This is one of those afternoons in which—"

"There is an atmosphere."

"There is—an atmosphere."

"The sun, nevertheless, is—"

"There has conceivably never *been* less sun. As our nameless mystery writer wrote about winter in New York, *Mithras walks nowhere nearby*. This unremitting rain. Us indoors without vistas, behind weeping windows at the other end of the Atlantic from the gorgeous golden autumn of Central Park. It'd drive you mad. And yet, as Orphrey is fond of saying, it could have been worse in the long run, we might all have been Welsh."

" 'Sing, O let man learn liberty
From crashing wind and lasting sea.' "

“That’s rich—you singing that song.”

“Sure, it’s what I’m paid to do ma’am, sing a song.”

“The parlors, turf-fire suffocating against damp. The walls split by the dado rail: dark green below and pale yellow above. The whisperings after chant . . . the scene of instruction with no instruction. Everything I’d burst away from just as soon as I could walk well enough to sneak out through the kitchen garden, heading out beyond the tall ferns to sit on the rocks to escape. Or down to the *cimitiere marin*.

“You realize the whole time we were there nobody mentioned going down there, even the odd time when the skies cleared. The place was never mentioned, and yet it must be there that Old Maev is buried, because she’s not down in the crypt, I went looking: it was like being in the cave under Orphrey’s kitchen. Unless they put her out to sea on a raft. I thought about asking about it this morning, just before we left for Galway, but something prevented me. What? Brain fog. And for the love of God would you ever not call me *ma’am*!”

“Promise. What did you say that redheaded witch was called—in *Rusalka*?”

“Ježibaba—and *touche*. The rain’s had such an effect over these last three days that I kept being reminded of Thalia Bridgewood years ago, when I first came to New York. She did a revival of *Rain* down at the Cherry Lane. For the sound effects they had a garden hose and a sheet of corrugated tin backstage. The city closed the show for wasting water in a drought. All I’ve been thinking of these three days is that drought, and of Gene Moore’s always gorgeous windows at Tiffany featuring that month a cascade running over rocks: diamonds, rubies, emeralds, sapphires. The city cited them for having it, only Gene outwitted them by pumping gin through the display.

“Well, somebody suggested to Bridgewood they do the Gene Moore trick with the garden hose in the wings and the sprinklers high up in the flies—and the stage manager had actually gone to Marian Tanner on Bank Street, who was gone on the play—had seen it with Jeanne Eagels and it changed her life—and on Bridgewood, too, and was willing to underwrite the purchase of the gin and the device of recycling through tubing and troughs and great washtubs in the wings the enormous quantity required.

"However, the very *idea* of *spilling gin* to create a sound effect! Bridgewood said, 'I've got enough on my hands in this show placating the demon ghost of that Eagels woman. If she ever got wind of the fact they were pouring *gin* into roof gutters—and there are those in this town, *dahling*, who know *exactly* how to stir up that wind—she'd stage an apparition in the first act that would *ruin* me forever. Post the closing, *dahling*, and let's all head for the Adirondacks to shoot geese!'

"That's all I've had running through my mind—all the while we've been supposed to be in serious chin wag with Lady Abbess—that and the wild urge to re-create the finale of that first act, where Miss Sadie Thompson is upbraided by the preacher. Nobody was upbraiding us—quite the opposite the whole long while—but the cumulative effect of all that kindness and all those soulful susurruses was to make me very nearly stand up on the parlor table and *bellow* Sadie's curtain line, 'I have the right to stand here and to say to you, *to hell with you*—and be damned!' Orphrey is right, the country would drive you mad."

"Or to Gleann na nGealt—there to live on cresses."

"Not any more. It's Ballinasloe these days."

"Are sloes a cure?"

"I have no idea. Anyway, not Ballinasloe either, thanking you. Palm Springs. The man you call John Oak now, he has the right idea—and perhaps Orphrey is right, too, about scouting congruous locations in California. No conveniently situated entrances to the Underworld out there—except of course that the ground may open up at any moment and swallow the whole of everything.

"Have you noticed this train has now completely *halted*. I mean, the few times I rode around with Toscanini, he never let the train go any faster than fifty miles an hour, and he would go on talking and doing somersaults over the furniture and acting like something out of the Phoenix Park Zoo—or as they say in Dublin, the *a-zoo*—while the Pullman porters laughed themselves into uproars of glee. And now we idle here while some natural philosopher elaborates his argument or warms the pot for his tea or picks a horse out at the Curragh."

"I have noticed, and am reminded of the story of the celestial boat that unwittingly dropped anchor on one of the round towers of Clonmacnois, and of the angel who nearly drowned descending from the ether into the terrestrial atmosphere to release the anchor so it could proceed, but the monks came out and helped him unhook it and the boat went on its way. I wish I had a camera right this minute."

"One can hardly be surprised at the consternation of the angels. Any angel worth his clarity *would* drown in this atmosphere. You wouldn't get a picture through these windows."

" 'Farther, a little thought will discover to us that though we allow the existence of Matter or Corporeal Substance, yet it will unavoidably follow from the principles which are now generally admitted, that the particular bodies of what kind soever, do none of them exist whilst they are not perceived. So long as we attribute real existence to unthinking things, distinct from their being perceived, it is not only impossible to know with evidence the nature of any real unthinking being, but even that it exists.' Bishop Berkeley, *The Principles of Human Knowledge. Anyway, no,* to snap you this minute, in this very mood. Lady Abbess did say, 'Sure to look at, you are the very moral of herself!' "

"It's not even begun, and here I'm wishing it already over."

"Nothing is ever over."

"Actually, nothing's ever over easy—except Irving's Adam and Eve on a whiskey-down raft, slice of ham, side of French, served with love by Rhoe at the Burger Ranch."

"I shall tell a story instead, to further delay the waiting."

"I can taste it: ketchup, seltzer, black coffee."

"Saint Patrick and the ghost of Caeilte MacRonain were in a parlor so Patrick could learn the ways of Ireland when along came a lone woman, robed in a mantle of green, a smock of soft silk against her skin and a fillet of gold around her forehead. 'I've come, Caeilte, to require of thee my marriage gift, that once upon a time you promised me.' And Patrick parried, 'It's a wonder to me how I see you two: the young girl invested in all comeliness; but thou Caeilte, a withered ancient, bent in the back, and grown dingy.' 'Which is no wonder at all,' said Caeilte, 'for she is of the *Tuatha de Danaan*, who are unfading, and whose duration is perennial; I am of the sons of Finn, that are perishable, and fade away.' "

"I can *taste* it! It's not something else, yet, it fades away; it's perennial *and* perishable. Would there be a point at all to your story, or not?"

"No, it was Lady Abbess's. Your duration itself is pretty perennial—it's been called sempiternal in fact. But by the sidhe I believe she was referring to Maev, and by the Milesian I believe she was referring to your father. I believe she believes Maev's duration to be perennial, as I've heard one or more of your Secret Seven declare, *with gay knobs on*."

"Six feet under: pushing up the bluets. A goose just walked over my grave—hasn't happened since that time in Los Angeles."

"Where you've often said your grave is even now being prepared—in a studio on Formosa and Santa Monica."

"Just listen to you. I can tell by the way you *intone* the street names you're another lunatic for the place, in embryo. Of course it cast it's spell on me as well, as it must on anybody brought up on fables, on magic, on alchemical transformations."

"Nice to know if I go mad there, there's Palm Springs—or going upstate toward Santa Barbara, a place called Camarillo. You didn't tell me you'd been down to the Abbey crypt. I ought to have come. Lucan says that every power is impatient for a partner."

"There's a town called Lucan, not far from here. We could walk to it. It's a famous old spa town, whose waters, like the ones in Lisdoonvarna in County Clare vastly superior in sulfur content and curative minerals to anything in Bath or Leamington Spa, or Spa itself in Belgium, or Aix-les-Bains, Vichy, Karlsbad, Marienbad, Montecatini, or Nervi. The only equivalent to Lucan and Lisdoonvarna in Europe is Margareten Island in the Danube, between

Buda and Pest. There's a lovely old inn in Lucan, and the Irish who come for cures are infinitely more interesting than the chichi Continentals frequenting those other places—again excepting the Hungarians. And I confess a nice spa stay would be ever so preferable to what's in store for us in Dublin, because I shall confess it, that story about the marriage contract shook my nerves. I don't want us to be married. I was a bastard, and if I'm to have these boys of yours, they must of necessity be bastards born as well. Were we to marry, I should lose them—don't ask me how I know, I simply do."

"Not marriage bond, marriage gift. As Tacitus says, *quamquam severa illi matrimonia ecullam morum partem magis laudaveris*—a concept not so much to do with the essence of the act itself, or the affect arising from it, as with the formal aspects and entailments of it."

"Tacitus might have been talking of the Irish—were you?"

"No."

"Good."

"The story was you then married Czgowchwz and had his child."

"I never married anybody, nor was ever pregnant. That was a story contrived in some kind of reaction to our rescue of the Jewish boy, the direct male descendent of Rabbi Lowe on the night they burned the most important synagogue in Europe, the place the Emperor Rudolf went to learn the holy secrets of Kabbalah.

"We got him down through Slovakia to Bratislava on the Danube, then backtracking, to Budapest, then across the Hortobágy Plain to Debrecen, then into Ruthenia for the duration of the war, until the Russians were approaching, when I took the decision of my life. Rather than flee, I walked right into the Russian army, carrying the child in my arms—and this is where that fable strikes a uncannily true chord. 'She met a Russian soldier and loved him a little.' I did meet a Russian soldier, seventeen years old, wounded in the Ukraine, such a pure soul, so pale and ethereal with the epicene beauty only White Russians have. Not only a pure boy, but a very sick boy, who couldn't have possibly conceived of such a thing as carnal lust, and anyway I wasn't exactly in my

Grushenka phase—that had passed with the Nazi occupation of Prague. I was the equivalent for him of Florence Nightingale or Edith Cavell or Edith Wharton in the First War.

"And of course they could use every capable volunteer nurse who came along, and I had the cures in me from Connemara—although we had to make substitutions with local herb poultices and febrifuge mosses, which, unlike the spa waters of Karlsbad, Marienbad, Aix-les-Bains, etcetera, were perfectly adequate, except we could have used carrageen moss on the fever and knocked it out instantly. Not surprising any of it, since after all the Craft originated among the Celts on the plains of Scythia in the second millennium BC. Anyway, without the two of us—myself and the local cunning woman—he'd have been a goner; there was no penicillin and his throat was burning out of him and he'd got scarlet fever and rheumatic fever on top of it. Incipient tuberculosis as well in the freezing winter, but sphagnum moss and massive doses of vodka took care of that one, the vodka distilled from good stores of rye from the summer harvest.

"Then they were so grateful to have been taken back to Moscow, and by this time, the cunning woman gone, I was speaking Old Court Russian, intercut with the same amount of French and French-derived words used in Petersburg, which Leningrad had never purged with that insipid *Pravda* Newspeak that sounds more foreign to the Russian peasant than Ukrainian Polish or Latvian or Finnish—in the voice copied from Akhmatova, who I'd adored when she'd come to Prague before the Great Terror, a voice that always intimidated the Soviets. They hated and feared Leningrad—after all they murdered Kirov, and of course Stalin hated all Russians, down to the last kulak, general, Soviet Jewish intellectual follower of Lenin.

"So I'd gotten the soldier and the boy, the direct descendent of Rabbi Lowe, supreme master of Kabbalah and Arabic alchemy both, creator of the Golem, out of Prague. In the aftermath of incineration of the culturally most important synagogue in Central Europe to Moscow, and Dolukhanova got *me* overnight into the Bolshoi chorus, and into a secure billet across the hall from Ulanova, prima ballerina of all the Russias, in one of the Seven Sisters you know, those Stalin Gothic monstrosities, each exactly the same design and height, that give the Moscow skyline the most surreal contour in Europe.

"Whereupon together we hatched our plan. Without giving notice—a thing only she could do, Dolukhanova announced herself *souffrante* and unable to sing the role of Marina in *Boris Gudunov*, on the very night she knew Stalin would be attending, and the management, quaking in their boots announced me as the substitute, under the name Mardyushka Gordzyvadzne—obviously trying to pass me off as Georgian, so out came what seemed once it got on the hair had the sheen of black hat paint, but once set—and I mean set: the red hair was gone until I got back to Prague and took two full years to grow out while I wore Ljuba Welitsch wigs—which was funny, because Ljuba had, in Vienna, before the War, grabbed hold of a hank of my hair and declared 'I am going to have that color or die!'

"And all the while the hat paint and the lacquer treatments to give the hair shine were in progress, so was an intense phonetic crash course in the twenty best answers in Georgian to anything Comrade Stalin might say in the first hour at table, because he always said the same things, never really listened to anybody else, and after that first hour—you could set your watch by it—had turned so shitfaced you could answer him in Chinese, just like you could with Churchill, his only match on the world stage to drunken incoherence in the evening to the point of actual incontinence. So with either of them the canard about audience reactions to a knockabout farce, or a laugh riot situation comedy, *piss ran down legs*, might without notice take on a new meaning.

"It was very bold of me, but irresistible, so after the first hour, by my watch exactly, without the word of a lie I commenced answering his every declaration in the Irish. His eyes kept lighting up and he's kept grunting *Da, da, pravda, pravda*. Go figure."

"So you sang Marina, brought down the house, and had your dinner with Stalin."

"Yes, nothing less than a *success fou* would have done the trick—and there was Dolukhanova, eyes twinkling, explaining to an open-mouthed chorus that I was her secret protégée and the whole performance had been cooked up to bring me to the attention of the Little Father, Comrade Stalin. The woman had nerves of steel, as did Ulanova in the ballet."

"And did she mind the child, the descendent of Rabbi Lowe?"

"Oh, no, I took him with me. She said, 'Tell him the child is yours—but not by a Russian, by a Georgian. He'll believe you. He did, and the boy slept in a little basket right beside the table, waking only occasionally and smiling up at the man he later remembered as kindness itself, feeding him Russian sweetmeats with his fingers. You see, children had the most remarkable effect on Stalin. They made him human for the interval he was in their presence—because you know he wasn't human. Hitler was human, and horribly twisted and sociopathic, paranoid schizophrenic, ugly, self-loathing and self-destructive, the exact self-image of the German proletariat and middle class after the criminal idiocy of the Treaty of Versailles. Stalin wasn't remotely any of those things, least of all self-destructive. Gennaio once told, years after the event, actually when I sang my first Fricka at the Met, that Freud had told Smiley Blanton and Marie Bonaparte, as they were spiriting him out of Vienna first to Paris—"

"Rather like yourself, really."

"If you like, *yes*—and then to London, that he could not comprehend the truth of Stalin, and since the disappearance of Sabina Spielrein into the maw of the Soviet Great Terror, it had haunted him for more than a decade, but he knew Stalin could never be analyzed, never be helped by any form of psychiatry. He was what medieval man called a monster possessed by the devil, in effect the devil incarnate. Sounded more like Jung than Freud, what with Jung's ridiculous *Schnappsidee* that what was happening in Germany was that Wotan was walking the earth—that *really* pissed off George London that one. Gennaio then said that had Freud lived to hear the story of Jacob Ben-Yakov and the supper party, with the devil incarnate feeding sweetmeats for the direct descendent of Rabbi Lowe, legendary creator of the Golem, he might have despaired further.

"At any rate, Stalin gave me leave to travel with the boy to Odessa, on condition that I would return to the Bolshoi. I was terrified and told Dolukhanova so. She gave me that look which translates as *Feh*, and said there are very few people Comrade Stalin knows he can't touch. Ulanova is one, and I am another. Unhappily he can get to Akhmatova, because she is out to destroy his fantasies, while we, for better or worse, by dancing Juliet and Giselle and singing Marfa and Marina, cosset them.

"In Odessa, on board the ship bound for Jaifa through hostile waters, the boy and I bade farewell—we were mother and child in every moral way, and it was terrible for him. But in '48, after I'd flown to Paris, he showed up on a diplomatic flight from Beirut and he heard me sing Amneris. We've kept the secret between us since, although it's hardly unknown in Tel Aviv. It is what the French call *un secret de Pulchinelle*. He's a wonderful boy, plays the cello in the Israel Philharmonic, and the happiest moment I had before I found you was going to Tel Aviv and singing the *Bachianas Brasileiros*, the *Hafner on der Hirt*, the Rachmaninoff *Vocalise* and Falla's *Siete Canciones Populares Españoles* with him. You see, in Israel, they know Czgowchwz is a Czech Jewish name."

"And what is the cellist's name, if I may ask?"

"His name is Jacob Ben-Yakov."

"So that is the truth beyond the cover story. Tell me."

"Hence the story that arose of my having had a male child by Czgowchwz. But it wasn't a world into which a child could be in conscience brought, especially not into a partisan underground movement where the retaliation of the Nazis included, ironically enough, quite biblical gestures such as putting the firstborn to the sword—a practice unhappily not confined to Pharaoh's army or to Herod Antipas either, but upon occasion recorded by the Hebrews themselves as acts of their heroes, so long as they were under the thrall of the temple priests.

"You know the Jews never became truly humane until the rabbinical Reformation in Alexandria, and it is the clear references to barbaric practices no better than their enemies that a thousand years later fell on their heads with the notorious blood libels of the German High Middle Ages. I took Czgowchwz's name because of the Jews. I did not convert, but they had the temerity to call me righteous among the Gentiles, for which I felt entirely unworthy, and the only way out of it—and Mother Saint Mawrdew agreed when we hooked up years later for the flight out of Prague, was to take his name. And when he was killed, I kept it, and the truth is whatever of us—you and I together—he was a very great man and I cannot—at least not yet—take the name Beltane, or marry you."

"Yes. After all, look at it this way—if we *were* married, we might—not that I'd go jumping off the train into the mud—have had to admit by now the honeymoon was over."

"Or that after all, you prefer little boys."

"Only because they obey, as I might've—much to my subsequent chagrin—vowed to do for you."

"And what of my chagrin? Were we married, I'd have to say *I married a witch.* Anyway, I never where I came from heard that about little boys. Perhaps like all Englishmen for the past four hundred years, you've confused the monarch, the mistress, the mother and—I've lost my train."

"Of thought? Just stalled. But I know you're not my mother. For a start, darling, mother's voice never cracked."

Mawrdew Czgowchwz saw flashbulbs pop; she envisioned headlines in the English gutter press: *Diva Confesses Slaying Songbird/Mate On Galway Train / Dublin Agog/Weapon Sought: Did This Look Kill?*

The Galway express lurched forward at last, past the switch signal and into Kingsbridge Station, thus freeing the diva from the toils of an unwelcome fantasy, that of an endless journey in freezing conditions in a dilapidated wooden railway coach through a war-torn chaotic country, the dismal and prophetic silence broken only at impossibly long intervals by what might have been stages in a long and troubled life, the conductor calling out "Omsk!" "Tomsk!" "Irkutsk!" "Vitebsk!"

*

Having been received ceremonially at Dublin Castle (walk around the room, look at its ceiling, defined by the stucco masterpiece *Hibernia Welcoming the Arts and Sciences*, beneath which, in Easter Week 1916 James Connolly lay convalescing before his execution in Kilmainham Gaol), they moved along to City Hall for "a gawp at the civic paraphernalia." From there they proceeded in Hyperion Productions' spit-polished Armstrong-Siddeley ("What they *ought* to've done," offered Brendan, the driver, "was haul the great old coach out of the shed fer you, only it's *dis-throyed*."), followed by a small convoy of unprepossessing Austin Minors down Dame Street to College Green, and straight up Grafton Street—lined, it seemed, with speculators as concerned in one and the same moment with goods and stuffs in numbers of shops' vitrines as with the passengers in the outsize vehicle edging its way past them—in front of the Grafton Cinema (Bette Davis in *Wedding Breakfast*) past the black service van of the Swastika Laundry in Ballsbridge.

A late afternoon egg-yolk sun, characteristic of Dublin in October, coming forth through coal-smoke-streaked clouds lounging in a weak blue sky, splashed old gold in oak-leaf patterns across significant crumbling and refurbished facades, in through fan-light, demi-lunes, and long lace-curtained Georgian windows. The tricolor of the Republic, unfurled and billowing—without fear, without reproach, its orange band faded to the color of the sun—in the exalted-if-sooted company of Mercury, Hibernia, and Fidelity atop the General Post Office, heralded the procession of the devout, the dislocated, the doubting, and the distracted in and out below.

At the top of Grafton Street the reception committee and their guests turned a little way left along Stephen's Green, and then at Dawson Street left again down toward the Mansion House, to be received in to an "oyster" tea with the Lord Mayor—greatly pleased to share his reminiscences of his guest of honor's last visit to the capital and to welcome her companion on his arrival there for the first time—received from the New York diva a communique from her city's mayor, the Right Honorable Robert F. Wagner Jr., reading, in part, "Our people possess the same genuine ideals of liberty and equality, and our two cities play a great role in the activities of the world."

Mawrdew Czgowchwz, having put all considerations of uxoricide (as exhilarating as histrionics) behind her, had been treating her consort for nearly an hour to many of the same conspiratorial side glances he had come to find so nearly overwhelmingly erotic all through May, June, July, August and September—their entire time together—in New York and environs.

Leaving the Mansion House (where many—though not, she noted, the abstemius Lord Mayor, had grown maudlin from too many tumblers of noggin in the forenoon) they were driven down to Nassau Street, around the front of Trinity College, down Westmoreland Street and over O'Connell Bridge, past the General Post Office and Nelson's Pillar. (Orphrey Whither scowled up at the landmark, even as sightseers climbed out onto the viewing platform at Nelson's impassive feet: "An outrage—an *anomaly*: wants to be blown off the street!" Brendan nodded in grim assent, waving to idling jarvey acquaintances.) They turned the corner of Parnell Square and met the facade of the Rotunda ("the second-oldest lying-in hospital in Europe; the oldest is in Vienna"), the marquee of the Ambassador Cinema (showing *The Solid Gold Cadillac*) and the front steps of the Gate Theatre (placards to the side advertizing *Nude With Violin*), before turning back down O'Connell Street to the front door of the Gresham.

Orphrey Whither, bounding out on the left side, spoke his mind.

"Having all grown antlers in the interim, Brendan, we will not *skulk* into the place through the garage, thanking-*you*. It is enough to know we are booked in *en camouflage*, in the ridiculous manner ordained by the necessities of kowtowing to this priest-ridden so-called Republic of theirs. The fact that there are thirty-two counties in the whole of Ireland, and thirty-two points in the compass, apparently leads the Irish to conclude that Ireland itself somehow abides in contingent relation to the great world entire—who are we then to wake them rudely from their dream?"

Mawrdew Czgowchwz looked at Jacob Beltane and then, removing a glove as she did so, leaned forward to address the manly driver.

"Actually, Brendan, the weather's turned so fine at that, that if you'd ever give us a moment—there suddenly being so much room back here in the saloon—we might just as well slip out of these rather confining garments and walk stark naked together into the lobby. As we're prebooked, *en camouflage*, I presume there'll be no necessity so to engage in any formalities—and in any event it might, don't you think, be of some importance to disconvey the impression we like to stand to them, particularly."

Leaving Brendan's eyes "stuck out on stalks" in the rearview mirror, they climbed, clothed, out of the car and ascended the steps. (Orphrey Whither was already on the sidewalk ahead of them, gesticulating, doing show business, recruiting citizens for *Pilgrim Soul*. "Tonight at Johnny Farrell's—open call!")

Remembering Consuelo Gilligan's parting dictum ("Lola Montez was Irish"), Mawrdew Czgowchwz wondered whether at that very hour (around midnight), somewhere chic and indoors in New York, her pet seer in snood of lace might not be gazing rapt into a certain compact mirror—the way the woman trying not to peer directly at the entourage, now crossing from the hotel lobby toward the lifts, was using hers: strategically angled to the mirrored wall of the lounge bar, so as not to miss a twist of the progress.

The diva had certainly become accustomed to being noticed in the cluttered and unfettered postwar world—where the barriers had come down in the same proletarian blitz with the baroque ceilings—but this, the scrutiny of the Dubliners was what the nuns had gone in for countering (all those years ago and only last week, with their *custody of the eyes*). What the Ruthenian Gypsy partisans had tried to school her in. What she had failed to carry off on that inhospitable plane on which the world was, if a stage, then one in a new (or old, blitzed) theater: without a wall to back against, without wings to dart into. One moreover entirely overlit, and so she seemed molested from no source. Yet, in the face now reflected in the lift interior's mirrored wall, she saw indeed—she would have said for the first time—the face of *one of their own*: a kind of cross between a recipient of absolution and a werewolf cornering its prey. ("Would y'ever get a gander at all the *hair!*") The face of the idler, the ogler, the *streeler*, and strait-gaiter (taking the holy hour) keen for info (to garner, as they would say, *the syllabus and rights of it*.)

"This is a scream," Mawrdew Czgowchwz said, the moment the door closed between them and their triumphant hosts.

"Being thought of as English, I, of course, am expected to take no particular notice." Jacob went to the long window and looked down, from the highest indoor vantage on O'Connell Street. "Remarkable race—most interesting, the voices, the replies. The Inquiring Photographer would do well hereabouts."

She sat down in an armchair opposite him and looked past him down into O'Connell Street. Then she stood and walked up to the window, looking across at Hibernia, illuminated atop the General Post Office, then turned back. Pivoting on his fixed, attentive position, she began a circuit of the room.

"Eyes everywhere—and no custody of them!"

"Talking eyes. Good God, they've laid on a cream tea!"

The holy hour having a while since ended, Orphrey Whither had gone down to work the bustling thoroughfares—and spike the talk—and spot-check the stringers engaged—for all along the winding route they'd lately motored along (and from the queue for returns at the Gaiety Theatre in South King Street, anticipating the evening's performance of *Bad Seed*, to the lounges of the Shelbourne on Stephen's Green, the Royal Hibernian in Dawson Street and the Moira, hard by Mercer's Hospital; and in the green room at the Queen's where the Abbey players lounged comfortably, prior to essaying *The Quare Fella*, while outside in Pearse Street Johnny Forty Coats, sausaged into his many layers—smock, gansey, shawl, rug, chasuble, blanket, weatherproof, cope—ran toward the Antient Concert Rooms as if the programme were about to commence. And in conversation at Grogan's in Leeson Street, Farrell's in South King Street, opposite the Gaiety, and McDaid's in Harry Street; at the Palace Bar in Westmoreland Street among the battered-black-hatted literati, and at Bewleys in Grafton Street among "The Handbags" bivouacked on the long banquettes discoursing in the smoky mirrors; and in sibilant whispers in the Long Room at Trinity, and in corridors of the National Library, and from armchair to armchair at the National Arts Club, and on the staircases at Newman House, and at the city desk of the *Irish Times* on D'Olier Street), there would be undulating the news that Herself-the-Wild-Goose had reached them, and, having assumed an attitude of grand repose, was situated, in the company of her paramour ("a scandalous international adultery that shocks the watching world" the archdiocese gave out, in confidence, but unable, owing to the Gresham's far-sighted booking arrangements—Jacob Beltane and Orphrey Whither sharing the back suite on the fifth floor, Mawrdew Czgowchwz occupying, alone, the front, offering full panoramic views of O'Connell Street, Nelson's Pillar and the General Post Office), the notorious songbird couple already in the short space of time since their arrival having been re-christened "Nedso" and "Nuala."

"Not," mewed the famously onomastic Brian O'Nolan, or was it Flann O'Brien, or was it Myles na gCopaleen that time, elaborating this conceit over a rake of drink as if he'd fashioned it—to assembled cronies at the Palace Bar, "Yer only man's no pint of plain a-*tall*, but a great strapping lad nearly the size of Clara Butt, and he makes a sound they tell me like a cross—y'know the *way*—between herself and John McCormack and *nuthin a-tall all* like that common squawk soundin' like the suicidal gurgle out of the dyin' Judas that's the common run of the English *contra-tenore*. I'm tellin' yiz all, now, there's a fella with not a bother on him and the one eye fixed on the score and the other *cocked* to the main chance—in the form of the *connectin' door* between the fifth floor *back* and the fifth floor *front* over at Maeve and Paddy O'Sullivan's place, that I have it from the boots is no longer fast-bolted, and he's only dyin' to see in the mornin' the disposition of the shoes left out, will they carry the charade that far. I tell yiz all, there is a fella poised on the *fair-tyle vairge!*"

"The *boots?*"

"No, not the boots, *y' eejit*—not unless there's *kinks afoot*."

"Hah, hah."

"Annyway, the fair-tyle *what?*"

"The fair-tyle *vairge*—y'know, the place of *encounter* between somethin' and somethin' *else*. Not unlike our own *James Jyece*—y'know the writer fella driven from our shores by the *hee*-pocrisy of us all, and obliged in his own words to practice his art in *sighin', in exhalation and in cunnilingus*. Sure the consort's name ought to be *Fergus*, who stood gar-*deen* fer Queen Maev when she went off in private to make her great water, but Nedso will do."

"*Jeeziz!*"

"Sure ain't they just come from America—a land of verges—and *vergers* too!"

"And like every fella on the *verge*, prone to exaggerated self-awareness."

"As well y'moight be yerself, *mar dhea*, was it yer own picture, portrait, and description along with that of herself the prodigal that was broadcasted and inseminated to every nook and corner of the counthry. Sure there was talk goin' around in Marlborough Street of great consternation in the corridors of Maynooth and in the Phoenix Park itself that the the two of them's behavior together was significant of the worst excesses of *courtly love* and the Albigensian *Cattarrhs*. 'And whose wouldn't be now,' sez yer man at Trinity, with a wee twinkle in the eye, 'in all this changeable weather with the rain pelting down and the nights drawn in so fierce and with terrible chills in the air and the coal fires an' everythin', is it anybody ye know that isn't on the old pastilles?' "

"Would ye say the fella'd be on starter's orders *per diem*?"

"I would not, so. The oul' wheeze that he presented himself for tuition to Dame Eva Turner dressed as a girleen is *entoirely* without foundation, and that's a fact."

"Izzit."

"It is, and in doin' the full dekko on the fella, she had the opportunity y'see when *pokin'* his *doy-a-phragm* ta *ascertain* he was wearing nothin' in the pelvic *orea!*"

"*Jeeziz!*""

"So 'tis sairtin he's got the apparatus below, but does he know what he's got it *for?*"

"T' serve the porpose like, y' mean besides stirrin' the tea. Sure and the seam in his bollocks is particular hand-stitched."

"*Jeeziz!*"

"Sure it's the times that's in it is what it is."

" 'Tis—and you're me ould segocia, wide as a gate, so y'are. 'Airm in airm,' he cried, 'fer Oive come t' lead yiz, fer Oirland's freedom we'll foight and doye! For the cause that called youse may call tomorra, in one last foight fer the ghreen aghain!' "

*

There being no necessity of a press conference to enlighten the paying public ("And what would I say to them anyway? That after all the pope gave Ireland to Henry II, in 1155, in the bull *Laudabiliter?*"), the impresario charged his prize attractions (over the house phone adjacent to the newsagents, stockpiling the Dublin and London evening papers) to be at the ready at half-seven for eight: to be transported up to Jammet's, in Nassau Street, for dinner, and then off at ten to the opening of the second half at the Olympia, a special gala organized on the theater's dark night (John Gielgud's night off in *Nude With Violin*: the actor would be in attendance to greet them in the Hyperion box) featuring Jimmy O'Dea's immortal turn as Biddy Mulligan, the Pride of the Coombe. Thence to supper at Farrell's, in the premises' *chambre séparée* (the snug, closed-off by folding, though not soundproof—doors).

"Not in the *Upper Room*, so?" one apprentice wit, auditioning to Micheál MacLíammóir, had cooed exiting the gents' lavatory at Harcourt Street Station, only moments before the exchange was recounted in its every acoustic nuance to Orphrey Whither by qui-vivacious tattlers in the Gresham's lobby (just then riveted by the following aperçu on himself in *An Irishman's Diary*).

"Whither is, we are assured, one of the triad (with Ophuls and Renoir) who have most effectively, through the mastery of deep-focus, tracking, and multiple action within the shot *socialized* space."

That'll get the free extras, he mused, in their droves.

"No indeed," the lordly intendant of the Gate Theatre's *art* seasons had replied. "This evening's entertainment is the publican *descends* to meet the Phari-*see!*" Orphrey Whither, spoiling for altercation, headed out, dispelling air in prodigal multiplicities of counterblast, into the quickly darkening Dublin streets.

As he barreled again up Grafton Street, ignoring the brightly lit shop windows, the Angelus rang out. Many devout citizens, moving lips, touching crooked forefingers to foreheads and cap brims—nodded near the Carmelite Church of Saint Theresa. Meanwhile, over on the North Side, in Morning Star

Street, prayer commenced as usual, its intention the cause of the Marian legionnaire Edel Quinn, dead these twelve years in Nairobi. Orphrey Whither, passing Johnny Forty Coats—deep in metaphysical rumination—thought *I shall engage the creature—for good measure, sure nineteen-sixteen was a time of allegorical excess.*

*

They lay together in the windowless room. He touched her hair.

"Gone missing?"

"Just name the place."

"And win the trip?"

"It all seems *ridiculous!*"

"Who exactly *is* this geezer we've been hoodwinked into being convenient to tonight after the show?"

"I've heard every identification from one-of-Maev's-first-lovers to her natural father—and back."

"Then possibly your *grandfather?*"

"Or some like contributor."

"I don't know what you mean by that. We've come to know in recent millennia which of the men a woman takes—"

"I've heard tell of it; and what have you done with the information?"

"Nomenclature, I believe it's—"

"Not, in my experience, the most trustworthy indicator."

"*Mens scia, conscia recti*. How did you first meet Orphrey Whither?"

"No, we have not."

"Pardon, I was merely—and anyway, what is it Milanov says?"

" '*Zo? Vot?*' But for the record, no, we have not. He first approached me at the Hollywood Bowl, an all-aria concert I didn't love doing but in which I did get a big kick out of giving as an encore Bernard Herrmann's *Salaambo* aria from *Citizen Kane*. He proposed a film on Malibran—said he could make what he liked, had dippers into pots of the earth's own money. Old family of pirates dating back to the days of the Muscovy trade. Sounded like another version of the O'Maurigan Spanish Armada legend. Already wildly famous for *The Day That Dawns* and *The Night of the End of Time*. I listened—said the Malibran *rediviva* was called Maria Callas. Said he'd encountered her; too corpulent for the screen. (I wasn't myself in those days scarce of weight.) He'd thought of using her voice dubbed over Jennifer Jones. I said I didn't imagine that together or separately either cared to impersonate a legend who fell off a horse and broke her neck at twenty-six. He confessed to a Performing Woman obsession. I asked him what else he did about it besides cruise dressing rooms.

"*Mens scia conscia recti*."

"Sounds obscene. Whenever I saw *mens* in the lesson, I only ever thought of where—you're a boon comrade, *there's* no mistake. At any rate, 1923 was the year I was spirited away from this dark, cold place and sent to Prague. Do you realize they'd shot my father right there across the street, and might have me? Not that they'd have done it in public, shot me in the—"

When she started laughing, he looked worried.

"It's nothing—about being shot. In the Dardanelles. They may have brought him into the lobby downstairs, dead, or dying."

"The Troubles seem to have stopped. What's that other hotel—the one up on The Green?"

"That would be either the Shelbourne or the Russell. It's better we're here, around the corner from the Pro-Cathedral, in the thick. Avoidance is a blunder, always was."

"Cast a cold eye—but not my way."

A note from The O'Maurigan had advised them on the walks to be taken in and around the capital. ("Go and sit in front of the blood and the bones too of Saint Valentine, in Whitefriars Chapel. A turn in the same Holy Den to the cult of Saint Jude you may omit: the pieties observed there are somewhat too sensational.")

At the Gaiety Theatre, Miko Riordan not only remembered the diva Mawrdew Czgowchwz as well as, upon waking sober in his chair at dawn each day to the grating noises of Potterton's milk float and Boland's bread van rattling together over the cobblestones, he would recall himself to himself and the waking world's dilemmas, but had in fact only just returned to his night watch and his *News of the Word* through the back alley to the stage door from Farrell's, having devoured the talk and the turn, "Love's Old Sweet Song" (dropping consequently, a tear of his own into the ecumenical pool). Sensible, courteous, full of pleasure in having such illustrious guests thus beholden to himself in the dark dead of the Dublin night, he slipped them in through the pass door to the ghostly stage, lit by a single standing work lamp. He walked them out onto the apron under the proscenium arch and, retiring to his post, his paper and his tea kettle, left them alone together.

Standing smote by recollection, onstage in the darkened empty theater, Mawrdew Czgowchwz attempted to convey some notion of what it had been like playing in elaborately mounted shows like *Carmen, Samson et Dalila* and *Aida* to sold-out standing-room-only houses in the confines of a Victorian music hall.

"I was apprehensive owing to the fact I hadn't sung in Dublin before, and to follow Stignani in the role was, I felt, asking for it, in the form of the big raspberry. New York hadn't had an Amneris of any really great stature since Louise Homer, but Ebe had sung here just the year before. It turned out such footling matters as comparison were the least ot it.

"Lord, that Triumphal Scene! Madness and mayhem. They'd recruited about a hundred supernumeraries, put them in woad cloaks and tin halberds from old Celtic-revival designs of *The Immortal Hour* and set them to marching around the place in twin circles, clockwise and counter-so across the stage and out into the alley in back of Neary's pub we've just come through, past the windows of the snug we've just been wedged into these four hours, and back again across the stage.

"The entry into the bullring in Seville was managed in much the same way and dressed in oddments I couldn't begin to describe to you, and the bacchanal in the temple of Dagon the same again, only this time the *Fianna* kit was worn inside out and upside down and torn in places—evidently to suggest that the Philistines were a that much more unruly crowd than the Egyptians.

"Unruly! Imagine the slapstick collisions between participants and the belting back of the drams against the perishing cold and the shivering wet—quids worths passed out through the snug's one window as if from the Hall of Healing—into outreached trembling hands—desperate clutches. Make you think you were in the Bastille courtyard the hour the day-old bread crusts were tossed in.

"During the Nile Scene—and especially on the closing night of the season—it was impossible to keep them out of Neary's, and they were by then breaking into ribald ballads about Little Egypt, and into renditions of 'Ol' Man River' and what not else, that you could hear across at the Royal College of Surgeons if not down Stephen's Green to the Holles Street Lying-in Hospital. It was no inconvenience to me, who had nothing to sing in the Act but *tradditor!* but the poor Aida, a misguided lyric as I remember called Serafina Something—disintegrated entirely, cracking of course on the C in '*O patria mia*,' and finally—before Radames could enter for the duet—abdicating the *palco scenico* in favor of a bewildered Amonasro, colliding with him in her flight as he, bounding onstage to discover neither confederate nor scapegoat, dashed to the apron here where we're standing and sang '*di Napata le gole*' straight up at the gods, thus leaving *me* to enter, thundering my *tradditor!*' at *him* rather than at Radames.

"Finally, as things were getting more and more out of hand, with the Judgment Scene upon us, the Madge, Maggie Burke-Sheridan and Micheál MacLíammóir—himself brandishing the cat-o-nine-tails they'd given me to torment the poor Seraphina Something with in the Boudoir Scene—'*Trema, vil schiava! In cor ti lessi—tu l'ami!'—tore* into Neri's and *lit into* into such malefactors who had not seen him coming and scampered out the back door into the alley and across South King Street to the sanctuary of Farrell's. 'Haven't ye disgraced yerselves *enough*? Will there never be an *end* to it in Ireland?!' Whereupon he was then and there bestowed with a new soubriquet."

"Wait, don't tell me, let me guess. *Il Bonzo Furibondo*."

"Bravo, you got it in one. Then there I was singing the whole of the Radames duet with Achille, who'd interrupted his Paris season and come over to a place he wasn't even sure was concrete on the earth, against the offstage sound of a ruckus the two of us decided to imagine a spontaneous rising of the populace of Memphis, protesting the condemnation of Radames. Because did we know even whether the Aida would come back to be entombed—and if not, then perhaps the opera's finale would have to be hastily rewritten, and we perhaps required to interpolate some other appropriate Verdian music, such as '*Ai nostri monti*.'

"Achille had arrived apologizing: he only knew Radames in French. 'Sure, misther, y'could sing it in *Choinese*,' he was informed, 'fer all the diff'rence it'd make—but isn't it *darlin' mew-sic annehway*? Im-*mor*-tal!'

"We did the *Carmen* together and the *Samson*, too. I spent *that* entire evening in opulent, if somewhat sluttish repose, lounging downstage—over there —under a canopy—never budged—the while everybody else either filed in and filed out solemnly or danced around upstage as though the whole sacred and profane melodrama were Dalila's dream. Samson came and went like a yokel sent to a fortune-teller at a carnival or, say, like on the pier at Yarmouth. The incestuous *poule de luxe* bedchamber in old Gaza—a sturdy bog-oak four-poster canopied in Brown Thomas tiger-print chintz—became, with the addition of a few symbolic papier-mâché stones clamped on between the acts, and rolled upstage on casters, the seductress's loge in the temple of Dagon, and therein I lay, never shifting the weight of my body around on my bones until from out of the flies there was dropped a single lightweight papier-mâché *col-ume* as they call them here, accompanied by the recorded sound of a wardrobe being knocked over, and the scene blacked out.

"The *Carmen* was abstract—locations stained onto assorted flats that didn't always in performance contrive to match up as conceived, so that one wound up, for example, being gashed open in public before the panorama of a mountain pass that looked suspiciously like the Sally Gap, into which a posse of shawlies, smoking cigars, had wandered, or else singing the '*Chanson Boheme*' out in front of the Four Courts.

"But *The Mikado* was a *very* classy affair, because Sibyl insisted on adherence, and saw to it that adherence was the outcome. And, as MacLíammóir pointed out, the Dubs prefer Gilbert and Sullivan to almost anything else—it was Gilbert and Sullivan that was playing nightly all through the Easter Rising, to full houses. The audience sang along at every performance, and I enjoyed Katisha immensely. I did her as a sort of frump Turandot in my own hair, which one critic called 'perverse' as what Japanese woman's hair is flaming red? We did have fun."

"Then as now," Jacob rejoined, gazing at the weird shadows cast by the work lamp here and there in the auditorium's hollows. "You are having something like fun hereabouts, I think."

"I *am*! What're you having?"

"Hallucinations. I agree completely with Plonque. Dublin, legend that it is, isn't concrete on the earth."

"True. You know I don't know why, but *Aida* here is like *Aida* in New York, even more important than in Italy—it's reckoned the definitive grand opera."

"To me it conjurs up Morgana Neri—and I think of Neri as the Nosferatu."

"Poor Morgana. Always claimed to be detached. The awful truth was she was unhinged. Yet, really, in spite of everything, there was something ... almost.

"No, it's the *effect* of *Aida* on the midwinter Family Circle. Really, there's nothing like it anywhere else—not now. I suppose it's like the erotic effect Korngold's *Violanta* had on the old Statsoper gallery. The thing it really is most like, though, is Radio City Music Hall's Christmas Show. That's really what *Aida* is—the secular Christmas show at the Met. How I miss New York! The only comfort is to say *this time next year*—and never mind what my father insisted, or Wittgenstein either. There can be no this time next year—God, the pair of them with their Viennese *mots*. I greatly prefer David Papers's insistence on propositions like the present is big with striving possibles. After all, my poor father ended up facedown in the gutter at twenty-six—like Malibran off her horse. And his friend—well, that life was grim, by all accounts."

"You're big enough with the only striving possibility I care to envision. I can't be sorry either that I missed the Neri Era, but, crazy as it sounds, I—it's like what you hear people say about the Blitz. 'Mind-*you*, I wouldn't *'ve missed it!*' In any case, it's over now: they've heard the last of Morgana Neri in New York."

"You know, I have the weird feeling *we* haven't."

*

Curate on the premises (and in his own mind—if not yet that of a certain recalcitrant party upstairs—lieutenant publican) John-John Farrell ("*Seanin Og*") pulled on his pint while examining his conscience and reckoning his turf accounts. Mainstay on the pumps since that June night during the Emergency when the elder John, called "Johnny" (then aged sixty-nine by his own account, and therefore how far in reality from four-score you couldn't get decent odds on anywhere in Dublin), too, "a wee episode for himself," pitching forward down the cellar stairs—a seeming "Olympic nosedive fairy stroke." (Merely to bolt back upright on a pallet at the Royal College of Surgeons up the street, to report Tír Na nÓg in the light at the end of the tunnel "an immortal after hours: ferocious great crack, and *nobody* callin' *time!*")

The son awaited his celebs, due in from the Olympia any minute, as audience present at the shenanigans there had already transferred en masse to Farrell's, a most unusual turn of event, remarked upon as a *slide*. Word was obviously out as to who might—and who with her besides—be as soon as not half seen hare-ing into the place—itself all glowing brass fixtures and fittings, worked bog-oak long bar, inlaid and stained leather-topped tables and long oval mirrors, composing a setting that pulsed in the dim gold smoky light of the late evening situation. John-John, dedicated to his vocation: to superintending the cessation of need and fret, prepared himself for his work on the late shift—dispensing consolation, corroboration, counsel, and comfort to punters determined to tell lies and celebrate credence.

Deliberately slowing her pace, balking shy as if maladroitly conducted, Mawrdew Czgowchwz entered the public house, to find herself surveying one long crowded room of her mother's bygone world and time. There was not a free barstool, an empty table or an uninhabited corner in view, nor, one would have testified, in the available floor space the makings of so much as the narrowest corridor through which a woman might progress; nevertheless, the crowd parted as first she stood a moment on the top step of three leading down into the lounge, and then, inhaling as if to produce a column of air with which to sing (or scream), descended.

Jacob Beltane stood partly to one side and observed the scene (coolly, rehearsing his part, as outlined by Orphrey Whither, in the next day's *Pilgrim Soul*). It was as if someone, releasing a spinning top, had directed it into the very center of the cleared expanse. Following a signal from John-John Farrell, another table and three chairs were lifted over the heads of the patrons in the rear, to give Mawrdew Czgowchwz the (necessary, it was whispered) time off her feet: an interval for questions from the floor, the while final preparations were being made in the snug for the main event, the diva's reception by the publican.

"Do you prefer being called Miss Cohalen or Madame Czgowchwz?"

"The latter, if the former doesn't object. It's the correct professional billing, only 'Miss' is preferable to 'Madame,' I feel, in places where varieties of English are freely spoken."

"Is this doubling a case of what's called the Identity Crisis?"

"I've been told there's a prayer in Old Irish that translates as *and God protect me from my double*. Whoever we each are, we'd both been around the block often enough—in opposite directions—and had never met. If that's what you mean. Is it, or not?"

"You're now evolving singly?"

"Quite frankly, one's not exactly single—or Rossetti's *Ancilla Domini* either."

"You are well in your health so."

"Be sure of it—but you'd want to be in the whole of your health before taking the star part in a motion picture, never mind one set in Dublin itself at the time of the Rising."

"What are your impressions of your native town?"

"Well, as to that, I was actually born near Clifton, in Galway. Yet there is an *atmosphere* in Dublin which leads me to expect each moment to be my next."

"Do you have a favorite air?"

"Well, I don't know if you'd call it an air, but I'm very fond of 'Dicey Riley.' "

"*Really?*"

"And of course 'Love's Old Sweet Song.' "

"How do you feel about playing your mother—a legend, an immortal, whom you never knew—in a fillim?"

"Insufficient."

"And what do you hope to gain by this arduous endeavor?"

"In the first place? The Academy Award."

Either as if that idea were being seconded by Providence, or as if the enquiry below had gone on long enough: busily characterizing the principals unnecessarily further, at the expense of plot headway, three thuds, resembling muffled stage thunder in a Mummers' pageant (or, more, to the mind of Mawrdew Czgowchwz, the three reports of clapper on mallet with which the French theater announces the commencement of its spectacles) resounded from above, and, as the ceiling lighting fixture (all brass) quivered in the sudden hush, the commotion in the barroom stopped short.

After a moment of silence, a light appeared in the doorway, sufficiently illuminating from the top the narrow back stairs, and, alone and unsupported by walking sticks, the proprietor, rubicund Johnny Farrell, dressed in dun tweeds in the Edwardian fashion, collared in cellulose, waistcoated, sporting a dark green silk tie, and fingering the old gold watch he checked in a swift glance against the back wall clock, descended in his own person to greet and be received by his illustrious and (he admitted it straight out to his guardian angel and the ghosts that fell in line behind) alluring guest—a signal honor, according to the report of common memory accorded no prior visitor other than the present Uachtaráin na hÉireann for his pains and courtesy in respect of Irishry and the Republic. He approached Mawrdew Czgowchwz.

" 'Tis yizzer, the progeny?"

"Are we sub judice?"

"Sub judice? Sure we're no such thing as sub judice."

"Then that I am—the progeny in question. And who's this you are yourself?"

"Who's *this?* Are yiz *delirious mental?* The divvil a *thulamawn*, woman, the bold strap of yiz! Fer yer own information and enlightenment—fer yizz've a poor grasp of the proceedings and could use a good bit of each—'tis *Johnny Farrell*, as such and in his own right on his own premises, *vee-day-lee-chet*—and he after comin' directly down those stairs there from above in the plain view and cognizance of the public and not up from under through the *cabuis* either, like the divil in the pantomime over t'the Gaiety Theatre at Christmas. And no matter fer your bold cheek yizz are welcome in this place, so y'are and yer companion with yiz."

"And a good man, too, is what they said you were, for there's nothing like the interviews to put the drouth on a woman—and whatever you're having yourself. They told me this would be the right place—so it is, and it's charming to know so."

"Jesus, *Mary*, and holy Saint Joseph the bold-particle mother incarnate! D'y'sing a-tall, additional?"

"I have done so."

"*Have* ye! Sinners, they say, have always the best voices. 'T was yerself, they tell me, in the opera next door—was it—of a Tuesdeh or a leftover Mondeh—when?"

"The years—the years—the one much the same as—until just this: and now—"

"*Were* ye daft, so?"

"Not entirely within the compass of the mentis so they say."

"Yizzer oulwan was *hatcha*, daft. There's ones were hatcha from the Great War, from the trenches and the boom-boom and them fallin' out of their standin' altogether, so, and some was hatcha from the Troubles, brother against brother, diehards and Free Staters, but your oulwen, now, she was hatcha entirely in her own right.

"Still, a fine figure of a woman she was, as evidently fer all t'see y'are yerself, t' get the *plamas* out of the way, and she boxed clever fer all that she was hatcha, and prospered, so she did. And you're like her, so, I can tell that. A fine figure of a woman t' whip them all up inta a wild frenzy, same as she did, put them on the point of heroic deeds—and they'd be comin' in here after the show, the same as they did then, ta *irrigate* matters and make their lives general once more."

"I shall consider what you have just said in my preparation."

"And don't be long about it either, fer we have here no lasting city. So yiz can sing still after all, the way yiz did the last time, so."

"I can sing if there's a reason, and a tune."

"I remember hearin' yiz sing when yiz first blew in here—with no tale of Flamin' Maev er annybody. Brahms it was, with a piano and fiddle behind yiz."

"Brahms's two songs for alto, piano and viola—indeed."

"Yizz'r very precise, are yiz not. Yizzer oulwan was a hard chaw like yer-self—on the perpetual up and down the length and breadth of the country, terrible to the world with the fierce harangues against the Sassanach, able to drive the heart crossways in the people. And she wouldn't stand for to be chuffed up by any oul shleeveen. 'Go way with yer *plamas* and yer *grah-mo-crees*,' she tell them all."

"Not all, I think."

"Yiz have a point there sure enough. She was ferocious until she met the Bohemian lad."

"Love's old sweet song."

"Well long ago there was a woman, as often there was, and always will ever be, but never was there another one like yizzer oulwan. Sure they'd stand on snow, the people t' hear her. Now there was many a sturdy man of mind and heart in them days, along with a whole class o' slopers that won out in the end, on account of all the good men went down. And the slopers were dead set against a woman puttin' in with them.

"And none moreso than the so-called Long Fella, that's been sniffin' at every arse that'll be sniffed at t'get the *taoiseach* back and likely he will, too, and I'd be aware of him, so I would, fer he's the most *hatcha* of all the *hatchas* that ever was. Sure there's dire possibilities afoot whenever that fella's around the place, hear me tell yiz. Y'wouldn't be safe to have hand, act or part, or to meet him on the road even. Only the Yanks ever outsmarted him, with the mountains of extorted pelf out of the thousands of poor boxes collected, and they wouldn't give the likes him a shilling of it, so they would not. They read him aright, d'y'see—a fella called Cohalen, too, a bigwig on the bench in New York. Saw him fer what he was, saw *to* it he went away with an empty purse and no promise or guarantee of anything but a few novenas here and there, and that was it.

"And he bore no love in his black heart fer herself I can promise y' that, but she was well able fer him, no fear—sure wouldn't she be all over the bastard while he was countin' one. He'd be on after her in all his devious and unaccountable ways and there she was gone.

"Did y' know she spat, so? She was a great one fer spittin'. 'T was her spittle would relieve you of your warts. She'd toot her slip-jigs on the tin whistle and spit, and the upshot cured you without recurrence.

"Now, she was no *oil paintin'* or *bathin' beauty* either, if y'take my meanin', and after a come-all-ye with her in it given out t' the world and its dog, she'd come in with the sweat pourin' off her and y'd want t' tell her to give the oul' oxters a good swipe at least, but she'd rip inta ya on the slightest provocation in that state—and there was many feared she had the heavy eye on her. Whatever of that, she'd tear a strip out of y'sure there'd be holy open murder in it 'til she steadied herself with a dram and before y'could say how are ye yerself things'd be quieted down and back t' normal almost."

"You knew her then?"

"*Knew* her! *Jaysus, Joseph, and all the weepin Marys*! And wasn't she another of 'em, too. Sure wasn't she only found by the tinkers at the roadside around Knock, in the County Mayo, on Hallow's Eve, wailin' away, and called Mary so to nullify the changeling's curse? And she did herself outfox the fairies all right."

("For," as she'd been told by Orphrey Whither, "she passed from the tinkers soon enough by the greatest stroke of fortune into the arms of the lady of the big house. Sure she came in through the front door that way, and so despite she spat—and long before the spittle cure was found in her to attest the origins she came from—did she learn to play the piano and the harp, and sing and grow up as well into a great immortal beauty and give herself the name of the High Queen of Ireland.")

"But I'll say not a word more," Johnny Farrell then avowed, "on that I've sworn my oath, only that she was Mary first, then May, and in the end, when thoughts in the posterity department evidently reared up, Maev, a class of name among neither Christians nor gyppos then current—although more frequently encountered along the banks of the Dodder than the banks of the Tolka, if ye take my meaning on the point."

"I think I do."

"Well, she was a good bit of rump now and never a scrag end, and didn't she fire the hearts of the men who rose for Ireland—something, now I look at ye in me own light, and rememberin' certain turns ye took the while previous in the music hall next door, when ye assumed the part of the cigarette-smokin' gyppo woman in Seville where the oranges originate, I might commence t' believe ye could in certain fortunate and preordained circumstances, chancin' yer arm so—*simulate* yourself!"

"Thanks," Mawrdew Czgowchwz replied, with equanimity. "I realize you do, from your own expression, sound familiar. The Countess Madge O'Meaghre Gautier assured me, before I left New York, that we've met."

"Y'd be speaking now of yet another—of Mary O'Meagher that was with the theatricals in North Abbey Street. I knew her."

"Mary Magdalen O'Meagher I believe was her full maiden name."

"Mary *Magdalen*? Aw, *whisht*!! Mary *Magdalen*, my lumbago—wouldn't it give ye identical pain! Sure there was never a woman in Ireland—in church nor chapel—christened Mary *Magdalen*!'

"Be that as it may—and may come out—what song shall I sing to you?"

"Y' were speakin' just now of 'Love's Old Sweet Song.' Can y' sing that?"

"I can. If somebody would please sit down to that piano? I'll sing that song for your, for I've suddenly a great yearning to get my supper into me."

*

It was late the next afternoon and Jacob was again alone in the bedroom, writing in his diary. The telephone rang again outside, discontinuing whatever had been going on.

An interval of a certain length ensued. A buzzer sounded; a door opened. Voices in the vestibule. Another door opened, then closed; the voices resumed, rising, separately, in volume.

Send not to know—

Mawrdew Czgowchwz entered the bedroom in haste.

"What's been going on out there?" Jacob asked, looking up from the diary. "Besides, that is, the politics of attraction. You have the wild look of a messenger whose one long speech he's terrified of bungling. Speak out."

"Are you sitting down—in the metaphorical sense?"

"I'm something like supine—will that do you?"

Dropping backward on the bed across his outstretched legs, she lay staring up at the ceiling (as if an allegorical figure, like Hibernia, were carved there, or as if the chandelier were a camera).

"Why do you keep on looking at the ceiling?"

"We always did that in the convent dormitory, whenever there was a moon: looked up at the white ceiling in the moonlight. It was a kind of tabula rasa; it helped your flow, and anyway, you weren't allowed to look across, you see, from bed to bed."

"Haven't you noticed there's only the one bed?"

"I have—and so apparently has the rest of the nation. That among other things is what the delegation is doing outside, waiting for me get out of this wrapper, throw on that pale green wool Georgette suit with the Empire line jacket, and tuck up my chevelure under some sort of headgear, in order to go along with the Taoiseach, Mr. Costello and the Leader of the Opposition—I give you, Mr. de Valera himself—and a posse of what Orphrey refers to as *doilies*—to meet the Uachtaráin, Mr. O'Kelly, up in the Phoenix Park."

“And what business of ours is it that Mr. O’Kelly—whoever he is when he’s at home up in the Phoenix Park—is an octoroon? Is he some local tinker, some conjur man?”

“*Oochta-royn*—that’s the President of the Republic. The Áras an Uachtaráin is in the Phoenix Park—not far from your obelisk, incidentally. It’s the former Viceregal Lodge, and resembles the White House in Washington. Mr. O’Kelly is, by the way a rather diminutive personage. There’s a story the Countess relates of his going to a hurling match up in Croke Park and as he crossed the field one of the Dubs is heard to complain, ‘Jee-siz, wouldn’t y’ think they’d cut the grass and give us a look at him!’ ”

“Hmm. I still don’t see in all this what business of all theirs is it that we share one bed? Still, you might want to mention the way this mattress *sags* down the middle. Or is the point that we are to move *into* the Octoroon’s White House? Into separate rooms—eight sixty-four and eight sixty-five? Is that the drill?”

“It is not. ‘The Long Fella just wants a word with ye, missus, citizen t’ citizen.’ Really—how am I supposed to know what Maev told the nuns about him? What hat should I go in? I can’t be bold and bareheaded, and anyway in this damp I’d catch my death.”

“What did you make of Johnny Farrell’s version of the changeling Maev?”

“I don’t know. Odd isn’t is that we’ve both issued forth from Gypsies? Anyway, now I know a little better why I was doing what I was in Ruthenia. I don’t know that it’s going to help me play Maev, however. Moreover, I know he’s holding something back—in fact, he said so, didn’t he. Whether *it* would have helped me play—I don’t really think I *can* play Maev. I could play Theda Bara in *A Fool There Was*. . . . I can play Amneris—still—”

“Your father’s successor wrote ‘Of that which we cannot speak, we must perforce remain silent.’ Unlike Garbo, unlike Geraldine Farrar, you’ve never been required to play silent. I should love to see your Theda Bara in *A Fool There Was*. I am that fool. I’ve seen your Amneris. It was your Covent Garden debut. As you were telling me how you did it here, I was hearing it then, and trying to imagine it in New York. That's because you gave that interview and said, 'Unless you heard my Amneris at the Metropolitan in New York, you didn't really hear my Amneris.' Did you mean that?"

"Well, yes I did. But let's to business now—which hat?"

"Hmm. In spite of the mutations mutating, and the fact that you hate the character and will never sing the part, it sounds to me very like yet another version of Floria Tosca going to—in which case, since *Vissi d'Arte* is out, what will you sing? Why don't you wear the forbidding cloche you let Consuelo Gilligan talk you into that rainy afternoon at Henri Bendel's hat rack. You know what Emerson said: '*The sense of being perfectly dressed gives a feeling of tranquility religion is powerless to bestow.*' "

"Sounds more like Ronald Firbank. Actually, Violetta Valery says—but she changes her mind in the last act. The cloche *is* the perfect choice, only it wasn't Bendel's, it was the *salon moderne* at Saks. It's a Tatianan original; she started *out* at Bendel's—Oh, but listen, would you by any chance be up to escorting Miranda down to her audition with Orphrey? I'm with the delegation down the back stair. I shall sing 'Love's Old Sweet Song'—the Octoroon will not have heard my rendition—and would I encore with 'Danny Boy.' Why not?"

"Skulking *out* through the *garage*! I'm commencing to believe there is espionage in the very marrow of your gorgeous bones."

"Be that as it may, you *are* a genius: this is the *only* hat!"

*

At Farrell's a catechetical exchange had been under way for some time, since report had been delivered there of the progress of a certain official vehicle bearing a bipartisan legislative assortment of some distinction and a helmeted woman of somewhat more up Marlborough Street past the Pro-Cathedral, down Mary Street to Capel Street, left to the quays, down Ormond Quay past the Ormond Hotel and the Four Courts themselves, past the barracks, on toward the Strawberry Beds and the Phoenix Park.

"What Saint Patrick would have to say to De Valera! Chroist! He'd've said, like Peader O'Donnell, that a million people have left Ireland, and Dev, slaverin' over the lickin' of his shoes would've pleaded, but are they not the *right* million?"

"*Not* Chroist—only a Fenian would call that old hoor Chroist. He'd say, 'Would'j'ever *disclose*, Eamon, what *exactly occurred* prior to the liberatin' of the dogs' and cats' home?' "

"Go on a way out of that—yizzer all on the pig's back and yiz haven't a sniff or a smell of the political astitutes of the man that built this country out of nuthin' inta what it is t'day, the man that plowed the fields and scattered liberty, and that'll be goin' up t' the Phoenix Park to get back the taoiseach in the spring, and that's a definite, so yizz'd be doin' a smart thing now t' be mindin' yerselves."

"Wise counsel, Oi warrant, for wasn't he, faith, the Long Fella, the plow and the stars and all of it else besides."

"What is the *pleow*, what is the *staaars*?"

"Aw, sure they's all hoors fer that the wide boys are—and long have been—and long more will be, them and all their hire-*archies*, until the last Irish heart is broken or the last British garrison is ripped from Oireland's soil and cast into the Oirish Sea."

"As to that *neow*—say what y'loike about the *commodius vivendi*, but in these premises y'll keep yer tongue off free Oireland and her hallowed martyrs of Sixteen, *mar dhea!*"

"*Moor-i-are*. Would that be Latin, now, or Oirish y'r talkin?' "

"As the milk woman asked Stephen Dedalus?"

"Who?"

"A character in a *buuk* called *Ulysses*."

"Oi haired of it."

"Are y'there Moore-i-are-eye-ty?"

"And that wasn't *moor-i-are*, it was *muy-er*."

"Well, that to me, now sounds Spanish, so it does."

"Does it."

"It does—are yiz not aware of the Spanish influence?"

"We're aware of the Spanish *influenza*, so, that came in follyin' the Great War."

"Och, would ye shut yer cake hole, ye bollocks ye, and not be talkin' of the martyrs of nointeen sixten! Sure and wasn't Oi, moyself up bright and *airly* ta foight the British on that fatal Easter Sondeh?"

"*Broight* and *airly*, and so it was on the Sundeh, and you in yer good stiches, and what of it, when the foightin' itself only *started* on the *Mondeh*?"

"*Who're ya tellin?*"

"Or maybe that should better be who's the *hoor* y're tellin—for faith, wasn't he up on the Sondeh, *and stayin'* up all the night long inta the very Mondeh itself when the balloon went up fer sairtin!"

"That Oi did *so*."

"Roight. A great verterbrate relic of the ould daycency out of the Eucharistic Congress is yourself, and in respect of th' events of Sixteen, a martyr t' the subject. Sure doesn't the whole of the Coombe know it well, and be damned to hell whosoever says otherwise—that yiz is a roight *shpalpeen* fer instance—and next we'll be hearin' it's a *pioneer* y'are as well, stood fer the pledge and foresworn in perpetuity the gargle, and on the foot of that that yiz did yerself assist at the borth of yerwoman that's after arrivin' even as we speak, in the day that's in it, at the Áras an Uachtaráin in the Phoenix Park fer tay and brack, talkin of the hire-*arky*!"

"Oi am not a pioneer . . . as *such*. Oi *am* Feena-Fawl, as is every daycint man in the place. And 'twas me *sister* that did that y'speak of, now—called out inta the cowld night from this same lounge bar here, fer they had the woman scourged and wouldna take her in at the Mater nor at the Rotunda either. *Because* of the hire-*arky* and thems the whole true facts of the case."

"Jeesiz, isn't a good thing, now, that Mamie Cadden wasn't on that night."

"Go on a way out of that, now!"

"I'll not so—for they're out to get the poor woman, all the bloody hypocrites, to cruci-*fy* her upside down like Saint Peter himself on the Hill of Howth."

"Saint Peter and Saint Vincent de Barfly, too—and yer woman in that play at the Gate, *The Cocktail Paarty*, d'yiz not remember that, in the last act? Cruci-*fied* offstage she was, upside down on an anthill, how-are-ye—and they'd do the same t' Mamie Cadden so they would if they could."

"Jaysiz, if that isn't one on me now—I never real-*ized* Saint Peter was crufi-*fied* on the Hill of Howth!"

"Feena-Fawl, Feena-Fawl—yiz are all of yiz Feena-fallin' down *drunk*, that's what. There's nothin in the wurld like youse ones fer sourcin' the drunk—sure yizz'd suck it off a sore leg, so yiz would."

"*Brack*. Would they not give toasted sliced pan, buttered?"

"They'd not; they'd lay on barm brack. Sure isn't brack the stuff of Holy Ireland, beyond the Pale?"

"Beyond the pale what?"

"Beyond the pale moon was shinin' across the green *meddah. Jeesiz!*"

"Sure there's no green meddah in Dublin, anyway."

"That is a stupid ole calumny and ye haven't a breeze—what d'ye think is the Phoenix Park, so, a *bog*?"

"The next question is, who gets the sixpence stuck in their brack, who the bit o' cloth, who the ring and who the matchstick—for sure this is a Samhain party, and them all dressed up as apparitions—"

"Or *sows*!"

"—for apparitions is all they are, any of 'em, so far as the plain people of Ireland is concerned!"

"Sure there was nature in the days when people had nuthin'."

"And a bit of an stager she well may be—a bit of a bounced Czech—though she has the look surely of a mare thrown from a Thoroughbred an'ed make any man's privates that was in it go *sprong*. And, speakin' of *commodius vicus*, a bit of an oul' *bike*, and barred, too, Oim towld, from the Pro-Cateee-thadril on Marlborough Street, the archbishop bein' a stickler fer the sacramental matrimonial."

"Oi herd she was permitted, in principle, t'attend the mass of the Magdie-*lanes*."

"Singin' a new *choon*—a new *ohria*—by herself. *Casti-gated Diva!*"

"Well to *me* now, the name itself's *peculiar*."

"*Mardah* Gorgeous. It is that—put ye in mind, *mar dhea*, of Dublin's own the ancient Gorgeous Rex."

"Except in this case, surely, it ought to be gorgeous *Regina*?"

"Well, he was a bold man who first ate an oyster, and she a bolder woman still."

"Go on away out of *that* with yer filthy oul talk!"

"Even so, now, would yiz ask yerselfs if except in the shining case of Ireland's own Maggie Sheridan of Castlebar, in the County Mayo, isn't divas and free *wheelin'* and behavior relatin' to matters of conciupi-science and cartwheels characterized as *flaithiulach*, virtually synonymous? Oi mentioned this very thing t' Myles himself t'other day, along with the *notion* that they might write an *opera*, d'y'see for *herself* along them lines."

"Along them *wash* lines."

"Y'know the *way*! An opera, now, on the Magdee-*lanes* that work in the diocesan *laundry*. She qualifies, surely on her own testi-*mony*, wasn't I just hearin' it read out loud. The armies of Europe, *mar dhea*! It couldn't've sounded grander in the Irish itself."

"Ye don't say."

"I do at that."

"And what answer did he give you?"

"Wait till I tell ya. '*Well*,' sez he, 'in the furst place there so happens to already *be* an opera that happens in a laundry and it's called *Ear-eece*, by that Mass-Cagney fella, who put inta his *Calvery-a Rooster-i-ca-na* that hymn rendered so gorgeous of a Sundeh by the Palestrina Boys' Choir at the High Mass at the Pro-*Cateeth-adril on* Marlborough Street—and in the second place them Magd-*lanes* is in moy opinion a collective *misnomer*, as while there is surely the well-attested story that Mary Magd-lane did wash the feet of the yer man with her own sorry tears and dried them with own her long red hair—and there y've got somethin' t' go on, now, in respect of herself the diva of the moment—there is absolutely *no record* of her ever washin' out the fella's smalls or any of the apostles either."

"Couldn't have sounded grander in the *Oirsh*? Wirrah, it isn't the *Oirish* that's in the back of that brain at all, but the *Gammon* or the Shelta or the *Cant*, or whatever this it is the Gyppos call their lingo, for wasn't the mother cast out of a Gyppo camp on the road inta Castlebar and taken into Moore Hall for a skivvy."

"Who're ya tellin? But there's a moral t' the story, for didn't they burn down Moore Hall, and didn't she retorn t' the West in a koind o' triumph with not one but two fellas—people said t' the Gore-Booths at Lissadell it was, and others bark about how it was t' the Gogartys in Renvyle, t' the place built fer them stuck out there on the point by some fella *Loo-teens*, but the fact *is* it wasn't the *O'Morachains* at Poulaphouca—and there's irony in that. Yes, with *two* fellas, one under each oxter—the *Ger*-man fella.

"Annaway the *Ger*-man and his little butty the Hungarian fella, and the wheeze is that the Gerr-man is aidin' and abettin' the cause in exactly the manner that got Sir Roger Casement his dire end, and *prolix* as well to the same *proclivities*, as many *Ger*-mans, and Roger Casement besides, were in them days, and many British, *mar dhea*, right down t'now. Only he wasn't Gerr-man at all, the one with the guile inim but an *Osterichan*, but it wasn't the bird that sticks his head in the sand anyway, an' y' said it the same way—said he come from the Osterichan and Hungarian Empire, not to be confused with the British Empire of which Ireland was a part and Dublin by roights the second city, so.

"Only the butty that's with the Gerr-man isn't Hungarian, but Bohemian, 'r as they say in mod'ren toimes, *Czech*—like y' was saying before, and so yer man wants t' know, well is he a *blank* check 'er a check fer a *fixed amount*? And yer Osterichan fella foinds this terrible rich—and terrible rich is what he is, and as it turns out trailin' after the butty and yerwoman the Flame Eater in the Circus that was Sixteen, all right.

"And then y'know the Osterichan, who was turned British by then come back t' Gahlway, t' the Killeries there by Lennane and talked t' the *bords* and charmed them so they ate out of the fella's hand, and then when the fella went away fer t' die in England, the *bords pined* and never flew again and the cats of Leenane ate them all up."

"Pine boards is called *deal*—did ye know that, Pasty?"

"Anyway good luck to Herself, for there's many a man'ed do jail time for a ride around the North Circular Road on that particular bicycle built fer two."

"Y've a *low drop*—d'ye know that?"

"Sure and to her amphibious Tommy, too, fer we're *civiloized* people here and wish no harm to the Sassenach that comes softly. Enjoy long amity, and rest in one peace when the hurry of the world is *threw*, and the fever of life, and what they call down in Limerick the ex-*coite*-ment is broke and the life of the corpus itself done with!"

"Nonetheless, a finer man never shat behind two heels, and that's the truth in a nutshell."

"Och, stoppit, now—yer makin' me all *scarleh*!"

"*Slainte!*"

"*Slainte!*"

"*Brack*, how-are-ye. Sure, with all them things in it, wouldn't it give y' the gawks, like and y'd crack a tooth and choke t'death on it' "

"Not if y'd gone along and had yer throat blessed on Saint Blazes Day."

"Whatever of that devotional lark, thanks be t' God for Boland's bread, ev'ry mornin."

"Oi'll decisively second that."

"They say Staleen ate black bread made of y' wouldn't know what at all."

"Jeesiz, wouldn't ye want a long spoon and yer wits about you, now, t' be goin' inta supper with that the likes of that fella, as yer woman supposedly did."

"Y' would—and as for yer higher-*armies*, there's the One True Holy Roman Catholic and Apostolic Church of the Nicerian Creed, and there was the Free State and now there's the Republic of Ireland and the Gaelic Athletic Association itself, but at the end of the day it's your man J.J. & S., so it is, that's got the ultimate *power* over *Paddy*."

"Oi don't think that's at *awl* true down in Limerick."

"The only thing that's at *awl* true down in Limerick, Patsy, is that if you keep on *goin'* you'll get to Killarney!"

"*Slainte!*"

"That hits the spot, now, does it not?"

"Serves the purpose, if y' like."

"Oh? Meanin' what, exactly?"

"Nuthin' only what is the spot."

"*Jeesiz!*"

"What is the *mune*? What is the stars? What is the spot?"

"Sure, Spot is the dog—see Spot run."

"But ye wouldn't hit a dog—sure only a terrible oul sinner would hit a dog."

"*Jeesiz!*"

"I'll tell yiz awl one thing fer free, speakin' of the J.J. and S. , and that's this. Without the word of a lie, and in plain sight of the customary, yer woman downed three drams of the crayture, follied by a pint of what they give at the Mater t' norsin' mothers, and when she stood herself up t' be goin' she made straight fer the door, sober as the Queen of England, and that is certifiable."

"Sure y' can drink away a fortune, but y'cant drink away a trade."

"A *trade!*"

"Sure isn't she a tradeswoman—a hawker—the same as oul' Molly Malone, minus if y' like the *cockles* and the *muscles*—"

"The *meowth* on ye!"

"—and a regular ate-the-bolts at that, what with the singin' and the filmin' of the life and times of her oulwen and everythin' else that's in it."

"Anyway she's got muscles all right fer all that—it's the muscles of the diaphragm that controls the air that passes through the vocal chords to—"

"Go on a way out of that, now—isn't all discussion of doia-*phragms* and berth control strictly *taboo* in Holy Ireland."

"*Jeesiz!*"

"Well neow, moy cuzzin' the priesht that's in the Pope's retina was back from Rome fer his holidays, musta been the summer afore this last one that's just gone, and sez he t'me that he went t' hear yer woman at the Baths of Carrycalla in that one about the Druids and the Romans and that she goes inta the fire at the end and the Roman fella goes in right after her—"

"*Norma*."

"That's the one now—and he said in the scene with the wee chislers where she intends to morder them and she can't that there wasn't a dry eye in the whole of the arena that's twice the size of Croke Park, he never heard the like—sure it would bring wather out of yer teeth."

"Well, isn't that pushin' the boat out now—*and* puttin' a tin hat on it additional."

"Making yer boat, so, some class of *submarine*."

"*Slainte!*"

"*Slainte!*"

"Yiz have a disthurbin' way in yer gabble of pilin' pelicans on Oscar, d'yiz know that?"

". . . so these pocketbooks y'see is thick at it, wrists flappin' in confabulation. So says the wan t' t'other, 'Moy *deer*, Shakespeare wuz *not* Oirish, and Queen Gertrude is not Mother Mo-chree.' 'Who're ya tellin'?' says t'other t' yer man, 'Don't Oi know that Mother Mo-chree was the *nun* founded the *Sisters o' Mare-cie* in Lower Baggot Street!' *Jaysus*, I thought I'd *doy* laffin', so I did."

*

Orphrey Whither stalked through the Gresham's lobby into the lounge, where he encountered the Manahans having afternoon tea.

"*Where* did they take her—how many of them *were* there?"

"What?" replied Manahan. "*Who?*"

"In the window of the car, in that hat, she looked like Mata Hari—and not like Garbo *as* Mata Hari either—like herself, Mata Hari! They wouldn't *dare* deport her—I *defy* them to!"

"We've been somewhat cryptically advised," said Maire Manahan, "to meet her here, with you, in order to discuss something to do with Miranda—who is, so far as we know, being given a vocal lesson this afternoon. We have no reason to think otherwise, unless O'Connell Street has lately become the Bandon Road."

The producer-director of *Pilgrim Soul* dropped into an ample armchair, letting fall floorward a folded, torn copy of *The Irish Times*. His head fell into his hand, and bobbed there.

"Is she trying to *wreck* me altogether?"

A waitress, arrived to clear the remains of the tea, stood over Orphrey Whither, looking down at the cast-off newspaper.

"You done with that, an' yew tron it on th' *floor*?"

"So I am *not*. Kindly leave it and get on, so, about your business, which is bringing here to me, before you betake yourself over to Marlborough Street for Solemn Benediction, a hot dish of your drisheen, and a cool pint of porter, straight off the wood. On second thought, come here to me a minute."

"Yes?"

"Do you smoke—on your own time?"

"I do that, yes."

"What brand?"

"Woodbines."

"Indeed." He produced a flat packet of cigarettes. "Here, try these next time, why don't you."

The waitress looked skeptical. "Are these American ones?"

"No, they are *not*, they are Balkan Sobranies. Try them—share them with the Boots, so."

"The *Boots*!"

"Be adventurous, why not? Good practice for the day democracy finally comes to Ireland. You're young, and may live to see it."

He turned back to the Manahans, somewhat soothed.

"On foot of these effusions," he continued, pointing down at the newspaper opened to the page under review, "The diocese now imagines *Pilgrim Soul* a combination of *The Song of Bernadette, Shadow and Substance The Righteous Are Bold* and *Joan of Arc*, with Ingrid Bergman—apparently conveniently ignoring the fact that *she'd* been denounced both on the floor of the United States House of Representatives *and* from the very venue alluded to by myself here not a minute ago, they have called for her in an official car, and taken her—"

"Surely not," said Manahan, "to Solemn Benediction."

"They warned me when I signed her," Orphrey Whither moaned, as the waitress returned with his food and drink on a tray, "she would have her way. It's all that time she spent in Hungary; she's mastered their approach. Were she to go into a revolving door behind you, she'd come out in front. You might just as well step aside gallantly hoping merely that you get through to the other side, and don't wind up back where you started. "Nigidius Figulus maintained there could be no peace without a tyrant. I've been too lenient with her. God send my leniency may not destroy my picture. She simply doesn't know what she's up against. The Taoiseach Costello is all right, and O'Kelly up in the Park is an amiable cipher, but that bastard son of a Cuban weasel, that tin-whistle Savonarola, that murderer and psychotic, is more powerful in Opposition that all of them put together. Thinks he's *Charles de Gaulle*—and him the Liberator of the feckin' Dogs and Cats Home—he's got that other bastard McQuaid right in his pocket and if he gets back in in the next elections, he'll shut us down as quick and as sure as he personally ordered Mick Collins's death of the Bandon Road, so he will! He'll poison the minds of the public against her until they'll be calling her the most ferocious immoral woman in Ireland, not excepting poor oul' Mamie Cadden!"

29 October 1956
Magwyck (The Snug)

My dearest Mawrdew Czgowchwz,

In deepest gratitude for (and in consternation and chagrin at the tardy response to) yours of the 29th ultimo.

As Malevich has written, the airplane was not contrived in order to carry business letters from Berlin to Moscow (or the diplomatic pouch either from New York to Dublin) but rather in obedience to the irresistible drive of this yearning for speed to take on external form. In this line, *Fama Volat*: the Meneghini has sung. More later: it was more than just a night out.

I am off tomorrow to windy, rainy, rocky, Manitoy (the storms of life pass harmless over the Valley of Seclusion) to work in sea-girt sequestration on the outdoor-summer-night-*son-et-lumiere*-with-thunderous-recitation spectacle, *The Archons*. (Attending to *seditiosi voci* who fain would set themselves to summer's work in winter, especially when the work in question is, well, seditious, featuring, as did Massine's ballet of Beethoven's Seventh Symphony, the Creation of the World, the Destruction of the World and the Descent from the Cross in between.)

"For a while." wrote Hart Crane, "I want to keep immune from beckoning and all that draws you into doorways, subways, sympathies, rapports and the City's complicated devastation." And Albertus Magnus, no less, directs "those wishing to reminisce, should withdraw from the public light into obscure privacy: in the public light the images of sensible things are scattered and their movement is confused; in obscurity however they are unified."

Added to which, Aquinas says Prudence has eight parts: *memoria, ratio, intellectus, docilitas, solertia, providentia, circumspectio*, and *cautio*. All of which now boils down to two words: *skip town*. Skip town, stay off the telephone and catch up on De Koven on Saturday nights over the short wave. Resignation is sublime: adopt it. And so, forth.

I don't plan to be back in New York making the rounds rigged out in me fancy Dan until the New Year. ("*Where* does he go?" one line-backer asked another, I was told. "Oh, you know my dear, that island, somewhere off Massachusetts." "Hm. He ought to be going to one off New Hampshire, called *Smuttynose*.") Except of course to check one or more further Meneghini apparitions—the Tosca, the Lucia—and perhaps to spend an afternoon with her and Leo Lerman. (She's not much for the *passagiata*: the publicity has been wormy—the *Time* cover, Dolores, the coy attentions commencing to be paid, we are told in appalled whispers, by "The Old Oaken Bucket in the Well of Loneliness"—and *really*, what a vicious parody of the divine Marie Dressler that old slag has turned into: Cole Porter is one ailing, disillusioned cookie to think her fun; Johnny Donovan, drunk at Madame Spivvy's, doing imitations of the Hy Gardner interview—like that.)

The Archons. That's the epic-allegory one I warned you about—the two-hour gnostic version of the War Between the East Side and the West Side that we're thinking of staging in the park and videotaping (television in the middle fifties having become, thanks to the likes of you, something more than auditions).

You remember, it came to me that time we visited Teotihuacán with Victoria after your Mexico City Amneris and Delilah. (I can still quote the review: "*Una mujer de peso* [with flaming red hair lay extended, half disrobed, in a dark fur cloak, upon a red ottoman, bent smiling over Samson, bound by the Philistines . . .]

It's a little like a shorter version of *The Mahabarata* cut into Hardy's *The Dynasts*, with a nod to Monsignor Hugh Benson's 1907 fable *Lord of the World*, a peppering of Plautus's *Arsinaria* (much with restless plebs) admixed with *Coriolanus*—the Voices, as in the Cigarettes: lines to cleave the general air with horrid speech, boasting as it does, in addition to principals, a large cast of character men and women—Sixth Avenue will be put to work—bawds, grooms, bravos, duennas, domestics, porters, *alquazils*, *alcaldes*, night watchmen, municipal sanitation workers, and all the other forces of apparent good and obscure evil to be found in a great metropolis.

We in the ages lying
In the buried past of the earth
Built Nineveh with our sighing
And Babel itself in our mirth

Basically, the good archons occupy the East Side—headquarters the Sherry Netherland, and the bad the West—headquarters the Dakota, and the theater of war is the Park. Except that the bad are in secret possession of the cathedral and Fanny Spellbound. I see him sitting under a hair dryer in the shape of the papal tiara. (And ye, ye unknown latencies shall thrill to every innuendo, and after all how desperately *lèse majesté* is it? Monsignor Benson has the Satanic airships destroy Rome and the pope with it.) Should I give our *strategia* control in return of Saint John the Divine? Do we want it? They do, of course, have control of the Met, Carnegie, and City Center, but the Dr. Mabuse of Thirty-ninth Street is in secret league with the enemy.

The one that started out as a comic rewrite of the *Bacchae*—you remember, it was called *The Revelers* until Paranoy, peering over my shoulder at the premiere of NOIA at the program in my lap to see written the line "Mother, *stop* it, you're tearing me to *pieces!*"—then veered off in the direction of the *Troades*. (You can blame your-pal-my-auntie for all this—it was *she* who insisted fifteen years ago I come back to my birthplace, go to the Jesuits at Regis and learn Greek.) It's the one that now bears the epigraph from Ezekiel 9: *Cause them that have charge over the city to draw near each with his destroying weapon in his hand.*

You can see I'm hellbent on being the next Maxwell Anderson / Christopher Fry: weighty themes/elevated expression of same—particularly the warning that New York could well disappear, exactly the way Byzantium did, and become the sore point of stories with morals in them. (Serve everybody right, too: New Yorkers, amateurs of Byzantine melodrama and *Befreiungskrieg*.) And which due to the success of the carnival shindig of Equinox last, and to the warm relations obtaining between (the aforementioned) Herself The Madge and Hizzoner, the mayor, late of Yorkville, we can get the City to let us put it on—or photograph it, anyway, at the Bethesda Fountain.

It's the one, in which, if she takes a shine to it (or they, *my* archons the angels of the Rialto, offer her a whole lot of money, whichever ever happens first in the order of consequence), or remind her that Shaw wrote *Major Barbara* for Eleanor Robson and she became Mrs. August Belmont, is designed for Thalia Bridgewood. Perhaps I'd better not all the same try on the last—the Miss Robson that was got took care of by the august August because she turned Shaw *down*. Still, Bridgewood is more likely to think of capturing a Texas millionaire through her art, through spectacle (even filmed) like the one the Redactor has made up for you in his pages, called Tulsa Buck O'Fogatry. Not bad. I'll find out who the little bastard is if it takes overtures to the FBI and its twisted *Gauleiter* through the very famous twisted eminence I'm planning to excoriate in said undertaking. Perhaps Strange will help me: I know these, boys, they end up telling *everything* in confession.

La Bridgewood will be playing a cross between Mnesilochus, protaginist (in drag) of Aristophanes' *Thesmophoriazousai* (and like him/her required to speak in hendacasyllables, but I think she does that already) Ezekial (aforementioned) and the Chrysler Building—all lit *up*, the way it was to have been originally, when they molded all that shining Krupp steel into New York's signal cathedral facade, and to have a high priest consort called "Nimrod." (After all, I tell myself, and I've told Bridgewood, Bernhardt, *La Divine Horizontale* in the Great War, carried over the trenches in a litter to give performances of the last act of *La dame aux camellias* by calcium light at night, played Strasbourg Cathedral in a pageant. "Let's make a name for ourselves!"—she, La Bridgewood, will announce (in imitation of Praxagora) to the assembled throng of chic refugees speaking all the tongues of the earth, the redistribution of all wealth and influence in the metropolis, while being ferried across from the Ramble in a poop.

Am hoping to feature opposite Bridgewood somebody beautiful. (There are no more at home of course like your former Carnegie hall-mate. Percase whimsically did wonder were I to offer the Graybar Building to Cornell, and play John Alden Carpenter's *Skyscrapers* in the dual-piano version, might Marlon Man come back to be in it with her, as Grand Central Terminal, but we know, don't we, he has bid *sayonara* to the stage.

Some body beautiful, because the part is suggested by the career of Alcibiades, of whom Aristophanes (my predecessor) wrote, "A lion should not be raised in the city, but it you decide to do so, you must cater to his ways. (Sounds like *Bringing Up Baby*, no?) What we need here is somebody who can act at the level of—oh, I don't know, Tony Perkins?

What *about* Tony? The career of Alcibiades and the melodrama of his being accused of throwing a raucous party on the eve of the disastrous Sicilian expedition that defiled the Eleusinian mysteries. The one, finally, that contains that vaudeville of elements from Greek tragedy and comedy both: Oedipus, Orestes, Elektra, Antigone; Philoctetes, Ion, Io, Hecuba; Tieresias, Pentheus, Medea, etc. Plus the Bacchae as nuns—remember I told you what I thought nuns were, and how they arose out of the cult of Isis, the Magdalen, and Maria Egiziaca. They are the Christ's bacchantes, and instead of tearing Dionysus to bits, they "receive" bits of their, etc. Just so you know.

You wouldn't tear a beloved to pieces of stale pressed white bread, would you? Anyway in the normal order of things a nun is not, despite the honorific title, a mother—pace Heloise—only I was thinking: you can always take the girl away from the nuns, but can you take the—but you took yourself away, didn't you? Anyway, Tynan, next time he comes to town nosing for a job, will be sure to say I've been influenced by Giradoux and by John Whiting. He's probably right.

Speaking of French influence, one wag said he heard it was going to be a sort of American *Soulier de Satin* spanning over a decade, and that the arguments starts when Bridgewood loses one of her fuck-me pumps at El Morocco. Not bad. I'd sooner be compared aforehand to Claudel, who even if he was a Nazi sympathizer, was also a diplomat (and used the diplomatic pouch as we do for his correspondence) than to Fry, who is really only a schoolmaster trading in on the myth that Shakespeare was one, too, which is ridiculous, because Shakespeare, the start of him anyway was the terrible Edward de Vere, the Seventeenth Earl of Oxford, who may have run a little lyceum for young men, as in *Love's Labours Lost*.

And the rest of him was Mary Sydney, Countess of Pembroke, and other members of her circle including her brother Henry Howard, Earl of Surrey, but you knew that.

And then, at the opposite end of the spectrum to Claudel, somebody at the archdiocese told Kilgallen (who printed it) that what it is is a recreation of the cast-of-4000 epic *son et lumiere* enacting the downfall of capitalism in the Prater Stadium in 1931. Question: Will we, come next year, be finding *The Archons* (Belvedere Lawn; 2 performances) anthologized in the 1956-57 Burns Mantle? Quite possibly, as he never omits a Bridgewood vehicle, some of which have actually run only 1½ performances.

Meanwhile, speaking of lyceums, everywhere one goes in New York this instant October one hears talk of everything under the sun, much of it revolving around you: it is the truth. A book about you would have to include hundreds of examples—an enormous kick line of them, as in the play *Waiting for Mawrdew Czgowchwz*. (Peep this: the Voices of the New York night "scripting" the book of Mawrdew Czgowchwz, *The Archons*, their lives, art politics, music politics, world politics, Destiny itself in the long run. Samples overheard and copied down—everybody taping everybody at home—and between the Inquiring Photographer and roving reporters on radio and television Everyman is a player.)

If it is a defeating thing to insist on producing Art or Nothing (a new dramatic experiment, replete with *progression d'effet, charpente, facade, cadences*—and at military funerals there's always one to count the cadence—not a morality for ranted recitation), then I shall go down howling. Or perhaps, better advised, instead, and better put in the words of my favorite extinct Ulster bard, the blind Seamus MacCuarta, to the people of the Cooley peninsula, for not properly recognizing his literary worth, I shall let them be—as badgers living underground their narrow lives, gorging themselves on the sweetmeats of innutritive illusion (as in any bawdy house on any sidestreet north of Forty-second Street between Sixth and Eighth avenues you care to name).

The *Under Nephin* caper went well. Funny the way they think they *owe* me something for cutting me out of the Sitwell picture. They cut Jimmy Merrill out, too, and I don't think either of us is going to suffer much from it. (If only it *were* a sign of some transaction or other, but I can't imagine it is.)

Now to the news. There was a gag going around that the ghost of Toscanini had appeared to the Meneghini the night before the opening, wailing, "The music is too great—it is beyond human powers. Cancel!" In any event, it was not a great official triumph, but details anon. One interesting theory had it that it is the *only* role she will not have a great success in at the Metropolitan, because the gods (which is to say the Elohim, dear, and not merely the Family Circle) will not have it. They will have it that Rosa's triumph in her greatest role will here and only here go uncontested—her statue up on the I. Miller Building and all. I'm reminded of what you said of MMC, quoting Chorley wasn't it, on Malibran, that nature had given her a rebel to subdue and not a vessel to command. I'm going to the second one, of course—we all are. Shame about her and New York—even about her and the Met. After having been treated as an acronym of Scala itself, and breezing of an aftermath into Biffi to be met as if she were *Iside stessa* by those gaggles of gorgeous and ecstatic *melochecche*—well, schlepping it with Tony Arturi and Frances Moore from the Old Brewery across to the Burger Ranch, or down to Macy's could hardly have been her idea of fan romance, and the Gotham City High Life, though it may attract her attention, can never do for her what the Milanese have done, for she lacks your (and Milanov's) flair for the Ringling Brothers aspect of *thuh opra*, and for corralling private citizens in significant numbers (and Leo could make her welcome *anywhere* that mattered in New York, save Nuncle's elevator at the Chelsea).

As a matter of fact, at Herbert Weinstock's party for her last week (full of those people from the kick line, momentarily diverted from talking about you to talking about her) she was terribly quiet and shy—and when I mentioned you (I had to: she wasn't wearing glasses and didn't know who I was, not that it's in her interest to recall me, especially from three years ago in Mexico City) she gave that odd look composed of complicity and awe: the awe I saw on her face onstage when in the boudoir scene you downwinded her with that open chest "*figlia di Faraoni!*" Open chest, incidentally, is something she should give up using: she is of breath too short for the gesture. So there.

Meanwhile, the *father* pulled us into the kitchen and announced summarily, "In my daughter's breast there beats the spirit of Thermopylae!" (Not to be confused with the Spirit of Marathon—q.v. *Under Nephin*—who was in fact the Pythia herself—of Delphi—who raised a fog that confused the invader under Brennus—a Celt, by the way, but not a *Boi*—most likely Illyrian—so that they fell about, and taking one another for the enemy, slew their own in overwhelming numbers. "I don't know if *he* knows what he means, dear," I heard Leo L. whisper to Robert Giroux, "but I hope to God nobody tries to convince Maria to sing *Xerxes!*" I thought to myself, self-immolation at the hot gates of hell?

Absit omen. Sounds to me like her fantasy runs to mass suicide after her final performance—and to think that this underground epic accuses *you* of *Stuvwxyzchina*—with notes left all over town, reading, "Go stranger this mystery and tell the *Times*, the *Tribune*, the *Journal American*, the *World Telegram and Sun* the *News* the *Mirror* and the *Post* that here, obeying her behests we fell." (Or were burnt to crisps. Really, she should leave Marfa's scene to you, even if you have poached on her Violetta.) Whereas you're content with bringing them screaming to their feet, she must have them paroxysmal, fetal, trussed in straitjackets, begging for surcease of sorrow and for merciful death—and you never know: if the kick line runs out of steam, if you stay away more than a single season, if you retire to have children, she could prevail—which after all, might be, well, as the Princeton boys are said to say, *only fair*—because as for life as you—and I, sometimes, construe it, she is, I'm afraid maladapted. Which leaves her high and dry on Art's cushioned pinnacle. I prefer your approach; I do. But I have an idea she'll never be happy here, never can be; it's my belief that something very Greek happened to her with daddy, and that all this with the mother is, truly, the cover story.

The *Time* cover story was vile and obviously threw her. (She is *a very nervous woman, pace*, spirit of Thermopylae, and it ought to be remembered that the *size* of New York, compared to that of Milan, or Chicago even, is enough to throw anybody, not to mention somebody it's already thrown out, so to speak.) Neither is she terribly well educated—but you knew that. She is witty—or caustic—but for instance, she missed the point entirely when, in some banter at Herbert W.'s about the fee controversy, it was mentioned that Tucker was reportedly outraged and might not do the *Tosca* because she was getting secret outside help, as it were, Leo Lerman snapped, "Doesn't he realize Maria wishes to emulate the virtuous woman of the Bible whose price is above Ruby's?" One thinks of what you yourself might have said of the Meneghini (in relation to the Frankly Dowdy Diva From Above the *Gelateria* in Parma) countering the charge that the fondness for luxury and couture seemed to sit ill on a supposedly dedicated artist. "Sure, where's the harm at all—and a bit of class."

And, after all, although it's a shameful truth, *Time* is a big part of New York: a vile part, but a significant one. I must tell you, it did occur to me that, feeling the way you've felt all these years about her, we might have mobilized something preemptive—but who knew that Luce would do what he did, in the holy name of motherhood? (And he likely entertains some confused notions about her premature antifascist activities during the war.) He would have done the same thing to you, you realize, when you landed here—unable as he was to disentangle the skein of your story, buying the story that you had been singing in Omsk, in Minsk (as opposed to Minsky's, in Jersey City; it is known you went there with Auntie, Consuelo Gilligan, and Grainne de Paor, but whether of not you gave them a song is not recorded), in Vitebsk (and probably convinced in his own alleged mind that you pushed Masaryk out the window like some Bohunk Tosca), had you not *known what you know*: had you not given that private warble over in Jersey, and enjoyed that fortuitous deep dish tea with Lucy Moses and Lila Tyng, who'd so adored you that winter in Paris as Amneris, as to the true authorship—and the exact remuneration involved in the transaction—of *The Women*. I remember how you said, "But there is a copy of the script in the Library of Congress with her handwritten corrections," and Paranoy's pointing out how easy it was to sit at rehearsals and transcribe the action of director and rethinking and cast rethinking and rewriting to keep the audience from leaving the theater. And you said it seemed so much her story and how hard it was to imagine a man writing it. Well, perhaps now, in the light of what's been coming to light you wonder what *your* story is, in relation to the said text—and so perhaps does Neri (see below).

Pity all the same we couldn't have foreseen the attack this fall on your friend—or the remake of *The Women* as *The Opposite Sex* (and the *Variety* headline Ralph made up trumpeting the hoax: LUCE LIP-SYNC

GYPS). She might well have paid a courtesy call on the American ambassadress in Rome, sipped a companionable Campari or two, and spoken a few straight words—delivered a few home truths (as Dawn Powell says), something like, "Listen, bitch, we *know* who wrote it, and for how much." George S. Kaufman for forty thousand bucks.

Notes from the Hotel Chelsea: Uncle Virgil, Lone Defender of the Mitigated (a.k.a. The Countess Razumovsky) wasn't there—or claims not. (Paranoy said, "No, he wasn't there; Nuncle prefers—*trahit sua nunque voluptas*—to fall asleep nine stories up at home on Twenty-third Street these days rather than in public parterres on Thirty-ninth and Fifty-seventh streets—where love no longer beckons. Not to mention the fact that some people are beginning to say 'Who?' and even to confuse him with the *other* T., the one with the P up in Cambridge who writes those chorales and sanguine, gusty symphonies that flirt with dissonance but are not besmirched." He, Nunc, has, however, *heard she's a hoax* and has apparently written to—get *this*—Mary Garden (they being '*on s'en passerait*'). Yes, dear old Mary, that pillar of strength, sanity, and perspicacity, known to the world, as was Jenny Lind, for piety, modesty, charitable good works, intrinsic worth of heart and delicacy of mind, and a spotless private life—a.k.a. to her intimates "Little Egypt" and "Isadora"—She learned dancin' in a hurry *'fore the days of* Arthur Murray. Written to say so (she is a hoax) in so many words: apparently he is in his own mind the *Flugelman* of that small band of vocal connoisseurs convinced that the rising tide of superstition and Kabbalism is too damaging to society to be ignored. This gives him a *cause* to which he can append his energies, lest he subside altogether, like any number of old bags around town, into beadwork pillows, sailor's valentines, gin, and jigsaw puzzles.

(Not to mention the fact that he would much rather dish with Mary over some really *significant* and *timeless* issue involving, for instance, her art versus that of Povla Frisch or the realization at long last of her ambition to sing Kundry—which he could easy arrange with a single phone call to Josephine La Puma and what better venue after all for *Parsifal* than the Palm Gardens [Madame Middleton would surely graciously demur] than deal with these upstart blow-ins—except to point out, of course, the fact that Sabatini, after all, did create *frissons* in her, Mary's, honor at the Ambassador, whereas what has been created for this Callas at the Ritz, only some new kind of greasy doughnut.)

Remember, Nunc was all set to denounce *you*, in *Aida* (probably for waking him up so rudely in the boudoir scene, with '*figlia di Faraoni!*'—for that and the unfortunate contretemps with the Neri transformation). "Nothing, I fear," he was heard to whisper to Olin Downes in the can after the Triumphal Scene, "but a rather more hysterical Herta Glaz, costumed in an overexuberant and yet, for a royal personage, surely under-clad manner, fielding a performing style and a blazing pyrean headdress together suggestive less of Miss Gladys Swarthout than of, say, Miss Margie Hart—and reminiscent of that of the gigantic red-haired harlot impersonated by Bert Savoy." (*Did* they run that back to you, at the interval to send you into V-8 overdrive in the Judgment Scene, reducing the presbyter to a mass of quivering mandarin jelly? *He* later denied saying it at all—claimed he was maliciously misquoted by a rival; that what he'd actually said was, "An uncanny portrait of a mysterious heart: she is a fiery Amneris who calls to mind no earlier exponent of the role, but rather the greatest of all Aidas, Teresa Stolz, the toast of the House of Savoy."

"A likely story," Paranoy was heard to comment. "The raddled old iniquity *was* probably *at* La Stolz's debut in that role, at Scala, on his Italian journeys. It's certain he was, with Walt Whitman, an Alboni fanatic—went to *both* of *her* Normas!")

Nunc is of course most famous—apart from giving Lou Harrison a nervous breakdown—for his pronouncement on another of your favorite pieces of Americana, recently re-immortalized by your favorite new American soprano. "A libretto," he said of *Porgy and Bess*, "that should never have been accepted, on a subject that should never have been treated, by a composer who should never have attempted it." (Clearly, he was aching for two more *nevers* to make up a resounding Lear-like crescendo, but Rhetoric, the tease, failed him.)

And I can't remember what he wrote—neither apparently can the author(s) of MNOPQR *STUVWXYZ*, who have unnerved me—apart from depicting me in general like a Cruikshank dandy or an exquisite in fits—by putting me in the mask of Menander at the party—because, if you remember Menander's boast was mine—or mine is his: that we make up the whole of what we write in our heads ahead on putting it on the page.

Of course, had even a close approximation of said scandalous text been produced, Nunc would have ferreted out—sending out Indian runners to barrooms and steam rooms, etc. , and sued to the tune of selected church hymns, you can bet your abovementioned *voce di petto* on it, Pet-o, for neither are the godly gladly mocked. Paranoy says Nunc has become like an old Roman *principessa* (perhaps he's been influenced by the creation of the mythical "Principessa Oriana Incantevole, the ancient of days, known to be stone-deaf since the bombing of Rome," in MNOPQR *STUVWXYZ*), living on the *piano nobile* of her mind's crumbling *palazzo*, amid the fantastic wreckage left behind in the wake of bands of maurading visitors (which gave me the shivers, for I've always liked the Chelsea).

This you will like. I heard one old dear say to another on the way out, "It's true, life is like that. She makes you see it." And Frances Moore said something I might have said as well of you, had I thought to: "When Maria sings, the painted scene clouds *move* across the painted moon!"

Many things said to have happened never did. This, for example, so eerily reminiscent of exaggerations published in the aforementioned text relating to yourself and companions as to invite.

"The whole theater was an insane asylum—fists waving, pummeling, hoarse guttural exclamations and anguished cries filling the auditorium. Strangers fell sobbing into one another's arms; delirious women clinging to one another staggered toward the exit doors. There was an undeniable sense of a universal chaos out of which some entirely new era was being created."

Paranoy said, "Sounds like Marcia Davenport losing her broadcast mind at Gina Cigna's debut" (which of course really *did happen*, on WOR).

Somebody said Marcia Davenport *was* there, telling everbody who would listen that this woman was a flash in the pan and that the real news was Jolanda Menneguzzer. Paranoy said, "That wasn't Marcia Davenport, that was Rodney Bergamot's new drag." But we know for a fact it was the only child of Alma Gluck, not merely from the way she sat out the intermissions in the stark attitude Dostoyevsky (who really should be raised to render the scene) made the derisive mouth of Nastasya Filipnova decry, to wit: "If I sit in a box in the French theater like the incarnation of some inapproachable dress-circle virtue . . . etc." Not only, but also because she dropped her program on the steps leading down from Sherry's on the way out during the final curtain uproar and some deft queen retrieving it for her and spying script, *pulled a quick switch*, then disappeared up the secret Thirty-ninth Street side stairway to the Family Circle. (It all came out the next day on the Line, along with the following:

"Marcia Davenport? She claims to have once been a member of the highest councils of state."

"Surely more a membrane than a member, no?")

What was written in the white space in the Steinway ad opposite the billing page went something like this:

Bellini.

Suddenly, Vincenzo began to sob. He doubled over and buried his head of golden curls in the bent crook of his arm. All of Paris was humming out the window. "*Qu'a-tu cheri?*" the Countess whispered, putting down her needlepoint and turning to him in sudden alarm. "What is it? *Que fait-tu mal*? What has disturbed you so?" "*Niente . . . niente*," he muttered desolately (for though joy is a convulsion, grief is a habit, and emotions had long since become his events), his lovely face wet with tears. "*Sono triste—e straniero!*"

And yes, your pet lunatic standee (or is that *slandee*?) was there for the seasonal opening: the one we call Bartleby; the one you and the Countess maintain lives in a broom closet at Patelson's and forges antique Baroque scores. Dressed in the usual semiclerical black, with the worn collar reversed. Listened, as always, to everything from the Fortieth Street lobby, sitting under the bust of Caruso, clutching *Fear and Trembling* and *The Sickness Unto Death*, reading from them at intermission, acknowledging (in the piercing and haughty luster of that gaze enjoining any notion of fraternity) *nessuno*.

Then a snatch of dialogue: "The *theater*? Please, my dear; the lights go down, the curtain goes up; people are *talking*. Boring."

When "Dolores" and "Gloria Gotham" walked down separate aisles and greeted one another, one wag was remarked, "The meeting of Erys and Enyo." (In the Irish these ones—Strife and Battle Axe—are called Nemain and Babh. They, with the Morrigan, constitute the Major Triad in Big Earth Trouble. O.W. will expatiate for you.)

Whereupon I myself saw, wreathed in blue cigarette smoke, either Dalí or the false Dalí (the latter I'm inclined to think, as there was no version true or false either of Gala at his side, only a gaggle of the living foredoomed). Whoever he was he was heard to proclaim, much to the consternation of the score desk gnomes, "The music is *irrelevant* with Callas—she is *elsewhere* from the first measure. I have in my life in the theater come upon only three incarnations of the tragic muse, this woman, Duse, and Margarita Xirgu." "*Who*?" one score desk gnome wailed.

(I might have told him, but Lorca's ghost came floating at just that moment out of the men's room, flashed his eyes, put a finger to his lips, and yet I heard him say, "You know how I have suffered in this city, I cannot bear to be here, I don't know why, but do not allow this terrible man to profane by speaking it the divine name of Margarita Xirgu!" I promised him I would prevent all further discourse of the only woman he could ever love, and then I felt his chill ameliorate and indeed his dark and diminutive ectoplasmic form dissolve in the light of Sherry's chandelier.)

There also appeared on Saturday a notice in the *Times*.

"Concerning the public circulation for profit of a certain literary enterprise known as MNOPQR *STUVWXYZ*, as the the gist there are parts more or less accurately representative of what may be called real life, transparently veiled, of a true living woman. . ."

Transparently veiled. Like something wrapped in cellophane—but then you *are*, as Cole would have it (and you know, you just might get a kick out of doing *Kiss Me, Kate* in summer stock) cellophane—the top, like La Gioconda's smile, Marilyn's salary, and the Leaning Tower). The author (or more likely authors) seem to have taken Raleigh's boast to heart, that *by filling up the Blanks of old Histories, we need not be so scrupulous. For it is not to be feared that Time should run backward, and by restoring all things themselves to knowledge, make our conjecture appear ridiculous.*

(That's what *he* thought. We Irish, who go to sea in the good ships Memory, Dream, and Reflection, to discover under the polestar's navigational sway old lands anew, have always known that Time curves as does the earth beyond the horizon—and if it is true, as it is said, that Death approaches, it can *only* do so in a direction of time *opposite* to that in which we approach that time when we shall go and live with the Morning Star. Didn't Einstein tell you likewise at Princeton, talking of time, of the drift of—*fado, fado*—the ages?)

Besides, is not the hole greater than the mass of its dug-out dirt? And has not the Irishman Lochlainn O'Raifeartaigh enlightened us all concerning nonperturbative and symmetrical methods of field theory? Do remember, these ones we're tracking down are quite possibly pass remarkable in subjects other than literature, for as Auden has pointed out, the years of grotesque force-feeding of college and university boys are, by virtue of the young's ability to commit *anything* to memory for a season, coupled with the voltaic intensity of the neurotic verve they both habitually and offhandedly display, quite frightening to behold.

(We have tested and tasted too much, lover,
Through a chink too wide there comes in no wonder.")

Ralph nearly slugged some old transparency on Saturday. "To produce and perfect the voice they want and know they can have, these women must first conceal or remake an obscure or troubled past to reinvent themselves as strong and independent." "Czgowchwz conceals *nothing*, remakes *nothing*. It's *all* on tape!"

(He missed the one who cackled, "Darling, when Bellini said *bring death by means of song*, do you suppose he meant *this*?")

In the meantime, may I tell you that earlier in the month, the only woman you ever though made *Tosca* interesting, Miss Price, has sung a glorious Cleopatra in *Giulio Cesare* at Carnegie Hall.

All right, I can't not talk about it all night. She may have three voices, all of them archetypes capable of defining for a generation the music she sings, but for me—to keep the triad argument going—she is everything in *two* of the three great essential manifestations of the Triple Goddess as envisioned by Mozart in the letter to his father wondering if he could snag Da Ponte after Salieri was through with him. That is to say the *seria* and the *mezzo carattere*. I don't see that she can ever be the *buffa*, which you can and have been. I'm sorry, but there it is.

The immediate problem, according to one seer, is: she is at the Met up against the psychic remnant of the greatest Norma of the early century and cannot, for all her genius, best it. (She's even known to have given out on the subject of the sometime vaudevillian who once gave voice lessons and sang a piece of the Verdi Requiem with Joan Crawford, "with her voice you can't compare us—it's *not fair*." *Fair*? Sounds like the canard about Princeton boys and a certain specified reciprocal erotic configuration.) Whatever the reason, this *Norma*, unless it undergoes a metamorphosis (or unless she starts some class of blazing affair in Gotham) is not going to be the one. Anyway according to everybody that's already happened, yes? In London—twice: and that's the second part of the argument, that having done *that*, she simply will not be given what she was given there: so that the two great Normas of the century as it turns out will have been Ponselle here and her there. You know how people go on. (It's true, life is like that.)

Fortuna favet fortibus. (Aloha.)

"This is not a job for a music critic," one vilificator avowed, "this is a job for a *plumber*! When she did *Butterfly* in Chicago, I said I'd rather be listening to Ganna Walska. Tonight I'd rather be listening to Ina Souez singing with Spike Jones! I am inclined after hearing this performance to believe the rumor that it was this voice—this woman—who gave Anita Cerquetti a nervous breakdown! I mean *really*. What has issued from those distended jaws is a voice such as it would be madness to attempt describing. There are, indeed, two or three epithets that might be applicable to it in art. One might say, for instance, that the sound was harsh and broken and hollow, but the hideous whole is indescribable, for the simple reason that no similar sound can ever have scorched the ears of humanity.

"There are two particulars, nevertheless which may be called characteristic of the tonal impact. In the first place the voice seemed to reach one's ears from a vast distance—as from some deep cavern under Broadway. In the second place, it impresses itself upon the hearing sense as sulfuric acid does upon the sense of touch."

(I did think that was evil; it reminded me quite uncannily of a similar calumny charged to a certain Hibernian-Czech-naturalized-by-act-of-Congress-American-operatic-eminence in the vexing case of an—almost certainly illegal, for there *are* standards—immigrant Sicilian psychotic called Cedrioli.)

An even more coquettish but equally cringe-making exchange took place outside Sherry's between two gentlemen unlikely ever to marry. "Obviously a reputation as full of hot air as the Hindenberg, and likely to meet a similar end." Pause. "Oh, I don't know, darling, not unless she gets *really* desperate and tries dropping anchor in Jersey."

And then a knowing—maddeningly knowing—appraisal. "Shot to shit in seven years; terrifying!"

For my part, I'll tell you that I have *never—not even from you,* not even from Lady Day (who is the only one finally to compare either of you with) heard emotional deprivation voiced with more molten anguish, whether in one voice stressed into three folds, as you insist, or from the three voices the Italians proclaim, whichever. At white heat, which I felt she reached nearly as often here as at Covent Garden, she is the end of the known histrionic world. The mint of the musical genius—the way, like you, she does her count from within, and is so always and never marking; the way her preemptive attack and swell to full volume in next to no time allows for split-second, almost improvisatory variation from phrase to phrase within the context of the line ... all that exquisite finesse that gives *bel canto* the stamp of a particular performer in a particular strait. She is with you and Victoria one of the trinity of exponents of that *ars subtilior* in which the giddy pleasure of rhythmic invention explodes. Such amazing, hard-won control veils only somewhat her dangerous and forbidding affect: a raging, and not so musical torrent (hence the "argument" in performance between her art and her ballistics) in contrast to your dark still well that could make me lose my mind, were it not lost.

(In fact there is some confusion of effect between you. One knows that a voice is as distinct as a fingerprint, but were not the grain of your instruments so nearly opposite—were not her voice so *molten* and yours so *radioactive*—one might be forgiven for arraigning you in the court prosecuting her for mass audience illusion-homicide, and vice versa.) If I found any fault at all, it was in the occasional end phrase: she tends nowadays to run out of steam (the operative word, I'm afraid among the naysayers was *scrannel*) certainly in relation to London, in '52, and the consequence seems to be that she dwells a fraction of a second too long on final notes, until the fevered brain refires. That and (I know we don't talk about wobble, but) the wobble you can at times now indeed play jump rope with, and the undeniable fact that she sometimes sounds absolutely like a *coyote*. (Somebody cackled, a propos the much-mooted Dallas engagements, "They are gonna *love* her out there—she *yodels!*") Like a coyote or like an egregious example of the notorious *bad fifth* (of which I know something myself, coming from a family of *poitin* distillers) in Henri Arnaut's fifteenth-century treatise on the Pythagorean tuning—and that is frightening (and reminds me, though I never thought I would be reminded, of Mark Twain's description of that animal as "a living, breathing allegory of Want"). But she knows the part front, back, and sideways, as I said to Kolodin—called by our author(s) *Kölnischwasser*: he is not amused—and he agreed—none of the morons in the dailies will get the message.

During the first intermission a combustible discussion of the sort much valued nowadays in existentialist New York got going at the bar in Sherry's—not over anything so insignificant and *contingent* as Divina's wobble: rather over the question of Norma and motherhood. One or two loons posited that you had to have been a mother, and three or four more took the opposite view—the Golgotha Church organist (redolent of vetiver and inhaling Benedictine like Vicks) going even so far as to insist you shouldn't even have *had* one. Team A cited Ponselle and the big Z. as non-moms, and Neri and thee as moms (both with lost children). I thought Ralph would choke to death on rage and spit. I found it riveting: in my experience it was the first time in the history of categories that you and the Old Foghorn have ever been put in the same file, except as *women* or as members of the cast of *Aida*.

I of course could only think of the truth of the matter, of that boy in Tel Aviv, who has certainly passed the age of the bar mitzvah. Will he remember you? Does he realize who you are? You never said you were his mother, only the neighbor, fair enough, but he must remember his years with you, your tutoring him in the Torah, like a Deborah in the wilds of Ruthenia. Deborah is "swarm of bees." "Busy little bees full of stings, making honey." You could never have stung the boy, only fed him on honey. I wonder do I sound jealous when I speak of this great work of yours. No, I don't think so, only mindful that I myself was in another context a boy fed on honey.

Incidentally, a propos *lineups*, I thought you might want to know where they put her in the rogues' gallery in the lobby. Right next to *you*, flush left of the north box office window. It took me a while to realize whom they'd moved: Mary C-V, who's now jauntily positioned between Milanov and Blanche Thebom.

Electing to abjure the felicities of the recessional (the gangways were, as Ralph declared, "*imbedded* crowded"), I cut out through pass door to the Executive Offices, my prerogative now I am an employee of the place—if that's what the translator of *Salome* is entitled to call himself (and what else can I call myself, "Bosey"? Or put another way—the way of wit—"I never call myself, dear; I'm always in; Too bad. I'd like to be able to give myself a piece of my mind once in a while, but my answering service is down on strong language.").

Whereupon, The big Z., with that ample vestal Mary Hanlon in tow, loomed in the prospect (having just come from the Del Monaco dressing room, where God knows *what*...) very like the *Queen Mary* emerging from a North River morning fog into her North River berth.

"Zo—*vot* are you doink smilink like it vuz your vedding? I'm cabeling Mawrdew Czgowchwz on you." "Madame, don't bother, I'm confessing. How could I live with myself and keep such a passion secret?" She looked balefully from Maisie to me. "You Irish could do anything." Poor Maisie looked *pilloried* (after decades of selfless toil organizing socials, and especially after the latest salvo against Z. by the Callas lobby in *Opera*, calling Mama's Aida in particular ridiculous, and excoriating the Slavic pitch. Mary was heard *screaming* only last weekend, "She's the *only*

Aida in *history* who sounds *Egyptian*! She *researched* that pitch—it's the way they *sounded*!!)."

Ralph said later, "I love her like a two-reel silent, but meanwhile in the first place Aida isn't Egyptian, she's Ehtiopian, so unless anybody's heard any Haile Selassie records lately ... and in the second place she died on G in the nineteen fifty-four *Normas* and she walked in here tonight like she had outdone Ponselle."

(It's true: the uproar when she entered must have unnerved the debutante: you could've heard it at Carnegie. It's a good thing the still young Miss Price—Madame's obvious successor as *prima Verdista*, if and when she is ever contracted, is busy elsewhere and could not attend.)

However, concerning the woman, she is a primitive woman, for all that she is a musical genius and for all that she has fallen in love with the Audrey Hepburn look and means to achieve it. A poorly educated, self-doubting (and therefore in respect of the genius perhaps all the more touching) primitive woman who has been terribly punished, whose overriding idea of stark retribution makes her finally less compelling than a woman like you (well, there are no other women like you, so you) who having gone through hell is able to find a kind of restoration through benevolence.

I could say more—all the nasty speculation about the weight loss—tape worms, surgery, etcetera—from devotees of warblers at least four axe handles across the pistol pockets. Let suffice that everything you've held about the woman all these years is still true, and the only thing to be done about it (at least until the pope opens the Letter from Fatima in 1960) is to put the two of you back together and charge a hundred dollars a ticket to raise cash to elect the first American president who likes to go to thuh opra. *Herodiade* alternating the mother and the daughter? Or are you currently so steeped in mother/daughter cross-referential melodrama that all you yearn to do is—but you declined *Dialogues des Carmelites*, didn't you. (It's going to be a succès fou, but I never did see you in it. It would be a kind of disloyalty to the Blue Nuns, no?)

Aftermaths and postmortems: this morning, on the line (reported on the telephone by Ralph and Alice):

"Did you love it, dear, love it *live*?"

"I loved it."

"Were you *moved*?"

"I *wuz*, deah—so moved they had to move me back."

One last detail, a propos Marcia Davenport. The on-dit somewhere in New York is that she is thinking of getting out a search warrant for this *author* creature, whom she has been advised, has, with his MNOPQR STUVWXYZ plagiarized *Of Lena Geyer*. (Too bad Max Perkins is dead: *he* wrote the thing for her, as sure as Kauffman wrote *The Women*. These women!) Anyway, Ralph said he thought *Of Lena Geyer* about Alma Gluck and the Marx Brothers, and somebody said *they* thought "The Secret Seven" was the Marx Brothers plus the Three Stooges. On and on. No word yet from the estates of either Huneker or Willa Cather. (I mean, if you're going to be *copied* from somebody, I'd prefer Huneker's Ishtar/Easter or Cather's Thea. Goddessy names, like your own. Lena is strictly the *Putzfrau*'s moniker, *nicht war?*)

First, the last First Friday of 1956. They'll just have to do without their December: those who have not already made nine in a row must begin again. As for me, I'm off again, as declared. I do hate leaving town, just in case Winchell does decide to blow his brains out on television: it would give me as much joy to behold as did the public humiliation and unmasking of the junior Senator from Wisconsin. I know, hatred is malignant, and I pray to have it lifted . . . one day. In the meantime I am so delighted with the sponsors of his vile show for canceling him that I may take up smoking Old Gold *and* give myself a Toni ("which twin?").

I could go on in this vein, but I'd best abrupt myself if I'm to regroup my forces for the day and face life (as in *In This Our*). I wonder will it ever get to the stage again when I sit down and look at that thing the way we did last winter?

Best of luck with *Pilgrim Soul* and the ways of *Eire-wohn mo bhron*. As to the floating-crap-game festivities here, and also a propos writing up the lives of people, here is a famous piece from the "Irish gossip game" from *What Shall We Do Tonight? or Social Amusements for Evening Parties*, the work of one Leger D. Mayne, published in New York by Dick & Fitzgerald in 1873. "One of the company invents a short striking narrative and writes it down, passing it verbally to the next in a circle, to his left. The next repeats it to the next on his left, and so on until the story returns to the originator. Example: 'Oliver Wendell Holmes, who has written so eloquently in the American Atlantic Monthly for the cause of the suffering freedmen, is about to relate the life of Snubbs, who has a commission and a fortune of fifteen thousand pounds.' By the time the story returns to its originator, it has become the following. 'Across the Atlantic, it is eloquently related that the cause of the suffering of the American monthlies is about a commissioned freedman taking the life of Snobbs, who had given permission and a fortune of fifty thousand pounds.' "

You will see the relevance to nearly everything detailed above, from the suffering monthlies to Clare Boothe Luce, Marcia Davenport, the snobs—the all of it. Not to mention what might become (by way, I must allow of improvement) to the originator's work by having it rewritten all over Dublin homes, and why so he the undersigned must do the best thing and skedaddle—not crossing the American Atlantic at all, as month by month the budget for *Pilgrim Soul* mounts by at least fifty thousand pounds, but only to its windy verge.

A brief word about the *Salome*. Apparently Vortice is under the impression (i.e., has gotten wind of the fact) that I am in correspondence with Peter Brook. Not convinced that P. is doing theater now, and still listening to people talk about the Bjoerling–de los Angeles *Faust*—how many—six or seven seasons past?—plus the gossip about Herbert Graf having been the original of Freud's Little Hans ... well, bother (or as they say in certain quarters in Perfidious Albion's smutty-seductive capital *bovver*). But I've got Regina R. on my side, and Valerio is already so terrified of her Herodias in the old production—well, he knows very little English, true, but if he hears her say to him from the original Wilde text (as she is quite capable of doing on behalf of the singers for instance—and why on earth do they keep insisting I've *translated* the thing, when all I've done is restore it?) "And as for you, you are *ridiculous!*" Well, he will have met his match in temperament, in spades, because as you've always said when Regina gets into a part, she *gets into a part.*

At any rate one's done one's best, following the directive of Joan Crawford to Scott Fitzgerald on the lot at MGM some time before the last war, and *written hard.* Or would one rather say with Kavanagh *God further the work,* reminding you that *the axle-roll of a rut-locked cart / Broke the burnt stick of noon in two* is not at all unlike the camera on its track, nor are the moments of sowing the character unlike potato drills—for we too have walked as he did and our talk too has been *a theme of kings, / a theme for strings.*

And when we put our ears to the paling-post / The music that came out was magical.

Remember what Maev means. Intoxication. And don't worry about playing your own mother; Gloria DeHaven did it with no aftereffect (that one can detect).

Do write c/o General Delivery, Neaport, or telephone the general store. (Massachusetts is a far cry from New York, but not so far as that from Dublin.) After last summer, they'd send out Indian runners in the winter storm to fetch the eremite off his lonely hill down from his own Tor Ballyhoo where on the widow's walk in the howling nor'easter, Calliope is right at home amid the travails and flails of any number of wailing whaling widows, see above.

Si da mi stesso diviso
e fattto singular di l'altra gente
to talk to you.

Your ever-loving pal
S.D.J. (The) O'Maurigan (Fitz)

P.S. Chin up, you're only having twins. Mr. Bloom had octuplets.

P.P.S. You know what they say—Orphrey always brings back the picture.

P.P.P.S. Lavinia has decided to go to *law school*. (And why not?) And I have taken up smoking (a young man should have an occupation of some kind). Lucky Strikes. We used to sneak them at Regis. I remember telling them there I'd smoked in England. Passing Clouds—Ferrier's brand. (*Nuvole Legere* as they might be called in Italy, lyrics from that opera which shall remain nameless in which you have so pointedly disdained to appear.) They all thought I was lying ("Liar! *Liar!*").

*

The night drawn in, Jacob was sitting at the long window, looking down into the populous, illuminated thoroughfare, listening to the traffic noise, and holding in his lap an unopened parcel, come in the diplomatic pouch from New York. The diva entered alone (looking he thought in some way implicated), sat down, and removed her hat.

The telephone rang; he quickly snatched it up.

"Yes?"

"Sorry, Madame, your New York call isn't on. Your woman is at the opera."

"Thank you."

"Was that New York?"

"It was. She's at the opera, will you try back later."

"What opera is she at at five o'clock in the afternoon—and it's not a Saturday, and All Hallows' Eve at that? I shall have to wait until tomorrow to give her the latest earful about the country she's abandoned. It's pointless getting overwrought in my condition."

"Your condition is perfect."

"These godawful headlines about Budapest—what's going to happen? As if we didn't know, as if we could *do* anything—"

"You can do anything you like—including quit, order up from room service, marry me, call a taxi for the airport, go to sleep, and dream of Bohemia, tell me what they wanted with you at the Octoroon's, sing 'Danny Boy'—or have you just done that?"

" 'Are you trying to tell me,' I asked them all, 'that my mother was a whore, and I myself by inevitable declension, in consequence, yet another whoring beggar's get?' "

"I see. *Were* they?"

"One would've thought so. Well, I nearly ate the faces off the lot of them—at first. Then I calmed down and listened."

"As I'm doing right here right now."

"Yes."

She sat down in an armchair opposite him and looked with him down into O'Connell Street.

"Fitz has a poet pal who works at the Museum of Modern Art and once told him, 'You enable me by your least remark, to unclutter myself, and my nerves. Thank you for not always laughing.' He told me that once and now I tell you, truly."

"The taciturn one—Auden's amanuensis or words to that effect on Ischia. Went with the old thing in his carpet slippers to the opening night of *The Cocktail Party*. Had a case on Lina Paliughi and Povla Frisch. He'd heard your *Fricka* at the Fenice, when Callas sang Brünnhilde."

"No, the other one—slender, terribly intense—assistant curator, big on Pollock, Kline, de Kooning, and Krasner. Fitz had acted with him in Cambridge. We all had coffee that afternoon and gossiped about Garbo after she'd left the screening of *Anna Christie and* strolled off home.

"I remember—with the chin, the broken nose and the immense Bette Davis eyes. By the way, your champion poet has written, at some length from the heft of the communique. Arrived while you were out in the diplomatic pouch—by messenger, riding a bicycle from Iveagh House right in to this room. Directly you tell me what the faces said to you, it's yours. I call that fair, don't you?"

She stood and walked up to the window, looking across at Hibernia, illuminated atop the General Post Office, and then turned back. Pivoting on his fixed, attentive position, she began a circuit of the room.

"Somebody—a person or persons unknown—is attempting to blackmail the government, claiming to be able to furnish in the event of any crisis in the already-unstable *Dail*, already in an uproar concerning certain documents said to prove that the thirty-two counties of Ireland are symbolic of the degrees in Scottish Rite Masonry and therefore by sacred secret definition an affront to the Roman Church, conclusive proof that might provoke a vote of no-confidence-in-anybody. Also proof positive of Maev Cohalen as prototype of Cissy Caffrey of Nighttown, in *Ulysses* said on this same unimpeachable authority to have gone from the whorehouse in Mabbot Street to Liverpool on the morning mail boat, thence to London where she set up in the afternoons her dispensary at an address in Gerrard Street, Soho, where today ironically may be found the offices and casting studios of the majority of film distribution companies—Hyperion included—in operation in the United Kingdom, and in the evenings at the Trocadero on Shaftesbury Avenue—climbing like the intrepid liana westward to Mayfair—Number 7 Curzon Street—under the patronage of none-other-than H. R. H. Edward, Prince of Wales, with whom she had taken the devilishly farsighted and imaginative liberty of having herself secretly photographed, in compromising positions from the *Kama Sutra*, in the *Benares* suite of the premises earlier mentioned."

"Gosh."

"And it went on from there—including some sly reference to her being perhaps the only woman prototype not merely of Cissey Caffrey, but one of H.R.H.'s *other mounts*.

"This a joke in a discussion of the horses hanging on the wall of a club. 'Why not the women he mounted as well as the horses?' Sniggering response: 'Question of space.' I remembered the passage as Fitz read the entire book out loud to me last spring, adding his own gloss at that point: did I know the definition of an Irish queer? One who prefers women to horses. I found the whole of it—not the book, the discussion of the committee—rather more

Lulu-esque than Ulyssean, in spite of Maev *not* being murdered by Jack the Ripper. Who was, wasn't he, a cousin of the Prince of Wales?

"The government consequently feel we must tread softly on the gone-missing business, and certainly not place our woman anywhere in Albion. They suggested an interval—'loike in *Gone With the Wind*, after Scarlett's been down on the ground gnawin' at the spuds'—then show her entering New York harbor. I said I liked intervals in the theater, that in Italy we're paid for the performance during the first one. They didn't get it—and I got nothing to eat."

"Let me call down for supper."

"Please. I could eat the horse she rode down O'Connell Street—either end."

"Actually, I think it's mutton they're giving. 'Do yiz grand,' as the kitchen assured me this morning of the pig's liver in place of the veal kidneys, while you were diving into those whatchmacallim pigs' feet."

"*Crubbeens*. Delicious they were."

XI

Back to 47 Gramercy

The Last First Friday of 1956 from which Madge departs for Dublin. Narrated in reminiscence by SDJO'M and MC in terms of Fitz's idea of the recording of the First Fridays on the the 3-D wheel viewer in terms of "talking pictures," etc. Also reviewing the situation in crossword puzzle fashion thus:

The Galway Express, An Domain Thair,
with Hyperion
drizzle and the
continued the sentiment
signaling memories too
ambivalent
progressive evocation often at
odds
discontent of
which
a
compound
of
the
outdoor
landscape
and
the
inner
state

Then back to Halloween at Magwyck.

They hurried in out of the cold; somebody lit a cigarette.

!@#$%^&*

And the eleventh and last First Friday of nineteen fifty-six got under way.

"I wanted to talk about Pollock, Rothko, de Kooning, and Kline, he wanted to talk about Lovis Corinth—the notorious *hidden* period, in which he supposedly painted among other things a nude self-portrait, supine, bent over like a pretzel, having just reached masturbatory climax, the ejaculate falling into his open mouth. Called *Saturn Devouring His Children*. I didn't buy it."

"It was for *sale*?"

"You could say so, in a manner of speaking. No, we didn't quite mesh."

!@#$%^&*

"*Mildred Pierce*—an opera? Set in a restaurant?"

"I don't know what you mean by that. I suppose the Pierces went out to restaurants—whatever restaurants there were in those days. But I was thinking of the whole thing from the wifely—or you might these days say the *feminist* point of view."

"Are we talking about the same Mildred Pierce?"

"I don't know. *I'm* talking about Franklin's wife—as fascinating a woman when you look into it as Mary Todd Lincoln. She thought it was perfectly unconscionable the way Franklin when he made the deal resettling the Omaha betrayed them by withholding protection from their sworn enemy the Sioux—in spite of the fact she thought the Omaha when they showed up in the Oval Office smelled perfectly horrid and had been assured the Sioux smelled no better—"

"Excuse me, there was no Oval Office in the White House in the period you're talking about."

"Really not? Well, in any case a fascinating period you will agree—something of an allegory of our own, really, and nobody's ever really done the Washington and the White House on the operatic stage—you know, sort of a Yankee *Khovanshchina*."

"An allegory of our own time?"

"They did that show on Broadway twenty-five years ago; it was called *Of Thee I Sing*."

"Yes, Pierce was personally a charming army factotum, politically unobjectionable to Southerners, whose campaign biography, you may care to know, was undertaken by no less an eminence than Nathaniel Hawthorne—that connoisseur of rectitude and genius. Under his not very scrutinous gaze—Pierce's, that is, not Hawthorne's—although it ought to be remarked here that in the years immediately following the Pierce administration, both men started drinking together in protracted bouts at regular intervals, observed by serving people rolling around together on the floor in varying states of déshabillé. Of which circumstance it is possible to make too much since riotous drinking inevitably leads at the very least to the loosening of collars, and yet . . . and yet the experience did, it is commonly agreed, lead directly to Hawthorne's perhaps premature demise—whether a case of Puritan remorse or merely a severe chill is up for argument.

"As to the Pierce administration, it was characterized by vigorous expansionist foreign policy which failed in most of its objectives—as indeed must most of those, overt and covert, currently being pursued by the Dulleses and their mandarins operating in closets, cabinets, corridors, and attics the world over, even as we speak."

"Sounds thrilling, darling, but perhaps more like an American *Ring*, no? Czgowchwz as Mildred Pierce, a sort of combination Freia, Fricka, Erda, *and* Waltraute."

"Excuse me, but was Franklin Pierce's wife's name really Mildred?"

"Yes. And of course, she drank. She opened a French restaurant in the Crystal Palace. The Maud Chez Elle of its day. Also a little boutique, the first to market the Tara brooch in America. Yes, a great entrepreneur, until she met her match . . . the bottle. The Crystal Palace burned down spectacularly in an afternoon—cause, it was rumored of her too exuberant presentation of the *crêpes flambées*. In that she and her lordly democrat were well matched."

"He too was a drunk, you mean."

"He was was referred to as the hero of many a well-fought bottle. A slobbering sot was once arrested in Washington for going amok on horseback on a public street, knocking a woman down and killing her. It was Franklin Pierce in office. Yes, they were a pair, if you like."

"Well, that *is* like the *Ring*, isn't it. Human frailty in high places, *horses*—and the great fire in the end!"

"Except of course, the Crystal Palace was in New York, and as you may know, the nation's capital is Washington, D.C."

"A mere detail of staging—allegory."

!@#$%^&*

"Darling, come into the music room and play that passage from the Saint-Saëns Fifth—so *Gaza*."

!@#$%^&*

"I quite like the Jesuit Strange—although they do say there are venues in which he's been seen distinctly off the beaten path of the Way of the Cross."

"I believe that in humble imtation of his Lord he has been known from time to time to consort with sinners—in dark haunts and in rather *steamy* situations."

"Chinese laundries?"

"Not quite. It is my sincere hope he is not found out and defrocked."

"How odd—I was always told priests could hear confessions anywhere."

"And there are eight million of them in the naked city."

"Mascagni's *Iris* is set in a *laundry*. I know somebody who heard Magda Olivero in it last summer in Pesaro—apparently divine."

"You know, there was a defrocked priest named Driscol, in early nineteenth-century New York—the editor of *The Temple of Reason*. This Jesuit lurking about the corners tonight puts me in mind of him, and of such terms as *malversation* and the like."

"Malversation? Corruption in office? I don't think they have production kickbacks per se in the archdiocese."

"Is that so. What about bingo and sale of indulgences?"

"Oh, *really*!"

!@#$%^&*

"It would be an eerie kind of feminist opera, but I do think *Double Indemnity*—"

"I can see your point, *if* it could be done with a New York setting, ending with 'Vamp fries in chair,' you know, like *Machinal*."

"I don't see that it makes any difference at all that the thing is sung by a chorus in an insane asylum, I think 'The Very Moment of Love' is a beautiful song."

"So it is—and you know, I was just thinking, that the Mary Cedrioli story —told from her point of view—might be an absolutely riveting—you know, Faustian—"

"She hasn't exactly got a point of view, has she, out there in Creedmoor in the *abbazzateria*."

"No, I suppose not—looking for a corner in the roundhouse to hunker down in and eat her gruel."

"As a chamber opera . . . a girl *Wozzeck*."

!@#$%^&*

"Look, it's a trade-off. Milton can't write a Broadway musical and Lenny's so-called serious music is all crap. Not everybody in the music business is a Mozart, get me?"

!@#$%^&*

"She is right to want to play Grushenka, it's a great book—this émigré pornographer is absurdly off the mark. The great question, of course, is its changing face: it is like those Catalan Trinities with three faces in one. Who is its hero? Boys in their teens know it is Alyosha. Men in their twenties, thirties, and forties know it is Dmitri. Only readers in their fifties know it is, irrefutably, Ivan. And finally, if we live past the allotted biblical span into our eighties and are still eating *blini* like they are inside, we discover the truth . . . it was Alyosha all along."

!@#$%^&*

"Yes, Socrates went right on learning—everything, it seems, except when to keep his mouth shut."

"No, no, my dear, there is no Grecian remnant whatever in plainchant—

which is, you know, only the extension of druidic psalmody: of those barbarities howled at Odin by lunatics running in circles around old oaks."

!@#$%^&*

"When I speak of Europe, I speak of *our hermaphroditic* Europe . . . exclusive of the Iberian and Scandinavian peninsulas, to say nothing of what lies beyond the *Manche*. Of that Europe of which Paris is the brain, Berlin the brawn, Vienna the dark heart, and all of Italy the stomach and sexual organs . . . the boot a penis hanging down over the vagina that is Rome. And the bowels and the asshole of our Europe, are, you understand, the Balkans."

!@#$%^&*

*

Sound asleep, Mawrdew Czgowchwz dreamed a Night-Sea Journey—in the sun boat of Amon-Ra, renamed *Scourge of Malice*—which embarked at twilight on a distant uncharted tributary of the eternal Nile—a little brook at the foot of Cleopatra's Needle in Central Park—and after a drift under the bridge in the Ramble floated out onto the boat lake behind the Bethesda Fountain over which the Angel of the Waters stood sentinel.

The ship itself sang out at first
Io no hol'ali, eppur quando dal molo
Lancio la prora al mar,
Fermi gli alcioni sul potente volo
Si librabo a guardar.
Io no ho pinne, eppur quando in marosi
Niun legno osa affrontar,
Trepidando, gli squali ardimentosi
Mi guardano passar!
Silime al mio signor,
Mite d'aspetto quanto e forte in cuor
Le fiamme ho anch'io nel petto,
Anch'io di spazio

Anch'io di gloria ho smania
Avanti—evviva Urania!
And the helmsman sang out a lamenting refrain.
Ci spinge il vento
Al patria suoi,
D'Irlanda O' figlia
Dove vai tu?

"Where do I come from? Where am I bound?" she begged.

The helmsman, in his argonaut's voice, announced the itinerary with satisfaction.

"Aegyptus, Syria, Mesopotamia, Cappadocia, Tuscia, Parvasia, Concavia, Hyrcania.

"Thracia, Gosnam, Thebaidi, Parsadal, India, Bactriane, Cilicia, Oxiana.

"Numidia, Cyprus, Parthia, Getulia, Arabia, Phalagon, Mantiana, Soxia.

"Gallia, Illyria, Sogdiana, Lydia, Caspis, Germania, Trenam, Bithynia, Graecia, Licia, Onigap.

"Candia, Orcheny, Achaia, Armenia, Cilicia, Paphlagonia, Phasiana, Chaldei.

"Itergi, Macedonia, Garamantica, Sauromatica, Aethiopia, Fiacim, Colchis, Cireniaca.

"Nasamonia, Carthago, Coxlant, Idumea, Parstavia, Vinsam, Tolpam, Carcedonia, Italia, Brytania, Phenices.

"Comaginem, Achronia, Marmarica, Idumia, Gebal, Elam, Nod.

"Media, Chaldea, Sericipopuli, Persia, Gongatha, Gorsim, Hispania.

"Pamphilia, Oacidi, Babylonia, Serendip, Felixia, Assyria, Metagonitidim, Cathay.

"Umbilica, Phrygia, Mauritania, Hibernia."

"By and large, no ports of call: no safe harbors."

Under Bow Bridge, around the western bend of the Ramble promontory and suddenly into a cove that had never been there before—through an open cavern like the one at Tintagel, the names carved on the tunnel walls:

Aegyptus, Thracia, Numidia, Gallia, Candia, Itergi, Phenices, Nod, Hispania, Cathay, Hibernia.

"Friends, have I been whirled around at the shift in the crossroads, though I went the right way before? Has some gale driven me from my course, like a boat on the sea?"

The current carried them westward into one of nineteenth-century Manhattan's underground streams, under the Dakota Apartments, spilling them dream-minutes later into the North River and down past the Scandinavian Lines, Cunard Line, French Line, United States Lines, Italian Lines, North German-Lloyd, Circle Line, and Holland-America Line piers; past the abandoned Weehauken, Jersey City, and Hoboken ferry terminals, past the freight depots and waterfront shanties, past The Battery and out into The Narrows, past the Statue of Liberty (Mae West, wrapped in Old Glory, singing "My Old Flame—I can't even think of his name.") and out into a dead calm Atlantic, underneath a full blood moon. Jacob sang Cavalli, "*Lucidissima face!*" and the moon, like Violetta's red camellia—*quando sara apassito* were the code words—turned cadmium white.

They passed the *Arcadia* on its east-west crossing, and waved.

Meanwhile, as the dreamer became aware, Mawrdew Czgowchwz as the "lost" Moby Diva, and, after a sermon by Leo Lerman delivered from the pulpit at Saint Patrick's (shaped like the prow of the *Andrea Doria* the *Arcadia* will be sent back out to rescue her from the *antipodes* before she is "laid out to whale shit" in NYC by the Neriacs). "Europe is *not* the antipodes!" "It is if you turn the world on its ear, as Mawrdew Czgowchwz's absence does. She is in the Land Goneunder we are all the young men from Nantucket. All these matters must be explicated—literally, analogically, tropologically, anagogically, for they are nowhat less crucial than Holy Writ!"

*

Halloween at the Everard.

Moriarty.

It is Halloween, featuring every manner of rampageous violation of propriety, including wigs and false locks, particularly among the Sorority of Withered Sibyls, which calls this dump its headquarters—*abeunt studia in mores*, say-so of Ovidius Naso. They of whom it may be said without exaggeration that the combinations of the locks on their twats are posted in every subway men's toilet, East Side-West Side, all around the town, from Coney Island to the Bronx Zoo.

It's quite a mixed bag, as Grand Guignol generally is, tending to the literary and historical, but also illustrative of the present. There are pairs of competing Grendel and Grendel's Dams, trio upon trio of weird sisters off the blasted heath, more Brides of Frankenstein than you can shake a crucifix at, and three or four of *the* most hideous impersonatons of Miss Bettie Paige you could ever in your worst moments imagine. It might be said one is spoiled for choice.

But let us hear from a constituent concessionaire, relpying directly to the vociferous inquiry.

!@#$%^&*

"Actually, if any of you would care to know the truth, what's going on in there is a succession of tarot readings being given by Miss Claire Voyante, the once-famous fortune-teller. She is known to have a *penchant* for the older civilizations and time was she could *unearth* things—indeed, she once had a great deal of foresight and enjoyed the custom of a great many sophisticates. She has far fewer now than formerly, which points to a moral retrogression—nevertheless she is a turn that still pulls them in."

"That one! Did I hear somebody whisper *withered sybils*—all pointing the way into the Underworld, whose Gotham gate this shithole is, day in, day out? If I didn't, I ought to have, for here grief and avenging care have bedded down with malady and grieving age—all the old bags descended from that first old bag of Cumae, many of whose true sequences cannot be established and for whose lives there are only the palest hints of chronology; and dread and hunger and depraved yearning that drives men to degradation and to crime and death and toil and death's own little sister sleep—oh, why go on!"

"Ya got me, dear—God, talk about *unhappy*!"

!@#$%^&*

"What is life? 'Tis not hereafter. Present mirth—"

"Life, dear, is whatever story you care to tell about life—our little—make that *littered*—lives all rounded with a *schlepp*."

"Ah, well, 'twas ever thus."

" '*Twasn't* ever thus. I didn't look like this in the beginning."

"What can be done, dear? Anyway it's all right on Halloween."

"And I'm not even wearing a mask. It's *catastrophic*!"

!@#$%^&*

"I wanna tell you they filled that girl so full of lead she gave birth to *a kitchen sink pipe*—in the morgue at Saint Vincent's, by Cesarean section."

"So I heard. In Catholic hospitals they always save the child instead of the mother don't they."

"You must admit, there is something terribly—I hesitate to say appropriate, but terribly poignant—especially in here, tonight—about the director of *Nosferatu* choking to death on cock."

"I'm lush, I'm gay, I'm wicked—I am everything that flames!"

"Nice to meet ya, dear, I'm the Wali of Swat."

"The Wali of Swat? What is that—is that like the Wizard of Oz? What?"

"No, it's like a sultan, I think, or a maharajah."

"Nonsense, we all know who the Sultan of Swat is, and it ain't her. She's more the Maharani type—at least in her own mind . . . the Maharani of Twat."

"She is an ample woman—but unfriendly. Do not attempt to trick her for any treat."

"She is, dear, an *unsanitary* woman. I said to her, 'This is a *bathhouse*, you know.' And you know what? She *sang* back at me—sang:

'Yo' cock is made of whale bone
Yo' balls is made of brass
Mah cunt is made fo' fuckin' men—two dollars
You could toyn me 'round and kiss mah ass!'

Imagine!"

"Differing natures find their tongues in the presence of differing spectacles!"

"Really? Well, honey, if you want to find that slattern's tongue, you better check the *proctoscope* lab, if you take my meaning. Such malisons do pour from that mouth, scandalizing every name—fulminations of a truly darkened mind. Indeed, her entire career has been one of affrays and resistings of arrest for behavior liable—a constant whirl of rage and futile storming. She revolts the young and mortifies the old. And that's the truth."

"Excuse me, isn't that behavior labile?"

!@#$%^&*

"Talk about no dots on her dice, some queen last left upstairs on the floor thirty-two ivory *teeth* in *gold plates*."

"That is Miss Tick, the renowned rice queen—ardent lover of the inscrutable and the epicanthic fold. She is inclined to moments of mental abstraction. Truth is, her ideation never did quite reach tournament level. She brings her own white sheets in to hang up on the wall with white tacks so that in her all-white cubicle she may have visions like Mabel Dodge did in her white apartment on lower Fifth Avenue.

"The cyclotron force of Miss Tick's subconscious spits this, that, and whatnot in the world's blank face. In Miss Tick's world things happen either more often than always or less often than never. We do not know how to reach her to tell her the truth. Or to give her back her teeth—better leave them at the desk and be done with it."

"But who is she? The teeth must be expensive."

"Miss Tick has a long and very sad story. Miss Tick is in reality called George—the fourth of that name in what as it happens is a very distinguished old New York family. Well, as she was a fat boy, they stopped calling her George the Fourth—if you know your English history, you will know why—but the rather uncanny thing in addition to that is, the family telephone exchange was *Regent*.

"Anyway, they stared calling poor Miss Tick *I.V.* Well, when she came out—not in a cotillion, dear, like the girls in her family, but, you know, in the Life, she was of course called 'Ivy.' But the 'I.V.' proved in the event too prescient, as she succumbed, first to faithless love, then to heroin, much in the manner of that Wilma Burroughs woman, but without the talent for self-display that has put that walking cadaver in the Heinous Hall of Fame. Miss Tick now lives on Chinese food delivered to her suite at the Broadway Central and takes paraldehyde for her nerves and comes in here to fright the populace—a power of example, you might say."

!@#$%^&*

At a doorway, looking in, two Cigarettes.

"The way Reparata lies there like some wounded antelope, upon which hunters have exhausted their spears and spent their strength, she seems no longer to have her predicament clearly in mind."

"Do not wake her—do not rip her from her dreams. The rumor circulating downstairs is that sometime earlier this day she did actually experience some kind of orgasm."

"No!"

"Yes. Somebody seems to have heard a distinctly *sanglier* sort of grunt, or roar, sometime earlier, perhaps as early as late afternoon the report goes, since when she has lain there in the condition which you now observe. Her time is long elapsed, but the management has wisely decided in consideration of Halloween not to press the issue. She may lie there yet awhile, for in a case like hers, a strenuous orgasm, no matter how induced, will resemble of all things most a power surge which has blown the main fuse."

"To me she seems kind—like she was nursing someone's baby."

Enter others.

"See how you are, Thymiane? You just *try* milkin' that borderline troll's bitch tits fo' human kindness—see what rancid nuh-ish-ment you receive. Be advised and be *passin'* for she is the more dreadful and the more hideous because there are no such creatures as she seems to be in nate-cha, and she has come to us deliberately, and there is some kind of awful mystery in that very fact itself! *Lasciala regnare nel silencio, nel silencio della tomba,* and pass on by fo' the good of yo' soul."

"It certainly does look, does it not, like she's busy making friends with the necessity of dying—a wise move, for she has no surviving friends in town. A compassionate soul might be moved to call out '*Talitha cumi!*' or 'Lazarus, come forth!' but gay prudence dictates reserve. Upon her demise, however, be assured the cry for celebration will ring out on the town, and many a toast to salvation be proposed. As the divine Horace proclaimed upon the death of Cleopatra, Serpent of the Nile,

Nunc est bibendum, nunc pede libero
pulsanda tellus, nunc Saliaribus
ornare pulvinar deorum
temous erat dapidus, sodales
antehac nefas depromere Caecubum
cellis avigtis dum Capitolio
regina dementes ruinas,
funus et imperio parabat . . . et cetera"

"And the *size* she is becoming at that. She is truly like the facts of life, you simply cannot get around her!"

"It's the truth, she is more than that she was when she was simply a well-padded woman with a wary eye—but becoming it ain't. Quoth the chronicler, '*Now the vast dusk bulk that is the whale's. . .*'

Beneath the thunders of the upper deep
Far, far beneath in the abysmal sea,
Her ancient, dreamless, uninvaded sleep . . ."

"I'll just whisper something kindly in her ear."

"Warily, Abadessa! Though she lies so sleepy and so sluggish, like the interval of stillness before the Apocalypse, yet the tap of her flukes is gay death. Leave her be now, until the wakeful trump of doom. I tell you she is something famous to be shunned. She ought to be spoken to only of sacred things and only through a grille at that.

"Mulier notata, oculis orbata,
aure mutilata, cornu ventilata,
vultu deformata et morbo vexata!"

"Dear me!"

"Oh, yes. Many there are among us, dear, who still remember the famous night she came in, took a room as usual, threw herself down on the bed, and—as was revealed in the ensuing uproar—lubricated what she called her love tunnel with something so foul-smelling it was stinking out the hall. Turned out in a moment of haste, she'd put in her carry-all not her KY but her Preparation H.

"Soon enough a customer was heard fleeing the room screaming, 'They've let a *woman* in—a *woman*! I have been asked to have carnal knowledge of a *woman* clearly involved in her *menses! Do* something with her!'

"Clearly she wasn't turning the poor boy on."

"My darling, Reparata couldn't turn a faucet on. Moments later the customer was found collapsed in the coffee shop—and no wonder, for he was a young seminarian—Episcopal, from that place over on Tenth Avenue. With faculties so delicately balanced, a constitution so tenderly organized—no sensitive boy could possibly come out of *that* unaffected.

"The news spread like, you should excuse the expression, wildfire, until finally the French navy arrived, all smoking Gauloises and the floor was fumigated, the while she the offender fled into the night, not to return for a *full year*, darling—a year spent in exile at the St. Mark's, which smells like a sewer full of drowned and decomposing rats morning noon and night until the end of time."

!@#$%^&*

"Lizards will brag to other lizards when they have found a particularly lovely rock."

"What if Amyntas is dark, I always say—and lilies that fester smell far worse than weeds."

"You're an understanding woman."

"It's terribly, terribly true—I have been dreaming one long dream my whole life though, praying, praying for it to turn wet."

!@#$%^&*

"Oh, Lord, why can't homosexual love be chaste, like in Dickens?"

"And Whitman, dear—do you find homosexual love in Whitman chaste? What about in Hart Crane? What about Brick and Skipper in *Cat on a Hot Tin Roof*? What about Leonardo Da Vinci—six-four, golden blond, and to hear the official noise, celibate. Hah-*hah*! Anyway, for the same reason Oscar couldn't read the death of Little Nell without breaking out into uncontrollable laughter."

"Excuse me, I daresay it is very wrong and very discreditable to eavesdrop, but—"

"Relax yourself, Miss Haversham—after all, what else is an old bat to do?"

"—but where is the woman who can so regulate her actions by the abstract principles of honor when those principles point one way and when her affections and the interests that grow out of them point the other?"

"That is true—when you come to a fork in the road, take it."

"You see, as I recall it now, he talked on in that same complimentary strain with a fluency that left me no exertion to make beyond the effort of maintaining my own composure. I was wise enough, under the circumstances, not to attempt to deceive him by plausible explanations, and woman enough, notwithstanding my dread of him, to feel my hand would be tainted by..."

"And you were right to feel so—I'm sure of it."

"I remained standing alone in the hallway with my heart beating in my breast—and now I must go on to the staircase and ascend slowly to my room."

"Good night, Miss Haversham—thanks for dropping by."

"I do think cutting people is wicked, don't you? Good night."

"And what was *that* all about, if I may ask politely."

"You mean you don't know? Chaste homosexual love—like in Dickens."

!@#$%^&*

"Miss Aubergine, I have been puttin' up with your lips since the minute I walked in here—nor enuf is *enuf*! When I tell you Miss Mattiwilde Dobbs is a *royal* singer from high-born Darktown society folk in Atlanta, and this Callas woman an *upstaht* from a New York immigrant *slum*, you *pay attention* tah me!"

"Yazz'm."

!@#$%^&*

"Darling, I do know what you mean, but an offstage entrance is technically impossible."

"Wait a minute, I think there's a point being made here—a Zen point. It must certainly be the offstage entrance that occasions the sound of one hand clapping."

"Joe, you're coming back. You want to know how I know? Two days ago when you arrived in this city, you didn't know anybody—didn't know me, and now we're married. Don't you see? Whoever it is makes arrangements for people is doing pretty well for us."

"Hickory, dickery, dock, the mouse ran up—"

"What did people do in New York before the visionaries?"

"Oh, New Yorkers have always been visionary. In the early nineteenth century they were greatly taken up with things like the Humane Society, the Free School Society, the New York Tract Society, the Erie Canal—"

"Indeed the New York waterfront has ever been of the greatest interest and importance."

"Speaking of which, *Der Frist ist um*! Seafood! There is more of it in here tonight than on Fridays at McGinnis of Sheepshead Bay! The *Queen Mary* has just docked again, the French and Italian navies are in full sail, scoring as trade, the Germans and Dutch are giving it away. The crews of the *Ile de France*, the *Nieuw Amsterdam*, the *Vulcania* and the *Mauritania*, all doing it together."

"I can't wait until they repair the *Stockholm*, though—those Swedes!"

'What is that chirping sound?"

"Abadessa is humming 'The Entry of the Sailors' from *Les Troyens*—a trifle sharp."

!@#$%^&*

"Darling, one has only to *glance* at Jane Austen's novels for evidence that maritime men-at-arms have tended to enjoy quite a different reputation from their land-based counterparts. The warmth with which she treats Captain Wentworth and his brother sailors in *Persuasion*—which is her masterpiece—derived in part from the fact that she had brothers in the Royal Navy, but her attitude had deeper, broader roots, ones with which we who call her the divine Jane are in total sympathy."

"Pleasure hearin' yer talk, Professor, but daddy's gotta get back t' work—there's mouths t' feed."

"There's all kinds of expressions for it, *n'est-ce pas*?. I had a guy last week worked me over something luscious, lapping away like a golden retriever, and then he put his *yard* into my *fundament*—that's *exactly* what he said. Isn't that *darling*? I thought it was."

"It is. Tell me dear, was he wearing Old Spice?"

!@#$%^&*

"Ask yourself this, will he be with you at Christmas?"

"Probably not, but so what, somebody will."

!@#$%^&*

"He even claims he was the one who operated the harpoon."

"It could be true."

"I was like Odysseus wandering all over the seven seas, marooned for a long season by the nymph Calypso, then released on order of Zeus and come to roost among the Phacians, the men who love long oars. As Odysseus himself said, 'What hard labor, queen, to tell you the story of my troubles start to finish!' "

"In that event, Miss Hush, do please spare yourself the effort. In the first place, *what* seven seas could Odysseus have traversed? And in the second place, I keep thinking of Kirk Douglas naked and that is disconcerting—even more disconcerting than peg-legged Gregory Peck lashed to that big white whale."

"Lordy *Lord*—you church choir girls are so *mean*!"

"—then hit the Penn Post where many a wanton forelock she might happily tug."

!@#$%^&*

"No, dear, she's not costumed as a heavy predator of hedge-bottom and ground-nesting species, that's what she *looks* like—and you're better off without your contact lenses."

"Virtue is knowledge; sin arises only from ignorance; the virtuous person is the happy person. In these three basic forms of optimistim lies the death of tragedy. It's tragic."

Anonymous to Soterius (whispered):

"Isn't that a paradox?"

"Ah learned much about paradox, chile, growin' up black in the South, and let me tell you somethin', honey mine, clarity along those particular lines did not come cheap, or easy either. Mine has been no cushioned past. Ah have lived hard and fast and furiously, without shame. Ah have drunk life to the lees. All times have Ah endured, some greatly enjoyed, many greatly suffered, both with those that loved me and alone."

"But it was worth it, wasn't it," a sudden intruder hissed. "Because now you're a regular *suppository* of hard-knock wisdom. Well, cry me a river, sister—and rattle that old tin can!"

"My, what hard and calloused hearts some women have! Yes, at times Ah have felt trapped, like a fly in blue amber, chile—*ath-ool* the Spanish say—yes, trapped."

"But now you're free."

"We are *awl* free, chile, thanks to Mister Lincoln. Mister Lincoln, you know had a male lovuh—"

!@#$%^&*

"And also of course the Golden Section. You know Leonardo's Vinci's famous drawing of Man as the Measure of All Things—the male figure rendered in two positions within the circumference of a circle—one at rest, arms at his sides, feet together, and the other as it were spread-eagled, the lines connecting arms and legs—"

"Oh, don't talk of it—spread-eagled. Do you realize that kind of thing used to *go on in here* in the twenties and thirties, before La Guardia came in."

"La Guardia came in *here*? When?"

"No, you fool—came into the mayoralty. There were reforms in the police, and by extension—well, you understand, I suppose; it really shouldn't have to be spelled out."

"I am sure The O'Maurigan could be persuaded in the right circumstances to pose, to prove a point. He is so rhetorical."

"You'd love that, wouldn't you, dear—tonight, in the charades room, as the next attraction, after Madame Twat's read her last card. You'd like to slip the boy a silly pill and see what you can get him to do in the name of art and science."

"Lil's a great one for breakin' down the doors of perception."

"It isn't just the Golden Section. He says the true method for assessing beauty is to measure the distance between the nipples—"

"Yes!"

"—and compare it to that between the middle of the breast and the navel—"

"Yes!"

"—and then to that between the navel and the—"

"*Yes*, I *will—yes!*"

"And tell me this, where does the penis fit in?"

"The penis doesn't come into it, my dear."

"Oh, *please!*"

"Then why are we talking about it here? And it must—otherwise why would Freud have bothered?"

"Darling, sometimes a salami is just a salami."

"I think it must come into it—as plumb line possibly."

"You may have something there—for instance, if you were to put Rubirosa or Milton Berle into that Da Vinci position, well—"

"*Milton Berle?*"

"Didn't you know, my dear? Monumental. Listen, you want to talk about measuring *things*—"

!@#$%^&*

A customer approaches the Triple Threat, a.k.a. The Appellate Court, at their open door.

UNA. Private party! Private party! Desist, Wart-Hog! Just because it's Halloween, do not believe you can get away with moral outrage. Duessa, you who are the connoisseur of Monstrosity, who is this besides the oldest and the ugliest he-whore in creation?

DUESSA. You leave her be, Una, pass her by with a shiver—for she has been turned out of every house in town.

TREZZA. It is too true, Duessa;, this is her last refuge; the last haven to which, having covered the waterfront in peacoat mufti, she may safely repair to labor over her manifests and correspondences.

UNA. *Repair!* I have never in my born days seen *anything* so *beyond* repair!

DUESSA. She is the white witch of Narnia—she dreams of devouring teenage boys in one great gulp.

TREZZA. Then she must beware the lion.

UNA. Which lion is that, the Cowardly Lion?

TREZZA. Of course not! The lion of Narnia—you aren't thinking straight.

UNA. And where exactly would *that* get me? Anyway the only lion I care about is the lion at Metro—*Ars Gratia Artis*."

DUESSA. *Just resting* is all you ever hear her say from deep in her cave. She lies in there, seeming to us like the spirit of some long dead thing pleading from the tomb to passersby to give her a word of greeting or a little wine, but thinking to herself that she looks like Goya's *Naked Maja*—whereas what she looks like when dawn's light comes to reveal her is a color reproduction of something that was never needed in the first place.

TREZZA. *Just resting*? They should hang the sign on *her*.

UNA. Maybe not *just resting*—better *jest rusting*.

DUESSA. It would be truth in advertising—for she is one old lawn mower!

TREZZA. *Ravissante*, she is hardly.

DUESSA. Older than the face she sits upon. It is a *long time* since she made her last john so nervous spinnin' out of private control right into public service. In those days, she had a career—welcome the coming, and speed the parting guest.

UNA. Can it be true?

DUESSA. Oh yes, Miss Girl! Why, she hardly let them wipe themselves off before she had them out the door—oh, she was Miss Turnstiles in those days, dear, when the subway was a nickel and she took in little more per trick! Of course she was had up on charges, but always got off somehow—in fact, she used to say that her absolute favorite sight in life was a *hung jury* of twelve angry men.

Suddenly a passing robe assaulted the judgmental trio.

"Cease and *desist*! You are three women of sin, whom Destiny that hath to instrument this lower world and what's in't the never surfeited sea hath caused to belch up . . . and so forth."

"Jeremiah thirty-two, seventeen, darling—Jeremiah thirty-two, seventeen—"

"*Hike!*"

"Impious child—you dream of making the team."

"One by one, and then . . . and in Technicolor."

"*For your body is like a common shore, that still receives*
All the town's filth! The sin of many men is within you!"

"Yeah, and not one at a time either—so eat your fuckin' heart out."

"This is all Duessa's doing—Duessa discord sows."

"And Trezza *abbazzata* goes—on a *dime*."

"And sex pig Una *wart hogs* blows—if not exclusively, often."

"Do your worst, the lot of you, for that is your seeming destiny, but I say unto you that we are all of us shocked and saddened by the sudden, violent lives of colleagues in this tragic and senseless way, and that of the countless many you have caused to weep, not a single tear shed by a broken heart among them shall there be that does not fall like a little rhinestone at the feet of the King of Glory in his royal seat in the splendor of heaven. And by the way, Una, your dwarf just came rollicking in."

"*Rollicking?*"

"That's what I said, bub—firewater to the Navaho, big time."

"*Caramba!* No good deed goes unpunished—well that is absolutely the last mercy fuck I throw. Now please get out—*am*-scray. I've got lots of things to do."

"Oh yeah—like what?"

"Throw up."

"What a place—what a place! We are all doomed—*doomed!*"

!@#$%^&*

*

They sailed past Connemara, past Mizen Head, past Cobh.

"I must sail up to Dublin!" Mawrdew Czgowchwz called out to the helmsman, "they're waiting for me there." The helmsman, in the voice of Orphrey Whither called down, "you are about to remember a pressing subsequent engagement," and continued, singing "Oh Inishfree my isle, I am returning/ From wasted years across the wintry sea!"

Past Finisterre into the Bay of Biscay, and down the coast past Biarritz and San Sebastián to Santander. Skirting Asturias around the horn of Galicia. Down past Lisbon and Faro to Gibraltar—along the coast of Andalucía, past Málaga, Valencia, Barcelona; past Marseilles and the Château d'If. Past Corsica and Sardinia and into the Tyrrhenian Sea. Past Ogygia where in the morning mist the nymph Calypso lounged on the shore, complaining,

> *T.S. Eliot writes books for me,*
> *Chiang-Kai-Shek sends me pots of tea,*
> *Harry S. Truman plays bop for me*—monotonous!

Through the Strait of Messina, down the Trinacrian coast past Aci Trezza, with Etna smoldering in the middle distance on one side, and on the other a vision of SDJO'M, dressed in his father's wartime overcoat and Marlon Brando as Alcibiades, together on the bridge of a destroyer approaching Scylla and Charybdis. Suddenly—as the morning mist burned off—there was Morgana Neri (Morgana: born of the sea) draping laundry on a rock in the sun at the wall of a crumbling seaside villa, a neon sign *Cave Canem*, flashing over the gate as a great vicious mastiff appeared and commenced barking.

She heard the voice of Mother St. Mawrdew, Latin Mistress of the St. Vitus Convent School in Prague. "This well-known phrase is a famous pun every student of Latin learns, for it can be also construed as 'Beware, lest I sing!' " Morgana Neri commenced singing in the appalling *vox stridula* reserved only for the appearance in nightmares of heifers, "*Io sono l'umile ancella del geni creator.*" The helmsman, in the frantic voice of Merovig Creplaczx, assailed her. *Wo weilest du mein irisch Kind?* Morgana Neri, sticking her middle finger into her mouth, and then waving it in the air, rose up above the boat, circling it, and taunting back: "*Maestro Merdacazzo, vostri tempi fanno schiffo!*" She disappeared, howling maledictions, into the whirlpool. "*E loro fanno di cul il trombetta.*"

They sailed up the heel of Italy and along the Adriatic coast, past Otranto, Brindisi, Termoli, Ravenna—toward Venice. As they approached the Lagoon, the head of Orpheus, on its route from Thrace, bobbed up and down on the wavelets, singing "Ev'ry Time We Say Goodbye."

Mawrdew Czgowchwz fell asleep in her dream (as always in the morning, after waking at first light and noting the fact she was still alive), reawakening as her boat was sailing past Chioggia into the Venetian Lagoon, to hear vaparetto voices chanting, "*Signori e signore, se vuole prendere delle precauzione: le onde si accavallano!*"

A howling chorus from the madhouse on Isola la Grazia cried despairingly, "*Oime, morrir' mi sento!*"

The vaparetto voices continued implacably. "*Lido! San Lazzaro degli Armeni! Arsenale! Fondamenta Nuova! San Girogio Maggiore! Zattere! Acc-ademia! San Marco!*"

They drifted under the Ponte dei Sospiri to the Fondamenta dela Fenice. A voice she recognized as that of Eugenio Montale, poet and music critic of Milan's *Corriere della Sera* crooned, "*Arrema su a strinata proda, O amoretti, la nave vaghegiatta! E dormite—che non oda a vostri malevoli spiriti che veleggiano a stormi!*"

Jacob, bearing aloft the immortal *Dioscouros's* torch of ingress and protection (an amber lantern of spectacular Venetian design) led the way into the theater. In her *camerino* at the Fenice (which was doubled in her dream by the Memory Theatre of Giulio Camillo as described on seven successive mornings to Girolamo Muzio in Milan in the middle of the sixteenth century) were hung the costumes of all the roles Mawrdew Czgowchwz had ever sung. She saw herself in these former incarnations, hanging up in each of them, like the mummies in the catacombs of the Carmelites of Palermo. She cried out in her dream, and the figures in the costumes flew up to the ceiling like Tiepolos, the faces on each of them exploding like balloons.

She was helped by wardrobe women into a black Venetian gown, slung with ropes of baroque paste pearls, sleeves slashed in pink, the while the voice of Maria Meneghini Callas, coming through the walls from the soprano *camerino* next door, repeated again and again "*fra le tenebre... fra le tenebre!*"

"I get it," said Mawrdew Czgowchwz to herself. "We're here at the Fenice together again, Maria and I, in *Gioconda*; I'm singing Laura."

Jacob Beltane appeared at the door, like Dana Andrews in *Laura*, in a wet raincoat and a dripping fedora. He looked across at her, and gasped. "But you're *dead*! Shot full in the face—your head blown off! Ivy Grudget found you on the floor."

He took a step closer to her. "They sent me to find the—" He turned away. "Oh, I get it—the brush-off. You committed suicide! You don't love me!"

"No!" she cried, "it's *Gioconda*! Laura *fakes* the suicide. I'm here at the Fenice, in *Gioconda*, with *Maria*!"

Jacob slumped in a chair, staring up at the portrait of Mawrdew Czgowchwz, as Laura, in Ponchielli's *La Gioconda*, and weeping, the while his voice crooned over the theater's loud-speaker system.

> *"Laura—is a voice on a windy hill,*
> *Footsteps that you hear down the hall...*
> *She gave her very first kiss to you*
> *That was Laura—but she's only a dream!"*

"That's not Ponchielli," a strident voice cried merrily, "that's David Raksin."

"Will you *wake up!*" cried Mawrdew Czgowchwz. "I'm only *playing* Laura! I *do* love you—I'm carrying your *children!*"

(She heard the voice of Ruth Draper. "Ought to be enough for anybody.")

Morgani Neri looked in at the open *camerino* door.

"Io non sono una donna gentile, Laura."

"I tell you," cried Mawrdew Czgowchwz. "I *love* him!"

Suddenly she was onstage at the Teatro della Fenice Di Memoria—blazingly footlighted by a ring of torches, beyond which, Halcyon Paranoy advised, "Everyone you've ever known" stood, sat, and lounged in stalls, banquettes, and tiers of boxes—cast opposite Maria Meneghini Callas in the second act of Amilcare Ponchielli's operatic masterpiece, *La Gioconda*, singing the duet.

"Io l'amo come il fulgor del creato!"

Looking out over the torch fires, she recognized Ghiringhelli and Rudolf Bing, sitting together in a stage box.

"Vedi," hissed her friend and colleague, squinting characteristically, *"il palco funesto!"*

A wipe. Mawrdew Czgowchwz stood in the wings the coryphees *en jetee*, in "The Dance of the Hours," landing on both sides of her, waddling off. Onstage Laura lay on a catafalque, suddenly exposed, while Jacob's sobbing voice—curious imitation, she thought, of Mario Lanza—led the entire audience in a chorus of *"Tu sei morta!"*

"This is a great pity," said Ghiringhelli to Rudolf Bing, standing in the shadows behind her. "The poor man's lost his children and his wife, too!"

"Never his wife," Bing replied. "And he can have children by himself. Do you not know Paracelsus's recipe for male children? In the dark of the moon draw a man's semen and place it in a retort, hermetically sealed. Bury in horse manure for forty days and magnetize—the manikin will form."

"There are many retorts to be found in Venice," said Ghiringhelli, "of exquisite amethystine glass—but to have intercourse with a *bottle!* And where in Venice are there horses to be found today?"

"I have found such intercourse amusing," said Rudolf Bing, "and am a great admirer of Theophrastus Bombastus von Hohenheim, whom the world calls Philippus Aureolus Paracelsus."

"Philippus—hence the horse pucky."

"Exactly. Because of his researches into kidney stones—the most hellish pain known to man, of far greater intensity than childbirth—and his construction of the man-shaped glass retort in which all processes of male life were, as in a crystal ball, made manifest, we have come to understand much."

"It would be a pity for a man, thinking himself in childbed to deliver kidney stones, *non e vero*?"

"You Italians are amusing—si, *molto divertente*. These things we speak of he learned at the illustrious academy of the Fuggers at Schwaze, and in his extended travels through Germany, Italy—to the old school of Arab medicine at Salerno—France, Russia, and beyond . . . together with all the steps of the holy science of alchemy as transmitted down the ages from Hermes Trismegistus and Maria the Jewess to Pico della Mirandola. These are distillation—"

"No mystery to you yourself, *Signore*!"

"Ahem. Along with solution, putrefaction, extraction, calcination, reverberation, sublimation, fixation, separation, reduction, coagulation, tinction, and so on. I never conclude a contract without a run-through of them all. Yes, there is a great opera to be written on Paracelsus—and I think I have found the singer to create him. Nothing like work to sop up grief. And as for the horses—well, you are surely not forgetting the bronze horses of San Marco?"

"But," quizzed Ghiringhelli, "do these horses *defecate*?"

"Most certainly," chortled Rudolf Bing triumphantly. "That is the secret of the procedure, and it is why Venice is the alchemist's paradise. At the dark of the moon, my dear Ghiringhelli, the bronze horses of San Marco defecate mercury."

"Ah!" said Ghiringhelli, nodding.

"*Precisely*," rasped Bing. "Whereupon, after forty days, you must feed the transparent *homunculus*, or *twin homunculi*, with the arcanum of human blood, maintaining the retort at the constant temperature of a mare's womb for a period of forty weeks. This is crucial."

"And what," asked Ghiringhelli, "is the temperature of a mare's womb?"

"It is the same as that of a contralto's throat in the aftermath of singing '*Stride la vampa*.' The point is, no woman is necessary to bear a cunning man's children."

"Oh, really?" Musicry's premiere oltrano challenged her tormentors over her shoulder (as she ascended in an arc, drawn into the energy vacuum left from the last coryphee's passage). "*That* is a matter of opinion—*and we shall see!*"

To assist her passage, seven angels came whirling down in spirals (the way her costumes had gone up). Michael, Gabriel, Vadriel, Raphael, Camael, and Zadchiel and Zaphkiel (the twins). Looking to the stage box, where Ghiringhelli and Rudolf Bing had been stationed prior to their translation to the wings, she saw in their places the benign aspects of Girolamo Muzio and his descendant Claudia. Claudia Muzio blew her a kiss.

"*Misterioso altero!*" Michael mused.

"*Libiam' ai dolci fremitti!*" Gabriel urged. "Here's how."

She sat up on the catafalque. Tearing the baroque paste pearls off her neck, flinging them into the air, she sang to the *galleria* with all her legendary force, "*Follie! Follie!*"

"*Dio mio!*" cried Girolamo Muzio, lurching forward recklessly.

"*Ben detto, nonno*," Claudia marveled, tapping his head with her fan. "*E una voce sovrumana venuta dal tempo immemoribile!*"

"*Tutto vanna e questo—povera donna—sola, abbondonata, in questo popoloso deserto chi s'appellano Venezia!*"

And why not, Mawrdew Czgowchwz demanded, taking her breath for the first ascent. It was the scene of the work's premiere.

"*Gioioooir! Gioioooir!*" The voice grew; it's sides fell off. Mawrdew Czgowchwz said "They want the portals of doom? All right, I'll give them the portals of doom—with gay knobs on."

> *"Sempre libera degg'io*
> *Folleggiare di gioia in gioia*
> *Vo' che scorra il vivo mio*

Pei sentieri del piacer.
Nasca il giorno, o il giorno muoia,
Sempre lieta ne' ritrovi.
A diletti sempre nuovi
Dee volare il mio pensier."

Jacob's voice—his own—cut in imploringly.

"Ah, quel amor, amore che palpito,
d'all'universo, dal universo intero . . . etc."
Misterioso, misterioso eterno,
Croce, croc'e delizia . . . delizia al cuor.

"No *schlag*, nuts and fruit on top this time around," Mawrdew Czgowchwz ordered herself. "Give 'em the E-flat-*e basta*."

"*Il mio pensier . . . il mio pensier . . . Ah! Ah!*"

When the E-flat *in alt* exploded from the singing mask the seven angels swooped into its center to ride it on the spotlight home (each ascending a half tone: Michael to E, Gabriel from there to F, Raphael to F, Vadriel to G, Camael to Ab, and the twins, in unison arriving at A-natural—so that they who'd dreamed of hearing Mawrdew Czgowchwz lose her mind would get their dream money's worth and not complain).

"*Beh, grazie, ragazzi!*" Mawrdew Czgowchwz, heading for the wings, saluted her departing angels, as the ovation erupted in the auditorium. "That will be the price of *that* in the big town."

"But this is *heresy*!" cried Ghiringhelli, a failed priest. "Sheer *heresy*! The angels, removed from the flow of time are forever suspended between one note and another!"

"Heresy, hearsay," snorted Bing, in reply, "if it's not the one it's the other! *Die Czgowchwz* was heretical from the outset—and it got worse. Violetta . . . Isolde . . . my hand was forced."

"But Madame Czgowchwz," exclaimed Rudolf Bing, blocking her way, holding out a one-page contract vouching her appearance at the Metropolitan on any convenient night in any role of her choice (with conductor, *regisseur* costume and set approval) in perpetuity.

"Your *ovation!*" exclaimed Ghiringhelli, holding out a transparent sack full of gleaming twenty-dollar gold pieces.

"Take it yourselves," she advised them, briskly signing the contract (with her right hand) and grabbing the sack (with her left), as scene dock doors opened onto the *canbaletto* behind the theater, revealing her boat (and Jacob faithful at his helmsman's post), idling in the dark water. "I'm indisposed."

*

!@#$%^&*

"Yes, Esclarmonde is in at dark and stormy rage tonight."

"*Or piombe essausta fra le tenebere.*"

"The curse'll do it to you every time. I remember the boy in question very well. Impenetrable, but hardly meaningless. The poor thing had a rear end pustulant with roaring clap. We sent him up to good Doctor Brown. Thank God for Lone Rangers and their silver bullets."

"Esclarmonde will soldier on."

"I underwrote Esclarmonde's interior swerves, for ages and ages—we all did; we really did think her interesting—compelling as we said then—back in the Helen Vinson days."

"Helen Vinson—an actress . . ."

"Before your time, dear, yes, and a good one, too, specializing in the kinds of very teary dramatic roles Miss Foye—for that was and is Esclarmonde's name . . . et cetera. Well, she got the Camp name because she'd been on the USS *Vinson* in the war, and when she first started coming in here she was famous for bringing in an old U.S. Navy recruiting poster showing a lot of sailors loading a long gun and reading, 'These men came across—they joined the Navy and are at the front now. Enlist today!' And all around the edges Polaroids of all these gorgeous numbers she claimed to have had in the North Atlantic—although they all, shirtless, blonde and tanned, almost to a man looked suspiciously *South Pacific* to us—and the road show at that, not even the original."

"*Tanned to a man*—you realize that could be—"

"What dear, a slogan for the Coppertone ads?"

"Well, think of it."

"You think of it, Mae, I'm thinkin' of Christmas. Anyway that routine went on for *eons*, and then suddenly she began to search for a situation, or the simulation of one, that would match the increasing severity of her features, and one night thought to herself, *The Blue Grotto*! She'd been to Ischia, y'know, after the war, in that little Auden clutch with Fiordiligi and Dorabella and the The Queen of the Night herself."

!@#$%^&*

"The hubris, dear, is to expect an answer."

"At all."

"At all."

"Got it."

!@#$%^&*

"So anyway in she comes this one night with *grotto paper*, dear, all *ruched* into *rocks*, and up she sticks it, and on the bare light bulb in the cell she always takes a blue gel she mopped from backstage at some Thalia Bridgewood open-and-shut case or other. And there she stands under the blue light, and I swear to God she throws the robe over her head to look mysterious, and not a minute later some queen screams, 'It's *Lourdes*—it's *The Song of Bernadette*!' And Miss Helen Earth goes all rancid and awful on the spot . . . *and stays that way*. She's carrying on next morning—which came about a half hour later—like a starched white woman in the Marmador, ranting about her people, all originally French, the lords of Foix, if you don't mind, so Sister Mary Manon-Charlotte Herodiade-Thais, the Massenet queen of all time names her Esclarmonde then and there and Esclarmonde she has remained. She took it as a tribute to her nobility of soul; nobody had the nerve to tell her the original was burned at the stake as a heretic."

!@#$%^&*

"There are no fire exits, darling, in hell."

"You seem to know a lot about the next life, Rose."

"The unexamined life after death will not have been worth living."

"I'm going to find that priest and sic him on you."

!@#$%^&*

"Come on, Audrey, you sing the '*Libiamo!*' Stella, you sing that thing from *The Student Prince* like you do, as good as Mario Lanza any night, and I'll sing 'It Might as Well Be Spring.' It *works*, darling, I tell you, better than the *Rosenkavalier* trio."

"*Etwas neues angefallen?*"

"*Bleib aus den Spiele, Wellgunde!*"

"*Guten Abend, mein Herr—hier is Fasching, so?*"

"Not unless we've come under surveillance by the FBI, sailor boy."

"Now was that *necessary?*"

"Germans. I have never been able to get over my mistrust."

"*Raffiniert ist der Herr Gott, Schatze, aber boshaft is Er nicht.*"

"Huh?"

"Something I heard once, dear, in the prisoner-of-war camp."

"I have always cultivated a feeling of humane indulgence for foreigners."

"I suppose working all day long in currency exchange does that."

"*Fresh!*"

!@#$%^&*

"I never asked was I going to be condemned to lie on my back for the rest of my life—I was afraid of one of those awful hockey-mistress reassurances from Sister. 'Come now, ensign, *what* a question to ask! We don't let our patients go talking in that way. Why just think of all those poor men—your shipmates—lying there together at the bottom of the sea—not that it will do to go all morbid about it. What I say is you've got a lot to be *grateful for!*' "

"I think all you British boys were *wonderful* through it all!"

!@#$%^&*

"I will tell you a little fable, darling, appropriate to Halloween. The story goes that King Midas—he of the touch—for ages hunted the wise old fuck Silenus, daemon of Dionysius, in the forests, unsuccessfully. When Silenus finally fell into Midas's grasp, the king demanded to know what was the very best thing of all for man—the epitome. After a long, pregnant pause, the daemon broke out into hysterical, screeching laughter, then cried out, 'O suffering creature, born for a day, child of accident and mishap, why must you force me to say that which is the worst thing for you to hear? The very best thing for you is forever unreachable—not to have been born, not to exist, to be nothing. The second best thing for you, however, is this: to die soon.' "

"I don't dig the Greeks. All that sunshine and blood—depressing. I like hopeful stories—like *The Divine Comedy*. Dante makes Purgatory a hopeful place; I can dig that."

"Purgatory is not a *place*, sweetheart. Purgatory is that spiritual condition of restless yearning in which the dead, having in the moment of death caught as it were a first-last instantaneous glimpse of the face of God, are denied a second look—which will distinguish them—so long as a single living soul *remembers them*—as they actually were, that is to say, not as represented in—

"A book or a play or a set of blueprints?"

"Exactly. You're very clever."

"Am I? Not clever enough to *atone*, though."

!@#$%^&*

"She is a beast, given to terrible deeds. Married men are her chosen prey. Just last week one came in drunk, passed out in his room leaving the door quite shut, and nevertheless woke with her voracious mouth working away with a purpose demented. She demanded he fuck her, but he said he did not do that, on account of his marriage vows. 'Finger-fuck me then, you heavenly boy-man,' she brayed to be heard in the hall, and the poor thing started in. 'No, lover, with your *left* hand—I know you're left-handed, I watched you check in.' So lover gets three fingers in and so tangled that with her gyrations she manages to *suck the wedding band off his left hand*, which he doesn't notice right away, but when he does, she pretends he doesn't know what he's talking about. She has him reduced to tears until she finally relents, retrieves the ring, and sends him out the door with, 'There take it; it's good for one free ride on the merry-go-round. See ya around, Galahad.' "

!@#$%^&*

"Death is not an event in life; it is not lived through. Well, I *ask* you!"

"Darling, when you read Wittgenstein you simply must suspend all disbelief—and it helps to have a picture of him to hand. The famous one in the open-necked shirt for instance is quite enough to keep any serious-minded woman on course, for an evening anyway."

!@#$%^&*

"Yes, she lies, she lies all the time, but that her stories are untrue does not mean they lack any representative value."

"Let no driven soul this low samootch explore
Thoughtless yet of those left dead upon the floor."
" 'She dealt her pretty words like Blades—
How glittering they shone—
And every One unbared a Nerve
Or wantoned with a Bone.' "

"I knew the very woman; she went to hell with herself."

"Not without trying—vainly, it happened—to get up a party."

"Sucked into the vortex of a highball glass."

"Just so—to the wail of the theremin. *The Lost Weekend.*"

"You were there? I never saw you."

"It was dark in the theater."

!@#$%^&*

"It was the *third* floor, dear, and not the second you looked into when you rode the El and looked out the window into people's lives in the tenements."

"Oh, well, that makes all the difference, doesn't it."

!@#$%^&*

"She is an old, ailing buzzard, with the croaks. Plus which, for all these many years, she's been convinced that none but the lonely hearts whose company she frequents has even read her—ever been as *le Maitre* says '*fixe a son compte*.' What a hilarious camp."

" '*Fix a son compte*.' I don't seem to remember reading that in Henry James."

"It's Glenway Wescott's *The Pilgrim Hawk*, dear, speaking of Bible study. Dear

Glinda dropped in for a visit once just after the war, and Madame thinks if she reads that same passage every week, perhaps—although if you ask me, it's hardly an inviting one, brilliant allegory it may be of what awaits the predatory homosexual.

"'She informed us, for example, that in a state of nature hawks rarely die of disease, they starve to death. Their eyesight fails, some of their flight feathers break off or fall out, and their talons get frail or broken. They cease to be able to judge what quarry is worth flying at, or their flight slows up so that even the likely quarry gets away. Or because they have lost weight, the victim is not stunned by their swooping down on it. Or when they have clutched it, they cannot hang on long enough to kill. Day after day they make fools of themselves. Then they have to depend upon very young birds, or sick birds, or little animals on the ground, which are the hardest of all to see, and in any case there are not enough of these easy conquests to keep them in flesh. The hungrier they get, the more wearily and weakly they hunt. And the weaker they get, the more often they go hungry, in a miserable confusion of cause and effect. Finally what appears to be shame and morbid discouragement overcomes them. They simply sit on the rocks or in a tree somewhere waiting to die, as you might say philosophically, letting themselves die.'"

"Generalizations are hazardous, and ambiguities abound."

"What *can* you do?"

"Talk about something else."

"We're already doing that."

!@#$%^&*

"Why do you know that a site in Georgia has yielded images in copper of dancing shamans in elaborate divine disguises—masked and winged, working up ecstasy with the noise of rattles made of human skulls? It's true!"

"A boy who supplies comfort of a morning—there's a boy!"

"Confucius say, darling, that that which cannot be pummeled by fists may be deflected by fingertips."

"And did you know the Polynesians navigate with their *balls*? True."

"Fascinating, dear. *Bali-Hai may find you*—"

"At the posttraditional level of justification, the only legitimate laws are those that can be rationally accepted by everyone in a discursive process of opinion and will formation."

"Says who?"

"Well, that's just it."

"Yes, it would be."

"*Tough*? The woman chews old rusty nails and spits out bullets!"

". . . redeemed from sins bemoaned but never detailed."

"You like that, huh?"

"Oh, honey, *fork tender*."

"Many are called, darling—"

"In here, too, many are called *darling*, including some of the meanest women on God's earth; there is a want of *standards*."

!@#$%^&*

Strange reappeared.

"Kindly watchmen out of Seir, what of the night?"

"Out of the sewer more likely—while lightning slashes the midnight sky."

The priest yawned. "Indeed. Meanwhile the god-sent night has ebbed away and grasping dawn in all her damp ambition once more holds the cards—and you two boys make lovely doormen both, to welcome the coming and to speed the parting guest in this twenty-four-hour-a-day year-round emporium-cum-sanitarium-cum-morgue."

*

Mawrdew Czgowchwz and her consort resumed their voyage, crossing the lagoon to Mestre and entering the inland waterway there. The Orient Express, with everyone she'd ever known aboard—all of them waving good-bye out the windows—passed overhead across a viaduct, on its way back to Paris.

Through the *navigle* across the Veneto to Milan, then into Cisalpine caves, whose subterranean streams carried them to the intersection of a tributary of the Rhine. Surfacing, they could hear the Rhinemaidens singing "*Wehw! Wehe!*" and then

"Es braust ein Ruf wie Donnerhall
Wie Schwertgeklirr un Wogen prall,
Zum Rhein, zum deutschen Rhein
We will des Stormes Huter sein."

They sailed past the Lorelei to Köln, where atop the cathedral roof Hildegard von Bingen stood singing "*Columba aspexit*" a capella to a parting sky.

At the antiphon, she paused, nodded down at the voyagers, and continued.

Then past, to Utrecht and into the Crooked Rhine, to be carried down into the North Sea. Crossing it, they sailed past the iron-bound coasts of the Orkneys and the Hebrides, past Antrim and Derry, and Lough Swilly, around Donegal, down the Mayo coast, again past Connemara the Aran Islands and the Cliffs of Moher, into the Shannon's mouth at Killimer. Jacob sang as they sailed up the Shannon.

"*Che ouro ciel, che chiaro il sol!*'

A warning voice descended at the bend in the river where the monastery ruin of Clonmacnoise gleamed in the sunlight. *Beware lest like Palinarus you fall from the helm to be murdered, Sannanach that you are, by the dwellers ashore, wild in their fury against you!*

At Athlone they entered the Grand Canal and left it as the Liffey cut across them at Chapelizod and they joined its flow, while the washerwomen greeted them. "Sure an' haven't ye heard it a *deluge* of toimes!" Mawrdew Czgowchwz advised herself: "It's up to me to wake me."

The boat of Amon-Ra anchored under O'Connell Bridge. Disembarking, its passengers mounted the quayside steps into the deserted metropolis. They walked up O'Connell Street and into the Gresham, without incident. They took the lift to the top floor and entered their suite as they had done all week. Mawrdew Czgowchwz walked ahead of Jacob Beltane into the bedroom. There they both were, in bed. She looked down at herself.

She lies *in un sonno fastidioso*. I could live in such sleep with him sounding that way, and all my ideation chordal, all my intrigues operative.

I'm not awake; evidently not time; in the event—all told. Are they awake down there—his double darlings in their swim? Are they ever not awake? Which:—increasing a millimeter a day, apiece. Enough for anybody? On the thirty-third day, says he, the eyes are dark for the first time and the brains are a quarter each larger than they were on day thirty-one. "That must be," I said to him, "a quarter of what was there—whatever if anything that was—and not a quarter that's the next thing bigger than a dime?"

"Exactly."

"And how do you—"

"I see—when I look in at them; it's the least I can do, look in at them."

What am I to do for them? What not? Not ride horses down O'Connell Street from either end, whatsoever—Miss O'Callaghan of Blackrock can do that thing for me; didn't she tell me so.

We are the creation each of strife itself; whereupon, presumably, strife breaks the mold—or would that be whereafter?

Daft she was the way they say, to ride in that condition, never knowing what it might—and what did it anyway? One thing at least: made it difficult for the Gypsies on the Hortobágy to trust me, shying away that way I did from their steeds. . . .

When will I wake from—best not wake him just yet. He's had a long hard day or two—and a long night, too, into the bargain, rowing that barge around the planet Earth with me in it.

Will I tell him—best not. Who's best to tell? Madge.

But where is she? Where are they all—I once knew. New York, New York—never far from the mind, even asleep.

What tale will I tell them, so, how will it go? In any version, vigorous as they all are, it's bound to sound, in any but the times it happened in, just about as remote from everyday life—poets, Gypsies, noblemen, and adversary thugs who have the absolute power of life and death over incalculable numbers of people. People are already behaving as if none of it ever happened.

"Your life is your life," Gennaio said; "it isn't a libretto."

"And yet," I said, "I've sometimes thought it was—as if."

"*Isn't* isn't the same as *as if*. It might well have been *as if*. How so?"

"What comes to mind?"

"Yes."

"Well," I said, "it's sometimes *as if*, having sought the company of Devilshoof and his Gypsies, sprung the locks on the dungeon *and* kidnapped the nobleman's child to hide her among them, *some one* of my progenitors—having sung rousing renditions of *'Tis Sad to Leave the Fatherland* and *A Heart Bowed Down*—succeeded in the course of his or her subsequent adventures in arousing the wrath of the Romany queen—a wrath that but for the discovery of a tell-tale scar somewhere or other on my anatomy, and the great luck I had when the bullet aimed at me by said selfsame ricochets, killing her who . . . you get the picture."

She fell again into half-sleep, Laura on the catafalque and heard a kind of universal *crocchio ristretto* (resembling the improvisations of *comprimarii* from guests her roiling undermind.

"*Quelle vie de* dog!"

"*Ma dimi. . .*"

"*Sage-mir, Josef, is die Grafin schon?*"

"*Aber wass hab ich getan das ich muss leiden so?*"

"Say what you will, he's nobody's fool."

"I'd heard he was out of work. . . ."

"It was, dear, a deep heart bruise."

"She is a hardworking woman, and no scholar."

Turning over, protesting, she moaned aloud, trying to force herself awake, but a voice protested, "*Abbondarmi cosi?*" How long must I put up with this?

Another voice, beyond the rim of sleep, cut in, commanding

"Come now, darling, wake up; it's morning, nearly."

Suddenly there was the Madge, in an enormous mushroom hat.

"God, where did you get that hat?"

(The world's best hats were once made in Bruges; no more.)

"Jacques Fath. What *have* you been up to in your sleep?"

(*Dentro di me?*)

"Well, everybody was talking; it was hard—listen, I *called* you last evening and you weren't—"

"No, dear, I was in Gander—ferocious storms."

"I've been dreaming—about life and death and Venice—the *undertow!*"

"I hope you've worked up an appetite, so—I surely have."

"Well, I'm awfully glad you've come."

"Not more than I. God forgive me, I can't think what I've been up to myself—leaving you alone with these hooligans, to be passed around like snuff at a wake. Never mind, I'm here now, and I'll not go back until I take you both with me."

"That may be some time—and what will New York be without your First Fridays?"

"What is was before them all the same. If you put your ear to it, you can still hear them at it. But never mind, word's been sent ahead to Merrion Square, where you'll be stopping from this out."

The *coup de maitresse*, the awakened reflected, there's nothing like it.

*

Delancey and The O'Maurigan sat together in the coffee shop, the latter smoking a Pall Mall while outlining his Freudian *Salome* as a riff on *The Interpretation of Dreams*. The poet crossed his legs, ash fell on the protruding knee, making of it a smudged face. As the recitation ended, he stubbed out the cigarette.

"*La commeddia e finita*. As for us, what's our next move?"

"Checking out seems to be the inevitable one."

Soon enough the two companions, relieved of the burden of the long dark night, were making their way down the white marble steps and out into Twenty-eighth Street.

"The morning suddens," the poet declared, looking east. "Oh, the *relief*! Every time I leave that place and walk like this into the hosed-down light of a

New York morning, I think I'm some survivor of a shipwreck on some long Night Sea Journey. It's the dream of the oarsman rowing away from some *Titanic*, as it goes down with everybody singing 'Nearer My God to Thee.' "

"Or maybe," Delancey offered, "the *Andrea Doria*, and everybody's singing '*Arrivederci, Roma*', and '*Volare*.' You should write about the place," he suggested, as they headed west down the block to The O'Maurigan's loft.

"Not up to it. Doubt either I shall ever write about anybody I fell in love with crossing a bridge. '*Fidadomi di altri piu che dime*.' All the same, the relief!"

At the iron steps up to his loft, The O'Maurigan turned to say good night.

"A few yards along he stopped under a lamp post and laughed in the hearty noiseless way which was peculiar to him."

"Who did?"

"Moriarty."

"Oh, is he back?"

"Yes, he needs me."

"So do a fair number of us. Well," Delancey concluded, taking his friend's hand, "see you in the funny papers. You know, if you're serious about going up to your rocky promontory like an Irish monk, I'd really like to come see you off at Grand Central, so when you've slept and dreamed and come wide awake again and it's midafternoon and you've got the sleeper to Boston to catch, call me, Ishmael."

*

The woman who had been Mawrdew Czgowchwz turned from the window to find the poet asleep in his chair, and as it was a warm June night, and close to dawn, she left him there without a coverlet, put out the lights and went up to bed, anticipating a deep and dreamless sleep ashore. Reliving any portion of one's life she thought merited no less.

And as each slept, the city went on about its errands.